Collected Fiction: 1926–1930

H. P. LOVECRAFT

Collected Fiction

A VARIORUM EDITION

VOLUME 2: 1926–1930

Edited by S. T. Joshi

Hippocampus Press

New York

First Paperback Edition.

Published by Hippocampus Press
P.O. Box 641, New York, NY 10156.
http://www.hippocampuspress.com

Cover design and cover artwork by Fergal Fitzpatrick. For the cover of
volume two, Mr. Fitzpatrick has used *abstract truth and scientific logic* as his
conceptual departure.

"I should describe mine own nature as tripartite, my interests consisting of
three parallel and dissociated groups—(a) Love of the strange and the
fantastic. (b) Love of the abstract truth and of scientific logick. (c) Love of
the ancient and the permanent. Sundry combinations of these three strains
will probably account for all my odd tastes and eccentricities."
—H. P. Lovecraft to Rheinhart Kleiner (7 March 1920)

Portrait of H. P. Lovecraft, c 1930.
Photo of S. T. Joshi by Emily Marija Kurmis.

Hippocampus Press logo designed by Anastasia Damianakos.

1 3 5 7 9 8 6 4 2

ISBN: 978-1-61498-110-7

Contents

Introduction

The stories in this volume constitute, on the whole, a body of work that first appeared in pulp magazines without initial publication in amateur journals. As a result, Lovecraft did not have much of an opportunity to revise these texts, as he had done for many of the stories that had first appeared in amateur periodicals. Two exceptions to this rule are "Pickman's Model" (which was slightly revised for its second appearance in *Weird Tales*) and "The Colour out of Space" (which was revised for a proposed book publication by F. Lee Baldwin that never eventuated).

Lovecraft's two short novels, *The Dream-Quest of Unknown Kadath* and *The Case of Charles Dexter Ward*, lay unpublished at the time of his death. He made no effort to prepare these texts for publication, although R. H. Barlow prepared partial typescripts of them (both of which contain slight revisions and corrections by Lovecraft). It would, however, be inaccurate to say that these stories are mere first drafts; the extent to which Lovecraft revised them in the course of composition bespeaks considerable care in matters of structure and style. *Dream-Quest* is slightly less revised than *Ward*, true to its nature as a "practice" novel (*SL* 2.95).

The two humorous squibs, "History of the 'Necronomicon'" and "Ibid," also remained unpublished until after Lovecraft's death, as did the fragment "The Descendant." "Ibid" is the only work in this volume for which a manuscript has not come to light. It was presumably sent to Maurice W. Moe, and its whereabouts among Moe's effects are unknown. For "The Colour out of Space," we do not have Lovecraft's original A.Ms. or T.Ms., but a T.Ms. presumably prepared by Baldwin, revised by the author.

Of the texts in this volume, "The Call of Cthulhu" and the two short novels were very poorly printed by Arkham House, because it unwisely chose (in the case of "The Call of Cthulhu") to follow the poor *Weird Tales* text, and (in the case of the novels) because whoever transcribed the texts exhibited a poor ability to read Lovecraft's hand-writing. Such major stories as "The Colour out of Space," "The Dun-wich Horror," and "The Whisperer in Darkness" were well printed by Arkham House because it followed Lovecraft's T.Ms.

The dream-account later titled "The Very Old Folk" was written in late 1927, embodied in a letter to Donald Wandrei. It appears in the Ap-pendix to Volume 3.

Abbreviations used in the notes are as follows:

A.Ms.   autograph manuscript
JHL   John Hay Library, Brown University (Providence, RI)
om.   omitted
SL   *Selected Letters* (1965–76; 5 vols.)
T.Ms.   typed manuscript

—S. T. JOSHI

Collected Fiction: 1926–1930

Cool Air

You ask me to explain why I am afraid of a draught[a] of cool air; why I shiver more than others upon entering a cold room, and seem nauseated and repelled when the chill of evening creeps through the heat of a mild autumn day. There are those who say I respond to cold as others do to a bad odour,[b] and I am the last to deny the impression. What I will do is to relate the most horrible circumstance[c] I ever encountered, and leave it to you to judge whether or not this forms a suitable explanation of my peculiarity.

It is a mistake to fancy that horror is associated inextricably with darkness, silence, and solitude. I found it in the glare of mid-afternoon,[d] in the clangour of a[e] metropolis, and in the teeming midst of a shabby and commonplace rooming-house with a prosaic landlady and two stalwart men by my side. In the spring of 1923 I had secured some dreary and unprofitable magazine work in the city of New York; and being unable to pay any substantial rent, began drifting from one cheap boarding establishment to another in search of a room which might combine the qualities of decent cleanliness, endurable furnishings, and very reasonable price. It soon developed that I had only a choice between

Editor's Note: The surviving T.Ms. was prepared by HPL. The first appearance (*Tales of Magic and Mystery,* March 1928) followed the T.Ms., but made some curious editorial alterations of phrases. The Arkham House editions follow the T.Ms. but also make some alterations. The posthumous *Weird Tales* appearance (September 1939) is not relevant to the tale's textual history.

Texts: A = T.Ms. (JHL); B = *Tales of Magic and Mystery* 1, No. 4 (March 1928): 29–34; C = *The Dunwich Horror and Others* (Arkham House, 1963), 203–11. Copytext: A.

[a] draught] draft B
[b] odour,] odor, B
[c] circumstance] circumstances C
[d] mid-afternoon,] midafternoon, C
[e] clangour of a] clangor of B

different evils, but after a time I came upon a house in West Fourteenth Street which disgusted me much less than the others I had sampled.

The place was a four-story mansion of brownstone, dating apparently from the late 'forties,[a] and fitted with woodwork and marble whose stained and sullied splendor[b] argued a descent from high levels of tasteful opulence. In the rooms, large and lofty, and decorated with impossible paper and ridiculously ornate stucco cornices, there lingered a depressing mustiness and hint of obscure cookery; but the floors were clean, the linen tolerably regular,[c] and the hot water not too often cold or turned off, so that I came to regard it as at least a bearable place to hibernate till[d] one might really live again. The landlady, a slatternly, almost bearded Spanish woman named Herrero, did not annoy me with gossip or with criticisms[e] of the late-burning electric light in my third-floor[f] front hall room; and my fellow-lodgers were as quiet and uncommunicative as one might desire, being mostly Spaniards a little above the coarsest and crudest grade. Only the din of street cars in the thoroughfare below proved a serious annoyance.

I had been there about three weeks when the first odd incident occurred. One evening at about eight I heard a spattering on the floor and became suddenly aware that I had been smelling the pungent odour[g] of ammonia for some time. Looking about, I saw that the ceiling was wet and dripping; the soaking apparently proceeding from a corner on the side toward the street. Anxious to stop the matter at its source, I hastened to the basement to tell the landlady; and was assured by her that the trouble would quickly be set right.

"Doctair Muñoz," she cried as she rushed upstairs ahead of me, "he have speel hees chemicals. He ees too seeck for doctair heemself—seecker and seecker all the time—but he weel not have no othair for help. He ees vairy queer in hees seeckness—all day he take funnee-smelling baths, and he cannot get excite or warm. All hees own

<hr>

[a] 'forties,] forties, A, B, C
[b] splendour] splendor B
[c] regular,] regularly, B
[d] till] 'til C
[e] criticisms] criticism B
[f] third-floor] third floor A, B, C
[g] odour] odor B

housework he do—hees leetle room are full of bottles and machines, and he do not work as doctair. But[a] he was great once—my fathair in Barcelona have hear of heem—and only joost now he feex a[b] arm of the plumber that get hurt of sudden. He nevair go out, only on roof, and my boy Esteban[c] he breeng heem hees food and laundry and mediceens and chemicals. My Gawd,[d] the sal-ammoniac[e] that man use for[f] keep heem cool!"

Mrs. Herrero disappeared up the staircase to the fourth floor, and I returned to my room. The ammonia ceased to drip, and as I cleaned up what had spilled and opened the window for air, I heard the landlady's heavy footsteps above me. Dr. Muñoz I had never heard, save for certain sounds as of some gasoline-driven mechanism; since his step was soft and gentle. I wondered for a moment what the strange affliction of this man might be, and whether his obstinate refusal of outside aid were not the result of a rather baseless eccentricity. There is, I reflected tritely, an infinite deal of pathos in the state of an eminent person who has come down in the world.

I might never have known Dr. Muñoz had it not been for the heart attack that suddenly seized me one forenoon as I sat writing in my room. Physicians had told me of the danger of those spells, and I knew there was no time to be lost; so[g] remembering what the landlady had said about the invalid's help of the injured workman, I dragged myself upstairs and knocked feebly at the door above mine. My knock was answered in good English by a curious voice some distance to the right, asking my name and business; and these things being stated, there came an opening of the door next to the one I had sought.

A rush of cool air greeted me; and though the day was one of the hottest of late June, I shivered as I crossed the threshold into a large apartment whose rich and tasteful decoration surprised me in this nest of squalor and seediness. A folding couch now filled its diurnal role of

[a] But] But, B
[b] a] *om.* B
[c] Esteban] Estaban C
[d] Gawd,] God, C
[e] sal-ammoniac] salammoniac C
[f] for] for to C
[g] so] so, C

sofa, and the mahogany furniture, sumptuous hangings, old paintings, and mellow bookshelves all bespoke a gentleman's study rather than a boarding-house bedroom. I now saw that the hall room above mine—the "leetle room" of bottles and machines which Mrs. Herrero had mentioned—was merely the laboratory of the doctor; and that his main living quarters lay in the spacious adjoining room whose convenient alcoves and large contiguous bathroom permitted him to hide all dressers and obtrusive utilitarian devices. Dr. Muñoz, most certainly, was a man of birth, cultivation, and discrimination.

The figure before me was short but exquisitely proportioned, and clad in somewhat formal dress of perfect cut and fit.[a] A high-bred face of masterful though not arrogant expression was adorned by a short iron-grey full beard, and an old-fashioned pince-nez shielded the full, dark eyes and surmounted an aquiline nose which gave a Moorish touch to a physiognomy otherwise dominantly Celtiberian. Thick, well-trimmed hair that argued the punctual calls of a barber was parted gracefully above a high forehead; and the whole picture was one of striking intelligence and superior blood and breeding.

Nevertheless, as I saw Dr. Muñoz in that blast of cool air, I felt a repugnance which nothing in his aspect could justify. Only his lividly inclined complexion and coldness of touch could have afforded a physical basis for this[b] feeling, and even these things should have been excusable considering the man's known invalidism. It might, too, have been the singular cold that alienated me; for such chilliness was abnormal on so hot a day, and the abnormal always excites aversion, distrust, and fear.

But repugnance was soon forgotten in admiration, for the strange physician's extreme skill at once became manifest despite the ice-coldness and shakiness of his bloodless-looking hands. He clearly understood my needs at a glance, and ministered to them with a master's deftness; the while reassuring me in a finely modulated though oddly hollow and timbreless voice that he was the bitterest of sworn enemies to death, and had sunk his fortune and lost all his friends in a lifetime[c]

[a] cut and fit.] fit and cut. C
[b] this] his B
[c] lifetime] life-time C

of bizarre experiment devoted to its bafflement and extirpation. Something of the benevolent fanatic seemed to reside in him, and he rambled on almost garrulously as he sounded my chest and mixed a suitable draught[a] of drugs fetched from the smaller laboratory room. Evidently he found the society of a well-born man a rare novelty in this dingy environment, and was moved to unaccustomed speech as memories of better days surged over him.

His voice, if queer, was at least soothing; and I could not even perceive that he breathed as the fluent sentences rolled urbanely out. He sought to distract my mind from my own seizure by speaking of his theories and experiments; and I remember his tactfully consoling me about my weak heart by insisting that will and consciousness are stronger than organic life itself, so that if a bodily frame be but originally healthy and carefully preserved, it may through a scientific enhancement of these qualities retain a kind of nervous animation despite the most serious impairments, defects, or even absences in the battery of specific organs. He might, he half-jestingly[b] said, some day teach me to live—or at least to possess some kind of conscious existence—without any heart at all! For his part, he was afflicted with a complication of maladies requiring a very exact regimen which included constant cold. Any marked rise in temperature might, if prolonged, affect him fatally; and the frigidity of his habitation—some 55 or 56[c] degrees Fahrenheit—was maintained by an absorption system of ammonia cooling, the gasoline engine of whose pumps I had often heard in my own room below.

Relieved of my seizure in a marvellously short while, I left the shivery place a disciple and devotee of the gifted recluse. After that I paid him frequent overcoated calls; listening while he told of secret researches and almost ghastly results, and trembling a bit when I examined the unconventional and astonishingly ancient volumes on his shelves. I was eventually, I may add, almost cured of my disease for all time by his skilful ministrations. It seems that he did not scorn the

[a] draught] draft B
[b] half-jestingly] half jestingly C
[c] 55 or 56] fifty-five or fifty-six C

incantations of the mediaevalists,[a] since he believed these cryptic formulae to contain rare psychological stimuli which might conceivably have singular effects on the substance of a nervous system from which organic pulsations had fled. I was touched by his account of the aged Dr. Torres of Valencia, who had shared his earlier experiments and nursed him through the great illness of eighteen years before, whence his present disorders proceeded. No sooner had the venerable practitioner saved his colleague than he himself succumbed to the grim enemy he had fought. Perhaps the strain had been too great; for Dr. Muñoz made it whisperingly clear—though not in detail—that the methods of healing had been most extraordinary, involving scenes and processes not welcomed by elderly and conservative Galens.

As the weeks passed, I observed with regret that my new friend was indeed slowly but unmistakably losing ground physically, as Mrs. Herrero had suggested. The livid aspect of his countenance was intensified, his voice became more hollow and indistinct, his muscular motions were less perfectly coördinated, and his mind and will displayed less resilience and initiative. Of this sad change he seemed by no means unaware, and little by little his expression and conversation both took on a gruesome irony which restored in me something of the subtle repulsion I had originally felt.[b]

He developed strange caprices, acquiring a fondness for exotic spices and Egyptian incense till[c] his room smelled like the vault of a sepulchred Pharaoh in the Valley of Kings. At the same time[d] his demands for cold air increased, and with my aid he amplified the ammonia piping of his room and modified the pumps and feed of his refrigerating machine till he could keep the temperature as low as 34° or 40°,[e] and finally even 28°;[f] the bathroom and laboratory, of course, being less chilled, in order that water might not freeze, and that chemical processes might not be impeded. The tenant adjoining him

[a] mediaevalists,] medievalists, B
[b] I . . . felt.] *om.* B
[c] till] 'til C
[d] time] time, C
[e] 34° or 40°,] thirty-four or forty degrees, C
[f] 28°;] twenty-eight degrees; C

complained of the icy air from around the connecting door,[a] so I helped him fit heavy hangings to obviate the difficulty. A kind of growing horror, of outré and morbid cast, seemed to possess him. He talked of death incessantly, but laughed hollowly when such things as burial or funeral arrangements were gently suggested.

All in all, he became a disconcerting and even gruesome companion; yet in my gratitude for his healing[b] I could not well abandon him to the strangers around him, and was careful to dust his room and attend to his needs each day, muffled in a heavy ulster which I bought especially for the purpose. I likewise did much of his shopping, and gasped in bafflement at some of the chemicals he ordered from druggists and laboratory supply houses.

An increasing and unexplained atmosphere of panic seemed to rise around his apartment. The whole house, as I have said, had a musty odour;[c] but the smell in his room was worse—[d]and in spite of all the spices and incense, and the pungent chemicals of the now incessant baths which he insisted on taking unaided.[e] I perceived that it must be connected with his ailment, and shuddered when I reflected on what that ailment might be. Mrs. Herrero crossed herself when she looked at him, and gave him up unreservedly to me; not even letting her son Esteban continue to run errands for him. When I suggested other physicians, the sufferer would fly into as much of a rage as he seemed to dare to entertain. He evidently feared the physical effect of violent emotion, yet his will and driving force waxed rather than waned, and he refused to be confined to his bed. The lassitude of his earlier ill days gave place to a return of his fiery purpose, so that he seemed about to hurl defiance at the death-daemon[f] even as that ancient enemy seized him. The pretence of eating, always curiously like a formality with him, he virtually abandoned; and mental power alone appeared to keep him from total collapse.

[a] door,] door; C
[b] healing] healing, C
[c] odour;] odor; B
[d] worse—] worse, C
[e] unaided.] unaided, C
[f] death-daemon] death-demon B

He acquired a habit of writing long documents of some sort, which he carefully sealed and filled with injunctions that I transmit them after his death to certain persons whom he named—for the most part lettered East Indians, but including a once celebrated French physician now generally thought dead, and about whom the most inconceivable things had been whispered. As it happened, I burned all these papers undelivered and unopened. His aspect and voice became utterly frightful, and his presence almost unbearable. One September day an unexpected glimpse of him induced an epileptic fit in a man who had come to repair his electric desk lamp; a fit for which he prescribed effectively whilst keeping himself well out of sight. That man, oddly enough, had been through the terrors of the Great War [a] without having incurred any fright so thorough.

Then, in the middle of October, the horror of horrors came with stupefying suddenness. One night about eleven the pump of the refrigerating machine broke down, so that within three hours the process of ammonia cooling became impossible. Dr. Muñoz summoned me by thumping on the floor, and I worked desperately to repair the injury while my host cursed in a tone whose lifeless, rattling hollowness surpassed description. My amateur efforts, however, proved of no use; and when I had brought in a mechanic from a neighbouring all-night garage we learned that nothing could be done till[b] morning, when a new piston would have to be obtained. The moribund hermit's rage and fear, swelling to grotesque proportions, seemed likely to shatter what remained of his failing physique; and once a spasm caused him to clap his hands to his eyes and rush into the bathroom. He groped his way out with face tightly bandaged, and I never saw his eyes again.

The frigidity of the apartment was now sensibly diminishing, and at about 5 a.m.[c] the doctor retired to the bathroom, commanding me to keep him supplied with all the ice I could obtain at all-night drug stores and cafeterias. As I would return from my sometimes discouraging trips and lay my spoils before the closed bathroom door, I could hear a restless splashing within, and a thick voice croaking out the order for

[a] Great War] great war C
[b] till] until C
[c] 5 a.m.] 5 A.M. B; five in the morning, C

"More—more!" At length a warm day broke, and the shops opened one by one. I asked Esteban either to help with the ice-fetching whilst[a] I obtained the pump piston, or to order the piston while I continued with the ice; but[b] instructed by his mother, he absolutely refused.

Finally I hired a seedy-looking[c] loafer whom I encountered on the corner of Eighth Avenue to keep the patient supplied with ice from a little shop where I introduced him, and applied myself diligently to the task of finding a pump piston and engaging workmen competent to install[d] it. The task seemed interminable, and I raged almost as violently as the hermit when I saw the hours slipping by in a breathless, foodless round of vain telephoning, and a hectic quest from place to place, hither and thither by subway and surface car. About noon I encountered a suitable supply house far downtown, and at approximately 1:30 p.m.[e] arrived at my boarding-place with the necessary paraphernalia and two sturdy and intelligent mechanics. I had done all I could, and hoped I was in time.

Black terror, however, had preceded me. The house was in utter turmoil, and above the chatter of awed voices I heard a man praying in a deep basso. Fiendish things were in the air, and lodgers told over the beads of their rosaries as they caught the odour[f] from beneath the doctor's closed door. The lounger I had hired, it seems, had fled screaming and mad-eyed not long after his second delivery of ice;[g] perhaps as a result of excessive curiosity. He could not, of course, have locked the door behind him; yet it was now fastened, presumably from the inside. There was no sound within save a nameless sort of slow, thick dripping.

Briefly consulting with Mrs. Herrero and the workmen despite a fear that gnawed my inmost soul, I advised the breaking down of the door; but the landlady found a way to turn the key from the outside with some wire device. We had previously opened the doors of all the other

[a] whilst] while B, C
[b] but] but, C
[c] seedy-looking] seedy looking A, B
[d] install] instill B
[e] 1:30 p.m.] 1:30 P.M. B; one-thirty that afternoon C
[f] odour] odor B
[g] ice;] ice: C

rooms on that hall, and flung all the windows to the very top. Now, noses protected by handkerchiefs, we tremblingly invaded the accursed south room which blazed with the warm sun of early afternoon.

A kind of dark, slimy trail led from the open bathroom door to the hall door, and thence to the desk, where a terrible little pool had accumulated. Something was scrawled there in pencil in an awful, blind hand on a piece of paper hideously smeared as though by the very claws that traced the hurried last words. Then the trail led to the couch and ended unutterably.

What was, or had been, on the couch I cannot and dare not say here. But this is what I shiveringly puzzled out on the stickily smeared paper before I drew a match and burned it to a crisp; what I puzzled out in terror as the landlady and two mechanics rushed frantically from that hellish place to babble their incoherent stories at the nearest police station. The nauseous words seemed well-nigh incredible in that yellow sunlight, with the clatter of cars and motor trucks ascending clamorously from crowded Fourteenth Street, yet I confess that I believed them then. Whether I believe them now I honestly do not know. There are things about which it is better not to speculate, and all that I can say is that I hate the smell of ammonia, and grow faint at a draught of unusually cool air.[a]

"The end," ran that noisome scrawl, "is here. No more ice—the man looked and ran away. Warmer every minute, and the tissues can't last. I fancy you know—what I said about the will and the nerves and the preserved body after the organs ceased to work. It was good theory, but couldn't keep up indefinitely. There was a gradual deterioration I had not foreseen. Dr. Torres knew, but the shock killed him. He couldn't stand what he had to do—[b]he had to get me in a strange, dark place[c] when he minded my letter and nursed me back. And the organs never would work again. It had to be done my way—artificial preservation—*for you see I died that time eighteen years ago.*"

[a] and all . . . air.] and I sure hate the smell of ammonia. B
[b] do—] do; C
[c] place] place, C

The Call of Cthulhu

(Found Among the Papers of the Late
Francis Wayland Thurston, of Boston)[a]

"Of such great powers or beings there may be conceivably a survival
. . . a survival of a hugely remote period when . . . consciousness was
manifested, perhaps, in shapes and forms long since withdrawn before the
tide of advancing humanity . . . forms of which poetry and legend alone
have caught a flying memory and called them gods, monsters, mythical
beings of all sorts and kinds. . . ."[b]

—Algernon Blackwood.[c]

I.

THE HORROR IN CLAY.

The most merciful thing in the world, I think, is the inability of
the human mind to correlate all its contents. We live on a
placid island of ignorance in the midst of black seas of infinity,
and it was not meant that we should voyage far. The sciences, each
straining in its own direction, have hitherto harmed us little; but some

Editor's Note: The surviving T.Ms. is by HPL. It was not followed very accurately by
Weird Tales (February 1928), as a number of paragraphing changes and other
alterations were made. Regrettably, the Arkham House editions followed *Weird
Tales.* Arkham House would have been better off following the reprint of the story
in T. Everett Harré's *Beware After Dark!* (1929), as HPL had supplied the editor with
a carbon of the T.Ms. The readings from this appearance are recorded here, even
though they are not strictly speaking relevant to the textual history of the tale.
  Texts: A = T.Ms. (JHL); B = *Weird Tales* 11, No. 2 (February 1928): 157–78,
287; C = T. Everett Harré, ed., *Beware After Dark!* (New York: Macauley, 1929), 223–
59; D = *The Dunwich Horror and Others* (Arkham House, 1963), 130–59. Copy-text: A.

[a] (Found . . . Boston)] Found . . . Boston. B [*as footnote*]; (Found . . . Boston.) C [*as
footnote*]; *om.* D
[b] "Of . . . kinds. . . ."] *om.* C; *Of . . . kinds* . . . D
[c] *—Algernon Blackwood.*] *om.* C; —ALGERNON BLACKWOOD D

day the piecing together of dissociated knowledge will open up such terrifying vistas of reality, and of our frightful position therein, that we shall either go mad from the revelation or flee from the deadly light into the peace and safety of a new dark age.

Theosophists have guessed at the awesome grandeur of the cosmic cycle wherein our world and human race form transient incidents. They have hinted at strange survivals in terms which would freeze the blood if not masked by a bland optimism. But it is not from them that there came the single glimpse of forbidden aeons[a] which chills me when I think of it and maddens me when I dream of it. That glimpse, like all dread glimpses of truth, flashed out from an accidental piecing together of separated things—in this case an old newspaper item and the notes of a dead professor. I hope that no one else will accomplish this piecing out; certainly, if I live, I shall never knowingly supply a link in so hideous a chain. I think that the professor, too, intended to keep silent regarding the part he knew, and that he would have destroyed his notes had not sudden death seized him.

My knowledge of the thing began in the winter of 1926–27 with the death of my grand-uncle[b] George Gammell Angell, Professor Emeritus of Semitic Languages[c] in Brown University, Providence, Rhode Island. Professor Angell was widely known as an authority on ancient inscriptions, and had frequently been resorted to by the heads of prominent museums; so that his passing at the age of ninety-two may be recalled by many. Locally, interest was intensified by the obscurity of the cause of death. The professor had been stricken whilst returning from the Newport boat; falling suddenly, as witnesses said, after having been jostled by a nautical-looking negro who had come from one of the queer dark courts on the precipitous hillside which formed a short cut from the waterfront to the deceased's home in Williams Street. Physicians were unable to find any visible disorder, but concluded after perplexed debate that some obscure lesion of the heart, induced by the brisk ascent of so steep a hill by so elderly a man, was responsible for the end. At the time I saw no reason to dissent from this dictum, but latterly I am inclined to wonder—and more than wonder.

[a] aeons] eons B, D
[b] grand-uncle] grand-uncle, B, C; granduncle, D
[c] Languages] languages B

As my grand-uncle's[a] heir and executor, for he died a childless widower, I was expected to go over his papers with some thoroughness; and for that purpose moved his entire set of files and boxes to my quarters in Boston. Much of the material which I correlated will be later published by the American Archaeological[b] Society, but there was one box which I found exceedingly puzzling, and which I felt much averse from shewing[c] to other eyes. It had been locked, and I did not find the key till it occurred to me to examine the personal ring which the professor carried always in his pocket. Then indeed[d] I succeeded in opening it, but when I did so seemed only to be confronted by a greater and more closely locked barrier. For what could be the meaning of the queer clay bas-relief and the disjointed jottings, ramblings, and cuttings which I found? Had my uncle, in his latter years, become credulous of the most superficial impostures? I resolved to search out the eccentric sculptor responsible for this apparent disturbance of an old man's peace of mind.

The bas-relief was a rough rectangle less than an inch thick and about five by six inches in area; obviously of modern origin. Its designs, however, were far from modern in atmosphere and suggestion; for[e] although the vagaries of cubism and futurism are many and wild, they do not often reproduce that cryptic regularity which lurks in prehistoric writing. And writing of some kind the bulk of these designs seemed certainly to be; though my memory, despite much familiarity with the papers and collections of my uncle, failed in any way to identify this particular species, or even to[f] hint at its remotest affiliations.

Above these apparent hieroglyphics was a figure of evidently pictorial intent, though its impressionistic execution forbade a very clear idea of its nature. It seemed to be a sort of monster, or symbol representing a monster, of a form which only a diseased fancy could conceive. If I say that my somewhat extravagant imagination yielded simultaneous pictures of an octopus, a dragon, and a human caricature,

[a] grand-uncle's] granduncle's B, D
[b] Archaeological] Archeological B
[c] shewing] showing A, B, C, D
[d] Then indeed] Then, indeed, B, C, D
[e] for] for, B, D
[f] to] *om.* B, D

I shall not be unfaithful to the spirit of the thing. A pulpy, tentacled head surmounted a grotesque and scaly body with rudimentary wings; but it was the *general outline* of the whole which made it most shockingly frightful. Behind the figure was a vague suggestion of a Cyclopean architectural background.

The writing accompanying this oddity was, aside from a stack of press cuttings, in Professor Angell's most recent hand; and made no pretence[a] to literary style. What seemed to be the main document was headed "CTHULHU CULT"[b] in characters painstakingly printed to avoid the erroneous reading of a word so unheard-of. The manuscript was divided into two sections, the first of which was headed "1925—Dream and Dream Work of H. A. Wilcox, 7 Thomas St., Providence, R.I.",[c] and the second, "Narrative of Inspector John R. Legrasse, 121 Bienville St., New Orleans, La.,[d] at 1908 A. A. S. Mtg.—Notes on Same, & Prof. Webb's Acct." The other manuscript papers were all brief notes, some of them accounts of the queer dreams of different persons, some of them citations from theosophical books and magazines (notably W. Scott-Elliot's[e] "Atlantis and the Lost Lemuria"[f]),[g] and the rest comments on long-surviving secret societies and hidden cults, with references to passages in such mythological and anthropological source-books as Frazer's "Golden Bough"[h] and Miss Murray's "Witch-Cult in Western Europe".[i] The cuttings largely alluded to outré mental illnesses[j] and outbreaks of group folly or mania in the spring of 1925.

The first half of the principal manuscript told a very peculiar tale. It appears that on March 1st, 1925, a thin, dark young man of neurotic and excited aspect had called upon Professor Angell bearing the singular clay bas-relief, which was then exceedingly damp and fresh.

---

[a] pretence] pretense B, C, D

[b] "CTHULHU CULT"] *"CTHULHU CULT"* B

[c] I.",] I.," B, C, D

[d] La.,] La. A, C

[e] Scott-Elliot's] Scott-Eliott's A, B, C; Scott-Elliott's D

[f] "Atlantis . . . Lemuria"] *Atlantis . . . Lemuria* A, B, C, D

[g] magazines (. . .),] magazines, (. . .) A

[h] "Golden Bough"] *Golden Bough* A, B, C, D

[i] "Witch-Cult . . . Europe".] *Witch-Cult . . . Europe.* A, B, C, D

[j] illnesses] illness D

His card bore the name of Henry Anthony Wilcox, and my uncle had recognised[a] him as the youngest son of an excellent family slightly known to him, who had latterly been studying sculpture at the Rhode Island School of Design and living alone at the Fleur-de-Lys Building near that institution. Wilcox was a precocious youth of known genius but great eccentricity, and had from childhood excited attention through the strange stories and odd dreams he was in the habit of relating. He called himself "psychically hypersensitive",[b] but the staid folk of the ancient commercial city dismissed him as merely "queer".[c] Never mingling much with his kind, he had dropped gradually from social visibility, and was now known only to a small group of aesthetes[d] from other towns. Even the Providence Art Club, anxious to preserve its conservatism, had found him quite hopeless.

On the occasion of the visit, ran the professor's manuscript, the sculptor abruptly asked for the benefit of his host's archaeological[e] knowledge in identifying the hieroglyphics on the bas-relief. He spoke in a dreamy, stilted manner which suggested pose and alienated sympathy; and my uncle shewed[f] some sharpness in replying, for the conspicuous freshness of the tablet implied kinship with anything but archaeology.[g] Young Wilcox's rejoinder, which impressed my uncle enough to make him recall and record it verbatim, was of a fantastically poetic cast which must have typified his whole conversation, and which I have since found highly characteristic of him. He said, "It is new, indeed, for I made it last night in a dream of strange cities; and dreams are older than brooding Tyre, or the contemplative Sphinx, or garden-girdled Babylon."

It was then that he began that rambling tale which suddenly played upon a sleeping memory and won the fevered interest of my uncle. There had been a slight earthquake tremor the night before, the most considerable felt in New England for some years; and Wilcox's

[a] recognised] recognized B, C, D
[b] hypersensitive",] hypersensitive," C, D
[c] queer".] queer." C, D
[d] aesthetes] esthetes B, D
[e] archaeological] archeological B, D
[f] shewed] showed A, B, C, D
[g] archaeology.] archeology. B, D

imagination had been keenly affected. Upon retiring, he had had an unprecedented dream of great Cyclopean cities of titan[a] blocks and sky-flung monoliths, all dripping with green ooze and sinister with latent horror. Hieroglyphics had covered the walls and pillars, and from some undetermined point below had come a voice that was not a voice; a chaotic sensation which only fancy could transmute into sound, but which he attempted to render by the almost unpronounceable jumble of letters, *"Cthulhu fhtagn"*.[b]

This verbal jumble was the key to the recollection which excited and disturbed Professor Angell. He questioned the sculptor with scientific minuteness; and studied with almost frantic intensity the bas-relief on which the youth had found himself working, chilled and clad only in his night-clothes,[c] when waking had stolen bewilderingly over him. My uncle blamed his old age, Wilcox afterward said, for his slowness in recognising[d] both hieroglyphics and pictorial design. Many of his questions seemed highly out-of-place[e] to his visitor, especially those which tried to connect the latter with strange cults or societies; and Wilcox could not understand the repeated promises of silence which he was offered in exchange for an admission of membership in some widespread mystical or paganly religious body. When Professor Angell became convinced that the sculptor was indeed ignorant of any cult or system of cryptic lore, he besieged his visitor with demands for future reports of dreams. This bore regular fruit, for after the first interview the manuscript records daily calls of the young man, during which he related startling fragments of nocturnal imagery whose burden was always some terrible Cyclopean vista of dark and dripping stone, with a subterrene voice or intelligence shouting monotonously in enigmatical sense-impacts uninscribable save as gibberish. The two sounds most frequently repeated are those rendered by the letters *"Cthulhu"* and *"R'lyeh"*.[f]

On March 23d,[g] the manuscript continued, Wilcox failed to appear;

---

[a] titan] Titan A, B, C, D

[b] *fhtagn".] fhtagn."* C, D

[c] night-clothes,] night-/clothes, A; nightclothes, B, C, D

[d] recognising] recognizing B, C, D

[e] out-of-place] out of place B, D

[f] *"R'lyeh".] "R'lyeh."* C, D

[g] 23d,] 23rd, B; 23, D

and inquiries at his quarters revealed that he had been stricken with an obscure sort of fever and taken to the home of his family in Waterman Street. He had cried out in the night, arousing several other artists in the building, and had manifested since then only alternations of unconsciousness and delirium. My uncle at once telephoned the family, and from that time forward kept close watch of the case; calling often at the Thayer Street office of Dr. Tobey, whom he learned to be in charge. The youth's febrile mind, apparently, was dwelling on strange things; and the doctor shuddered now and then as he spoke of them. They included not only a repetition of what he had formerly dreamed, but touched wildly on a gigantic thing "miles high" which walked or lumbered about. He at no time fully described this object,[a] but occasional frantic words, as repeated by Dr. Tobey, convinced the professor that it must be identical with the nameless monstrosity he had sought to depict in his dream-sculpture. Reference to this object, the doctor added, was invariably a prelude to the young man's subsidence into lethargy. His temperature, oddly enough, was not greatly above normal; but his[b] whole condition was otherwise such as to suggest true fever rather than mental disorder.

On April 2nd[c] at about 3 p.m.[d] every trace of Wilcox's malady suddenly ceased. He sat upright in bed, astonished to find himself at home and completely ignorant of what had happened in dream or reality since the night of March 22nd.[e] Pronounced well by his physician, he returned to his quarters in three days; but to Professor Angell he was of no further assistance. All traces of strange dreaming had vanished with his recovery, and my uncle kept no record of his night-thoughts after a week of pointless and irrelevant accounts of thoroughly usual visions.

Here the first part of the manuscript ended, but references to certain of the scattered notes gave me much material for thought—so much, in fact, that only the ingrained scepticism[f] then forming my

[a] object,] object D
[b] his] the B, C, D [his *typed over* the *in A*]
[c] 2nd] 2 D
[d] p.m.] p. m. B, C; P.M. D
[e] 22nd.] 22. D
[f] scepticism] skepticism B, C, D

philosophy can account for my continued distrust of the artist. The notes in question were those descriptive of the dreams of various persons covering the same period as that in which young Wilcox had had his strange visitations. My uncle, it seems, had quickly instituted a prodigiously far-flung body of inquiries amongst nearly all the friends whom he could question without impertinence, asking for nightly reports of their dreams, and the dates of any notable visions for some time past. The reception of his request seems to have been varied; but he must, at the very least, have received more responses than any ordinary man could have handled without a secretary. This original correspondence was not preserved, but his notes formed a thorough and really significant digest. Average people in society and business— New England's traditional "salt of the earth"—gave an almost completely negative result, though scattered cases of uneasy but formless nocturnal impressions appear here and there, always between March 23d and April 2nd[a]—the period of young Wilcox's delirium. Scientific men were little more affected, though four cases of vague description suggest fugitive glimpses of strange landscapes, and in one case there is mentioned a dread of something abnormal.

It was from the artists and poets that the pertinent answers came, and I know that panic would have broken loose had they been able to compare notes. As it was, lacking their original letters, I half suspected the compiler of having asked leading questions, or of having edited the correspondence in corroboration of what he had latently resolved to see. That is why I continued to feel that Wilcox, somehow cognisant[b] of the old data which my uncle had possessed, had been imposing on the veteran scientist. These responses from aesthetes[c] told a disturbing tale. From February 28th to April 2nd[d] a large proportion of them had dreamed very bizarre things, the intensity of the dreams being immeasurably the stronger during the period of the sculptor's delirium. Over a fourth of those who reported anything, reported scenes and half-sounds not unlike those which Wilcox had described; and some of

[a] 23d . . . 2nd] 23d . . . 2d. A; 23rd . . . 2nd. B; 23 . . . 2 D
[b] cognisant] cognizant B, C, D
[c] aesthetes] esthetes B, D
[d] 28th . . . 2nd] 28 . . . 2 D

the dreamers confessed acute fear of the gigantic nameless thing visible toward the last. One case, which the note describes with emphasis, was very sad. The subject, a widely known architect with leanings toward theosophy and occultism, went violently insane on the date of young Wilcox's seizure, and expired several months later after incessant screamings to be saved from some escaped denizen of hell. Had my uncle referred to these cases by name instead of merely by number, I should have attempted some corroboration and personal investigation; but as it was, I succeeded in tracing down only a few. All of these, however, bore out the notes in full. I have often wondered if all the objects of the professor's questioning felt as puzzled as did this fraction. It is well that no explanation shall ever reach them.

The press cuttings, as I have intimated, touched on cases of panic, mania, and eccentricity during the given period. Professor Angell must have employed a cutting bureau, for the number of extracts was tremendous[a] and the sources scattered throughout the globe. Here was a nocturnal suicide in London, where a lone sleeper had leaped from a window after a shocking cry. Here likewise a rambling letter to the editor of a paper in South America, where a fanatic deduces a dire future from visions he has seen. A despatch[b] from California describes a theosophist colony as donning white robes en masse for some "glorious fulfilment" which never arrives, whilst items from India speak guardedly of serious native unrest toward the end of March. Voodoo orgies multiply in Hayti,[c] and African outposts report ominous mutterings. American officers in the Philippines find certain tribes bothersome about this time, and New York policemen are mobbed by hysterical Levantines on the night of March 22–23. The west of Ireland, too, is full of wild rumour[d] and legendry, and a fantastic painter named Ardois-Bonnot hangs a blasphemous "Dream Landscape"[e] in the Paris spring salon of 1926. And so numerous are the recorded troubles in insane asylums,[f] that only a miracle can have stopped the

[a] tremendous] tremendous, B, D
[b] despatch] dispatch B, D
[c] Hayti,] Haiti, B, D
[d] rumour] rumor B, D
[e] "Dream Landscape"] *Dream Landscape* B, D
[f] asylums,] asylums B, D

medical fraternity from noting strange parallelisms and drawing mystified conclusions. A weird bunch of cuttings, all told; and I can at this date scarcely envisage the callous rationalism with which I set them aside. But I was then convinced that young Wilcox had known of the older matters mentioned by the professor.

II.
THE TALE OF INSPECTOR LEGRASSE.

The older matters which had made the sculptor's dream and bas-relief so significant to my uncle formed the subject of the second half of his long manuscript. Once before, it appears, Professor Angell had seen the hellish outlines of the nameless monstrosity, puzzled over the unknown hieroglyphics, and heard the ominous syllables which can be rendered only as "*Cthulhu*"; and all this in so stirring and horrible a connexion[a] that it is small wonder he pursued young Wilcox with queries and demands for data.

The earlier experience had come in 1908, seventeen years before, when the American Archaeological Society held its annual meeting in St. Louis. Professor Angell, as befitted one of his authority and attainments, had had a prominent part in all the deliberations; and was one of the first to be approached by the several outsiders who took advantage of the convocation to offer questions for correct answering and problems for expert solution.

The chief of these outsiders, and in a short time the focus of interest for the entire meeting, was a commonplace-looking middle-aged man who had travelled[b] all the way from New Orleans for certain special information unobtainable from any local source. His name was John Raymond Legrasse, and he was by profession an Inspector of Police.[c] With him he bore the subject of his visit, a grotesque, repulsive, and apparently very ancient stone statuette whose origin he was at a loss to determine.[d] It must not be fancied that Inspector Legrasse had the least

---

[a] connexion] connection B, C, D
[b] travelled] traveled B, D
[c] Inspector of Police.] inspector of police. B, D
[d] determine.] determine. ¶ B, D

interest in archaeology.[a] On the contrary, his wish for enlightenment was prompted by purely professional considerations. The statuette, idol, fetish, or whatever it was, had been captured some months before in the wooded swamps south of New Orleans during a raid on a supposed voodoo meeting; and so singular and hideous were the rites connected with it, that the police could not but realise[b] that they had stumbled on a dark cult totally unknown to them, and infinitely more diabolic than even the blackest of the African voodoo circles. Of its origin, apart from the erratic and unbelievable tales extorted from the captured members, absolutely nothing was to be discovered; hence the anxiety of the police for any antiquarian lore which might help them to place the frightful symbol, and through it track down the cult to its fountain-head.

Inspector Legrasse was scarcely prepared for the sensation which his offering created. One sight of the thing had been enough to throw the assembled men of science into a state of tense excitement, and they lost no time in crowding around him to gaze at the diminutive figure whose utter strangeness and air of genuinely abysmal antiquity hinted so potently at unopened and archaic vistas. No recognised[c] school of sculpture had animated this terrible object, yet centuries and even thousands of years seemed recorded in its dim and greenish surface of unplaceable stone.

The figure, which was finally passed slowly from man to man for close and careful study, was between seven and eight inches in height, and of exquisitely artistic workmanship. It represented a monster of vaguely anthropoid outline, but with an octopus-like[d] head whose face was a mass of feelers, a scaly, rubbery-looking body, prodigious claws on hind and fore feet, and long, narrow wings behind. This thing, which seemed instinct with a fearsome and unnatural malignancy, was of a somewhat bloated corpulence, and squatted evilly on a rectangular block or pedestal covered with undecipherable characters. The tips of the wings touched the back edge of the block, the seat occupied the centre,[e] whilst the long, curved claws of the doubled-up, crouching hind legs gripped the front edge and extended a quarter of the way down toward the bottom

[a] archaeology.] archeology. B, D
[b] realise] realize B, C, D
[c] recognised] recognized B, C, D
[d] octopus-like] octopuslike B, D
[e] centre,] center, B, C, D

of the pedestal. The cephalopod head was bent forward, so that the ends of the facial feelers brushed the backs of huge fore-paws[a] which clasped the croucher's elevated knees. The aspect of the whole was abnormally lifelike, and the more subtly fearful because its source was so totally unknown. Its vast, awesome, and incalculable age was unmistakable; yet not one link did it shew[b] with any known type of art belonging to civilisation's[c] youth—or indeed to any other time.[d] Totally separate and apart, its very material was a mystery; for the soapy, greenish-black stone with its golden or iridescent flecks and striations resembled nothing familiar to geology or mineralogy. The characters along the base were equally baffling; and no member present, despite a representation of half the world's expert learning in this field, could form the least notion of even their remotest linguistic kinship. They, like the subject and material, belonged to something horribly remote and distinct from mankind as we know it; something frightfully suggestive of old and unhallowed cycles of life in which our world and our conceptions have no part.

And yet, as the members severally shook their heads and confessed defeat at the Inspector's[e] problem, there was one man in that gathering who suspected a touch of bizarre familiarity in the monstrous shape and writing, and who presently told with some diffidence of the odd trifle he knew. This person was the late William Channing Webb, Professor of Anthropology[f] in Princeton University, and an explorer of no slight note.[g] Professor Webb had been engaged, forty-eight years before, in a tour of Greenland and Iceland in search of some Runic inscriptions which he failed to unearth; and whilst high up on the West Greenland coast had encountered a singular tribe or cult of degenerate Esquimaux[h] whose religion, a curious form of devil-worship, chilled him with its deliberate bloodthirstiness and repulsiveness. It was a faith of which

[a] fore-paws] forepaws B; fore-/paws D
[b] shew] show A, B, C, D
[c] civilisation's] civilization's B, C, D
[d] time.] time. ¶ B, D
[e] Inspector's] inspector's B, D
[f] Professor of Anthropology] professor of anthropology B, D
[g] note.] note. ¶ B, D
[h] Esquimaux] Eskimos B, D

other Esquimaux[a] knew little, and which they mentioned only with shudders, saying that it had come down from horribly ancient aeons[b] before ever the world was made. Besides nameless rites and human sacrifices there were certain queer hereditary rituals addressed to a supreme elder devil or *tornasuk;* and of this Professor Webb had taken a careful phonetic copy from an aged *angekok* or wizard-priest, expressing the sounds in Roman letters as best he knew how. But just now of prime significance was the fetish which this cult had cherished, and around which they danced when the aurora leaped high over the ice cliffs. It was, the professor stated, a very crude bas-relief of stone, comprising a hideous picture and some cryptic writing. And so[c] far as he could tell, it was a rough parallel in all essential features of the bestial thing now lying before the meeting.

This data,[d] received with suspense and astonishment by the assembled members, proved doubly exciting to Inspector Legrasse; and he began at once to ply his informant with questions. Having noted and copied an oral ritual among the swamp cult-worshippers[e] his men had arrested, he besought the professor to remember as best he might the syllables taken down amongst the diabolist Esquimaux.[f] There then followed an exhaustive comparison of details, and a moment of really awed silence when both detective and scientist agreed on the virtual identity of the phrase common to two hellish rituals so many worlds of distance apart. What, in substance, both the Esquimau[g] wizards and the Louisiana swamp-priests had chanted to their kindred idols was something very like this—the word-divisions being guessed at from traditional breaks in the phrase as chanted aloud:

"Ph'nglui mglw'nafh Cthulhu R'lyeh wgah'nagl fhtagn."

Legrasse[h] had one point in advance of Professor Webb, for several among his mongrel prisoners had repeated to him what older celebrants

---

[a] Esquimaux] Eskimos B, D
[b] aeons] eons B, D
[c] so] as B, D
[d] This data,] These data, B, D
[e] cult-worshippers] cult-worshipers B, C, D
[f] Esquimaux.] Eskimos. B, D
[g] Esquimau] Eskimo B, D
[h] Legrasse] ¶ Legrasse B, C, D

had told them the words meant. This text, as given, ran something like this:

"In his house at R'lyeh dead Cthulhu waits dreaming."[a]

And now, in response to a general and[b] urgent demand, Inspector Legrasse related as fully as possible his experience with the swamp worshippers;[c] telling a story to which I could see my uncle attached profound significance. It savoured[d] of the wildest dreams of myth-maker and theosophist, and disclosed an astonishing degree of cosmic imagination among such half-castes and pariahs as might be least expected to possess it.

On November 1st,[e] 1907, there had come to the[f] New Orleans police a frantic summons from the swamp and lagoon country to the south. The squatters there, mostly primitive but good-natured descendants of Lafitte's men, were in the grip of stark terror from an unknown thing which had stolen upon them in the night. It was voodoo, apparently, but voodoo of a more terrible sort than they had ever known; and some of their women and children had disappeared since the malevolent tom-tom had begun its incessant beating far within the black haunted woods where no dweller ventured. There were insane shouts and harrowing screams, soul-chilling chants and dancing devil-flames; and, the frightened messenger added, the people could stand it no more.

So a body of twenty police, filling two carriages and an automobile, had set out in the late afternoon with the shivering squatter as a guide. At the end of the passable road they alighted, and for miles splashed on in silence through the terrible cypress woods where day never came. Ugly roots and malignant hanging nooses of Spanish moss beset them, and now and then a pile of dank stones or fragment[g] of a rotting wall intensified by its hint of morbid habitation a depression which every malformed tree and every fungous islet combined to create. At length the squatter settlement, a miserable huddle of huts, hove in sight;

[a] *"In . . . dreaming."*] "In . . . dreaming." B, D

[b] and] *om.* B, D

[c] worshippers;] worshipers; B, C, D

[d] savoured] savored B, C, D

[e] 1st,] 1, D

[f] the] *om.* B, D

[g] fragment] fragments B, D

and hysterical dwellers ran out to cluster around the group of bobbing lanterns. The muffled beat of tom-toms was now faintly audible far, far ahead; and a curdling shriek came at infrequent intervals when the wind shifted. A reddish glare, too, seemed to filter through the pale undergrowth beyond endless avenues of forest night. Reluctant even to be left alone again, each one of the cowed squatters refused point-blank to advance another inch toward the scene of unholy worship, so Inspector Legrasse and his nineteen colleagues plunged on unguided into black arcades of horror that none of them had ever trod before.

The region now entered by the police was one of traditionally evil repute, substantially unknown and untraversed by white men. There were legends of a hidden lake unglimpsed by mortal sight, in which dwelt a huge, formless white polypous thing with luminous eyes; and squatters whispered that bat-winged devils flew up out of caverns in inner earth to worship it at midnight. They said it had been there before D'Iberville, before La Salle, before the Indians, and before even the wholesome beasts and birds of the woods. It was nightmare itself, and to see it was to die. But it made men dream, and so they knew enough to keep away. The present voodoo orgy was, indeed, on the merest fringe of this abhorred area, but that location was bad enough; hence perhaps the very place of the worship had terrified the squatters more than the shocking sounds and incidents.

Only poetry or madness could do justice to the noises heard by Legrasse's men as they ploughed[a] on through the black morass toward the red glare and the muffled tom-toms. There are vocal qualities peculiar to men, and vocal qualities peculiar to beasts; and it is terrible to hear the one when the source should yield the other. Animal fury and orgiastic licence[b] here whipped themselves to daemoniac[c] heights by howls and squawking ecstasies that tore and reverberated through those nighted woods like pestilential tempests from the gulfs of hell. Now and then the less organised ululation[d] would cease, and from

---

[a] ploughed] plowed B, C, D
[b] licence] license B, C, D
[c] daemoniac] demoniac B, D
[d] organised ululation] organized ululations B, D; organized ululation C

what seemed a well-drilled chorus of hoarse voices would rise in sing-song[a] chant that hideous phrase or ritual:

"Ph'nglui mglw'nafh Cthulhu R'lyeh wgah'nagl fhtagn."

Then[b] the men, having reached a spot where the trees were thinner, came suddenly in sight of the spectacle itself. Four of them reeled, one fainted, and two were shaken into a frantic cry which the mad cacophony of the orgy fortunately deadened. Legrasse dashed swamp water on the face of the fainting man, and all stood trembling and nearly hypnotised[c] with horror.

In a natural glade of the swamp stood a grassy island of perhaps an acre's extent, clear of trees and tolerably dry. On this now leaped and twisted a more indescribable horde of human abnormality than any but a Sime or an Angarola could paint. Void of clothing, this hybrid spawn were braying, bellowing,[d] and writhing about a monstrous ring-shaped[e] bonfire; in the centre[f] of which, revealed by occasional rifts in the curtain of flame, stood a great granite monolith some eight feet in height; on top of which, incongruous with its diminutiveness, rested the noxious carven statuette. From a wide circle of ten scaffolds set up at regular intervals with the flame-girt monolith as a centre[g] hung, head downward, the oddly marred bodies of the helpless squatters who had disappeared. It was inside this circle that the ring of worshippers[h] jumped and roared, the general direction of the mass motion being from left to right in endless Bacchanale[i] between the ring of bodies and the ring of fire.

It may have been only imagination and it may have been only echoes which induced one of the men, an excitable Spaniard, to fancy he heard antiphonal responses to the ritual from some far and unillumined spot deeper within the wood of ancient legendry and horror. This man, Joseph D. Galvez, I later met and questioned; and

[a] sing-song] singsong B, D
[b] Then] ¶ Then B, C, D
[c] hypnotised] hypnotized B, C, D
[d] bellowing,] bellowing A, B, C, D
[e] ring-shaped] ring-/shaped B; ringshaped D
[f] centre] center B, C, D
[g] centre] center B, C, D
[h] worshippers] worshipers B, C, D
[i] Bacchanale] bacchanale B, D

he proved distractingly imaginative. He indeed went so far as to hint of the faint beating of great wings, and of a glimpse of shining eyes and a[a] mountainous white bulk beyond the remotest trees—but I suppose he had been hearing too much native superstition.

Actually, the horrified pause of the men was of comparatively brief duration. Duty came first; and although there must have been nearly a hundred mongrel celebrants in the throng, the police relied on their firearms and plunged determinedly into the nauseous rout. For five minutes the resultant din and chaos were beyond description. Wild blows were struck, shots were fired, and escapes were made; but in the end Legrasse was able to count some forty-seven sullen prisoners, whom he forced to dress in haste and fall into line between two rows of policemen. Five of the worshippers[b] lay dead, and two severely wounded ones were carried away on improvised stretchers by their fellow-prisoners. The image on the monolith, of course, was carefully removed and carried back by Legrasse.

Examined at headquarters after a trip of intense strain and weariness, the prisoners all proved to be men of a very low, mixed-blooded, and mentally aberrant type. Most were seamen, and a sprinkling of negroes and mulattoes, largely West Indians or Brava Portuguese[c] from the Cape Verde Islands, gave a colouring[d] of voodooism to the heterogeneous cult. But before many questions were asked, it became manifest that something far deeper and older than negro fetichism[e] was involved. Degraded and ignorant as they were, the creatures held with surprising[f] consistency to the central idea of their loathsome faith.

They worshipped,[g] so they said, the Great Old Ones who lived ages before there were any men, and who came to the young world out of the sky. Those[h] Old Ones were gone now, inside the earth and under the sea; but their dead bodies had told their secrets in dreams to

---

[a] a] *om.* D
[b] worshippers] worshipers B, C, D
[c] Portuguese] Portugese A
[d] colouring] coloring B, C, D
[e] fetichism] fetishism B, D
[f] surprising] surprizing B
[g] worshipped,] worshiped, B, C, D
[h] Those] These D

the first men,[a] who formed a cult which had never died. This was that cult, and the prisoners said it had always existed and always would exist, hidden in distant wastes and dark places all over the world until the time when the great priest Cthulhu, from his dark house in the mighty city of R'lyeh under the waters, should rise and bring the earth again beneath his sway. Some day he would call, when the stars were ready, and the secret cult would always be waiting to liberate him.

Meanwhile no more must be told. There was a secret which even torture could not extract. Mankind was not absolutely alone among the conscious things of earth, for shapes came out of the dark to visit the faithful few. But these were not the Great Old Ones. No man had ever seen the Old Ones. The carven idol was great Cthulhu, but none might say whether or not the others were precisely like him. No one could read the old writing now, but things were told by word of mouth. The chanted ritual was not the secret—that was never spoken aloud, only whispered. The chant meant only this: "In his house at R'lyeh dead Cthulhu waits dreaming."

Only two of the prisoners were found sane enough to be hanged, and the rest were committed to various institutions. All denied a part in the ritual murders, and averred that the killing had been done by Black Winged[b] Ones which had come to them from their immemorial meeting-place in the haunted wood. But of those mysterious allies no coherent account could ever be gained. What the police did extract,[c] came mainly from an immensely aged mestizo named Castro, who claimed to have sailed to strange ports and talked with undying leaders of the cult in the mountains of China.

Old Castro remembered bits of hideous legend that paled the speculations of theosophists and made man and the world seem recent and transient indeed. There had been aeons[d] when other Things ruled on the earth, and They had had great cities. Remains of Them, he said the deathless Chinamen[e] had told him, were still to be found as

---

[a] men,] man, B, D
[b] Black Winged] Black-winged B, D
[c] extract,] extract B, C, D
[d] aeons] eons B, D
[e] Chinamen] Chinaman A

Cyclopean stones on islands in the Pacific. They all died vast epochs of time before men[a] came, but there were arts which could revive Them when the stars had come round again to the right positions in the cycle of eternity. They had, indeed, come themselves from the stars, and brought Their images with Them.

These Great Old Ones, Castro continued, were not composed altogether of flesh and blood. They had shape—for did not this star-fashioned image prove it?—but that shape was not made of matter. When the stars were right, They could plunge from world to world through the sky; but when the stars were wrong, They could not live. But although They no longer lived, They would never really die. They all lay in stone houses in Their great city of R'lyeh, preserved by the spells of mighty Cthulhu for a glorious resurrection when the stars and the earth might once more be ready for Them. But at that time some force from outside must serve to liberate Their bodies. The spells that preserved Them intact likewise prevented Them from making an initial move, and They could only lie awake in the dark and think whilst uncounted millions of years rolled by. They knew all that was occurring in the universe, but Their mode of speech was transmitted thought. Even now They talked in Their tombs. When, after infinities of chaos, the first men came, the Great Old Ones spoke to the sensitive among them by moulding[b] their dreams; for only thus could Their language reach the fleshly[c] minds of mammals.

Then, whispered Castro, those first men formed the cult around small idols which the Great Ones shewed[d] them; idols brought in dim aeras[e] from dark stars. That cult would never die till the stars came right again, and the secret priests would take great Cthulhu from His tomb to revive His subjects and resume His rule of earth. The time would be easy to know, for then mankind would have become as the Great Old Ones; free and wild and beyond good and evil, with laws and morals thrown aside and all men shouting and killing and revelling[f]

[a] men] man B, D
[b] moulding] molding B, C, D
[c] fleshly] fleshy D
[d] shewed] showed A, B, C, D
[e] aeras] eras B, C, D
[f] revelling] reveling B, C, D

in joy. Then the liberated Old Ones would teach them new ways to shout and kill and revel and enjoy themselves, and all the earth would flame with a holocaust of ecstasy and freedom. Meanwhile the cult, by appropriate rites, must keep alive the memory of those ancient ways and shadow forth the prophecy of their return.

In the elder time chosen men had talked with the entombed Old Ones in dreams, but then something had happened. The great stone city R'lyeh, with its monoliths and sepulchres,[a] had sunk beneath the waves; and the deep waters, full of the one primal mystery through which not even thought can pass, had cut off the spectral intercourse. But memory never died, and high-priests[b] said that the city would rise again when the stars were right. Then came out of the earth the black spirits of earth, mouldy[c] and shadowy, and full of dim rumours[d] picked up in caverns beneath forgotten sea-bottoms. But of them old Castro dared not speak much. He cut himself off hurriedly, and no amount of persuasion or subtlety could elicit more in this direction. The *size* of the Old Ones, too, he curiously declined to mention. Of the cult, he said that he thought the centre[e] lay amid the pathless deserts of Arabia, where Irem, the City of Pillars, dreams hidden and untouched. It was not allied to the European witch-cult, and was virtually unknown beyond its members. No book had ever really hinted of it, though the deathless Chinamen[f] said that there were double meanings in the "Necronomicon"[g] of the mad Arab Abdul Alhazred which the initiated might read as they chose, especially the much-discussed couplet:

"That is not dead which can eternal lie,
 And with strange aeons[h] even death may die."[i]

[a] sepulchres,] sepulchers, B, C, D
[b] high-priests] high priests A, B, C, D
[c] mouldy] moldy B, D
[d] rumours] rumors B, C, D
[e] centre] center B, C, D
[f] Chinamen] Chinaman A
[g] "Necronomicon"] Necronomicon A, C; *Necronomicon* B, D
[h] aeons] eons B, D
[i] "That . . . die."] That . . . die. D

Legrasse, deeply impressed and not a little bewildered, had inquired in vain concerning the historic affiliations of the cult. Castro, apparently, had told the truth when he said that it was wholly secret. The authorities at Tulane University could shed no light upon either cult or image, and now the detective had come to the highest authorities in the country and met with no more than the Greenland tale of Professor Webb.

The feverish interest aroused at the meeting by Legrasse's tale, corroborated as it was by the statuette, is echoed in the subsequent correspondence of those who attended; although scant mention occurs in the formal publications[a] of the society. Caution is the first care of those accustomed to face occasional charlatanry and imposture. Legrasse for some time lent the image to Professor Webb, but at the latter's death it was returned to him and remains in his possession, where I viewed it not long ago. It is truly a terrible thing, and unmistakably akin to the dream-sculpture of young Wilcox.

That my uncle was excited by the tale of the sculptor I did not wonder, for what thoughts must arise upon hearing, after a knowledge of what Legrasse had learned of the cult, of a sensitive young man who had *dreamed* not only the figure and exact hieroglyphics of the swamp-found image and the Greenland devil tablet, but had come *in his dreams* upon at least three of the precise words of the formula uttered alike by Esquimau[b] diabolists and mongrel Louisianans? Professor Angell's instant start on an investigation of the utmost thoroughness was eminently natural; though privately I suspected young Wilcox of having heard of the cult in some indirect way, and of having invented a series of dreams to heighten and continue the mystery at my uncle's expense. The dream-narratives and cuttings collected by the professor were, of course, strong corroboration; but the rationalism of my mind and the extravagance of the whole subject led me to adopt what I thought the most sensible conclusions. So, after thoroughly studying the manuscript again and correlating the theosophical and anthropological notes with the cult narrative of Legrasse, I made a trip to Providence to see the sculptor and give him the rebuke I thought proper for so boldly imposing upon a learned and aged man.

[a] publications] publication B, D
[b] Esquimau] Eskimo B, D

Wilcox still lived alone in the Fleur-de-Lys Building in Thomas Street, a hideous Victorian imitation of seventeenth-century[a] Breton architecture which flaunts its stuccoed front amidst the lovely colonial[b] houses on the ancient hill, and under the very shadow of the finest Georgian steeple in America. I found him at work in his rooms, and at once conceded from the specimens scattered about that his genius is indeed profound and authentic. He will, I believe, some time be heard from[c] as one of the great decadents; for he has crystallised[d] in clay and will one day mirror in marble those nightmares and phantasies[e] which Arthur Machen evokes in prose, and Clark Ashton Smith makes visible in verse and in painting.

Dark, frail, and somewhat unkempt in aspect, he turned languidly at my knock and asked me my business without rising. When I told him who I was, he displayed some interest; for my uncle had excited his curiosity in probing his strange dreams, yet had never explained the reason for the study. I did not enlarge his knowledge in this regard, but sought with some subtlety to draw him out.[f] In a short time I became convinced of his absolute sincerity,[g] for he spoke of the dreams in a manner none could mistake. They and their subconscious residuum had influenced his art profoundly, and he shewed[h] me a morbid statue whose contours almost made me shake with the potency of its black suggestion. He could not recall having seen the original of this thing except in his own dream bas-relief, but the outlines had formed themselves insensibly under his hands. It was, no doubt, the giant shape he had raved of in delirium. That he really knew nothing of the hidden cult, save from what my uncle's relentless catechism had let fall, he soon made clear; and again I strove to think of some way in which he could possibly have received the weird impressions.

He talked of his dreams in a strangely poetic fashion; making me see

[a] seventeenth-century] Seventeenth Century B, D
[b] colonial] Colonial A, B, C, D
[c] some time be heard from] be heard from sometime B, D
[d] crystallised] crystallized B, C, D
[e] phantasies] fantasies B, D
[f] out.] out. ¶ B, D
[g] sincerity,] sincerity D
[h] shewed] showed A, B, C, D

with terrible vividness the damp Cyclopean city of slimy green stone—whose *geometry,* he oddly said, was *all wrong*—and hear with frightened expectancy the ceaseless, half-mental calling from underground: *"Cthulhu fhtagn"*, *"Cthulhu fhtagn"*.[a] These words had formed part of that dread ritual which told of dead Cthulhu's dream-vigil in his stone vault at R'lyeh, and I felt deeply moved despite my rational beliefs. Wilcox, I was sure, had heard of the cult in some casual way, and had soon forgotten it amidst the mass of his equally weird reading and imagining. Later, by virtue of its sheer impressiveness, it had found subconscious expression in dreams, in the bas-relief, and in the terrible statue I now beheld; so that his imposture upon my uncle had been a very innocent one. The youth was of a type, at once slightly affected and slightly ill-mannered, which I could never like; but I was willing enough now to admit both his genius and his honesty. I took leave of him amicably, and wish him all the success his talent promises.

The matter of the cult still remained to fascinate me, and at times I had visions of personal fame from researches into its origin and connexions.[b] I visited New Orleans, talked with Legrasse and others of that old-time raiding-party, saw the frightful image, and even questioned such of the mongrel prisoners as still survived. Old Castro, unfortunately, had been dead for some years. What I now heard so graphically at first-hand,[c] though it was really no more than a detailed confirmation of what my uncle had written, excited me afresh; for I felt sure that I was on the track of a very real, very secret, and very ancient religion whose discovery would make me an anthropologist of note. My attitude was still one of absolute materialism,[d] *as I wish it still were,* and I discounted with almost[e] inexplicable perversity the coincidence of the dream notes and odd cuttings collected by Professor Angell.

One thing[f] I began to suspect, and which I now fear I *know,* is that my uncle's death was far from natural. He fell on a narrow hill street leading up from an ancient waterfront swarming with foreign

---

[a] *fhtagn", . . . fhtagn".*] *fhtagn, ". . . fhtagn."* ¶ B, D; *fhtagn, ". . . fhtagn."* C

[b] connexions.] connections. B, C, D

[c] first-hand,] first hand, B, D

[d] materialism,] materialism D

[e] almost] a most D

[f] thing] thing which B, D

mongrels, after a careless push from a negro sailor. I did not forget the mixed blood and marine pursuits of the cult-members in Louisiana, and would not be surprised to learn of secret methods and poison needles as ruthless and as anciently known as the cryptic rites and beliefs. Legrasse and his men, it is true, have been let alone; but in Norway a certain seaman who saw things is dead. Might not the deeper inquiries of my uncle after encountering the sculptor's data have come to sinister ears? I think[a] Professor Angell died because he knew too much, or because he was likely to learn too much. Whether I shall go as he did remains to be seen, for I have learned much now.

III.
THE MADNESS FROM THE SEA.

If heaven[b] ever wishes to grant me a boon, it will be a total effacing of the results of a mere chance which fixed my eye on a certain stray piece of shelf-paper. It was nothing on which I would naturally have stumbled in the course of my daily round, for it was an old number of an Australian journal, the[c] *Sydney Bulletin* for April 18, 1925. It had escaped even the cutting bureau which had at the time of its issuance been avidly collecting material for my uncle's research.

I had largely given over my inquiries into what Professor Angell called the "Cthulhu Cult",[d] and was visiting a learned friend in[e] Paterson, New Jersey; the curator of a local museum and a mineralogist of note. Examining one day the reserve specimens roughly set on the storage shelves in a rear room of the museum, my eye was caught by an odd picture in one of the old papers spread beneath the stones. It was the *Sydney Bulletin* I have mentioned, for my friend has wide affiliations in all conceivable foreign parts; and the picture was a half-tone cut of a hideous stone image almost identical with that which Legrasse had found in the swamp.

Eagerly clearing the sheet of its precious contents, I scanned the item

[a] think] thing B
[b] heaven] Heaven A, C
[c] the] *om.* B, D
[d] Cult",] Cult," B, C, D
[e] in] of B, D

in detail; and was disappointed to find it of only moderate length. What it suggested, however, was of portentous significance to my flagging quest; and I carefully tore it out for immediate action. It read as follows:

MYSTERY DERELICT FOUND AT SEA

Vigilant[a] Arrives With[b] Helpless Armed New Zealand Yacht in Tow.
One Survivor and Dead Man Found Aboard. Tale of
Desperate Battle and Deaths at Sea.
Rescued Seaman Refuses
Particulars of Strange Experience.
Odd Idol Found in His Possession. Inquiry
to Follow.[c]

The Morrison Co.'s freighter *Vigilant,* bound from Valparaiso, arrived this morning at its wharf in Darling Harbour, having in tow the battled and disabled but heavily armed steam yacht *Alert* of Dunedin, N. Z., which was sighted April 12th in S. Latitude 34° 21′, W. Longitude 152° 17′[d] with one living and one dead man aboard.

The *Vigilant* left Valparaiso March 25th, and on April 2nd[e] was driven considerably south of her course by exceptionally heavy storms and monster waves. On April 12th the derelict was sighted; and though apparently deserted, was found upon boarding to contain one survivor in a half-delirious condition and one man who had evidently been dead for more than a week.[f] The living man was clutching a horrible stone idol of unknown origin, about a foot in height, regarding whose nature authorities at Sydney University, the Royal Society, and the Museum in College Street all profess complete bafflement, and which the survivor says he found in the cabin of the yacht, in a small carved shrine of common pattern.

This man, after recovering his senses, told an exceedingly strange story of piracy and slaughter. He is Gustaf Johansen, a Norwegian of some intelligence, and had been second mate of the two-masted schooner *Emma*

---

[a] Vigilant] *Vigilant* B, C, D
[b] With] with C, D
[c] Vigilant ... Follow.] [*printed in paragraph form in B, D*]; *Vigilant* ... One / Survivor ... Battle / and ... His / Possession. ... Follow. C
[d] 17′] 17′, B, D
[e] 2nd] 2 A, C; 2d B, D
[f] week.] week. ¶ B, D

COLLECTED FICTION: 1926–1930

of Auckland, which sailed for Callao February 20th[a] with a complement of eleven men.[b] The *Emma*, he says, was delayed and thrown widely south of her course by the great storm of March 1st, and on March 22nd,[c] in S. Latitude 49° 51′, W. Longitude 128° 34′, encountered the *Alert*, manned by a queer and evil-looking crew of Kanakas and half-castes. Being ordered peremptorily to turn back, Capt. Collins refused; whereupon the strange crew began to fire savagely and without warning upon the schooner with a peculiarly heavy battery of brass cannon forming part of the yacht's equipment.[d] The *Emma*'s men shewed[e] fight, says the survivor, and though the schooner began to sink from shots beneath the waterline they managed to heave alongside their enemy and board her, grappling with the savage crew on the yacht's deck, and being forced to kill them all, the number being slightly superior, because of their particularly abhorrent and desperate though rather clumsy mode of fighting.

Three of the *Emma*'s men, including Capt. Collins and First Mate Green, were killed; and the remaining eight under Second Mate Johansen proceeded to navigate the captured yacht, going ahead in their original direction to see if any reason for their ordering back had existed.[f] The next day, it appears, they raised and landed on a small island, although none is known to exist in that part of the ocean; and six of the men somehow died ashore, though Johansen is queerly reticent about this part of his story,[g] and speaks only of their falling into a rock chasm.[h] Later, it seems, he and one companion boarded the yacht and tried to manage her, but were beaten about by the storm of April 2nd.[i] From that time till his rescue on the 12th[j] the man remembers little, and he does not even recall when William Briden, his companion, died. Briden's death reveals no apparent cause, and was probably due to excitement or exposure.[k] Cable advices from Dunedin report that the *Alert* was well known there as an island trader, and bore an evil reputation along the waterfront. It was owned by a curious group of

[a] 20th] 20th, B, D
[b] men.] men. ¶ B, D
[c] 22nd,] 22d, B, D
[d] equipment.] equipment. ¶ B, D
[e] shewed] showed A, B, C, D
[f] existed.] existed. ¶ B, D
[g] story,] story B, D
[h] chasm.] chasm. ¶ B, D
[i] 2nd.] 2nd. ¶ B; 2d. ¶ D
[j] 12th] 12th, B, D
[k] exposure.] exposure. ¶ B, D

half-castes whose frequent meetings and night trips to the woods attracted no little curiosity; and it had set sail in great haste just after the storm and earth tremors of March 1st.[a] Our Auckland correspondent gives the *Emma* and her crew an excellent reputation, and Johansen is described as a sober and worthy man.[b] The admiralty will institute an inquiry on the whole matter beginning tomorrow, at which every effort will be made to induce Johansen to speak more freely than he has done hitherto.

This was all, together with the picture of the hellish image; but what a train of ideas it started in my mind! Here were new treasuries of data on the Cthulhu Cult, and evidence that it had strange interests at sea as well as on land. What motive prompted the hybrid crew to order back the *Emma* as they sailed about with their hideous idol? What was the unknown island on which six of the *Emma*'s crew had died, and about which the mate Johansen was so secretive? What had the vice-admiralty's investigation brought out, and what was known of the noxious cult in Dunedin? And most marvellous[c] of all, what deep and more than natural linkage of dates was this which gave a malign and now undeniable significance to the various turns of events[d] so carefully noted by my uncle?

March 1st—our February 28th according to the International Date Line—the earthquake and storm had come. From Dunedin the *Alert* and her noisome crew had darted eagerly forth as if imperiously summoned, and on the other side of the earth poets and artists had begun to dream of a strange, dank Cyclopean city whilst a young sculptor had moulded[e] in his sleep the form of the dreaded Cthulhu. March 23d[f] the crew of the *Emma* landed on an unknown island and left six men dead; and on that date the dreams of sensitive men assumed a heightened vividness and darkened with dread of a giant monster's malign pursuit, whilst an architect had gone mad and a sculptor had lapsed suddenly into delirium! And what of this storm of April 2nd—the date on which all dreams of the dank city ceased, and Wilcox emerged unharmed from the bondage of strange fever? What of all this—and of those

[a] 1st.] 1st. ¶ B, D
[b] man.] man. ¶ B, D
[c] marvellous] marvelous B, C, D
[d] events] event D
[e] moulded] molded B, C, D
[f] 23d] 23rd B, D

hints of old Castro about the sunken, star-born Old Ones and their coming reign; their faithful cult *and their mastery of dreams?* Was I tottering on the brink of cosmic horrors beyond man's power to bear? If so, they must be horrors of the mind alone, for in some way the second of April had put a stop to whatever monstrous menace had begun its siege of mankind's soul.

That evening, after a day of hurried cabling and arranging, I bade my host adieu and took a train for San Francisco. In less than a month I was in Dunedin;[a] where, however, I found that little was known of the strange cult-members who had lingered in the old sea-taverns.[b] Waterfront scum was far too common for special mention; though there was vague talk about one inland trip these mongrels had made, during which faint drumming and red flame were noted on the distant hills.[c] In Auckland I learned that Johansen had returned *with yellow hair turned white* after a perfunctory and inconclusive questioning at Sydney, and had thereafter sold his cottage in West Street and sailed with his wife to his old home in Oslo. Of his stirring experience he would tell his friends no more than he had told the admiralty officials, and all they could do was to give me his Oslo address.

After that I went to Sydney and talked profitlessly with seamen and members of the vice-admiralty court. I saw the *Alert,* now sold and in commercial use, at Circular Quay in Sydney Cove, but gained nothing from its non-committal[d] bulk. The crouching image with its cuttlefish head, dragon body, scaly wings, and hieroglyphed pedestal, was preserved in the Museum at Hyde Park; and I studied it long and well, finding it a thing of balefully exquisite workmanship, and with the same utter mystery, terrible antiquity, and unearthly strangeness of material which I had noted in Legrasse's smaller specimen. Geologists, the curator told me, had found it a monstrous puzzle; for they vowed that the world held no rock like it. Then I thought with a shudder of what old Castro had told Legrasse about the primal Great Ones: "They had come from the stars, and had brought Their images with Them."

[a] Dunedin;] Dunedin: D
[b] sea-taverns.] sea taverns. A, B, C, D
[c] hills.] hills. ¶ B, D
[d] non-committal] noncommittal D

Shaken with such a mental revolution as I had never before known, I now resolved to visit Mate Johansen in Oslo. Sailing for London, I reëmbarked[a] at once for the Norwegian capital; and one autumn day landed at the trim wharves in the shadow of the Egeberg.[b] Johansen's address, I discovered, lay in the Old Town of King Harold Haardrada, which kept alive the name of Oslo during all the centuries that the greater city masqueraded as "Christiania".[c] I made the brief trip by taxicab, and knocked with palpitant heart at the door of a neat and ancient building with plastered front. A sad-faced woman in black answered my summons, and I was stung with disappointment when she told me in halting English that Gustaf Johansen was no more.

He had not survived his return, said his wife, for the doings at sea in 1925 had broken him. He had told her no more than he had told the public, but had left a long manuscript—of "technical matters" as he said—written in English, evidently in order to safeguard her from the peril of casual perusal. During a walk through a narrow lane near the Gothenburg dock, a bundle of papers falling from an attic window had knocked him down. Two Lascar sailors at once helped him to his feet, but before the ambulance could reach him he was dead. Physicians found no adequate cause for the end, and laid it to heart trouble and a weakened constitution.

I now felt gnawing at my vitals that dark terror which will never leave me till I, too, am at rest; "accidentally" or otherwise. Persuading the widow that my connexion[d] with her husband's "technical matters" was sufficient to entitle me to his manuscript, I bore the document away and began to read it on the London boat.[e] It was a simple, rambling thing—a naive[f] sailor's effort at a post-facto diary—and strove to recall day by day that last awful voyage. I cannot attempt to transcribe it verbatim in all its cloudiness and redundance, but I will tell its gist enough to shew[g] why the sound of the water against the vessel's sides

[a] reëmbarked] re-embarked B, D
[b] Egeberg.] Egeberg. ¶ B, D
[c] "Christiania".] "Christiania." B, C, D
[d] connexion] connection B, C, D
[e] boat.] boat. ¶ B, D
[f] naive] naïve C, D
[g] shew] show A, B, C, D

became so unendurable to me that I stopped my ears with cotton.

Johansen, thank God, did not know quite all, even though he saw the city and the Thing, but I shall never sleep calmly again when I think of the horrors that lurk ceaselessly behind life in time and in space, and of those unhallowed blasphemies from elder stars which dream beneath the sea, known and favoured[a] by a nightmare cult ready and eager to loose them on the world whenever another earthquake shall heave their monstrous stone city again to the sun and air.

Johansen's voyage had begun just as he told it to the vice-admiralty. The *Emma,* in ballast, had cleared Auckland on February 20th, and had felt the full force of that earthquake-born tempest which must have heaved up from the sea-bottom the horrors that filled men's dreams. Once more under control, the ship was making good progress when held up by the *Alert* on March 22nd, and I could feel the mate's regret as he wrote of her bombardment and sinking. Of the swarthy cult-fiends on the *Alert* he speaks with significant horror. There was some peculiarly abominable quality about them which made their destruction seem almost a duty, and Johansen shews[b] ingenuous wonder at the charge of ruthlessness brought against his party during the proceedings of the court of inquiry. Then, driven ahead by curiosity in their captured yacht under Johansen's command, the men sight a great stone pillar sticking out of the sea, and in S. Latitude 47° 9', W. Longitude 126° 43'[c] come upon a coast-line[d] of mingled mud, ooze, and weedy Cyclopean masonry which can be nothing less than the tangible substance of earth's supreme terror—the nightmare corpse-city of R'lyeh, that was built in measureless aeons[e] behind history by the vast, loathsome shapes that seeped down from the dark stars. There lay great Cthulhu and his hordes, hidden in green slimy vaults and sending out at last, after cycles incalculable, the thoughts that spread fear to the dreams of the sensitive and called imperiously to the faithful to come on a pilgrimage of liberation and restoration. All this Johansen did not suspect, but God knows he soon saw enough!

[a] favoured] favored B, C, D
[b] shews] shows A, B, C, D
[c] 43'] 43', D
[d] coast-line] coastline A, B, C, D
[e] aeons] eons B, D

I suppose that only a single mountaintop,[a] the hideous monolith-crowned citadel whereon great Cthulhu was buried, actually emerged from the waters. When I think of the *extent* of all that may be brooding down there I almost wish to kill myself forthwith. Johansen and his men were awed by the cosmic majesty of this dripping Babylon of elder daemons,[b] and must have guessed without guidance that it was nothing of this or of any sane planet. Awe at the unbelievable size of the greenish stone blocks, at the dizzying height of the great carven monolith, and at the stupefying identity of the colossal statues and bas-reliefs with the queer image found in the shrine on the *Alert*, is poignantly visible in every line of the mate's frightened description.

Without knowing what futurism is like, Johansen achieved something very close to it when he spoke of the city; for instead of describing any definite structure or building, he dwells only on[c] broad impressions of vast angles and stone surfaces—surfaces too great to belong to any thing right or proper for this earth, and impious with horrible images and hieroglyphs. I mention his talk about *angles* because it suggests something Wilcox had told me of his awful dreams. He had said that the *geometry* of the dream-place he saw was abnormal, non-Euclidean, and loathsomely redolent of spheres and dimensions apart from ours. Now an unlettered seaman felt the same thing whilst gazing at the terrible reality.

Johansen and his men landed at a sloping mud-bank on this monstrous Acropolis,[d] and clambered slipperily up over titan oozy blocks which could have been no mortal staircase. The very sun of heaven seemed distorted when viewed through the polarising[e] miasma welling out from this sea-soaked perversion, and twisted menace and suspense lurked leeringly in those crazily elusive angles of carven rock where a second glance shewed concavity after the first shewed[f] convexity.

Something very like fright had come over all the explorers before anything more definite than rock and ooze and weed was seen. Each

[a] mountaintop,] mountain-top, A, B, C, D
[b] daemons,] demons, B, D
[c] on] on the A [the *crossed out*], B, D
[d] Acropolis,] acropolis, D
[e] polarising] polarizing B, C, D
[f] shewed . . . shewed] showed . . . showed A, B, C, D

would have fled had he not feared the scorn of the others, and it was only half-heartedly that they searched—vainly, as it proved—for some portable souvenir to bear away.

It was Rodriguez the Portuguese[a] who climbed up the foot of the monolith and shouted of what he had found. The rest followed him, and looked curiously at the immense carved door with the now familiar squid-dragon bas-relief. It was, Johansen said, like a great barn-door; and they all felt that it was a door because of the ornate lintel, threshold, and jambs around it, though they could not decide whether it lay flat like a trap-door[b] or slantwise like an outside cellar-door. As Wilcox would have said, the geometry of the place was all wrong. One could not be sure that the sea and the ground were horizontal, hence the relative position of everything else seemed phantasmally[c] variable.

Briden pushed at the stone in several places without result. Then Donovan felt over it delicately around the edge, pressing each point separately as he went. He climbed interminably along the grotesque stone moulding[d]—that is, one would call it climbing if the thing was not after all horizontal—and the men wondered how any door in the universe could be so vast. Then, very softly and slowly, the acre-great panel began to give inward at the top; and they saw that it was balanced.[e] Donovan slid or somehow propelled himself down or along the jamb and rejoined his fellows, and everyone watched the queer recession of the monstrously carven portal. In this phantasy[f] of prismatic distortion it moved anomalously in a diagonal way, so that all the rules of matter and perspective seemed upset.

The aperture was black with a darkness almost material. That tenebrousness was indeed a *positive quality;* for it obscured such parts of the inner walls as ought to have been revealed, and actually burst forth like smoke from its aeon-long[g] imprisonment, visibly darkening the sun as it slunk away into the shrunken and gibbous sky on flapping

---

[a] Portuguese] Portugese A
[b] trap-door] trap door A, D
[c] phantasmally] fantasmally B, D
[d] moulding] molding B, C, D
[e] balanced.] balanced. ¶ B, D
[f] phantasy] fantasy B, D
[g] aeon-long] eon-long B, D

membraneous[a] wings. The odour[b] arising from the newly opened depths was intolerable, and at length the quick-eared Hawkins thought he heard a nasty, slopping sound down there. Everyone listened, and everyone was listening still when It lumbered slobberingly into sight and gropingly squeezed Its gelatinous green immensity through the black doorway into the tainted outside air of that poison city of madness.

Poor Johansen's handwriting almost gave out when he wrote of this. Of the six men who never reached the ship, he thinks two perished of pure fright in that accursed instant. The Thing cannot[c] be described—there is no language for such abysms of shrieking and immemorial lunacy, such eldritch contradictions of all matter, force, and cosmic order. A mountain walked or stumbled. God! What wonder that across the earth a great architect went mad, and poor Wilcox raved with fever in that telepathic instant? The Thing of the idols, the green, sticky spawn of the stars, had awaked to claim his own. The stars were right again, and what an age-old cult had failed to do by design, a band of innocent sailors had done by accident. After vigintillions of years great Cthulhu was loose again, and ravening for delight.

Three men were swept up by the flabby claws before anybody turned. God rest them, if there be any rest in the universe. They were Donovan, Guerrera,[d] and Ångstrom.[e] Parker slipped as the other three were plunging frenziedly over endless vistas of green-crusted rock to the boat, and Johansen swears he was swallowed up by an angle of masonry which shouldn't have been there; an angle which was acute, but behaved as if it were obtuse. So only Briden and Johansen reached the boat, and pulled desperately for the *Alert* as the mountainous monstrosity flopped down the slimy stones and hesitated[f] floundering at the edge of the water.

Steam had not been suffered to go down entirely, despite the departure of all hands for the shore; and it was the work of only a few

[a] membraneous] membranous A, B, C, D
[b] odour] odor B, C, D
[c] cannot] can not B, D
[d] Guerrera,] Guerrera B, D
[e] Ångstrom.] Angstrom. B, C, D
[f] hesitated] hesitated, D

moments of feverish rushing up and down between wheel[a] and engines to get the *Alert* under way. Slowly, amidst the distorted horrors of that indescribable scene, she began to churn the lethal waters; whilst on the masonry of that charnel shore that was not of earth the titan Thing from the stars slavered and gibbered like Polypheme cursing the fleeing ship of Odysseus. Then, bolder than the storied Cyclops, great Cthulhu slid greasily into the water and began to pursue with vast wave-raising strokes of cosmic potency. Briden looked back and went mad, laughing shrilly as he kept on[b] laughing at intervals till death found him one night in the cabin whilst Johansen was wandering deliriously.

But Johansen had not given out yet. Knowing that the Thing could surely overtake the *Alert* until steam was fully up, he resolved on a desperate chance; and, setting the engine for full speed, ran lightning-like on deck and reversed the wheel. There was a mighty eddying and foaming in the noisome brine, and as the steam mounted higher and higher the brave Norwegian drove his vessel head on against the pursuing jelly which rose above the unclean froth like the stern of a daemon[c] galleon. The awful squid-head with writhing feelers came nearly up to the bowsprit of the sturdy yacht, but Johansen drove on relentlessly.[d] There was a bursting as of an exploding bladder, a slushy nastiness as of a cloven sunfish, a stench as of a thousand opened graves, and a sound that the chronicler would not put on paper. For an instant the ship was befouled by an acrid and blinding green cloud, and then there was only a venomous seething astern; where—God in heaven![e]—the scattered plasticity of that nameless sky-spawn was nebulously *recombining* in its hateful original form, whilst its distance widened every second as the *Alert* gained impetus from its mounting steam.

That was all. After that Johansen only brooded over the idol in the cabin and attended to a few matters of food for himself and the laughing maniac by his side. He did not try to navigate after the first bold flight,[f] for the reaction had taken something out of his soul. Then

---

[a] wheel] wheels B, D
[b] laughing shrilly as he kept on] laughing shrilly, as he kept on C; *om*. D
[c] daemon] demon B, D
[d] relentlessly.] relentlessly. ¶ B, D
[e] heaven!] Heaven! A, C
[f] flight,] flight; D

came the storm of April 2nd, and a gathering of the clouds about his consciousness. There is a sense of spectral whirling through liquid gulfs of infinity, of dizzying rides through reeling universes on a comet's tail, and of hysterical plunges from the pit to the moon and from the moon back again to the pit, all livened by a cachinnating chorus of the distorted, hilarious elder gods and the green, bat-winged mocking imps of Tartarus.

Out of that dream came rescue—the *Vigilant,* the vice-admiralty court, the streets of Dunedin, and the long voyage back home to the old house by the Egeberg. He could not tell—they would think him mad. He would write of what he knew before death came, but his wife must not guess. Death would be a boon if only it could blot out the memories.

That was the document I read, and now I have placed it in the tin box beside the bas-relief and the papers of Professor Angell. With it shall go this record of mine—this test of my own sanity, wherein is pieced together that which I hope may never be pieced together again. I have looked upon all that the universe has to hold of horror, and even the skies of spring and the flowers of summer must ever afterward be poison to me. But I do not think my life will be long. As my uncle went, as poor Johansen went, so I shall go. I know too much, and the cult still lives.

Cthulhu still lives, too, I suppose, again in that chasm of stone which has shielded him since the sun was young. His accursed city is sunken once more, for the *Vigilant* sailed over the spot after the April storm; but his ministers on earth still bellow and prance and slay around idol-capped monoliths in lonely places. He must have been trapped by the sinking whilst within his black abyss, or else the world would by now be screaming with fright and frenzy. Who knows the end? What has risen may sink, and what has sunk may rise. Loathsomeness waits and dreams in the deep, and decay spreads over the tottering cities of men. A time will come—but I must not and cannot[a] think! Let me pray that, if I do not survive this manuscript, my executors may put caution before audacity and see that it meets no other eye.

[a] cannot] can not B, D

Pickman's Model

You needn't think I'm crazy, Eliot—plenty of others have queerer prejudices than this. Why don't you laugh at Oliver's grandfather, who won't ride in a motor? If I don't like that damned subway, it's my own business; and we got here more quickly anyhow in the taxi. We'd have had to walk up the hill from Park Street if we'd taken the car.

I know I'm more nervous than I was when you saw me last year, but you don't need to hold a clinic over it. There's plenty of reason, God knows, and I fancy I'm lucky to be sane at all. Why the third degree? You didn't use to be so inquisitive.

Well, if you must hear it, I don't know why you shouldn't. Maybe you ought to, anyhow, for you kept writing me like a grieved parent when you heard I'd begun to cut the Art Club and keep away from Pickman. Now that he's disappeared I go around to the club once in a while, but my nerves aren't what they were.

Editor's Note: HPL's original A.Ms. turned up some time ago; it is held by private hands. It is of interest in recording a passage toward the end that was excised. (HPL curiously suggests that he had destroyed this A.Ms. [*OFF* 85].) The T.Ms. was prepared by HPL. It was followed by *Weird Tales* (October 1927), with the usual editorial alterations; the Arkham House editions also follow the T.Ms., with some alterations. One revision—the alteration of "Marlborough Street" to "Newbury Street," occurring three times in the text—appears in the T.Ms. in pencil, but not in HPL's hand; the handwriting may be Barlow's. This revision, along with several others, appears in the *Weird Tales* reprint (November 1936), meaning that HPL provided a revised text for the reprint (probably a tearsheet of the original appearance with revisions in pen). Other variants in the reprint are, however, probably editorial.

Texts: A = A.Ms. (private hands); B = T.Ms. (JHL); C = *Weird Tales* 10, No. 4 (October 1927): 505–14; D = *Weird Tales* 28, No. 4 (November 1936): 495–505; E = *The Dunwich Horror and Others* (Arkham House, 1963), 19–32. Copy-text: B (with some readings from D).

No, I don't know what's become of Pickman, and I don't like to guess. You might have surmised I had some inside information when I dropped him—and that's why I don't want to think where he's gone. Let the police find what they can—it won't be much, judging from the fact that they don't know yet of the old North End place he hired under the name of Peters. I'm not sure that I could find it again myself—not that I'd ever try, even in broad daylight! Yes, I do know, or am afraid I know, why he maintained it. I'm coming to that. And I think you'll understand before I'm through why I don't tell the police. They would ask me to guide them, but I couldn't go back there even if I knew the way. There was something there—and now I can't use the subway or (and you may as well have your laugh at this, too) go down into cellars any more.

I should think you'd have known I didn't drop Pickman for the same silly reasons that fussy old women like Dr. Reid or Joe Minot or Bosworth[a] did. Morbid art doesn't shock me, and when a man has the genius Pickman had I feel it an honour[b] to know him, no matter what direction his work takes. Boston never had a greater painter than Richard Upton Pickman. I said it at first and I say it still, and I never swerved an inch, either, when he shewed[c] that "Ghoul Feeding".[d] That, you remember, was when Minot cut him.

You know, it takes profound art and profound insight into Nature[e] to turn out stuff like Pickman's. Any magazine-cover hack can splash paint around wildly and call it a nightmare or a Witches' Sabbath[f] or a portrait of the devil, but only a great painter can make such a thing really scare or ring true. That's because only a real artist knows the actual anatomy of the terrible or the physiology of fear—the exact sort of lines and proportions that connect up with latent instincts or hereditary memories of fright, and the proper colour[g] contrasts and lighting effects to stir the dormant sense of strangeness. I don't have to tell you why a

[a] Bosworth] Rosworth E
[b] honour] honor C, D
[c] shewed] showed B, C, D, E
[d] "Ghoul Feeding".] *Ghoul Feeding.* C, D; "Ghoul Feeding." D, E
[e] Nature] nature C, D
[f] Witches' Sabbath] *Witches' Sabbath* D
[g] colour] color C, D

Fuseli really brings a shiver while a cheap ghost-story frontispiece merely makes us laugh. There's something those fellows catch—beyond life—that they're able to make us catch for a second. Doré had it. Sime has it. Angarola of Chicago has it. And Pickman had it as no man ever had it before or—I hope to heaven[a]—ever will again.

Don't ask me what it is they see. You know, in ordinary art, there's all the difference in the world between the vital, breathing things drawn from Nature[b] or models and the artificial truck that commercial small fry reel off in a bare studio by rule. Well, I should say that the really weird artist has a kind of vision which makes models, or summons up what amounts to actual scenes from the spectral world he lives in. Anyhow, he manages to turn out results that differ from the pretender's mince-pie dreams in just about the same way that the life painter's results differ from the concoctions of a correspondence-school cartoonist. If I had ever seen what Pickman saw—but no! Here, let's have a drink before we get any deeper. Gad, I wouldn't be alive if I'd ever seen what that man—if he was a man—saw!

You recall that Pickman's forte was faces. I don't believe anybody since Goya could put so much of sheer hell into a set of features or a twist of expression. And before Goya you have to go back to the mediaeval[c] chaps who did the gargoyles and chimaeras[d] on Notre Dame and Mont Saint-Michel. They believed all sorts of things—and maybe they saw all sorts of things, too, for the Middle Ages had some curious phases. I remember your asking Pickman yourself once, the year before you went away, wherever in thunder he got such ideas and visions. Wasn't that a nasty laugh he gave you? It was partly because of that laugh that Reid dropped him. Reid, you know, had just taken up comparative pathology, and was full of pompous "inside stuff" about the biological or evolutionary significance of this or that mental or physical symptom. He said Pickman repelled him more and more every day, and almost frightened him toward the last—that the fellow's features and expression were slowly developing in a way he didn't like; in a way

[a] heaven] Heaven A, B, E
[b] Nature] nature C, D
[c] mediaeval] medieval C, D
[d] chimaeras] chimeras C, D

that wasn't human. He had a lot of talk about diet, and said Pickman must be abnormal and eccentric to the last degree. I suppose you told Reid, if you and he had any correspondence over it, that he'd let Pickman's paintings get on his nerves or harrow up his imagination. I know I told him that myself—then.

But keep in mind that I didn't drop Pickman for anything like this. On the contrary, my admiration for him kept growing; for that "Ghoul Feeding"[a] was a tremendous achievement. As you know, the club wouldn't exhibit it, and the Museum of Fine Arts wouldn't accept it as a gift; and I can add that nobody would buy it, so Pickman had it right in his house till he went. Now his father has it in Salem—you know Pickman comes of old Salem stock, and had a witch ancestor hanged in 1692.

I got into the habit of calling on Pickman quite often, especially after I began making notes for a monograph on weird art. Probably it was his work which put the idea into my head, and anyhow, I found him a mine of data and suggestions when I came to develop it. He shewed[b] me all the paintings and drawings he had about;[c] including some pen-and-ink sketches that would, I verily believe, have got him kicked out of the club if many of the members had seen them. Before long I was pretty nearly a devotee, and would listen for hours like a schoolboy to art theories and philosophic speculations wild enough to qualify him for the Danvers asylum. My hero-worship, coupled with the fact that people generally were commencing to have less and less to do with him, made him get very confidential with me; and one evening he hinted that if I were fairly close-mouthed and none too squeamish, he might shew[d] me something rather unusual—something a bit stronger than anything he had in the house.

"You know," he said, "there are things that won't do for Newbury[e] Street—things that are out of place here, and that can't be conceived here, anyhow. It's my business to catch the overtones of the soul, and you won't find those in a parvenu set of artificial streets on made land.

[a] "Ghoul Feeding"] *Ghoul Feeding* C, D
[b] shewed] showed B, C, D, E
[c] about;] about, D
[d] shew] show B, C, D, E
[e] Newbury] Marlborough A, B, C [*altered in B in pencil, but not in HPL's handwriting*]

Back Bay isn't Boston—it isn't anything yet, because it's had no time to pick up memories and attract local spirits. If there are any ghosts here, they're the tame ghosts of a salt marsh and a shallow cove; and I want human ghosts—the ghosts of beings highly organised[a] enough to have looked on hell and known the meaning of what they saw.

"The place for an artist to live[b] is the North End. If any aesthete[c] were sincere, he'd put up with the slums for the sake of the massed traditions. God, man! Don't you realise[d] that places like that weren't merely *made,* but actually *grew?* Generation after generation lived and felt and died there, and in days when people weren't afraid to live and feel and die. Don't you know there was a mill on Copp's Hill in 1632, and that half the present streets were laid out by 1650? I can shew[e] you houses that have stood two centuries and a half and more; houses that have witnessed what would make a modern house crumble into powder. What do moderns know of life and the forces behind it? You call the Salem witchcraft a delusion, but I'll wager my four-times-great-grandmother could have told you things. They hanged her on Gallows Hill, with Cotton Mather looking sanctimoniously on. Mather, damn him, was afraid somebody might succeed in kicking free of this accursed cage of monotony—I wish someone had laid a spell on him or sucked his blood in the night!

"I can shew you a house he lived in, and I can shew[f] you another one he was afraid to enter in spite of all his fine bold talk. He knew things he didn't dare put into that stupid 'Magnalia'[g] or that puerile 'Wonders of the Invisible World'.[h] Look here, do you know the whole North End once had a set of tunnels that kept certain people in touch with each other's houses, and the burying-ground,[i] and the sea? Let them prosecute and persecute above ground—things went on every day that

[a] organised] organized C, D
[b] live] love D
[c] aesthete] esthete C, D
[d] realise] realize C, D
[e] shew] show A, B, C, D, E
[f] shew . . . shew] show . . . show A, B, C, D, E
[g] 'Magnalia'] *Magnalia* A, B, C, D, E
[h] 'Wonders . . . World'.] *Wonders . . . World.* A, B, C, D, E
[i] burying-ground,] burying ground, A, B, C, E

they couldn't reach, and voices laughed at night that they couldn't place!

"Why, man, out of ten surviving houses built before 1700 and not moved since,[a] I'll wager that in eight I can shew[b] you something queer in the cellar. There's hardly a month that you don't read of workmen finding bricked-up arches and wells leading nowhere in this or that old place as it comes down—you could see one near Henchman Street from the elevated last year. There were witches and what their spells summoned; pirates and what they brought in from the sea; smugglers; privateers—and I tell you, people knew how to live, and how to enlarge the bounds of life, in the old times![c] This wasn't the only world a bold and wise man could know—faugh! And to think of today in contrast, with such pale-pink brains that even a club of supposed artists gets shudders and convulsions if a picture goes beyond the feelings of a Beacon Street tea-table![d]

"The only saving grace of the present is that it's too damned stupid to question the past very closely. What do maps and records and guide-books[e] really tell of the North End? Bah! At a guess I'll guarantee to lead you to thirty or forty alleys and networks of alleys north of Prince Street that aren't suspected by ten living beings outside of the foreigners that swarm them. And what do those Dagoes know of their meaning? No, Thurber, these ancient places are dreaming gorgeously and overflowing with wonder and terror and escape[f] from the commonplace, and yet there's not a living soul to understand or profit by them. Or[g] rather, there's only one living soul—for I haven't been digging around in the past for nothing!

"See here, you're interested in this sort of thing. What if I told you that I've got another studio up there, where I can catch the night-spirit of antique horror and paint things that I couldn't even think of in Newbury[h] Street? Naturally I don't tell those cursed old maids at the

[a] since,] since A, B, C, E
[b] shew] show B, C, D, E
[c] times!] time! E
[d] tea-table!] teatable! E
[e] guide-books] guidebooks A, B, C, E
[f] escape] escapes A, B, C, E
[g] Or] Or, D
[h] Newbury] Marlborough A, B, C [*altered in B as above*]

club—with Reid, damn him, whispering even as it is that I'm a sort of monster bound down the toboggan of reverse evolution. Yes, Thurber, I decided long ago that one must paint terror as well as beauty from life, so I did some exploring in places where I had reason to know terror lives.

"I've got a place that I don't believe three living Nordic men besides myself have ever seen. It isn't so very far from the elevated as distance goes, but it's centuries away as the soul goes. I took it because of the queer old brick well in the cellar—one of the sort I told you about. The shack's almost tumbling down, so that nobody else would live there, and I'd hate to tell you how little I pay for it. The windows are boarded up, but I like that all the better, since I don't want daylight for what I do. I paint in the cellar, where the inspiration is thickest, but I've other rooms furnished on the ground floor. A Sicilian owns it, and I've hired it under the name of Peters.

"Now if you're game, I'll take you there tonight. I think you'd enjoy the pictures, for as I said, I've let myself go a bit there. It's no vast tour—I sometimes do it on foot, for I don't want to attract attention with a taxi in such a place. We can take the shuttle at the South Station for Battery Street, and after that the walk isn't much."

Well, Eliot, there wasn't much for me to do after that harangue but to keep myself from running instead of walking for the first vacant cab we could sight. We changed to the elevated at the South Station, and at about twelve[a] o'clock had climbed down the steps at Battery Street and struck along the old waterfront past Constitution Wharf. I didn't keep track of the cross streets, and can't tell you yet which it was we turned up, but I know it wasn't Greenough Lane.

When we did turn, it was to climb through the deserted length of the oldest and dirtiest alley I ever saw in my life, with crumbling-looking gables, broken small-paned windows, and archaic chimneys that stood out half-disintegrated against the moonlit sky. I don't believe there were three houses in sight that hadn't been standing in Cotton Mather's time—certainly I glimpsed at least two with an overhang, and once I thought I saw a peaked roof-line of the almost forgotten pre-gambrel type, though antiquarians tell us there are none left in Boston.

---

[a] twelve] 12 C

From that alley, which had a dim light, we turned to the left into an equally silent and still narrower alley with no light at all;[a] and in a minute made what I think was an obtuse-angled bend toward the right in the dark. Not long after this Pickman produced a flashlight and revealed an antediluvian ten-panelled[b] door that looked damnably worm-eaten. Unlocking it, he ushered me into a barren hallway with what was once splendid dark-oak panelling[c]—simple, of course, but thrillingly suggestive of the times of Andros and Phipps[d] and the witchcraft.[e] Then he took me through a door on the left, lighted an oil lamp, and told me to make myself at home.

Now, Eliot, I'm what the man in the street would call fairly "hard-boiled",[f] but I'll confess that what I saw on the walls of that room gave me a bad turn. They were his pictures, you know—the ones he couldn't paint or even shew[g] in Newbury[h] Street—and he was right when he said he had "let himself go".[i] Here—have another drink—I need one anyhow!

There's no use in my trying to tell you what they were like, because the awful, the blasphemous horror[j] and the unbelievable loathsomeness and moral foetor[k] came from simple touches quite beyond the power of words to classify. There was none of the exotic technique you see in Sidney Sime, none of the trans-Saturnian landscapes and lunar fungi that Clark Ashton Smith uses to freeze the blood. The backgrounds were mostly old churchyards, deep woods, cliffs by the sea, brick tunnels, ancient panelled[l] rooms, or simple vaults of masonry. Copp's Hill

[a] all;] all: E
[b] ten-panelled] ten-paneled C, D
[c] panelling] paneling C, D
[d] Phipps] Phips C, D
[e] witchcraft.] Witchcraft. A, B, C, E
[f] "hard-boiled",] "hard-boiled," C, D, E
[g] shew] show B, C, D, E
[h] Newbury] Marlborough A, B, C [*altered in B as above*]
[i] go".] go." A, B, C, D, E
[j] horror] horror, A, B, C, E
[k] foetor] fetor C, D
[l] panelled] paneled C, D

Burying-Ground,[a] which could not be many blocks away from this very house, was a favourite[b] scene.

The madness and monstrosity lay in the figures in the foreground—for Pickman's morbid art was preëminently[c] one of daemoniac[d] portraiture. These figures were seldom completely human, but often approached humanity in varying degree.[e] Most of the bodies, while roughly bipedal, had a forward-slumping[f] and a vaguely canine cast. The texture of the majority was a kind of unpleasant rubberiness. Ugh! I can see them now! Their occupations—well, don't ask me to be too precise. They were usually feeding—I won't say on what. They were sometimes shewn[g] in groups in cemeteries or underground passages, and often appeared to be in battle over their prey—or rather, their treasure-trove. And what damnable expressiveness Pickman sometimes gave the sightless faces of this charnel booty! Occasionally the things were shewn[h] leaping through open windows at night, or squatting on the chests of sleepers, worrying at their throats. One canvas shewed[i] a ring of them baying about a hanged witch on Gallows Hill, whose dead face held a close kinship to theirs.

But don't get the idea that it was all this hideous business of theme and setting which struck me faint. I'm not a three-year-old kid, and I'd seen much like this before. It was the *faces*, Eliot, those accursed *faces,* that leered and slavered out of the canvas with the very breath of life! By God,[j] man, I verily believe they *were* alive! That nauseous wizard had waked the fires of hell in pigment, and his brush had been a nightmare-spawning wand. Give me that decanter, Eliot!

[a] Burying-Ground,] Burying Ground, A, B, C, E
[b] favourite] favorite C, D
[c] preëminently] pre-/eminently C; pre-eminently D
[d] daemoniac] demoniac C, D
[e] degree.] degrees. C, D
[f] forward-slumping] forward slumping, A, B, C, E
[g] shewn] shown A, B, C, D, E
[h] shewn] shown B, C, D, E
[i] shewed] showed A, B, C, D, E
[j] God,] heaven, D

There was one thing called "The Lesson"[a]—heaven[b] pity me, that I ever saw it! Listen—can you fancy a squatting circle of nameless dog-like[c] things in a churchyard teaching a small child how to feed like themselves? The price of a changeling, I suppose—you know the old myth about how the weird people leave their spawn in cradles in exchange for the human babes they steal. Pickman was shewing[d] what happens to those stolen babes—how they grow up—and then I began to see a hideous relationship in the faces of the human and non-human figures. He was, in all his gradations of morbidity between the frankly non-human[e] and the degradedly human, establishing a sardonic linkage and evolution. The dog-things were developed from mortals!

And no sooner had I wondered what he made of their own young as left with mankind in the form of changelings, than my eye caught a picture embodying that very thought. It was that of an ancient Puritan interior—a heavily beamed room with lattice widows, a settle, and clumsy seventeenth-century[f] furniture, with the family sitting about while the father read from the Scriptures. Every face but one shewed[g] nobility and reverence, but that one reflected the mockery of the pit. It was that of a young man in years, and no doubt belonged to a supposed son of that pious father, but in essence it was the kin of the unclean things. It was their changeling—and in a spirit of supreme irony Pickman had given the features a very perceptible resemblance to his own.

By this time Pickman had lighted a lamp in an adjoining room and was politely holding open the door for me,[h] asking me if I would care to see his "modern studies".[i] I hadn't been able to give him much of my opinions—I was too speechless with fright and loathing—but I think he fully understood and felt highly complimented. And now I want to assure you again, Eliot, that I'm no mollycoddle to scream at anything

[a] "The Lesson"] *The Lesson* C, D
[b] heaven] Heaven A, B, E
[c] dog-like] doglike A, B, C, D, E
[d] shewing] showing A, B, C, D, E
[e] non-human] nonhuman E
[f] seventeenth-century] Seventeenth Century C, D
[g] shewed] showed B, C, D, E
[h] me,] me; A, B, C, E
[i] studies".] studies." E

which shews[a] a bit of departure from the usual. I'm[b] not easily knocked out. Remember, too, that I'd just about recovered my wind and gotten used to those frightful pictures which turned colonial[c] New England into a kind of annex of hell. Well, in spite of all this, that next room forced a real scream out of me, and I had to clutch at the doorway to keep from keeling over. The other chamber had shewn[d] a pack of ghouls and witches overrunning[e] the world of our forefathers, but this one brought the horror right into our own daily life!

Gad, how that man could paint! There was a study called "Subway Accident",[f] in which a flock of the vile things were clambering up from some unknown catacomb through a crack in the floor of the Boylston Street subway and attacking a crowd of people on the platform. Another shewed[g] a dance on Copp's Hill among the tombs with the background of today. Then there were any number of cellar views, with monsters creeping in through holes and rifts in the masonry and grinning as they squatted behind barrels or furnaces and waited for their first victim to descend the stairs.

One disgusting canvas seemed to depict a vast cross-section of Beacon Hill, with ant-like[h] armies of the mephitic monsters squeezing themselves through burrows that honeycombed the ground. Dances in the modern cemeteries were freely pictured, and another conception somehow shocked me more than all the rest—a scene in an unknown vault, where scores of the beasts crowded about one who held a well-known Boston guide-book[i] and was evidently reading aloud. All were pointing to a certain passage, and every face seemed so distorted with epileptic and reverberant laughter that I almost thought I heard the

---

[a] shews] shows A, B, C, D, E
[b] I'm] I'm middle-aged and decently sophisticated, and I guess you saw enough of me in France to know I'm A, B, C, E
[c] colonial] Colonial D
[d] shewn] shown B, C, D, E
[e] overrunning] over-running E
[f] "Subway Accident",] *Subway Accident,* C, D; "Subway Accident," E
[g] shewed] showed B, C, D, E
[h] ant-like] antlike C
[i] guide-book] guidebook A, B, C, E; guide-/book D

fiendish echoes. The title of the picture was, "Holmes, Lowell, and Longfellow Lie Buried in Mount Auburn".[a]

As I gradually steadied myself and got readjusted to this second room of deviltry and morbidity, I began to analyse[b] some of the points in my sickening loathing. In the first place, I said to myself, these things repelled because of the utter inhumanity and callous cruelty they shewed[c] in Pickman. The fellow must be a relentless enemy of all mankind to take such glee in the torture of brain and flesh and the degradation of the mortal[d] tenement. In the second place, they terrified because of their very greatness. Their art was the art that convinced— when we saw the pictures we saw the daemons[e] themselves and were afraid of them. And the queer part was, that Pickman got none of his power from the use of selectiveness or bizarrerie. Nothing was blurred, distorted, or conventionalised;[f] outlines were sharp and lifelike,[g] and details were almost painfully defined. And the faces!

It was not any mere artist's interpretation that we saw; it was pandemonium[h] itself, crystal clear[i] in stark objectivity. That was it, by heaven![j] The man was not a fantaisiste or romanticist at all—he did not even try to give us the churning, prismatic ephemera of dreams, but coldly and sardonically reflected some stable, mechanistic, and well-established horror-world which he saw fully, brilliantly, squarely, and unfalteringly. God knows what that world can have been, or where he ever glimpsed the blasphemous shapes that loped and trotted and crawled through it; but whatever the baffling source of his images, one thing was plain. Pickman was in every sense—in conception and in execution—a thorough, painstaking, and almost scientific *realist*.

---

[a] "Holmes, . . . Auburn".] "Holmes, . . . Auburn." A, B, D, E; *Holmes, . . . Auburn.* C
[b] analyse] analyze C, D
[c] shewed] showed B, C, D, E
[d] mortal] moral D
[e] daemons] demons C, D
[f] conventionalised;] conventionalized; C, D
[g] lifelike,] life-like, D
[h] pandemonium] pandaemonium A, B, E
[i] crystal clear] crystal-clear C, D
[j] heaven!] Heaven! A, B, E

My host was now leading the way down-cellar[a] to his actual studio, and I braced myself for some hellish effects among the unfinished canvases. As we reached the bottom of the damp stairs he turned his flashlight to a corner of the large open space at hand, revealing the circular brick curb of what was evidently a great well in the earthen floor. We walked nearer, and I saw that it must be five feet across, with walls a good foot thick and some six inches above the ground level— solid work of the seventeenth century,[b] or I was much mistaken. That, Pickman said, was the kind of thing he had been talking about—an aperture of the network of tunnels that used to undermine the hill. I noticed idly that it did not seem to be bricked up, and that a heavy disc[c] of wood formed the apparent cover. Thinking of the things this well must have been connected with if Pickman's wild hints had not been mere rhetoric, I shivered slightly; then turned to follow him up a step and through a narrow door into a room of fair size, provided with a wooden floor and furnished as a studio. An acetylene gas outfit gave the light necessary for work.

The unfinished pictures on easels or propped against the walls were as ghastly as the finished ones upstairs, and shewed[d] the painstaking methods of the artist. Scenes were blocked out with extreme care, and pencilled[e] guide-lines[f] told of the minute exactitude which Pickman used in getting the right perspective and proportions. The man was great—I say it even now, knowing as much as I do. A large camera on a table excited my notice, and Pickman told me that he used it in taking scenes for backgrounds, so that he might paint them from photographs in the studio instead of carting his outfit around the town for this or that view. He thought a photograph quite as good as an actual scene or model for sustained work, and declared he employed them regularly.

There was something very disturbing about the nauseous sketches and half-finished monstrosities that leered around from every side of

[a] down-cellar] down cellar A, B, C, E
[b] seventeenth century,] Seventeenth Century, C, D
[c] disc] disk C, D
[d] shewed] showed B, C, D, E
[e] pencilled] penciled C, D
[f] guide-lines] guide lines A, B, C, E

the room, and when Pickman suddenly unveiled a huge canvas on the side away from the light I could not for my life keep back a loud scream—the second I had emitted that night. It echoed and re-echoed[a] through the dim vaultings of that ancient and nitrous cellar, and I had to choke back a flood of reaction that threatened to burst out as hysterical laughter. Merciful Creator,[b] Eliot, but I don't know how much was real and how much was feverish fancy![c] It doesn't seem to me that earth can hold a dream like that!

It was a colossal and nameless blasphemy with glaring red eyes, and it held in bony claws a thing that had been a man, gnawing at the head as a child nibbles at a stick of candy. Its position was a kind of crouch, and as one looked one felt that at any moment it might drop its present prey and seek a juicier morsel. But[d] damn it all, it wasn't even the fiendish subject that made it such an immortal fountain-head of all panic—not that, nor the dog face with its pointed ears, bloodshot eyes, flat nose, and drooling lips. It wasn't the scaly claws nor the mould-caked[e] body nor the half-hooved feet—none of these, though any one of them might well have driven an excitable man to madness.

It was the technique, Eliot—the cursed, the impious, the unnatural technique! As I am a living being, I never elsewhere saw the actual breath of life so fused into a canvas. The monster was there—it glared and gnawed and gnawed and glared—and I knew that only a suspension of Nature's[f] laws could ever let a man paint a thing like that without a model—without some glimpse of the nether world which no mortal unsold to the fiend[g] has ever had.

Pinned with a thumb-tack to a vacant part of the canvas was a piece of paper,[h] now badly curled up—probably, I thought, a photograph from which Pickman meant to paint a background as hideous as the nightmare it was to enhance. I reached out to uncurl and look at it,

[a] re-echoed] echoed A, B, C, E
[b] Creator,] Creator! A, B, C, E
[c] fancy!] fancy. A, B, C, E
[d] But] But, D
[e] mould-caked] mold-caked C, D
[f] Nature's] nature's C, D
[g] fiend] Fiend A, B, C, D, E
[h] paper,] paper A, B, C, E

when suddenly I saw Pickman start as if shot. He had been listening with peculiar intensity ever since my shocked scream had waked unaccustomed echoes in the dark cellar, and now he seemed struck with a fright which, though not comparable to my own, had in it more of the physical than of the spiritual. He drew a revolver and motioned me to silence, then stepped out into the main cellar and closed the door behind him.

I think I was paralysed[a] for an instant. Imitating Pickman's listening, I fancied I heard a faint scurrying sound somewhere, and a series of squeals or bleats[b] in a direction I couldn't determine. I thought of huge rats and shuddered. Then there came a subdued sort of clatter which somehow set me all in gooseflesh[c]—a furtive, groping kind of clatter, though I can't attempt to convey what I mean in words. It was like heavy wood falling on stone or brick—wood on brick— what did that make me think of?

It came again, and louder. There was a vibration as if the wood had fallen farther than it had fallen before.[d] After that followed a sharp grating noise, a shouted gibberish from Pickman, and the deafening discharge of all six chambers of a revolver, fired spectacularly as a lion-tamer might fire in the air for effect. A muffled squeal or squawk, and a thud. Then more wood and brick grating, a pause, and the opening of the door—at which I'll confess I started violently. Pickman reappeared with his smoking weapon, cursing the bloated rats that infested the ancient well.

---

[a] paralysed] paralyzed C, D
[b] squeals or bleats] squeals, or bleats, D; squeals or beats E
[c] gooseflesh] goose-flesh D
[d] before.] before. What ~~did it~~ was it that gripped malignly at my memory, playing with it as a cat plays with a mouse or a ghoul plays with a corpse? God!—Yes— that was it! The wooden cover on that well—the ancient brick well that reached to the labyrinth of witchcraft tunnels to graveyard & den & sea! *It had been pushed up from beneath by something trying to get out.* And even as I reeled from the impact of that idea I heard a steady grating sound. The cover was coming off! ¶ A shot broke the spell. ~~My eyes, released from the hypnosis of fear,~~ Whether it was followed by a muffled squawk & a thud I can't be sure; for my eyes, released from the fright-hypnosis, were focussing all my remaining faculties in a search for a means of escape. I spied a narrow window over the table, & leaping up, was fumbling with the rusty hasp when another shot sounded from the main cellar. A [*excised*]

"The deuce knows what they eat, Thurber," he grinned, "for those archaic tunnels touched graveyard and witch-den and seacoast.[a] But whatever it is, they must have run short, for they were devilish anxious to get out. Your yelling stirred them up, I fancy. Better be cautious in these old places—our rodent friends are the one drawback, though I sometimes think they're a positive asset by way of atmosphere and colour."[b]

Well, Eliot, that was the end of the night's adventure. Pickman had promised to shew[c] me the place, and heaven[d] knows he had done it. He led me out of that tangle of alleys in another direction, it seems, for when we sighted a lamp post[e] we were in a half-familiar street with monotonous rows of mingled tenement blocks and old houses. Charter Street, it turned out to be, but I was too flustered to notice just where we hit it. We were too late for the elevated, and walked back downtown through Hanover Street. I remember that walk. We switched from Tremont up Beacon, and Pickman left me at the corner of Joy, where I turned off. I never spoke to him again.

Why did I drop him? Don't be impatient. Wait till I ring for coffee. We've had enough of the other stuff, but I for one need something. No—it wasn't the paintings I saw in that place; though I'll swear they were enough to get him ostracised[f] in nine-tenths of the homes and clubs of Boston, and I guess you won't wonder now why I have to steer clear of subways and cellars. It was—something I found in my coat the next morning. You know, the curled-up paper tacked to that frightful canvas in the cellar; the thing I thought was a photograph of some scene he meant to use as a background for that monster. That last scare had come while I was reaching to uncurl it, and it seems I had vacantly crumpled it into my pocket. But here's the coffee—take it black, Eliot, if you're wise.

---

[a] seacoast.] sea-coast. E
[b] colour."] color." C, D
[c] shew] show B, C, D, E
[d] heaven] Heaven A, B, E
[e] lamp post] lamp-post C, D
[f] ostracised] ostracized C, D

Yes, that paper was the reason I dropped Pickman; Richard Upton Pickman, the greatest artist I have[a] ever known—and the foulest being that ever leaped the bounds of life into the pits of myth and madness. Eliot,[b] old Reid was right. He wasn't strictly human. Either he was born in strange shadow, or he'd found a way to unlock the forbidden gate. It's all the same now, for he's gone—back into the fabulous darkness he loved to haunt. Here, let's have the chandelier going.

Don't ask me to explain or even conjecture about what I burned. Don't ask me, either, what lay behind that mole-like scrambling Pickman was so keen to pass off as rats. There are secrets, you know, which might have come down from old Salem times, and Cotton Mather tells even stranger things. You know how damned lifelike[c] Pickman's paintings were—how we all wondered where he got those faces.

Well—that paper wasn't a photograph of any background, after all. What it shewed[d] was simply the monstrous being he was painting on that awful canvas. It was the model he was using—and its background was merely the wall of the cellar studio in minute detail. But by God,[e] Eliot, *it was a photograph from life.*

[a] have] had D
[b] Eliot,] Eliot— A, B, C, E
[c] lifelike] life-like D
[d] shewed] showed B, C, D, E
[e] God,] heaven, D

The Silver Key

When Randolph Carter was thirty he lost the key of[a] the gate of dreams. Prior to that time he had made up for the prosiness of life by nightly excursions to strange and ancient cities beyond space, and lovely, unbelievable garden lands across ethereal seas; but as middle age hardened upon him he felt these[b] liberties slipping away little by little, until at last he was cut off altogether. No more could his galleys sail up the river Oukranos past the gilded spires of Thran, or his elephant caravans tramp through perfumed jungles in Kled, where forgotten palaces with veined ivory columns sleep lovely and unbroken under the moon.

He had read much of things as they are, and talked with too many people. Well-meaning philosophers had taught him to look into the logical relations of things, and analyse[c] the processes which shaped his thoughts and fancies. Wonder had gone away, and he had forgotten that all life is only a set of pictures in the brain, among which there is no difference betwixt those born of real things and those born of inward dreamings, and no cause to value the one above the other. Custom had dinned into his ears a superstitious reverence for that which tangibly and physically exists, and had made him secretly ashamed to dwell in visions. Wise men told him his simple fancies

Editor's Note: The T.Ms. is by HPL, and it was followed with the customary alterations in the only appearance in HPL's lifetime: *Weird Tales* (January 1929). The Arkham House editions also follow the T.Ms., but the 1964 edition leaves out a significant passage in the second paragraph.

Texts: A = T.Ms. (JHL); B = *Weird Tales* 13, No. 1 (January 1929): 41–49, 144; C = *The Outsider and Others* (Arkham House 1939), 32–39; D = *At the Mountains of Madness and Other Novels* (Arkham House, 1964), 386–97. Copy-text: A.

[a] of] to B
[b] these] those C, D
[c] analyse] analyze B

were inane and childish, and he believed it because he could see that they might easily be so. What he failed to recall was that the deeds of reality are just as inane and[a] childish, and even more absurd because their actors persist in fancying them full of meaning and purpose as the blind cosmos grinds aimlessly on from nothing to something and from[b] something back to nothing again, neither heeding nor knowing the wishes or existence of the minds that flicker for a second now and then in the darkness.

They had chained him down to things that are, and had then explained the workings of those things till mystery had gone out of the world. When he complained, and longed to escape into twilight realms where magic moulded[c] all the little vivid fragments and prized associations of his mind into vistas of breathless expectancy and unquenchable delight, they turned him instead toward the new-found[d] prodigies of science, bidding him find wonder in the atom's vortex and mystery in the sky's dimensions. And when he had failed to find these boons in things whose laws are known and measurable, they told him he lacked imagination, and was immature because he preferred dream-illusions to the illusions of our physical creation.

So Carter had tried to do as others did, and pretended that the common events and emotions of earthy minds were more important than the fantasies of rare and delicate souls. He did not dissent when they told him that the animal pain of a stuck pig or dyspeptic ploughman[e] in real life is a greater thing than the peerless beauty of Narath with its hundred carven gates and domes of chalcedony, which he dimly remembered from his dreams; and under their guidance he cultivated a painstaking sense of pity and tragedy.

Once in a while, though, he could not help seeing how shallow, fickle, and meaningless all human aspirations are, and how emptily our real impulses contrast with those pompous ideals we profess to hold. Then he would have recourse to the polite laughter they had taught

[a] childish, and . . . and] *om.* D
[b] something and from] *om.* B
[c] moulded] molded B
[d] new-found] new-/found C; newfound D
[e] ploughman] plowman B

him to use against the extravagance and artificiality of dreams; for he saw that the daily life of our world is every inch as extravagant and artificial, and far less worthy of respect because of its poverty in beauty and its silly reluctance to admit its own lack of reason and purpose. In this way he became a kind of humorist, for he did not see that even humour[a] is empty in a mindless universe devoid of any true standard of consistency or inconsistency.

In the first days of his bondage he had turned to the gentle churchly faith endeared to him by the naive[b] trust of his fathers, for thence stretched mystic avenues which seemed to promise escape from life. Only on closer view did he mark the starved fancy and beauty, the stale and prosy triteness, and the owlish gravity and grotesque claims of solid truth which reigned boresomely and overwhelmingly among most of its professors; or feel to the full the awkwardness with which it sought to keep alive as literal fact the outgrown fears and guesses of a primal race confronting the unknown. It wearied Carter to see how solemnly people tried to make earthly reality out of old myths which every step of their boasted science confuted, and this misplaced seriousness killed the attachment he might have kept for the ancient creeds had they been content to offer the sonorous rites and emotional outlets in their true guise of ethereal fantasy.

But when he came to study those who had thrown off the old myths, he found them even more ugly than those who had not. They did not know that beauty lies in harmony, and that loveliness of life has no standard amidst an aimless cosmos save only its harmony with the dreams and the feelings which have gone before and blindly moulded our little spheres out of the rest of chaos. They did not see that good and evil and beauty and ugliness are only ornamental fruits of perspective, whose sole value lies in their linkage to what chance made our fathers think and feel, and whose finer details are different for every race and culture. Instead, they either denied these things altogether or transferred them to the crude, vague instincts which they shared with the beasts and peasants; so that their lives were dragged malodorously out in pain, ugliness, and disproportion, yet filled with a

[a] humour] humor B
[b] naive] naïve C, D

ludicrous pride at having escaped from something no more unsound than that which still held them. They had traded the false gods of fear and blind piety for those of licence[a] and anarchy.

Carter did not taste deeply of these modern freedoms; for their cheapness and squalor sickened a spirit loving beauty alone,[b] while his reason rebelled at the flimsy logic with which their champions tried to gild brute impulse with a sacredness stripped from the idols they had discarded. He saw that most of them, in common with their cast-off priestcraft, could not escape from the delusion that life has a meaning apart from that which men dream into it; and could not lay aside the crude notion of ethics and obligations beyond those of beauty, even when all Nature shrieked of its unconsciousness and impersonal unmorality in the light of their scientific discoveries. Warped and bigoted with preconceived illusions of justice, freedom, and consistency, they cast off the old lore and the old ways[c] with the old beliefs; nor ever stopped to think that that lore and those ways were the sole makers of their present thoughts and judgments, and the sole guides and standards in a meaningless universe without fixed aims or stable points of reference. Having lost these artificial settings, their lives grew void of direction and dramatic interest; till at length they strove to drown their ennui in bustle and pretended usefulness, noise and excitement, barbaric display and animal sensation. When these things palled, disappointed, or grew nauseous through revulsion, they cultivated irony and bitterness, and found fault with the social order. Never could they realise[d] that their brute foundations were as shifting and contradictory as the gods of their elders, and that the satisfaction of one moment is the bane of the next. Calm, lasting beauty comes only in dream, and this solace the world had thrown away when in its worship of the real it threw away the secrets of childhood and innocence.

Amidst this chaos of hollowness and unrest Carter tried to live as befitted a man of keen thought and good heritage. With his dreams fading under the ridicule of the age he could not believe in anything,

[a] licence] license B, C, D
[b] alone,] alone D
[c] ways] way D
[d] realise] realize B, C, D

but the love of harmony kept him close to the ways of his race and station. He walked impassive through the cities of men, and sighed because no vista seemed fully real; because every flash of yellow sunlight on tall roofs and every glimpse of balustraded plazas in the first lamps of evening served only to remind him of dreams he had once known, and to make him homesick for ethereal lands he no longer knew how to find. Travel was only a mockery; and even the Great War stirred him but little, though he served from the first in the Foreign Legion of France. For a while he sought friends, but soon grew weary of the crudeness of their emotions, and the sameness and earthiness of their visions. He felt vaguely glad that all his relatives were distant and out of touch with him, for they could[a] not have understood his mental life. That is, none but his grandfather and great-uncle Christopher could, and they were long dead.

Then he began once more the writing of books, which he had left off when dreams first failed him. But here, too, was there no satisfaction or fulfilment;[b] for the touch of earth was upon his mind, and he could not think of lovely things as he had done of yore. Ironic humour[c] dragged down all the twilight minarets he reared, and the earthy fear of improbability blasted all the delicate and amazing flowers in his faery[d] gardens. The convention of assumed pity spilt mawkishness on his characters, while the myth of an important reality and significant human events and emotions debased all his high fantasy into thin-veiled allegory and cheap social satire. His new novels were successful as his old ones had never been; and because he knew how empty they must be to please an empty herd, he burned them and ceased his writing. They were very graceful novels, in which he urbanely laughed at the dreams he lightly sketched; but he saw that their sophistication had sapped all their life away.

It was after this that he cultivated deliberate illusion, and dabbled in the notions of the bizarre and the eccentric as an antidote for the

[a] could] would C, D
[b] fulfilment;] fulfillment; C, D
[c] humour] humor B, D
[d] faery] faëry C

commonplace. Most of these, however, soon shewed[a] their poverty and barrenness; and he saw that the popular doctrines of occultism are as dry and inflexible as those of science, yet without even the slender palliative of truth to redeem them. Gross stupidity, falsehood, and muddled thinking are not dream; and form no escape from life to a mind trained above their[b] level. So Carter bought stranger books and sought out deeper and more terrible men of fantastic erudition; delving into arcana of consciousness that few have trod, and learning things about the secret pits of life, legend, and immemorial antiquity which disturbed him ever afterward. He decided to live on a rarer plane, and furnished his Boston home to suit his changing moods; one room for each, hung in appropriate colours,[c] furnished with befitting books and objects, and provided with sources of the proper sensations of light, heat, sound, taste, and odour.[d]

Once he heard of a man in the South[e] who was shunned and feared for the blasphemous things he read in prehistoric books and clay tablets smuggled from India and Arabia. Him he visited,[f] living with him and sharing his studies for seven years, till horror overtook them one midnight in an unknown and archaic graveyard, and only one emerged where two had entered. Then he went back to Arkham, the terrible witch-haunted old town of his forefathers in New England, and had experiences in the dark, amidst the hoary willows and tottering gambrel roofs, which made him seal for ever[g] certain pages in the diary of a wild-minded ancestor. But these horrors took him only to the edge of reality, and were not of the true dream country he had known in youth; so that at fifty he despaired of any rest or contentment in a world grown too busy for beauty and too shrewd for dream.[h]

Having perceived at last the hollowness and futility of real things, Carter spent his days in retirement, and in wistful disjointed memories

[a] shewed] showed A, B, C, D
[b] their] their own C, D
[c] colours,] colors, B
[d] odour.] odor. B
[e] South] south D
[f] visited,] visited D
[g] for ever] forever D
[h] dream.] dreams. D

of his dream-filled youth. He thought it rather silly that he bothered[a] to keep on living at all, and got from a South American acquaintance a very curious liquid to take him to oblivion without suffering. Inertia and force of habit, however, caused him to defer action; and he lingered indecisively among thoughts of old times, taking down the strange hangings from his walls and refitting the house as it was in his early boyhood—purple panes,[b] Victorian furniture, and all.

With the passage of time he became almost glad he had lingered, for his relics of youth and his cleavage from the world made life and sophistication seem very distant and unreal; so much so that a touch of magic and expectancy stole back into his nightly slumbers. For years those slumbers had known only such twisted reflections of every-day things as the commonest slumbers know, but now there returned a flicker of something stranger and wilder; something of vaguely awesome immanence[c] which took the form of tensely clear pictures from his childhood days, and made him think of little inconsequential things he had long forgotten. He would often awake calling for his mother and grandfather, both in their graves a quarter of a century.

Then one night his grandfather reminded him of a key. The grey[d] old scholar, as vivid as in life, spoke long and earnestly of their ancient line, and of the strange visions of the delicate and sensitive men who composed it. He spoke of the flame-eyed Crusader who learnt wild secrets of the Saracens that held him captive; and of the first Sir Randolph Carter who studied magic when Elizabeth was queen. He spoke, too, of that Edmund Carter who had just escaped hanging in the Salem witchcraft, and who had placed in an antique box a great silver key handed down from his ancestors. Before Carter awaked, the gentle visitor had told him where to find that box; that carved oak box of archaic wonder whose grotesque lid no hand had raised for two centuries.

In the dust and shadows of the great attic he found it, remote and forgotten at the back of a drawer in a tall chest. It was about a foot square, and its Gothic carvings were so fearful that he did not marvel

[a] bothered] bother B
[b] panes,] panes. D
[c] immanence] imminence C, D
[d] grey] gray B

no person since Edmund Carter had dared to[a] open it. It gave forth no noise when shaken, but was mystic with the scent of unremembered spices. That it held a key was indeed only a dim legend, and Randolph Carter's father had never known such a box existed. It was bound in rusty iron, and no means was provided for working the formidable lock. Carter vaguely understood that he would find within it some key to the lost gate of dreams, but of where and how to use it his grandfather had told him nothing.

An old servant forced the carven lid, shaking as he did so at the hideous faces leering from the blackened wood, and at some unplaced familiarity. Inside, wrapped in a discoloured[b] parchment, was a huge key of tarnished silver covered with cryptical arabesques; but of any legible explanation there was none. The parchment was voluminous, and held only the strange hieroglyphs of an unknown tongue written with an antique reed. Carter recognised[c] the characters as those he had seen on a certain papyrus scroll belonging to that terrible scholar of the South who had vanished one midnight in a nameless cemetery. The man had always shivered when he read this scroll, and Carter shivered now.

But he cleaned the key, and kept it by him nightly in its aromatic box of ancient oak. His dreams were meanwhile increasing in vividness, and though shewing[d] him none of the strange cities and incredible gardens of the old days, were assuming a definite cast whose purpose could not be mistaken. They were calling him back along the years, and with the mingled wills of all his fathers were pulling him toward some hidden and ancestral source. Then he knew he must go into the past and merge himself with old things, and day after day he thought of the hills to the north where haunted Arkham and the rushing Miskatonic[e] and the lonely rustic homestead of his people lay.

In the brooding fire of autumn Carter took the old remembered way past graceful lines of rolling hill and stone-walled meadow, distant vale and hanging woodland, curving road and nestling farmstead, and the

[a] to] *om.* B
[b] discoloured] discolored B
[c] recognised] recognized B, C, D
[d] shewing] showing A, B, C, D
[e] Miskatonic] Miskantonic D

crystal windings of the Miskatonic, crossed here and there by rustic bridges of wood or stone. At one bend he saw the[a] group of giant elms among which an ancestor had oddly vanished a century and a half before, and shuddered as the wind blew meaningly through them. Then there was the crumbling farmhouse of old Goody Fowler the witch, with its little evil windows and great roof sloping nearly to the ground on the north side. He speeded up his car as he passed it, and did not slacken till he had mounted the hill where his mother and her fathers before her were born, and where the old white house still looked proudly across the road at the breathlessly lovely panorama of rocky slope and verdant valley, with the distant spires of Kingsport on the horizon, and hints of the archaic, dream-laden sea in the farthest background.

Then came the steeper slope that held the old Carter place he had not seen in over forty years. Afternoon was far gone when he reached the foot, and at the bend half way[b] up he paused to scan the outspread countryside golden and glorified in the slanting floods of magic poured out by a western sun. All the strangeness and expectancy of his recent dreams seemed present in this hushed and unearthly landscape, and he thought of the unknown solitudes of other planets as his eyes traced out the velvet and deserted lawns shining undulant between their tumbled walls, the[c] clumps of faery[d] forest setting off far lines of purple hills beyond hills, and the spectral wooded valley dipping down in shadow to dank hollows where trickling waters crooned and gurgled among swollen and distorted roots.

Something made him feel that motors did not belong in the realm he was seeking, so he left his car at the edge of the forest, and putting the great key in his coat pocket walked on up the hill. Woods now engulfed him utterly, though he knew the house was on a high knoll that cleared the trees except to the north. He wondered how it would look, for it had been left vacant and untended through his neglect since the death of his strange great-uncle Christopher thirty years

[a] the] a B
[b] half way] half-way B
[c] the] and D
[d] faery] faëry C

before. In his boyhood he had revelled[a] through long visits there, and had found weird marvels in the woods beyond the orchard.

Shadows thickened around him, for the night was near. Once a gap in the trees opened up to the right, so that he saw off across leagues of twilight meadow and spied the old Congregational steeple on Central Hill in Kingsport; pink with the last flush of day, the panes of the little round windows blazing with reflected fire. Then, when he was in deep shadow again, he recalled with a start that the glimpse must have come from childish memory alone, since the old white church had long been torn down to make room for the Congregational Hospital. He had read of it with interest, for the paper had told about some strange burrows or passages found in the rocky hill beneath.

Through his puzzlement a voice piped, and he started again at its familiarity after long years. Old Benijah Corey had been his Uncle Christopher's hired man, and was aged even in those far-off times of his boyhood visits. Now he must be well over a hundred, but that piping voice could come from no one else. He could distinguish no words, yet the tone was haunting and unmistakable. To think that "Old Benijy" should still be alive!

"Mister Randy! Mister Randy! Whar be[b] ye? D'ye want to skeer yer Aunt Marthy plumb to death? Hain't she tuld ye to keep nigh the place in the arternoon an' git back afur dark? Randy! Ran . . . dee![c] . . . He's the beatin'est boy fer runnin' off in the woods I ever see; haff the time a-settin' moonin' raound that snake-den in the upper timber-lot![d] . . . Hey,[e] yew, Ran . . . dee!"[f]

Randolph Carter stopped in the pitch darkness and rubbed his hand across his eyes. Something was queer. He had been somewhere he ought not to be; had strayed very far away to places where he had not belonged, and was now inexcusably late. He had not noticed the time on the Kingsport steeple, though he could easily have made it out with his pocket telescope; but he knew his lateness was something very

[a] revelled] reveled B
[b] Whar be] Wharbe D
[c] Ran . . . dee!] Ran—dee! B
[d] timber-lot!] timberlot! D
[e] Hey,] Hey D
[f] Ran . . . dee!"] Ran—dee!" B

strange and unprecedented. He was not sure he had his little telescope with him, and put his hand in his blouse pocket to see. No, it was not there, but there was the big silver key he had found in a box somewhere. Uncle Chris had told him something odd once about an old unopened box with a key in it, but Aunt Martha had stopped the story abruptly, saying it was no kind of thing to tell a child whose head was already too full of queer fancies. He tried to recall just where he had found the key, but something seemed very confused. He guessed it was in the attic at home in Boston, and dimly remembered bribing Parks with half his week's allowance to help him open the box and keep quiet about it; but when he remembered this, the face of Parks came up very strangely, as if the wrinkles of long years had fallen upon the brisk little Cockney.[a]

"Ran . . . dee! Ran . . . dee![b] Hi! Hi! Randy!"

A swaying lantern came around the black bend, and old Benijah pounced on the silent and bewildered form of the pilgrim.

"Durn ye, boy, so thar ye be! Ain't ye got a tongue in yer head, that ye can't answer a body? I ben callin' this haff hour, an' ye must a heerd me long ago! Dun't[c] ye know yer Aunt Marthy's all a-fidget over yer bein' off arter dark? Wait till I tell yer Uncle Chris when he gits hum! Ye'd orta know these here woods ain't no fitten place to be traipsin' this hour! They's things abroad what dun't do nobody no good, as my gran'sir'[d] knowed afur me. Come, Mister Randy, or Hannah wun't[e] keep supper no longer!"

So Randolph Carter was marched up the road where wondering stars glimmered through high autumn boughs. And dogs barked as the yellow light of small-paned windows shone out at the farther turn, and the Pleiades[f] twinkled across the open knoll where a great gambrel roof stood black against the dim west. Aunt Martha in the doorway, and did not scold too hard when Benijah shoved the truant in. She knew Uncle Chris well enough to expect such things of the

---

[a] Cockney.] cockney. B

[b] "Ran . . . dee! Ran . . . dee!] "Ran—dee! Ran—dee! B

[c] Dun't] Don't B [Don't *changed to* Dun't *in A*]

[d] gran'sir'] gran'-sir' C, D

[e] wun't] wunt A, C, D

[f] Pleiades] Pleiads A

Carter blood. Randolph did not shew[a] his key, but ate his supper in silence and protested only when bedtime came. He sometimes dreamed better when awake, and he wanted to use that key.

In the morning Randolph was up early, and would have run off to the upper timber-lot if Uncle Chris had not caught him and forced him into his chair by the breakfast table. He looked impatiently around the low-pitched room with the rag carpet and exposed beams and corner-posts, and smiled only when the orchard boughs scratched at the little[b] leaded panes of the rear window. The trees and the hills were close to him, and formed the gates of that timeless realm which was his true country.

Then, when he was free, he felt in his blouse pocket for the key; and being reassured, skipped off across the orchard to the rise beyond, where the wooded hill climbed again to heights above even the treeless knoll. The floor of the forest was mossy and mysterious, and great lichened rocks rose vaguely here and there in the dim light like Druid[c] monoliths among the swollen and twisted trunks of a sacred grove. Once in his ascent Randolph crossed a rushing stream whose falls a little way off sang runic incantations to the lurking fauns and Ægipans[d] and dryads.

Then he came to the strange cave in the forest slope, the dreaded "snake-den" which country folk shunned, and away from which Benijah had warned him again and again. It was deep; far deeper than anyone but Randolph suspected, for the boy had found a fissure in the farthermost black corner that led to a loftier grotto beyond—a haunting sepulchral place whose granite walls held a curious illusion of conscious artifice. On this occasion he crawled in as usual, lighting his way with matches filched from the sitting-room match-safe, and edging through the final crevice with an eagerness hard to explain even to himself. He could not tell why he approached the farther wall so confidently, or why he instinctively drew forth the great silver key as he did so. But on he went, and when he danced back to the house that

[a] shew] show A, B, C, D
[b] little] om. D
[c] Druid] druid B
[d] Ægipans] aegipans A, B, C, D

night he offered no excuses for his lateness, nor heeded in the least the reproofs he gained for ignoring the noontide dinner-horn altogether.

Now it is agreed by all the distant relatives of Randolph Carter that something occurred to heighten his imagination in his tenth year. His cousin, Ernest B. Aspinwall, Esq., of Chicago, is fully ten years his senior;[a] and distinctly recalls a change in the boy after the autumn of 1883. Randolph had looked on scenes of fantasy that few others can ever have beheld, and stranger still were some of the qualities which he shewed[b] in relation to very mundane things. He seemed, in fine, to have picked up an odd gift of prophecy; and reacted unusually to things which, though at the time without meaning, were later found to justify the singular impressions. In subsequent decades as new inventions, new names, and new events appeared one by one in the book of history, people would now and then recall wonderingly how Carter had years before let fall some careless word of undoubted connexion[c] with what was then far in the future. He did not himself understand these words, or know why certain things made him feel certain emotions; but fancied that some unremembered dream must be responsible. It was as early as 1897 that he turned pale when some traveller[d] mentioned the French town of Belloy-en-Santerre, and friends remembered it when he was almost mortally wounded there in 1916, while serving with the Foreign Legion in the Great War.

Carter's relatives talk much of these things because he has lately disappeared. His little old servant Parks, who for years bore patiently with his vagaries, last saw him on the morning he drove off alone in his car with a key he had recently found. Parks had helped him get the key from the old box containing it, and had felt strangely affected by the grotesque carvings on the box, and by some other odd quality he could not name. When Carter left, he had said he was going to visit his old ancestral country around Arkham.

[a] senior;] senior B
[b] shewed] showed A, B, C, D
[c] connexion] connection B, C, D
[d] traveller] traveler B

Half way[a] up Elm Mountain, on the way to the ruins of the old Carter place, they found his motor set carefully by the roadside; and in it was a box of fragrant wood with carvings that frightened the countrymen who stumbled on it. The box held only a queer parchment whose characters no linguist or palaeographer[b] has been able to decipher or identify. Rain had long effaced any possible footprints, though Boston investigators had something to say about evidences of disturbances among the fallen timbers of the Carter place. It was, they averred, as though someone had groped about the ruins at no distant period. A common white handkerchief found among forest rocks on the hillside beyond cannot be identified as belonging to the missing man.

There is talk of apportioning Randolph Carter's estate among his heirs, but I shall stand firmly against this course because I do not believe he is dead. There are twists of time and space, of vision and reality, which only a dreamer can divine; and from what I know of Carter I think he has[c] merely found a way to traverse these mazes. Whether or not he will ever come back, I cannot[d] say. He wanted the lands of dream he had lost, and yearned for the days of his childhood. Then he found a key, and I somehow believe he was able to use it to strange advantage.

I shall ask him when I see him, for I expect to meet him shortly in a certain dream-city we both used to haunt. It is rumoured[e] in Ulthar, beyond the river[f] Skai, that a new king reigns on the opal throne of Ilek-Vad, that fabulous town of turrets atop the hollow cliffs of glass overlooking the twilight sea wherein the bearded and finny Gnorri build their singular labyrinths, and I believe I know how to interpret this rumour.[g] Certainly, I look forward impatiently to the sight of that great silver key, for in its cryptical arabesques there may stand symbolised[h] all the aims and mysteries of a blindly impersonal cosmos.

[a] Half way] Half-way B

[b] palaeographer] paleographer B

[c] has] had D

[d] cannot] can not B

[e] rumoured] rumored B

[f] river] River A, B, C, D

[g] rumour.] rumor. B

[h] symbolised] symbolized B

The Strange High House in the Mist

In the morning mist comes up from the sea by the cliffs beyond Kingsport. White and feathery it comes from the deep to its brothers the clouds, full of dreams of dank pastures and caves of leviathan. And later, in still summer rains on the steep roofs of poets, the clouds scatter bits of those dreams, that men shall not live without rumour[a] of old,[b] strange secrets, and wonders that planets tell planets alone in the night. When tales fly thick in the grottoes of tritons, and conches[c] in seaweed cities blow wild tunes learned from the Elder Ones, then great eager mists flock to heaven laden with lore, and oceanward eyes on the rocks see only a mystic whiteness, as if the cliff's rim were the rim of all earth, and the solemn bells of buoys tolled free in the aether of faery.[d]

Editor's Note: The surviving ms. is a strange compendium of the original autograph draft (pp. 1–7, 10) and a T.Ms. (pp. 8–9) extensively revised by HPL in pen. The ms. has been revised in pencil; some of these revisions must date after the first appearance (*Weird Tales*, October 1931), since that publication prints those phrases in the text in their unrevised state. Moreover, at least one phrase was probably revised as HPL prepared a clean T.Ms. to send to *Weird Tales*. Arkham House editions derive from the *Weird Tales* text, hence do not incorporate these revisions (of which there are comparatively few).

On a page prefacing the text, and written in a much later hand than the A.Ms. part of the text, HPL has written: "A fantastic short story by me, entitled 'The Strange High House in the Mist', was to have appeared in the second number of *The Recluse*. The rough draught is no longer in existence, & no proofs were furnished. Several carbon copies of the typed ms. remain, & the story was later printed in *Weird Tales*."

Texts: A = A.Ms./T.Ms. (JHL); B = *Weird Tales* 18, No. 3 (October 1931): 394–400; C = *Dagon and Other Macabre Tales* (Arkham House, 1965), 260–68. Copy-text: A.

[a] rumour] rumor B, C
[b] old,] old B, C
[c] conches] conchs B, C
[d] faery.] faëry. B, C

Now north of archaic Kingsport the crags climb lofty and curious, terrace on terrace, till the northernmost hangs in the sky like a grey[a] frozen wind-cloud. Alone it is, a bleak point jutting in limitless space, for there the coast turns sharp where the great Miskatonic pours out of the plains past Arkham, bringing woodland legends and little quaint memories of New England's hills. The sea-folk in Kingsport look up at that cliff as other sea-folk look up at the pole-star, and time the night's watches by the way it hides or shews[b] the Great Bear, Cassiopeia, and the Dragon. Among them it is one with the firmament, and truly, it is hidden from them when the mist hides the stars or the sun. Some of the cliffs they love, as that whose grotesque profile they call Father Neptune, or that whose pillared steps they term The Causeway;[c] but this one they fear because it is so near the sky. The Portuguese[d] sailors coming in from a voyage cross themselves when they first see it, and the old Yankees believe it would be much graver matter than[e] death to climb it, if indeed that were possible. Nevertheless there is an ancient house on that cliff, and at evening men see lights in the small-paned windows.

The ancient house has always been there, and people say One dwells therein[f] who talks with the morning mists that come up from the deep, and perhaps sees singular things oceanward at those times when the cliff's rim becomes the rim of all earth, and solemn buoys toll free in the white aether of faery.[g] This they tell from hearsay, for that forbidding crag is always unvisited, and natives dislike to train telescopes on it. Summer boarders have indeed scanned it with jaunty binoculars, but have never seen more than the grey[h] primeval roof, peaked and shingled, whose eaves come nearly to the grey[i] foundations, and the dim yellow light of the little windows peeping out from under those eaves in the dusk. These summer people do not believe that the

---

[a] grey] gray B, C
[b] shews] shows A, B, C
[c] The Causeway;] "The Causeway;" B; "The Causeway"; C
[d] Portuguese] Portugese A
[e] than] then B
[f] therein] within B, C
[g] faery.] faëry. B, C
[h] grey] gray B, C
[i] grey] gray B, C

same One has lived in the ancient house for hundreds of years, but cannot[a] prove their heresy to any real Kingsporter. Even the Terrible Old Man who talks to leaden pendulums in bottles, buys groceries with centuried Spanish gold, and keeps stone idols in the yard of his antediluvian cottage in Water Street can only say these things were the same when his grandfather was a boy, and that must have been inconceivable ages ago, when Belcher or Shirley or Pownall or Bernard was Governor of His Majesty's Province of the Massachusetts-Bay.

Then one summer there came a philosopher into Kingsport. His name was Thomas Olney, and he taught ponderous things in a college by Narragansett Bay. With stout wife and romping children he came, and his eyes were weary with seeing the same things for many years, and thinking the same well-disciplined thoughts. He looked at the mists from the diadem of Father Neptune, and tried to walk into their white world of mystery along the titan steps of The Causeway. Morning after morning he would lie on the cliffs and look over the world's rim at the cryptical aether beyond, listening to spectral bells and the wild cries of what might have been gulls. Then, when the mist would lift and the sea stand out prosy with the smoke of steamers, he would sigh and descend to the town, where he loved to thread the narrow olden lanes up and down hill, and study the crazy tottering gables and odd pillared[b] doorways which had sheltered so many generations of sturdy sea-folk. And he even talked with the Terrible Old Man, who was not fond of strangers, and was invited into his fearsomely archaic cottage where low ceilings and wormy panelling hear the echoes of disquieting soliloquies in the dark small hours.

Of course it was inevitable that Olney should mark the grey[c] unvisited cottage in the sky, on that sinister northward crag which is one with the mists and the firmament. Always over Kingsport it hung, and always its mystery sounded in whispers through Kingsport's crooked alleys. The Terrible Old Man wheezed a tale that his father had told him, of lightning that shot one night *up from*[d] that peaked cottage

[a] cannot] can not B, C
[b] odd pillared] odd-pillared B, C
[c] grey] gray B, C
[d] *up from*] up from C

to the clouds of higher heaven; and Granny Orne, whose tiny gambrel-roofed abode in Ship Street is all covered with moss and ivy, croaked over something her grandmother had heard at second-hand, about shapes that flapped out of the eastern mists straight into the narrow single door of that unreachable place—for the door is set close to the edge of the crag toward the ocean, and glimpsed only from ships at sea.

At length, being avid for new strange things and held back by neither the Kingsporter's fear nor the summer boarder's usual indolence, Olney made a very terrible resolve. Despite a conservative training—or because of it, for humdrum lives breed wistful longings for[a] the unknown—he swore a great oath to scale that avoided northern cliff and visit the abnormally antique grey[b] cottage in the sky. Very plausibly his saner self argued that the place must be tenanted by people who reached it from inland along the easier ridge beside the Miskatonic's estuary. Probably they traded in Arkham, knowing how little Kingsport liked their habitation, or perhaps being unable to climb down the cliff on the Kingsport side. Olney walked out along the lesser cliffs to where the great crag leaped insolently up to consort with celestial things, and became very sure that no human feet could mount it or descend it on that beetling southern slope. East and north it rose thousands of feet vertically[c] from the water, so only the western side, inland and toward Arkham,[d] remained.

One early morning in August Olney set out to find a path to the inaccessible pinnacle. He worked northwest along pleasant back roads, past Hooper's Pond and the old brick powder house[e] to where the pastures slope up to the ridge above the Miskatonic and give a lovely vista of Arkham's white Georgian steeples across leagues of river and meadow. Here he found a shady road to Arkham, but no trail at all in the seaward direction he wished. Woods and fields crowded up to the high bank of the river's mouth, and bore not a sign of man's presence; not even a stone wall or a straying cow, but only the tall grass and giant

---

[a] for] of C
[b] grey] gray B, C
[c] vertically] perpendicular A, B, C [*revised in pencil in A*]
[d] Arkham,] Arkham C
[e] powder house] powder-house B, C

trees and tangles of briers[a] that the first Indian might have seen. As he climbed slowly east, higher and higher above the estuary on his left and nearer and nearer the sea, he found the way growing in difficulty;[b] till he wondered how ever the dwellers in that disliked place managed to reach the world outside, and whether they came often to market in Arkham.

Then the trees thinned, and far below him on his right he saw the hills and antique roofs and spires of Kingsport. Even Central Hill was a dwarf from this height, and he could just make out the ancient graveyard by the Congregational Hospital, beneath which rumour[c] said some terrible caves or burrows lurked. Ahead lay sparse grass and scrub blueberry bushes, and beyond them the naked rock of the crag and the thin peak of the dreaded grey[d] cottage. Now the ridge narrowed, and Olney grew dizzy at his loneness in the sky. South[e] of him the frightful precipice above Kingsport, north of him the vertical drop of nearly a mile to the river's mouth. Suddenly a great chasm opened before him, ten feet deep, so that he had to let himself down by his hands and drop to a slanting floor, and then crawl perilously up a natural defile in the opposite wall. So this was the way the folk of the uncanny house journeyed betwixt earth and sky!

When he climbed out of the chasm a morning mist was gathering, but he clearly saw the lofty and unhallowed cottage ahead; walls as grey[f] as the rock, and high peak standing bold against the milky white of the seaward vapours.[g] And he perceived that there was no door on this landward end, but only a couple of small lattice windows with dingy bull's-eye panes leaded in seventeenth-century[h] fashion. All around him was cloud and chaos, and he could see nothing below but[i] the whiteness of illimitable space. He was alone in the sky with this queer and very disturbing house; and when he sidled around to the

---

[a] briers] briars B, C
[b] difficulty;] difficulty B, C
[c] rumour] rumor B, C
[d] grey] gray B, C
[e] sky. South] sky, south C
[f] grey] gray B, C
[g] vapours.] vapors. B, C
[h] seventeenth-century] Seventeenth Century B, C
[i] but] *om.* C

front and saw that the wall stood flush with the cliff's edge, so that the single narrow door was not to be reached save from the empty aether, he felt a distinct terror that altitude could not wholly explain. And it was very odd that shingles so worm-eaten could survive, or bricks so crumbled still form a standing chimney.

As the mist thickened, Olney crept around to the windows on the north and west and south sides, trying them but finding them all locked. He was vaguely glad they were locked, because the more he saw of that house the less he wished to get in. Then a sound halted him. He heard a lock rattle and bolt shoot, and a long creaking follow as if a heavy door were slowly and cautiously opened. This was on the oceanward side that he could not see, where the narrow portal opened on blank space thousands of feet in the misty sky above the waves.

Then there was heavy, deliberate tramping in the cottage, and Olney heard the windows opening, first on the north side opposite him, and then on the west just around the corner. Next would come the south windows, under the great low eaves on the side where he stood; and it must be said that he was more than uncomfortable as he thought of the detestable house on one side and the vacancy of upper air on the other. When a fumbling came in the nearer casements he crept around to the west again, flattening himself against the wall beside the now opened windows. It was plain that the owner had come home; but he had not come from the land, nor from any balloon or airship that could be imagined. Steps sounded again, and Olney edged round to the north; but before he could find a haven a voice called softly, and he knew he must confront his host.

Stuck out of a[a] west window was a great black-bearded face whose eyes were phosphorescent[b] with the imprint of unheard-of sights. But the voice was gentle, and of a quaint olden kind, so that Olney did not shudder when a brown hand reached out to help him over the sill and into that low room of black oak wainscots and carved Tudor furnishings. The man was clad in very ancient garments, and had about him an unplaceable nimbus of sea-lore and dreams of tall galleons. Olney does not recall many of the wonders he told, or even who he

[a] a] the C
[b] were phosphorescent] shone phosphorescently A

was; but says that he was strange and kindly, and filled with the magic of unfathomed voids of time and space. The small room seemed green with a dim aqueous light, and Olney saw that the far windows to the east were not open, but shut against the misty aether with dull thick panes like the bottoms of old bottles.

That bearded host seemed young, yet looked out of eyes steeped in the elder mysteries; and from the tales of marvellous[a] ancient things he related, it must be guessed that the village folk were right in saying he had communed with the mists of the sea and the clouds of the sky ever since there was any village to watch his taciturn dwelling from the plain below. And the day wore on, and still Olney listened to rumours[b] of old times and far places, and heard how the Kings[c] of Atlantis fought with the slippery blasphemies that wriggled out of rifts in ocean's floor, and how the pillared and weedy temple of Poseidonis is still glimpsed at midnight by lost ships, who know by its sight that they are lost. Years of the Titans were recalled, but the host grew timid when he spoke of the dim first age of chaos before the gods or even the Elder Ones were born, and when only[d] *the other gods* came to dance on the peak of Hatheg-Kla in the stony desert near Ulthar, beyond the river[e] Skai.

It was at this point that there came a knocking on the door; that ancient door of nail-studded oak beyond which lay only the abyss of white cloud. Olney started in fright, but the bearded man motioned him to be still, and tiptoed to the door to look out through a very small peep-hole.[f] What he saw he did not like, so pressed his fingers to his lips and tiptoed around to shut and lock all the windows before returning to the ancient settle beside his guest. Then Olney saw lingering against the translucent squares of each of the little dim windows in succession a queer black outline as the caller moved inquisitively about before leaving; and he was glad his host had not answered the knocking. For there are strange objects in the great abyss, and the seeker of dreams must take care not to stir up or meet the wrong ones.

[a] marvellous] marvelous B, C
[b] rumours] rumors B, C
[c] Kings] kings B, C
[d] only] *om.* B, C
[e] river] River A, B, C
[f] peep-hole.] peephole. B, C

Then the shadows began to gather; first little furtive ones under the table, and then bolder ones in the dark panelled corners. And the bearded man made enigmatical gestures of prayer, and lit tall candles in curiously wrought brass candlesticks.[a] Frequently he would glance at the door as if he expected someone,[b] and at length his glance seemed answered by a singular rapping which must have followed some very ancient and secret code. This time he did not even glance through the peep-hole,[c] but swung the great oak bar and shot the bolt, unlatching the heavy door and flinging it wide to the stars and the mist.

And then to the sound of obscure harmonies there floated into that room from the deep all the dreams and memories of earth's sunken Mighty Ones. And golden flames played about weedy locks, so that Olney was dazzled as he did them homage. Trident-bearing Neptune was there, and sportive tritons and fantastic nereids, and upon dolphins' backs was balanced a vast crenulate shell wherein rode the grey[d] and awful form of primal Nodens, Lord of the Great Abyss. And the conches[e] of the tritons gave weird blasts, and the nereids made strange sounds by striking on the grotesque resonant shells of unknown lurkers in black sea-caves. Then hoary Nodens reached forth a wizened hand and helped Olney and his host into the vast shell, whereat the conches[f] and the gongs set up a wild and awesome clamour.[g] And out into the limitless aether reeled that fabulous train, the noise of whose shouting was lost in the echoes of thunder.

All night in Kingsport they watched that lofty cliff when the storm and the mists gave them glimpses of it, and when toward the small hours the little dim windows went dark they whispered of dread and disaster. And Olney's children and stout wife prayed to the bland proper god of Baptists, and hoped that the traveller would borrow an umbrella and rubbers unless the rain stopped by morning. Then dawn swam dripping and mist-wreathed out of the sea, and the buoys tolled

[a] candlesticks.] candle-sticks. C
[b] someone,] some one, B, C
[c] peep-hole,] peephole, B; peep-/hole, C
[d] grey] gray B, C
[e] conches] conchs B
[f] conches] conchs B, C
[g] clamour.] clamor. B, C

solemn in vortices of white aether. And at noon elfin horns rang over the ocean as Olney, dry and light-footed, climbed down from the cliffs to antique Kingsport with the look of far places in his eyes. He could not recall what he had dreamed in the sky-perched hut of that still nameless hermit, or say how he had crept down that crag untraversed by other feet. Nor could he talk of these matters at all save with the Terrible Old Man, who afterward mumbled queer things in his long white beard; vowing that the man who came down from that crag was not wholly the man who went up, and that somewhere under that grey[a] peaked roof, or amidst inconceivable reaches of that sinister white mist, there lingered still the lost spirit of him who was Thomas Olney.

And ever since that hour, through dull dragging years of greyness[b] and weariness, the philosopher has laboured[c] and eaten and slept and done uncomplaining the suitable deeds of a citizen. Not any more does he long for the magic of farther hills, or sigh for secrets that peer like green reefs from a bottomless sea. The sameness of his days no longer gives him sorrow, and well-disciplined thoughts have grown enough for his imagination. His good wife waxes stouter and his children older and prosier and more useful, and he never fails to smile correctly with pride when the occasion calls for it. In his glance there is not any restless light, and if he ever listens for solemn bells or far elfin horns it is only at night when old dreams are wandering. He has never seen Kingsport again, for his family disliked the funny old houses,[d] and complained that the drains were impossibly bad. They have a trim bungalow now at Bristol Highlands, where no tall crags tower, and the neighbours[e] are urban and modern.

But in Kingsport strange tales are abroad, and even the Terrible Old Man admits a thing untold by his grandfather. For now, when the wind sweeps boisterous out of the north past the high ancient house that is one with the firmament, there is broken at last that ominous[f] brooding silence ever before the bane of Kingsport's maritime cotters.

[a] grey] gray B, C
[b] greyness] grayness B, C
[c] laboured] labored B, C
[d] houses,] houses B, C
[e] neighbours] neighbors B, C
[f] ominous] ominous, B, C

And old folk tell of pleasing voices heard singing there, and of laughter that swells with joys beyond earth's joys; and say that at evening the little low windows are brighter than formerly. They say, too, that the fierce aurora comes oftener to that spot, shining blue in the north with visions of frozen worlds while the crag and the cottage hang black and fantastic against wild coruscations. And the mists of the dawn are thicker, and sailors are not quite so sure that all the muffled seaward ringing is that of the solemn buoys.

Worst of all, though, is the shrivelling of old fears in the hearts of Kingsport's young men, who grow prone to listen at night to the north wind's faint distant sounds. They swear no harm or pain can inhabit that high peaked cottage, for in the new voices gladness beats, and with them the tinkle of laughter and music. What tales the sea-mists may bring to that haunted and northernmost pinnacle they do not know, but they long to extract some hint of the wonders that knock at the cliff-yawning door when clouds are thickest. And patriarchs dread lest some day one by one they seek out that inaccessible peak in the sky, and learn what centuried secrets hide beneath the steep shingled roof which is part of the rocks and the stars and the ancient fears of Kingsport. That those venturesome youths will come back they do not doubt, but they think a light may be gone from their eyes, and a will from their hearts. And they do not wish quaint Kingsport with its climbing lanes and archaic gables to drag listless down the years while voice by voice the laughing chorus grows stronger and wilder in that unknown and terrible eyrie where mists and the dreams of mists stop to rest on their way from the sea to the skies.

They do not wish the souls of their young men to leave the pleasant hearths and gambrel-roofed taverns of old Kingsport, nor do they wish the laughter and song in that high rocky place to grow louder. For as the voice which has come has brought fresh mists from the sea and from the north fresh lights, so do they say that still other voices will bring more mists and more lights, till perhaps the olden gods (whose existence they hint only in whispers for fear the Congregational parson shall hear) may come out of the deep and from unknown Kadath in the cold waste and make their dwelling on that evilly appropriate crag so close to the gentle hills and valleys of quiet simple fisherfolk.[a] This they do not wish, for to plain people things not of earth are unwelcome; and besides, the Terrible Old Man often recalls what Olney said about a knock that the lone dweller feared, and a shape seen black and inquisitive against the mist through those queer translucent windows of leaded bull's-eyes.

All these things, however, the Elder Ones only may decide; and meanwhile the morning mist still comes up by that lonely vertiginous peak with the steep ancient house, that grey[b] low-eaved house where none is seen but where evening brings furtive lights while the north wind tells of strange revels. White and feathery it comes from the deep to its brothers the clouds, full of dreams of dank pastures and caves of leviathan. And when tales fly thick in the grottoes of tritons, and conches[c] in seaweed cities blow wild tunes learned from the Elder Ones, then great eager vapours[d] flock to heaven laden with lore; and Kingsport, nestling uneasy on its lesser cliffs below that awesome hanging sentinel of rock, sees oceanward only a mystic whiteness, as if the cliff's rim were the rim of all earth, and the solemn bells of the buoys tolled free in the aether of faery.[e]

---

[a] quiet . . . fisherfolk.] quiet, . . . fisher folk. B, C
[b] grey] gray, B, C
[c] conches] conchs B
[d] vapours] vapors B, C
[e] faery.] faëry. B, C

The Dream-Quest of Unknown Kadath

Three times Randolph Carter dreamed of the marvellous city, and three times was he snatched away while still he paused on the high terrace above it. All golden and lovely it blazed in the sunset, with walls, temples, colonnades,[a] and arched bridges of veined marble, silver-basined fountains of prismatic spray in broad squares and perfumed gardens, and wide streets marching between delicate trees and blossom-laden urns and ivory statues in gleaming rows; while on steep northward slopes climbed tiers of red roofs and old peaked gables harbouring little lanes of grassy cobbles. It was a fever of the gods;[b] a fanfare of supernal trumpets and a clash of immortal cymbals. Mystery hung about it as clouds about a fabulous unvisited mountain; and as Carter stood breathless and expectant on that balustraded parapet there swept up to him the poignancy and suspense of almost-

Editor's Note: The surviving A.Ms. is HPL's original draft; it is not as extensively revised and interlined as that of *The Case of Charles Dexter Ward*, indicating that less polishing was done on what HPL regarded as "practice in carrying plot threads for a considerable distance" (*SL* 2.99). Barlow prepared a T.Ms. of just over half the text; it contains a few corrections by HPL, including the alteration of some names (e.g., "Thok" for "Throk"). HPL was, however, markedly inconsistent in the recording of species names of his imagined creatures; in my judgment these should be lower-cased (by analogy with the later use of "shoggoth" in *At the Mountains of Madness*), even when HPL has indicated on the T.Ms. that they should be capitalised. HPL is also inconsistent in other usages as well as in the spelling of some proper names. In the first published appearance (*Beyond the Wall of Sleep* [Arkham House, 1943]), the editors followed the T.Ms. until it left off, then worked from the A.Ms.

Texts: A = A.Ms. (JHL); B = T.Ms. (by Barlow); C = *At the Mountains of Madness and Other Novels* (Arkham House, 1965). Copy-text: A (with a few readings from B).

[a] colonnades,] colonnades A, B, C
[b] gods;] gods, B, C

vanished memory, the pain of lost things,[a] and the maddening need to place again what once had[b] an awesome and momentous place.

He knew that for him its meaning must once have been supreme; though in what cycle or incarnation he had known it, or whether in dream or in waking, he could not tell. Vaguely it called up glimpses of a far,[c] forgotten first youth, when wonder and pleasure lay in all the mystery of days, and dawn and dusk alike strode forth prophetick[d] to the eager sound of lutes and song;[e] unclosing faery[f] gates toward further and surprising marvels. But each night as he stood on that high marble terrace with the curious urns and carven rail and looked off over that hushed sunset city of beauty and unearthly immanence,[g] he felt the bondage of dream's tyrannous gods; for in no wise could he leave that lofty spot, or descend the wide marmoreal flights flung endlessly down to where those streets of elder witchery lay outspread and beckoning.

When for the third time he awaked[h] with those flights still undescended and those hushed sunset streets still untraversed, he prayed long and earnestly to the hidden gods of dream that brood capricious above the clouds on unknown Kadath, in the cold waste where no man treads. But the gods made no answer and shewed no relenting, nor did they give any favouring sign when he prayed to them in dream, and invoked them sacrificially through the bearded priests[i] Nasht and Kaman-Thah, whose cavern-temple with its pillar of flame lies not far from the gates of the waking world. It seemed, however, that his prayers must have been adversely heard, for after even the first of them he ceased wholly to behold the marvellous city; as if his three glimpses from afar had been mere accidents or oversights,[j] and against some hidden plan or wish of the gods.

[a] things,] things A, B, C
[b] had] had been B, C
[c] far,] far B, C
[d] prophetick] prophetic C
[e] song;] song, C
[f] faery] fiery B, C
[g] immanence,] imma B; immanence C
[h] awaked] awakened B, C
[i] priests] priests of B, C
[j] oversights,] over-/sights, B; over-sights, C

At length, sick with longing for those glittering sunset streets and cryptical hill lanes among ancient tiled roofs, nor able sleeping or waking to drive them from his mind, Carter resolved to go with bold entreaty whither no man had gone before, and dare the icy deserts through the dark to where unknown Kadath, veiled in cloud and crowned with unimagined stars, holds secret and nocturnal the onyx castle of the Great Ones.

In light slumber he descended the seventy steps to the cavern of flame and talked of this design to the bearded priests Nasht and Kaman-Thah. And the priests shook their pshent-bearing heads and vowed it would be the death of his soul. They pointed out that the Great Ones had shewn[a] already their wish, and that it is not agreeable to them to be harassed by insistent pleas. They reminded him, too, that not only had no man ever been to unknown[b] Kadath, but no man had ever suspected in what part of space it may lie; whether it be in the dreamlands around our[c] world, or in those surrounding some unguessed companion of Fomalhaut or Aldebaran. If in our dreamland, it might conceivably be reached; but[d] only three fully human souls since time began had ever crossed and re-crossed[e] the black impious gulfs to other dreamlands, and of that three[f] two had come back quite mad. There were, in such voyages, incalculable local dangers; as well as that shocking final peril which gibbers unmentionably outside the ordered universe, where no dreams reach; that last amorphous blight of nethermost confusion which blasphemes and bubbles at the centre of all infinity—the boundless daemon-sultan[g] Azathoth, whose name no lips dare speak aloud, and who gnaws hungrily in inconceivable, unlighted chambers beyond time amidst the muffled, maddening beating of vile drums and the thin, monotonous whine of accursed flutes; to which detestable pounding and piping dance slowly, awkwardly, and absurdly the gigantic

---

[a] shewn] shown C
[b] unknown] *om.* B, C
[c] our] our own B, C
[d] reached; but] reached B; reached, but C
[e] re-crossed] recrossed C
[f] three] three, C
[g] daemon-sultan] daemon sultan A, B, C

ultimate[a] gods, the blind, voiceless, tenebrous, mindless Other Gods whose soul and messenger is the crawling chaos Nyarlathotep.

Of these things was Carter warned by the priests Nasht and Kaman-Thah in the cavern of flame, but still he resolved to find the gods on unknown Kadath in the cold waste, wherever that might be, and to win from them the sight and remembrance and shelter of the marvellous sunset city. He knew that his journey would be strange and long, and that the Great Ones would be against it; but being old in the land of dream he counted on many useful memories and devices to aid him. So asking a farewell[b] blessing of the priests and thinking shrewdly on his course, he boldly descended the seven hundred steps to the Gate of Deeper Slumber and set out through the enchanted wood.[c]

In the tunnels of that twisted wood, whose low prodigious oaks twine groping boughs and shine dim with the phosphorescence of strange fungi, dwell the furtive and secretive zoogs;[d] who know many obscure secrets of the dream-world[e] and a few of the waking world, since the wood at two places touches the lands of men, though it would be disastrous to say where. Certain unexplained rumours, events,[f] and vanishments occur among men where the zoogs[g] have access, and it is well that they cannot travel far outside the world of dream. But over the nearer parts of the dream-world[h] they pass freely, flitting small and brown and unseen and bearing back piquant tales to beguile the hours around their hearths in the forest they love. Most of them live in burrows, but some inhabit the trunks of the great trees; and although they live mostly on fungi it is muttered that they have also a slight taste for meat, either physical or spiritual, for certainly many dreamers have entered that wood who have not come out. Carter, however, had no fear; for he was an old dreamer and had learnt their fluttering language and made many a treaty with them; having found through their help

[a] ultimate] Ultimate B, C
[b] farewell] formal B, C
[c] enchanted wood.] Enchanted Wood. B, C
[d] zoogs;] Zoogs; B, C
[e] dream-world] dream world A, B, C
[f] events,] events A
[g] zoogs] Zoogs B, C
[h] dream-world] dream world A, B, C

the splendid city of Celephaïs[a] in Ooth-Nargai beyond the Tanarian Hills, where reigns half the year the great King[b] Kuranes, a man he had known by another name in life. Kuranes was the one soul who had been to the star-gulfs and returned free from madness.

Threading now the low phosphorescent aisles between those gigantic trunks, Carter made fluttering sounds in the manner of the zoogs,[c] and listened now and then for responses. He remembered one particular village of the creatures near[d] the centre of the wood, where a circle of great mossy stones in what was once a clearing tells of older and more terrible dwellers long forgotten, and toward this spot he hastened. He traced his way by the grotesque fungi, which always seem better nourished as one approaches the dread circle where elder beings danced and sacrificed. Finally the greater[e] light of those thicker fungi revealed a sinister green and grey vastness pushing up through the roof of the forest and out of sight. This was the nearest of the great ring of stones, and Carter knew he was close to the zoog[f] village. Renewing his fluttering sound, he waited patiently; and was at length[g] rewarded by an impression of many eyes watching him. It was the zoogs,[h] for one sees their weird eyes long before one can discern their small, slippery brown outlines.

Out they swarmed, from hidden burrow and honeycombed[i] tree, till the whole dim-litten region was alive with them. Some of the wilder ones brushed Carter unpleasantly, and one even nipped loathsomely at his ear; but these lawless spirits were soon restrained by their elders. The Council of Sages, recognising the visitor, offered a gourd of fermented sap from a haunted tree unlike the others, which had grown from a seed dropt down by someone on the moon; and as Carter

[a] Celephaïs] Celephais B, C
[b] King] king B
[c] zoogs,] Zoogs, B, C
[d] near] was in B, C
[e] greater] great B, C
[f] zoog] Zoog B, C
[g] length] last B, C
[h] zoogs,] Zoogs, B, C
[i] honeycombed] honeycomed A, B

drank it ceremoniously a very strange colloquy began. The zoogs[a] did not, unfortunately, know where the peak of Kadath lies, nor could they even say whether the cold waste is in our dream-world[b] or in another. Rumours of the Great Ones came equally from all points; and one might only say that they were likelier to be seen on high mountain peaks than in valleys, since on such peaks they dance reminiscently when the moon is above and the clouds beneath.

Then one very ancient zoog[c] recalled a thing unheard-of by the others; and said that in Ulthar, beyond the river[d] Skai, there still lingered the last copy of those inconceivably old Pnakotic Manuscripts made by waking men in forgotten boreal kingdoms and borne into the land of dreams when the hairy cannibal Gnophkehs overcame many-templed Olathoë[e] and slew all the heroes of the land of Lomar. Those manuscripts,[f] he said, told much of the gods;[g] and besides, in Ulthar there were men who had seen the signs of the gods, and even one old priest who had scaled a great mountain to behold them dancing by moonlight. He had failed, though his companion had succeeded and perished namelessly.

So Randolph Carter thanked the zoogs,[h] who fluttered amicably and gave him another gourd of moon-tree wine to take with him, and set out through the phosphorescent wood for the other side, where the rushing Skai flows down from the slopes of Lerion, and Hatheg and Nir and Ulthar dot the plain. Behind him, furtive and unseen, crept several of the curious zoogs;[i] for they wished to learn what might befall him, and bear back the legend to their people. The vast oaks grew thicker as he pushed on beyond the village, and he looked sharply for a certain spot where they would thin somewhat, standing quite dead or dying among the unnaturally dense fungi and the rotting mould and

[a] zoogs] Zoogs B, C
[b] dream-world] dream world A, B, C
[c] zoog] Zoog B, C
[d] river] River A, B, C
[e] Olathoë] Olathoe B, C
[f] manuscripts,] manuscripts B, C
[g] gods;] gods, B, C
[h] zoogs,] Zoogs, B, C
[i] zoogs;] Zoogs; B, C

mushy logs of their fallen brothers. There he would turn sharply aside, for at that spot a mighty slab of stone rests on the forest floor; and those who have dared approach it say that it bears an iron ring three feet wide. Remembering the archaic circle of great mossy rocks, and what it was possibly set up for, the zoogs[a] do not pause near that expansive slab with its huge ring; for they realise that all which is forgotten need not necessarily be dead, and they would not like to see the slab rise slowly and deliberately.

Carter detoured at the proper place, and heard behind him the frightened fluttering of some of the more timid zoogs.[b] He had known they would follow him, so he was not disturbed; for one grows accustomed to the anomalies of these prying creatures. It was twilight when he came to the edge of the wood, and the strengthening glow told him it was the twilight of morning. Over fertile plains rolling down to the Skai he saw the smoke of cottage chimneys, and on every hand were the hedges and ploughed fields and thatched roofs of a peaceful land. Once he stopped at a farmhouse well for a cup of water, and all the dogs barked affrightedly at the inconspicuous zoogs[c] that crept through the grass behind. At another house, where people were stirring, he asked questions about the gods, and whether they danced often upon Lerion; but the farmer and his wife would only make the Elder Sign and tell him the way to Nir and Ulthar.

At noon he walked through the one broad high street of Nir, which he had once visited and which marked his farthest former travels in this direction; and soon afterward he came to the great stone bridge across the Skai, into whose central pier[d] the masons had sealed a living human sacrifice when they built it thirteen-hundred years before. Once on the other side, the frequent presence of cats (who all arched their backs at the trailing zoogs)[e] revealed the near neighbourhood of Ulthar; for in Ulthar, according to an ancient and significant law, no man may kill a cat. Very pleasant were the suburbs of Ulthar, with their little green

---

[a] zoogs] Zoogs B, C
[b] zoogs.] Zoogs. B, C
[c] zoogs] Zoogs B, C
[d] pier] piece B, C
[e] zoogs)] Zoogs) B, C

cottages and neatly fenced farms; and still pleasanter was the quaint town itself, with its old peaked roofs and overhanging upper stories and numberless chimney-pots and narrow hill streets where one can see old cobbles whenever the graceful cats afford space enough. Carter, the cats being somewhat dispersed by the half-seen zoogs,[a] picked his way directly to the modest Temple of the Elder Ones where the priests and old records were said to be; and once within that venerable circular tower of ivied stone—which crowns[b] Ulthar's highest hill—he sought out the patriarch Atal, who had been up the forbidden peak Hatheg-Kla in the stony desert and had come down again alive.

Atal, seated on an ivory dais in a festooned shrine at the top of the temple, was fully three centuries old; but still very keen of mind and memory. From him Carter learned many things about the gods, but mainly that they are indeed only earth's[c] gods, ruling feebly our own dreamland and having no power or habitation elsewhere. They might, Atal said, heed a man's prayer if in good humour; but one must not think of climbing to their onyx stronghold atop Kadath in the cold waste. It was lucky that no man knew where Kadath towers, for the fruits of ascending it would be very grave. Atal's companion Barzai the Wise had been drawn screaming into the sky for climbing merely the known peak of Hatheg-Kla. With unknown Kadath, if ever found, matters would be much worse; for although earth's[d] gods may sometimes be surpassed by a wise mortal, they are protected by the Other Gods from Outside, whom it is better not to discuss. At least twice in the world's history the Other Gods set their seal upon earth's[e] primal granite; once in antediluvian times, as guessed from a drawing in those parts of the Pnakotic Manuscripts too ancient to be read, and once on Hatheg-Kla when Barzai the Wise tried to see earth's[f] gods dancing by moonlight. So, Atal said, it would be much better to let all gods alone except in tactful prayers.

[a] zoogs,] Zoogs, A, B, C
[b] crowns] crown C
[c] earth's] Earth's B, C
[d] earth's] Earth's B, C
[e] earth's] Earth's B, C
[f] earth's] Earth's B, C

Carter, though disappointed by Atal's discouraging advice and by
the meagre help to be found in the Pnakotic Manuscripts and the
Seven Cryptical Books of Hsan, did not wholly despair. First he
questioned the old priest about that marvellous sunset city seen from
the railed terrace, thinking that perhaps he might find it without the
gods'[a] aid; but Atal could tell him nothing. Probably, Atal said, the
place belonged to his especial dream-world[b] and not to the general
land of vision that many know; and conceivably it might be on another
planet. In that case earth's[c] gods could not guide him if they would.
But this was not likely, since the stopping of the dreams shewed pretty
clearly that it was something the Great Ones wished to hide from him.

Then Carter did a wicked thing, offering his guileless host so many
draughts of the moon-wine[d] which the zoogs[e] had given him that the
old man became irresponsibly talkative. Robbed of his reserve, poor
Atal babbled freely of forbidden things; telling of a great image
reported by travellers as carved on the solid rock of the mountain
Ngranek, on the isle of Oriab in the Southern Sea, and hinting that it
may be a likeness which earth's gods once wrought of their own
features in the days when they danced by moonlight on that mountain.
And he hiccoughed likewise that the features of that image are very
strange, so that one might easily recognise[f] them, and that they are
signs of the authentic race of the gods.

Now the use of all this in finding the gods became at once apparent
to Carter. It is known that in disguise the younger among the Great
Ones often espouse the daughters of men, so that around the borders
of the cold waste wherein stands Kadath the peasants must all bear
their blood. This being so, the way to find that waste must be to see
the stone face on Ngranek[g] and mark the features; then, having noted
them with care, to search for such features among living men. Where
they are plainest and thickest, there must the gods dwell nearest; and

[a] gods'] god's B, C
[b] dream-world] dream world A, B, C
[c] earth's] Earth's B, C
[d] moon-wine] moon-vine C
[e] zoogs] Zoogs B, C
[f] recognise] recognize C
[g] Ngranek] Ngranck C

whatever stony waste lies back of the villages in that place must be that wherein stands Kadath.

Much of the Great Ones might be learnt in such regions, and those with their blood might inherit little memories very useful to a seeker. They might not know their parentage, for the gods so dislike to be known among men that none can be found who has seen their faces wittingly; a thing which Carter realised even as he sought to scale Kadath. But they would have queer lofty thoughts misunderstood by their fellows, and would sing of far places and gardens so unlike any known even in[a] dreamland that common folk would call them fools; and from all this one could perhaps learn old secrets of Kadath, or gain hints of the marvellous sunset city which the gods held secret. And more, one might in certain cases seize some well-loved child of a god as hostage; or even capture some young god himself, disguised and dwelling amongst men with a comely peasant maiden as his bride.

Atal, however, did not know how to find Ngranek on its isle of Oriab; and recommended that Carter follow the singing Skai under its bridges down to the Southern Sea; where no burgess of Ulthar has ever been, but whence the merchants come in boats or with long caravans of mules and two-wheeled carts. There is a great city there, Dylath-Leen, but in Ulthar its reputation is bad because of the black three-banked galleys that sail to it with rubies from no clearly named shore. The traders that come from those galleys to deal with the jewellers are human, or nearly so, but the rowers are never beheld; and it is not thought wholesome in Ulthar that merchants should trade with black ships from unknown places whose rowers cannot be exhibited.

By the time he had given this information Atal was very drowsy, and Carter laid him gently on a couch of inlaid ebony and gathered his long beard decorously on his chest. As he turned to go, he observed that no suppressed fluttering followed him, and wondered why the zoogs[b] had become so lax in their curious pursuit. Then he noticed all the sleek complacent cats of Ulthar licking their chops with unusual gusto, and recalled the spitting and caterwauling he had faintly heard[c]

[a] in] in the C
[b] zoogs] Zoogs C
[c] heard] heard, B, C

in lower parts of the temple while absorbed in the old priest's conversation. He recalled, too, the evilly hungry way in which an especially impudent young zoog[a] had regarded a small black kitten in the cobbled street outside. And because he loved nothing on earth more than small black kittens, he stooped and petted the sleek cats of Ulthar as they licked their chops, and did not mourn because those inquisitive zoogs[b] would escort him no farther.

It was sunset now, so Carter stopped at an ancient inn on a steep little street overlooking the lower town. And as he went out on the balcony of his room and gazed down at the sea of red tiled roofs and cobbled ways and the pleasant fields beyond, all mellow and magical in the slanted light, he swore that Ulthar would be a very likely place to dwell in always, were not the memory of a greater sunset city ever goading one on[c] toward unknown perils. Then twilight fell, and the pink walls of the plastered gables turned violet and mystic, and little yellow lights floated up one by one from old lattice windows. And sweet bells pealed in the temple tower above, and the first star winked softly above the meadows across the Skai. With the night came song, and Carter nodded as the lutanists praised ancient days from beyond the filigreed balconies and tessellated[d] courts of simple Ulthar. And there might have been sweetness even in the voices of Ulthar's many cats, but that they were mostly heavy and silent from strange feasting. Some of them stole off to those cryptical realms which are known only to cats and which villagers say are on the moon's dark side, whither the cats leap from tall housetops, but one small black kitten crept upstairs and sprang in Carter's lap to purr and play, and curled up near his feet when he lay down at last on the little couch whose pillows were stuffed with fragrant, drowsy herbs.

In the morning Carter joined a caravan of merchants bound for Dylath-Leen with the spun wool of Ulthar and the cabbages of Ulthar's busy farms. And for six days they rode with tinkling bells on the smooth road beside the Skai; stopping some nights at the inns of

[a] zoog] Zoog C
[b] zoogs] Zoogs C
[c] on] onward B, C
[d] tessellated] tesselated B, C

little quaint fishing towns, and on other nights camping under the stars while snatches of boatmen's songs came from the placid river. The country was very beautiful, with green hedges and groves and picturesque peaked cottages and octagonal windmills.

On the seventh day a blur of smoke arose[a] on the horizon ahead, and then the tall black towers of Dylath-Leen, which is built mostly of basalt. Dylath-Leen with its thin angular towers looks in the distance like a bit of the Giants'[b] Causeway, and its streets are dark and uninviting. There are many dismal sea-taverns[c] near the myriad wharves, and all the town is thronged with the strange seamen of every land on earth and of a few which are said to be not on earth. Carter questioned the oddly robed men of that city about the peak of Ngranek on the isle of Oriab, and found that they knew of it well. Ships came from Baharna on that island, one being due to return thither in only a month, and Ngranek is but two days' zebra-ride from that port. But few had seen the stone face of the god, because it is on a very difficult side of Ngranek, which overlooks only sheer crags and a valley of sinister lava. Once the gods were angered with men on that side, and spoke of the matter to the Other Gods.

It was hard to get this information from the traders and sailors in Dylath-Leen's sea-taverns,[d] because they mostly preferred to whisper of the black galleys. One of them was due in a week with rubies from its unknown shore, and the townsfolk dreaded to see it dock. The mouths of the men who came from it to trade were too wide, and the way their turbans were humped up in two points above their foreheads was in especially bad taste. And their shoes were the shortest and queerest ever seen in the Six Kingdoms. But worst of all was the matter of the unseen rowers. Those three banks of oars moved too briskly and accurately and vigorously to be comfortable, and it was not right for a ship to stay in port for weeks while the merchants traded, yet to give no glimpse of its crew. It was not fair to the tavern-keepers of Dylath-Leen, or to the grocers and butchers, either; for not a scrap

---

[a] arose] rose B, C
[b] Giants'] Giant's B, C
[c] sea-taverns] sea taverns A, B, C
[d] sea-taverns,] sea taverns, A, B, C

of provisions was ever sent aboard. The merchants took only gold and stout black slaves from Parg across the river. That was all they ever took, those unpleasantly featured merchants and their unseen rowers; never anything from the butchers and grocers, but only gold and the fat black men of Parg whom they bought by the pound. And the odours from those galleys which the south wind blew in from the wharves are not to be described. Only by constantly smoking strong thagweed could even the hardiest denizen of the old sea-taverns[a] bear them. Dylath-Leen would never have tolerated the black galleys had such rubies been obtainable elsewhere, but no mine in all earth's dreamland was known to produce their like.

Of these things Dylath-Leen's cosmopolitan folk chiefly gossiped whilst Carter waited patiently for the ship from Baharna,[b] which might bear him to the isle whereon carven Ngranek towers lofty and barren. Meanwhile he did not fail to seek through the haunts of far travellers for any tales they might have concerning Kadath in the cold waste or a marvellous city of marble walls and silver fountains seen below terraces in the sunset. Of these things, however, he learned nothing; though he once thought that a certain old slant-eyed merchant looked queerly intelligent when the cold waste was spoken of. This man was reputed to trade with the horrible stone villages on the icy desert plateau of Leng, which no healthy folk visit and whose evil fires are seen at night from afar. He was even rumoured to have dealt with that high-priest not to be described, which wears a yellow silken mask over its face and dwells all alone in a prehistoric stone monastery. That such a person might well have had nibbling traffick with such beings as may conceivably dwell in the cold waste was not to be doubted, but Carter soon found that it was no use questioning him.

Then the black galley slipped into the harbour past the basalt mole[c] and the tall lighthouse, silent and alien, and with a strange stench that the south wind drove into the town. Uneasiness rustled through the taverns along that waterfront, and after a while the dark wide-mouthed merchants with humped turbans and short feet clumped stealthily

[a] sea-taverns] sea taverns A, B, C
[b] Baharna,] Barharna, A, B
[c] mole] _ale B; wale C

ashore to seek the bazaars of the jewellers. Carter observed them closely, and disliked them more the longer he looked at them. Then he saw them drive the stout black men of Parg up the gangplank[a] grunting and sweating into that singular galley, and wondered in what lands—or if in any lands at all—those fat pathetic creatures might be destined to serve.

And on the third evening of that galley's stay one of the uncomfortable merchants spoke to him, smirking sinfully and hinting of what he had heard in the taverns of Carter's quest. He appeared to have knowledge too secret for public telling; and though[b] the sound of his voice was unbearably hateful, Carter felt that the lore of so far a traveller must not be overlooked. He bade him therefore be his own[c] guest in locked chambers above, and drew out the last of the zoogs'[d] moon-wine[e] to loosen his tongue. The strange merchant drank heavily, but smirked unchanged by the draught. Then he drew forth a curious bottle with wine of his own, and Carter saw that the bottle was a single hollowed ruby, grotesquely carved in patterns too fabulous to be comprehended. He offered his wine to his host, and though Carter took only the least sip, he felt the dizziness of space and the fever of unimagined jungles. All the while the guest had been smiling more and more broadly, and as Carter slipped into blankness the last thing he saw was that dark odious face convulsed with evil laughter,[f] and something quite unspeakable where one of the two frontal puffs of that orange turban had become disarranged with the shakings of that epileptic mirth.

Carter next had consciousness amidst horrible odours beneath a tent-like awning on the deck of a ship, with the marvellous coasts of the Southern Sea flying by in unnatural swiftness. He was not chained, but three of the dark sardonic merchants stood grinning nearby, and the sight of those humps in their turbans made him almost as faint as did the stench that filtered up through the sinister hatches. He saw slip past him the glorious lands and cities of which a fellow-dreamer of earth—a lighthouse-keeper in ancient Kingsport—had often discoursed

[a] gangplank] gang-/plank B; gang-plank C
[b] though] although B, C
[c] own] *om.* B, C
[d] zoogs'] Zoogs' A; zoog's B; Zoog's C
[e] moon-wine] moon-/wine B; moonwine C
[f] laughter,] laughter B, C

in the old days, and recognised[a] the templed terraces of Zar,[b] abode of forgotten dreams; the spires of infamous Thalarion, that daemon-city of a thousand wonders where the eidolon Lathi reigns; the charnel gardens of Xura,[c] land of pleasures unattained, and the twin headlands of crystal, meeting above in a resplendent arch, which guard the harbour of Sona-Nyl, blessed land of fancy.

Past all these gorgeous lands the malodorous[d] ship flew unwholesomely, urged by the abnormal strokes of those unseen rowers below. And before the day was done Carter saw that the steersman could have no other goal than the Basalt Pillars of the West, beyond which simple folk say splendid Cathuria lies, but which wise dreamers well know are the gates of a monstrous cataract wherein the oceans of earth's dreamland drop wholly to abysmal nothingness and shoot through the empty spaces toward other worlds and other stars and the awful voids outside the ordered universe where the daemon-sultan Azathoth gnaws hungrily in chaos amid pounding and piping and the hellish dancing of the Other Gods, blind, voiceless, tenebrous, and mindless, with their soul and messenger Nyarlathotep.

Meanwhile the three sardonic merchants would give no word of their intent, though Carter well knew that they must be leagued with those who wished to hold him from his quest. It is understood in the land of dream that the Other Gods have many agents moving among men; and all these agents, whether wholly human or slightly less than human, are eager to work the will of those blind and mindless things in return for the favour of their hideous soul and messenger, the crawling chaos Nyarlathotep. So Carter inferred that the merchants of the humped turbans, hearing of his daring search for the Great Ones in their castle on[e] Kadath, had decided to take him away and deliver him to Nyarlathothep for whatever nameless bounty might be offered for such a prize. What might be the land of those merchants, in our known universe or in the eldritch spaces outside, Carter could not

---

[a] recognised] recognized B, C
[b] Zar,] Zak, B, C
[c] Xura,] Zura, C
[d] malodorous] malodourous B, C
[e] on] of B, C

guess; nor could he imagine at what hellish trysting-place they would meet the crawling chaos to give him up and claim their reward. He knew, however, that no beings as nearly human as these would dare approach the ultimate nighted throne of the daemon Azathoth in the formless central void.

At the set of sun the merchants licked their excessively wide lips and glared hungrily,[a] and one of them went below and returned from some hidden and offensive cabin with a pot and basket of plates. Then they squatted close together beneath the awning and ate the smoking meat that was passed around. But when they gave Carter a portion, he found something very terrible in the size and shape of it; so that he turned even paler than before and cast that portion into the sea when no eye was on him. And again he thought of those unseen rowers beneath, and of the suspicious nourishment from which their far too mechanical strength was derived.

It was dark when the galley passed betwixt the Basalt Pillars of the West and the sound of the ultimate cataract swelled portentous from ahead. And the spray of that cataract rose to obscure the stars, and the deck grew damp, and the vessel reeled in the surging current of the brink. Then with a queer whistle and plunge the leap was taken, and Carter felt the terrors of nightmare as earth fell away and the great boat shot silent and comet-like into planetary space. Never before had he known what shapeless black things lurk and caper and flounder all through the aether, leering and grinning at such voyagers as may pass, and sometimes feeling about with slimy paws when some moving object excites their curiosity. These are the nameless larvae of the Other Gods, and like them are blind and without mind, and possessed of singular hungers and thirsts.

But that offensive galley did not aim as far as Carter had feared, for he soon saw that the helmsman was steering a course directly for the moon. The moon was a crescent,[b] shining larger and larger as they approached it, and shewing its singular craters and peaks uncomfortably. The ship made for the edge, and it soon became clear that its destination was that secret and mysterious side which is always

[a] hungrily,] hungrily B, C
[b] crescent,] crescent B, C

turned away from the earth, and which no fully human person, save perhaps the dreamer Snireth-Ko, has ever beheld. The close aspect of the moon as the galley drew near proved very disturbing to Carter, and he did not like the size and shape of the ruins which crumbled here and there. The dead temples on the mountains were so placed that they could have glorified no wholesome or suitable[a] gods, and in the symmetries of the broken columns there seemed to lurk[b] some dark and inner meaning which did not invite solution. And what the structure and proportions of the olden worshippers could have been, Carter steadily refused to conjecture.

When the ship rounded the edge, and sailed over those lands unseen by man, there appeared in the queer landscape certain signs of life, and Carter saw many low, broad, round cottages in fields of grotesque whitish fungi. He noticed that these cottages had no windows, and thought that their shape suggested the huts of Esquimaux. Then he glimpsed the oily waves of a sluggish sea, and knew that the voyage was once more to be by water—or at least through some liquid. The galley struck the surface with a peculiar sound, and the odd elastic way the waves received it was very perplexing to Carter. They now slid along at great speed, once passing and hailing another galley of kindred form, but generally seeing nothing but that curious sea and a sky that was black and star-strown[c] even though the sun shone scorchingly in it.

There presently rose ahead the jagged hills of a leprous-looking coast, and Carter saw the thick unpleasant grey[d] towers of a city. The way they leaned and bent, the manner in which they were clustered, and the fact that they had no windows at all, was very disturbing to the prisoner; and he bitterly mourned the folly which had made him sip the curious wine of that merchant with the humped turban. As the coast drew nearer, and the hideous stench of that city grew stronger, he saw upon the jagged hills many forests, some of whose trees he recognised[e]

---

[a] wholesome or suitable] suitable or wholesome B, C
[b] lurk] be B, C
[c] star-strown] star-strewn C
[d] grey] gray C
[e] recognised] recognized B, C

as akin to that solitary moon-tree in the enchanted wood of earth, from whose sap the small brown zoogs[a] ferment their peculiar[b] wine.

Carter could now distinguish moving figures on the noisome wharves ahead, and the better he saw them the worse he began to fear and detest them. For they were not men at all, or even approximately men, but great greyish-white slippery things which could expand and contract at will, and whose principal shape—though it often changed—was that of a sort of toad without any eyes, but with a curiously[c] vibrating mass of short pink tentacles on the end of its blunt, vague snout. These objects were waddling busily about the wharves, moving bales and crates and boxes with preternatural strength, and now and then hopping on or off some anchored galley with long oars in their fore-paws.[d] And now and then one would appear driving a herd of clumping slaves, which indeed were approximate human beings with wide mouths like those merchants who traded in Dylath-Leen; only these herds, being without turbans or shoes or clothing, did not seem so very human after all. Some of these[e] slaves— the fatter ones, whom a sort of overseer would pinch experimentally— were unloaded from ships and nailed in crates which workers pushed into[f] low warehouses or loaded on great lumbering vans.

Once a van was hitched up[g] and driven off, and the fabulous thing which drew it was such that Carter gasped, even after having seen the other monstrosities of that hateful place. Now and then a small herd of slaves dressed and turbaned like the dark merchants would be driven aboard a galley, followed by a great crew of the slippery grey[h] toad-things as officers, navigators, and rowers. And Carter saw that the almost-human creatures were reserved for the more ignominious kinds of servitude which required no strength, such as steering and cooking, fetching and carrying, and bargaining with men on the earth or other

---

[a] zoogs] Zoogs C
[b] peculiar] curious B, C
[c] curiously] curious B, C
[d] fore-paws.] forepaws. B, C
[e] these] the C
[f] into] into the C
[g] up] *om.* B, C
[h] grey] *om.* B, C

planets where they traded. These creatures must have been convenient on earth, for they were truly not unlike men when dressed and carefully shod and turbaned, and could haggle in the shops of men without embarrassment or curious explanations. But most of them, unless lean and[a] ill-favoured, were unclothed and packed in crates and drawn off in lumbering lorries by fabulous things. Occasionally other beings were unloaded and crated; some very like these semi-humans, some not so similar, and some not similar at all. And he[b] wondered if any of the poor stout black men of Parg were left to be unloaded and crated and shipped inland in those obnoxious drays.

When the galley landed at a greasy-looking quay of spongy rock a nightmare horde of toad-things wriggled out of the hatches, and two of them seized Carter and dragged him ashore. The smell and aspect of that city are beyond telling, and Carter held only scattered images of the tiled streets and black doorways and endless precipices of grey vertical walls without windows. At length he was dragged within a low doorway and made to climb infinite steps in pitch blackness. It was, apparently, all one to the toad-things whether it were light or dark. The odour of the place was intolerable, and when Carter was locked into a chamber and left alone he scarcely had strength to crawl around and ascertain its form and dimensions. It was circular, and about twenty feet across.

From then on time ceased to exist. At intervals food was pushed in, but Carter would not touch it. What his fate would be, he did not know; but he felt that he was held for the coming of that frightful soul and messenger of infinity's Other Gods, the crawling chaos Nyarlathotep. Finally, after an unguessed span of hours or days, the great stone door swung wide again[c] and Carter was shoved down the stairs and out into the red-litten streets of that fearsome city. It was night on the moon, and all through the town were stationed slaves bearing torches.

In a destestable square a sort of procession was formed; ten of the toad-things and twenty-four almost-human[d] torch-bearers, eleven on either side, and one each before and behind. Carter was placed in the

---

[a] and] or B, C
[b] he] I A
[c] again] again, B, C
[d] almost-human] almost human A, B, C

middle of the line; five toad-things ahead and five behind, and one almost-human torch-bearer on each[a] side of him. Certain of the toad-things produced disgustingly carven flutes of ivory and made loathsome sounds. To that hellish piping the column advanced out of the tiled streets and into nighted plains of obscene fungi, soon commencing to climb one of the lower and more gradual hills that lay behind the city. That on some frightful slope or blasphemous plateau the crawling chaos waited, Carter could not doubt; and he wished that the suspense might soon be over. The whining of those impious flutes was shocking, and he would have given worlds for some even half-normal sound; but these toad-things had no voices, and the slaves did not talk.

Then through that star-specked darkness there did come a normal sound. It rolled from the higher hills, and from all the jagged peaks around it was caught up and echoed in a swelling pandaemoniac chorus. It was the midnight yell of the cat, and Carter knew at last that the old village folk were right when they made low guesses about the cryptical realms which are known only to cats, and to which the elders among cats repair by stealth nocturnally, springing from high housetops. Verily, it is to the moon's dark side that they go to leap and gambol on the hills and converse with ancient shadows, and here amidst that column of foetid things Carter heard their homely, friendly cry, and thought of the steep roofs and warm hearths and little lighted windows of home.

Now much of the speech of cats was known to Randolph Carter, and in this far,[b] terrible place he uttered the cry that was suitable. But that he need not have done, for even as his lips opened he heard the chorus wax and draw nearer, and saw swift shadows against the stars as small graceful shapes leaped from hill to hill in gathering legions. The call of the clan had been given, and before the foul procession had time even to be frightened a cloud of smothering fur and a phalanx of murderous claws were tidally and tempestuously upon it. The flutes stopped, and there were shrieks in the night. Dying almost-humans screamed, and cats spit and yowled and roared, but the toad-things

[a] each] either B, C
[b] far,] far C

made never a sound as their stinking green ichor oozed fatally onto[a] that porous earth with the obscene fungi.

It was a stupendous sight while the torches lasted, and Carter had never before seen so many cats. Black, grey, and white; yellow, tiger, and mixed; common, Persian, and Manx;[b] Thibetan, Angora, and Egyptian; all were there in the fury of battle, and there hovered over them some trace of that profound and inviolate sanctity which made their goddess great in the temples of Bubastis. They would leap seven strong at the throat of an almost-human or the pink tentacled snout of a toad-thing and drag it down savagely to the fungous plain, where myriads of their fellows would surge over it and into it with the frenzied claws and teeth of a divine battle-fury. Carter had seized a torch from a stricken slave, but was soon overborne by the surging waves of his loyal defenders. Then he lay in the utter blackness hearing the clangour of war and the shouts of the victors, and feeling the soft paws of his friends as they rushed to and fro over him in the fray.

At last awe and exhaustion closed his eyes, and when he opened them again it was upon a strange scene. The great shining disc of the earth, thirteen times greater than that of the moon as we see it, had risen with floods of weird light over the lunar landscape; and across all those leagues of wild plateau and ragged crest there squatted one endless sea of cats in orderly array. Circle on circle they reached, and two or three leaders out of the ranks were licking his face and purring to him consolingly. Of the dead slaves and toad-things[c] there were not many signs, but Carter thought he saw one bone a little way off in the open space between him and the beginning of the solid circles of[d] the warriors.

Carter now spoke with the leaders in the soft language of cats, and learned that his ancient friendship with the species was well known and often spoken of in the places where cats congregate. He had not been unmarked in Ulthar when he passed through, and the sleek old cats had remembered how he petted them after they had attended to

---

[a] onto] upon B, C
[b] Manx;] Manx, B, C
[c] toad-things] toad things A
[d] the beginning . . . of] *om.* B, C

the hungry zoogs[a] who looked evilly at a small black kitten. And they recalled, too, how he had welcomed the very little kitten who came to see him at the inn, and how he had given it a saucer of rich cream in the morning before he left. The grandfather of that very little kitten was the leader of the army now assembled, for he had seen the evil procession from a far hill and recognised[b] the prisoner as a sworn friend of his kind on earth and in the land of dream.

A yowl now came from a farther peak, and the old leader paused abruptly in his conversation. It was one of the army's outposts, stationed on the highest of the mountains to watch the one foe which earth's[c] cats fear; the very large and peculiar cats from Saturn, who for some reason have not been oblivious of the charm of our moon's dark side. They are leagued by treaty with the evil toad-things, and are notoriously hostile to our earthly cats; so that at this juncture a meeting would have been a somewhat grave matter.

After a brief consultation of generals, the cats rose and assumed a closer formation, crowding protectingly around Carter and preparing to take the great leap through space back to the housetops of our earth and its dreamland. The old field-marshal advised Carter to let himself be borne along smoothly and passively in the massed ranks of furry leapers, and told him how to spring when the rest sprang and land gracefully when the rest landed. He also offered to deposit him in any spot he desired, and Carter decided on the city of Dylath-Leen whence the black galley had set out; for he wished to sail thence for Oriab and the carven crest of[d] Ngranek, and also to warn the people of the city to have no more traffick with black galleys, if indeed that traffick could be tactfully and judiciously broken off. Then, upon a signal, the cats all leaped gracefully with their friend packed securely in their midst; while in a black cave on a far[e] unhallowed summit of the moon-mountains still vainly waited the crawling chaos Nyarlathotep.

The leap of the cats through space was very swift; and being

---

[a] zoogs] Zoogs C
[b] recognised] recognized C
[c] earth's] Earth's B, C
[d] of] *om.* B, C
[e] a far] an B, C

surrounded by his companions,[a] Carter did not see this time the great black shapelessnesses that lurk and caper and flounder in the abyss. Before he fully realised what had happened he was back in his familiar room at the inn at Dylath-Leen, and the stealthy, friendly[b] cats were pouring out of the window in streams. The old leader from Ulthar was the last to leave, and as Carter shook his paw he said he would be able to get home by cockcrow. When dawn came, Carter went downstairs and learned that a week had elapsed since his capture and leaving. There was still nearly a fortnight to wait for the ship bound toward Oriab, and during that time he said what he could against the black galleys and their infamous ways. Most of the townsfolk believed him; yet so fond were the jewellers of great rubies that none would wholly promise to cease trafficking with the wide-mouthed merchants. If aught of evil ever befalls Dylath-Leen through such traffick, it will not be his fault.

In about a week the desiderate ship put in by the black mole[c] and tall lighthouse, and Carter was glad to see that she was a barque of wholesome men, with painted sides and yellow lateen sails and a grey[d] captain in silken robes. Her cargo was the fragrant resin of Oriab's inner groves, and the delicate pottery baked by the artists of Baharna, and the strange little figures carved from Ngranek's ancient lava. For this they were paid in the wool of Ulthar and the iridescent textiles of Hatheg and the ivory that the black men carve across the river in Parg. Carter made arrangements with the captain to go to Baharna and was told that the voyage would take ten days. And during his week of waiting he talked much with that captain of Ngranek, and was told that very few had seen the carven face thereon; but that most travellers are content to learn its legends from old people and lava-gatherers and image-makers in Baharna and afterward say in their far homes that they have indeed beheld it. The captain was not even sure that any person now living had beheld that carven face, for the wrong side of Ngranek is very difficult and barren and sinister, and there are rumours of caves near the peak wherein dwell the night-gaunts. But the captain

[a] companions,] companions B, C
[b] friendly] friendly, A, B
[c] mole] __le B; wale C
[d] grey] gray C

did not wish to say just what a night-gaunt might be like, since such cattle are known to haunt most persistently the dreams of those who think too often of them. Then Carter asked that captain about unknown Kadath in the cold waste, and the marvellous sunset city, but of these the good man could truly tell nothing.

Carter sailed out of Dylath-Leen one early morning when the tide turned, and saw the first rays of sunrise on the thin angular towers of that dismal basalt town. And for two days they sailed eastward in sight of green coasts, and saw often the pleasant fishing towns that climbed up steeply with their red roofs and chimney-pots from old dreaming wharves and beaches where nets lay drying. But on the third day they turned sharply south where the roll of the water was stronger, and soon passed from sight of any land. On the fifth day the sailors were nervous, but the captain apologised for their fears, saying that the ship was about to pass over the weedy walls and broken columns of a sunken city too old for memory, and that when the water was clear one could see so many moving shadows in that deep place that simple folk disliked it. He admitted, moreover, that many ships had been lost in that part of the sea; having been hailed when quite close to it, but never seen again.

That night the moon was very bright, and one could see a great way down in the water. There was so little wind that the ship could not move much, and the ocean was very calm. Looking over the rail Carter saw many fathoms deep the dome of a great temple, and in front of it an avenue of unnatural sphinxes leading to what was once a public square. Dolphins sported merrily in and out of the ruins, and porpoises revelled clumsily here and there, sometimes coming to the surface and leaping clear out of the sea. As the ship drifted on a little the floor of the ocean rose in hills, and one could clearly mark the lines of ancient climbing streets and the washed-down walls of myriad little houses.

Then the suburbs appeared, and finally a great lone building on a hill, of simpler architecture than the other structures, and in much better repair. It was dark and low and covered four sides of a square, with a tower at each corner, a paved court in the centre, and small curious round windows all over it. Probably it was of basalt, though weeds draped the greater part; and such was its lonely and impressive place on that far hill that it may have been a temple or monastery. Some phosphorescent fish inside it gave the small round windows an aspect of shining, and Carter did not blame the sailors much for their fears. Then by the watery moonlight he noticed an odd high monolith in the middle of that central court, and saw that something was tied to it. And when after getting a telescope from the captain's cabin he saw that that bound thing was a sailor in the silk robes of Oriab, head downward and without any eyes, he was glad that a rising breeze soon took the ship ahead to more healthy parts of the sea.

The next day they spoke[a] a ship with violet sails bound for Zar, in the land of forgotten dreams, with bulbs of strange-coloured[b] lilies for cargo. And on the evening of the eleventh day they came in sight of the isle of Oriab,[c] with Ngranek rising jagged and snow-crowned in the distance. Oriab is a very great isle, and its port of Baharna a mighty city. The wharves of Baharna are of porphyry, and the city rises in great stone terraces behind them, having streets of steps that are frequently arched over by buildings and the bridges between buildings. There is a great canal which goes under the whole city in a tunnel with granite gates and leads to the inland lake of Yath, on whose farther shore are the vast clay-brick ruins of a primal city whose name is not remembered. As the ship drew into the harbour at evening the twin beacons Thon and Thal gleamed a welcome, and in all the million windows of Baharna's terraces mellow lights peeped out quietly and gradually as the stars peep out overhead in the dusk, till that steep and climbing seaport became a glittering constellation hung between the stars of heaven and the reflections of those stars in the still harbour.

The captain, after landing, made Carter a guest in his own small house on the shore[d] of Yath where the rear of the town slopes down to it; and his wife and servants brought strange toothsome foods for the traveller's delight. And in the days after that Carter asked for rumours and legends of Ngranek in all the taverns and public places where lava-gatherers and image-makers meet, but could find no one who had been up the higher slopes or seen the carven face. Ngranek was a hard mountain with only an accursed valley behind it, and

---

[a] spoke] spoke with B, C
[b] strange-coloured] strange coloured A, B, C
[c] Oriab,] Oriab C
[d] shore] shores B, C

besides, one could never depend on the certainty that night-gaunts are altogether fabulous.

When the captain sailed back to Dylath-Leen Carter took quarters in an ancient tavern opening on an alley of steps in the original part of the town, which is built of brick and resembles the ruins of Yath's farther shore. Here he laid his plans for the ascent of Ngranek, and correlated all that he had learned from the lava-gatherers about the roads thither. The keeper of the tavern was a very old man, and had heard so many legends that he was a great help. He even took Carter to an upper room in that ancient house and shewed him a crude picture which a traveller had scratched on the clay wall in the olden[a] days when men were bolder and less reluctant to visit Ngranek's higher slopes. The old tavern-keeper's great-grandfather had heard from his great-grandfather that the traveller who scratched that picture had climbed Ngranek and seen the carven face, here drawing it for others to behold; but Carter had very great doubts, since the large rough features on the wall were hasty and careless, and wholly overshadowed by a crowd of little companion shapes in the worst possible taste, with horns and wings and claws and curling tails.

At last, having gained all the information he was likely to gain in the taverns and public places of Baharna, Carter hired a zebra and set out one morning on the road by Yath's shore for those inland parts wherein towers stony Ngranek. On his right were rolling hills and pleasant orchards and neat little stone farmhouses, and he was much reminded of those fertile fields that flank the Skai. By evening he was near the nameless ancient ruins on Yath's farther shore, and though old lava-gatherers had warned him not to camp there at night, he tethered his zebra to a curious pillar before a crumbling wall and laid his blanket in a sheltered corner beneath some carvings whose meaning none could decipher. Around him he wrapped another blanket, for the nights are cold in Oriab; and when upon awaking once he thought he felt the wings of some insect brushing his face he covered his head altogether and slept in peace till roused by the magah birds in distant resin groves.

The sun had just come up over the great slope whereon leagues of

[a] olden] old B, C

primal brick foundations and worn walls and occasional cracked pillars
and pedestals stretched down desolate to the shore of Yath, and Carter
looked about for his tethered zebra. Great was his dismay to see that
docile beast stretched prostrate beside the curious pillar to which it had
been tied, and still greater was he vexed on finding that the steed was
quite dead, with its blood all sucked away through a singular wound in
its throat. His pack had been disturbed, and several shiny knickknacks[a] taken away, and all around[b] on the dusty soil were great
webbed footprints for which he could not in any way account. The
legends and warnings of lava-gatherers occurred to him[c] and he
thought of what had brushed his face in the night. Then he shouldered
his pack and strode on toward Ngranek, though not without a shiver
when he saw close to him as the highway passed through the ruins a
great gaping arch low in the wall of an old temple, with steps leading
down into darkness farther than he could peer.

His course now led[d] uphill through wilder and partly wooded
country, and he saw only the huts of charcoal-burners and the camps[e]
of those who gathered resin from the groves. The whole air was
fragrant with balsam, and all the magah birds sang blithely as they
flashed their seven colours in the sun. Near sunset he came on a new
camp of lava-gatherers returning with laden sacks from Ngranek's
lower slopes; and here he also camped, listening to the songs and tales
of the men, and overhearing what they whispered about a companion
they had lost. He had climbed high to reach a mass of fine lava above
him, and at nightfall did not return to his fellows. When they looked
for him the next day they found only his turban, nor was there any sign
on the crags below that he had fallen. They did not search any more,
because the old men[f] among them said it would be of no use. No one
ever found what the night-gaunts took, though those beasts themselves
were so uncertain as to be almost fabulous. Carter asked them if night-
gaunts sucked blood and liked shiny things and left webbed footprints,

[a] knick-knacks] knicknacks A, B; knickknacks C
[b] around] round B, C
[c] him] him, B, C
[d] led] lay B, C
[e] camps] camp B, C
[f] men] man C

but they all shook their head negatively and seemed frightened at his making such an inquiry. When he saw how taciturn they had become he asked them no more, but went to sleep in his blanket.

The next day he rose with the lava-gatherers and exchanged farewells as they rode west and he rode east on a zebra he had bought of them. Their older men gave him blessings and warnings, and told him he had better not climb too high on Ngranek, but while he thanked them heartily he was in no wise dissuaded. For still did he feel that he must find the gods on unknown Kadath,[a] and win from them a way to that haunting and marvellous city in the sunset. By noon, after a long uphill ride, he came upon some abandoned brick villages of the hill-people who had once dwelt thus close to Ngranek and carved images from its smooth lava. Here they had dwelt till the days of the old tavern-keeper's[b] grandfather, but about that time they felt that their presence was disliked. Their homes had crept even up the mountain's slope, and the higher they built the more people they would miss when the sun rose. At last they decided it would be better to leave altogether, since things were sometimes glimpsed in the darkness which no one could interpret favourably; so in the end all of them went down to the sea and dwelt in Baharna,[c] inhabiting a very old quarter and teaching their sons the old art of image-making which to this day they carry on. It was from these children of the exiled hill-people that Carter had heard the best tales about Ngranek when searching through Baharna's ancient taverns.

All this time the great gaunt side of Ngranek was looming up higher and higher as Carter approached it. There were sparse trees on the lower slope,[d] and feeble shrubs above them, and then the bare hideous rock rose spectral into the sky[e] to mix with frost and ice and eternal snow. Carter could see the rifts and ruggedness of that sombre stone, and did not welcome the prospect of climbing it. In places there were solid streams of lava, and scoriac heaps that littered slopes and ledges. Ninety aeons[f] ago, before even the gods had danced upon its

[a] Kadath,] Kadath; B, C
[b] tavern-keeper's] tavernkeeper's C
[c] Baharna,] Barharna, A
[d] slope,] slopes C [B has s typed over comma]
[e] sky] sky, B, C
[f] aeons] acons C

pointed peak, that mountain had spoken with fire and roared with the voices of the inner thunders. Now it towered all silent and sinister, bearing on the hidden side that secret titan image whereof rumour told. And there were caves in that mountain, which might be empty and alone with elder darkness, or might—if legend spoke truly—hold horrors of a form not to be surmised.

The ground sloped upward to the foot of Ngranek, thinly covered with scrub oaks and ash trees, and strown[a] with bits of rock, lava, and ancient cinder. There were the charred embers of many camps, where the lava-gatherers were wont to stop, and several rude altars which they had built either to propitiate the Great Ones or to ward off what they dreamed of in Ngranek's high passes and labyrinthine caves. At evening Carter reached the farthermost pile of embers and camped for the night, tethering his zebra to a sapling and wrapping himself well in his blanket[b] before going to sleep. And all through the night a voonith howled distantly from the shore of some hidden pool, but Carter felt no fear of that amphibious terror, since he had been told with certainty that not one of them dares even approach the slopes[c] of Ngranek.

In the clear sunshine of morning Carter began the long ascent, taking his zebra as far as that useful beast could go, but tying it to a stunted ash tree when the floor of the thin road[d] became too steep. Thereafter he scrambled up alone; first through the forest with its ruins of old villages in overgrown clearings, and then over the tough grass where anaemic shrubs grew here and there. He regretted coming clear of the trees, since the slope was very precipitous and the whole thing rather dizzying. At length he began to discern all the countryside spread out beneath him whenever he looked around;[e] the deserted huts of the image-makers, the groves of resin trees and the camps of those who gathered from them, the woods where prismatic magahs nest and sing, and even a hint very far away of the shores of Yath and of those forbidding ancient ruins whose name is forgotten. He found it best not to look around, and

[a] strown] strewn B, C
[b] blanket] blankets B, C
[c] slopes] slope B, C
[d] road] wood B, C
[e] around;] about; B, C

kept on climbing and climbing till the shrubs became very sparse and there was often nothing but the tough grass to cling to.

Then the soil became meagre, with great patches of bare rock cropping out, and now and then the nest of a condor in a crevice. Finally there was nothing at all but the bare rock, and had it not been very rough and weathered, he could scarcely have ascended farther. Knobs, ledges, and pinnacles, however, helped greatly; and it was cheering to see occasionally the sign of some lava-gatherer scratched clumsily in the friable stone, and know that wholesome human creatures had been there before him. After a certain height the presence of man was further shewn by handholds and footholds hewn where they were needed, and by little quarries and excavations where some choice vein or stream of lava had been found. In one place a narrow ledge had been chopped artificially to an especially rich deposit far to the right of the main line of ascent. Once or twice Carter dared to look around, and was almost stunned by the spread of landscape below. All the island betwixt him and the coast lay open to his sight, with Baharna's stone terraces and the smoke of its chimneys mystical in the distance. And beyond that the illimitable Southern Sea[a] with all its curious secrets.

Thus far there had been much winding around the mountain, so that the farther and carven side was still hidden. Carter now saw a ledge running upward and to the left which seemed to head the way he wished, and this course he took in the hope that it might prove continuous. After ten minutes he saw it was indeed no cul-de-sac, but that it led steeply on in an arc which would, unless suddenly interrupted or deflected, bring him after a few hours' climbing to that unknown southern slope overlooking the desolate crags and the accursed valley of lava. As new country came into view below him he saw that it was bleaker and wilder than those seaward lands he had traversed. The mountain's side, too, was somewhat different; being here pierced by curious cracks and caves not found on the straighter route he had left. Some of these were above him and some beneath him, all opening on sheerly perpendicular cliffs and wholly unreachable by the feet of man. The air was very cold now, but so hard was the climbing that he did not mind it. Only the increasing rarity bothered

[a] Southern Sea] southern sea B, C

him, and he thought that perhaps it was this which had turned the heads of other travellers and excited those absurd tales of night-gaunts whereby they explained the loss of such climbers as fell from these perilous paths. He was not much impressed by travellers'[a] tales, but had a good curved scimitar in case of any trouble. All lesser thoughts were lost in the wish to see that carven face which might set him on the track of the gods atop unknown Kadath.

At last, in the fearsome iciness of upper space, he came round fully to the hidden side of Ngranek and saw in infinite gulfs below him the lesser crags and sterile abysses of lava which marked the olden wrath of the Great Ones. There was unfolded, too, a vast expanse of country to the south; but it was a desert land without fair fields or cottage chimneys, and seemed to have no ending. No trace of the sea was visible on this side, for Oriab is a great island. Black caverns and odd crevices were still numerous on the sheer vertical cliffs, but none of them was accessible to a climber. There now loomed aloft a great beetling mass which hampered the upward view, and Carter was for a moment shaken with doubt lest it prove impassable. Poised in windy insecurity miles above earth, with only space and death on one side and only slippery walls of rock on the other, he knew for a moment the fear that makes men shun Ngranek's hidden side. He could not turn round, yet the sun was already low. If there were no way aloft, the night would find him crouching there still, and the dawn would not find him at all.

But there was a way, and he saw it in due season. Only a very expert dreamer could have used those imperceptible footholds, yet to Carter they were sufficent. Surmounting now the outward-hanging rock, he found the slope above much easier than that below, since a great glacier's melting had left a generous space with loam and ledges. To the left a precipice dropped straight from unknown heights to unknown depths, with a cave's dark mouth just out of reach above him. Elsewhere, however, the mountain slanted back strongly, and even gave him space to lean and rest.

He felt from the chill that he must be near the snow line, and looked up to see what glittering pinnacles might be shining in that late

---

[a] travellers'] traveller's B, C

ruddy sunlight. Surely enough, there was the snow uncounted thousands of feet above, and below it a great beetling crag like that he had just climbed; hanging for ever[a] in bold outline, black against the white of the frozen peak.[b] And when he saw that crag he gasped and cried out aloud, and clutched at the jagged rock in awe; for the titan bulge had not stayed as earth's dawn had shaped it, but gleamed red and stupendous in the sunset with the carved and polished features of a god.

Stern and terrible shone that face that the sunset lit with fire. How vast it was no mind can ever measure, but Carter knew at once that man could never have fashioned it. It was a god chiselled by the hands of the gods, and it looked down haughty and majestic upon the seeker. Rumour had said it was strange and not to be mistaken, and Carter saw that it was indeed so; for those long narrow eyes and long-lobed ears, and that thin nose and pointed chin, all spoke of a race that is not of men but of gods.[c] He clung overawed in that lofty and perilous eyrie, even though it was this which he had expected and come to find; for there is in a god's face more of marvel than prediction can tell, and when that face is vaster than a great temple and seen looking down[d] at sunset in the cryptic silences of that upper world from whose dark lava it was divinely hewn of old, the marvel is so strong that none may escape it.

Here, too, was the added marvel of recognition; for although he had planned to search all dreamland over for those whose likeness to this face might mark them as the gods'[e] children, he now knew that he need not do so. Certainly, the great face carven on that mountain was of no strange sort, but the kin of such as he had seen often in the taverns of the seaport Celephaïs[f] which lies in Ooth-Nargai beyond the Tanarian Hills and is ruled over by that King Kuranes whom Carter once knew in waking life. Every year sailors with such a face came in dark ships from the north to trade their onyx for the carved jade and spun gold and little red singing birds of Celephaïs,[g] and it was clear

---

[a] for ever] forever A, B, C

[b] outline, . . . peak.] outline. B, C

[c] gods.] gods. ¶ B, C

[d] down] downward B, C

[e] gods'] god's B, C

[f] Celephaïs] Celephais B, C

[g] Celephaïs,] Celephais, B, C

that these could be no others than the half-gods he sought. Where they dwelt, there must the cold waste lie close, and within it unknown Kadath and its onyx castle for the Great Ones. So to Celephaïs[a] he must go, far distant from the isle of Oriab, and in such parts as would take him back to Dylath-Leen and up the Skai to the bridge by Nir, and again into the enchanted wood of the zoogs,[b] whence the way would bend northward through the garden lands by Oukranos to the gilded spires of Thran, where he might find a galleon bound over the Cerenerian Sea.[c]

But dusk was now thick, and the great carven face looked down even sterner in shadow. Perched on that ledge night found the seeker; and in the blackness he might neither go down nor go up, but only stand and cling and shiver in that narrow place till the day came, praying to keep awake lest sleep loose[d] his hold and send him down the dizzy miles of air to the crags and sharp rocks of the accursed valley. The stars came out, but save for them there was only black nothingness in his eyes; nothingness leagued with death, against whose beckoning he might do no more than cling to the rocks and lean back away from an unseen brink. The last thing of earth that he saw in the gloaming was a condor soaring close to the westward precipice beside him, and darting screaming away when it came near the cave whose mouth yawned just out of reach.

Suddenly, without a warning sound in the dark, Carter felt his curved scimitar drawn stealthily out of his belt by some unseen hand. Then he heard it clatter down over the rocks below. And between him and the Milky Way he thought he saw a very terrible outline of something noxiously thin and horned and tailed and bat-winged. Other things, too, had begun to blot out patches of stars west of him, as if a flock of vague entities were flapping thickly and silently out of that inaccessible cave in the face of the precipice. Then a sort of cold rubbery arm seized his neck and something else seized his feet, and he was lifted inconsiderately up and swung about in space. Another minute and the

[a] Celephaïs] Celephais B, C
[b] zoogs,] Zoogs, B, C
[c] Cerenerian Sea.] Cerenarian Sea. A; Cerenarian sea. B, C
[d] loose] lose C

stars were gone, and Carter knew that the night-gaunts had got him.

They bore him breathless into that cliffside cavern and through monstrous labyrinths beyond. When he struggled, as at first he did by instinct, they tickled him with deliberation. They made no sound at all themselves, and even their membraneous wings were silent. They were frightfully cold and damp and slippery, and their paws kneaded one detestably. Soon they were plunging hideously downward through inconceivable abysses in a whirling, giddying, sickening rush of dank, tomb-like air; and Carter felt that they were shooting into the ultimate vortex of shrieking and daemonic madness. He screamed again and again, but whenever he did so the black paws tickled him with greater subtlety. Then he saw a sort of grey phosphorescence about, and guessed they were coming even to that inner world of subterrene horror of which dim legends tell, and which is litten only by the pale death-fire wherewith reeks the ghoulish air and the primal mists of the pits at earth's core.

At last far below him he saw the faint lines of grey and ominous pinnacles which he knew must be the fabled Peaks of Thok.[a] Awful and sinister they stand in the haunted dusk[b] of sunless and eternal depths; higher than man may reckon, and guarding terrible valleys where the bholes[c] crawl and burrow nastily. But Carter preferred to look at them than at his captors, which were indeed shocking and uncouth black beings[d] with smooth, oily, whale-like surfaces, unpleasant horns that curved inward toward each other, bat-wings whose beating made no sound, ugly prehensile paws, and barbed tails that lashed needlessly and disquietingly. And worst of all, they never spoke or laughed, and never smiled because they had no faces at all to smile with, but only a suggestive blankness where a face ought to be. All they ever did was clutch and fly and tickle; that was the way of night-gaunts.

As the band flew lower the Peaks of Thok[e] rose grey and towering on all sides, and one saw clearly that nothing lived on that austere and

[a] Thok.] Throk. A, B [*revised by HPL*], C
[b] dusk] disk B, C
[c] bholes] dholes C
[d] beings] things B, C
[e] Thok] Throk A, B [*revised by HPL*], C

impassive[a] granite of the endless twilight. At still lower levels the death-fires in the air gave out, and one met only the primal blackness of the void save aloft where the thin peaks stood out goblin-like. Soon the peaks were very far away, and nothing about but great rushing winds with the dankness[b] of nethermost grottoes in them. Then in the end the night-gaunts landed on a floor of unseen things which felt like layers of bones, and left Carter all alone in that black valley. To bring him thither was the duty of the night-gaunts that guard Ngranek; and this done, they flapped away silently. When Carter tried to trace their flight he found he could not, since even the Peaks of Thok[c] had faded out of sight. There was nothing anywhere but blackness and horror and silence and bones.

Now Carter knew from a certain source that he was in the vale of Pnath,[d] where crawl and burrow the enormous bholes;[e] but he did not know what to expect, because no one has ever seen a bhole[f] or even guessed what such a thing may be like. Bholes[g] are known only by dim rumour, from the rustling they make amongst mountains of bones and the slimy touch they have when they wriggle past one. They cannot be seen because they creep only in the dark. Carter did not wish to meet a bhole,[h] so listened intently for any sound in the unknown depths of bones about him. Even in this fearsome place he had a plan and an objective, for whispers of Pnath[i] and its approaches[j] were not unknown to one with whom he had talked much in the old days. In brief, it seemed fairly likely that this was the spot into which all the ghouls of the waking world cast the refuse of their feastings; and that if he but had good luck he might stumble upon that mighty crag taller

---

[a] impassive] impressive B, C
[b] dankness] darkness B, C
[c] Thok] Throk A, B [*revised by HPL*], C
[d] Pnath,] Pnoth, B [*revised by HPL*], C
[e] bholes;] dholes; C
[f] bhole] dhole C
[g] Bholes] Dholes C
[h] bhole,] dhole, C
[i] Pnath] Pnoth B [*revised by HPL*], C
[j] and its approaches] *om.* B, C

even than Thok's[a] peaks which marks the edge of their domain. Showers of bones would tell him where to look, and once found he could call to a ghoul to let down a ladder; for strange to say, he had a very singular link with these terrible creatures.

A man he had known in Boston—a painter of strange pictures with a secret studio in an ancient and unhallowed alley near a graveyard—had actually made friends with the ghouls and had taught him to understand the simpler part of their disgusting meeping and glibbering. This man had vanished at last, and Carter was not sure but that he might find him now, and use for the first time in dreamland that far-away English of his dim waking life. In any case, he felt he could persuade a ghoul to guide him out of Pnath;[b] and it would be better to meet a ghoul, which one can see, than a bhole,[c] which one cannot see.

So Carter walked in the dark, and ran when he thought he heard something among the bones underfoot. Once he bumped into a stony slope, and knew it must be the base of one of Thok's[d] peaks. Then at last he heard a monstrous rattling and clatter which reached far up in the air, and became sure he had come nigh the crag of the ghouls. He was not sure he could be heard from this valley miles below, but realised that the inner world has strange laws. As he pondered he was struck by a flying bone so heavy that it must have been a skull, and therefore realising his nearness to the fateful crag he sent up as best he might that meeping cry which is the call of the ghoul.

Sound travels slowly, so that it was some time before he heard an answering glibber. But it came at last, and before long he was told that a rope ladder would be lowered. The wait for this was very tense, since there was no telling what might not have been stirred up among those bones by his shouting. Indeed, it was not long before he actually did hear a vague rustling afar off. As this thoughtfully approached, he became more and more uncomfortable; for he did not wish to move away from the spot where the ladder would come. Finally the tension

---

[a] Thok's] Throk's A, B [*revised by HPL*], C
[b] Pnath;] Pnoth; B [*revised by HPL*], C
[c] bhole,] dhole, C
[d] Thok's] Throk's A, B [*revised by HPL*], C

grew almost unbearable, and he was about to flee in panic when the thud of something on the newly heaped bones nearby drew his notice from the other sound. It was the ladder, and after a minute of groping he had it taut in his hands. But the other sound did not cease, and followed him even as he climbed. He had gone fully five feet from the ground when the rattling beneath waxed emphatic, and was a good ten feet up when something swayed the ladder from below. At a height which must have been fifteen or twenty feet he felt his whole side brushed by a great slippery length which grew alternately convex and concave with wriggling, and thereafter[a] he climbed desperately to escape the unendurable nuzzling of that loathsome and overfed bhole[b] whose form no man might see.

For hours he climbed with aching arms and blistered hands, seeing again the grey death-fire and Thok's[c] uncomfortable pinnacles. At last he discerned above him the projecting edge of the great crag of the ghouls, whose vertical side he could not glimpse; and hours later he saw a curious face peering over it as a gargoyle peers over a parapet of Notre Dame. This almost made him lose his hold through faintness, but a moment later he was himself again; for his vanished friend Richard Pickman had once introduced him to a ghoul, and he knew well their canine faces and slumping forms and unmentionable idiosyncrasies. So he had himself well under control when that hideous thing pulled him out of the dizzy emptiness over the edge of the crag, and did not scream at the partly consumed refuse heaped at one side or at the squatting circles of ghouls who gnawed and watched curiously.

He was now on a dim-litten plain whose sole topographical features were great boulders and the entrances of burrows. The ghouls were in general respectful, even if one did attempt to pinch him while several others eyed his leanness speculatively. Through patient glibbering he made inquiries regarding his vanished friend, and found he had become a ghoul of some prominence in abysses nearer the waking world. A greenish elderly ghoul offered to conduct him to Pickman's present habitation, so despite a natural loathing he followed the

[a] wriggling, and thereafter] wriggling; and hereafter C
[b] bhole] dhole C
[c] Thok's] Throk's A, B [*revised by HPL*], C

creature into a capacious burrow and crawled after him for hours in the blackness of rank mould. They emerged on a dim plain strown[a] with singular relics of earth—old gravestones, broken urns, and grotesque fragments of monuments—and Carter realised with some emotion that he was probably nearer the waking world than at any other time since he had gone down the seven hundred steps from the cavern of flame to the Gate of Deeper Slumber.

There, on a tombstone of 1768 stolen from the Granary Burying Ground in Boston, sat the ghoul which was once the artist Richard Upton Pickman. It was naked and rubbery, and had acquired so much of the ghoulish physiognomy that its human origin was already obscure. But it still remembered a little English, and was able to converse with Carter in grunts and monosyllables, helped out now and then by the glibbering of ghouls. When it learned that Carter wished to get to the enchanted wood and from there to the city Celephaïs[b] in Ooth-Nargai beyond the Tanarian Hills, it seemed rather doubtful; for these ghouls of the waking world do no business in the graveyards of upper dreamland (leaving that to the web-footed[c] wamps that are spawned in dead cities),[d] and many things intervene betwixt their gulf and the enchanted wood, including the terrible kingdom of the gugs.[e]

The gugs,[f] hairy and gigantic, once reared stone circles in that wood and made strange sacrifices to the Other Gods and the crawling chaos Nyarlathotep, until one night an abomination of theirs reached the ears of earth's gods and they were banished to caverns below. Only a great trap-door[g] of stone with an iron ring connects the abyss of the earth-ghouls with the enchanted wood, and this the gugs[h] are afraid to open because of a curse. That a mortal dreamer could traverse their cavern realm and leave by that door is inconceivable; for mortal dreamers were their former food, and they have legends of the

[a] strown] strewn B, C
[b] Celephaïs] Celephais C
[c] web-footed] red-footed B, C
[d] cities),] cities A, B [*comma added by HPL in B*]
[e] gugs.] Gugs. A, B, C
[f] gugs,] Gugs, A, B, C
[g] trap-door] trap door A, B, C
[h] gugs] Gugs A, B, C

toothsomeness of such dreamers even though banishment has restricted their diet to the ghasts, those repulsive beings which die in the light, and which live in the vaults of Zin and leap on long hind legs like kangaroos.

So the ghoul that was Pickman advised Carter either to leave the abyss at Sarkomand, that deserted city in the valley below Leng where black nitrous stairways guarded by winged diorite[a] lions lead down from dreamland to the lower gulfs, or to return through a churchyard to the waking world and begin the quest anew down the seventy steps of light slumber to the cavern of flame and the seven hundred steps to the Gate of Deeper Slumber and the enchanted wood. This, however, did not suit the seeker; for he knew nothing of the way from Leng to Ooth-Nargai, and was likewise reluctant to awake lest he forget all he had so far gained in this dream. It were disastrous to his quest to forget the august and celestial faces of those seamen from the north who traded onyx in Celephaïs,[b] and who, being the sons of gods, must point the way to the cold waste and Kadath where the Great Ones dwell.

After much persuasion the ghoul consented to guide his guest inside the great wall of the gugs'[c] kingdom. There was one chance that Carter might be able to steal through that twilight realm of circular stone towers at an hour when the giants would be all gorged and snoring indoors, and reach the central tower with the sign of Koth upon it, which has the stairs leading up to that stone trap-door[d] in the enchanted wood. Pickman even consented to lend three ghouls to help with a tombstone lever in raising the stone door; for of ghouls the gugs[e] are somewhat afraid, and they often flee from their own colossal graveyards when they see feasting there.

He also advised Carter to disguise as a ghoul himself; shaving the beard he had allowed to grow (for ghouls have none),[f] wallowing naked in the mould to get the correct surface, and loping in the usual slumping way, with his clothing carried in a bundle as if it were a

[a] diorite] diarote C
[b] Celephaïs,] Celephais, B, C
[c] gugs'] Gugs' A, B, C
[d] trap-door] trap door A, B, C
[e] gugs] Gugs A, B, C
[f] grow (. . .),] grow, (. . .) A, B [*revised by HPL*]

choice morsel from a tomb. They would reach the city of the gugs[a]—which is coterminous[b] with the whole kingdom—through the proper burrows, emerging in a cemetery not far from the stair-containing Tower of Koth. They must beware, however, of a large cave near the cemetery; for this is the mouth of the vaults of Zin, and the vindictive ghasts are always on watch there murderously for those denizens of the upper abyss who hunt and prey on them. The ghasts try to come out when the gugs[c] sleep,[d] and they attack ghouls as readily as gugs,[e] for they cannot discriminate. They are very primitive, and eat one another. The gugs[f] have a sentry at a narrow place in the vaults of Zin, but he is often drowsy and is sometimes surprised by a party of ghasts. Though ghasts cannot live in real light, they can endure the grey twilight of the abyss for hours.

So at length Carter crawled through endless burrows with three helpful ghouls bearing the slate gravestone of Col. Nehemiah[g] Derby, obiit[h] 1719, from the Charter Street Burying Ground in Salem. When they came again into open twilight they were in a forest of vast lichened monoliths reaching nearly as high as the eye could see and forming the modest gravestones of the gugs.[i] On the right of the hole out of which they wriggled, and seen through aisles of monoliths, was a stupendous vista of Cyclopean[j] round towers mounting up illimitable into the grey air of inner earth. This was the great city of the gugs,[k] whose doorways are thirty feet high. Ghouls come here often, for a buried gug[l] will feed a community for almost a year, and even with the added peril it is better to burrow for gugs[m] than to bother with the

[a] gugs] Gugs A, B, C
[b] coterminous] conterminous C
[c] gugs] Gugs A, B, C
[d] sleep,] sleep C
[e] gugs,] Gugs, A, B, C
[f] gugs] Gugs A, B, C
[g] Nehemiah] Nepemiah B [*corrected by HPL*], C
[h] obiit] obit B, C
[i] gugs.] Gugs. A, B, C
[j] Cyclopean] cyclopean A, B, C
[k] gugs,] Gugs, A, B, C
[l] gug] Gug A, B, C
[m] gugs] Gugs A, B, C

graves of men. Carter now understood the occasional titan bones he had felt beneath him in the vale of Pnath.[a]

Straight ahead, and just outside the cemetery, rose a sheer perpendicular cliff at whose base an immense and forbidding cavern yawned. This the ghouls told Carter to avoid as much as possible, since it was the entrance to the unhallowed vaults of Zin where gugs[b] hunt ghasts in the darkness.[c] And truly, that warning was soon well justified; for the moment a ghoul began to creep toward the towers to see if the hour of the gugs'[d] resting had been rightly timed, there glowed in the gloom of that great cavern's mouth first one pair of yellowish-red eyes and then another, implying that the gugs[e] were one sentry less, and that ghasts have indeed an excellent sharpness of smell. So the ghoul returned to the burrow and motioned his companions to be silent. It was best to leave the ghasts to their own devices, and there was a possibility that they might soon withdraw, since they must naturally be rather tired after coping with a gug[f] sentry in the black vaults. After a moment something about the size of a small horse hopped out into the grey twilight, and Carter turned sick at the aspect of that scabrous and unwholesome beast, whose face is so curiously human despite the absence of a nose, a forehead, and other important particulars.

Presently three other ghasts hopped out to join their fellow, and a ghoul glibbered softly at Carter that their absence of battle-scars was a bad sign. It proved that they had not fought the gug[g] sentry at all, but[h] merely slipped past him as he slept, so that their strength and savagery were still unimpaired and would remain so till they had found and

[a] Pnath.] Pnoth. B [*revised by HPL*], C
[b] gugs] Gugs A, B, C
[c] darkness.] darkness. One ghoul now crept ahead to see if the hour of the Gug's resting had been correctly timed; upon returning with an affirmative nod, the whole party shambled along in the manner of ghouls, Carter imitating the gait of his companions with much skill. They went very silently, but such is the sharpness of smell among the ghasts that their progress was not long unmarked. Almost as soon A [*excised*]
[d] gugs'] Gugs' A, B, C
[e] gugs] Gugs A, B, C
[f] gug] Gug A, B, C
[g] gug] Gug A, B, C
[h] but] but had B, C

disposed of a victim. It was very unpleasant to see those filthy and disproportioned animals,[a] which soon numbered about fifteen, grubbing about and making their kangaroo leaps in the grey twilight where titan towers and monoliths arose, but it was still more unpleasant when they spoke among themselves in the coughing gutturals of ghasts. And yet, horrible as they were, they were not so horrible as what presently came out of the cave after them with disconcerting suddenness.

It was a paw, fully two feet and a half across, and equipped with formidable talons. After it came another paw, and after that a great black-furred arm to which both of the paws were attached by short forearms. Then two pink eyes shone, and the head of the awakened gug[b] sentry, large as a barrel, wobbled[c] into view. The eyes jutted two inches from each side, shaded by bony protuberances overgrown with coarse hairs. But the head was chiefly terrible because of the mouth. That mouth had great yellow fangs and ran from the top to the bottom of the head, opening vertically instead of horizontally.

But before that unfortunate gug[d] could emerge from the cave and rise to his full twenty feet, the vindictive ghasts were upon him. Carter feared for a moment that he would give an alarm and arouse all his kin, till a ghoul softly glibbered that gugs[e] have no voice,[f] but talk by means of facial expression. The battle which then ensued was truly a frightful one. From all sides the venomous ghasts rushed feverishly at the creeping gug,[g] nipping and tearing with their muzzles, and mauling murderously with their hard pointed hooves. All the time they coughed excitedly, screaming when the great vertical mouth of the gug would occasionally bite into one of their number, so that the noise of the combat would surely have aroused the sleeping city had not the weakening of the sentry begun to transfer the action farther and farther within the cavern. As it was, the tumult soon receded altogether from sight in the blackness, with only occasional evil echoes to mark its continuance.

[a] animals,] animals B, C
[b] gug] Gug A, B, C
[c] wobbled] wabbled B [*corrected by HPL*], C
[d] gug] Gug A, B, C
[e] gugs] Gugs A, B, C
[f] voice,] voice C
[g] gug,] Gug, A, B, C

Then the most alert of the ghouls gave the signal for all to advance, and Carter followed the loping three out of the forest of monoliths and into the dark noisome streets of that awful city whose rounded towers of Cyclopean[a] stone soared up beyond the sight. Silently they shambled over that rough rock pavement, hearing with disgust the abominable muffled snortings from great black doorways which marked the slumber of the gugs.[b] Apprehensive of the ending of the rest hour, the ghouls set a somewhat rapid pace; but even so the journey was no brief one, for distances in that town of giants are on a great scale. At last, however, they came to a somewhat open space before a tower even vaster than the rest, above whose colossal doorway was fixed a monstrous symbol in bas-relief which made one shudder without knowing its meaning. This was the central tower with the sign of Koth, and those huge stone steps just visible through the dusk within were the beginning of the great flight leading to upper dreamland and the enchanted wood.

There now began a climb of interminable length in utter blackness;[c] made almost impossible by the monstrous size of the steps, which were fashioned for gugs,[d] and were therefore nearly a yard high. Of their number Carter could form no just estimate, for he soon became so worn out that the tireless and elastic ghouls were forced to aid him. All through the endless climb there lurked the peril of detection and pursuit; for though no gug[e] dares lift the stone door to the forest because of the Great Ones'[f] curse, there are no such restraints concerning the tower and the steps, and escaped ghasts are often chased[g] even to the very top. So sharp are the ears of gugs,[h] that the bare feet and hands of the climbers might readily be heard when the city awoke; and it would of course take but little time for the striding giants, accustomed from their ghast-hunts in the vaults of Zin to

[a] Cyclopean] cyclopean A, B, C
[b] gugs.] Gugs. C
[c] blackness;] blackness B, C
[d] gugs,] Gug C [*capitalised in B by HPL*]
[e] gug] Gug C [*capitalised in B by HPL*]
[f] Ones'] One's B, C
[g] chased] chased, B, C
[h] gugs,] Gugs, C [*capitalised in B by HPL*]

seeing without light, to overtake their smaller and slower quarry on those Cyclopean[a] steps. It was very depressing to reflect that the silent pursuing gugs[b] would not be heard at all, but would come very suddenly and shockingly in the dark upon the climbers. Nor could the traditional fear of gugs[c] for ghouls be depended upon in that peculiar place where the advantages lay so heavily with the gugs.[d] There was also some peril from the furtive and venomous ghasts, which frequently hopped up into[e] the tower during the sleep hour of the gugs.[f] If the gugs[g] slept long, and the ghasts returned soon from their deed in the cavern, the scent of the climbers might easily be picked up by those loathsome and ill-disposed things; in which case it would almost be better to be eaten by a gug.[h]

Then, after aeons of climbing, there came a cough from the darkness above; and matters assumed a very grave and unexpected turn. It was clear that a ghast, or perhaps even more, had strayed into that tower before the coming of Carter and his guides; and it was equally clear that this peril was very close. After a breathless second the leading ghoul pushed Carter to the wall and arranged his two kinsfolk[i] in the best possible way, with the old slate tombstone raised for a crushing blow whenever the enemy might come in sight. Ghouls can see in the dark, so the party was not as badly off as Carter would have been alone. In another moment the clatter of hooves revealed the downward hopping of at least one beast, and the slab-bearing ghouls poised their weapon for a desperate blow. Presently two yellowish-red eyes flashed into view, and the panting of the ghast became audible above its clattering. As it hopped down to the step just above the ghouls, they wielded the ancient gravestone with prodigious force, so that there was only a wheeze and a choking before the victim collapsed

[a] Cyclopean] cyclopean A, B, C
[b] gugs] Gugs C [*capitalised in B by HPL*]
[c] gugs] Gugs C [*capitalised in B by HPL*]
[d] gugs.] Gugs. C [*capitalised in B by HPL*]
[e] into] onto C
[f] gugs.] Gugs. C [*capitalised in B by HPL*]
[g] gugs] Gugs C [*capitalised in B by HPL*]
[h] gug.] Gug. C [*capitalised in B by HPL*]
[i] two kinsfolk] kinsfolk B; kinfolk C

in a noxious heap. There seemed to be only this one animal, and after a moment of listening the ghouls tapped Carter as a signal to proceed again. As before, they were obliged to aid him; and he was glad to leave that place of carnage where the ghast's uncouth remains sprawled invisible in the blackness.

At last the ghouls brought their companion to a halt; and feeling above him, Carter realised that the great stone trap-door[a] was reached at last. To open so vast a thing completely was not to be thought of, but the ghouls hoped to get it up just enough to slip the gravestone under as a prop, and permit Carter to escape through the crack. They themselves planned to descend again and return through the city of the gugs,[b] since their elusiveness was great, and they did not know the way overland to spectral Sarkomand with its lion-guarded gate to the abyss.

Mighty was the straining of those three ghouls at the stone of the door above them, and Carter helped push with as much strength as he had. They judged the edge next the top of the staircase to be the right one, and to this they bent all the force of their disreputably nourished muscles. After a few moments a crack of light appeared; and Carter, to whom that task had been entrusted, slipped the end of the old gravestone in the aperture. There now ensued a mighty heaving; but progress was very slow, and they had of course to return to their first position every time they failed to turn the slab and prop the portal open.

Suddenly their desperation was magnified a thousandfold[c] by a sound on the steps below them. It was only the thumping and rattling of the slain ghast's hooved body as it rolled down to lower levels; but of all the possible causes of that body's dislodgment and rolling, none was in the least reassuring. Therefore, knowing the ways of gugs,[d] the ghouls set to with something of a frenzy; and in a surprisingly short time had the door so high that they were able to hold it still whilst Carter turned the slab and left a generous opening. They now helped Carter through, letting him climb up to their rubbery shoulders and later guiding his feet as he clutched at the blessed soil of the upper

[a] trap-door] trap door A, B, C
[b] gugs,] Gugs, C [*capitalised by HPL in B*]
[c] thousandfold] thousand fold C
[d] gugs,] Gugs, C [*capitalised by HPL in B*]

dreamland outside. Another second and they were through themselves, knocking away the gravestone and closing the great trap-door[a] while a panting became audible beneath. Because of the Great Ones' curse[b] no gug[c] might ever emerge from that portal, so with a deep relief and sense of repose Carter lay quietly on the thick grotesque fungi of the enchanted wood while his guides squatted near in the manner that ghouls rest.

Weird as was that enchanted wood through which he had fared so long ago, it was verily a haven and a delight after the[d] gulfs he had now left behind. There was no living denizen about, for zoogs[e] shun the mysterious door in fear, and Carter at once consulted with his ghouls about their future course. To return through the tower they no longer dared, and the waking world did not appeal to them when they learned that they must pass the priests Nasht and Kaman-Thah in the cavern of flame. So at length they decided to return through Sarkomand and its gate of the abyss,[f] though of how to get there they knew nothing. Carter recalled that it lies in the valley below Leng, and recalled likewise that he had seen in Dylath-Leen a sinister, slant-eyed old merchant reputed to trade on Leng. Therefore[g] he advised the ghouls to seek out Dylath-Leen, crossing the fields to Nir and the Skai and following the river to its mouth. This they at once resolved to do, and lost no time in loping off, since the thickening of the dusk promised a full night ahead for travel. And Carter shook the paws of those repulsive beasts, thanking them for their help and sending his gratitude to the beast which once was Pickman; but could not help sighing with pleasure when they left. For a ghoul is a ghoul, and at best an unpleasant companion for man. After that Carter sought a forest pool and cleansed himself of the mud of nether earth, thereupon reassuming the clothes he had so carefully carried.

[a] trap-door] trap door A, B, C
[b] Ones' curse] One's curse B; One's curst C
[c] gug] Gug C [*capitalised by HPL in B*]
[d] the] these B, C
[e] zoogs] Zoogs C
[f] abyss,] abysss, C
[g] Leng. Therefore] Leng, therefore B, C

It was now night in that redoubtable wood of monstrous trees, but because of the phosphorescence one might travel as well as by day; wherefore Carter set out upon the well-known route toward Celephaïs,[a] in Ooth-Nargai[b] beyond the Tanarian Hills. And as he went he thought of the zebra he had left tethered to an ash tree[c] on Ngranek in far-away Oriab so many aeons ago, and wondered if any lava-gatherer[d] had fed and released it. And he wondered, too, if he would ever return to Baharna and pay for the zebra that was slain by night in those ancient ruins by Yath's shore, and if the old tavern-keeper would remember him. Such were the thoughts that came to him in the air of the regained upper dreamland.

But presently his progress was halted by a sound from a very large hollow tree. He had avoided the great circle of stones, since he did not care to speak with zoogs[e] just now; but it appeared from the singular fluttering in that huge tree that important councils were in session elsewhere. Upon drawing nearer he made out the accents of a tense and heated discussion; and before long became conscious of matters which he viewed with the greatest concern. For a war on the cats was under debate in that sovereign assembly of zoogs.[f] It all came from the loss of the party which had sneaked after Carter to Ulthar, and which the cats had justly punished for unsuitable intentions. The matter had long rankled; and now, or within at least[g] a month, the marshalled zoogs[h] were about to strike the whole feline tribe in a series of surprise attacks, taking individual cats or groups of cats unawares, and giving not even the myriad cats of Ulthar a proper chance to drill and mobilise. This was the plan of the zoogs,[i] and Carter saw that he must foil it before leaving on[j] his mighty quest.

[a] Celephaïs,] Celephais, B [*corrected by HPL*], C
[b] Ooth-Nargai] Oooth-Nargai C
[c] ash tree] ash-tree A, B, C
[d] lava-gatherer] lava-gatherers B, C
[e] zoogs] Zoogs C
[f] zoogs.] Zoogs. C
[g] within at least] at least within B, C
[h] zoogs] Zoogs C
[i] zoogs,] Zoogs, C
[j] on] upon B, C

Very quietly therefore did Randolph Carter steal to the edge of the wood and send the cry of the cat over the starlit fields. And a great grimalkin in a nearby cottage took up the burden and relayed it across leagues of rolling meadow to warriors large and small, black, grey, tiger, white, yellow, and mixed; and it echoed through Nir and beyond the Skai even into Ulthar, and Ulthar's numerous cats called in chorus and fell into a line of march. It was fortunate that the moon was not up, so that all the cats were on earth. Swiftly and silently leaping, they sprang from every hearth and housetop and poured in a great furry sea across the plains to the edge of the wood. Carter was there to greet them, and the sight of shapely, wholesome cats was indeed good for his eyes after the things he had seen and walked with in the abyss. He was glad to see his venerable friend and one-time rescuer at the head of Ulthar's detachment, a collar of rank around his sleek neck, and whiskers bristling at a martial angle. Better still, as a sub-lieutenant in that army was a brisk young fellow who proved to be none other than the very little kitten at the inn to whom Carter had given a saucer of rich cream on that long-vanished morning in Ulthar. He was a strapping and promising cat now, and purred as he shook hands with his friend. His grandfather said he was doing very well in the army, and that he might well expect a captaincy after one more campaign.

Carter now outlined the peril of the cat tribe, and was rewarded by deep-throated purrs of gratitude from all sides. Consulting with the generals, he prepared a plan of instant action which involved marching at once upon the zoog[a] council and other known strongholds of zoogs;[b] forestalling their surprise attacks and forcing them to terms before the mobilisation of their army of invasion. Thereupon without a moment's loss that great ocean of cats flooded the enchanted wood and surged around the council tree and the great stone circle. Flutterings rose to panic pitch as the enemy saw the newcomers,[c] and there was very little resistance among the furtive and curious brown zoogs.[d] They saw that they were beaten in advance, and turned from

---

[a] zoog] Zoog C
[b] zoogs;] Zoogs; C
[c] newcomers,] newcomers B [*corrected by HPL*], C
[d] zoogs.] Zoogs. C

thoughts of vengeance to thoughts of present self-preservation.

Half the cats now seated themselves in a circular formation with the captured zoogs[a] in the centre, leaving open a lane down which were marched the additional captives rounded up by the other cats in other parts of the wood. Terms were discussed at length, Carter acting as interpreter, and it was decided that the zoogs[b] might remain a free tribe on condition of rendering to the cats a large annual[c] tribute of grouse, quail, and pheasants from the less fabulous parts of their[d] forest. Twelve young zoogs[e] of noble families were taken as hostages to be kept in the Temple of the[f] Cats at Ulthar, and the victors made it plain that any disappearances of cats on the borders of the zoog[g] domain would be followed by consequences highly disastrous to zoogs.[h] These matters disposed of, the assembled cats broke ranks and permitted the zoogs[i] to slink off one by one to their respective homes, which they hastened to do with many a sullen backward glance.

The old cat general now offered Carter an escort through the forest to whatever border he wished to reach, deeming it likely that the zoogs[j] would harbour dire resentment against him for the frustration of their warlike enterprise. This offer he welcomed with gratitude; not only for the safety it afforded, but because he liked the graceful companionship of cats. So in the midst of a pleasant and playful regiment, relaxed after the successful performance of its duty, Randolph Carter walked with dignity through that enchanted and phosphorescent wood of titan trees, talking of his quest with the old general and his grandson whilst others of the band indulged in fantastic gambols or chased fallen leaves that the wind drove among

[a] zoogs] Zoogs C
[b] zoogs] Zoogs C
[c] annual] om. B, C
[d] their] the C
[e] zoogs] Zoogs C
[f] the] om. B, C
[g] zoog] Zoog C
[h] zoogs.] Zoogs. C
[i] zoogs] Zoogs C
[j] zoogs] Zoogs C

the fungi of the[a] primeval floor. And the old cat said that he had heard much of unknown Kadath in the cold waste, but did not know where it was. As for the marvellous sunset city, he had not even heard of that, but would gladly relay to Carter anything he might later learn.

He gave the seeker some passwords of great value among the cats of dreamland, and commended him especially to the old chief of the cats in Celephaïs,[b] whither he was bound. That old cat, already slightly known to Carter, was a dignified Maltese;[c] and would prove highly influential in any transaction. It was dawn when they came to the proper edge of the wood, and Carter bade his friends a reluctant farewell. The young sub-lieutenant he had met as a small kitten would have followed him had not the old general forbidden it, but that austere patriarch insisted that the path of duty lay with the tribe and the army. So Carter set out alone over the golden fields that stretched mysterious beside a willow-fringed river, and the cats went back into the wood.

Well did the traveller know those garden lands that lie betwixt the wood and[d] the Cererenerian Sea, and blithely did he follow the singing river Oukranos that marked his course. The sun rose higher over gentle slopes of grove and lawn, and heightened the colours of the thousand flowers that starred each knoll and dingle. A blessed haze lies upon all this region, wherein is held a little more of the sunlight than other places hold, and a little more of the summer's humming music of birds and bees; so that men walk through it as through a faery place, and feel greater joy and wonder than they ever afterward remember.

By noon Carter reached the jasper terraces of Kiran which slope down to the river's edge and bear that temple of loveliness wherein the King of Ilek-Vad comes from his far realm on the twilight sea once a year in a golden palanquin to pray to the god of Oukranos, who sang to him in youth when he dwelt in a cottage by its banks. All of jasper is that temple, and covering an acre of ground with its walls and courts, its seven pinnacled towers, and its inner shrine where the river enters through hidden channels and the god sings softly in the night. Many

[a] the] that B, C [*B apparently corrected by Barlow*]
[b] and] of A, B, C
[c] Maltese;] maltese, C
[d] Celephaïs,] Celephais, B [*corrected by HPL*], C

times the moon hears strange music as it shines on those courts and terraces and pinnacles, but whether that music be the song of the god or the chant of the cryptical priests, none but the King of Ilek-Vad may say; for only he has[a] entered the temple or seen the priests. Now, in the drowsiness of day, that carven and delicate fane was silent, and Carter heard only the murmur of the great stream and the hum of the birds and bees as he walked onward under an enchanted sun.

All that afternoon the pilgrim wandered on through perfumed meadows and in the lee of gentle riverward hills bearing peaceful thatched cottages and the shrines of amiable gods carven from jasper or chrysoberyl. Sometimes he walked close to the bank of Oukranos and whistled to the sprightly and iridescent fish of that crystal stream, and at other times he paused amidst the whispering rushes and gazed at the great dark wood on the farther side, whose trees came down clear to the water's edge. In former dreams he had seen quaint lumbering buopoths come shyly out of that wood to drink, but now he could not glimpse any. Once in a while he paused to watch a carnivorous fish catch a fishing bird, which it lured to the water by shewing[b] its tempting scales in the sun, and grasped by the beak with its enormous mouth as the winged hunter sought to dart down upon it.

Toward evening he mounted a low grassy rise and saw before him flaming in the sunset the thousand gilded spires of Thran. Lofty beyond belief are the alabaster walls of that incredible city, sloping inward toward the top and wrought in one solid piece by what means no man knows, for they are more ancient than memory. Yet lofty as they are with their hundred gates and two hundred turrets, the clustered towers within, all white beneath their golden spires, are loftier still; so that men on the plain around see them soaring into the sky, sometimes shining clear, sometimes caught at the top in tangles of cloud and mist, and sometimes clouded lower down with their utmost pinnacles blazing free above the vapours. And where Thran's gates open on the river are great wharves of marble, with ornate galleons of fragrant cedar and calamander riding gently at anchor, and strange bearded sailors sitting on casks and bales with the hieroglyphs of far

[a] has] had B, C
[b] shewing] showing A, B, C

places. Landward beyond the walls lies the farm country, where small white cottages dream between little hills, and narrow roads with many stone bridges wind gracefully among streams and gardens.

Down through this verdant land Carter walked at evening, and saw twilight float up from the river to the marvellous golden spires of Thran. And just at the hour of dusk he came to the southern gate, and was stopped by a red-robed sentry till he had told three dreams beyond belief, and proved himself a dreamer worthy to walk up Thran's steep mysterious streets and linger in[a] bazaars where the wares of the ornate galleons were sold. Then into that incredible city he walked; through a wall so thick that the gate was a tunnel, and thereafter amidst curved and undulant ways winding deep and narrow between the heavenward towers. Lights shone through grated and balconied windows, and the sound of lutes and pipes stole timid from inner courts where marble fountains bubbled. Carter knew his way, and edged down through darker streets to the river, where at an old sea-tavern[b] he found the captains and seamen he had known in myriad other dreams. There he bought his passage to Celephaïs on a great green galleon, and there he stopped for the night after speaking gravely to the venerable cat of that inn, who blinked dozing before an enormous hearth and dreamed of old wars and forgotten gods.

In the morning Carter boarded the galleon bound for Celephaïs,[c] and sat in the prow as the ropes were cast off and the long sail down to the Cerenerian Sea began. For many leagues the banks were much as they were above Thran, with now and then a curious temple rising on the farther hills toward the right, and a drowsy village on the shore, with steep red roofs and nets spread in the sun. Mindful of his search, Carter questioned all the mariners closely about those whom they had met in the taverns of Celephaïs,[d] asking the names and ways of the strange men with long, narrow eyes, long-lobed ears, thin noses, and pointed chins who came in dark ships from the north and traded onyx for the carved jade and spun gold and little red singing birds of

[a] in] in the B, C
[b] sea-tavern] sea tavern A, B, C
[c] Celephaïs,] Celephais, B [*corrected by HPL*], C
[d] Celephaïs,] Celephais, B [*corrected by HPL*], C

Celephaïs.[a] Of these men the sailors knew not much, save that they talked but seldom and spread a kind of awe about them.

Their land, very far away, was called Inganok,[b] and not many people cared to go thither because it was a[c] cold twilight land, and said to be close to unpleasant Leng; although high impassable mountains towered on the side where Leng was thought to lie, so that none might say whether this evil plateau with its horrible stone villages and unmentionable monastery were really there, or whether the rumour were only a fear that timid people felt in the night when those formidable barrier peaks loomed black against a rising moon. Certainly, men reached Leng from very different oceans. Of other boundaries of Inganok[d] those sailors had no notion, nor had they heard of the cold waste and unknown Kadath save from vague unplaced report. And of the marvellous sunset city which Carter sought they knew nothing at all. So the traveller asked no more of far things, but bided his time till he might talk with those strange men from cold and twilight Inganok[e] who are the seed of such gods as carved their features on Ngranek.

Late in the day the galleon reached those bends of the river which traverse the perfumed jungles of Kled. Here Carter wished he might disembark, for in those tropic tangles sleep wondrous palaces of ivory, lone and unbroken, where once dwelt fabulous monarchs of a land whose name is forgotten. Spells of the Elder Ones keep those places unharmed and undecayed, for it is written that there may one day be need of them again; and elephant caravans have glimpsed them from afar by moonlight, though none dares approach them closely because of the guardians to which their wholeness is due. But the ship swept on, and dusk hushed the hum of the day, and the first stars above blinked answers to the early fireflies on the banks as that jungle fell far behind, leaving only its fragrance as a memory that it had been. And all through the night that galleon floated on past mysteries unseen and

---

[a] Celephaïs.] Celephais. B [*corrected by HPL*], C
[b] Inganok,] Inqanoth, B; Inquanok, C
[c] a] *om.* C
[d] Inganok] Inquanok B, C
[e] Inganok] Inquanok B, C

unsuspected. Once a lookout reported fires on the hills to the east, but the sleepy captain[a] said they had better not be looked at too much, since it was highly uncertain just who or what had lit them.

In the morning the river had broadened out greatly, and Carter saw by the houses along the banks that they were close to the vast trading city of Hlanith on the Cerenerian Sea. Here the walls are of rugged granite, and the houses peakedly fantastic with beamed and plastered gables. The men of Hlanith are more like those of the waking world than any others in dreamland; so that the city is not sought except for barter, but is prized for the solid work of its artisans. The wharves of Hlanith are of oak, and there the galleon made fast while the captain traded in the taverns. Carter also went ashore, and looked curiously upon the rutted streets where wooden ox-carts[b] lumbered and feverish merchants cried their wares vacuously in the bazaars. The sea-taverns[c] were all close to the wharves on cobbled lanes salt with the spray of high tides, and seemed exceedingly ancient with their low black-beamed ceilings and casements of greenish bull's-eye panes. Ancient sailors in those taverns talked much of distant ports, and told many stories of the curious men from twilight Inganok,[d] but had little to add to what the seamen of the galleon had told. Then, at last, after much unloading and loading, the ship set sail once more over the sunset sea, and the high walls and gables of Hlanith grew less as the last golden light of day lent them a wonder and beauty beyond any that men had given them.

Two nights and two days the galleon sailed over the Cerenerian Sea, sighting no land and speaking but one other vessel. Then near sunset of the second day there loomed up ahead the snowy peak of Aran with its gingko-trees swaying on the lower slopes,[e] and Carter knew that they were come to the land of Ooth-Nargai and the marvellous city of Celephaïs.[f] Swiftly there came into sight the glittering minarets of that fabulous town, and the untarnished marble

[a] captain] Captain B, C
[b] ox-carts] ox carts A, B, C
[c] sea-taverns] sea taverns A, B, C
[d] Inganok,] Inquanok, B, C
[e] slopes,] slope, B, C
[f] Celephaïs.] Celephais. B, C

walls with their bronze statues, and the great stone bridge where Naraxa joins the sea. Then rose the green[a] gentle hills behind the town, with their groves and gardens of asphodels and the small shrines and cottages upon them; and far in the background the purple ridge of the Tanarians, potent and mystical, behind which lay forbidden ways into the waking world and toward other regions of dream.

The harbour was full of painted galleys, some of which were from the marble cloud-city of Serannian, that lies in ethereal space beyond where the sea meets the sky, and some of which were from more substantial ports on the oceans[b] of dreamland. Among these the steersman threaded his way up to the spice-fragrant wharves, where the galleon made fast in the dusk as the city's million lights began to twinkle out over the water. Ever new seemed this deathless city of vision, for here time has no power to tarnish or destroy. As it has always been is still the turquoise of Nath-Horthath, and the eighty orchid-wreathed priests are the same who builded it ten thousand years ago. Shining still is the bronze of the great gates, nor are the onyx pavements ever worn or broken. And the great bronze statues on the walls look down on merchants and camel drivers older than fable, yet without one grey hair in their forked beards.

Carter did not at once seek out the temple or the palace or the citadel, but stayed by the seaward wall among traders and sailors. And when it was too late for rumours and legends he sought out an ancient tavern he knew well, and rested with dreams of the gods on unknown Kadath whom he sought. The next day he searched all along the quays for some of the strange mariners of Inganok,[c] but was told that none were now in port, their galley not being due from the north for full two weeks. He found, however, one Thorabonian sailor who had been to Inganok[d] and had worked in the onyx quarries of that twilight place; and this sailor said there was certainly a desert[e] to the north of the peopled region, which everybody seemed to fear and shun. The

[a] green] *om.* C
[b] ports on the oceans] parts B, C
[c] Inganok,] Inkanok, A; Inquanok, B, C
[d] Inganok] Inquanok B, C
[e] desert] descent B, C

Thorabonian opined that this desert led around the utmost rim of impassable peaks into Leng's horrible plateau, and that this was why men feared it; though he admitted there were other vague tales of evil presences and nameless sentinels. Whether or not this could be the fabled waste wherein unknown Kadath stands he did not know; but it seemed unlikely that those presences and sentinels, if indeed they truly[a] existed, were stationed for naught.[b]

On the following day Carter walked up the Street of the Pillars to the turquoise temple and talked with the high-priest.[c] Though Nath-Horthath is chiefly worshipped in Celephaïs,[d] all the Great Ones are mentioned in diurnal prayers; and the priest was reasonably versed in their moods. Like Atal in distant Ulthar, he strongly advised against any attempt[e] to see them; declaring that they are testy and capricious, and subject to strange protection from the mindless Other Gods from Outside, whose soul and messenger is the crawling chaos Nyarlathotep. Their jealous hiding of the marvellous sunset city shewed clearly that they did not wish Carter to reach it, and it was doubtful how they would regard a guest whose object was to see them and plead before them. No man had ever found Kadath in the past, and it might be just as well if none ever found it in the future. Such rumours as were told about that onyx castle of the Great Ones were not by any means reassuring.

Having thanked the orchid-crowned high-priest,[f] Carter left the temple and sought[g] the bazaar of the sheep-butchers, where the old chief of Celephaïs'[h] cats dwelt sleek and contented. That grey and dignified being was sunning himself on the onyx pavement, and extended a languid paw as his caller approached. But when Carter repeated the passwords and introductions furnished him by the old cat general of Ulthar, the furry patriach became very cordial and

---

[a] truly] *om.* B, C

[b] naught.] nought. C

[c] high-priest.] High Priest. A, B, C

[d] Celephaïs,] Celephais, B [*corrected by HPL*], C

[e] attempt] attempts B, C

[f] high-priest,] High Priest, A, B, C

[g] sought] sought out B, C

[h] Celephaïs'] Celephais' B [*corrected by HPL*], C

communicative; and told much of the secret lore known to cats on the seaward slopes of Ooth-Nargai. Best of all, he repeated several things told him furtively by the timid waterfront cats of Celephaïs[a] about the men of Inganok,[b] on whose dark ships no cat will go.

It seems that these men have an aura not of earth about them, though that is not the reason why no cat will sail on their ships. The reason for this is that Inganok[c] holds shadows which no cat can endure, so that in all that cold twilight realm there is never a cheering purr or a homely mew. Whether it be because of things wafted over the impassable peaks from hypothetical Leng, or because of things filtering down from the chilly desert to the north, none may say; but it remains a fact that in that far land there broods a hint of outer space which cats do not like, and to which they are more sensitive than men. Therefore they will not go on the dark ships that seek the basalt quays of Inganok.[d]

The old chief of the cats also told him where to find his friend King Kuranes, who in Carter's latter dreams had reigned alternately in the rose-crystal Palace of the Seventy Delights at Celephaïs[e] and in the turreted cloud-castle of sky-floating Serannian. It seems[f] that he could no more find content in those places, but had formed a mighty longing for the English cliffs and downlands of his boyhood; where in little dreaming villages England's old songs hover at evening behind lattice windows, and where grey church towers peep lovely through the verdure of distant valleys. He could not go back to these things in the waking world because his body was dead; but he had done the next best thing and dreamed a small tract of such countryside in the region east of the city,[g] where meadows roll gracefully up from the sea-cliffs to the foot of the Tanarian Hills. There he dwelt in a grey Gothic manor-house of stone looking on the sea, and tried to think it was ancient Trevor Towers, where he was born and where thirteen generations of his forefathers had first seen the light. And on the coast

[a] Celephaïs] Celephais B [*corrected by HPL*], C
[b] Inganok,] Inquanok, B, C
[c] Inganok] Inquanok B, C
[d] Inganok.] Inkanok. A; Inquanok. B, C
[e] Celephaïs] Celephais B [*corrected by HPL*], C
[f] seems] seemed C
[g] city,] city C

nearby he had built a little Cornish fishing village with steep cobbled ways, settling therein such people as had the most English faces, and seeking ever to teach them the dear remembered accents of old Cornwall fishers. And in a valley not far off he had reared a great Norman Abbey whose tower he could see from his window, placing around it in the churchyard grey stones with the names of his ancestors carved thereon, and with a moss somewhat like Old England's moss. For though Kuranes was a monarch in the land of dream, with all imagined pomps and marvels, splendours and beauties, ecstasies[a] and delights, novelties[b] and excitements at his command, he would gladly have resigned for ever the whole of his power and luxury and freedom for one blessed day as a simple boy in that pure and quiet England, that ancient, beloved England which had moulded his being and of which he must always be immutably a part.

So when Carter bade that old grey chief of the cats adieu, he did not seek the terraced palace of rose-crystal[c] but walked out the eastern gate and across the daisied fields toward a peaked gable which he glimpsed through the oaks of a park sloping up to the sea-cliffs. And in time he came to a great hedge and a gate with a little brick lodge, and when he rang the bell there hobbled to admit him no robed and anointed[d] lackey of the palace, but a small stubbly[e] old man in a smock who spoke as best he could in the quaint tones of far Cornwall. And Carter walked up the shady path between trees as near as possible to England's trees, and climbed[f] the terraces among gardens set out as in Queen Anne's time. At the door, flanked by stone cats in the old way, he was met by a whiskered butler in suitable livery; and was presently taken to the library where Kuranes, Lord of Ooth-Nargai and the Sky around Serannian, sat pensive in a chair by the window looking on his little seacoast village and wishing that his old nurse would come in and scold him because he was not ready for that hateful lawn-party at the vicar's, with the carriage waiting and his mother nearly out of patience.

[a] ecstasies] extasies A
[b] novelties] novelies A
[c] rose-crystal] rose crystal B, C
[d] anointed] annointed B [*corrected by HPL*]; an-/nointed C
[e] stubbly] stubby C
[f] climbed] clumbed C

Kuranes, clad in a dressing-gown of the sort favoured by London tailors in his youth, rose eagerly to meet his guest; for the sight of an Anglo-Saxon from the waking world was very dear to him, even if it was a Saxon from Boston, Massachusetts, instead of from Cornwall. And for long they talked of old times, having much to say because both were old dreamers and well versed in the wonders of incredible places. Kuranes, indeed, had been out beyond the stars in the ultimate void, and was said to be the only one who had ever returned sane from such a voyage.

At length Carter brought up the subject of his quest, and asked of his host those questions he had asked of so many others. Kuranes did not know where Kadath was, or the marvellous sunset city; but he did know that the Great Ones were very dangerous creatures to seek out, and that the Other Gods had strange ways of protecting them from impertinent curiosity. He had learned much of the Other Gods in distant parts of space, especially in that region where form does not exist, and coloured gases study the innermost secrets. The violet gas S'ngac had told him terrible things of the crawling chaos Nyarlathotep, and had warned him never to approach the central void where the daemon-sultan[a] Azathoth gnaws hungrily in the dark. Altogether, it was not well to meddle with the Elder Ones; and if they persistently denied all access to the marvellous sunset city, it were better not to seek that city.

Kuranes furthermore doubted whether his guest would profit aught by coming to the city even were he to gain it. He himself had dreamed and yearned long years for lovely Celephaïs[b] and the land of Ooth-Nargai, and for the freedom and colour and high experience of life devoid of its chains, conventions, and stupidities. But now that he was come into that city and that land, and was the king thereof, he found the freedom and the vividness all too soon worn out, and monotonous for want of linkage with anything firm in his feelings and memories. He was a king in Ooth-Nargai, but found no meaning therein, and drooped always for the old familiar things of England that had shaped his youth. All his kingdom would he give for the sound of Cornish church bells over the downs, and all the thousand minarets of

[a] daemon-sultan] daemon sultan A, B, C
[b] Celephaïs] Celephais B [*corrected by HPL*], C

Celephaïs[a] for the steep homely roofs of the village near his home. So
he told his guest that the unknown sunset city might not hold quite
the[b] content he sought, and that perhaps it had better remain a
glorious and half-remembered dream. For he had visited Carter often
in the old waking days, and knew well the lovely New England slopes
that had given him birth.

At the last, he was very certain, the seeker would long only for the
early remembered scenes; the glow of Beacon Hill at evening, the tall
steeples and winding hill streets of quaint Kingsport, the hoary
gambrel roofs of ancient and witch-haunted Arkham, and the blessed
miles of[c] meads and valleys where stone walls rambled and white
farmhouse gables peeped out from bowers of verdure. These things he
told Randolph Carter, but still the seeker held to his purpose. And in
the end they parted each with his own conviction, and Carter went
back through the bronze gate into Celephaïs[d] and down the Street of
the[e] Pillars to the old sea-wall,[f] where he talked more with the mariners
of far ports and waited for the dark ship from cold and twilight
Inganok,[g] whose strange-faced sailors and onyx-traders had in them
the blood of the Great Ones.

One starlight[h] evening when the Pharos shone splendid over the
harbour the longed-for ship put in, and strange-faced sailors and
traders appeared one by one and group by group in the ancient taverns
along the sea-wall. It was very exciting to see again those living faces so
like the godlike features on Ngranek, but Carter did not hasten to
speak with the silent seamen. He did not know how much of pride and
secrecy and dim supernal memory might fill those children of the
Great Ones, and was sure it would not be wise to tell them of his quest
or ask too closely of that cold desert stretching north of their twilight

[a] Celephaïs] Celephais B [*corrected by HPL*], C
[b] the] that B, C
[c] miles of] *om.* B, C
[d] Celephaïs] Celephais B [*corrected by HPL*], C
[e] the] *om.* C
[f] sea-wall,] sea wall, A, B, C
[g] Inganok,] Inquanok, B, C
[h] starlight] starlit B, C

land. They talked little with the other folk in those ancient sea-taverns;[a] but would gather in groups in remote corners and sing among themselves the haunting airs of unknown places, or chant long tales to one another in accents alien to the rest of dreamland. And so rare and moving were those airs and tales,[b] that one might guess their wonders from the faces of those who listened, even though the words came to common ears only as strange cadence and obscure melody.

For a week the strange seamen lingered in the taverns and traded in the bazaars of Celephaïs,[c] and before they sailed Carter had taken passage on their dark ship, telling them that he was an old onyx-miner[d] and wishful to work in their quarries. That ship was very lovely and cunningly wrought, being of teakwood with ebony fittings and traceries of gold, and the cabin in which the traveller lodged had hangings of silk and velvet. One morning at the turn of the tide the sails were raised and the anchor lifted, and as Carter stood on the high stern he saw the sunrise-blazing walls and bronze statues and golden minarets of ageless Celephaïs[e] sink into the distance, and the snowy peak of Mount Aran grow smaller and smaller. By noon there was nothing in sight save the gentle blue of the Cerenerian Sea, with one painted galley afar off bound for that cloud-hung[f] realm of Serannian where the sea meets the sky.

And night came with gorgeous stars, and the dark ship steered for Charles' Wain and the Little Bear as they swung slowly round the pole. And the sailors sang strange songs of unknown places, and then[g] stole off one by one to the forecastle while the wistful watchers murmured old chants and leaned over the rail to glimpse the luminous fish playing in bowers beneath the sea. Carter went to sleep at midnight, and rose in the glow of a young morning, marking that the sun seemed farther south than was its wont. And all through that second day he made progress in knowing the men of the ship, getting them little by little to

[a] sea-taverns;] sea taverns; A, B, C
[b] tales,] tales B, C
[c] Celephaïs,] Celephais, B [*corrected by HPL*], C
[d] onyx-miner] onyx miner A, B, C
[e] Celephaïs] Celephais B [*corrected by HPL*], C
[f] cloud-hung] *om.* B, C
[g] then] they B, C

talk of their cold twilight land, of their exquisite onyx city, and of their fear of the high and impassable peaks beyond which Leng was said to be. They told him how sorry they were that no cats would stay in the land of Inganok,[a] and how they thought the hidden nearness of Leng was to blame for it. Only of the stony desert to the north they would not talk. There was something disquieting about that desert, and it was thought expedient not to admit its existence.

On later days they talked of the quarries in which Carter said he was going to work. There were many of them, for all the city of Inganok[b] was builded of onyx, whilst great polished blocks of it were traded in Rinar, Ogrothan, and Celephaïs,[c] and at home with the merchants of Thraa, Ilarnek, and Kadatheron, for the beautiful wares of those fabulous ports. And far to the north, almost in that[d] cold desert whose existence the men of Inganok[e] did not care to admit, there was an unused quarry greater than all the rest; from which had been hewn in forgotten times such prodigious lumps and blocks that the sight of their chiselled vacancies struck terror to all who beheld. Who had mined those incredible blocks, and whither they had been transported, no man might say; but it was thought best not to trouble that quarry, around which such inhuman memories might conceivably cling. So it was left all alone in the twilight, with only the raven and the rumoured shantak-bird[f] to brood on its immensities. When Carter heard of this quarry he was moved to deep thought, for he knew from old tales that the Great Ones' castle atop unknown Kadath is of onyx.

Each day the sun wheeled lower and lower in the sky, and the mists overhead grew thicker and thicker. And in two weeks there was not any sunlight at all, but only a weird grey twilight shining through a dome of eternal cloud by day, and a cold starless phosphorescence from the under side of that cloud by night. On the twentieth day a great jagged rock in the sea was sighted from afar, the first land glimpsed since Aran's snowy peak had dwindled behind the ship.

[a] Inganok,] Inquanok, B, C
[b] Inganok] Inqanok B, C
[c] Celephaïs,] Celephais, B [*corrected by HPL*]; Celephais C
[d] that] the B, C
[e] Inganok] Inquanok B, C
[f] shantak-bird] Shantak-bird C

Carter asked the captain the name of that rock, but was told that it had no name and had never been sought by any vessel because of the sounds that came from it at night. And when, after dark, a dull and ceaseless howling arose from that jagged granite place, the traveller was glad that no stop had been made, and that the rock had no name. The seamen prayed and chanted till the noise was out of earshot, and Carter dreamed terrible dreams within dreams in the small hours.

Two mornings after that there loomed far ahead and to the east a line of great grey peaks whose tops were lost in the changeless clouds of that twilight world. And at the sight of them the sailors sang glad songs, and some knelt down on the deck to pray; so that Carter knew they were come to the land of Inganok[a] and would soon be moored to the basalt quays of the great town bearing that land's name. Toward noon a dark coast-line appeared, and before three o'clock there stood out against the north the bulbous domes and fantastic spires of the onyx city. Rare and curious did that archaic city rise above its walls and quays, all of delicate black with scrolls, flutings, and arabesques of inlaid gold. Tall and many-windowed were the houses, and carved on every side with flowers and patterns whose dark symmetries dazzled the eye with a beauty more poignant than light. Some ended in swelling domes that tapered to a point, others in terraced pyramids whereon rose clustered minarets displaying every phase of strangeness and imagination. The walls were low, and pierced by frequent gates, each under a great arch rising high above the general level and capped by the head of a god chiselled with that same skill displayed in the monstrous face on distant Ngranek. On a hill in the centre rose a sixteen-angled tower greater than all the rest and bearing a high pinnacled belfry resting on a flattened dome. This, the seamen said, was the Temple of the Elder Ones, and was ruled by an old high-priest[b] sad with inner secrets.

At intervals the clang of a strange bell shivered over the onyx city, answered each time by a peal of mystic music made up of horns, viols, and chanting voices. And from a row of tripods on a gallery round the high dome of the temple there burst flares of flame at certain

[a] Inganok] Inquanok B, C
[b] high-priest] High-Priest A, B, C

moments; for the priests and people of that city were wise in the primal mysteries, and faithful in keeping the rhythms of the Great Ones as set forth in scrolls older than the Pnakotic Manuscripts. As the ship rode past the great basalt breakwater into the harbour the lesser noises of the city grew manifest, and Carter saw the slaves, sailors, and merchants on the docks. The sailors and merchants were of the strange-faced race of the gods, but the slaves were squat, slant-eyed folk said by rumour to have drifted somehow across or around the impassable peaks from[a] valleys beyond Leng. The wharves reached wide outside the city wall and bore upon them all manner of merchandise from the galleys anchored there, while at one end were great piles of onyx both carved and uncarved awaiting shipment to the far markets of Rinar, Ogrothan,[b] and Celephaïs.[c]

It was not yet evening when the dark ship anchored beside a jutting quay of stone, and all the sailors and traders filed ashore and through the arched gate into the city. The streets of that city were paved with onyx,[d] and some of them were wide and straight whilst others were crooked and narrow. The houses near the water were lower than the rest, and bore above their curiously arched doorways certain signs of gold said to be in honour of the respective small gods that favoured each. The captain of the ship took Carter to an old sea-tavern[e] where flocked the mariners of quaint countries, and promised that he would next day shew him the wonders of the twilight city, and lead him to the taverns of the onyx-miners by the northern wall. And evening fell, and little bronze lamps were lighted, and the sailors in that tavern sang songs of remote places. But when from its high tower the great bell shivered over the city, and the peal of the horns and viols and voices rose cryptical in answer thereto, all ceased their songs or tales and bowed silent till the last echo died away. For there is a wonder and a strangeness on the twilight city of Inganok,[f] and men fear to be lax in its rites lest a doom and a vengeance lurk unsuspectedly close.

[a] from] from the C
[b] Ogrothan,] Ogrothan A, B; Ograthan C
[c] Celephaïs.] Celephais. B [*corrected by HPL*], C
[d] onyx,] onyx B, C
[e] sea-tavern] sea tavern A, B, C
[f] Inganok,] Inquanok, B, C

Far in the shadows of that tavern Carter saw a squat form he did not like, for it was unmistakably that of the old slant-eyed merchant he had seen so long before in the taverns of Dylath-Leen, who was reputed to trade with the horrible stone villages of Leng which no healthy folk visit and whose evil fires are seen at night from afar, and even to have dealt with that high-priest not to be described, which wears a yellow silken mask over its face and dwells all alone in a prehistoric stone monastery. This man had seemed to shew a queer gleam of knowing when Carter asked the traders of Dylath-Leen about the cold waste and Kadath; and somehow his presence in dark and haunted Inganok,[a] so close to the wonders of the north, was not a reassuring thing. He slipped wholly out of sight before Carter could speak to him, and sailors later said that he had come with a yak caravan from some point not well determined, bearing the colossal and rich-flavoured eggs of the rumoured shantak-bird[b] to trade for the dexterous[c] jade goblets that merchants brought from Ilarnek.

On the following morning the ship-captain led Carter through the onyx streets of Inganok,[d] dark under their twilight sky. The inlaid doors and figured house-fronts, carven balconies and crystal-paned oriels, all gleamed with a sombre and polished loveliness; and now and then a plaza would open out with black pillars, colonnades, and the statues of curious beings both human and fabulous. Some of the vistas down long and unbending streets, or through side alleys and over bulbous domes, spires, and arabesqued roofs, were weird and beautiful beyond words; and nothing was more splendid than the massive height[e] of the great central Temple of the Elder Ones[f] with its sixteen carven sides, its flattened dome, and its lofty pinnacled belfry, overtopping all else, and majestic whatever its foreground. And always to the east, far beyond the city walls and the leagues of pasture land, rose the gaunt grey sides of those topless and impassable peaks across which hideous Leng was said to lie.

[a] Inganok,] Inquanok, B, C
[b] shantak-bird] Shantak-bird C
[c] dexterous] dextrous C
[d] Inganok,] Inquanok, B, C
[e] height] heights C
[f] Ones] *end of* B

The captain took Carter to the mighty temple, which is set with its walled garden in a great round plaza whence the streets go as spokes from a wheel's hub. The seven arched gates of that garden, each having over it a carven face like those on the city's gates, are always open;[a] and the people roam reverently at will down the tiled paths and through the little lanes lined with grotesque termini and the shrines of modest gods. And there are fountains, pools, and basins there to reflect the frequent blaze of the tripods on the high balcony, all of onyx and having in them small luminous fish taken by divers from the lower bowers of ocean. When the deep clang from the temple's[b] belfry shivers over the garden and the city, and the answer of the horns and viols and voices peals out from the seven lodges by the garden gates, there issue from the seven doors of the temple long columns of masked and hooded priests in black, bearing at arm's length before them great golden bowls from which a curious steam rises. And all the seven columns strut peculiarly in single file, legs thrown far forward without bending the knees, down the walks that lead to the seven lodges, wherein they disappear and do not appear again. It is said that subterrene paths connect the lodges with the temple, and that the long files of priests return through them; nor is it unwhispered that deep flights of onyx steps go down to mysteries that are never told. But only a few are those who hint that the priests in the masked and hooded columns are not human priests.[c]

Carter did not enter the temple, because none but the Veiled King is permitted to do that. But before he left the garden the hour of the bell came, and he heard the shivering clang deafeningly above him, and the wailing of the horns and viols and voices loud from the lodges by the gates. And down the seven great walks stalked the long files of bowl-bearing priests in their singular way, giving to the traveller a fear which human priests do not often give. When the last of them had vanished he left that garden, noting as he did so a spot on the pavement over which the bowls had passed. Even the ship-captain did

---

[a] open;] open, C
[b] temple's] temple C
[c] priests.] beings. C

not like that spot, and hurried him on toward the hill whereon the Veiled King's palace rises many-domed and marvellous.

The ways to the onyx palace are steep and narrow, all but that[a] broad curving one where the king and his companions ride on yaks or in yak-drawn chariots. Carter and his guide climbed up an alley that was all steps, between inlaid walls bearing strange signs in gold, and under balconies and oriels whence sometimes floated soft strains of music or breaths of exotic fragrance. Always ahead loomed those titan walls, mighty buttresses, and clustered and bulbous domes for which the Veiled King's palace is famous; and at length they passed under a great black arch and emerged in the gardens of the monarch's pleasure. There Carter paused in faintness at so much of[b] beauty; for the onyx terraces and colonnaded walks, the gay parterres[c] and delicate flowering trees espaliered to golden lattices, the brazen urns and tripods with cunning bas-reliefs, the pedestalled and almost breathing statues of veined black marble, the basalt-bottomed lagoons and[d] tiled fountains with luminous fish, the tiny temples of iridescent singing birds atop carven columns, the marvellous scrollwork of the great bronze gates, and the blossoming vines trained along every inch of the polished walls all joined to form a sight whose loveliness was beyond reality, and half-fabulous even in the land of dream. There it shimmered like a vision under that grey twilight sky, with the domed and fretted magnificence of the palace ahead, and the fantastic silhouette of the distant impassable peaks on the right. And ever the small birds and the fountains sang, while the perfume of rare blossoms spread like a veil over that incredible garden. No other human presence was there, and Carter was glad it was so. Then they turned and descended again the onyx alley of steps, for the palace itself no visitor may enter; and it is not well to look too long and steadily at the great central dome, since it is said to house the archaic father of all the rumoured shantak-birds,[e] and to send out queer dreams to the curious.

[a] that] the C
[b] of] *om.* C
[c] parterres] porterres C
[d] lagoons and] lagoon's C
[e] shantak-birds,] Shantak-birds, C

After that the captain took Carter to the north quarter of the town, near the Gate of the Caravans, where are the taverns of the yak-merchants and the onyx-miners. And there, in a low-ceiled inn of quarrymen, they said farewell; for business called the captain whilst Carter was eager to talk with miners about the north. There were many men in that inn, and the traveller was not long in speaking to some of them; saying that he was an old miner of onyx, and anxious to know somewhat of Inganok's[a] quarries. But all that he learnt[b] was not much more than he knew before, for the miners were timid and evasive about the cold desert to the north and the quarry that no man visits. They had fears of fabled emissaries from around the mountains where Leng is said to lie, and of evil presences and nameless sentinels far north among the scattered rocks. And they whispered also that the rumoured shantak-birds[c] are no wholesome things; it being indeed for the best that no man has ever truly seen one (for that fabled father of shantaks[d] in the king's dome is fed in the dark).

The next day, saying that he wished to look over all the various mines for himself and to visit the scattered farms and quaint onyx villages of Inganok,[e] Carter hired a yak and stuffed great leathern saddle-bags for a journey. Beyond the Gate of the Caravans the road lay straight betwixt tilled fields, with many odd farmhouses crowned by low domes. At some of these houses the seeker stopped to ask questions; once finding a host so austere and reticent, and so full of an unplaced majesty like to that in the huge features on Ngranek, that he felt certain he had come at last upon one of the Great Ones themselves, or upon one with full nine-tenths of their blood, dwelling amongst men. And to that austere and reticent cotter he was careful to speak very well of the gods, and to praise all the blessings they had ever accorded him.

That night Carter camped in a roadside meadow beneath a great lygath-tree to which he tied his yak, and in the morning resumed his

[a] Inganok's] Inquanok's C
[b] learnt] learned C
[c] shantak-birds] Shantak-birds C
[d] shantaks] Shantaks C
[e] Inganok,] Inquanok, C

northward pilgrimage. At about ten o'clock he reached the small-domed village of Urg, where traders rest and miners tell their tales, and paused in its taverns till noon. It is here that the great caravan road turns west toward Selarn, but Carter kept on north by the quarry road. All the afternoon he followed that rising road, which was somewhat narrower than the great highway, and which now led through a region with more rocks than tilled fields. And by evening the low hills on his left had risen into sizeable black cliffs, so that he knew he was close to the mining country. All the while the great gaunt sides of the impassable mountains towered afar off at his right, and the farther he went, the worse tales he heard of them from the scattered farmers and traders and drivers of lumbering onyx-carts along the way.

On the second night he camped in the shadow of a large black crag, tethering his yak to a stake driven in the ground. He observed the greater phosphorescence of the clouds at this northerly point, and more than once thought he saw dark shapes outlined against them. And on the third morning he came in sight of the first onyx quarry, and greeted the men who there laboured with picks and chisels. Before evening he had passed eleven quarries; the land being here given over altogether to onyx cliffs and boulders, with no vegetation at all, but only great rocky fragments scattered about a floor of black earth, with the grey impassable peaks always rising gaunt and sinister on his right. The third night he spent in a camp of quarry men whose flickering fires cast weird reflections on the polished cliffs to the west. And they sang many songs and told many tales, shewing such strange knowledge of the olden days and the habits of gods that Carter could see they held many latent memories of their sires the Great Ones. They asked him whither he went, and cautioned him not to go too far to the north; but he replied that he was seeking new cliffs of onyx, and would take no more risks than were common among prospectors. In the morning he bade them adieu and rode on into the darkening north, where they had warned him he would find the feared and unvisited quarry whence hands older than men's hands had wrenched prodigious blocks. But he did not like it when, turning back to wave a last farewell, he thought he saw approaching the camp that squat and evasive old merchant with slanting eyes, whose conjectured traffick with Leng was the gossip of distant Dylath-Leen.

After two more quarries the inhabited part of Inganok[a] seemed to end, and the road narrowed to a steeply rising yak-path among forbidding black cliffs. Always on the right towered the gaunt and distant peaks, and as Carter climbed farther and farther into this untraversed realm he found it grew darker and colder. Soon he perceived that there were no prints of feet or hooves on the black path beneath, and realised that he was indeed come into strange and deserted ways of elder time. Once in a while a raven would croak far overhead, and now and then a flapping behind some vast rock would make him think uncomfortably of the rumoured shantak-bird.[b] But in the main he was alone with his shaggy steed, and it troubled him to observe that this excellent yak became more and more reluctant to advance, and more and more disposed to snort affrightedly at any small noise along the route.

The path now contracted between sable and glistening walls, and began to display an even greater steepness than before. It was a bad footing, and the yak often slipped on the stony fragments strown[c] thickly about. In two hours Carter saw ahead a definite crest, beyond which was nothing but dull grey sky, and blessed the prospect of a level or downward course. To reach this crest, however, was no easy task; for the way had grown nearly perpendicular, and was perilous with loose black gravel and small stones. Eventually Carter dismounted and led his dubious yak; pulling very hard when the animal balked or stumbled, and keeping his own footing as best he might. Then suddenly he came to the top and saw beyond, and gasped at what he saw.

The path indeed led straight ahead and slightly down, with the same lines of high natural walls as before; but on the left hand there opened out a monstrous space, vast acres in extent, where some archaic power had riven and rent the native cliffs of onyx in the form of a giants' quarry. Far back into the solid precipice ran that Cyclopean[d] gouge, and deep down within earth's bowels its lower delvings yawned. It was no quarry of man, and the concave sides were scarred with great

[a] Inganok] Inkanok A; Inquanok C
[b] shantak-bird.] Shantak-bird. C
[c] strown] strewn C
[d] Cyclopean] cyclopean A, C

squares yards wide[a] which told of the size of the blocks once hewn by nameless hands and chisels. High over its jagged rim huge ravens flapped and croaked, and vague whirrings in the unseen depths told of bats or urhags or less mentionable presences haunting the endless blackness. There Carter stood in the narrow way amidst the twilight with the rocky path sloping down before him; tall onyx cliffs on his right that led on as far as he could see,[b] and tall cliffs on the left chopped off just ahead to make that terrible and unearthly quarry.

All at once the yak uttered a cry and burst from his control, leaping past him and darting on in a panic till it vanished down the narrow slope toward the north. Stones kicked by its flying hooves fell over the brink of the quarry and lost themselves in the dark without any sound of striking bottom; but Carter ignored the perils of that scanty path as he raced breathlessly after the flying steed. Soon the left-hand cliffs resumed their course, making the way once more a narrow lane; and still the traveller leaped on after the yak whose great wide prints told of its desperate flight.

Once he thought he heard the hoofbeats of the frightened beast, and doubled his speed from this encouragement. He was covering miles, and little by little the way was broadening in front till he knew he must soon emerge on the cold and dreaded desert to the north. The gaunt grey flanks of the distant impassable peaks were again visible above the right-hand[c] crags, and ahead were the rocks and boulders of an open space which was clearly a foretaste of the dark and limitless plain. And once more those hoofbeats sounded in his ears, plainer than before, but this time giving terror instead of encouragement because he realised that they were not the frightened hoofbeats of his fleeing yak. These[d] beats were ruthless and purposeful, and they were behind him.

Carter's pursuit of the yak became now a flight from an unseen thing, for though he dared not glance over his shoulder he felt that the presence behind him could be nothing wholesome or mentionable. His yak must have heard or felt it first, and he did not like to ask himself

[a] squares yards wide] squares, yards wide, C
[b] see,] see C
[c] right-hand] right hand C
[d] These] The C

whether it had followed him from the haunts of men or had floundered up out of that black quarry pit. Meanwhile the cliffs had been left behind, so that the oncoming night fell over a great waste of sand and spectral rocks wherein all paths were lost. He could not see the hoofprints of his yak, but always from behind him there came that detestable clopping; mingled now and then with what he fancied were titanic flappings and whirrings. That he was losing ground seemed unhappily clear to him, and he knew he was hopelessly lost in this broken and blasted desert of meaningless rocks and untravelled sands. Only those remote and impassable peaks on the right gave him any sense of direction, and even they were less clear as the grey twilight waned and the sickly phosphorescence of the clouds took its place.

Then dim and misty in the darkling north before him he glimpsed a terrible thing. He had thought it for some moments a range of black mountains, but now he saw it was something more. The phosphorescence of the brooding clouds shewed it plainly, and even silhouetted parts of it as low[a] vapours glowed behind. How distant it was he could not tell, but it must have been very far. It was thousands of feet high, stretching in a great concave arc from the grey impassable peaks to the unimagined westward spaces, and had once indeed been a ridge of mighty onyx hills. But now those[b] hills were hills no more, for some hand greater than man's had touched them. Silent they squatted there atop the world like wolves or ghouls, crowned with clouds and mists and guarding the secrets of the north for ever. All in a great half circle they squatted, those dog-like mountains carven into monstrous watching statues, and their right hands were raised in menace against mankind.

It was only the flickering light of the clouds that made their mitred[c] double heads seem to move, but as Carter stumbled on he saw arise from their shadowy laps[d] great forms whose motions were no delusion. Winged and whirring, those forms grew larger each moment, and the traveller knew his stumbling was at an end. They were not any birds or bats known elsewhere on earth or in dreamland, for they were

[a] low] *om.* C
[b] those] these C
[c] mitred] pitred C
[d] laps] caps C

larger than elephants and had heads like a horse's. Carter knew that they must be the shantak-birds[a] of ill rumour, and wondered no more what evil guardians and nameless sentinels made men avoid the boreal rock desert. And as he stopped in final resignation he dared at last to look behind him;[b] where indeed was trotting the squat slant-eyed trader of evil legend, grinning astride a lean yak and leading on a noxious horde of leering shantaks[c] to whose wings still clung the rime and nitre of the nether pits.

Trapped though he was by fabulous and hippocephalic winged nightmares that pressed around in great unholy circles, Randolph Carter did not lose consciousness. Lofty and horrible those titan gargoyles towered above him, while the slant-eyed merchant leaped down from his yak and stood grinning before the captive. Then the man motioned Carter to mount one of the repugnant shantaks,[d] helping him up as his judgment struggled with his loathing. It was hard work ascending, for the shantak-bird[e] has scales instead of feathers, and those scales are very slippery. Once he was seated, the slant-eyed man hopped up behind him, leaving the lean yak to be led away northward toward the ring of carven mountains by one of the incredible bird colossi.

There now followed a hideous whirl through frigid space, endlessly up and eastward toward the gaunt grey flanks of those impassable mountains beyond which Leng was said to lie.[f] Far above the clouds they flew, till at last there lay beneath them those fabled summits which the folk of Inganok[g] have never seen, and which lie always in high vortices of gleaming mist. Carter beheld them very plainly as they passed below, and saw upon their topmost peaks strange caves which made him think of those on Ngranek; but he did not question his captor about these things when he noticed that both the man and the horse-headed shantak[h] appeared oddly fearful of them, hurrying past

[a] shantak-birds] Shantak-birds C
[b] him;] him, C
[c] shantaks] Shantaks C
[d] shantaks,] Shantaks, C
[e] shantak-bird] Shantak-bird C
[f] lie.] be. C
[g] Inganok] Inquanok C
[h] shantak] Shantak C

nervously and shewing great tension until they were left far in the rear.

The shantak[a] now flew lower, revealing beneath the canopy of cloud a grey barren plain whereon at great distances shone little feeble fires. As they descended there appeared at intervals lone huts of granite and bleak stone villages whose tiny windows glowed with pallid light. And there came from those huts and villages a shrill droning of pipes and a nauseous rattle of crotala which proved at once that Inganok's[b] people are right in their geographick[c] rumours. For travellers have heard such sounds before, and know that they float only from that cold desert plateau which healthy folk never visit; that haunted place of evil and mystery which is Leng.

Around the feeble fires dark forms were dancing, and Carter was curious as to what manner of beings they might be; for no healthy folk have ever been to Leng, and the place is known only by its fires and stone huts as seen from afar. Very slowly and awkwardly did those forms leap, and with an insane twisting and bending not good to behold; so that Carter did not wonder at the monstrous evil imputed to them by vague legend, or the fear in which all dreamland holds their abhorrent frozen plateau. As the shantak[d] flew lower, the repulsiveness of the dancers became tinged with a certain hellish familiarity; and the prisoner kept straining his eyes and racking his memory for clues to where he had seen such creatures before.

They leaped as though they had hooves instead of feet, and seemed to wear a sort of wig or headpiece with small horns. Of other clothing they had none, but most of them were quite furry. Behind they had dwarfish tails, and when they glanced upward he saw the excessive width of their mouths. Then he knew what they were, and that they did not wear any wigs or headpieces after all. For the cryptic folk of Leng were of one race with the uncomfortable merchants of the black galleys that traded rubies at Dylath-Leen; those not quite human merchants who are the slaves of the monstrous moon-things! They were indeed the same dark folk who had shanghaied Carter on

[a] shantak] Shantak C
[b] Inganok's] Inquanok's C
[c] geographick] geographic C
[d] shantak] Shantak C

their noisome galley so long ago, and whose kith he had seen driven in herds about the unclean wharves of that accursed lunar city, with the leaner ones toiling and the fatter ones taken away in crates for other needs of their polypous and amorphous masters. Now he saw where such ambiguous creatures came from, and shuddered at the thought that Leng must be known to these formless abominations from the moon.

But the shantak[a] flew on past the fires and the stone huts and the less than human dancers, and soared over sterile hills of grey granite and dim wastes of rock and ice and snow. Day came, and the phosphorescence of low clouds gave place to the misty twilight of that northern world, and still the vile bird winged meaningly through the cold and silence. At times the slant-eyed man talked with his steed in a hateful and guttural language, and the shantak[b] would answer with tittering tones that rasped like the scratching of ground glass. All this while the land was getting higher, and finally they came to a windswept[c] table-land which seemed the very roof of a blasted and tenantless world. There, all alone in the hush and the dusk and the cold, rose the uncouth stones of a squat windowless building, around which a circle of crude monoliths stood. In all this arrangement there was nothing human, and Carter surmised from old tales that he was indeed come to that most dreadful and legendary of all places, the remote and prehistoric monastery wherein dwells uncompanioned the high-priest[d] not to be described, which wears a yellow silken mask over its face and prays to the Other Gods and their crawling chaos Nyarlathotep.

The loathsome bird now settled to the ground, and the slant-eyed man hopped down and helped his captive alight. Of the purpose of his seizure Carter now felt very sure; for clearly the slant-eyed merchant was an agent of the darker powers, eager to drag before his masters a mortal whose presumption had aimed at the finding of unknown Kadath and the saying of a prayer before the faces of the Great Ones in their onyx castle. It seemed likely that this merchant had caused his former capture by the slaves of the moon-things in Dylath-Leen, and

[a] shantak] Shantak C
[b] shantak] Shantak C
[c] windswept] wind-swept A, C
[d] high-priest] High-Priest A, C

that he now meant to do what the rescuing cats had baffled; taking the victim to some dread rendezvous with monstrous Nyarlathotep and telling with what boldness the seeking of unknown Kadath had been tried. Leng and the cold waste north of Inganok[a] must be close to the Other Gods, and there the passes to Kadath are well guarded.

The slant-eyed man was small, but the great hippocephalic bird was there to see he was obeyed; so Carter followed where he led, and passed within the circle of standing rocks and into the low arched doorway of that windowless stone monastery. There were no lights inside, but the evil merchant lit a small clay lamp bearing morbid bas-reliefs and prodded his prisoner on through mazes of narrow winding corridors. On the walls of the corridors were painted frightful scenes older than history, and in a style unknown to the archaeologists of earth. After countless aeons their pigments were brilliant still, for the cold and dryness of hideous Leng keep alive many primal things. Carter saw them fleetingly in the rays of that dim and moving lamp, and shuddered at the tale they told.

Through those archaic frescoes Leng's annals stalked; and the horned, hooved, and wide-mouthed almost-humans danced evilly amidst forgotten cities. There were scenes of old wars, wherein Leng's almost-humans fought with the bloated purple spiders of the neighbouring vales; and there were scenes also of the coming of the black galleys from the moon, and of the submission of Leng's people to the polypous and amorphous blasphemies that hopped and floundered and wriggled out of them. Those slippery greyish-white blasphemies they worshipped as gods, nor ever complained when scores of their best and fatted males were taken away in the black galleys. The monstrous moonbeasts[b] made their camp on a jagged isle in the sea, and Carter could tell from the frescoes that this was none other than the lone nameless rock he had seen when sailing to Inganok;[c] that grey accursed rock which Inganok's[d] seamen shun, from which vile howlings reverberate all through the night.

[a] Inganok] Inkanok A; Inquanok C
[b] moonbeasts] moon-beasts A, C
[c] Inganok;] Inquanok; C
[d] Inganok's] Inquanok's C

And in those frescoes was shewn the great seaport and capital of the almost-humans; proud and pillared betwixt the cliffs and the basalt wharves, and wondrous with high fanes and carven places. Great gardens and columned streets led from the cliffs and from each of the six sphinx-crowned gates to a vast central plaza, and in that plaza was a pair of winged colossal lions guarding the top of a subterrene staircase. Again and again were those huge winged lions shewn, their mighty flanks of diorite[a] glistening in the grey twilight of the day and the cloudy phosphorescence of the night. And as Carter stumbled past their frequent and repeated pictures it came to him at last what indeed they were, and what city it was that the almost-humans had ruled so anciently before the coming of the black galleys. There could be no mistake, for the legends of dreamland are generous and profuse. Indubitably that primal city was no less a place than storied Sarkomand, whose ruins had bleached for a million years before the first true human saw the light, and whose twin titan lions guard eternally the steps that lead down from dreamland to the Great Abyss.[b]

Other views shewed the gaunt grey peaks dividing Leng from Inganok,[c] and the monstrous shantak-birds[d] that build nests on the ledges half way up. And they shewed likewise the curious caves near the very topmost pinnacles, and how even the boldest of the shantaks[e] fly screaming away from them. Carter had seen those caves when he passed over them, and had noticed their likeness to the caves on Ngranek. Now he knew that the likeness was more than a chance one, for in these pictures were shewn their fearsome denizens; and those bat-wings, curving horns, barbed tails, prehensile paws,[f] and rubbery bodies were not strange to him. He had met those silent, flitting,[g] and clutching creatures before; those mindless guardians of the Great Abyss whom even the Great Ones fear, and who own not Nyarlathotep but hoary Nodens as their lord. For they were the

---

[a] diorite] diarite C
[b] Great Abyss.] great abyss. A
[c] Inganok,] Inquanok, C
[d] shantak-birds] Shantak-birds C
[e] shantaks] Shantaks C
[f] paws,] paws A, C
[g] flitting,] flitting A, C

dreaded night-gaunts, who never laugh or smile because they have no faces, and who flop unendingly in the dark betwixt the Vale of Pnath and the passes to the outer world.

The slant-eyed merchant had now prodded Carter into a great domed space whose walls were carved in shocking bas-reliefs, and whose centre held a gaping circular pit surrounded by six malignly stained stone altars in a ring. There was no light in this vast and[a] evil-smelling crypt, and the small lamp of the sinister merchant shone so feebly that one could grasp details only little by little. At the farther end was a high stone dais reached by five steps; and there on a golden throne sat a lumpish figure robed in yellow silk figured with red and having a yellow silken mask over its face. To this being the slant-eyed man made certain signs with his hands, and the lurker in the dark replied by raising a disgustingly carven flute of ivory in silk-covered paws and blowing certain loathsome sounds from beneath its flowing yellow mask. This colloquy went on for some time, and to Carter there was something sickeningly familiar in the sound of that flute and the stench of the malodorous place. It made him think of a frightful red-litten city and of the revolting procession that once filed through it; of that, and of an awful climb through lunar countryside beyond, before the rescuing rush of earth's friendly cats. He knew that the creature on the dais was without doubt the high-priest not to be described, of which legend whispers such fiendish and abnormal possibilities, but he feared to think just what that abhorred high-priest might be.

Then the figured silk slipped a trifle from one of the greyish-white paws, and Carter knew what the noisome high-priest was. And in that hideous second stark fear drove him to something his reason would never have dared to attempt, for in all his shaken consciousness there was room only for one frantic will to escape from what squatted on that golden throne. He knew that hopeless labyrinths of stone lay betwixt him and the cold table-land outside, and that even on that table-land the noxious shantak[b] still waited; yet in spite of all this there was in his mind only the instant need to get away from that wriggling, silk-robed monstrosity.

[a] and] *om.* C
[b] shantak] Shantak C

The slant-eyed man had set his[a] curious lamp upon one of the high and wickedly stained altar-stones by the pit, and had moved forward somewhat to talk to the high-priest with his hands. Carter, hitherto wholly passive, now gave that man a terrific push with all the wild strength of fear, so that the victim toppled at once into that gaping well which rumour holds to reach down to the hellish Vaults of Zin where gugs hunt ghasts[b] in the dark. In almost the same second he seized the lamp from the altar and darted out into the frescoed labyrinths, racing this way and that as chance determined and trying not to think of the stealthy padding of shapeless paws on the stones behind him, or of the silent wrigglings and crawlings which must be going on back there in lightless corridors.

After a few moments he regretted his thoughtless haste, and wished he had tried to follow backward the frescoes he had passed on the way in. True, they were so confused and duplicated that they could not have done him much good, but he wished none the less he had made the attempt. Those he now saw were even more horrible than those he had seen then, and he knew he was not in the corridors leading outside. In time he became quite sure he was not followed, and slackened his pace somewhat; but scarce had he breathed in half relief when a new peril beset him. His lamp was waning, and he would soon be in pitch blackness with no means of sight or guidance.

When the light was all gone he groped slowly in the dark, and prayed to the Great Ones for such help as they might afford. At times he felt the stone floor sloping up or down, and once he stumbled over a step for which no reason seemed to exist. The farther he went the damper it seemed to be, and when he was able to feel a junction or the mouth of a side passage he always chose the way which sloped downward the least. He believed, though, that his general course was down; and the vault-like smell and incrustations on the greasy walls and floor alike warned him he was burrowing deep in Leng's unwholesome table-land. But there was not any warning of the thing which came at last; only the thing itself with its terror and shock and breath-taking[c]

---

[a] his] the C
[b] ghasts] shasts C
[c] breath-taking] breath-/taking A

chaos. One moment he was groping slowly over the slippery floor of an almost level place, and the next he was shooting dizzily downward in the dark through a burrow which must have been well-nigh vertical.

Of the length of that hideous sliding he could never be sure, but it seemed to take hours of delirious nausea and ecstatic frenzy. Then he realised[a] he was still, with the phosphorescent clouds of a northern night shining sickly above him. All around were crumbling walls and broken columns, and the pavement on which he lay was pierced by straggling grass and wrenched asunder by frequent shrubs and roots. Behind him a basalt cliff rose topless and perpendicular; its dark side sculptured into repellent scenes, and pierced by an arched and carven entrance to the inner blacknesses out of which he had come. Ahead stretched double rows of pillars, and the fragments and pedestals of pillars, that spoke of a broad and bygone street; and from the urns and basins along the way he knew it had been a great street of gardens. Far off at its end the pillars spread to mark a vast round plaza, and in that open circle there loomed gigantic under the lurid night clouds a pair of monstrous things. Huge winged lions of diorite[b] they were, with blackness and shadow between them. Full twenty feet they reared their grotesque and unbroken heads, and snarled derisive on the ruins around them. And Carter knew right well what they must be, for legend tells of only one such twain. They were the changeless guardians of the Great Abyss,[c] and these dark ruins were in truth primordial Sarkomand.

Carter's first act was to close and barricade the archway in the cliff with fallen blocks and odd debris that lay around. He wished no follower from Leng's hateful monastery, for along the way ahead would lurk enough of other dangers. Of how to get from Sarkomand to the peopled parts of dreamland he knew nothing at all; nor could he gain much by descending to the grottoes of the ghouls, since he knew they were no better informed than he. The three ghouls which had helped him through the city of gugs to the outer world had not known how to reach Sarkomand in their journey back, but had planned to ask old traders in Dylath-Leen. He did not like to think of going again to

[a] realised] realized C
[b] diorite] diarite C
[c] Great Abyss,] great abyss, A

the subterrene world of gugs and risking once more that hellish tower
of Koth with its Cyclopean steps leading to the enchanted wood, yet
he felt he might have to try this course if all else failed. Over Leng's
plateau past the lone monastery he dared not go unaided; for the high-
priest's emissaries must be many, while at the journey's end there
would no doubt be the shantaks[a] and perhaps other things to deal
with. If he could get a boat he might sail back to Inganok[b] past the
jagged and hideous rock in the sea, for the primal frescoes in the
monastery labyrinth had shewn that this frightful place lies not far
from Sarkomand's basalt quays. But to find a boat in this aeon-
deserted city was no probable thing, and it did not appear likely that he
could ever make one.

Such were the thoughts of Randolph Carter when a new
impression began beating upon his mind. All this while there had
stretched before him the great corpse-like width of fabled Sarkomand
with its black broken pillars and crumbling sphinx-crowned gates and
titan stones and monstrous winged lions against the sickly glow of
those luminous night clouds. Now he saw far ahead and on the right a
glow that no clouds could account for, and knew he was not alone in
the silence of that dead city. The glow rose and fell fitfully, flickering
with a greenish tinge which did not reassure the watcher. And when he
crept closer, down the littered street and through some narrow gaps
between tumbled walls, he perceived that it was a campfire near the
wharves with many vague forms clustered darkly around it,[c] and a
lethal odour hanging heavily over all. Beyond was the oily lapping of
the harbour water with a great ship riding at anchor, and Carter paused
in stark terror when he saw that the ship was indeed one of the
dreaded black galleys from the moon.

Then, just as he was about to creep back from that detestable
flame, he saw a stirring among the vague dark forms and heard a
peculiar and unmistakable sound. It was the frightened meeping of a
ghoul, and in a moment it had swelled to a veritable chorus of anguish.
Secure as he was in the shadow of monstrous ruins, Carter allowed his

[a] shantaks] Shantaks C
[b] Inganok] Inquanok C
[c] it,] it; C

curiosity to conquer his fear, and crept forward again instead of retreating. Once in crossing an open street he wriggled worm-like on his stomach, and in another place he had to rise to his feet to avoid making a noise among heaps of fallen marble. But always he succeeded in avoiding discovery, so that in a short time he had found a spot behind a titan pillar whence[a] he could watch the whole green-litten scene of action. There,[b] around a hideous fire fed by the obnoxious stems of lunar fungi, there squatted a stinking circle of the toad-like[c] moonbeasts and their almost-human[d] slaves. Some of these slaves were heating curious iron spears in the leaping flames, and at intervals applying their white-hot points to three tightly trussed prisoners that lay writhing before the leaders of the party. From the motions of their tentacles Carter could see that the blunt-snouted moonbeasts were enjoying the spectacle hugely, and vast was his horror when he suddenly recognised the frantic meeping and knew that the tortured ghouls were none other than the faithful trio which had guided him safely from the abyss[e] and had thereafter set out from the enchanted wood to find Sarkomand and the gate to their native deeps.

The number of malodorous moonbeasts about that greenish fire was very great, and Carter saw that he could do nothing now to save his former allies. Of how the ghouls had been captured he could not guess; but fancied that the grey toad-like[f] blasphemies had heard them inquire in Dylath-Leen concerning the way to Sarkomand and had not wished them to approach so closely the hateful plateau of Leng and the high-priest not to be described. For a moment he pondered on what he ought to do, and recalled how near he was to the gate of the ghouls' black kingdom. Clearly it was wisest to creep east to the plaza of twin lions and descend at once to the gulf, where assuredly he would meet no horrors worse than those above, and where he might soon find ghouls eager to rescue their brethren and perhaps to wipe out the moonbeasts from the black galley. It occured to him that the portal, like other gates

[a] whence] where C
[b] There,] There C
[c] toad-like] toadlike A, C
[d] almost-human] almost human C
[e] abyss] abyss, C
[f] toad-like] toadlike A, C

to the abyss, might be guarded by flocks of night-gaunts; but he did not fear these faceless creatures now. He had learned that they are bound by solemn treaties with the ghouls, and the ghoul which was Pickman had taught him how to glibber a password they understood.

So Carter began another silent crawl through the ruins, edging slowly toward the great central plaza and the winged lions. It was ticklish work, but the moonbeasts were pleasantly busy and did not hear the slight noises which he twice made by accident among the scattered stones. At last he reached the open space and picked his way among the stunted trees and briers[a] that had grown up therein. The gigantic lions loomed terrible above him in the sickly glow of the phosphorescent night clouds, but he manfully persisted toward them and presently crept round to their faces, knowing it was on that side he would find the mighty darkness which they guard. Ten feet apart crouched the mocking-faced beasts of diorite,[b] brooding on Cyclopean pedestals[c] whose sides were chiselled into[d] fearsome bas-reliefs. Betwixt them was a tiled court with a central space which had once been railed with balusters of onyx. Midway in this space a black well opened, and Carter soon saw that he had indeed reached the yawning gulf whose crusted and mouldy stone steps lead down[e] to the crypts of nightmare.

Terrible is the memory of that dark descent,[f] in which hours wore themselves away whilst Carter wound sightlessly round and round down a fathomless spiral of steep and slippery stairs. So worn and narrow were the steps, and so greasy with the ooze of inner earth, that the climber never quite knew when to expect a breathless fall and hurtling down to the ultimate pits; and he was likewise uncertain just when or how the guardian night-gaunts would suddenly pounce upon him, if indeed there were any stationed in this primeval passage. All about him was a stifling odour of nether gulfs, and he felt that the air of these choking depths was not made for mankind. In time he became very numb and somnolent, moving more from automatic impulse than

[a] briers] vines C
[b] diorite,] diarite, C
[c] pedestals] pedastals C
[d] into] in C
[e] down] do C
[f] descent,] descent C

from reasoned will; nor did he realise[a] any change when he stopped moving altogether as something quietly seized him from behind. He was flying very rapidly through the air before a malevolent tickling told him that the rubbery night-gaunts had performed their duty.

Awaked to the fact that he was in the cold, damp clutch of the faceless flutterers, Carter remembered the password of the ghouls and glibbered it as loudly as he could amidst the wind and chaos of flight. Mindless though night-gaunts are said to be, the effect was instantaneous; for all tickling stopped at once, and the creatures hastened to shift their captive to a more comfortable position. Thus encouraged,[b] Carter ventured some explanations; telling of the seizure and torture of three ghouls by the moonbeasts, and of the need of assembling a party to rescue them. The night-gaunts, though inarticulate, seemed to understand what was said; and shewed greater haste and purpose in their flight. Suddenly the dense blackness gave place to the grey twilight of inner earth, and there opened up ahead one of those flat sterile plains on which ghouls love to squat and gnaw. Scattered tombstones and osseous fragments told of the denizens of that place; and as Carter gave a loud meep of urgent summons, a score of burrows emptied forth their leathery, dog-like tenants. The night-gaunts now flew low and set their passenger upon his feet, afterward withdrawing a little and forming a hunched semicircle on the ground while the ghouls greeted the newcomer.

Carter glibbered his message rapidly and explicitly to the grotesque company, and four of them at once departed through different burrows to spread the news to others and gather such troops as might be available for the rescue. After a long wait a ghoul of some importance appeared, and made significant signs to the night-gaunts, causing two of the latter to fly off into the dark. Thereafter there were constant accessions to the hunched flock of night-gaunts on the plain, till at length the slimy soil was fairly black with them. Meanwhile fresh ghouls crawled out of the burrows one by one, all glibbering excitedly and forming in crude battle array not far from the huddled night-gaunts. In time there appeared that proud and influential ghoul which

---

[a] realise] realize C
[b] encouraged,] encouraged C

was once the artist Richard Pickman of Boston, and to him Carter glibbered a very full account of what had occurred. The erstwhile Pickman, surprised[a] to greet his ancient friend again, seemed very much impressed, and held a conference with other chiefs a little apart from the growing throng.

Finally, after scanning the ranks with care, the assembled chiefs all meeped in unison and began glibbering orders to the crowds of ghouls and night-gaunts. A large detachment of the horned flyers vanished at once, while the rest grouped themselves two by two on their knees with extended fore legs,[b] awaiting the approach of the ghouls one by one. As each ghoul reached the pair of night-gaunts to which he was assigned, he was taken up and borne away into the blackness; till at last the whole throng had vanished save for Carter, Pickman, and the other chiefs, and a few pairs of night-gaunts. Pickman explained that night-gaunts are the advance guard and battle steeds of the ghouls, and that the army was issuing forth to Sarkomand to deal with the moonbeasts. Then Carter and the ghoulish chiefs approached the waiting bearers and were taken up by the damp, slippery paws. Another moment and all were whirling in wind and darkness; endlessly up, up, up to the gate of the winged lions and the spectral ruins of primal Sarkomand.

When, after a great interval, Carter saw again the sickly light of Sarkomand's nocturnal sky, it was to behold the great central plaza swarming with militant ghouls and night-gaunts. Day, he felt sure, must be almost due; but so strong was the army that no surprise of the enemy would be needed. The greenish flare near the wharves still glimmered faintly, though the absence of ghoulish meeping shewed that the torture of the prisoners was over for the nonce. Softly glibbering directions to their steeds,[c] and to the flock of riderless night-gaunts ahead, the ghouls presently rose in wide whirring columns and swept on over the bleak ruins toward the evil flame. Carter was now beside Pickman in the front rank of ghouls, and saw as they approached the noisome camp that the moonbeasts were totally unprepared. The

[a] surprised] pleased C
[b] fore legs,] forelegs, A, C
[c] steeds,] steeds C

three prisoners lay bound and inert beside the fire, while their toad-like[a] captors slumped drowsily about in no certain order. The almost-human slaves were asleep, even the sentinels shirking a duty which in this realm must have seemed to them merely perfunctory.

The final swoop of the night-gaunts and mounted ghouls was very sudden, each of the greyish toad-like[b] blasphemies and their almost-human slaves being seized by a group of night-gaunts before a sound was made. The moonbeasts, of course, were voiceless; and even the slaves had little chance to scream before rubbery paws choked them into silence. Horrible were the writhings of those great jellyish abnormalities as the sardonic night-gaunts clutched them, but nothing availed against the strength of those black prehensile talons. When a moonbeast writhed too violently, a night-gaunt would seize and pull its quivering pink tentacles; which seemed to hurt so much that the victim would cease its struggles. Carter expected to see much slaughter, but found that the ghouls were far subtler in their plans. They glibbered certain simple orders to the night-gaunts which held the captives,[c] trusting the rest to instinct; and soon the hapless creatures were borne[d] silently away into the Great Abyss, to be distributed impartially amongst the bholes,[e] gugs, ghasts,[f] and other dwellers in darkness whose modes of nourishment are not painless to their chosen victims. Meanwhile the three bound ghouls had been released and consoled by their conquering kinsfolk, whilst various parties searched the neighbourhood for possible remaining moonbeasts, and boarded the evil-smelling black galley at the wharf to make sure that nothing had escaped the general defeat. Surely enough, the capture had been thorough;[g] for not a sign of further life could the victors detect. Carter, anxious to preserve a means of access to the rest of dreamland, urged them not to sink the anchored galley; and this request was freely granted out of gratitude for his act in reporting the plight of the

[a] toad-like] toadlike A, C
[b] toad-like] toadlike A, C
[c] captives,] captives C
[d] borne] born C
[e] bholes,] dholes, C
[f] ghasts,] ghasts A, C
[g] thorough;] thorough, C

captured trio. On the ship were found some very curious objects and decorations, some of which Carter cast at once into the sea.

Ghouls and night-gaunts now formed themselves in separate groups, the former questioning their rescued fellows anent past happenings. It appeared that the three had followed Carter's directions and proceeded from the enchanted wood to Dylath-Leen by way of Nir and the Skai, stealing human clothes at a lonely farmhouse and loping as closely as possible in the fashion of a man's walk. In Dylath-Leen's taverns their grotesque ways and faces had aroused much comment; but they had persisted in asking the way to Sarkomand until at last an old traveller was able to tell them. Then they knew that only a ship for Lelag-Leng would serve their purpose, and prepared to wait patiently for such a vessel.

But evil spies had doubtless reported much; for shortly a black galley put into port, and the wide-mouthed ruby merchants invited the ghouls to drink with them in a tavern. Wine was produced from one of those sinister bottles grotesquely carved from a single ruby, and after that the ghouls found themselves prisoners on the black galley as Carter had once found himself. This time, however, the unseen rowers steered not[a] for the moon but for antique Sarkomand; bent evidently on taking their captives before the high-priest not to be described. They had touched at the jagged rock in the northern sea which Inganok's[b] mariners shun, and the ghouls had there seen for the first time the real[c] masters of the ship; being sickened despite their own callousness by such extremes of malign shapelessness and fearsome odour. There, too, were witnessed the nameless pastimes of the toad-like[d] resident garrison—such pastimes as give rise to the night-howlings which men fear. After that had come the landing at ruined Sarkomand and the beginning of the tortures, whose continuance the present rescue had prevented.

Future plans were next discussed, the three rescued ghouls suggesting a raid on the jagged rock and the extermination of the toad-

---

[a] not] nor C
[b] Inganok's] Inquanok's C
[c] real] red C
[d] toad-like] toadlike A, C

like[a] garrison there. To this, however, the night-gaunts objected; since the prospect of flying over water did not please them. Most of the ghouls favoured the design, but were at a loss how to follow it without the help of the winged night-gaunts. Thereupon Carter, seeing that they could not navigate the anchored galley, offered to teach them the use of the great banks of oars; to which proposal they eagerly assented. Grey day had now come, and under that leaden northern sky a picked detachment of ghouls filed into the noisome ship and took their seats on the rowers' benches. Carter found them fairly apt at learning, and before night had risked several experimental trips around the harbour. Not till three days later, however, did he deem it safe to attempt the voyage of conquest. Then, the rowers trained and the night-gaunts safely stowed in the forecastle, the party set sail at last; Pickman and the other chiefs gathering on deck and discussing modes of approach and procedure.

On the very first night the howlings from the rock were heard. Such was their timbre that all the galley's crew shook visibly; but most of all trembled the three rescued ghouls who knew precisely what those howlings meant. It was not thought best to attempt an attack by night, so the ship lay to under the phosphorescent clouds to wait for the dawn of a greyish day. When the light was ample and the howlings still the rowers resumed their strokes, and the galley drew closer and closer to that jagged rock whose granite pinnacles clawed fantastically at the dull sky. The sides of the rock were very steep; but on ledges here and there could be seen the bulging walls of queer windowless dwellings, and the low railings guarding travelled high roads.[b] No ship of men had ever come so near the place, or at least, had never come so near and departed again; but Carter and the ghouls were void of fear and kept inflexibly on, rounding the eastern face of the rock and seeking the wharves which the rescued trio described as being on the southern side within a harbour formed of steep headlands.

The headlands were prolongations of the island proper, and came so closely together that only one ship at a time might pass between them. There seemed to be no watchers on the outside, so the galley was steered boldly through the flume-like strait and into the stagnant

---

[a] toad-like] toadlike A, C
[b] high roads.] highroads. C

foetid[a] harbour beyond. Here, however, all was bustle and activity; with several ships lying at anchor along a forbidding stone quay, and scores of almost-human slaves and moonbeasts by the waterfront handling crates and boxes or driving nameless and fabulous horrors hitched to lumbering lorries. There was a small stone town hewn out of the vertical cliff above the wharves, with the start of a winding road that spiralled out of sight toward higher ledges of the rock. Of what lay inside that prodigious peak of granite none might say, but the things one saw on the outside were far from encouraging.

At sight of the oncoming galley the crowds on the wharves displayed much eagerness; those with eyes staring intently, and those without eyes wriggling their pink tentacles expectantly. They did not, of course, realise[b] that the black ship had changed hands; for ghouls look much like the horned and hooved almost-humans, and the night-gaunts were all out of sight below. By this time the leaders had fully formed a plan; which was to loose the night-gaunts as soon as the wharf was touched, and then to sail directly away, leaving matters wholly to the instincts of those almost mindless[c] creatures. Marooned on the rock, the horned flyers would first of all seize whatever living things they found there, and afterward, quite helpless to think except in terms of the homing instinct, would forget their fear[d] of water and fly swiftly back to the abyss; bearing their noisome prey to appropriate destinations in the dark, from which not much would emerge alive.

The ghoul that was Pickman now went below and gave the night-gaunts their simple instructions, while the ship drew very near to the ominous and malodorous wharves. Presently a fresh stir rose along the waterfront, and Carter saw that the motions of the galley had begun to excite suspicion. Evidently the steersman was not making for the right dock, and probably the watchers had noticed the difference between the hideous ghouls and the almost-human slaves whose places they were taking. Some silent alarm must have been given, for almost at once a horde of the mephitic moonbeasts began to pour from the little

[a] foetid] putrid C
[b] realise] realize C
[c] almost mindless] almost-mindless C
[d] fear] fears C

black doorways of the windowless houses and down the winding road at the right. A rain of curious javelins struck the galley as the prow hit the wharf, felling two ghouls and slightly wounding another; but at this point all the hatches were thrown open to emit a black cloud of whirring night-gaunts which swarmed over the town like a flock of horned and Cyclopean bats.

The jellyish moonbeasts had procured a great pole and were trying to push off the invading ship, but when the night-gaunts struck them they thought of such things no more. It was a very terrible spectacle to see those faceless and rubbery ticklers at their pastime, and tremendously impressive to watch the dense cloud of them spreading through the town and up the winding roadway to the reaches above. Sometimes a group of the black flutterers would drop a toad-like[a] prisoner from aloft by mistake, and the manner in which the victim would burst was highly offensive to the sight and smell. When the last of the night-gaunts had left the galley the ghoulish leaders glibbered an order of withdrawal, and the rowers pulled quietly out of the harbour between the grey headlands while still the town was a chaos of battle and conquest.

The Pickman ghoul allowed several hours for the night-gaunts to make up their rudimentary minds and overcome their fear of flying over the sea, and kept the galley standing about a mile off the jagged rock while he waited[b] and dressed the wounds of the injured men. Night fell, and the grey twilight gave place to the sickly phosphorescence of low clouds, and all the while the leaders watched the high peaks of that accursed rock for signs of the night-gaunts' flight. Toward morning a black speck was seen hovering timidly over the topmost pinnacle, and shortly afterward the speck had become a swarm. Just before daybreak the swarm seemed to scatter, and within a quarter of an hour it had vanished wholly in the distance toward the northeast. Once or twice something seemed to fall from the thinning swarm into the sea; but Carter did not worry, since he knew from observation that the toad-like[c] moonbeasts cannot swim. At[d] length,

---

[a] toad-like] toadlike A, C
[b] waited] waited, C
[c] toad-like] toadlike A, C
[d] At] A t C

when the ghouls were satisfied that all the night-gaunts had left for Sarkomand and the Great Abyss with their doomed burdens, the galley put back into the harbour betwixt the grey headlands; and all the hideous company landed and roamed curiously over the denuded rock with its towers and eyries and fortresses chiselled from the solid stone.

Frightful were the secrets uncovered in those evil and windowless crypts; for the remnants of unfinished pastimes were many, and in various stages of departure from their primal state. Carter put out of the way certain things which were after a fashion alive, and fled precipitately from a few other things about which he could not be very positive. The stench-filled houses were furnished mostly with grotesque stools and benches carven from moon-trees, and were painted inside with nameless and frantic designs. Countless weapons, implements, and ornaments lay about;[a] including some large idols of solid ruby depicting singular beings not found on the earth. These latter did not, despite their material, invite either appropriation or long inspection; and Carter took the trouble to hammer five of them into very small pieces. The scattered spears and javelins he collected, and with Pickman's approval distributed among the ghouls. Such devices were new to the dog-like[b] lopers, but their relative simplicity made them easy to master after a few concise hints.

The upper parts of the rock held more temples than private homes, and in numerous hewn chambers were found terrible carven altars and doubtfully stained fonts and shrines for the worship of things more monstrous than the mild[c] gods atop Kadath. From the rear of one great temple stretched a low black passage which Carter followed far into the rock with a torch till he came to a lightless domed hall of vast proportions, whose vaultings were covered with daemoniac[d] carvings and in whose centre yawned a foul and bottomless well like that in the hideous monastery of Leng where broods alone the high-priest not to be described. On the distant shadowy side, beyond the noisome well, he thought he discerned a

[a] about;] about, C
[b] dog-like] doglike A, C
[c] mild] wild C
[d] daemoniac] demoniac A, C

small door of strangely wrought bronze; but for some reason he felt an unaccountable dread of opening it or even approaching it, and hastened back through the cavern to his unlovely allies as they shambled about with an ease and abandon he could scarcely feel. The ghouls had observed the unfinished pastimes of the moonbeasts, and had profited in their fashion. They had also found a hogshead of potent moon-wine, and were rolling it down to the wharves for removal and later use in diplomatic dealings, though the rescued trio, remembering its effect on them in Dylath-Leen, had warned their company to taste none of it. Of rubies from lunar mines there was a great store, both rough and polished, in one of the vaults near the water; but when the ghouls found they were not good to eat they lost all interest in them. Carter did not try to carry any away, since he knew too much about those which had mined them.

Suddenly there came an excited meeping from the sentries on the wharves, and all the loathsome foragers turned from their tasks to stare seaward and cluster round the waterfront. Betwixt the grey headlands a fresh black galley was rapidly advancing, and it could[a] be but a moment before the almost-humans on deck would perceive the invasion of the town and give the alarm to the monstrous things below. Fortunately the ghouls still bore the spears and javelins which Carter had distributed amongst them; and at his command, sustained by the being that was Pickman, they now formed a line of battle and prepared to prevent the landing of the ship. Presently a burst of excitement on the galley told of the crew's discovery of the changed state of things, and the instant stoppage of the vessel proved that the superior numbers of the ghouls had been noted and taken into account. After a moment of hesitation the newcomers silently turned and passed out between the headlands again, but not for an instant did the ghouls imagine that the conflict was averted. Either the dark ship would seek reinforcements,[b] or the crew would try to land elsewhere on the island; hence a party of scouts was at once sent up toward the pinnacle to see what the enemy's course would be.

[a] could] would C
[b] reinforcements,] reinforcements C

In a very few minutes a[a] ghoul returned breathless to say that the moonbeasts and almost-humans were landing on the outside of the more easterly of the rugged grey headlands, and ascending by hidden paths and ledges which a goat could scarcely tread in safety. Almost immediately afterward the galley was sighted again through the flume-like[b] strait, but only for a second. Then,[c] a few moments later, a second messenger panted down from aloft to say that another party was landing on the other headland; both being much more numerous than the size of the galley would seem to allow for. The ship itself, moving slowly with only one sparsely manned tier of oars, soon hove in sight betwixt the cliffs, and lay to in the foetid harbour as if to watch the coming fray and stand by for any possible use.

By this time Carter and Pickman had divided the ghouls into three parties, one to meet each of the two invading columns and one to remain in the town. The first two at once scrambled up the rocks in their respective directions, while the third was subdivided into a land party and a sea party. The sea party, commanded by Carter, boarded the anchored galley and rowed out to meet the undermanned galley of the newcomers; whereat the latter retreated through the strait to the open sea. Carter did not at once pursue it, for he knew he might be needed more acutely near the town.

Meanwhile the frightful detachments of the moonbeasts and almost-humans had lumbered up to the top of the headlands and were shockingly silhouetted on either side against the grey twilight sky. The thin hellish flutes of the invaders had now begun to whine, and the general effect of those hybrid, half-amorphous processions was as nauseating as the actual odour given off by the toad-like[d] lunar blasphemies. Then the two parties of the ghouls swarmed into sight and joined the silhouetted panorama. Javelins began to fly from both sides, and the swelling meeps of the ghouls and the bestial howls of the almost-humans gradually joined the hellish whine of the flutes to form a frantick and indescribable chaos of daemon cacophony. Now

[a] a] the C
[b] flume-like] flumelike A
[c] Then,] Then C
[d] toad-like] toadlike A, C

and then bodies fell from the narrow ridges of the headlands into the sea outside or the harbour inside, in the latter case being sucked quickly under by certain submarine lurkers whose presence was indicated only by prodigious bubbles.

For half an hour this dual battle raged in the sky, till upon the west cliff the invaders were completely annihilated. On the east cliff, however, where the leader of the moonbeast party appeared to be present, the ghouls had not fared so well; and were slowly retreating to the slopes of the pinnacle proper. Pickman had quickly ordered reinforcements for this front from the party in the town, and these had helped greatly in the earlier stages of the combat. Then, when the western battle was over, the victorious survivors hastened across to the aid of their hard-pressed fellows; turning the tide and forcing the invaders back again along the narrow ridge of the headland. The almost-humans were by this time all slain, but the last of the toad-like[a] horrors fought desperately with the great spears clutched in their powerful and disgusting paws. The time for javelins was now nearly past, and the fight became a hand-to-hand contest of what few spearmen could meet upon that narrow ridge.

As fury and recklessness increased, the number falling into the sea became very great. Those striking the harbour met nameless extinction from the unseen bubblers, but of those striking the open sea some were able to swim to the foot of the cliffs and land on tidal rocks, while the hovering galley of the enemy rescued several moonbeasts. The cliffs were unscalable except where the monsters had debarked, so that none of the ghouls on the rocks could rejoin their battle-line. Some were killed by javelins from the hostile galley or from the moonbeasts above, but a few survived to be rescued. When the security of the land parties seemed assured, Carter's galley sallied forth between the headlands and drove the hostile ship far out to sea; pausing to rescue such ghouls as were on the rocks or still swimming in the ocean. Several moonbeasts washed on rocks or reefs were speedily put out of the way.

Finally, the moonbeasts'[b] galley being safely in the distance and the

---

[a] toad-like] toadlike A, C
[b] moonbeasts'] moonbeast's A; moonbeast C

invading land army concentrated in one place, Carter landed a considerable force on the eastern headland in the enemy's rear; after which the fight was short-lived indeed. Attacked from both sides, the noisome flounderers were rapidly cut to pieces or pushed into the sea, till by evening the ghoulish chiefs agreed that the island was again clear of them. The hostile galley, meanwhile, had disappeared; and it was decided that the evil jagged rock had better be evacuated before any overwhelming horde of lunar horrors might be assembled and brought against the victors.

So by night Pickman and Carter assembled all the ghouls and counted them with care, finding that over a fourth had been lost in the day's battles. The wounded were placed on bunks in the galley, for Pickman always discouraged the old ghoulish custom of killing and eating one's own wounded, and the able-bodied troops were assigned to the oars or to such other places as they might most usefully fill. Under the low phosphorescent clouds of night the galley sailed, and Carter was not sorry to be departing from that[a] island of unwholesome secrets, whose lightless domed hall with its bottomless well and repellent bronze door lingered restlessly in his fancy. Dawn found the ship in sight of Sarkomand's ruined quays of basalt, where a few night-gaunt sentries still waited, squatting like black horned gargoyles on the broken columns and crumbling sphinxes of that fearful city which lived and died before the years of man.

The ghouls made camp amongst the fallen stones of Sarkomand, despatching a messenger for enough night-gaunts to serve them as steeds. Pickman and the other chiefs were effusive in their gratitude for the aid Carter had lent them; and[b] Carter now began to feel that his plans were indeed maturing well, and that he would be able to command the help of these fearsome allies not only in quitting this part of dreamland, but in pursuing his ultimate quest for the gods atop unknown Kadath, and the marvellous sunset city they so strangely withheld from his slumbers. Accordingly he spoke of these things to the ghoulish leaders; telling what he knew of the cold waste wherein Kadath stands and of

---

[a] that] the C
[b] them; and] them. C

the monstrous shantaks[a] and the mountains carven into double-headed images which guard it. He spoke of the fear of shantaks[b] for night-gaunts, and of how the vast hippocephalic birds fly screaming from the black burrows high up on the gaunt grey peaks that divide Inganok[c] from hateful Leng. He spoke, too, of the things he had learnt[d] concerning night-gaunts from the frescoes in the windowless monastery of the high-priest not to be described; how even the Great Ones fear them, and how their ruler is not the crawling chaos Nyarlathotep at all, but hoary and immemorial Nodens, Lord of the Great Abyss.

All these things Carter glibbered to the assembled ghouls, and presently outlined that request which he had in mind,[e] and which he did not think extravagant considering the services he had so lately rendered the rubbery, dog-like[f] lopers. He wished very much, he said, for the services of enough night-gaunts to bear him safely through the air past the realm of shantaks[g] and carven mountains, and up into the cold waste beyond the returning tracks of any other mortal. He desired to fly to the onyx castle atop unknown Kadath in the cold waste to plead with the Great Ones for the sunset city they denied him, and felt sure that the night-gaunts could take him thither without trouble; high above the perils of the plain, and over the hideous double heads of those carven sentinel mountains that squat eternally in the grey dusk. For the horned and faceless creatures there could be no danger from aught of earth,[h] since the Great Ones themselves dread them. And even were unexpected things to come from the Other Gods, who are prone to oversee the affairs of earth's milder gods, the night-gaunts need not fear; for the outer hells are indifferent matters to such silent and slippery flyers as own not Nyarlathotep for their master, but bow only to potent and archaic Nodens.

A flock of ten or fifteen night-gaunts, Carter glibbered, would

[a] shantaks] Shantaks C
[b] shantaks] Shantaks C
[c] Inganok] Inquanok C
[d] learnt] learned C
[e] mind,] mind C
[f] rubbery, dog-like] rubbery, doglike A; rubbery doglike C
[g] shantaks] Shantaks C
[h] earth,] earth C

surely be enough to keep any combination of shantaks[a] at a distance;[b] though perhaps it might be well to have some ghouls in the party to manage the creatures, their ways being better known to their ghoulish allies than to men. The party could land him at some convenient point within whatever walls that fabulous onyx citadel might have, waiting in the shadows for his return or his signal whilst he ventured inside the castle to give prayer to the gods of earth. If any ghouls chose to escort him into the throne-room of the Great Ones, he would be thankful, for their presence would add weight and importance to his plea. He would not, however, insist upon this but merely wished transportation to and from the castle atop unknown Kadath; the final journey being either to the marvellous[c] sunset city itself, in case the gods proved favourable, or back to the earthward Gate of Deeper Slumber in the enchanted wood[d] in case his prayers were fruitless.

Whilst Carter was speaking all the ghouls listened with great attention, and as the moments advanced the sky became black with clouds of those night-gaunts for which messengers had been sent. The winged horrors settled in a semicircle around the ghoulish army, waiting respectfully as the dog-like[e] chieftains considered the wish of the earthly traveller. The ghoul that was Pickman glibbered gravely with its[f] fellows, and in the end Carter was offered far more than he had at most expected. As he had aided the ghouls in their conquest of the moonbeasts, so would they aid him in his daring voyage to realms whence none had ever returned; lending him not merely a few of their allied night-gaunts, but their entire army as they encamped, veteran fighting ghouls and newly assembled night-gaunts alike, save only a small garrison for the captured black galley and such spoils as had come from the jagged rock in the sea. They would set out through the air whenever he might wish, and once arrived on Kadath a suitable train of ghouls would attend him in state as he placed his petition before earth's gods in their onyx castle.

[a] shantaks] Shantaks C
[b] distance;] distance, C
[c] marvellous] marvelous C
[d] enchanted wood] Enchanted Wood C
[e] dog-like] doglike A, C
[f] its] his C

Moved by a gratitude and satisfaction beyond words, Carter made plans with the ghoulish leaders for his audacious voyage. The army would fly high, they decided, over hideous Leng with its nameless monastery and wicked stone villages; stopping only at the vast grey peaks to confer with the shantak-frightening[a] night-gaunts whose burrows honeycombed their summits. They would then, according to what advice they might receive from those denizens, choose their final course; approaching unknown Kadath either through the desert of carven mountains north of Inganok,[b] or through the more northerly reaches of repulsive Leng itself. Dog-like[c] and soulless as they are, the ghouls and the night-gaunts had no dread of what those untrodden deserts might reveal; nor did they feel any deterring awe at the thought of Kadath towering lone with its onyx castle of mystery.

About midday the ghouls and night-gaunts prepared for flight, each ghoul selecting a suitable pair of horned steeds to bear him. Carter was placed well up toward the head of the column beside Pickman, and in front of the whole a double line of riderless night-gaunts was provided as a vanguard. At a brisk meep from Pickman the whole shocking army rose in a nightmare cloud above the broken columns and crumbling sphinxes of primordial Sarkomand; higher and higher, till even the great basalt cliff behind the town was cleared, and the cold, sterile table-land of Leng's outskirts laid open to sight. Still higher flew the black host, till even this table-land grew small beneath them; and as they worked northward over the windswept[d] plateau of horror Carter saw once again with a shudder the circle of crude monoliths and the squat windowless building which he knew held that frightful silken-masked blasphemy from whose clutches he had so narrowly escaped.[e] This time no descent was made as the army swept bat-like[f] over the sterile landscape, passing the feeble fires of the unwholesome stone villages at a great altitude, and pausing not at all to mark the morbid twistings of the hooved, horned almost-humans that

[a] shantak-frightening] Shantak-frightening C
[b] Inganok,] Inquanok, C
[c] Dog-like] Doglike A, C
[d] windswept] wind-swept A, C
[e] escaped.] excaped. C
[f] bat-like] batlike A, C

dance and pipe eternally therein. Once they saw a shantak-bird[a] flying low over the plain, but when it saw them it screamed noxiously and flapped off to the north in grotesque panic.

At dusk they reached the jagged grey peaks that form the barrier of Inganok,[b] and hovered about those[c] strange caves near the summits which Carter recalled as so frightful to the shantaks.[d] At the insistent meeping of the ghoulish leaders there issued forth from each lofty burrow a stream of horned black flyers;[e] with which the ghouls and night-gaunts of the party conferred at length by means of ugly gestures. It soon became clear that the best course would be that over the cold waste north of Inganok,[f] for Leng's northward reaches are full of unseen pitfalls that even the night-gaunts dislike; abysmal influences centreing[g] in certain white hemispherical buildings on curious knolls, which common folklore associates unpleasantly with the Other Gods and their crawling chaos Nyarlathotep.

Of Kadath the flutterers of the peaks knew almost nothing, save that there must be some mighty marvel toward the north, over which the shantaks[h] and the carven mountains stand guard. They hinted at rumoured abnormalities of proportion in those trackless leagues beyond, and recalled vague whispers of a realm where night broods eternally; but of definite data they had nothing to give. So Carter and his party thanked them kindly; and, crossing the topmost granite pinnacles to the skies of Inganok,[i] dropped below the level of the phosphorescent night clouds and beheld in the distance those terrible squatting gargoyles that were mountains till some titan hand carved fright into their virgin rock.

There they squatted,[j] in a hellish half-circle, their legs on the desert

[a] shantak-bird] Shantak-bird C
[b] Inganok,] Inquanok, C
[c] those] these C
[d] shantaks.] Shantaks. C
[e] flyers;] flyers C
[f] Inganok,] Inquanok, C
[g] centreing] centering C
[h] shantaks] Shantaks C
[i] Inganok,] Inquanok, C
[j] squatted,] squatted C

sand and their mitres piercing the luminous clouds; sinister, wolf-like, and double-headed, with faces of fury and right hands raised, dully and malignly watching the rim of man's world and guarding with horror the reaches of a cold northern world that is not man's. From their hideous laps rose evil shantaks[a] of elephantine bulk, but these all fled with insane titters as the vanguard of night-gaunts was sighted in the misty sky. Northward above those gargoyle mountains the army flew, and over leagues of dim desert where never a landmark rose. Less and less luminous grew the clouds, till at length Carter could see only blackness around him; but never did the winged steeds falter, bred as they were in earth's blackest crypts, and seeing not with any eyes, but with the whole dank surface of their slippery forms. On and on they flew, past winds of dubious scent and sounds of dubious import; ever in thickest darkness, and covering such prodigious spaces that Carter wondered whether or not they could still be within earth's dreamland.

Then suddenly the clouds thinned and the stars shone spectrally above. All below was still black, but those pallid beacons in the sky seemed alive with a meaning and directiveness they had never possessed elsewhere. It was not that the figures of the constellations were different, but that the same familiar shapes now revealed a significance they had formerly failed to make plain. Everything focussed toward the north; every curve and asterism of the glittering sky became part of a vast design whose function was to hurry first the eye and then the whole observer to some secret and terrible goal of convergence beyond the frozen waste that stretched endlessly ahead. Carter looked toward the east where the great ridge of barrier peaks had towered along all the length of Inganok,[b] and saw against the stars a jagged silhouette which told of its continued presence. It was more broken now, with yawning clefts and fantastically erratic pinnacles; and Carter studied closely the suggestive turns[c] and inclinations of that grotesque outline, which seemed to share with the stars some subtle northward urge.

They were flying past at a tremendous speed, so that the watcher had to strain hard to catch details; when all at once he beheld just above

[a] shantaks] Shantaks C
[b] Inganok,] Inquanok, C
[c] turns] turnings C

the line of the topmost peaks a dark and moving object against the stars, whose course exactly paralleled[a] that of his own bizarre party. The ghouls had likewise glimpsed it, for he heard their low glibbering all about him, and for a moment he fancied the object was a gigantic shantak,[b] of a size vastly greater than that of the average specimen. Soon, however, he saw that this theory would not hold; for the shape of the thing above the mountains was not that of any hippocephalic bird. Its outline against the stars, necessarily vague as it was, resembled rather some huge mitred head[c] or pair of heads infinitely magnified; and its rapid bobbing flight through the sky seemed most peculiarly a wingless one. Carter could not tell which side of the mountains it was on, but soon perceived that it had parts below the parts he had first seen, since it blotted out all the stars in places where the ridge was deeply cleft.

Then came a wide gap in the range, where the hideous reaches of transmontane Leng were joined to the cold waste on this side by a low pass through which the stars shone wanly. Carter watched this gap with intense care, knowing that he might see outlined against the sky beyond it the lower parts of the vast thing that flew undulantly above the pinnacles. The object had now floated ahead a trifle, and every eye of the party was fixed on the rift where it would presently appear in full-length silhouette. Gradually the huge thing above the peaks neared the gap, slightly slackening its speed as if conscious of having outdistanced the ghoulish army. For another minute suspense was keen, and then the brief instant of full silhouette and revelation came; bringing to the lips of the ghouls an awed and half-choked meep of cosmic fear, and to the soul of the traveller a chill that has never wholly left it. For the mammoth bobbing shape that overtopped the ridge was only a head— a mitred double head—and below it in terrible vastness loped the frightful swollen body that bore it; the mountain-high monstrosity that walked in stealth and silence; the hyaena-like distortion of a giant anthropoid shape that trotted blackly against the sky, its repulsive pair of cone-capped heads reaching half way to the zenith.

Carter did not lose consciousness or even scream aloud, for he was

[a] paralleled] parallelled A
[b] shantak,] Shantak, C
[c] head] head, C

an old dreamer; but he looked behind him in horror and shuddered when he saw that there were other monstrous heads silhouetted above the level of the peaks, bobbing along stealthily after the first one. And straight in the rear were three of the mighty mountain shapes seen full against the southern stars, tiptoeing wolf-like and lumberingly, their tall mitres nodding thousands of feet in the air. The carven mountains, then, had not stayed squatting in that rigid semicircle north of Inganok[a] with right hands uplifted. They had duties to perform, and were not remiss. But it was horrible[b] that they never spoke, and never even made a sound in walking.

Meanwhile the ghoul that was Pickman had glibbered an order to the night-gaunts, and the whole army soared higher into the air. Up toward the stars the grotesque column shot, till nothing stood out any longer against the sky; neither the grey granite ridge that was still nor the carven and[c] mitred mountains that walked. All was blackness beneath as the fluttering legions[d] surged northward amidst rushing winds and invisible laughter in the aether, and never a shantak[e] or less mentionable entity rose from the haunted wastes to pursue them. The farther they went, the faster they flew, till soon their dizzying speed seemed to pass that of a rifle ball and approach that of a planet in its orbit. Carter wondered how with such speed the earth could still stretch beneath them, but knew that in the land of dream dimensions have strange properties. That they were in a realm of eternal night he felt certain, and he fancied that the constellations overhead had subtly emphasised[f] their northward focus; gathering themselves up as it were to cast the flying army into the void of the boreal pole, as the folds of a bag are gathered up to cast out the last bits of substance therein.

Then he noticed with terror that the wings of the night-gaunts were not flapping any more. The horned and faceless steeds had folded their membraneous appendages, and were resting quite passive in the chaos of wind that whirled and chuckled as it bore them on. A force not

[a] Inganok] Inquanok, C
[b] horrible] horrible, C
[c] and] *om.* C
[d] legions] legion C
[e] shantak] Shantak C
[f] emphasised] emphasized C

of earth had seized on the army, and ghouls and night-gaunts alike were powerless before a current which pulled madly and relentlessly into the north whence no mortal had ever returned. At length a lone pallid light was seen on the skyline ahead, thereafter rising steadily as they approached, and having beneath it a black mass that blotted out the stars. Carter saw that it must be some beacon on a mountain, for only a mountain could rise so vast as seen from so prodigious a height in the air.

Higher and higher rose the light and the blackness beneath it, till half the northern sky was obscured by the rugged conical mass. Lofty as the army was, that pale and sinister beacon rose above it, towering monstrous over all peaks and concernments of earth, and tasting the atomless aether where the cryptical moon and the mad planets reel. No mountain known of man was that which loomed before them. The high clouds far below were but a fringe for its foothills. The gasping[a] dizziness of topmost air was but a girdle for its loins. Scornful and spectral climbed that bridge betwixt earth and heaven, black in eternal night, and crowned with a pshent of unknown stars whose awful and significant outline grew every moment clearer. Ghouls meeped in wonder as they saw it, and Carter shivered in fear lest all the hurtling army be dashed to pieces on the unyielding onyx of that Cyclopean[b] cliff.

Higher and higher rose the light, till it mingled with the loftiest orbs of the zenith and winked down at the flyers with lurid mockery. All the north beneath it was blackness now; dread, stony blackness from infinite depths to infinite heights, with only that pale winking beacon perched unreachably at the top of all vision. Carter studied the light more closely, and saw at last what lines its inky background made against the stars. There were towers on that titan mountaintop; horrible domed towers in noxious and incalculable tiers and clusters beyond any dreamable workmanship of man; battlements and terraces of wonder and menace, all limned tiny and black and distant against the starry pshent that glowed malevolently at the uppermost rim of sight. Capping that most measureless of mountains was a castle beyond all mortal thought, and in it glowed the daemon-light. Then Randolph Carter knew that his quest was done, and that he saw above

[a] gasping] groping C
[b] Cyclopean] cyclopean A, C

him the goal of all forbidden steps and audacious visions; the fabulous, the incredible home of the Great Ones atop unknown Kadath.

Even as he realised[a] this thing, Carter noticed a change in the course of the helplessly wind-sucked party. They were rising abruptly now, and it was plain that the focus of their flight was the onyx castle where the pale light shone. So close was the great black mountain that its sides sped by them dizzily as they shot upward, and in the darkness they could discern nothing upon it. Vaster and vaster loomed the tenebrous towers of the nighted castle above, and Carter could see that it was well-nigh blasphemous in its immensity. Well might its stones have been quarried by nameless workmen in that horrible gulf rent out of the rock in the hill pass north of Inganok,[b] for such was its size that a man on its threshold stood even as an ant[c] on the steps of earth's loftiest fortress. The pshent of unknown stars above the myriad domed turrets glowed with a sallow, sickly flare, so that a kind of twilight hung about the murky walls of slippery onyx. The pallid beacon was now seen to be a single shining window high up in one of the loftiest towers, and as the helpless army neared the top of the mountain Carter thought he detected unpleasant shadows flitting across the feebly luminous expanse. It was a strangely arched window, of a design wholly alien to earth.

The solid rock now gave place to the giant foundations of the monstrous castle, and it seemed that the speed of the party was somewhat abated. Vast walls shot up, and there was a glimpse of a great gate through which the voyagers were swept. All was night in the titan courtyard, and then came the deeper blackness of inmost things as a huge arched portal engulfed the column. Vortices of cold wind surged dankly through sightless labyrinths of onyx, and Carter could never tell what Cyclopean[d] stairs and corridors lay silent along the route of his endless aërial twisting. Always upward led the terrible plunge in darkness, and never a sound, touch,[e] or glimpse broke the dense pall of mystery. Large as the army of ghouls and night-gaunts

[a] realised] realized C
[b] Inganok,] Inquanok, C
[c] an ant] air out C
[d] Cyclopean] cyclopean C
[e] touch,] touch A, C

was, it was lost in the prodigious voids of that more than earthly castle. And when at last there suddenly dawned around him the lurid light of that single tower room whose lofty window had served as a beacon, it took Carter long to discern the far walls and high, distant ceiling, and to realise[a] that he was indeed not again in the boundless air outside.

Randolph Carter had hoped to come into the throne-room of the Great Ones with poise and dignity, flanked and followed by impressive lines of ghouls in ceremonial order, and offering his prayer as a free and potent master among dreamers. He had known that the Great Ones themselves are not beyond a mortal's power to cope with, and had trusted to luck that the Other Gods and their crawling chaos Nyarlathotep would not happen to come to their aid at the crucial moment, as they had so often done before when men sought out earth's gods in their home or on their mountains. And with his hideous escort he had half hoped to defy even the Other Gods if need were, knowing as he did that ghouls have no masters, and that night-gaunts own not Nyarlathotep but only archaick Nodens for their lord. But now he saw that supernal Kadath in its cold waste is indeed girt with dark wonders and nameless sentinels, and that the Other Gods are of a surety vigilant in guarding the mild, feeble gods of earth. Void as they are of lordship over ghouls and night-gaunts, the mindless, shapeless blasphemies of outer space can yet control them when they must; so that it was not in state as a free and potent master of dreamers that Randolph Carter came into the Great Ones' throne-room with his ghouls. Swept and herded by nightmare tempests from the stars, and dogged by unseen horrors of the northern waste, all that army floated captive and helpless in the lurid light, dropping numbly to the onyx floor when by some voiceless order the winds of fright dissolved.

Before no golden dais had Randolph Carter come, nor was there any august circle of crowned and haloed beings with narrow eyes, long-lobed ears, thin nose, and pointed chin whose kinship to the carven face on Ngranek might stamp them as those to whom a dreamer might pray. Save for that[b] one tower room the onyx castle atop Kadath was dark, and the masters were not there. Carter had

[a] realise] realize C
[b] that] the C

come to unknown Kadath in the cold waste, but he had not found the gods. Yet still the lurid light glowed in that one tower room whose size was so little less than that of all outdoors, and whose distant walls and roof were so nearly lost to sight in thin, curling mists. Earth's gods were not there, it was true, but of subtler and less visible presences there could be no lack. Where the mild gods are absent, the Other Gods are not unrepresented; and certainly, the onyx castle of castles was far from tenantless. In what outrageous form or forms terror would next reveal itself,[a] Carter could by no means imagine. He felt that his visit had been expected, and wondered how close a watch had all along been kept upon him by the crawling chaos Nyarlathotep. It is Nyarlathotep, horror of infinite shapes and dread soul and messenger of the Other Gods, that the fungous moonbeasts serve; and Carter thought of the black galley that had vanished when the tide of battle turned against the toad-like[b] abnormalities on the jagged rock in the sea.

Reflecting upon these things, he was staggering to his feet in the midst of his nightmare company when there rang without warning through that pale-litten and limitless chamber the hideous blast of a daemon trumpet. Three times pealed that frightful brazen scream, and when the echoes of the third blast had died chucklingly away Randolph Carter saw that he was alone. Whither, why,[c] and how the ghouls and night-gaunts had been snatched from sight was not for him to divine. He knew only that he was suddenly alone, and that whatever unseen powers lurked mockingly around him were no powers of earth's friendly dreamland. Presently from the chamber's uttermost reaches a new sound came. This, too, was a rhythmic trumpeting; but of a kind far removed from the three raucous blasts which had dissolved his grisly[d] cohorts. In this low fanfare echoed all the wonder and melody of ethereal dream; exotic vistas of unimagined loveliness floating from each strange chord and subtly alien cadence. Odours of incense came to match the golden notes; and overhead a great light dawned, its colours changing in cycles unknown to earth's spectrum, and following the song of the trumpets in

[a] itself,] itself. C
[b] toad-like] toadlike A, C
[c] why,] why A, C
[d] grisly] goodly C

weird symphonic harmonies. Torches flared in the distance, and the beat of drums throbbed nearer amidst waves of tense expectancy.

Out of the thinning mists and the cloud of strange incense[a] filed twin columns of giant black slaves with loin-cloths of iridescent silk. Upon their heads were strapped vast helmet-like torches of glittering metal, from which the fragrance of obscure balsams spread in fumous spirals. In their right hands were crystal wands whose tips were carven into leering chimaeras, while their left hands grasped long,[b] thin silver trumpets which they blew in turn. Armlets and anklets of gold they had, and between each pair of anklets stretched a golden chain that held its wearer to a sober gait. That they were true black men of earth's dreamland was at once apparent, but it seemed less likely that their rites and costumes were wholly things of our earth. Ten feet from Carter the columns stopped, and as they did so each trumpet flew abruptly to its bearer's thick lips. Wild and ecstatic was the blast that followed, and wilder still the cry that chorused just after from dark throats somehow made shrill by strange artifice.

Then down the wide lane betwixt the two columns a lone figure strode; a tall, slim figure with the young face of an antique Pharaoh, gay with prismatic robes and crowned with a golden pshent that glowed with inherent light. Close up to Carter strode that regal figure; whose proud carriage and swart[c] features had in them the fascination of a dark god or fallen archangel, and around whose eyes there lurked the languid sparkle of capricious humour. It spoke, and in its mellow tones there rippled the mild[d] music of Lethean streams.

"Randolph Carter," said the voice, "you have come to see the Great Ones whom it is unlawful for men to see. Watchers have spoken of this thing, and the Other Gods have grunted as they rolled and tumbled mindlessly to the sound of thin flutes in the black ultimate void where broods the daemon-sultan whose name no lips dare speak aloud.

"When Barzai the Wise climbed Hatheg-Kla to see the Great Ones dance and howl above the clouds in the moonlight he never returned. The

---

[a] incense] incenses C
[b] long,] long C
[c] swart] smart C
[d] mild] wild C

Other Gods were there, and they did what was expected. Zenig of Aphorat sought to reach unknown Kadath in the cold waste, and his skull is now set in a ring on the little finger of one whom I need not name.

"But you, Randolph Carter, have braved all things of earth's dreamland, and burn still with the flame of quest. You came not as one curious, but as one seeking his due, nor have you failed ever in reverence toward the mild gods of earth. Yet have these gods kept you from the marvellous sunset city of your dreams, and wholly through their own small covetousness; for verily, they craved the weird loveliness of that which your fancy had fashioned, and vowed that henceforward no other spot should be their abode.

"They are gone from their castle on unknown Kadath to dwell in your marvellous city. All through its palaces of veined marble they revel by day, and when the sun sets they go out in the perfumed gardens and watch the golden glory on temples and colonnades, arched bridges and silver-basined fountains, and wide streets with blossom-laden urns and ivory statues in gleaming rows. And when night comes they climb tall terraces in the dew, and sit on carved benches of porphyry scanning the stars, or lean over pale balustrades to gaze at the town's steep northward slopes, where one by one the little windows in old peaked gables shine softly out with the calm yellow light of homely candles.

"The gods love your marvellous city, and walk no more in the ways of the gods. They have forgotten the high places of earth, and the mountains that knew their youth. The earth has no longer any gods that are gods, and only the Other Ones from outer space hold sway on unremembered Kadath. Far away in a valley of your own childhood, Randolph Carter, play the heedless Great Ones. You have dreamed too well, O wise arch-dreamer, for you have drawn dream's gods away from the world of all men's visions to that which is wholly yours; having builded out of your boyhood's small fancies a city more lovely than all the phantoms that have gone before.

"It is not well that earth's gods leave their thrones for the spider to spin on, and their realm for the Others to sway in the dark manner of Others. Fain would the powers from outside bring chaos and horror to you, Randolph Carter, who are the cause of their upsetting, but that they know it is by you alone that the gods may be sent back to their world.

In that half-waking dreamland which is yours, no power of uttermost night may pursue; and only you can send the selfish Great Ones gently out of your marvellous sunset city, back through the northern twilight to their wonted place atop unknown Kadath in the cold waste.

"So, Randolph Carter, in the name of the Other Gods I spare you and charge you to serve my will. I charge you to seek that sunset city which is yours, and to send thence the drowsy truant gods for whom the dream-world[a] waits. Not hard to find is that roseal fever of the gods, that fanfare of supernal trumpets and clash of immortal cymbals, that mystery whose place and meaning have haunted you through the halls of waking and the gulfs of dreaming, and tormented you with hints of vanished memory and the pain of lost things awesome and momentous. Not hard to find is that symbol and relic of your days of wonder, for truly, it is but the stable and eternal gem wherein all that wonder sparkles crystallised to light your evening path. Behold! It is not over unknown seas but back over well-known years that your quest must go; back to the bright strange things of infancy and the quick sun-drenched glimpses of magic that old scenes brought to wide young eyes.

"For know you, that your gold and marble city of wonder is only the sum of what you have seen and loved in youth. It is the glory of Boston's hillside roofs and western windows aflame with sunset; of the flower-fragrant Common and the great dome on the hill and the tangle of gables and chimneys in the violet valley where the many-bridged Charles flows drowsily. These things you saw, Randolph Carter, when your nurse first wheeled you out in the springtime, and they will be the last things you will ever see with eyes of memory and of love. And there is antique Salem with its brooding years, and spectral Marblehead scaling its rocky precipices into past centuries, and the glory of Salem's towers and spires seen afar from Marblehead's pastures across the harbour against the setting sun.

"There is Providence,[b] quaint and lordly on its seven hills over the blue harbour, with terraces of green leading up to steeples and citadels of living antiquity, and Newport climbing wraith-like[c] from its

[a] dream-world] dream world A, C
[b] Providence,] Providence C
[c] wraith-like] wraithlike A, C

dreaming breakwater. Arkham is there, with its moss-grown gambrel roofs and the rocky rolling meadows behind it; and antediluvian Kingsport hoary with stacked chimneys and deserted quays and overhanging gables, and the marvel of high cliffs and the milky-misted ocean with tolling buoys beyond.

"Cool vales in Concord, cobbled lanes in Portsmouth, twilight bends of rustic New-Hampshire[a] roads where giant elms half hide white farmhouse walls and creaking well-sweeps. Gloucester's salt wharves and Truro's windy willows. Vistas of distant steepled towns and hills beyond hills along the North Shore, hushed stony slopes and low ivied cottages in the lee of huge boulders in Rhode-Island's[b] back country. Scent of the sea and fragrance of the fields; spell of the dark woods and joy of the orchards and gardens at dawn. These, Randolph Carter, are your city; for they are yourself. New-England[c] bore you, and into your soul she poured a liquid loveliness which cannot die. This loveliness, moulded, crystallised, and polished by years of memory and dreaming, is your terraced wonder of elusive sunsets; and to find that marble parapet with curious urns and carven rail, and descend at last those[d] endless balustraded steps to the city of broad squares and prismatic fountains, you need only to turn back to the thoughts and visions of your wistful boyhood.

"Look! through that window shine the stars of eternal night. Even now they are shining above the scenes you have known and cherished, drinking of their charm that they may shine more lovely over the gardens of dream. There is Antares—he is winking at this moment over the roofs of Tremont Street, and you could see him from your window on Beacon Hill. Out beyond those stars yawn the gulfs from whence my mindless masters have sent me. Some day you too may traverse them, but if you are wise you will beware such folly; for of those mortals who have been and returned, only one preserves a mind unshattered by the pounding, clawing horrors of the void. Terrors and blasphemies gnaw at one another for space, and there is more evil in the lesser ones

[a] New-Hampshire] New Hampshire C
[b] Rhode-Island's] Rhode Island's C
[c] New-England] New England C
[d] those] these C

than in the greater; even as you know from the deeds of those who sought to deliver you into my hands, whilst I myself harboured no wish to shatter you, and would indeed have helped you hither long ago had I not been elsewhere busy, and certain that you would yourself find the way. Shun,[a] then, the outer hells, and stick to the calm, lovely things of your youth. Seek out your marvellous city and drive thence the recreant Great Ones, sending them back gently to those scenes which are of their own youth, and which wait uneasy for their return.

"Easier even than[b] the way of dim memory is the way I will prepare for you. See! There comes hither a monstrous shantak, led by a slave who for your peace of mind had best keep invisible. Mount and be ready—there! Yogash the black will help you on the scaly horror. Steer for that brightest star just south of the zenith—it is Vega, and in two hours will be just above the terrace of your sunset city. Steer for it only till you hear a far-off singing in the high aether. Higher than that lurks madness, so rein your shantak[c] when the first note lures. Look then back to earth, and you will see shining the deathless altar-flame of Ired-Naa from the sacred roof of a temple. That temple is in your desiderate sunset city, so steer for it before you heed the singing and are lost.

"When you draw nigh the city steer for the same high parapet whence of old you scanned the outspread glory, prodding the shantak[d] till he cry aloud. That cry the Great Ones will hear and know as they sit on their perfumed terraces, and there will come upon them such a homesickness that all of your city's wonders will not console them for the absence of Kadath's grim castle and the pshent of eternal stars that crowns it.

"Then must you land amongst them with the shantak,[e] and let them see and touch that noisome and hippocephalic bird; meanwhile discoursing to them of unknown Kadath, which you will so lately have left, and telling them how its boundless halls are lonely[f] and unlighted, where of old they used to leap and revel in supernal radiance. And the

[a] Shun,] Shun C
[b] than] then C
[c] shantak] Shantak C
[d] shantak] Shantak C
[e] shantak,] Shantak, C
[f] lonely] lovely C

shantak[a] will talk to them in the manner of shantaks,[b] but it will have no powers of persuasion beyond the recalling of elder days.

"Over and over must you speak to the wandering Great Ones of their home and youth, till at last they will weep and ask to be shewn the returning path they have forgotten. Thereat can you loose the waiting shantak,[c] sending him skyward with the homing cry of his kind; hearing which the Great Ones will prance and jump with antique mirth, and forthwith stride after the loathly bird in the fashion of gods, through the deep gulfs of heaven to Kadath's familiar towers and domes.

"Then will the marvellous sunset city be yours to cherish and inhabit for ever, and once more will earth's gods rule the dreams of men from their accustomed seat. Go now—the casement is open and the stars await outside. Already your shantak[d] wheezes and titters with impatience. Steer for Vega through the night, but turn when the singing sounds. Forget not this warning, lest horrors unthinkable suck you into the gulf of shrieking and ululant madness. Remember the Other Gods; they are great and mindless and terrible, and lurk in the outer voids. They are good gods to shun.

"*Hei! Aa-shanta 'nygh!* You are off! Send back earth's gods to their haunts on unknown Kadath, and pray to all space that you may never meet me in my thousand other forms. Farewell, Randolph Carter, and beware; *for I am Nyarlathotep, the Crawling Chaos!*"[e]

And Randolph Carter, gasping and dizzy on his hideous shantak,[f] shot screamingly into space toward the cold blue glare of boreal Vega; looking but once behind him at the clustered and chaotic turrets of the onyx nightmare wherein still glowed the lone lurid light of that window above the air and the clouds of earth's dreamland. Great polypous horrors slid darkly past, and unseen bat-wings[g] beat multitudinous around him, but still he clung to the unwholesome mane of that loathly and hippocephalic scaled bird. The stars danced mockingly,

[a] shantak] Shantak C
[b] shantaks,] Shantaks, C
[c] shantak,] Shantak, C
[d] shantak] Shantak C
[e] *Chaos!*"] *Chaos.*" C
[f] shantak,] Shantak, C
[g] bat-wings] bat wings A, C

almost shifting now and then to form pale signs of doom that one might wonder one had not seen and feared before; and ever the winds of aether[a] howled of vague blackness and loneliness beyond the cosmos.

Then through the glittering vault ahead there fell a hush of portent, and all the winds and horrors slunk away as night things slink away before the dawn. Trembling in waves that golden wisps of nebula made weirdly visible, there rose a timid hint of far-off melody, droning in faint chords that our own universe of stars knows not. And as that music grew, the shantak[b] raised its ears and plunged ahead, and Carter likewise bent to catch each lovely strain. It was a song, but not the song of any voice. Night and the spheres sang it, and it was old when space and Nyarlathotep and the Other Gods were born.

Faster flew the shantak,[c] and lower bent the rider, drunk with the marvels of strange gulfs, and whirling in the crystal coils of outer magic. Then came too late the warning of the evil one, the sardonic caution of the daemon legate who had bidden the seeker beware the madness of that song. Only to taunt had Nyarlathotep marked out the way to safety and the marvellous sunset city; only to mock had that black messenger revealed the secret of those[d] truant gods whose steps he could so easily lead back at will. For madness and the void's wild vengeance are Nyarlathotep's only gifts to the presumptuous; and frantick though the rider strove to turn his disgusting steed, that leering, tittering shantak[e] coursed on impetuous and relentless, flapping its great slippery wings in malignant joy, and headed for those unhallowed pits whither no dreams reach; that last amorphous blight of nethermost[f] confusion where bubbles and blasphemes at infinity's centre the mindless daemon-sultan Azathoth, whose name no lips dare speak aloud.

Unswerving and obedient to the foul legate's orders, that hellish bird plunged onward through shoals of shapeless lurkers and caperers in darkness, and vacuous herds of drifting entities that pawed and groped and groped and pawed; the nameless larvae of the Other Gods, that

[a] aether] nether C
[b] shantak] Shantak C
[c] shantak,] Shantak, C
[d] those] these C
[e] shantak] Shantak C
[f] nethermost] nether-most C

are like them blind and without mind, and possessed of singular hungers and thirsts.

Onward unswerving and relentless, and tittering hilariously to watch the chuckling and hysterics into which the siren[a] song of night and the spheres had turned, that eldritch scaly monster bore its helpless rider; hurtling and shooting, cleaving the uttermost rim and spanning the outermost abysses; leaving behind the stars and the realms of matter, and darting meteor-like through stark formlessness toward those inconceivable, unlighted chambers beyond Time[b] wherein black[c] Azathoth gnaws shapeless and ravenous amidst the muffled, maddening beat of vile drums and the thin, monotonous whine of accursed flutes.[d]

Onward—onward—through the screaming, cackling, and blackly populous gulfs—and then from some dim blessed distance there came an image and a thought to Randolph Carter the doomed. Too well had Nyarlathotep planned his mocking and his tantalising, for he had brought up that which no gusts of icy terror could quite efface. Home—New England—Beacon Hill—the waking world.

"For know you, that your gold and marble city of wonder is only the sum of what you have seen and loved in youth . . . the glory of Boston's hillside roofs and western windows aflame with sunset; of the flower-fragrant Common and the great dome on the hill and the tangle of gables and chimneys in the violet valley where the many-bridged Charles flows drowsily . . . this loveliness, moulded, crystallised, and polished by years of memory and dreaming, is your terraced wonder of elusive sunsets; and to find that marble parapet with curious urns and carven rail, and descend at last those endless balustraded steps to the city of broad squares and prismatic fountains, you need only to turn back to the thoughts and visions of your wistful boyhood."

[a] siren] risen C
[b] Time] time C
[c] black] *om.* C
[d] flutes.] flutes, to which detestable pounding and piping dance slowly, awkwardly, and absurdly the gigantic Ultimate Gods [*revised to lower-case*], the blind, voiceless, tenebrous, mindless Other Gods whose soul and messenger is the crawling chaos Nyarlathotep. A [*excised*]

Onward—onward—dizzily onward to ultimate doom through the blackness where sightless feelers pawed and slimy snouts jostled and nameless things tittered and tittered and tittered. But the image and the thought had come, and Randolph Carter knew clearly that he was dreaming and only dreaming, and that somewhere in the background the world of waking and the city of his infancy still lay. Words came again—"You need only turn back to the thoughts and visions of your wistful boyhood." Turn—turn—blackness on every side, but Randolph Carter could turn.

Thick though the rushing nightmare that clutched his senses, Randolph Carter could turn and move. He could move, and if he chose he could leap off the evil shantak[a] that bore him hurtlingly doomward at the orders of Nyarlathotep. He could leap off and dare those depths of night that yawned interminably down, those depths of fear whose terrors yet could not exceed the nameless doom that lurked waiting at chaos' core. He could turn and move and leap—he could— he would—he would—[b]

Off that vast hippocephalic abomination leaped the doomed and desperate dreamer, and down through endless voids of sentient blackness he fell. Aeons reeled, universes died and were born again, stars became nebulae and nebulae became stars, and still Randolph Carter fell through those endless voids of sentient blackness.

Then in the slow creeping course of eternity the utmost cycle of the cosmos churned itself into another futile completion, and all things became again as they were unreckoned kalpas before. Matter and light were born anew as space once had known them; and comets, suns,[c] and worlds sprang flaming into life, though nothing survived to tell that they had been and gone, been and gone, always and always, back to no first beginning.

And there was a firmament again, and a wind, and a glare of purple light in the eyes of the falling dreamer. There were gods and presences and wills; beauty and evil, and the shrieking of noxious night robbed of its prey. For through the unknown ultimate cycle had lived a thought

[a] shantak] Shantak C
[b] would—] would—. A, C
[c] suns,] suns A, C

and a vision of a dreamer's boyhood, and now there were re-made a waking world and an old cherished city to body and to justify these things. Out of the void S'ngac the violet gas had pointed the way, and archaic Nodens was bellowing his guidance from unhinted deeps.

Stars swelled to dawns, and dawns burst into fountains of gold, carmine, and purple, and still the dreamer fell. Cries rent the aether as ribbons of light beat back the fiends from outside. And hoary Nodens raised a howl of triumph when Nyarlathotep, close on his quarry, stopped baffled by a glare that seared his formless hunting-horrors to grey dust. Randolph Carter had indeed descended at last the wide marmoreal flights to his marvellous city, for he was come again to the fair New England world that had wrought him.

So to the organ chords of morning's myriad whistles, and dawn's blaze thrown dazzling through purple panes by the great gold dome of the State House on the hill, Randolph Carter leaped shoutingly awake within his Boston room. Birds sang in hidden gardens and the perfume of trellised vines came wistful from arbours his grandfather had reared. Beauty and light glowed from classic mantel and carven cornice and walls grotesquely figured, while a sleek black cat rose yawning from hearthside sleep that his master's start and shriek had disturbed. And vast infinities away, past the Gate of Deeper Slumber and the enchanted wood and the garden lands and the Cerenerian[a] Sea and the twilight reaches of Inganok,[b] the crawling chaos Nyarlathotep strode brooding into the onyx castle atop unknown Kadath in the cold waste, and taunted insolently the mild gods of earth whom he had snatched abruptly from their scented revels in the marvellous sunset city.

[a] Cerenerian] Cerenarian A, C
[b] Inganok,] Inquanok, C

The Case of Charles Dexter Ward

"The essential Saltes of Animals may be so prepared and preserved, that an ingenious Man may have the whole Ark of Noah in his own Studie,[a] and raise the fine Shape[b] of an Animal out of its Ashes at his Pleasure; and by the lyke Method[c] from the essential Saltes of humane Dust, a Philosopher may, without any criminal Necromancy, call up the Shape of any dead Ancestour from the Dust whereinto his Bodie has been incinerated."[d]

BORELLUS[e]

Editor's Note: HPL's autograph manuscript survives and has served as the basis of all published versions. R. H. Barlow began a typescript, but it barely constitutes a fifth of the complete text; it does, however, bear revisions by HPL that Arkham House failed to incorporate when it first published the text in *Beyond the Wall of Sleep* (1943). Incredible as it may seem, there is substantial evidence that the next Arkham House publication—*At the Mountains of Madness and Other Novels* (1964)—attempted to transcribe the text from the autograph manuscript rather than merely copying the *Beyond the Wall of Sleep* text. The number of significant variants, and the nature of some, clearly indicate that the divergences between the 1943 and 1964 texts are not the result of erroneous copying but of erroneous readings of the A.Ms. Neither text is particularly sound, but the 1943 text is slightly superior. The archaic documents are particularly difficult to transcribe properly, and the Arkham House texts make a number of systematic errors in these cases. The A.Ms., essentially a rough draft, contains numerous small internal inconsistencies of usage, some of which I have corrected. The passage in Saxon minuscules (p. 350) is a reproduction of HPL's handwritten draft; the page on which it appears contains numerous practice attempts to write the passage. (The Arkham House texts attempt to transcribe the passage by hand, resulting in incoherence.) The first published appearance of the novel—*Weird Tales* 35, No. 9 (May 1941): 8–40; No. 10 (July 1941): 64–121—was heavily abridged and was not followed by any later editions; there is no need to record its textual variants.

Texts: A = A.Ms. (JHL); B = T.Ms. (by Barlow) (JHL); C = *Beyond the Wall of Sleep* (Arkham House, 1943), 135–209; D = *At the Mountains of Madness and Other Novels* (Arkham House, 1964), 101–221. Copy-text: A (with some readings from B).

[a] owne Studie,] owne Studie C; own Studie D
[b] Shape] shape C, D
[c] Method] method C, D
[d] "The . . . incinerated."] The . . . incinerated. C, D
[e] BORELLUS] Borellus C

214

I. A RESULT AND A PROLOGUE

1.

From a private hospital for the insane near Providence, Rhode Island, there recently disappeared an exceedingly singular person. He bore the name of Charles Dexter Ward, and was placed under restraint most reluctantly by the grieving father who had watched his aberration grow from a mere eccentricity to a dark mania involving both a possibility of murderous tendencies and a profound and[a] peculiar change in the apparent contents of his mind. Doctors confess themselves quite baffled by his case, since it presented oddities of a general physiological as well as psychological character.

In the first place, the patient seemed oddly older than his twenty-six years would warrant. Mental disturbance, it is true, will age one rapidly; but the face of this young man had taken on a subtle cast which only the very aged usually[b] acquire. In the second place, his organic processes shewed[c] a certain queerness of proportion[d] which nothing in medical experience can parallel. Respiration and heart action had a baffling lack of symmetry; the voice was lost, so that no sounds above a whisper were possible;[e] digestion was incredibly prolonged and minimised, and neural reactions to standard stimuli bore no relation at all[f] to anything heretofore recorded, either normal or pathological. The skin had a morbid chill and dryness, and the cellular structure of the tissue seemed exaggeratedly coarse and loosely knit.[g] Even a large olive birthmark on the[h] right hip had disappeared, whilst[i] there had formed on the[j] chest a very peculiar mole or blackish spot of which no trace existed before. In

[a] profound and] *om.* D
[b] usually] normally D
[c] shewed] showed D
[d] proportion] proportion, D
[e] symmetry; . . . possible;] symmetry, . . . possible, A, B [*revised by HPL*], C, D
[f] at all] *om.* D
[g] loosely knit.] loosely-knit. A, B, C
[h] the] his A, B [*revised by HPL*], C, D
[i] whilst] while D
[j] the] his A, B [*revised by HPL*], C, D

general, all physicians agree that in Ward the processes of metabolism had become retarded to a degree beyond precedent.

Psychologically, too, Charles Ward was unique. His madness held no affinity to any sort recorded in even the latest and most exhaustive of treatises, and was conjoined to a mental force which would have made him a genius or a leader had it not been twisted into strange and grotesque forms. Dr. Willett, who was Ward's family physician, affirms that the patient's gross mental capacity, as gauged by his response to matters outside the sphere of his insanity, had actually increased since the seizure. Ward, it is true, was always a scholar and an antiquarian; but even his most brilliant early work did not shew[a] the prodigious grasp and insight displayed during his last examinations by the alienists. It was, indeed, a difficult matter to obtain a legal commitment to the hospital, so powerful and lucid did the youth's mind seem; and only on the evidence of others, and on the strength of many abnormal gaps in his stock of information as distinguished from his intelligence,[b] was he finally placed in confinement. To the very moment of his vanishment he was an omnivorous reader and as great a conversationalist as his poor voice permitted; and shrewd observers, failing to foresee his escape, freely predicted that he would not be long in gaining his discharge from custody.

Only Dr. Willett, who[c] brought Charles Ward into the world and had[d] watched his growth of body and mind ever since, seemed frightened at the thought of his[e] future freedom. He had had a terrible experience and had made a terrible discovery which he dared not reveal to his sceptical colleagues. Willett, indeed, presents a minor mystery all his own in his connexion[f] with the case. He was the last to see the patient before his flight, and emerged from that final conversation in a state of mixed horror and relief which several recalled when Ward's escape became known three hours later. That escape itself is one of the unsolved wonders of Dr. Waite's hospital. A

[a] shew] show D
[b] intelligence,] intelligence A, B, C, D
[c] who] who had D
[d] had] *om.* A, B [*revised by HPL*], C, D
[e] his] this D
[f] connexion] connection D

window open above a sheer drop of sixty feet could[a] hardly explain it, yet after that talk with Willett the youth was undeniably gone. Willett himself has no public explanations to offer, though he seems strangely easier in mind than before the escape. Many, indeed, feel that he would like to say more if he thought any considerable number would believe him. He had found Ward in his room, but shortly after his departure the attendants knocked in vain. When they opened the door the patient was not there, and all they found was the open window with a chill April breeze blowing in a cloud of fine bluish-grey dust that almost choked them. True, the dogs howled some time before;[b] but that was while Willett was still present, and they had caught nothing and shewn[c] no disturbance later on. Ward's father was told at once over the telephone, but he seemed more saddened than surprised. By the time Dr. Waite called in person, Dr. Willett had been talking with him, and both disavowed any knowledge or complicity in the escape. Only from certain closely confidential friends of Willett and the senior Ward have any clues been gained, and even these are too wildly fantastic for general credence. The one fact which remains is that up to the present time no trace of the missing madman has been unearthed.

Charles Ward was an antiquarian from infancy, no doubt gaining his taste from the venerable town around him, and from the relics of the past which filled every corner of his parents' old mansion in Prospect Street on the crest of the hill. With the years his devotion to ancient things increased; so that history, genealogy, and the study of colonial[d] architecture, furniture,[e] and craftsmanship at length crowded everything else from his sphere of interests. These tastes are important to remember in considering his madness; for although they do not form its absolute nucleus, they play a prominent part in its superficial form. The gaps of information which the alienists noticed were all related to modern matters,[f] and were invariably offset by a correspondingly excessive though outwardly concealed knowledge of bygone matters as

[a] could] would D
[b] before;] before, D
[c] shewn] shown D
[d] colonial] Colonial C, D
[e] furniture,] furniture D
[f] matters,] matters A, B [*revised by HPL*], C, D

brought out by adroit questioning;[a] so that one would have fancied the patient literally transferred to a former age through some obscure sort of auto-hypnosis. The odd thing was that Ward seemed no longer interested in the antiquities[b] he knew so well. He had, it appears, lost his regard for them through sheer familiarity; and all his final efforts were obviously bent toward mastering those common facts of the modern world which had been so totally and unmistakably expunged from his brain. That this wholesale deletion had occurred, he did his best to hide;[c] but it was clear to all who watched him that his whole programme of reading and conversation was determined by a frantic wish to imbibe such knowledge of his own life and of the ordinary practical and cultural background of the twentieth century as ought to have been his by virtue of his birth in 1902 and his education in the schools of our own[d] time. Alienists are now wondering how, in view of his vitally[e] impaired range[f] of data, the escaped patient manages to cope with the complicated world of today; the dominant opinion being that he is 'lying low'[g] in some humble and unexacting position till his stock of modern information can be brought up to the normal.

The beginning of Ward's madness is a matter of dispute among alienists. Dr. Lyman, the eminent Boston authority, places it in 1919 or 1920, during the boy's last year at the Moses Brown School, when[h] he suddenly turned from the study of the past to the study of the occult, and refused to qualify for college on the ground that he had individual researches of much greater importance to make. This is certainly borne[i] out by Ward's altered habits at the time, especially by his continual search through town records and among old burying-grounds[j] for a

[a] questioning;] questionings: C
[b] antiquities] antiquarities C
[c] hide;] hide, C
[d] own] *om.* C
[e] vitally] wholly C, D
[f] range] stock A, B [*revised by HPL*], C, D
[g] 'lying low'] "lying low" D
[h] when] where D
[i] borne] brought D
[j] burying-grounds] burying grounds A, B, C, D

certain grave dug in 1771;[a] the grave of an ancestor named Joseph Curwen, some of whose papers he professed to have found behind the panelling of a very old house in Olney Court, on Stampers'[b] Hill, which Curwen was known to have built and occupied.[c] It is,[d] broadly speaking, undeniable that the winter of 1919–20 saw a great change in Ward; whereby he abruptly dropped[e] his general antiquarian pursuits and embarked on a desperate delving into occult subjects both at home and abroad, varied only by this strangely persistent search for his forefather's grave.

From this opinion, however, Dr. Willett substantially dissents;[f] basing his verdict on his close and continuous knowledge of the patient, and on certain frightful investigations and discoveries which he made toward the last. Those investigations and discoveries have left their mark upon him; so that his voice trembles when he tells them, and his hand trembles when he tries to write of them. Willett admits that the change of 1919–20 would ordinarily appear to mark the beginning of a progressive decadence which culminated in the horrible and[g] uncanny alienation of 1928;[h] but believes from personal observation that a finer distinction must be made. Granting freely that the boy was always ill-balanced temperamentally, and prone to be unduly susceptible and enthusiastic in his responses to phenomena around him, he refuses to concede that the early alteration marked the actual passage from sanity to madness; crediting instead Ward's own statement that he had discovered or rediscovered something whose effect on human thought was likely to be marvellous and profound.[i] The true madness, he is certain, came with a later change;[j] after the Curwen portrait and the

[a] 1771;] 1741; C, D
[b] Stampers'] Stampers A, B [*revised by HPL*], C, D
[c] built and occupied.] built and occupied. ¶ C; occupied. ¶ D
[d] is,] is D
[e] dropped] stopped D
[f] dissents;] dissents, C, D
[g] and] sad D
[h] 1928;] 1928, C, D
[i] profound.] profound. ¶ C, D
[j] change;] change; after the horrible responses to the invocations began; when the patient's memory commenced to exclude contemporary images and when his

ancient papers had been unearthed; after a trip to strange foreign places had been made, and some terrible invocations chanted under strange and secret circumstances; after certain *answers* to these invocations had been plainly indicated, and a frantic letter penned under agonising and inexplicable conditions; after the wave of vampirism and the ominous Pawtuxet gossip; and after the patient's memory commenced to exclude contemporary images whilst his voice failed and his physical aspect underwent the subtle modification so many subsequently noticed.

It was only about this time, Willett points out with much acuteness, that the nightmare qualities became indubitably linked with Ward;[a] and the doctor feels shudderingly sure that enough solid evidence exists to sustain the youth's claim regarding his crucial discovery. In the first place, two workmen of high intelligence saw Joseph Curwen's ancient papers found. Secondly, the boy once shewed[b] Dr. Willett[c] those papers and a page of the Curwen diary, and each of the documents had every appearance of genuineness. The hole where Ward claimed to have found them was long[d] a visible reality, and Willett had a very convincing final glimpse of them in surroundings which can scarcely be believed and can never perhaps be proved. Then there were the mysteries and coincidences of the Orne and Hutchinson letters, and the problem of the Curwen penmanship and of what the detectives brought to light about Dr. Allen; these things, and the terrible message in mediaeval minuscules found in Willett's pocket when he gained consciousness after his shocking experience.

And most conclusive of all, there are the two hideous *results* which the doctor obtained from a certain pair of formulae during his final investigations; results which virtually proved the authenticity of the papers and of their monstrous implications at the same time that those papers were borne for ever from human knowledge.

---

voice failed and his physical aspect underwent the subtle modification so many subsequently noticed; A [*excised*]

[a] Ward;] Ward, C, D

[b] shewed] showed D

[c] Dr. Willett] him A, B [*revised by HPL*], C, D

[d] was long] is A, B [*revised by HPL*], C, D

2.

One must look back at Charles Ward's earlier life as at something belonging as much to the past as the antiquities he loved so keenly. In the autumn of 1918, and with a considerable show of zest in the military training of the period, he had begun his junior year at the Moses Brown School, which lies very near his home. The old main building, erected in 1819, had always charmed his youthful antiquarian sense; and the spacious park in which the academy[a] is set appealed to his sharp[b] eye for landscape. His social activities were few; and his hours were spent mainly at home, in rambling walks, in his classes and drills, and in pursuit of antiquarian and genealogical data at the City Hall, the State House, the Public Library, the Athenaeum, the Historical Society, the John Carter Brown and John Hay Libraries of Brown University, and the newly opened Shepley Library in Benefit Street. One may picture him yet as he was in those days; tall, slim, and blond,[c] with studious eyes and a slight stoop, dressed somewhat carelessly, and giving a dominant impression of harmless awkwardness rather than attractiveness.

His walks were always adventures in antiquity, during which he managed to recapture from the myriad relics of a glamorous old city a vivid and connected picture of the centuries before. His home was a great Georgian mansion atop the well-nigh precipitous hill that rises just east of the river;[d] and from the rear windows of its rambling wings he could look dizzily out over all the clustered spires, domes, roofs,[e] and skyscraper[f] summits of the lower town to the purple hills of the countryside beyond. Here he was born, and from the lovely classic porch of the double-bayed brick facade[g] his nurse had first wheeled him in his carriage; past the little white farmhouse of two hundred years before that the town had long ago[h] overtaken, and on toward the

[a] academy] Academy C, D
[b] sharp] *om.* C, D
[c] blond,] bland, C
[d] river;] river, A, B [*revised by HPL*], C, D
[e] roofs,] roofs A, B, C, D
[f] skyscraper] sky-scraper D
[g] facade] façade C, D
[h] ago] *om.* D

stately colleges along the shady,[a] sumptuous street, whose old square brick mansions and smaller wooden houses with narrow, heavy-columned Doric porches dreamed solid and exclusive amidst their generous yards and gardens.

He had been wheeled, too, along sleepy Congdon Street, one tier lower down on the steep hill, and with all its eastern homes[b] on high terraces. The small wooden houses averaged a greater age here, for it was up this hill that the growing town had climbed; and in these rides he had imbibed something of the colour of a quaint colonial[c] village. The nurse used to stop and sit on the benches of[d] Prospect Terrace to chat with policemen; and one of the child's first memories is[e] of the great westward sea of hazy roofs and domes and steeples and far hills which he saw one winter afternoon from that great railed embankment, all violet and mystic against a fevered,[f] apocalyptic sunset of reds and golds and purples and curious greens. The vast marble dome of the State House stood out in massive silhouette, its crowning statue haloed fantastically by a break in one of the tinted stratus clouds that barred the flaming sky.

When he was larger his famous walks began; first with his impatiently dragged nurse,[g] and then alone in dreamy meditation. Farther and farther down that almost perpendicular hill he would venture, each time reaching older and quainter levels of the ancient city. He would hesitate gingerly down vertical Jenckes Street with its bank[h] walls and colonial[i] gables to the shady Benefit Street corner, where before him was a wooden antique with an Ionic-pilastered pair of doorways, and beside him a prehistoric gambrel-roofer with a bit of primal farmyard remaining, and the great Judge Durfee house with its fallen vestiges of Georgian grandeur. It was getting to be a slum here;

[a] stately . . . shady,] shady . . . stately, C, D
[b] homes] houses C, D
[c] colonial] Colonial C, D
[d] of] on D
[e] is] was D
[f] fevered,] fevered D
[g] nurse,] nurse C, D
[h] bank] back D
[i] colonial] Colonial C, D

but the titan elms cast a restoring shadow over the place, and the boy used to stroll south past the long lines of the pre-Revolutionary homes with their great central chimneys and classic portals. On the eastern side they were set high over basements with railed double flights of stone steps, and the young Charles could picture them as they were when the street was new, and red heels and periwigs set off the painted pediments whose signs of wear were now becoming so visible.

Westward the hill dropped almost as steeply as above, down to the old "Town Street"[a] that the founders[b] had laid out at the river's edge in 1636. Here ran innumerable little lanes with leaning, huddled houses of immense antiquity; and[c] fascinated though he was, it was long before he dared to thread their archaic verticality for fear they would turn out[d] a dream or a gateway to unknown terrors. He found it much less formidable to continue along Benefit Street past the iron fence of St. John's hidden churchyard and the rear of the 1761 Colony House and the mouldering bulk of the Golden Ball Inn where Washington stopped. At Meeting Street—the successive Gaol Lane and King Street of other periods—he would look upward to the east and see the arched flight of steps to which the highway had to resort in climbing the slope, and downward to the west, glimpsing the old brick colonial[e] schoolhouse that smiles across the road at the ancient Sign[f] of Shakespear's Head where the *Providence Gazette and Country-Journal* was printed before the Revolution. Then came the exquisite First Baptist Church of 1775, luxurious with its matchless Gibbs steeple, and the Georgian roofs and cupolas hovering by. Here and to the southward the neighbourhood became better, flowering at last into a marvellous group of early mansions; but still the little ancient lanes led off down the precipice to the west,[g] spectral in their many-gabled[h] archaism, and dipping to a riot of iridescent decay where the wicked old waterfront

[a] "Town Street"] "town street" A, B [*revised by HPL*]
[b] founders] founder C
[c] and] and, D
[d] out] out to be D
[e] colonial] Colonial D
[f] Sign] sign D
[g] west,] west; A, B, C, D
[h] many-gabled] many-peaked A, B [*revised by HPL*], C, D

recalls its proud East India days amidst polyglot vice and squalor, rotting wharves,[a] and blear-eyed ship-chandleries, with[b] such surviving alley names as Packet, Bullion, Gold, Silver, Coin, Doubloon,[c] Sovereign, Guilder, Dollar, Dime,[d] and Cent.

Sometimes,[e] as he grew taller and more adventurous, young Ward would venture down into this maelstrom of tottering houses, broken transoms, tumbling steps, twisted balustrades, swarthy faces, and nameless odours; winding from South Main to South Water, searching out the docks where the bay and sound steamers still touched, and returning northward at this lower level past the steep-roofed 1816 warehouses and the broad square at the Great Bridge, where the 1773 Market House still stands firm on its ancient arches. In that square he would pause to drink in the bewildering beauty of the old town as it rises on its[f] eastward bluff, decked with its two[g] Georgian spires and crowned by the vast new Christian Science dome as London is crowned by St. Paul's. He liked mostly to reach this point in the late afternoon, when the slanting sunlight touches the Market House and the ancient hill roofs and belfries with gold, and throws magic around the dreaming wharves where Providence Indiamen used to ride at anchor. After a long look he would grow almost dizzy with a poet's love for the sight, and then he would scale the slope homeward in the dusk past the old white church and up the narrow precipitous ways where yellow gleams would begin to peep out in small-paned windows and through fanlights set high over double flights of steps with curious wrought-iron railings.

At other times, and in later years, he would seek for vivid contrasts; spending half a walk in the crumbling colonial regions northwest of his home, where the hill drops to the lower eminence of Stampers'[h] Hill with its ghetto and negro[i] quarter clustering round the

---

[a] wharves,] wharves A, B, C, D
[b] ship-chandleries, with] ship-chandleries and A, B [*revised by HPL*], C, D
[c] Doubloon,] Dubloon, C
[d] Dime,] Dime A, D; Dim B [*revised by HPL to* Dime,]; Dim, C
[e] Sometimes,] Sometimes C
[f] its] the C, D
[g] two] *om.* D
[h] Stampers'] Stampers A, B [*revised by HPL*], C, D
[i] negro] Negro D

place where the Boston stage coach[a] used to start before the Revolution, and the other half in the gracious southerly[b] realm about George, Benevolent, Power, and Williams Streets, where the old slope holds unchanged the fine estates and bits of walled garden and steep green lane in which so many fragrant memories linger. These rambles, together with the diligent studies which accompanied them, certainly account for a large amount of the antiquarian lore which at last crowded the modern world from Charles Ward's mind; and illustrate[c] the mental soil upon which fell, in that fateful winter of 1919–20, the seeds that came to such strange and terrible fruition.

Dr. Willett is certain that, up to this ill-omened winter of first change, Charles Ward's antiquarianism was free from every trace of the morbid. Graveyards held for him no particular attraction beyond their quaintness and historic value, and of anything like violence or savage instinct he was utterly devoid. Then, by insidious degrees, there appeared to develop a curious sequel to one of his genealogical triumphs of the year before; when he had discovered among his maternal ancestors a certain very long-lived man named Joseph Curwen, who had come from Salem in March of 1692, and about whom a whispered series of highly peculiar and disquieting stories clustered.

Ward's great-great-grandfather Welcome Potter had in 1785 married a certain "Ann Tillinghast, daughter to Mrs. Eliza, daughter to Capt.[d] James Tillinghast",[e] of whose paternity the family had preserved no trace. Late in 1918, whilst examining a volume of original town records in manuscript, the young genealogist encountered an entry describing a legal change of name, by which in 1772 a Mrs. Eliza Curwen, widow of Joseph Curwen, resumed, along with her seven-year-old daughter Ann, her maiden name of Tillinghast; on the ground 'that her Husband's name was become a publick Reproach by Reason of what was knowne after his Decease; the which confirming an antient common Rumour, tho' not to be credited by a loyall Wife till so proven as to be wholely past Doubting'.[a] This entry came to light upon the accidental separation of two leaves which had been carefully pasted together and treated as one by a laboured revision of the page numbers.

It was at once clear to Charles Ward that he had indeed discovered a hitherto unknown great-great-great-grandfather. The discovery doubly excited him because he had already heard vague reports and seen scattered allusions relating to this person;[b] about whom there remained so few publicly available records, aside from those becoming public only in modern times, that it almost seemed as if a conspiracy had existed to blot him from memory. What did appear, moreover, was of such a[c] singular and provocative nature that one could not fail to imagine curiously what it was that the colonial recorders were so anxious to conceal and forget;[d] or to suspect that the deletion had reasons all too valid.

Before this, Ward had been content to let his romancing about old Joseph Curwen remain in the idle stage; but having discovered his own relationship to this apparently "hushed-up" character, he proceeded to hunt out as systematically as possible whatever he might find concerning him. In this excited quest he eventually succeeded beyond his highest expectations;[e] for old letters, diaries,[f] and sheaves of unpublished memoirs in cobwebbed Providence garrets and elsewhere yielded many illuminating passages which their writers had not thought it worth their while[g] to destroy. One important sidelight came from a point as remote as New York, where some Rhode Island colonial correspondence was stored in the Museum at Fraunces' Tavern. The really crucial thing, though, and what in Dr. Willett's opinion formed the definite source of Ward's undoing, was the matter found in August 1919 behind the panelling of the crumbling house in Olney Court. It was that, beyond a doubt, which opened up those black vistas whose end was deeper than the pit.

---

[a] 'that . . . Doubting'.] 'that . . . Doubting.' C; "that . . . Doubting." D
[b] person;] person D
[c] a] *om.* D
[d] forget;] forget, A, B [*revised by HPL*], C, D
[e] expectations;] expectations, A, B [*revised by HPL*], C, D
[f] diaries,] diaries A, B, C, D
[g] worth their while] worthwhile D

II. An Antecedent and a Horror

1.

Joseph Curwen, as revealed by the rambling legends embodied in what Ward heard and unearthed, was a very astonishing, enigmatic, and[a] obscurely horrible individual. He had fled from Salem to Providence—that universal haven of the odd, the free, and the dissenting—at the beginning of the great witchcraft panic;[b] being in fear of accusation because of his solitary ways and queer chemical or alchemical experiments. He was a colourless-looking man of about thirty, and was soon found qualified to become a freeman of Providence;[c] thereafter buying a home lot just north of Gregory Dexter's at about the foot of Olney Street. His house was built on Stampers'[d] Hill west of the Town Street, in what later became Olney Court; and in 1761 he replaced this with a larger one, on the same site, which is still standing.

Now the first odd thing about Joseph Curwen was that he did not seem to grow much older than he had been on his arrival. He engaged in shipping enterprises, purchased wharfage near Mile-End Cove, helped rebuild the Great Bridge in 1713, and in 1723 was one of the founders of the Congregational Church on the hill; but always did he retain the nondescript aspect of a man not greatly over thirty or thirty-five. As decades mounted up, this singular quality began to excite wide notice; but Curwen always explained it by saying that he came of hardy forefathers, and practiced[e] a simplicity of living which did not wear him out. How such simplicity could be reconciled with the inexplicable comings and goings of the secretive merchant, and with the queer gleaming[f] of his windows at all hours of night, was not very clear to the townsfolk; and they were prone to assign other reasons for his continued youth and longevity. It was held, for the most part, that Curwen's incessant mixings and boilings of chemicals had much to do

[a] and] *om.* C, D
[b] panic;] panic, D
[c] Providence;] Providence, D
[d] Stampers'] Stampers A, B [*not revised by HPL*], C, D
[e] practiced] practised C, D
[f] gleaming] gleamings C, D

with his condition. Gossip spoke of the strange substances he brought from London and the Indies on his ships or purchased in Newport, Boston,[a] and New York; and when old Dr. Jabez Bowen came from Rehoboth[b] and opened his apothecary shop across the Great Bridge at the Sign of the Unicorn and Mortar, there was ceaseless talk of the drugs, acids, and metals that the taciturn recluse incessantly bought or ordered from him. Acting on the assumption that Curwen possessed a wondrous and secret medical skill, many sufferers of various sorts applied to him for aid; but though he appeared to encourage their belief in a non-committal way, and always gave them odd-coloured potions in response to their requests, it was observed that his ministrations to others seldom proved of benefit. At length, when over fifty years had passed since the stranger's advent, and without producing more than five years' apparent change in his face and physique, the people began to whisper more darkly; and to meet more than half way[c] that desire for isolation which he had always shewn.[d]

Private letters and diaries of the period reveal, too, a multitude of other reasons why Joseph Curwen was marvelled at, feared, and finally shunned like a plague. His passion for graveyards, in which he was glimpsed at all hours and under all conditions, was notorious; though no one had witnessed any deed on his part which could actually be termed ghoulish. On the Pawtuxet Road he had a farm, at which he generally lived during the summer, and to which he would frequently be seen riding at various odd times of the day or night. Here his only visible servants, farmers, and caretakers were a sullen pair of aged[e] Narragansett Indians; the husband dumb and curiously scarred, and the wife of a very repulsive cast of countenance, probably due to a mixture of negro[f] blood. In the lean-to of this house was the laboratory where most of the chemical experiments were conducted. Curious porters and teamers who delivered bottles, bags,[g] or boxes at the small rear

[a] Boston,] Boston A, B, C, D
[b] Rehoboth] Behoboth C
[c] half way] half-way D
[d] shewn.] shown. D
[e] aged] *om.* D
[f] negro] Negro D
[g] bags,] bags A, B, C, D

door would exchange accounts of the fantastic flasks, crucibles, alembics, and furnaces they saw in the low[a] shelved room; and prophesied in whispers that the close-mouthed "chymist"—by which they meant *alchemist*[b]—would not be long in finding the Philosopher's Stone. The nearest neighbours to this farm—the Fenners, a quarter of a mile away—had still queerer things to tell of certain sounds which they insisted came from the Curwen place in the night. There were cries, they said, and sustained howlings; and they did not like the large number of livestock which thronged the pastures, for no such amount was needed to keep a lone old man and a very few servants in meat, milk, and wool. The identity of the stock seemed to change from week to week as new droves were purchased from the Kingstown farmers. Then, too, there was something very obnoxious about a certain great stone outbuilding with only high narrow slits for windows.

Great Bridge idlers likewise[c] had much to say of Curwen's town house in Olney Court; not so much the fine new one built in 1761, when the man must have been nearly a century old, but the first low gambrel-roofed one with the windowless attic and shingled sides,[d] whose timbers he took the peculiar precaution of burning after its demolition. Here there was less mystery, it is true; but the hours at which lights were seen, the secretiveness of the two swarthy foreigners who comprised the only menservants, the hideous indistinct mumbling of the incredibly aged French housekeeper, the large amounts of food seen to enter a door within which only four persons lived, and the *quality* of certain voices often heard in muffled conversation at highly unseasonable times, all combined with what was known of the Pawtuxet farm to give the place a bad name.

In choicer circles, too, the Curwen home was by no means undiscussed; for[e] as the newcomer had gradually worked into the church and trading life of the town, he had naturally made acquaintances of the better sort, whose company and conversation he was well fitted

[a] low] low, D
[b] *alchemist*] alchemist C
[c] likewise] *om.* D
[d] sides,] sides D
[e] for] for, D

by education[a] to enjoy. His birth was known to be good, since the Curwens or Corwins[b] of Salem needed no introduction in New England. It developed that Joseph Curwen had travelled much in very early life, living for a time in England and making at least two voyages to the Orient; and his speech, when he deigned to use it, was that of a learned and cultivated Englishman. But for some reason or other Curwen did not care for society. Whilst never actually rebuffing a visitor, he always reared such a wall of reserve that few could think of anything to say to him which would not sound inane.

There seemed to lurk in his bearing some cryptic, sardonic arrogance, as if he had come to find all human beings dull through having moved among stranger and more potent entities. When Dr. Checkley the famous wit[c] came from Boston in 1738[d] to be rector of King's Church, he did not neglect calling on one of whom he soon[e] heard so much; but left in a very short while because of some sinister undercurrent he detected in his host's discourse. Charles Ward told his father, when they discussed Curwen one winter evening, that he would give much to learn what the mysterious old man had said to the sprightly cleric, but that all diarists agree concerning Dr. Checkley's reluctance to repeat anything he had heard. The good man had been hideously shocked, and could never recall Joseph Curwen without a visible loss of the gay urbanity for which he was famed.

More definite, however, was the reason why another man of taste and breeding avoided the haughty hermit. In 1746 Mr. John Merritt, an elderly English gentleman of literary and scientific leanings, came from Newport to the town which was so rapidly overtaking it in standing, and built a fine country seat on the Neck in what is now the heart of the best residence section. He lived in considerable style and comfort, keeping the first coach and liveried servants in town, and taking great pride in his telescope, his microscope, and his well-chosen library of English and Latin books. Hearing of Curwen as the owner of the best

---

[a] by education] *om.* D
[b] Corwins] Carwens C, D
[c] Checkley . . . wit] Checkley, . . . wit, C, D
[d] 1738] 1783 C, D
[e] soon] had D

library in Providence, Mr. Merritt early paid him a call, and was more cordially received than most other callers at the house had been. His admiration for his host's ample shelves, which besides the Greek, Latin, and English classics were equipped with a remarkable battery of philosophical, mathematical,[a] and scientific works including Paracelsus, Agricola, Van Helmont, Sylvius, Glauber, Boyle, Boerhaave, Becher, and Stahl, led Curwen to suggest a visit to the farmhouse and laboratory whither he had never invited anyone before; and the two drove out at once in Mr. Merritt's coach.

Mr. Merritt always confessed to seeing nothing really horrible at the farmhouse, but maintained that the titles of the books in the special library of thaumaturgical, alchemical, and theological subjects which Curwen kept in a front room were alone sufficient to inspire him with a lasting loathing. Perhaps, however, the facial expression of the owner in exhibiting them contributed much of the prejudice. The bizarre collection, besides a host of standard works which Mr. Merritt was not too alarmed to envy, embraced nearly all the cabbalists,[b] daemonologists,[c] and magicians known to man; and was a treasure-house of lore in the doubtful realms of alchemy and astrology. Hermes Trismegistus[d] in Mesnard's edition, the "Turba Philosophorum",[e] Geber's "Liber Investigationis",[f] and Artephius' "Key of Wisdom"[g] all were there;[h] with the cabbalistic "Zohar",[i] Peter Jammy's set of Albertus Magnus,[j] Raymond Lully's "Ars Magna et Ultima"[k] in Zetzner's[l] edition,

---

[a] mathematical,] mathematical A, B, D
[b] cabbalists,] cabalists, C, D
[c] daemonologists,] demonologists, A, B, C, D
[d] Trismegistus] Trismogistus C
[e] "Turba Philosophorum",] *Turba Philosophorum,* A, B; *Turba Philosopharum,* C, D
[f] "Liber Investigationis",] *Liber Investigationis* A; *Liber Investiagionis,* B; *Liber Investigationis;* C, D
[g] Artephius' "Key of Wisdom"] Artephius' *Key of Wisdom* A, B; Artephous' *Key of Wisdom;* C; Artephous' *Key of Wisdom,* D
[h] there;] here; D
[i] cabbalistic "Zohar",] cabalistic *Zohar,* A, B, C, D
[j] Jammy's . . . Albertus Magnus,] Jamm's . . . *Albertus Magnus,* D
[k] "Ars Magna et Ultima"] *Ars Magna et Ultima* A, B, C, D
[l] Zetzner's] Zetsner's C, D

Roger Bacon's "Thesaurus Chemicus",[a] Fludd's "Clavis Alchimiae",[b] and Trithemius' "De Lapide Philosophico"[c] crowding them close. Mediaeval Jews and Arabs were represented in profusion, and Mr. Merritt turned pale when,[d] upon taking down a fine volume conspicuously labelled as the "Qanoon-e-Islam",[e] he found it was in truth the forbidden "Necronomicon"[f] of the mad Arab Abdul Alhazred, of which he had heard such monstrous things whispered some years previously after the exposure of nameless rites at the strange little fishing village of Kingsport, in the Province of the Massachusetts-Bay.

But oddly enough, the worthy gentleman owned himself most impalpably disquieted by a mere minor detail. On the huge mahogany table there lay face downward a badly worn copy of Borellus, bearing many cryptical marginalia and interlineations in Curwen's hand. The book was open at[g] about its middle, and one paragraph displayed such thick and tremulous pen-strokes beneath the lines of mystic black-letter[h] that the visitor could not resist scanning it through. Whether it was the nature of the passage underscored, or the feverish heaviness of the strokes which formed the underscoring, he could not tell; but something in that combination affected him very badly and very peculiarly. He recalled it to the end of his days, writing it down from memory in his diary and once trying to recite it to his close friend Dr. Checkley till he saw how greatly it disturbed the urbane rector. It read:

> "The essential Saltes of Animals may be so prepared and preserved, that an ingenious Man may have the whole[i] Ark of Noah in his owne Studie, and raise the fine Shape of an Animal out of its Ashes at his Pleasure;[j] and by[k] the lyke Method from the essential Saltes of humane

---

[a] "Thesaurus Chemicus",] *Thesaurus Chemicus,* A, B, C, D
[b] "Clavis Alchimiae",] *Clavis Alchimiae,* A, B, C, D
[c] "De Lapide Philosophico"] *De Lapide Philosophico* A, B, C, D
[d] when,] when D
[e] "Qanoon-e-Islam",] *Qanoon-e-Islam,* A, B; *Qanoon-é-Islam,* C, D
[f] "Necronomicon"] *Necronomicon* A, B, C, D
[g] at] to D
[h] black-letter] black-letters D
[i] whole] Whole C
[j] Pleasure;] Pleasure, D
[k] by] of C

Dust, a Philosopher may, without any criminal Necromancy, call up the Shape of any dead Ancestour from the Dust whereinto his Bodie has been incinerated."[a]

It was near the docks along the southerly part of the Town Street, however, that the worst things were muttered about Joseph Curwen. Sailors are superstitious folk; and the seasoned salts who manned the infinite rum, slave,[b] and molasses sloops, the rakish privateers,[c] and the great brigs of the Browns, Crawfords, and Tillinghasts, all made strange furtive signs of protection when they saw the slim, deceptively young-looking figure with its yellow hair and slight stoop[d] entering the Curwen warehouse in Doubloon Street or talking with captains and supercargoes[e] on the long quay where the Curwen ships rode restlessly. Curwen's own clerks and captains hated and feared him, and all his sailors were mongrel riff-raff from Martinique, St. Eustatius, Havana, or Port Royal. It was, in a way, the frequency with which these sailors were replaced[f] which inspired the acutest and most tangible part of the fear in which the old man was held. A crew would be turned loose in the town on shore leave, some of its members perhaps charged with this errand or that; and when reassembled it would be almost sure to lack one or more men. That many of the errands had concerned the farm on the Pawtuxet Road, and that few of the sailors had ever been seen to return from that place, was not forgotten; so that in time it became exceedingly difficult for Curwen to keep his oddly assorted hands. Almost invariably several would desert soon after hearing the gossip of the Providence wharves, and their replacement in the West Indies became an increasingly great problem to the merchant.

In 1760 Joseph Curwen was virtually an outcast, suspected of vague horrors and daemoniac[g] alliances which seemed all the more menacing because they could not be named, understood, or even proved to exist. The last straw may have come from the affair of the

[a] "The . . . incinerated."] The . . . incinerated. C, D
[b] slave,] slave A, B, C, D
[c] privateers,] privateers A, B, C, D
[d] stoop] stoop, D
[e] supercargoes] supercargos C, D
[f] replaced] replaced, A, B, C, D
[g] daemoniac] demoniac D

missing soldiers in 1758, for in March and April of that year two Royal regiments on their way to New France were quartered in Providence, and depleted by an inexplicable process far beyond the average rate of desertion. Rumour dwelt on the frequency with which Curwen was wont to be seen talking with the red-coated strangers; and as several of them began to be missed, people thought of the odd conditions among his own seamen. What would have happened if the regiments had not been ordered on, no one can tell.

Meanwhile the merchant's worldly affairs were prospering. He had a virtual monopoly of the town's trade in saltpetre, black pepper, and cinnamon, and easily led any other one shipping establishment save the Browns in his importation of brassware, indigo, cotton, woollens, salt, rigging, iron, paper,[a] and English goods of every kind. Such shopkeepers as James Green, at the Sign of the Elephant in Cheapside, the Russells, at the Sign of the Golden Eagle across the Bridge, or Clark and Nightingale at the Frying-Pan and Fish near the New Coffee-House, depended almost wholly upon him for their stock; and his arrangements with the local distillers, the Narragansett dairymen and horse-breeders,[b] and the Newport candle-makers, made him one of the prime exporters of the Colony.

Ostracised though he was, he did not lack for civic spirit of a sort. When the Colony House burned down, he subscribed handsomely to the lotteries by which the new brick one—still standing at the head of its parade in the old main street—was built in 1761. In that same year, too, he helped rebuild the Great Bridge after the October gale. He replaced many of the books of the public library consumed in the Colony House[c] fire, and bought heavily in the lottery that gave the muddy Market Parade and deep-rutted Town Street their pavement of great round stones with a brick footwalk[d] or "causey" in the middle. About this time, also, he built the plain but excellent new house whose doorway is still[e] such a triumph of carving. When the Whitefield

[a] paper,] paper A, B, C, D
[b] horse-breeders,] horse breeders, C
[c] Colony House] Colony-house A
[d] brick footwalk] foot-walk C, D
[e] still] *om.* D

adherents broke off from Dr. Cotton's hill church in 1743 and founded Deacon Snow's church across the Bridge, Curwen had gone with them; though his zeal and attendance soon abated. Now, however, he cultivated piety once more; as if to dispel the shadow which had thrown him into isolation and would soon begin to wreck his business fortunes if not sharply checked.

2.

The sight of this strange, pallid man, hardly middle-aged in aspect[a] yet certainly not less than a full century old, seeking at last to emerge from a cloud of fright and detestation too vague to pin down or analyse, was at once a pathetic, a dramatic, and a contemptible thing. Such is the power of wealth and of surface gestures, however, that there came indeed a slight abatement in the visible aversion displayed toward him; especially after the rapid disappearances of his sailors abruptly ceased. He must likewise have begun to practice[b] an extreme care and secrecy in his graveyard expeditions, for he was never again caught at such wanderings; whilst the rumours of uncanny sounds and manoeuvres[c] at his Pawtuxet farm diminished in proportion. His rate of food consumption and cattle replacement remained abnormally high; but not until modern times, when Charles Ward examined a set of his accounts and invoices in the Shepley Library, did it occur to any person—save one embittered youth, perhaps—to make dark comparisons between the large number of Guinea blacks he imported until 1766, and the disturbingly small number for whom he could produce bona fide bills of sale either to slave-dealers at the Great Bridge or to the planters of the Narragansett Country. Certainly, the cunning and ingenuity of this abhorred character were uncannily profound, once the necessity for their exercise had become impressed upon him.

But of course the effect of all this belated mending was necessarily slight. Curwen continued to be avoided and distrusted, as indeed the one fact of his continued air of youth at a great age would have been enough

[a] aspect] aspect, C, D
[b] practice] practise D
[c] manoeuvres] maneuvers D

to warrant; and he could see that in the end his fortunes would be likely to suffer. His elaborate studies and experiments, whatever they may have been, apparently required a heavy income for their maintenance; and since a change of environment would deprive him of the trading advantages he had gained, it would not have profited him to begin anew in a different region just then. Judgment demanded that he patch up his relations with the townsfolk of Providence, so that his presence might no longer be a signal for hushed conversation, transparent excuses of errands elsewhere, and a general atmosphere of constraint[a] and uneasiness. His clerks, being now reduced to the shiftless and impecunious residue whom no one else would employ, were giving him much worry; and he held to his sea-captains and mates only by shrewdness in gaining some kind of ascendancy over them—a mortgage, a promissory note, or a bit of information very pertinent to their welfare. In many cases, diarists have recorded with some awe, Curwen shewed[b] almost the power of a wizard in unearthing family secrets for questionable use. During the final five years of his life it seemed as though only direct talks with the long-dead could possibly have furnished some of the data which he had so glibly at his tongue's end.

About this time the crafty scholar hit upon a last desperate expedient to regain his footing in the community. Hitherto a complete hermit, he now determined to contract an advantageous marriage;[c] securing as a bride some lady whose unquestioned position would make all ostracism of his home impossible. It may be that he also had deeper reasons for wishing an alliance; reasons so far outside the known cosmic sphere that only papers found a century and a half after his death caused anyone to suspect them; but of this nothing certain can ever be learned. Naturally he was aware of the horror and indignation with which any ordinary courtship of his would be received, hence he looked about for some likely candidate upon whose parents he might exert a suitable pressure. Such candidates, he found, were not at all easy to discover;[d] since he had very particular requirements in the way of

---

[a] constraint] restraint C, D
[b] shewed] showed D
[c] marriage;] marriage, D
[d] discover;] discover, D

beauty, accomplishments, and social security. At length his survey narrowed down to the household of one of his best and oldest ship-captains, a widower of high birth and unblemished standing named Dutee[a] Tillinghast, whose only daughter Eliza seemed dowered with every conceivable advantage save prospects as an heiress. Capt.[b] Tillinghast was completely under the domination of Curwen; and consented, after a terrible interview in his cupolaed house on Power's Lane hill, to sanction the blasphemous alliance.

Eliza Tillinghast was at that time eighteen years of age, and had been reared as gently as the reduced circumstances of her father permitted. She had attended Stephen Jackson's school opposite the Court-House Parade;[c] and had been diligently instructed by her mother, before the latter's death of smallpox[d] in 1757, in[e] all the arts and refinements of domestic life. A sampler of hers, worked in 1753 at the age of nine, may still be found in the rooms[f] of the Rhode Island[g] Historical Society. After her mother's death she had kept the house, aided only by one old black woman. Her arguments with her father concerning the proposed Curwen marriage must have been painful indeed; but of these we have no record. Certain it is that her engagement to young Ezra Weeden, second mate of the Crawford packet *Enterprise,* was dutifully broken off, and that her union with Joseph Curwen took place on the seventh[h] of March, 1763, in the Baptist church, in the presence of one of the most distinguished assemblages which the town could boast; the ceremony being performed by the younger Samuel Winsor.[i] The *Gazette* mentioned the event very briefly, and in most surviving copies the item in question seems to be cut or torn out. Ward found a single intact copy after much search in the archives of a private collector of note, observing with amusement the meaningless urbanity of the language:

[a] Dutee] Dutie C, D
[b] Capt.] Captain C, D
[c] Court-House Parade;] Court House Parade C, D
[d] smallpox] small-pox C, D
[e] in] on C
[f] rooms] room C
[g] Rhode Island] Rhode-Island A
[h] seventh] 7th A, B
[i] Winsor.] Winson. C, D

"Monday evening last, Mr. Joseph Curwen, of this Town, Merchant, was married to Miss Eliza Tillinghast, Daughter of Capt. Dutee[a] Tillinghast, a young Lady[b] who has real Merit, added to a beautiful Person, to grace the connubial State and perpetuate its Felicity."[c]

The collection of Durfee-Arnold letters,[d] discovered by Charles Ward shortly before his first reputed madness in the private collection of Melville F. Peters, Esq., of George St.,[e] and covering this and a somewhat antecedent period, throws vivid light on the outrage done to public sentiment by this ill-assorted match. The social influence of the Tillinghasts, however, was not to be denied; and once more Joseph Curwen found his house frequented by persons whom he could never otherwise have induced to cross his threshold. His acceptance was by no means complete, and his bride was socially the sufferer through her forced venture; but at all events the wall of utter[f] ostracism was somewhat worn down. In his treatment of his wife the strange bridegroom astonished both her and the community by displaying an extreme graciousness and consideration. The new house in Olney Court was now wholly free from disturbing manifestations, and although Curwen was much absent at the Pawtuxet farm which his wife never visited, he seemed more like a normal citizen than at any other time in his long years of residence. Only one person remained in open enmity with him, this being the youthful ship's officer whose engagement to Eliza Tillinghast had been so abruptly broken. Ezra Weeden had frankly vowed vengeance; and[g] though of a quiet and ordinarily[h] mild disposition, was now gaining a hate-bred,[i] dogged purpose which boded no good to the usurping husband.

On the seventh of May, 1765, Curwen's only child Ann was born;

---

[a] Capt. Dutee] Captain Dutie C, D
[b] Lady] lady C, D
[c] "Monday . . . Felicity."] Monday . . . Felicity. C, D
[d] letters,] letters A
[e] Peters, Esq., of George St.,] Peters of George Street, C, D
[f] utter] *end of* B
[g] vengeance; and] vengeance and, D
[h] ordinarily] originally C
[i] hate-bred,] hate-bred D

and was christened by the Rev.[a] John Graves of King's Church, of which both husband and wife had become communicants shortly after their marriage,[b] in order to compromise between their respective Congregational and Baptist affiliations. The record of this birth, as well as that of the marriage two years before, was stricken from most copies of the church and town annals where it ought to appear; and Charles Ward located both with the greatest difficulty after his discovery of the widow's change of name had apprised him of his own relationship, and engendered the feverish interest which culminated in his madness. The birth entry, indeed, was found very curiously through correspondence with the heirs of the loyalist Dr. Graves, who had taken with him a duplicate set of records when he left his pastorate at the outbreak of the Revolution. Ward had tried this source because he knew that his great-great-grandmother Ann Tillinghast Potter[c] had been an Episcopalian.

Shortly after the birth of his daughter, an event he seemed to welcome with a fervour greatly out of keeping with his usual coldness, Curwen resolved to sit for a portrait. This he had painted by a very gifted Scotsman named Cosmo Alexander, then a resident of Newport, and since famous as the early teacher of Gilbert Stuart. The likeness was said to have been executed on a wall-panel of the library of the house in Olney Court, but neither of the two old diaries mentioning it gave any hint of its ultimate disposition. At this period the erratic scholar shewed[d] signs of unusual abstraction, and spent as much time as he possibly could at his farm on the Pawtuxet Road. He seemed, it was stated, in a condition of suppressed excitement or suspense; as if[e] expecting some phenomenal thing or on the brink of some strange discovery. Chemistry or alchemy would appear to have played a great part, for he took from his house to the farm the greater number of his volumes on that subject.

His affectation of civic interest did not diminish, and he lost no opportunities for helping such leaders as Stephen Hopkins, Joseph

[a] Rev.] Reverend C, D
[b] marriage,] marriages D
[c] great-great-grandmother . . . Potter] great-great-grandmother, . . . Potter, D
[d] shewed] showed D
[e] if] *om.* A [*text originally read* as if on this; if on this *crossed out and* expecting *written over it—the omission of* if *being an apparent error*]

Brown, and Benjamin West in their efforts to raise the cultural tone of the town, which was then much below the level of Newport in its patronage of the liberal arts. He had helped Daniel Jenckes found his bookshop in 1763, and was thereafter his best customer;[a] extending aid likewise to the struggling *Gazette* that appeared each Wednesday at the Sign of Shakespear's Head. In politics he ardently supported Governor Hopkins against the Ward party whose prime strength was in Newport, and his really eloquent speech at Hacker's[b] Hall in 1765 against the setting off of North Providence as a separate town with a pro-Ward vote in the General Assembly did more than any other one thing to wear down the prejudice against him. But Ezra Weeden, who watched him closely, sneered cynically at all this outward activity; and freely swore it was no more than a mask for some nameless traffick[c] with the blackest gulfs of Tartarus. The revengeful youth began a systematic study of the man and his doings whenever he was in port; spending hours at night by the wharves with a dory in readiness when he saw lights in the Curwen warehouses, and following the small boat which would sometimes steal quietly off and down the bay. He also kept as close a watch as possible on the Pawtuxet farm, and was once severely bitten by the dogs the old Indian couple loosed upon him.

3.

In 1766 came the final change in Joseph Curwen. It was very sudden, and gained[d] wide notice amongst the curious townsfolk; for the air of suspense and expectancy dropped like an old cloak, giving instant place to an ill-concealed exaltation of perfect triumph. Curwen seemed to have difficulty in restraining himself from public harangues on what he had found or learned or made; but apparently the need of secrecy was greater than the longing to share his rejoicing, for no explanation was ever offered by him. It was after this transition, which appears to have come early in July, that the sinister scholar began to astonish

[a] customer;] customer, D
[b] Hacker's] Hacher's C, D
[c] traffick] traffic D
[d] gained] gained a D

people by his possession of information which only their long-dead ancestors would seem to be able to impart.

But Curwen's feverish secret activities by no means ceased with this change. On the contrary, they tended rather to increase; so that more and more of his shipping business was handled by the captains whom he now bound to him by ties of fear as potent as those of bankruptcy had been. He altogether abandoned the slave trade, alleging that its profits were constantly decreasing. Every possible moment was spent at the Pawtuxet farm; though there were rumours now and then of his presence in places which, though not actually near graveyards, were yet so situated in relation to graveyards that thoughtful people wondered just how thorough the old merchant's change of habits really was. Ezra Weeden, though his periods of espionage were necessarily brief and intermittent on account of his sea voyaging, had a vindictive persistence which the bulk of the practical townsfolk and farmers lacked; and subjected Curwen's affairs to a scrutiny such as they had never had before.

Many of the odd manoeuvres of the strange merchant's vessels had been taken for granted on account of the unrest of the times, when every colonist seemed determined to resist the provisions of the Sugar Act which hampered a prominent traffick.[a] Smuggling and evasion were the rule in Narragansett Bay, and nocturnal landings of illicit cargoes were continuous commonplaces. But Weeden, night after night[b] following the lighters or[c] small sloops which he saw steal off from the Curwen warehouses at the Town Street docks, soon felt assured that it was not merely His Majesty's armed ships which the sinister skulker was anxious to avoid. Prior to the change in 1766 these boats had for the most part contained chained negroes,[d] who were carried down and across the bay and landed at an obscure point on the shore just north of Pawtuxet; being afterward driven up the bluff and across country to the Curwen farm, where they were locked in that enormous stone outbuilding which had only high narrow slits for windows. After that

[a] traffick.] traffic. D
[b] night] night, D
[c] or] of C
[d] negroes,] Negroes, D

change, however, the whole programme was altered. Importation of slaves ceased at once, and for a time Curwen abandoned his midnight sailings. Then, about the spring of 1767, a new policy appeared. Once more the lighters grew wont to put out from the black,[a] silent docks, and this time they would go down the bay some distance, perhaps as far as Namquit[b] Point, where they would meet and receive cargo from strange ships of considerable size and widely varied appearance. Curwen's sailors would then deposit this cargo at the usual point on the shore, and transport it overland to the farm; locking it in the same cryptical stone building which had formerly received the negroes.[c] The cargo consisted almost wholly of boxes and cases, of which a large proportion were oblong and heavy and disturbingly suggestive of coffins.

Weeden always watched the farm with unremitting assiduity;[d] visiting it each night for long periods, and seldom letting a week go by without a sight except when the ground bore a footprint-revealing snow. Even then he would often walk as close as possible in the travelled road or on the ice of the neighbouring river[e] to see what tracks others might have left. Finding his own vigils interrupted by nautical duties, he hired a tavern companion named Eleazar Smith to continue the survey during his absences; and between them the two could have set in motion some extraordinary rumours. That they did not do so was only because they knew the effect of publicity would be to warn their quarry and make further progress impossible. Instead, they wished to learn something definite before taking any action. What they did learn must have been startling indeed, and Charles Ward spoke many times to his parents of his regret at Weeden's later burning of his notebooks. All that can be told of their discoveries is what Eleazar Smith jotted down in a none too coherent diary, and what other diarists and letter writers have timidly repeated from the statements which they finally made—and according to which the farm was only the outer shell of some vast and

[a] black,] black C, D
[b] Namquit] Nanquit C, D
[c] negroes.] Negroes. D
[d] assiduity;] assiduity, C, D
[e] river] river, C, D

revolting menace, of a scope and depth too profound and intangible for more than shadowy comprehension.

It is gathered that Weeden and Smith became early convinced that a great series of tunnels and catacombs, inhabited by a very sizeable staff of persons besides the old Indian and his wife, underlay the farm. The house was an old peaked relic of the middle seventeenth century with enormous stack chimney and diamond-paned lattice windows, the laboratory being in a lean-to toward the north, where the roof came nearly to the ground. This building stood clear of any other; yet[a] judging by the different voices heard at odd times within, it must have been accessible through secret passages beneath. These voices, before 1766, were mere mumblings and negro whimperings[b] and frenzied screams, coupled with curious chants or invocations. After that date, however, they assumed a very singular and terrible cast as they ran the gamut betwixt dronings of dull acquiescence and explosions of frantic pain or[c] fury, rumblings of conversation and whines of entreaty, pantings of eagerness and shouts of protest. They appeared to be in different languages, all known to Curwen, whose rasping accents were frequently distinguishable in reply, reproof, or threatening.[d] Sometimes it seemed that several persons must be in the house; Curwen, certain captives, and the guards of those captives. There were voices of a sort that neither Weeden nor Smith had ever heard before despite their wide knowledge of foreign parts,[e] and many that they did seem to place as belonging to this or that nationality. The nature of the conversations seemed always a kind of catechism, as if Curwen were extorting some sort of information from terrified or rebellious prisoners.

Weeden had many verbatim reports of overheard scraps in his notebook, for English, French, and Spanish, which he knew, were frequently used; but of these nothing has survived. He did, however, say that besides a few ghoulish dialogues in which the past affairs of Providence families were concerned, most of the questions and

---

[a] yet] but C; yet, D
[b] negro whimperings] Negro whisperings D
[c] pain or] *om.* D
[d] threatening.] threatening. ¶ C, D
[e] parts,] ports, C, D

answers he could understand were historical or scientific; occasionally pertaining to very remote places and ages. Once, for example, an alternately raging and sullen figure was questioned in French about the Black Prince's massacre at Limoges in 1370, as if there were some hidden reason which he ought to know. Curwen asked the prisoner— if prisoner it were—whether the order to slay was given because of the Sign of the Goat found on the altar in the ancient Roman crypt beneath the Cathedral,[a] or whether the Dark Man of the Haute Vienne Coven had spoken[b] the Three Words. Failing to obtain replies, the inquisitor had seemingly resorted to extreme means; for there was a terrific shriek followed by silence and muttering and a bumping sound.

None of these colloquies were[c] ever ocularly witnessed, since the windows were always heavily draped. Once, though, during a discourse in an unknown tongue, a shadow was seen on the curtain which startled Weeden exceedingly; reminding him of one of the puppets in a show he had seen in the autumn of 1764 in Hacker's[d] Hall, when a man from Germantown, Pennsylvania, had given a clever mechanical spectacle advertised as a "View of the Famous City of Jerusalem, in which are represented Jerusalem, the Temple of Solomon, his Royal Throne, the noted Towers, and Hills, likewise the Sufferings of Our Saviour from the Garden of Gethsemane to the Cross on the Hill of Golgotha; an artful piece of Statuary, Worthy to be seen by the Curious." It was on this occasion that the listener, who had crept close to the window of the front room whence the speaking proceeded, gave a start which roused the old Indian pair and caused them to loose the dogs on him. After that no more conversations were ever heard in the house, and Weeden and Smith concluded that Curwen had transferred his field of action to regions below.

That such regions in truth existed, seemed amply clear from many things. Faint cries and groans unmistakably came up now and then from what appeared to be the solid earth in places far from any structure;

[a] Cathedral,] cathedral, C, D
[b] spoken] spoke D
[c] were] was C
[d] Hacker's] Hacher's C, D

whilst hidden in the bushes along the river-bank[a] in the rear, where the high ground sloped steeply down to the valley of the Pawtuxet, there was found an arched oaken door in a frame of heavy masonry, which was obviously an entrance to caverns within the hill. When or how these catacombs could have been constructed, Weeden was unable to say; but he frequently pointed out how easily the place might have been reached by bands of unseen workmen from the river. Joseph Curwen put his mongrel seamen to diverse uses indeed! During the heavy spring rains of 1769 the two watchers kept a sharp eye on the steep river-bank[b] to see if any subterrene secrets might be washed to light, and were rewarded by the sight of a profusion of both human and animal bones in places where deep gullies had been worn in the banks. Naturally[c] there might be many explanations of such things in the rear of a stock farm, and in a locality where old Indian burying-grounds[d] were common, but Weeden and Smith drew their own inferences.

It was in January[e] 1770, whilst Weeden and Smith were still debating vainly on what, if anything, to think or do about the whole bewildering business, that the incident of the *Fortaleza* occurred. Exasperated by the burning of the revenue sloop *Liberty* at Newport during the previous summer, the customs fleet under Admiral Wallace had adopted an increased vigilance concerning strange vessels; and on this occasion His Majesty's armed schooner *Cygnet*, under Capt. Charles Leslie,[f] captured after a short pursuit one early morning[g] the snow[h] *Fortaleza* of Barcelona, Spain, under Capt.[i] Manuel Arruda, bound according to its log from Grand Cairo, Egypt, to Providence. When searched for contraband material, this ship revealed the astonishing fact that its cargo consisted exclusively of Egyptian mummies, consigned to "Sailor A. B. C.", who would come to remove

[a] river-bank] riverbank D
[b] river-bank] riverbank D
[c] Naturally] Naturally, C, D
[d] burying-grounds] burying grounds D
[e] January] January, D
[f] Capt. Charles Leslie,] Captain Charles Leshe, C; Captain Harry Leshe, D
[g] captured . . . morning] captured, . . . morning, D
[h] snow] scow C, D
[i] Capt.] Captain C, D

his goods in a lighter just off Namquit[a] Point and whose identity Capt.[b] Arruda felt himself in honour bound not to reveal. The Vice-Admiralty Court at Newport, at a loss what to do in view of the non-contraband nature of the cargo on the one hand and of the unlawful secrecy of the entry on the other hand, compromised on Collector Robinson's recommendation by freeing the ship but forbidding it a port in Rhode Island waters. There were later rumours of its having been seen in Boston Harbour, though it never openly entered the Port of Boston.

This extraordinary incident did not fail of wide remark in Providence,[c] and there were not many who doubted the existence of some connexion[d] between the cargo of mummies and the sinister Joseph Curwen. His exotic studies and his curious chemical importations being common knowledge, and his fondness for graveyards being common suspicion;[e] it did not take much imagination to link him with a freakish importation which could not conceivably have been destined for anyone else in the town. As if conscious of this natural belief, Curwen took care to speak casually on several occasions of the chemical value of the balsams found in mummies; thinking perhaps that he might make the affair seem less unnatural, yet stopping just short of admitting his participation. Weeden and Smith, of course, felt no doubt whatsoever of the significance of the thing; and indulged in the wildest theories concerning Curwen and his monstrous labours.

The following spring, like that of the year before, had heavy rains; and the watchers kept careful track of the river-bank behind the Curwen farm. Large sections were washed away, and a certain number of bones discovered; but no glimpse was afforded of any actual subterranean chambers of burrows. Something was rumoured, however, at the village of Pawtuxet about a mile below, where the river flows in falls over a rocky terrace to join the placid landlocked[f] cove. There, where quaint old cottages climbed the hill from the rustic

---

[a] Namquit] Nanquit C, D
[b] Capt.] Captain C, D
[c] Providence,] Providence A, C, D
[d] connexion] connection A, D
[e] suspicion;] suspicion, C
[f] landlocked] land-locked C

bridge, and fishing-smacks[a] lay anchored at their sleepy docks, a vague report went round of things that were floating down the river and flashing into sight for a minute as they went over the falls. Of course the Pawtuxet is a long river which winds through many settled regions abounding in graveyards, and of course the spring rains had been very heavy; but the fisherfolk about the bridge did not like the wild way that one of the things stared as it shot down to the still water below, or the way that another half cried out[b] although its condition had greatly departed from that of objects which normally cry out. That rumour sent Smith—for Weeden was just then at sea—in haste to the river-bank behind the farm; where surely enough there remained the evidences of an extensive cave-in. There was, however, no trace of a passage into the steep bank; for the miniature avalanche had left behind a solid wall of mixed earth and shrubbery from aloft. Smith went to the extent of some experimental digging, but was deterred by lack of success—or perhaps by fear of possible success. It is interesting to speculate on what the persistent and revengeful Weeden would have done had he been ashore at the time.

4.

By the autumn of 1770 Weeden decided that the time was ripe to tell others of his discoveries; for he had a large number of facts to link together, and a second eye-witness to refute the possible charge that jealousy and vindictiveness had spurred his fancy. As his first confidant he selected Capt.[c] James Mathewson of the *Enterprise,* who on the one hand knew him well enough not to doubt his veracity, and on the other hand was sufficiently influential in the town to be heard in turn with respect. The colloquy took place in an upper room of Sabin's Tavern near the docks, with Smith present to corroborate virtually every statement; and it could be seen that Capt.[d] Mathewson was tremendously impressed. Like nearly everyone else in the town,[e] he

[a] fishing-smacks] fishing smacks D
[b] out] out, D
[c] Capt.] Captain C, D
[d] Capt.] Captain C, D
[e] town,] town C, D

had had black suspicions of his own anent Joseph Curwen; hence it needed only this confirmation and enlargement of data to convince him absolutely. At the end of the conference he was very grave, and enjoined strict silence upon the two younger men. He would, he said, transmit the information separately to some ten or so of the most learned and prominent citizens of Providence; ascertaining their views and following whatever advice they might have to offer. Secrecy would probably be essential in any case, for this was no matter that the town constables or militia could cope with;[a] and above all else the excitable crowd must be kept in ignorance, lest there be enacted in these already troublous times a repetition of that frightful Salem panic of less than a century before which had first brought Curwen hither.

The right persons to tell, he believed, would be Dr. Benjamin West, whose pamphlet on the late transit of Venus proved him a scholar and keen thinker; Rev.[b] James Manning, President of the College[c] which had just moved up from Warren and was temporarily housed in the new King Street schoolhouse awaiting the completion of its building on the hill above Presbyterian-Lane;[d] ex-Governor Stephen Hopkins, who had been a member of the Philosophical Society at Newport, and was a man of very broad perceptions;[e] John Carter, publisher of the *Gazette;* all four of the Brown brothers, John, Joseph, Nicholas,[f] and Moses, who formed the recognised local magnates, and of whom Joseph was an amateur scientist of parts; old Dr. Jabez Bowen, whose erudition was considerable, and who had much first-hand knowledge of Curwen's odd purchases;[g] and Capt.[h] Abraham Whipple, a privateersman of phenomenal boldness and energy who could be counted on to lead in any active measures needed. These men, if favourable, might eventually be brought together for collective deliberation; and with them would rest the responsibility of deciding

[a] with;] with, D
[b] Rev.] Reverend C, D
[c] College] College, D
[d] Presbyterian-Lane;] Presbyterian Lane; D
[e] perceptions;] perception; C
[f] Nicholas,] Nicholas A, C, D
[g] purchases;] purchases, A, D
[h] Capt.] Captain C, D

whether or not to inform the Governor of the Colony, Joseph Wanton of Newport, before taking action.

The mission of Capt.[a] Mathewson prospered beyond his highest expectations; for whilst he found one or two of the chosen confidants somewhat sceptical of the possible ghastly[b] side of Weeden's tale, there was not one who did not think it necessary to take some sort of secret and coördinated[c] action. Curwen, it was clear, formed a vague potential menace to the welfare of the town and Colony; and must be eliminated at any cost. Late in December 1770[d] a group of eminent townsmen met at the home of Stephen Hopkins and debated tentative measures. Weeden's notes, which he had given to Capt.[e] Mathewson, were carefully read; and he and Smith were summoned to give testimony anent details. Something very like fear seized the whole assemblage before the meeting was over, though there ran through that fear a grim determination which Capt.[f] Whipple's bluff and resonant profanity best expressed. They would not notify the Governor, because a more than legal course seemed necessary. With hidden powers of uncertain extent apparently at his disposal, Curwen was not a man who could safely be warned to leave town. Nameless reprisals might ensue, and[g] even if the sinister creature complied, the removal would be no more than the shifting of an unclean burden to another place. The times were lawless, and[h] men who had flouted the King's revenue forces for years were not the ones to balk at sterner things when duty impelled. Curwen must be surprised at his Pawtuxet farm by a large raiding party[i] of seasoned privateersmen and given one decisive chance to explain himself. If he proved a madman, amusing himself with shrieks[j] and imaginary conversations in different voices, he would be properly

[a] Capt.] Captain C, D
[b] ghastly] ghostly C, D
[c] coördinated] co-ordinated D
[d] 1770] 1770, C, D
[e] Capt.] Captain C, D
[f] Capt.] Captain C, D
[g] and] and, D
[h] and] and the D
[i] raiding party] raiding-party A, C, D
[j] shrieks] shrieked C, D

confined. If something graver appeared,[a] and if the underground horrors indeed turned out to be real, he and all with him must die. It could be done quietly, and even the widow and her father need not be told how it came about.

While these serious steps were under discussion there occurred in the town an incident so terrible and inexplicable that for a time little else was mentioned for miles around. In the middle of a moonlight January night with heavy snow underfoot there resounded over the river and up the hill a shocking series of cries which brought sleepy heads to every window; and people around Weybosset Point saw a great white thing plunging frantically along the badly cleared space in front of the Turk's Head. There was a baying of dogs in the distance, but this subsided as soon as the clamour of the awakened town became audible. Parties of men with lanterns and muskets hurried out to see what was happening, but nothing rewarded their search. The next morning, however, a giant, muscular body, stark naked, was found on the jams of ice around the southern piers of the Great Bridge, where the Long Dock stretched out beside Abbott's distil-house, and the identity of this object became a theme for endless speculation and whispering. It was not so much the younger as the older folk who whispered, for only in the patriarchs did that rigid face with horror-bulging eyes strike any chord of memory. They, shaking as they did so, exchanged furtive murmurs of wonder and fear; for in those stiff, hideous features lay a resemblance so marvellous as to be almost an identity—and that identity was with a man who had died full fifty years before.

Ezra Weeden was present at the finding; and remembering the baying of the night before, set out along Weybosset Street and across Muddy Dock Bridge whence the sound had come. He had a curious expectancy, and was not surprised when, reaching the edge of the settled district where the street merged into the Pawtuxet Road, he came upon some very curious tracks in the snow. The naked giant had been pursued by dogs and many booted men, and the returning tracks of the hounds and their masters could be easily traced. They had given up the chase upon coming too near the town. Weeden smiled grimly, and as a perfunctory detail traced the footprints back to their source. It

[a] appeared,] appeared D

was the Pawtuxet farm of Joseph Curwen, as he well knew it would be; and he would have given much had the yard been less confusingly trampled. As it was, he dared not seem too interested in full daylight. Dr. Bowen, to whom Weeden went at once with his report, performed an autopsy on the strange corpse, and discovered peculiarities which baffled him utterly. The digestive tracts of the huge man seemed never to have been in use, whilst the whole skin had a coarse, loosely knit[a] texture impossible to account for. Impressed by what the old men whispered of this body's likeness to the long-dead blacksmith Daniel Green, whose great-grandson Aaron Hoppin was a supercargo in Curwen's employ, Weeden asked casual questions till he found where Green was buried. That night a party of ten visited the old North Burying Ground opposite Herrenden's Lane and opened a grave. They found it vacant, precisely as they had expected.

Meanwhile arrangements had been made with the post riders to intercept Joseph Curwen's mail, and shortly before the incident of the naked body there was found a letter from one Jedediah Orne of Salem which made the cooperating[b] citizens think deeply. Parts of it, copied and preserved in the private archives of the Smith[c] family where Charles Ward found it, ran as follows:

> "I delight that you continue in y[e] Gett'g[d] at Olde Matters in your Way, and doe not think better was done at Mr.[e] Hutchinson's in Salem-Village. Certainely, there was Noth'g butt y[e] liveliest Awfulness in that which H. rais'd upp from What he[f] cou'd gather onlie a part of. What you sente,[g] did not Worke, whether because of[h] Any Thing miss'g, or because y[e] Wordes were not Righte from my Speak'g or y[r] Copy'g. I alone[i] am at a Loss. I have not y[e] Chymicall art to followe Borellus, and owne my Self confounded by y[e] VII. Booke of y[e] Necronomicon[j] that you recommende.

---

[a] loosely knit] loosely-knit A, C, D
[b] coöperating] co-operating D
[c] Smith] *om.* D
[d] y[e] Gett'g] ye getting C, D [*All instances of* y[e] *and* y[r] *printed as* ye *and* yr *in C and D*]
[e] Mr.] Mr, D
[f] What he] what he C; what we D
[g] sente,] sente D
[h] of] *om.* C, D
[i] Copy'g. I alone] copy'g. Alone C, D
[j] Necronomicon] *Necronomicon* C, D

But I wou'd have you Observe what was tolde[a] to us aboute tak'g Care whom to calle up, for you are Sensible what Mr. Mather writ in ye Magnalia[b] of ————, and can judge how truely[c] that Horrendous thing is reported. I say to you againe, doe not call up[d] Any that you can not put downe; by the Which I meane, Any that can in Turne call up somewhat against you, whereby your Powerfullest Devices may not be of use. Ask of the Lesser, lest the Greater[e] shall not wish to Answer, and shall commande more than you. I was frighted when I read of your know'g what Ben Zariatnatmik[f] hadde in his ebony[g] Boxe, for I was conscious who must have tolde you. And againe I ask that you shalle write me as Jedediah and not Simon. In this Community a Man may not live too long, and you knowe my Plan by which I came back as my Son. I am desirous you will Acquaint me with what ye Blacke Man learnt from Sylvanus Cocidius in ye Vault, under ye Roman Wall,[h] and will be oblig'd for ye Lend'g[i] of ye MS. you speak of."[j]

Another and unsigned letter from Philadelphia provoked equal thought, especially for the following passage:

"I will observe what you say respecting the sending of Accounts only by y^r Vessels, but can not always be certain when to expect them. In the Matter spoke of, I require onlie[k] one more thing; but wish to be sure I apprehend you exactly. You inform me, that no Part must be missing if the finest Effects are to be had, but you can not but know how hard it is to be sure. It seems a great Hazard and Burthen to take away the whole Box, and in Town (i.e.[l] St. Peter's, St. Paul's, St. Mary's, or Christ Church) it can scarce be done at all. But I know what Imperfections were in the one I[m] rais'd up October last, and how many live Specimens you were

---

[a] tolde] told D
[b] Magnalia] Magnolia C
[c] truely] truly D
[d] up] upp C, D
[e] Greater] greater C, D
[f] Zariatnatmik] Zaristnatmik C, D
[g] ebony] Ebony C, D
[h] Wall,] wall, C, D
[i] Lend'g] lend'g A
[j] "I . . . of."] I . . . of. C, D
[k] onlie] only C, D
[l] i.e.] i. e., C; i.e., D
[m] I] om. C, D

forc'd to imploy[a] before you hit upon the right Mode in the year 1766; so will be guided by you in all Matters. I am impatient for y[r] Brig, and inquire daily at Mr. Biddle's Wharf."[b]

A third suspicious letter was in an unknown tongue and even an unknown alphabet. In the Smith diary found by Charles Ward a single oft-repeated combination of characters is clumsily copied; and authorities at Brown University have pronounced the alphabet Amharic or Abyssinian, although they do not recognise the word. None of these epistles was ever delivered to Curwen, though the disappearance of Jedediah Orne from Salem as recorded shortly afterward shewed[c] that the Providence men took certain quiet steps. The Pennsylvania Historical Society also has some curious letters received by Dr. Shippen regarding the presence of an unwholesome character in Philadelphia. But more decisive steps were in the air, and it is in the secret assemblages of sworn and tested sailors and faithful old privateersmen in the Brown warehouses by night that we must look for the main fruits of Weeden's disclosures. Slowly and surely a plan of campaign was under development which would leave no trace of Joseph Curwen's noxious mysteries.

Curwen, despite all precautions, apparently felt that something was in the wind; for he was now remarked to wear an unusually worried look. His coach was seen at all hours in the town and on the Pawtuxet Road,[d] and he dropped little by little the air of forced geniality with which he had latterly sought to combat the town's prejudice. The nearest neighbours to his farm, the Fenners, one night remarked a great shaft of light shooting into the sky from some aperture in the roof of that cryptical stone building with the high,[e] excessively narrow windows; an event which they quickly communicated to John Brown in Providence. Mr. Brown had become the executive leader of the select group bent on Curwen's extirpation, and had informed the Fenners that some action was about to be taken. This he deemed needful

---

[a] imploy] employ D
[b] "I . . . Wharf."] I . . . Wharf. C, D
[c] shewed] showed D
[d] Road,] road, C
[e] high,] high C

because of the impossibility of their not witnessing the final raid; and he explained his course by saying that Curwen was known to be a spy of the customs officers at Newport, against whom the hand of every Providence shipper, merchant, and farmer was openly or clandestinely raised. Whether the ruse was wholly believed by neighbours who had seen so many queer things is not certain;[a] but at any rate the Fenners were willing to connect any evil with a man of such queer ways. To them Mr. Brown had entrusted the duty of watching the Curwen farmhouse, and of regularly reporting every incident which took place there.

5.

The probability that Curwen was on guard and attempting unusual things, as suggested by the odd shaft of light, precipitated at last the action so carefully devised by the band of serious citizens. According to the Smith diary a company of about 100[b] men met at 10 p.m.[c] on Friday, April 12th,[d] 1771, in the great room of Thurston's Tavern at the Sign of the Golden Lion on Weybosset Point across the Bridge.[e] Of the guiding group of prominent men in addition to the leader John Brown[f] there were present Dr. Bowen,[g] with his case of surgical instruments, President Manning without the great periwig (the largest in the Colonies) for which he was noted, Governor Hopkins, wrapped in his dark cloak and accompanied by his seafaring brother Esek,[h] whom he had initiated at the last moment with the permission of the rest, John Carter, Capt.[i] Mathewson, and Capt.[j] Whipple, who was to lead the actual raiding party. These chiefs conferred apart in a rear

[a] certain;] certain, C, D
[b] 100] one hundred D
[c] 10 p.m.] ten P.M. C; ten p.m. D
[d] 12th,] twelfth, C, D
[e] Bridge.] bridge. D
[f] leader John Brown] leader, John Brown, C, D
[g] Bowen,] Brown, C
[h] Esek,] Eseh C; Eseh, D
[i] Capt.] Captain C, D
[j] Capt.] Captain C, D

chamber, after which Capt.[a] Whipple emerged to the great room and gave the gathered seamen their last oaths and instructions. Eleazar[b] Smith was with the leaders as they sat in the rear apartment awaiting the arrival of Ezra Weeden, whose duty was to keep track of Curwen and report the departure of his coach for the farm.

About 10:30[c] a heavy rumble was heard on the Great Bridge, followed by the sound of a coach in the street outside; and at that hour there was no need of waiting for Weeden in order to know that the doomed man had set out for his last night of unhallowed wizardry. A moment later, as the receding coach clattered faintly over the Muddy Dock Bridge, Weeden appeared; and the raiders fell silently into military order in the street, shouldering the firelocks, fowling-pieces, or whaling harpoons which they had with them. Weeden and Smith were with the party, and of the deliberating citizens there were present for active service Capt.[d] Whipple, the leader, Capt. Esek[e] Hopkins, John Carter, President Manning, Capt.[f] Mathewson, and Dr. Bowen; together with Moses Brown, who had come up at the eleventh hour though absent from the preliminary session in the tavern. All these freemen and their hundred sailors began the long march without delay, grim and a trifle apprehensive as they left the Muddy Dock behind and mounted the gentle rise of Broad Street toward the Pawtuxet Road. Just beyond Elder Snow's church some of the men turned back to take a parting look at Providence lying outspread under the early spring stars. Steeples and gables rose dark and shapely, and salt breezes swept up gently from the cove north of the Bridge. Vega was climbing above the great hill across the water, whose crest of trees was broken by the roof-line of the unfinished College edifice. At the foot of that hill, and along the narrow mounting lanes of its side,[g] the old town dreamed; Old Providence, for whose safety and sanity so monstrous and colossal a blasphemy was about to be wiped out.

[a] Capt.] Captain C, D
[b] Eleazar] Eleazer D
[c] 10:30] ten-thirty C, D
[d] Capt.] Captain C, D
[e] Capt. Esek] Captain Eseh C, D
[f] Capt.] Captain C, D
[g] hill, . . . side,] hill . . . side D

An hour and a quarter later the raiders arrived, as previously agreed, at the Fenner farmhouse;[a] where they heard a final report on their intended victim. He had reached his farm over half an hour before, and the strange light had soon afterward shot once into the sky. There[b] were no lights in any visible windows, but this[c] was always the case of late. Even as this news was given another great glare arose toward the south, and the party realised that they had indeed come close to the scene of awesome and unnatural wonders. Capt.[d] Whipple now ordered his force to separate into three divisions; one of twenty[e] men under Eleazar Smith to strike across to the shore and guard the landing-place[f] against possible reinforcements for Curwen[g] until summoned by a messenger for desperate service,[h] a second of twenty[i] men under Capt. Esek[j] Hopkins to steal down into the river valley behind the Curwen farm and demolish with axes or gunpowder the oaken door in the high, steep bank,[k] and the third to close in on the house and adjacent buildings themselves. Of this last[l] division one third was to be led by Capt.[m] Mathewson to the cryptical stone edifice with high narrow windows, another third to follow Capt.[n] Whipple himself to the main farmhouse, and the remaining third to preserve a circle around the whole group of buildings until summoned by a final emergency signal.

The river party would break down the hillside door at the sound of a single whistle-blast, then[o] waiting and capturing anything which might issue from the regions within. At the sound of two whistle-

---

[a] farmhouse;] farmhouse, D
[b] sky. There] sky but there D
[c] windows, but this] windows. This D
[d] Capt.] Captain C, D
[e] twenty] 20 A
[f] landing-place] landing place D
[g] Curwen] Curwen, D
[h] service,] service; C, D
[i] twenty] 20 A
[j] Capt. Esek] Captain Eseh C, D
[k] bank,] bank; C, D
[l] last] *om.* D
[m] Capt.] Captain C, D
[n] Capt.] Captain C, D
[o] then] *om.* C, D

blasts[a] it would advance through the aperture to oppose the enemy or join the rest of the raiding contingent. The party at the stone building would accept these respective signals in an analogous manner; forcing an entrance at the first, and at the second descending whatever passage into the ground might be discovered, and joining the general or focal warfare expected to take place within the caverns. A third or emergency signal of three blasts would summon the immediate reserve from its[b] general guard duty; its twenty men dividing equally and entering the unknown depths through both farmhouse and stone building. Capt.[c] Whipple's belief in the existence of catacombs was absolute, and he took no alternative into consideration when making his plans. He had with him a whistle of great power and shrillness,[d] and did not fear any missing[e] or misunderstanding of signals. The final reserve at the landing, of course, was nearly out of the whistle's range;[f] hence would require a special messenger if needed for help. Moses Brown and John Carter went with Capt.[g] Hopkins to the river-bank,[h] while Pres.[i] Manning was detailed with Capt.[j] Mathewson to the stone building. Dr. Bowen, with Ezra Weeden, remained in Capt.[k] Whipple's party which was to storm the farmhouse itself. The attack was to begin as soon as a messenger from Capt.[l] Hopkins had joined Capt.[m] Whipple to notify him of the river party's readiness. The leader would then deliver the loud single blast, and the various advance parties would commence their simultaneous attack on three points. Shortly before 1 a.m.[n] the three divisions left the Fenner farmhouse; one to guard the

[a] whistle-blasts] whistle blasts A, C, D
[b] its] the C
[c] Capt.] Captain C, D
[d] shrillness,] shrillness C, D
[e] missing] mistaking C; upsetting D
[f] range;] range, D
[g] Capt.] Captain C, D
[h] river-bank,] river bank, A; riverbank, C
[i] Pres.] President C, D
[j] Capt.] Captain C, D
[k] Capt.] Captain C, D
[l] Capt.] Captain C, D
[m] Capt.] Captain C, D
[n] 1 a.m.] one A.M. C; one a.m. D

landing, another to seek the river valley and the hillside door, and the third to subdivide and attend to the actual buildings of the Curwen farm.

Eleazar Smith, who accompanied the shore-guarding party, records in his diary an uneventful march and a long wait on the bluff by the bay; broken once by what seemed to be the distant sound of the signal whistle and again by a peculiar muffled blend of roaring and crying and a powder blast which seemed to come from the same direction. Later on one man thought he caught some distant gunshots, and still later Smith himself felt the throb of titanic and[a] thunderous words resounding in upper air. It was just before dawn that a single haggard messenger with wild eyes and a hideous unknown odour about his clothing appeared and told the detachment to disperse quietly to their homes and never again think or speak of the night's doings or of him who had been Joseph Curwen. Something about the bearing of the messenger carried a conviction which his mere words could never have conveyed; for though he was a seaman well[b] known to many of them, there was something obscurely lost or gained in his soul which set him for evermore[c] apart. It was the same later on when they met other old companions who had gone into that zone of horror. Most of them had lost or gained something imponderable and indescribable. They had seen or heard or felt something which was not for human creatures, and could not forget it. From them there was never any gossip, for to even the commonest of mortal instincts there are terrible boundaries. And from that single messenger the party at the shore caught a nameless awe which almost sealed their own lips. Very few are the rumours which ever came from any of them, and Eleazar Smith's diary is the only written record which has survived from that whole expedition which set forth from the Sign of the Golden Lion under the stars.[d]

Charles Ward, however, discovered another vague sidelight in some Fenner correspondence which he found in New London, where he knew another branch of the family had lived. It seems that the

---

[a] and] *om.* C, D
[b] well] *om.* D
[c] for evermore] for-/evermore D
[d] stars.] Stars. C, D

Fenners, from whose house the doomed farm was distantly visible, had watched the departing columns of raiders; and had heard very clearly the angry barking of the Curwen dogs, followed by the first shrill blast which precipitated the attack. This[a] blast had been followed by a repetition of the great shaft of light from the stone building, and in another moment, after a quick sounding of the second signal ordering a general invasion, there had come a subdued prattle of musketry followed by a horrible roaring cry which the correspondent Luke Fenner[b] had represented in his epistle by the characters *"Waaaahrrrrr— R'waaahrrr".*[c] This cry, however, had possessed a quality which no mere writing could convey, and the correspondent mentions that his mother fainted completely at the sound. It was later repeated less loudly, and further but more muffled evidences of gunfire ensued; together with a loud explosion of powder from the direction of the river. About an hour afterward all the dogs began to bark[d] frightfully, and there were vague ground rumblings so marked that the candlesticks tottered on the mantelpiece. A strong smell of sulphur was noted; and Luke Fenner's father declared that he heard the third or emergency whistle signal, though the others failed to detect it. Muffled musketry sounded again, followed by a deep scream less piercing but even more horrible than those which had preceded it; a kind of throaty, nastily plastic cough or gurgle whose quality as a scream must have come more from its continuity and psychological import than from its actual acoustic value.

Then the flaming thing burst into sight at a point where the Curwen farm ought to lie, and the human cries of desperate and frightened men were heard. Muskets flashed and cracked, and the flaming thing fell to the ground. A second flaming thing appeared, and a shriek of human origin[e] was plainly distinguished. Fenner wrote that he could even gather a few words belched in frenzy: "Almighty, protect thy lamb!" Then there were more shots, and the second flaming thing fell. After that came silence for about three-quarters of

---

[a] This] The first D [first *repeated from line above*]

[b] correspondent Luke Fenner] correspondent, Luke Fenner, D

[c] *"Waaaahrrrrr—R'waaahrrr".*] "Waaaarrr—R'waaahrr." C; "Waaaarrrr—R'waaahrrr". D

[d] bark] bay C

[e] origin] crying D

an hour; at the end of which time little Arthur Fenner, Luke's brother, exclaimed that he saw 'a red fog'[a] going up to the stars from the accursed farm in the distance. No one but the child can testify to this, but Luke admits the significant coincidence implied by the panic of almost convulsive fright which at the same moment arched the backs and stiffened the fur of the three cats then within the room.

Five minutes later a chill wind blew up, and the air became suffused with such an intolerable stench that only the strong freshness of the sea could have prevented its being noticed by the shore party or by any wakeful souls in Pawtuxet village. This stench was nothing which any of the Fenners had ever encountered before, and produced a kind of clutching, amorphous fear beyond that of the tomb or the charnel-house. Close upon it came the awful voice which no hapless hearer will ever be able to forget. It thundered out of the sky like a doom, and windows rattled as its echoes died away. It was deep and musical; powerful as a bass organ, but evil as the forbidden books of the Arabs. What it said no man can tell, for it spoke in an unknown tongue, but this is the writing Luke Fenner set down to portray the daemoniac[b] intonations: "DEESMEES—JESHET—BONE DOSEFE DUVEMA—ENITEMOSS."[c] Not till the year 1919 did any soul link this crude transcript with anything else in mortal knowledge, but Charles Ward paled as he recognised[d] what Mirandola had denounced in shudders as the ultimate horror among black magic's incantations.

An unmistakably human shout or deep chorused scream seemed to answer this malign wonder from the Curwen farm,[e] after which the unknown stench grew complex with an added odour equally intolerable. A wailing distinctly different from the scream now burst out,[f] and was protracted ululantly in rising and falling paroxysms. At times it became almost articulate, though no auditor could trace any definite words; and at one point it seemed to verge toward the confines of diabolic and hysterical laughter. Then a yell of utter, ultimate fright and stark madness

[a] 'a red fog'] "a red fog" D
[b] daemoniac] demoniac D
[c] BONE . . . ENITEMOSS."] BONEDOSEFEDUVEMA—ENITEMOSS." C, D
[d] recognised] recognized D
[e] farm,] farm D
[f] out,] out C

wrenched from scores of human throats; a yell which came strong and clear despite the depth from which it must have burst; after which darkness and silence ruled all things. Spirals of acrid smoke ascended to blot out the stars, though no flames appeared[a] and no buildings were observed to be gone or injured on the following day.

Toward dawn two frightened messengers with monstrous and unplaceable odours saturating their clothing knocked at the Fenner door and requested a keg of rum,[b] for which they paid very well indeed. One of them told the family that the affair of Joseph Curwen was over, and that the events of the night were not to be mentioned again. Arrogant as the order seemed, the aspect of him who gave it took away all resentment and lent it a fearsome authority; so that only these furtive letters of Luke Fenner, which he urged his Connecticut relative to destroy, remain to tell what was seen and heard. The non-compliance of that relative, whereby the letters were saved after all, has alone kept the matter from a merciful oblivion. Charles Ward had one detail to add as a result of a long canvass of Pawtuxet residents for ancestral traditions. Old Charles Slocum of that village said that there was known to his grandfather a queer rumour concerning a charred, distorted body found in the fields a week after the death of Joseph Curwen was announced. What kept the talk alive was the notion that this body, so far as could be seen in its burnt and twisted condition, was neither thoroughly human nor wholly allied to any animal which Pawtuxet folk had ever seen or read about.

6.

Not one man who participated in that terrible raid could ever be induced to say a word concerning it, and every fragment of the vague data which survives comes from those outside the final fighting party. There is something frightful in the care with which these actual raiders destroyed each scrap[c] which bore the least allusion to the matter.[d]

[a] appeared] appeared, C, D
[b] rum,] rum C, D
[c] each scrap] such scraps D
[d] matter.] matter. ¶ C, D

Eight sailors had been killed, but although their bodies were not produced their families were satisfied with the statement that a clash with customs officers had occurred. The same statement also covered the numerous cases of wounds, all of which were extensively bandaged and treated only by Dr. Jabez Bowen, who had accompanied the party. Hardest to explain was the nameless odour clinging to all the raiders, a thing which was discussed for weeks. Of the citizen leaders, Capt.[a] Whipple and Moses Brown were most severely hurt, and letters of their wives testify the bewilderment which their reticence and close guarding of their bandages produced. Psychologically every participant was aged, sobered, and shaken. It is fortunate that they were all strong men of action and simple, orthodox religionists, for with more subtle introspectiveness and mental complexity they would have fared ill indeed. President Manning was the most disturbed; but even he outgrew the darkest shadow, and smothered memories in prayers. Every man of those leaders had a stirring part to play in later years, and it is perhaps fortunate that this is so. Little more than a twelvemonth afterward Capt.[b] Whipple led the mob who burnt the revenue ship *Gaspee,* and in this bold act we may trace one step in the blotting out of unwholesome images.

There was delivered to the widow of Joseph Curwen a sealed leaden coffin of curious design, obviously found ready on the spot when needed, in which she was told her husband's body lay. He had, it was explained, been killed in a customs battle about which it was not politic to give details. More than this no tongue ever uttered of Joseph Curwen's end, and Charles Ward had only a single hint wherewith to construct a theory. This hint was the merest thread—a shaky underscoring of a passage in Jedediah Orne's confiscated letter to Curwen, as[c] partly copied in Ezra Weeden's handwriting. The copy was found in the possession of Smith's descendants; and we are left to decide whether Weeden gave it to his companion after the end, as a mute clue to the abnormality which had occurred, or whether, as is more probable, Smith had it before, and added the underscoring himself from

[a] Capt.] Captain C, D
[b] Capt.] Captain C, D
[c] as] *om.* C, D

what he had managed to extract from his friend by shrewd guessing and adroit cross-questioning. The underlined passage is merely this:

> *"I say to you againe, doe not call[a] up Any that you can not[b] put downe; by the Which[c] I meane, Any that can in Turne[d] call[e] up somewhat against you, whereby your Powerfullest[f] Devices may not be of use. Ask of the Lesser, lest the Greater shall not wish to Answer, and shall commande more than you."[g]*

In[h] the light of this passage, and reflecting on what last unmentionable allies a beaten man might try to summon in his direst extremity, Charles Ward may well have wondered whether any citizen of Providence killed Joseph Curwen.

The deliberate effacement of every memory of the dead man from Providence life and annals was vastly aided by the influence of the raiding leaders. They had not at first meant to be so thorough, and had allowed the widow and her father and child to remain in ignorance of the true conditions; but Capt.[i] Tillinghast was an astute man, and soon uncovered enough rumours to whet his horror and cause him to demand that his daughter and granddaughter change their name, burn the library and all remaining papers, and chisel the inscription from the slate slab above Joseph Curwen's grave. He knew Capt.[j] Whipple well, and probably extracted more hints from that bluff mariner than anyone else ever gained respecting the end of the accused sorcerer.

From that time on the obliteration of Curwen's memory became increasingly rigid, extending at last by common consent even to the town records and files of the *Gazette*. It can be compared in spirit only to the hush that lay on Oscar Wilde's name for a decade after his disgrace, and in extent only to the fate of that sinful King of Runazar[k]

[a] *call*] *calle* C

[b] *can not*] *cannot* C, D

[c] *Which*] *which* A, C, D

[d] *Turne*] *turn* A, C, D

[e] *call*] *calle* A

[f] *Powerfullest*] *powerfullest* A, C, D

[g] *"I...you."*] *I...you.* C, D

[h] In] ¶ In C, D

[i] Capt.] Captain C, D

[j] Capt.] Captain C, D

[k] Runazar] Runagur C, D

in Lord Dunsany's tale, whom the Gods[a] decided must not only cease to be, but must cease ever to have been.

Mrs. Tillinghast, as the widow became known after 1772, sold the house in Olney Court and resided with her father in Power's Lane till her death in 1817. The farm at Pawtuxet, shunned by every living soul, remained to moulder through the years; and seemed to decay with unaccountable rapidity. By 1780 only the stone and brickwork were standing, and by 1800 even these had fallen to shapeless heaps. None ventured to pierce the tangled shrubbery on the river-bank[b] behind which the hillside door may have lain, nor did any try to frame a definite image of the scenes amidst which Joseph Curwen departed from the horrors he had wrought.

Only robust old Capt.[c] Whipple was heard by alert listeners to mutter once in a while to himself, "Pox on that ———, but he had no business to laugh while he screamed. 'Twas as though the damn'd[d] ——— had some'at[e] up his sleeve. For half a crown I'd burn his ——— house."

III. A SEARCH AND AN EVOCATION

1.

Charles Ward, as we have seen, first learned in 1918 of his descent from Joseph Curwen. That he at once took an intense interest in everything pertaining to the bygone mystery is not to be wondered at; for every vague rumour that he had heard of Curwen now became something vital to himself, in whom flowed Curwen's blood. No spirited and imaginative genealogist could have done otherwise than begin forthwith an avid and systematic collection of Curwen data.

In his first delvings there was not the slightest attempt at secrecy; so that even Dr. Lyman hesitates to date the youth's madness from any period before the close of 1919. He talked freely with his family—

[a] Gods] gods C, D
[b] river-bank] river bank A, C, D
[c] Capt.] Captain C, D
[d] damn'd] damned D
[e] some'at] some 'at C

though his mother was not particularly pleased to own an ancestor like Curwen—and with the officials of the various museums and libraries he visited. In applying to private families for records thought to be in their possession he made no concealment of his object, and shared the somewhat amused scepticism with which the accounts of the old diarists and letter-writers were regarded. He often expressed a keen wonder as to what really had taken place a century and a half before at that Pawtuxet farmhouse whose site he vainly tried to find, and what Joseph Curwen really had been.

When he came across the Smith diary and archives and encountered the letter from Jedediah Orne he decided to visit Salem and look up Curwen's early activities and connexions[a] there, which he did during the Easter vacation of 1919. At the Essex Institute, which was well known to him from former sojourns in the glamorous old town of crumbling Puritan gables and clustered gambrel roofs, he was very kindly received, and unearthed there a considerable amount of Curwen data. He found that his ancestor was born in Salem-Village, now Danvers, seven miles from town, on the eighteenth[b] of February (O.S.)[c] 1662–3; and that he had run away to sea at the age of fifteen, not appearing again for nine years, when he returned with the speech, dress, and manners of a native Englishman and settled in Salem proper. At that time he had little to do with his family, but spent most of his hours with the curious books he had brought from Europe, and the strange chemicals which came for him on ships from England, France, and Holland. Certain trips of his into the country were the objects of much local inquisitiveness, and were whisperingly associated with vague rumours of fires on the hills at night.

Curwen's only close friends had been one Edward Hutchinson of Salem-Village and one Simon Orne of Salem. With these men he was often seen in conference about the Common, and visits among them were by no means infrequent. Hutchinson had a house well out toward the woods, and it was not altogether liked by sensitive people because of the sounds heard there at night. He was said to entertain strange

[a] connexions] connexions D
[b] eighteenth] 18th A
[c] (O.S.)] (O. S.) C

visitors, and the lights seen from his windows were not always of the same colour. The knowledge he displayed concerning long-dead persons and long-forgotten events was considered distinctly unwholesome, and he disappeared about the time the witchcraft panic began, never to be heard from again. At that time Joseph Curwen also departed, but his settlement in Providence was soon learned of. Simon Orne lived in Salem until 1720, when his failure to grow visibly old began to excite attention. He thereafter disappeared, though thirty years later his precise counterpart and self-styled son turned up to claim his property. The claim was allowed on the strength of documents in Simon Orne's known hand, and Jedediah Orne continued to dwell in Salem till 1771, when certain letters from Providence citizens to the Rev.[a] Thomas Barnard and others brought about his quiet removal to parts unknown.

Certain documents by and about all of these strange characters[b] were available at the Essex Institute, the Court House, and the Registry of Deeds,[c] and included both harmless commonplaces such as land titles and bills of sale, and furtive fragments of a more provocative nature. There were four or five unmistakable allusions to them on the witchcraft trial records; as when one Hepzibah Lawson swore on July 16,[d] 1692, at the Court of Oyer and Terminer[e] under Judge Hathorne, that 'fortie Witches and the Blacke Man were wont to meete[f] in the Woodes behind Mr. Hutchinson's house',[g] and one Amity How declared at a session of August 8th[h] before Judge Gedney that 'Mr. G. B. (Rev.[i]

---

[a] Rev.] Reverend C, D

[b] characters] matters C, D

[c] Deeds,] Deeds, and it took Ward but a short time to prove from identity of penmanship a theory he had already considered established from the text of the Curwen letter; namely, that Simon Orne and his supposed son Jedediah were one and the same person. As the man had said to his correspondent, it was hardly safe to live too long in Salem, hence he resorted to a period abroad and did not return except as a representative of a new generation. A [excised]

[d] 16,] sixteenth, C; tenth, D

[e] Terminer] Terminen C, D

[f] meete] meet D

[g] 'fortie . . . house',] 'fortie . . . house,' C; "fortie . . . house", D

[h] 8th] eighth C, D

[i] Rev.] om. C, D

George Burroughs) on that Nighte putt y^e ᵃ Divell his Marke upon Bridget S., Jonathan A., *Simon O.,* Deliverance W., *Joseph C.,* Susan P., Mehitable C., and Deborah B.ᵇ Then there was a catalogue of Hutchinson's uncanny library as found after his disappearance, and an unfinished manuscript in his handwriting, couched in a cipher none could read. Ward had a photostatic copy of this manuscript made, and began to work casually on the cipher as soon as it was delivered to him. After the following August his labours on the cipher became intense and feverish, and there is reason to believe from his speech and conduct that he hit upon the key before October or November. He never stated, though, whether or not he had succeeded.

But of the greatest immediate interest was the Orne material. It took Ward only a short time to prove from identity of penmanship a thing he had already considered established from the text of the letter to Curwen; namely, that Simon Orne and his supposed son were one and the same person. As Orne had said to his correspondent, it was hardly safe to live too long in Salem, hence he resorted to a thirty-year sojourn abroad, and did not return to claim his lands except as a representative of a new generation. Orne had apparently been careful to destroy most of his correspondence, but the citizens who took action in 1771 found and preserved a few letters and papers which excited their wonder. There were cryptic formulae and diagrams in his and other hands which Ward now either copied with care or had photographed, and one extremely mysterious letter in a chirography that the searcher recognised from items in the Registry of Deeds as positively Joseph Curwen's.

This Curwen letter, though undated as to the year, was evidently not the one in answer to which Orne had written the confiscated missive; and from internal evidence Ward placed it not much later than 1750. It may not be amiss to give the text in full, as a sample of the style of one whose history was so dark and terrible. The recipient is addressed as "Simon", but a line (whether drawn by Curwen or Orneᶜ Ward could not tell) is run through the word.

ᵃ y^e] the C, D
ᵇ 'Mr. . . . Deborah B.'] "Mr. . . . Deborah B." D
ᶜ Orne] Orne, C, D

Prouidence, I. May (Ut. vulgo)[a]

Brother:—

My honour'd Antient ffriende,[b] due Respects and earnest Wishes to Him whom we serve for y^r eternall[c] Power. I am just come upon That which[d] you ought to knowe, concern'g the Matter[e] of the Laste Extremitie and what[f] to doe regard'g[g] yt. I am not dispos'd to followe you in go'g Away on acct. of my Yeares,[h] for Prouidence[i] hath not y^e[j] Sharpeness of ye Bay in hunt'g oute uncommon Things and bringinge to Tryall. I am ty'd up in Shippes and Goodes, and cou'd not doe as you did, besides the Whiche[k] my ffarme at Patuxet[l] hath under it What[m] you Knowe,[n] that wou'd not waite[o] for my com'g Backe as an Other.

But I am not unreadie for harde ffortunes,[p] as I haue tolde you, and haue[q] longe work'd upon ye Way[r] of get'g Backe after ye Laste.[s] I laste Night[t] strucke on ye Wordes[u] that bringe up YOGGE-SOTHOTHE, and sawe for ye firste Time that fface[v] spoke of by Ibn Schacabac in ye ———. And IT said, that ye III Psalme in ye Liber-Damnatus holdes ye Clauicle.[w] With Sunne in V House, Saturne in Trine, drawe ye Pentagram of Fire, and saye ye ninth Uerse thrice. This Uerse[x] repeate eache Roodemas and

---

[a] Prouidence, . . . vulgo)] Providence, I May C; Providence, 1 May D
[b] ffriende,] friende, C, D
[c] eternall] Eternall C
[d] That which] That Which C; that which D
[e] Matter] matter D
[f] what] What C
[g] regard'g] regard' C, D
[h] Yeares,] yeares, C, D
[i] Prouidence] Providence C, D
[j] y^e] yet C
[k] Whiche] Which C; whiche D
[l] ffarme at Patuxet] Farme, at Patuxet C; farme at Pawtuxet D
[m] What] That D
[n] Knowe,] knowe, D
[o] wou'd not waite] Wou'd not Waite C
[p] ffortunes,] fortunes, C, D
[q] haue . . . haue] have . . . have C, D
[r] longe . . . Way] lone . . . Way C; long . . . way D
[s] Laste.] Loste. C, D
[t] Night] Nighte D
[u] Wordes] Words D
[v] fface] face C, D
[w] Clauicle.] Clavicle. C, D
[x] Uerse . . . Uerse] Verse . . . Verse C, D

Hallow's Eue,[a] and y[e] Thing[b] will breede in y[e] Outside Spheres.

And of[c] y[e] Seede of Olde shal One be borne who shal looke Backe, tho' know'g not what he seekes.

Yett will this availe Nothing if there be no Heir, and if the Saltes, or the Way to make the Saltes,[d] bee not Readie for his Hande; and[e] here I will owne, I have not taken needed Stepps nor founde[f] Much. Ye Process is plaguy[g] harde to come neare;[h] and it uses up such a Store of Specimens, I am harde putte to it to get Enough, notwithstand'g the Sailors I have from y[e] [i] Indies. Ye People aboute are become curious,[j] but I can stande them off. Ye Gentry[k] are worse than y[el] Populace, be'g more Circumstantiall in their Accts. and more believ'd in what they tell. That Parson and Mr. Merritt have talk'd some, I am fearfull, but no Thing soe far is Dangerous. Ye Chymical substances are easie of get'g, there be'g II. goode Chymists in Towne, Dr. Bowen and Sam:[m] Carew. I[n] am foll'g oute what Borellus saith, and haue[o] Helpe in Abdool Al-Hazred his VII. Booke. Whatever I gette, you shal haue.[p] And in y[e] meane while, do not neglect to make use of y[e] Wordes I haue here giuen.[q] I haue[r] them Righte, but if you Desire to see HIM, imploy the Writing on y[e] Piece of ————[s] that I am putt'g in this Packet. Saye y[e] Uerses[t] every Roodmas[u] and Hallow's Eue;[v]

---

[a] Eue,] Eve, C, D

[b] Thing] thing C, D

[c] *of*] *o* C

[d] Saltes,] Saltes D

[e] Hande; and] Hande. And C; Hands. And D

[f] founde] found D

[g] plaguy] plagney C; plaguey D

[h] neare;] neare, C, D

[i] y[e]] the C, D

[j] curious,] Curious, C

[k] Gentry] gentry C, D

[l] y[e]] the D

[m] Sam:] Sam C, D

[n] I] In C

[o] haue] have C, D

[p] haue.] have. C, D

[q] haue here giuen.] have here given. C, D

[r] haue] have C, D

[s] ————] ————, D

[t] Uerses] Verses C, D

[u] Roodmas] Roodemas C, D

[v] Eue;] Eve; C, D

and if y[r] Line runn out not, *one shal*[a] *bee in yeares to come that shal looke backe and use what Saltes or Stuff for Saltes you shal leaue*[b] *him.* Job XIV. XIV.

I rejoice you are again at Salem, and hope I may see you not longe hence. I have a goode Stallion, and am think'g of get'g a Coach, there be'g one (Mr. Merritt's) in Prouidence already,[c] tho' y[e] Roades are bad. If you are dispos'd to Travel,[d] doe not pass me bye. From Boston take y[e] Post[e] Rd. thro' Dedham, Wrentham, and Attleborough, goode Taverns be'g at all these Townes. Stop at Mr. Bolcom's in Wrentham, where y[e] Beddes are finer than Mr. Hatch's, but eate at y[e] other House for their Cooke[f] is better. Turne into Prou.[g] by Patucket ffalls,[h] and y[e] Rd. past Mr. Sayles's Tavern. My House opp. Mr. Epenetus Olney's Tavern off y[e] Towne Street, Ist on y[e] N. side of Olney's Court. Distance from Boston Stone[i] abt. XLIV Miles.[j]

Sir, I am y[r] olde and true ffriend[k] and Servt. in *Almousin-Metraton.*[l]

Josephus C.

To Mr. Simon Orne,
William's-Lane, in Salem.

This letter, oddly enough, was what first gave Ward the exact location of Curwen's Providence home; for none of the records encountered up to that time had been at all specific. The discovery was doubly striking because it indicated,[m] as the newer Curwen house[n] built in 1761 on the site of the old, a dilapidated building still standing in Olney Court[o] and well known to Ward in his antiquarian rambles over Stampers'[p] Hill. The place was indeed only a few squares from his

[a] *shal*] *shall* D
[b] *leaue*] *leave* C, D
[c] Prouidence already,] Providence already, C; Providence alreadie, D
[d] Travel,] travel, C, D
[e] Post] Poste D
[f] Cooke] cooke C, D
[g] Prou.] Prov. C; Providence D
[h] ffalls,] falls, C, D
[i] Stone] Store D
[j] Miles.] miles. C
[k] ffriend] friende C; friend D
[l] *Almousin-Metraton.*] Almonsin-Metraton. C, D
[m] indicated,] indicated D
[n] house] house, D
[o] Court] Curt D
[p] Stampers'] Stampers A, C, D

own home on the great hill's higher ground, and was now the abode of a negro[a] family much esteemed for occasional washing, housecleaning,[b] and furnace-tending services. To find, in distant Salem, such sudden proof of the significance of this familiar rookery in his own family history, was a highly impressive thing to Ward; and he resolved to explore the place immediately upon his return. The more mystical phases of the letter, which he took to be some extravagant kind of symbolism, frankly baffled him; though he noted with a thrill of curiosity that the Biblical passage referred to—Job 14, 14—was the familiar verse, "If a man die, shall he live again? All the days of my appointed time will I wait, till my change come."

2.

Young Ward came home in a state of pleasant excitement, and spent the following Saturday in a long and exhaustive study of the house in[c] Olney Court. The place, now crumbling with age, had never been a mansion; but was a modest two-and-a-half story[d] wooden town house of the familiar Providence colonial[e] type, with plain peaked roof, large central chimney,[f] and artistically carved doorway with rayed fanlight, triangular pediment, and trim Doric pilasters. It had suffered but little alteration externally, and Ward felt he was gazing on something very close to the sinister matters of his quest.

The present negro[g] inhabitants were known to him, and he was very courteously shewn[h] about the interior by old Asa and his stout wife Hannah. Here there was more change than the outside indicated, and Ward saw with regret that fully half of the fine scroll-and-urn overmantels and shell-carved cupboard linings were gone, whilst much of the fine wainscotting and bolection moulding was marked, hacked,

---

[a] negro] Negro D
[b] housecleaning,] house-/cleaning, C; house-cleaning, D
[c] in] of D
[d] story] storey D
[e] colonial] Colonial A, C, D
[f] chimney,] chimney D
[g] negro] Negro D
[h] shewn] shown C, D

and gouged, or covered up altogether with cheap wall-paper.[a] In general, the survey did not yield as much as Ward had somehow expected; but it was at least exciting to stand within the ancestral walls which had housed such a man of horror as Joseph Curwen. He saw with a thrill that a monogram had been very carefully effaced from the ancient brass knocker.

From then until after the close of school Ward spent his time on the photostatic copy of the Hutchinson cipher and the accumulation of local Curwen data. The former still proved unyielding; but of the latter he obtained so much, and so many clues to similar data elsewhere, that he was ready by July[b] to make a trip to New London and New York to consult old letters whose presence in those places was indicated. This trip was very fruitful, for it brought him the Fenner letters with their terrible description of the Pawtuxet farmhouse raid, and the Nightingale-Talbot letters in which he learned of the portrait painted on a panel of the Curwen library. This matter of the portrait interested him particularly, since he would have given much to know just what Joseph Curwen looked like; and he decided to make a second search of the house in Olney Court to see if there might not be some trace of the ancient features beneath peeling coats of later paint or layers of mouldy wall-paper.[c]

Early in August that search took place, and Ward went carefully over the walls of every room sizeable enough to have been by any possibility the library of the evil builder. He paid especial attention to the large panels of such overmantels as still remained; and was keenly excited after about an hour, when on a broad area above the fireplace in a spacious ground-floor room[d] he became certain that the surface brought out by the peeling of several coats of paint was sensibly darker than any ordinary interior paint or the wood beneath it was likely to have been. A few more careful tests with a thin knife, and he knew that he had come upon an oil portrait of great extent. With truly scholarly

[a] wall-paper.] wall paper. C, D
[b] by July] *om.* D
[c] wall-paper.] wall paper. D
[d] when . . . room] when, . . . room, D

restraint[a] the youth did not risk the damage which an immediate attempt to uncover the hidden picture with the knife might have done, but just retired from the scene of his discovery to enlist expert help. In three days he returned with an artist of long experience, Mr. Walter C.[b] Dwight, whose studio is near the foot of College Hill; and that accomplished restorer of paintings set to work at once with proper methods and chemical substances. Old Asa and his wife were duly excited over their strange visitors, and were properly reimbursed for this invasion of their domestic hearth.

As day by day the work of restoration progressed, Charles Ward looked on with growing interest at the lines and shades gradually unveiled after their long oblivion. Dwight had begun at the bottom; hence since the picture was a three-quarter-length one, the face did not come out for some time. It was meanwhile seen that the subject was a spare, well-shaped man with dark-blue coat, embroidered waistcoat, black satin small-clothes, and white silk stockings, seated in a carved chair against the background of a window with wharves and ships beyond. When the head came out it was observed to bear a neat Albemarle wig, and to possess a thin, calm, undistinguished face which seemed somehow familiar to both Ward and the artist. Only at the very last, though, did the restorer and his client begin to gasp with astonishment at the details of that lean, pallid visage, and to recognise with a touch of awe the dramatic trick which heredity had played. For it took the final bath of oil and the final stroke of the delicate scraper to bring out fully the expression which centuries had hidden; and to confront the bewildered Charles Dexter Ward, dweller in the past, with his own living features in the countenance of his horrible great-great-great-grandfather.

Ward brought his parents to see the marvel he had uncovered, and his father at once determined to purchase the picture despite its execution on stationary panelling. The resemblance to the boy, despite an appearance of rather greater age, was marvellous; and it could be seen that through some trick of atavism the physical contours of Joseph Curwen had found precise duplication after a century and a half. Mrs. Ward's resemblance to her ancestor was not at all marked,

[a] restraint] restraint, D
[b] C.] *om.* D

though she could recall relatives who had some of the facial characteristics shared by her son and by the bygone Curwen. She did not relish the discovery, and told her husband that he had better burn the picture instead of bringing it home. There was, she averred, something unwholesome about it; not only intrinsically, but in its very resemblance to Charles. Mr. Ward, however, was a practical man of power and affairs—a cotton manufacturer with extensive mills at Riverpoint in the Pawtuxet Valley—and not one to listen to feminine scruples. The picture impressed him mightily with its likeness to his son, and he believed the boy deserved it as a present. In this opinion, it is needless to say, Charles most heartily concurred; and[a] a few days later Mr. Ward located the owner of the house—a[b] small rodent-featured person with a guttural accent—and obtained the whole mantel and overmantel bearing the picture at a curtly fixed priced which cut short the impending torrent of unctuous haggling.

It now remained to take off the panelling and remove it to the Ward home, where provisions were made for its thorough restoration and installation with an electric[c] mock-fireplace in Charles's third-floor study or[d] library. To Charles was left the task of superintending this removal, and on the twenty-eighth[e] of August he accompanied two expert workmen from the Crooker decorating firm to the house in Olney Court, where the mantel and portrait-bearing overmantel were detached with great care and precision for transportation in the company's motor truck. There was left a space of exposed brickwork marking the chimney's course, and in this young Ward observed a cubical recess about a foot square, which must have lain directly behind the head of the portrait. Curious as to what such a space might mean or contain, the youth approached and looked within; finding beneath the deep coatings of dust and soot some loose yellowed papers, a crude,[f] thick copy-book, and a few mouldering textile shreds which may have formed the ribbon binding the rest together. Blowing away the bulk of the dirt and cinders,

[a] concurred; and] concurred;— C
[b] house—a] house and a C, D
[c] an electric] an electric or C; electric or D
[d] or] *om.* C, D
[e] twenty-eighth] 28th A
[f] crude,] crude C, D

he took up the book and looked at the bold inscription on its cover. It was in a hand which he had learned to recognise at the Essex Institute, and proclaimed the volume as the *"Journall* [a] *and Notes of Jos:* [b] *Curwen, Gent., of Providence-Plantations, Late of Salem."*

Excited beyond measure by his discovery, Ward shewed[c] the book to the two curious workmen beside him. Their testimony is absolute as to the nature and genuineness of the finding, and Dr. Willett relies on them to help establish his theory that the youth was not mad when he began his major eccentricities. All the other papers were likewise in Curwen's handwriting, and one of them seemed especially portentous because of its inscription: *"To Him Who Shal Come After, & How He May Gett Beyonde Time &*[d] *ye Spheres."* Another was in a cipher; the same, Ward hoped, as the Hutchinson cipher which had hitherto baffled him. A third, and here the searcher rejoiced, seemed to be a key to the cipher; whilst the fourth and fifth were addressed respectively to "Edw:[e] Hutchinson, Armiger" and "Jedediah Orne, Esq.",[f] 'or Their Heir or Heirs, or Those Represent'g Them'.[g] The sixth and last was inscribed: *"Joseph Curwen his Life and Travells Bet'n yf yeares 1678 and 1687: Of*[h] *Whither He Voyag'd, Where He Stay'd, Whom He Sawe, and What He Learnt."*[i]

3.

We have now reached the point from which the more academic school of alienists date Charles Ward's madness. Upon his discovery the youth had looked immediately at a few of the inner pages of the book and manuscripts, and had evidently seen something which impressed him tremendously. Indeed, in shewing[j] the titles to the workmen he appeared to guard the text itself with peculiar care, and to labour under

[a] *"Journall*] *"Journal* D
[b] *Jos:*] *Jos.* C, D
[c] shewed] showed D
[d] *&* . . . *&*] *and* . . . *and* C, D
[e] "Edw:] "Edw. C
[f] Esq.",] Esq.," D
[g] 'or . . . Them'.] 'or . . . Them.' C; "or . . . Them." D
[h] *Of*] *of* C, D
[i] *Learnt."*] *learnt."* C, D
[j] shewing] showing D

a perturbation for which even the antiquarian and genealogical significance of the find could hardly account. Upon returning home he broke the news with an almost embarrassed air, as if he wished to convey an idea of its supreme importance without having to exhibit the evidence itself. He did not even shew[a] the titles to his parents, but simply told them that he had found some documents in Joseph Curwen's handwriting, "mostly in cipher",[b] which would have to be studied very carefully before yielding up their true meaning. It is unlikely that he would have shewn[c] what he did to the workmen, had it not been for their unconcealed curiosity. As it was he doubtless wished to avoid any display of peculiar reticence which would increase their discussion of the matter.

That night Charles Ward sat up in his room reading the new-found book and papers, and when day came he did not desist. His meals, on his urgent request when his mother called to see what was amiss, were sent up to him; and in the afternoon he appeared only briefly when the men came to install the Curwen picture and mantelpiece[d] in his study. The next night he slept in snatches in his clothes, meanwhile wrestling feverishly with the unravelling of the cipher manuscript. In the morning his mother saw that he was at work on the photostatic copy of the Hutchinson cipher, which he had frequently shewn[e] her before; but in response to her query he said that the Curwen key could not be applied to it. That afternoon he abandoned his work and watched the men fascinatedly as they finished their installation of the picture with its woodwork above a cleverly realistic electric log, setting the mock-fireplace and overmantel a little out from the north wall as if a chimney existed, and boxing in the[f] sides with panelling to match the room's. The front panel holding the picture was sawn and hinged to allow cupboard space behind it. After the workmen went he moved his work into the study and sat down before it with his eyes half on the cipher and half on the portrait which stared back at him like a year-adding

[a] shew] show D
[b] cipher",] cipher," C, D
[c] shewn] shown D
[d] mantelpiece] mantlepiece D
[e] shewn] shewed C; shown D
[f] the] its C, D

and[a] century-recalling mirror.[b]

His parents,[c] subsequently recalling his conduct at this period, give interesting details anent the policy of concealment which he practiced.[d] Before servants he seldom hid any paper which he might be studying, since he rightly assumed that Curwen's intricate and archaic chirography would be too much for them. With his parents, however, he was more circumspect; and unless the manuscript in question were a cipher, or a mere mass of cryptic symbols and unknown ideographs (as that entitled *"To Him Who Shal Come After* etc."[e] seemed to be),[f] he would cover it with some convenient paper until his caller had departed. At night he kept the papers under lock and key in an antique cabinet of his, where he also placed them whenever he left the room. He soon resumed fairly regular hours and habits, except that his long walks and other outside interests seemed to cease. The opening of school, where he now began his senior year, seemed a great bore to him; and he frequently asserted his determination never to bother with college. He had, he said, important special investigations to make, which would provide him with more avenues toward knowledge and the humanities than any university which the world could boast.

Naturally, only one who had always been more or less studious, eccentric, and solitary could have pursued this course for many days without attracting notice. Ward, however, was constitutionally a scholar and a hermit; hence his parents were less surprised than regretful at the close confinement and secrecy he adopted. At the same time, both his father and mother thought it odd that he would shew[g] them no scrap of his treasure-trove, nor give any connected account of such data as he had deciphered. This reticence he explained away as due to a wish to wait until he might announce some connected revelation, but as the weeks passed without further disclosures there began to grow up between the youth and his family a kind of

[a] year-adding and] year-adding, C, D
[b] mirror. ¶] mirror. C, D
[c] parents,] parents C
[d] practiced.] practised. D
[e] *After* etc."] *After, etc."* D
[f] ideographs (. . .),] ideographs, (. . .) A; ideographs (. . .) D
[g] shew] show D

constraint; intensified in his mother's case by her manifest disapproval of all Curwen delvings.

During October Ward began visiting the libraries again, but no longer for the antiquarian matter of his former days. Witchcraft and magic, occultism and daemonology,[a] were what he sought now; and when Providence sources proved unfruitful he would take the train for Boston and tap the wealth of the great library in Copley Square, the Widener Library at Harvard, or the Zion Research Library in Brookline, where certain rare works on Biblical subjects are available. He bought extensively, and fitted up a whole additional set of shelves in his study for newly acquired works on uncanny subjects; while during the Christmas holidays he made a round of out-of-town trips including one to Salem to consult certain records at the Essex Institute.

About the middle of January, 1920, there entered Ward's bearing an element of triumph which he did not explain, and he was no more found at work upon the Hutchinson cipher. Instead, he inaugurated a dual policy of chemical research and record-scanning; fitting up for the one a laboratory in the unused attic of the house, and for the latter haunting all the sources of vital statistics in Providence. Local dealers in drugs and scientific supplies, later questioned, gave astonishingly queer and[b] meaningless catalogues of the substances and instruments he purchased; but clerks at the State House,[c] the City Hall, and the various libraries agree as to the definite object of his second interest. He was searching intensely and feverishly for the grave of Joseph Curwen, from whose slate slab an older generation had so wisely blotted the name.

Little by little there grew upon the Ward family the conviction that something was wrong. Charles had had freaks and changes of minor interests before, but this growing secrecy and absorption in strange pursuits was unlike even him. His school work was the merest pretence; and although he failed in no test, it could be seen that the old application had all vanished. He had other concernments now; and when not in his

---

[a] daemonology,] demonology, D
[b] queer and] queer, D
[c] State House,] State-House, A, C, D

new laboratory with a score of obsolete alchemical[a] books, could be found either poring over old burial records down town or glued to his volumes of occult lore in his study, where the startlingly—one almost fancied increasingly—similar features of Joseph Curwen stared blandly at him from the great overmantel on the north wall.

Late in March Ward[b] added to his archive-searching[c] a ghoulish series of rambles about the various ancient cemeteries of the city. The cause appeared later, when it was learned from City Hall clerks that he had probably found an important clue. His quest had suddenly shifted from the grave of Joseph Curwen to that of one Naphthali Field; and this[d] shift was explained when, upon going over the files that he had been over, the investigators actually found a fragmentary record of Curwen's burial which had escaped the general obliteration, and which stated that the curious leaden coffin had been interred "10 ft. S. and 5 ft. W. of Naphthali Field's grave in y[e] ————". The lack of a specified burying-ground[e] in the surviving entry greatly complicated the search, and Naphthali Field's grave seemed as elusive as that of Curwen;[f] but here no systematic effacement had existed, and one might reasonably be expected to stumble on the stone itself even if its record had perished. Hence the rambles—from which St. John's (the former King's) Churchyard[g] and the ancient Congregational burying-ground[h] in the midst of Swan Point Cemetery were excluded, since other statistics had shewn[i] that the only Naphthali Field (obiit[j] 1729) whose grave could have been meant had been a Baptist.

[a] alchemical] chemical C
[b] Ward] Ward underwent another period of apparent triumph or elation, and visited the public archives no more. He had found, it later appeared from the statements of a City Hall clerk, an obscure and trivial record which seemed to solve his problem [*several words deleted*] written directions [*one and a half lines deleted*] added to his archive A [*excised*]
[c] archive-searching] archives—searching C
[d] this] his D
[e] burying-ground] burying ground A, C, D
[f] Curwen;] Curwen's; C, D
[g] Churchyard] churchyard C
[h] burying-ground] burying ground A
[i] shewn] shown D
[j] obiit] obit. C, D

4.

It was toward May when Dr. Willett,[a] at the request of the senior Ward[b] and fortified with all the Curwen data which the family had gleaned from Charles in his non-secretive days, talked with the young man. The interview was of little value or conclusiveness, for Willett felt at every moment that Charles was thoroughly master of himself and in touch with matters of real importance; but it at least forced the secretive youth to offer some rational explanation of his recent demeanour. Of a pallid, impassive type not easily shewing[c] embarrassment, Ward seemed quite ready to discuss his pursuits, though not to reveal their object. He stated that the papers of his ancestor[d] had contained some remarkable secrets of early scientific knowledge, for the most part in cipher, of an apparent scope comparable only to the discoveries of Friar Bacon and perhaps surpassing even those. They were, however, meaningless except when correlated with a body of learning now wholly obsolete; so that their immediate presentation to a world equipped only with modern science would rob them of all impressiveness and dramatic significance. To take their vivid place in the history of human thought they must first be correlated by one familiar with the background out of which they evolved, and to this task of correlation Ward was now devoting himself. He was seeking to acquire as fast as possible those neglected arts of old which a true interpreter of the Curwen data must possess, and hoped in time to make a full announcement and presentation of the utmost interest to mankind and to the world of thought. Not even Einstein, he declared, could more profoundly revolutionise the current conception of things.

As to his graveyard search, whose object he freely admitted, but the details of whose progress he did not relate, he said he had reason to think that Joseph Curwen's mutilated headstone bore certain mystic symbols—carved from directions in his will and ignorantly spared by those who had effaced the name—which were absolutely essential to

[a] Willett,] Willett C
[b] Ward] Ward, D
[c] shewing] showing D
[d] ancestor] ancester C

the final solution of his cryptic system. Curwen, he believed, had wished to guard his secret with care; and had consequently distributed the data in an exceedingly curious fashion. When Dr. Willett asked to see the mystic documents, Ward displayed much reluctance and tried to put him off with such things as photostatic copies of the Hutchinson cipher and Orne formulae[a] and diagrams; but finally shewed[b] him the exteriors of some of the real Curwen finds—the *"Journal and Notes"*,[c] the cipher (title in cipher also),[d] and the formula-filled message *"To Him Who Shal Come After"*—and let him glance inside such as were in obscure characters.

He also opened the diary at a page carefully selected for its innocuousness and gave Willett a glimpse of Curwen's connected handwriting in English. The doctor noted very closely the crabbed and complicated letters, and the general aura of the seventeenth century which clung round both penmanship and style despite the writer's survival into the eighteenth century, and became quickly certain that the document was genuine. The text itself was relatively trivial, and Willett recalled only a fragment:

> "Wedn. 16 Octr. 1754. My Sloope the *Wakeful*[e] this Day[f] putt in from London with XX newe Men pick'd up in y[e] Indies, Spaniards from Martineco and 2[g] Dutch Men from Surinam. Ye Dutch Men are like to Desert from have'g[h] hearde Somewhat ill of these[i] Ventures, but I will see to y[e] Inducing[j] of them to Staye. ffor[k] Mr. Knight Dexter at y[e] Bay and Book 120 Pieces Camblets, 100 Pieces Assrtd.[l] Cambleteens, 20 Pieces blue Duffles, 100 Pieces Shalloons, 50 Pieces Calamancoes,[m] 300 Pieces

[a] formulae] formula D
[b] shewed] showed D
[c] *"Journal and Notes"*,] *"Journall and Notes,"* C; *"Journal and Notes,"* D
[d] cipher (. . .),] cipher, (. . .) A; cipher (. . .) C, D
[e] *Wakeful*] *Wahefal* C, D
[f] Day] day C, D
[g] 2] *om.* C, D
[h] have'g] hav'g D
[i] these] thse D
[j] Inducing] inducing D
[k] ffor] For C, D
[l] Assrtd.] Assrt. C
[m] Calamancoes,] Calamancocoes, C, D

each, Shendsoy and Humhums. ffor[a] Mr. Green at y[e] Elephant 50 Gallon[b] Cyttles, 20 Warm'g Pannes, 15 Bake Cyttles, 10 pr. Smoke'g Tonges.[c] ffor Mr. Perrigo[d] 1 Sett of Awles. ffor Mr. Nightingale[e] 50 Reames prime Foolscap. Say'd y[e] SABAOTH thrice last Nighte but None appear'd. I must heare more from Mr. H. in Transylvania, tho' it is Harde reach'g him and exceeding strange he can not give me the Use[f] of what he hath[g] so well us'd these hundred yeares. Simon hath not Writ these V. Weekes, but I expecte soon hear'g from him."

When upon reaching this point Dr. Willett turned the leaf he was quickly checked by Ward, who almost snatched the book from his grasp. All that the doctor had a chance to see on the newly opened page was a brief pair of sentences; but these, strangely enough, lingered tenaciously in his memory. They ran: "Ye Verse from Liber-Damnatus be'g spoke V Roodmasses[h] and IV[i] Hallows-Eves,[j] I am Hopeful y[e] Thing is breed'g Outside y[e] Spheres. It will drawe One who is to Come,[k] if I can make sure he shal bee, and he shall think on Past thinges and look back[l] thro' all y[e] yeares, against y[e] which I must have ready y[e] Saltes or That to make 'em with."

Willett saw no more, but somehow this small glimpse gave a new and vague terror to the painted features of Joseph Curwen which stared blandly down from the overmantel. Ever after that he entertained the odd fancy—which his medical skill of course assured him was only a fancy—that the eyes of the portrait had a sort of wish, if not an actual tendency, to follow young Charles Ward as he moved about the room. He stopped before leaving to study the picture closely, marvelling at its resemblance to Charles and memorising every

---

[a] ffor] For C, D
[b] Elephant 50 Gallon] Elephant 50 gallo C; Elephant, 50 gallon D
[c] Tonges.] Tongues. C
[d] ffor Mr. Perrigo] For Mr. Perrigo, C, D
[e] ffor Mr. Nightingale] For Mr. Nightingale C; For Mr. Nightingale, D
[f] can not . . . Use] cannot . . . use C, D
[g] hath] heath C
[h] Roodmasses] Roodemasses C, D
[i] V . . . IV] V. . . . IV. C
[j] Hallows-Eves,] Hallow's-Eves, C, D
[k] Come,] Come C, D
[l] look back] looke back C; looke backe D

minute detail of the cryptical, colourless face, even down to a slight scar or pit in the smooth brow above[a] the right eye. Cosmo Alexander, he decided, was a painter worthy of the Scotland that produced Raeburn, and a teacher worthy of his illustrious pupil[b] Gilbert Stuart.

Assured by the doctor that Charles's mental health was in no danger, but that on the other hand he was engaged in researches which might prove of real importance, the Wards were more lenient than they might otherwise have been when during the following June the youth made positive his refusal to attend college. He had, he declared, studies of much more vital importance to pursue; and intimated a wish to go abroad the following year in order to avail himself of certain sources of data not existing in America. The senior Ward, while denying this latter wish as absurd for a boy of only eighteen, acquiesced regarding the university; so that after a none too brilliant graduation from the Moses Brown School there ensued for Charles a three-year[c] period of intensive occult study and graveyard searching. He became recognised as an eccentric, and dropped even more completely from the sight of his family's friends than he had been before; keeping close to his work and only occasionally making trips to other cities to consult obscure records. Once he went south to talk with a strange old mulatto who dwelt in a swamp and about whom a newspaper had printed a curious article. Again he sought a small village in the Adirondacks whence reports of certain odd ceremonial practices had come. But still his parents forbade him the trip to the Old World which he desired.

Coming of age in April, 1923, and having previously inherited a small competence from his maternal grandfather, Ward determined at last to take the European trip hitherto denied him. Of his proposed itinerary he would say nothing save that the needs of his studies would carry him to many places,[d] but he promised to write his parents fully and faithfully. When they saw he could not be dissuaded, they ceased all opposition and helped as best they could; so that in June the young

[a] above] over D
[b] pupil] pupil, C
[c] three-year] three year C
[d] places,] places D

man sailed for Liverpool with the farewell blessings of his father and mother, who accompanied him to Boston and waved him out of sight from the White Star pier in Charlestown. Letters soon told of his safe arrival, and of his securing good quarters in Great Russell Street, London;[a] where he proposed to stay, shunning all family friends, till he had exhausted the resources of the British Museum in a certain direction. Of his daily life he wrote but little, for there was little to write. Study and experiment consumed[b] all his time, and he mentioned a laboratory which he had established in one of his rooms. That he said nothing of antiquarian rambles in the glamorous old city with its luring skyline of ancient domes and steeples and its tangles of roads and alleys whose mystic convolutions and sudden vistas alternately beckon and surprise, was taken by his parents as a good index of the degree to which his new interests had engrossed his mind.

In June, 1924, a brief note told of his departure for Paris, to which he had before made one or two flying trips for material in the Bibliothèque[c] Nationale. For three months thereafter he sent only postal cards,[d] giving an address in the Rue St. Jacques and referring to a special search among rare manuscripts in the library of an unnamed private collector. He avoided acquaintances, and no tourists brought back reports of having seen him. Then came a silence, and in October the Wards received a picture card from Prague, Czecho-Slovakia,[e] stating that Charles was in that ancient town for the purpose of conferring with a certain very aged man supposed to be the last living possessor of some very curious mediaeval information. He gave an address in the Neustadt, and announced no move till the following January;[f] when he dropped several cards from Vienna telling of his passage through that city on the way toward a more easterly region whither one of his correspondents and fellow-delvers into the occult had invited him.

The next card was from Klausenburg in Transylvania, and told of Ward's progress toward his destination. He was going to visit a Baron

[a] London;] London, D
[b] consumed] concerned D
[c] Bibliothèque] Bibliotheque A, C
[d] postal cards,] postal cards C; post-cards, D
[e] Czecho-Slovakia,] om. D
[f] January;] January, D

Ferenczy, whose estate lay in the mountains east of Rakus; and was to be addressed at Rakus in the care of that nobleman. Another card from Rakus a week later, saying that his host's carriage had met him and that he was leaving the village for the mountains, was his last message for a considerable time; indeed, he did not reply to his parents' frequent letters until May, when he wrote to discourage the plan of his mother for a meeting in London, Paris, or Rome during the summer, when the elder Wards were planning to travel in Europe. His researches, he said, were such that he could not leave his present quarters;[a] while the situation of Baron Ferenczy's castle did not favour visits. It was on a crag in the dark wooded mountains, and the region was so shunned by the country folk that normal people could not help feeling ill at ease. Moreover, the Baron was not a person likely to appeal to correct and conservative New England gentlefolk. His aspect and manners had idiosyncrasies, and his age was so great as to be disquieting. It would be better, Charles said, if his parents would wait for his return to Providence; which could scarcely be far distant.

That return did not, however, take place until May, 1926,[b] when after a few heralding cards[c] the young wanderer quietly slipped into New York on the *Homeric* and traversed the long miles to Providence by motor coach,[d] eagerly drinking in the green rolling hills, the fragrant, blossoming orchards, and the white steepled towns of vernal Connecticut; his first taste of ancient New England in nearly four years. When the coach crossed the Pawcatuck and entered Rhode Island amidst the faery goldenness of a late spring afternoon his heart beat with quickened force, and the entry to Providence along Reservoir and Elmwood avenues was a breathless and wonderful thing despite the depths of forbidden lore to[e] which he had delved. At the high square where Broad, Weybosset, and Empire Streets join, he saw before and below him in the fire of sunset the pleasant, remembered houses and domes and steeples of the old town; and his head swam

[a] quarters;] quarters, D
[b] 1926,] 1925, C, D
[c] when . . . cards] when, . . . cards, C, D
[d] coach,] coach C
[e] to] into D

curiously as the vehicle rolled down the terminal behind the Biltmore, bringing into view the great dome and soft, roof-pierced greenery of the ancient hill across the river, and the tall colonial[a] spire of the First Baptist Church limned pink in the magic evening light against the fresh springtime verdure of its precipitous background.

Old Providence! It was this place and the mysterious forces of its long, continuous history which had brought him into being, and which had drawn him back toward marvels and secrets whose boundaries no prophet might fix. Here lay the arcana, wondrous or dreadful as the case might be, for which all his years of travel and application had been preparing him. A taxicab whirled him through Post Office Square with its glimpse of the river, the old Market House, and the head of the bay, and up the steep curved slope of Waterman Street to Prospect, where the vast gleaming dome and sunset-flushed Ionic columns of the Christian Science Church beckoned northward. Then eight squares past the fine old estates his childish eyes had known, and the quaint brick sidewalks so often trodden by his youthful feet. And at last the little white overtaken farmhouse on the right, and[b] on the left the classic Adam porch and stately bayed facade[c] of the great brick house where he was born. It was twilight, and Charles Dexter Ward had come home.

5.

A school of alienists slightly less academic than Dr. Lyman's[d] assign to Ward's European trip the beginning of his true madness. Admitting that he was sane when he started, they believe that his conduct upon returning implies a disastrous change. But even to this claim Dr. Willett refuses to accede. There was, he insists, something later; and the queernesses of the youth at this stage he attributes to the practice of rituals learned abroad—odd enough things, to be sure, but by no means implying mental aberration on the part of their celebrant. Ward himself, though visibly aged and hardened, was still normal in his

[a] tall colonial] tall Colonial A; tall, colonial C, D
[b] and] *om.* D
[c] facade] façade C, D
[d] Lyman's] Lyman's, C

general reactions; and in several talks with Willett displayed a balance which no madman—even an incipient one—could feign continuously for long. What elicited the notion of insanity at this period were the *sounds* heard at all hours from Ward's attic laboratory, in which he kept himself most of the time. There were chantings and repetitions, and thunderous declamations in uncanny rhythms; and although these sounds were always in Ward's own voice, there was something in the quality of that voice,[a] and in the accents of the formulae it pronounced, which could not but chill the blood of every hearer. It was noticed that Nig, the venerable and beloved black cat of the household, bristled[b] and arched his back perceptibly when certain of the tones were heard.

The odours occasionally wafted from the laboratory were likewise exceedingly strange. Sometimes they were very noxious, but more often they were aromatic, with a haunting, elusive quality which seemed to have the power of inducing fantastic images. People who smelled them had a tendency to glimpse momentary mirages of enormous vistas, with strange hills or endless avenues of sphinxes and hippogriffs stretching off into infinite distance. Ward did not resume his old-time rambles, but applied himself diligently to the strange books he had brought home, and to equally strange delvings within his quarters; explaining that European sources had greatly enlarged the possibilities of his work, and promising[c] great revelations in the years to come. His older aspect increased to a startling degree his resemblance to the Curwen portrait in his library;[d] and Dr. Willett would often pause by the latter after a call, marvelling at the virtual identity, and reflecting that only the small pit above the picture's right eye now remained to differentiate the long-dead[e] wizard from the living youth. These calls of Willett's, undertaken at the request of the senior Wards, were curious affairs. Ward at no time repulsed the doctor, but the latter saw that he could never reach the young man's inner psychology.

[a] voice,] voice A, C
[b] bristled] brisked D
[c] promising] promised D
[d] library;] library D
[e] long-dead] long dead C, D

Frequently he noted peculiar things about; little wax images of grotesque design on the shelves or tables, and the half-erased remnants of circles, triangles, and pentagrams in chalk or charcoal on the cleared central space of the large room. And always in the night those rhythms and incantations thundered, till it became very difficult to keep servants or suppress furtive talk of Charles's madness.

In January, 1927, a peculiar incident occurred. One night about midnight, as Charles was chanting a ritual whose weird cadence echoed unpleasantly through the house below, there came a sudden gust of chill wind from the bay, and a faint, obscure trembling of the earth which everyone in the neighbourhood noted. At the same time the cat exhibited phenomenal traces of fright, while dogs bayed for as much as a mile around. This was the prelude to a sharp thunderstorm, anomalous for the season, which brought with it such a crash that Mr. and Mrs. Ward believed the house had been[a] struck. They rushed upstairs to see what damage had been done, but Charles met them at the door to the attic; pale, resolute, and portentous, with an almost fearsome combination of triumph and seriousness on his face. He assured them that the house had not really been struck, and that the storm would soon be over. They paused, and looking through a window saw that he was indeed right; for the lightning flashed farther and farther off, whilst the trees ceased to bend in the strange frigid gust from the water. The thunder sank to a sort of dull mumbling chuckle and finally died away. Stars came out, and the stamp of triumph on Charles Ward's face crystallised into a very singular expression.

For two months or more after this incident Ward was less confined than usual to his laboratory. He exhibited a curious interest in the weather, and made odd inquiries about the date of the spring thawing of the ground. One night late in March he left the house after midnight, and did not return till almost morning;[b] when his mother, being wakeful, heard a rumbling motor draw up to the carriage entrance. Muffled oaths could be distinguished, and Mrs. Ward, rising and going to the window, saw four dark figures removing a long, heavy box from a truck at Charles's direction and carrying it within by the

[a] had been] *om.* C
[b] morning;] morning, D

side door. She heard laboured breathing and ponderous footfalls on the stairs, and finally a dull thumping in the attic; after which the footfalls descended again, and the four men reappeared outside and drove off in their truck.

The next day Charles resumed his strict attic seclusion, drawing down the dark shades of his laboratory windows and appearing to be working on some metal substance. He would open the door to no one, and steadfastly refused all proffered food. About noon a wrenching sound followed by a terrible cry and a fall were heard, but when Mrs. Ward rapped at the door her son at length answered faintly, and told her that nothing had gone amiss. The hideous and indescribable stench now welling out was absolutely harmless and unfortunately necessary. Solitude was the one prime essential, and he would appear later for dinner. That afternoon, after the conclusion of some odd hissing sounds which came from behind the locked portal, he did finally appear;[a] wearing an extremely haggard aspect and forbidding anyone to enter the laboratory upon any pretext. This, indeed, proved the beginning of a new policy of secrecy; for never afterward was any other person permitted to visit either the mysterious garret workroom or the adjacent storeroom which he cleaned out, furnished roughly, and added to his inviolably private domain as a sleeping apartment. Here he lived, with books brought up from his library beneath, till the time he purchased the Pawtuxet bungalow and moved to it all his scientific effects.

In the evening Charles secured the paper before the rest of the family and damaged part of it through an apparent accident. Later on Dr. Willett, having fixed the date from statements by various members of the household, looked up an intact copy at the *Journal* office and found that in the destroyed section the following small item had occurred:

Nocturnal Diggers Surprised in
North Burial Ground

Robert Hart, night watchman at the North Burial Ground, this morning discovered a party of several men with a motor truck in the oldest part of

---

[a] appear;] appear, D

the cemetery, but apparently frightened them off before they had accomplished whatever their object may have been.

The discovery took place at about four[a] o'clock, when Hart's attention was attracted by the sound of a motor outside his shelter. Investigating, he saw a large truck on the main drive several rods away; but could not reach it before the sound of his feet on the gravel had revealed his approach. The men hastily placed a large box in the truck and drove away toward the street before they could be overtaken; and since no known grave was disturbed, Hart believes that this box was an object which they wished to bury.

The diggers must have been at work for a long while before detection, for Hart found an enormous hole dug at a considerable distance back from the roadway in the lot of Amasa[b] Field, where most of the old stones have long ago disappeared. The hole, a place as large and deep as a grave, was empty; and did not coincide with any interment mentioned in the cemetery records.

Sergt.[c] Riley of the Second Station viewed the spot and gave the opinion that the hole was dug by bootleggers rather gruesomely and ingeniously seeking a safe cache for liquor in a place not likely to be disturbed. In reply to questions Hart said he thought the escaping truck had headed up Rochambeau Avenue, though he could not be sure.

During the next few days Ward was seldom seen by his family. Having added sleeping quarters to his attic realm, he kept closely to himself there, ordering food brought to the door and not taking it in until after the servant had gone away. The droning of monotonous formulae and the chanting of bizarre rhythms recurred at intervals, while at other times occasional listeners could detect the sound of tinkling glass, hissing chemicals, running water, or roaring gas flames. Odours of the most unplaceable quality, wholly unlike any[d] before noted, hung at times around the door; and the air of tension observable in the young recluse whenever he did venture briefly forth was such as to excite the keenest speculation. Once he made a hasty trip to the Athenaeum for a book he required, and again he hired a messenger to fetch him a highly obscure volume from Boston.

[a] four] 4 A
[b] Amasa] Amosa C, D
[c] Sergt.] Sergeant C, D
[d] any] any other C

Suspense was written portentously over the whole situation, and both the family and Dr. Willett confessed themselves wholly at a loss what to do or think about it.

6.

Then on the fifteenth of April a strange development occurred. While nothing appeared to grow different in kind, there was certainly a very terrible difference in degree; and Dr. Willett somehow attaches great significance to the change. The day was Good Friday, a circumstance of which the servants made much, but which others quite naturally dismiss as an irrelevant coincidence. Late in the afternoon young Ward began repeating a certain formula in a singularly loud voice, at the same time burning some substance so pungent that its fumes escaped over the entire house. The formula was so plainly audible in the hall outside the locked door that Mrs. Ward could not help memorising it as she waited and listened anxiously, and later on she was able to write it down at Dr. Willett's request. It ran as follows, and experts have told Dr. Willett that its very close analogue can be found in the mystic writings of "Eliphas Levi",[a] that cryptic soul who crept through a crack in the forbidden door and glimpsed the frightful vistas of the void beyond:

> "Per Adonai Eloim, Adonai Jehova,
> Adonai Sabaoth, Metraton On[b] Agla Mathon,[c]
> verbum pythonicum, mysterium salamandrae,
> conventus[d] sylvorum, antra gnomorum,
> daemonia Coeli Gad, Almousin,[e] Gibor, Jehosua,[f]
> Evam, Zariatnatmik, veni,[g] veni, veni."[h]

[a] "Levi",] Levi," C
[b] On] Ou C; *Ou* D
[c] Mathon,] Methon, C; *Methonn,* D
[d] conventus] cenventus C; *cenventus* D
[e] Gad, Almousin,] God, Almonsin, C; *God, Almonsin,* D
[f] Gibor, Jehosua,] Gibor, / Jehosua, C; *Gibor, / Jehosua,* D
[g] Zariatnatmik, veni,] Zariathnatmik, Veni, C; *Zariathnatmik, Veni,* D
[h] "Per . . . veni."] Per . . . veni. C; *Per . . . veni.* D

This had been going on for two hours without change or intermission when over all the neighbourhood a pandaemoniac[a] howling of dogs set in. The extent of this howling can be judged from the space it received in the papers the next day, but to those in the Ward household it was overshadowed by the odour which instantly followed it; a hideous,[b] all-pervasive odour which none of them had ever smelt before or have ever smelt since. In the midst of this mephitic flood there came a very perceptible flash like that of lightning, which would have been blinding and impressive but for the daylight around; and then was heard *the voice* that no listener can ever forget because of its thunderous remoteness, its incredible depth, and its eldritch dissimilarity to Charles Ward's voice. It shook the house, and was clearly heard by at least two neighbours above the howling of the dogs. Mrs. Ward, who had been listening in despair outside her son's locked laboratory, shivered as she recognised its hellish import; for Charles had told her of its evil fame in dark books, and of the manner in which it had thundered, according to the Fenner letters, above the doomed Pawtuxet farmhouse on the night of Joseph Curwen's annihilation. There was no mistaking that nightmare phrase, for Charles had described it too vividly in the old days when he had talked frankly of his Curwen investigations. And yet it was only this fragment of an archaic[c] and forgotten language: "DIES MIES JESCHET BOENE DOESEF DOUVEMA ENITEMAUS."

Close upon this thundering there came a momentary darkening of the daylight, though sunset was still an hour distant, and then a puff of added odour[d] different from the first but equally unknown and intolerable. Charles was chanting again now and his mother could hear syllables that sounded like "Yi-nash-Yog-Sothoth-he-lgeb[e]-fi-throdog"[f]—ending in a "Yah!" whose maniacal force mounted in an ear-splitting[g] crescendo. A second later all previous memories were

---

[a] pandaemoniac] pandemoniac A, C, D
[b] hideous,] hideous C, D
[c] archaic] archaick A, C
[d] odour] odour, C, D
[e] lgeb] lglb C, D
[f] throdog"] throdag" C, D
[g] ear-splitting] earsplitting D

effaced by the wailing scream which burst out with frantic explosiveness and gradually changed form to a paroxysm of diabolic and hysterical laughter. Mrs. Ward, with the mingled fear and blind courage of maternity, advanced and knocked affrightedly at the concealing panels, but obtained no sign of recognition. She knocked again, but paused nervelessly as a second shriek arose, this one unmistakably in the familiar voice of her son, *and sounding concurrently with the still bursting*[a] *cachinnations of that other voice.* Presently she fainted, although she is still unable to recall the precise and immediate cause. Memory sometimes makes merciful deletions.[b]

Mr. Ward returned from the business section at about[c] quarter past six; and[d] not finding his wife downstairs, was told by the frightened servants that she was probably watching at Charles's door, from which the sounds had been far stranger than ever before. Mounting the stairs at once, he saw Mrs. Ward stretched at full length on the floor of the corridor outside the laboratory; and realising that she had fainted, hastened to fetch a glass of water from a set bowl[e] in a neighbouring alcove. Dashing the cold fluid in her face, he was heartened to observe an immediate response on her part, and was watching the bewildered opening of her eyes when a chill shot through him and threatened to reduce him to the very state from which she was emerging. For the seemingly silent laboratory was not as silent as it had appeared to be, but held the murmurs of a tense, muffled conversation in tones too low for comprehension, yet of a quality profoundly disturbing to the soul.

It was not, of course, new for Charles to mutter formulae; but this muttering was definitely different. It was so palpably a dialogue, or imitation of a dialogue, with the regular alternation[f] of inflections suggesting question and answer, statement and response. One voice

---

[a] *still bursting*] *still-bursting* D
[b] deletions.] deletions. ¶ When Mrs. Ward recovered consciousness it was dark, and she had not moved or been moved. Her own scream, if she had given one, could not have been heard above the other din to which the servants had been trained to pay not [*sic*] attention, and although she had A [*excised*]
[c] about] a D
[d] six; and] six, and, D
[e] set bowl] setbowl D
[f] of a . . . alternation] *om.* D

was undisguisedly that of Charles, but the other had a depth and hollowness which the youth's best powers of ceremonial mimicry had scarcely approached before. There was something hideous, blasphemous, and abnormal about it, and but for a cry from his recovering wife which cleared his mind by arousing his protective instincts[a] it is not likely that Theodore Howland Ward could have maintained for nearly a year more his old boast that he had never fainted. As it was, he seized his wife in his arms and bore her quickly downstairs before she could notice the voices which had so horribly disturbed him. Even so, however, he was not quick enough to escape catching something himself which caused him to stagger dangerously with his burden. For Mrs. Ward's cry had evidently been heard by others than he,[b] and there had come in response to it from behind the locked door the first distinguishable words which that hushed[c] and terrible colloquy had yielded. They were merely an excited caution in Charles's own voice, but somehow their implications held a nameless fright for the father who overheard them. The phrase was just this: *"Sshh!—write!"*[xd]

Mr. and Mrs. Ward conferred at some length after dinner, and the former resolved to have a firm and serious talk with Charles that very night. No matter how important the object, such conduct could no[e] longer be permitted; for these latest developments transcended every limit of sanity and formed a menace to the order and nervous well-being of the entire household. The youth must indeed have taken complete leave of his senses,[f] since only downright madness could have prompted the wild screams and imaginary conversations in assumed voices which the present day had brought forth. All this must be stopped,[g] or Mrs. Ward would be made ill and the keeping of servants become an impossibility.

[a] instincts] instincts, C, D
[b] he,] he C, D
[c] hushed] masked D
[d] *write!"*] *write"!* A; *Write!"* C, D
[e] no] not D
[f] senses,] sense, C
[g] stopped,] stopped D

Mr. Ward rose at the close of the meal and started upstairs for Charles's laboratory. On the third floor, however, he paused at the sounds which he heard proceeding from the now disused library of his son. Books were apparently being flung about and papers wildly rustled, and upon stepping to the door Mr. Ward beheld the youth within, excitedly assembling a vast armful of literary matter of every size and shape. Charles's aspect was very drawn and haggard, and he dropped his entire load with a start at the sound of his father's voice. At the elder man's command he sat down, and for some time listened to the admonitions he had so long deserved. There was no scene. At the end of the lecture he agreed that his father was right, and that his noises,[a] mutterings, incantations, and chemical odours were indeed inexcusable nuisances. He agreed to a policy of greater quiet, though insisting on a prolongation of his extreme privacy. Much of his future work, he said, was in any case purely book research; and he could obtain quarters elsewhere for any such vocal rituals as might be necessary at a later stage. For the fright and fainting of his mother he expressed the keenest contrition, and explained that the conversation later heard was part of an elaborate symbolism designed to create a certain mental atmosphere. His use of abstruse technical[b] terms somewhat bewildered Mr. Ward, but the parting impression was one of undeniable sanity and poise[c] despite a mysterious tension of the utmost gravity. The interview was really quite inconclusive, and as Charles picked up his armful and left the room Mr. Ward hardly knew what to make of the entire business. It was as mysterious as the death of poor old Nig, whose stiffening form had been found an hour before in the basement, with staring eyes and fear-distorted mouth.[d]

Driven by some vague detective instinct, the bewildered parent now glanced curiously at the vacant shelves to see what his son had taken up to the attic. The youth's library was plainly and rigidly classified, so that one might tell at a glance the books or at least the

[a] noises,] voices, D
[b] technical] chemical C, D
[c] poise] poise, C, D
[d] form . . . mouth.] form, with staring eyes and fear-distorted mouth, had been found an hour before in the basement. D

kind of books which had been withdrawn. On this occasion Mr. Ward was astonished to find that nothing of the occult or the antiquarian, beyond what had been previously removed, was missing. These new withdrawals were all modern items; histories, scientific treatises, geographies, manuals of literature, philosophic works, and certain contemporary newspapers and magazines. It was a very curious shift from Charles Ward's recent run of reading, and the father paused in a growing vortex of perplexity and an engulfing sense of strangeness. The strangeness was a very poignant sensation, and almost clawed at his chest as he strove to see just what was wrong around him. Something was indeed wrong, and tangibly as well as spiritually so. Ever since he had been in this room he had known that something was amiss, and at last it dawned upon him what it was.

On the north wall rose still the ancient carved overmantel from the house in Olney Court, but to the cracked and precariously restored oils of the large Curwen portrait disaster had come. Time and unequal heating had done their work at last, and at some time since the room's last cleaning the worst had happened. Peeling clear of the wood, curling tighter and tighter, and finally crumbling into small bits with what must have been malignly silent suddenness, the portrait of Joseph Curwen had resigned for ever[a] its staring surveillance of the youth it so strangely resembled, and now lay scattered on the floor as a thin coating of fine bluish-grey dust.

IV. A MUTATION AND A MADNESS

1.

In the week following that memorable Good Friday Charles Ward was seen more often than usual, and was continually carrying books between his library and the attic laboratory. His actions were quiet and rational, but he had a furtive, hunted look which his mother did not like, and developed an incredibly ravenous appetite as gauged by his demands upon the cook.[b] Dr. Willett had been told of those Friday

[a] for ever] forever C
[b] cook.] cook. ¶ C, D

noises and happenings, and on the following Tuesday had a long conversation with the youth in the library where the picture stared no more. The interview was, as always, inconclusive; but Willett is still ready to swear that the youth was sane and himself at the time. He held out promises of an early revelation, and spoke of the need of securing a laboratory elsewhere. At the loss of the portrait he grieved singularly little considering his first enthusiasm over it, but seemed to find something of positive humour in its sudden crumbling.[a]

About the second week Charles began to be absent from the house for long periods, and one day when good old black Hannah came to help with the spring cleaning she mentioned his frequent visits to the old house in Olney Court, where he would come with a large valise and perform curious delvings in the cellar. He was always very liberal to her and to old Asa, but seemed more worried than he used to be;[b] which grieved her very much, since she had watched him grow up from birth.[c] Another report of his doings came from Pawtuxet, where some friends of the family saw him at a distance a surprising number of times. He seemed to haunt the resort and canoe-house of Rhodes-on-the-Pawtuxet, and subsequent inquiries by Dr. Willett at that place brought out the fact that his purpose was always to secure access to the rather hedged-in river-bank, along which he would walk toward the north, usually not reappearing for a very long while.

Late[d] in May came a momentary revival of ritualistic sounds in the attic laboratory which brought a stern reproof from Mr. Ward and a

[a] crumbling.] crumbling. ¶ Also in this week was a very curious but no doubt irrelevant incident which one of the servants reported upon suddenly leaving without notice. She had been delivering food—an unholy lot of it, as she thought—at the locked attic door when Charles Ward had suddenly appeared at the other end of the corridor. He had said nothing and done nothing to frighten her, but she had been frightened none the less. He had been blundering along, she said, as if he did not know his way; and she had not liked his face at the moment. Mrs. Ward, upon hearing this plaint, at once summoned Charles; who treated the story with amused contempt. He did not seem to frighten the superstitious girl this time, but she nevertheless persisted in her determination to leave. The Charles in the hall upstairs, she insisted, 'wasn't the same'. A [*excised*]
[b] be;] be, D
[c] birth.] birth. ¶ C, D
[d] Late] Later C, D

somewhat distracted promise of amendment from Charles. It occurred one morning, and seemed to form a resumption of the imaginary conversation noted on that turbulent Good Friday. The youth was arguing or remonstrating hotly with himself, for there suddenly burst forth a perfectly distinguishable series of clashing shouts in differentiated tones like alternate demands and denials[a] which caused Mrs. Ward to run upstairs and listen at the door. She could hear no more than a fragment whose only plain words were "must have it red for three months",[b] and upon her knocking all sounds ceased at once.[c] When Charles was later questioned by his father he said that there were certain conflicts of spheres of consciousness which only great skill could avoid, but which he would try to transfer to other realms.

About the middle of June a queer nocturnal incident occurred. In the early evening there had been some noise and thumping in the laboratory upstairs, and Mr. Ward was on the point of investigating when it suddenly quieted down. That midnight, after the family had retired, the butler was nightlocking the front door when according to his statement Charles appeared somewhat blunderingly and uncertainly at the foot of the stairs with a large suitcase and made signs that he wished egress. The youth spoke no word, but the worthy Yorkshireman caught one sight of his fevered eyes and trembled causelessly. He opened the door and young Ward went out, but in the morning he presented his resignation to Mrs. Ward. There was, he said, something unholy in the glance Charles had fixed on him. It was no way for a young gentleman

---

[a] denials] denials, C, D

[b] months",] months," C

[c] once.] once. The shouting had been in the two distinct voices which Charles had used before; one his known tones, and the other a deep, hollow, and utterly disguised thing which somehow chilled her horribly. The strange voice had been demanding something, and the familiar voice kept replying, "I won't!", or "you shan't do that." It seemed easier to recall the familiar voice than the strange one, but Mrs. Ward kept one of the alien phrases in mind to tell her husband that evening. It was a sort of throaty gurgle which sounded like: "Where is that —— planted? You get that —— carcass or let me get it. I'll give ye a week, and then, by ——, I'll have him this way or that. And —— ye, I'll keep still no more nor I please!" Another one was approximately the following: "Ye fool, I tell un, dig in the *nor'east* corner." Still another was: "I'll wait no more, I must get there myself. Do you let me there, A [*excised*]

to look at an honest person, and he could not possibly stay another night. Mrs. Ward allowed the man to depart, but she did not value his statement highly. To fancy Charles in a savage state that night was quite ridiculous, for as long as she had remained awake she had heard faint sounds from the laboratory above; sounds as if of sobbing and pacing, and of a sighing which told only of despair's profoundest depths. Mrs. Ward had grown used to listening for sounds in the night, for the mystery of her son was fast driving all else from her mind.

The next evening, much as on another evening nearly three months before, Charles Ward seized the newspaper very early and accidentally lost the main section. This matter was not recalled till later, when Dr. Willett began checking up loose ends and searching out missing links here and there. In the *Journal* office he found the section which Charles had lost, and marked two items as of possible significance. They were as follows:

More Cemetery Delving

It was this morning discovered by Robert Hart, night watchman at the North Burial Ground, that ghouls were again at work in the ancient portion of the cemetery.[a] The grave of Ezra Weeden, who was born in 1740 and died in 1824 according to his uprooted and savagely splintered slate headstone, was found excavated and rifled, the work being evidently done with a spade stolen from an adjacent tool-shed.[b]

Whatever the contents may have been after more than a century of burial, all was gone except a few slivers of decayed wood. There were no wheel tracks, but the police have measured a single set of footprints which they found in the vicinity, and which indicate the boots of a man of refinement.

Hart is inclined to link this incident with the digging discovered last March, when a party in a motor truck were frightened away after making a deep excavation; but Sergt.[c] Riley of the Second Station discounts this theory and points to vital differences in the two cases. In March the digging had been in a spot where no grave was known; but this time a well-marked and cared-for grave had been rifled with every evidence of deliberate purpose, and with a conscious malignity expressed in the splintering of the slab which had been intact up to the day before.

[a] cemetery.] cemetary. D
[b] tool-shed.] tool shed. A, C, D
[c] Sergt.] Sergeant C, D

Members of the Weeden family, notified of the happening, expressed their astonishment and regret; and were wholly unable to think of any enemy who would care to violate the grave of their ancestor. Hazard Weeden of 598 Angell Street recalls a family legend according to which Ezra Weeden was involved in some very peculiar circumstances, not dishonourable to himself, shortly before the Revolution; but of any modern feud or mystery he is frankly ignorant. Inspector Cunningham has been assigned to the case, and hopes to uncover some valuable clues in the near future.

Dogs Noisy in Pawtuxet

Residents of Pawtuxet were aroused about 3 a.m.[a] today by a phenomenal baying of dogs which seemed to centre near the river just north of Rhodes-on-the-Pawtuxet.[b] The volume and quality of the howling were unusually odd, according to most who heard it; and Fred Lemdin, night watchman at Rhodes, declares it was mixed with something very like the shrieks of a man in mortal terror and agony. A sharp and very brief thunderstorm, which seemed to strike somewhere near the bank of the river, put an end to the disturbance. Strange and unpleasant odours, probably from the oil tanks along the bay, are popularly linked with this incident; and may have had their share in exciting the dogs.

The aspect of Charles now became very haggard and hunted, and all agree[c] in retrospect that he may have wished at this period to make some statement or confession from which sheer terror withheld him. The morbid listening of his mother in the night brought out the fact that he made frequent sallies abroad under cover of darkness, and most of the more academic alienists unite at present in charging him with the revolting cases of vampirism which the press so sensationally reported about this time, but which have not yet been definitely traced to any known perpetrator. These cases, too recent and celebrated to need detailed mention, involved victims of every age and type and seemed to cluster around two distinct localities; the residential hill and the North End, near the Ward home, and the suburban districts across the Cranston line near Pawtuxet. Both late wayfarers and sleepers with open windows were attacked, and those who lived to tell the tale spoke

[a] 3 a.m.] three A.M. C; three a.m. D
[b] Rhodes-on-the-Pawtuxet.] Rhodes-on-the Pawtuxet. D
[c] agree] agreed D

unanimously of a lean, lithe, leaping monster with burning eyes which fastened its teeth in the throat or upper arm and feasted ravenously.

Dr. Willett, who refuses to date the madness of Charles Ward as far back as even this, is cautious in attempting to explain these horrors. He has, he declares, certain theories of his own; and limits his positive statements to a peculiar kind of negation. "I will not," he says, "state who or what I believe perpetrated these attacks and murders, but I will declare that Charles Ward was innocent of them. I have reason to be sure he was ignorant of the taste of blood, as indeed his continued anaemic decline and increasing pallor prove better than any verbal argument. Ward meddled with terrible things, but he has paid for it, and he was never a monster or a villain. As for now—[a]I don't like to think. A change came, and I'm content to believe that the old Charles Ward died with it. His soul did, anyhow, for that mad flesh that vanished from Waite's hospital had another."

Willett speaks with authority, for he was often at the Ward home attending Mrs. Ward, whose nerves had begun to snap under the strain. Her nocturnal listening had bred some morbid hallucinations which she confided to the doctor with hesitancy, and which he ridiculed in talking to her, although they made him ponder deeply when alone. These delusions always concerned the faint sounds which she fancied she heard in the attic laboratory and bedroom, and emphasised the occurrence[b] of muffled sighs and sobbings at the most impossible times. Early in July Willett ordered Mrs. Ward to Atlantic City for an indefinite recuperative sojourn, and cautioned both Mr. Ward and the haggard and elusive Charles to write her only cheering letters. It is probably to this enforced and reluctant escape that she owes her life and continued sanity.

2.

Not long after his mother's departure Charles Ward began negotiating for the Pawtuxet bungalow. It was a squalid little wooden edifice with a concrete garage, perched high on the sparsely settled bank of the

---

[a] now—] now, C, D
[b] occurrence] occurrences D

river slightly above Rhodes, but for some odd reason the youth would have nothing else. He gave the real-estate agencies no peace till one of them secured it for him at an exorbitant price from a somewhat reluctant owner, and as soon as it was vacant he took possession under cover of darkness, transporting in a great closed van the entire contents of his attic laboratory, including the books both weird and modern which he had borrowed from his study. He had this van loaded in the black small hours, and his father recalls only a drowsy realisation of stifled oaths and stamping feet on the night the goods were taken away. After that Charles moved back to his own old[a] quarters on the third floor, and never haunted the attic again.

To the Pawtuxet bungalow Charles transferred all the secrecy with which he had surrounded his attic realm, save that he now appeared to have two sharers of his mysteries; a villainous-looking Portuguese[b] half-caste from the South Main St. waterfront[c] who acted as a servant, and a thin, scholarly stranger with dark glasses and a stubbly full beard of dyed aspect whose status was evidently that of a colleague. Neighbours vainly tried to engage these odd persons in conversation. The mulatto Gomes spoke very little English, and the bearded man, who gave his name as Dr. Allen,[d] voluntarily followed his example. Ward himself tried to be more affable, but succeeded only in provoking curiosity with his rambling accounts of chemical research. Before long queer tales began to circulate regarding the all-night burning of lights; and somewhat later, after this burning had suddenly ceased, there rose still queerer tales of disproportionate orders of meat from the butcher's and of the muffled shouting,[e] declamation, rhythmic chanting, and screaming supposed to come from some very deep cellar below the place. Most distinctly the new and strange household was bitterly disliked by the honest bourgeoisie of the vicinity, and it is not remarkable that dark hints were advanced connecting the hated establishment with the current epidemic of

[a] old] *om.* D
[b] Portuguese] Portugese A, C
[c] St. waterfront] Street Waterfront C, D
[d] man, . . . Allen,] man . . . Allen C, D
[e] shouting,] shouting C

vampiristic attacks and murders; especially since the radius of that plague seemed now confined wholly to Pawtuxet and the adjacent streets of Edgewood.

Ward spent most of his time at the bungalow, but slept occasionally at home and was still reckoned a dweller beneath his father's roof. Twice he was absent from the city on week-long trips, whose destinations have not yet been discovered.[a] He grew steadily paler and more emaciated even than before, and lacked some of his former assurance when repeating to Dr. Willett his old, old story of vital research and future revelations. Willett often waylaid him at his father's house, for the elder Ward was deeply worried and perplexed, and wished his son to get as much sound oversight as could be managed in the case of so secretive and independent an adult. The doctor still insists that the youth was sane even as late as this, and adduces many a conversation to prove his point.

About September the vampirism declined, but in the following January Ward almost became involved in serious trouble. For some time the nocturnal arrival and departure of motor trucks at the Pawtuxet bungalow had been commented upon, and at this juncture an unforeseen hitch exposed the nature of at least one item of their contents.[b] In a lonely spot near Hope Valley had occurred one of the frequent sordid waylayings[c] of trucks by "hi-jackers" in quest of liquor

[a] discovered.] discovered. About September the vampirism declined, and the public began to notice a prevailing mania for grave-robberies which seemed to develop out of the two old cases noted earlier in the year. The objects of this gruesome pilfering were mostly very old interments, and the methods were so rapid and efficient that no capture was ever made by the police; but several cemetery watchmen mentioned a small motor coupe with blurred number plates as the vehicle of the escaping ghouls, and at length the offences ceased as local graveyard protection became more and more adequate. The authorities formed no real suspicions as to the criminals; but Pawtuxet gossip hinted that Ward kept a Ford coupe in his concrete garage, and that it was often heard departing and arriving at the most unholy times of night. A [*excised*]
[b] contents.] contents. A party of "hi-jackers", those armed banditti who prey upon illicit carriers of liquor, had noted the steady traffic; and having drawn some very commonplace conclusions, had resolved to make a haul in their most approved manner. Learning to recognise [*new page:*] During one of the A [*excised*]
[c] waylayings] waylaying D

shipments, but this time the robbers had been destined to receive the greater shock. For the long cases they seized proved upon opening to contain some exceedingly gruesome things; so gruesome, in fact, that the matter could not be kept quiet amongst the denizens of the underworld. The thieves had hastily buried what they discovered, but when the State Police got wind of the matter a careful search was made. A recently arrested vagrant, under promise of immunity from prosecution on any additional charge, at last consented to guide a party of troopers to the spot; and there was found in that hasty cache a very hideous and shameful thing. It would not be well for the national—or even the international—sense of decorum if the public were ever to know what was uncovered by that awestruck party. There was no mistaking it, even by these far from studious officers; and telegrams to Washington ensued with feverish rapidity.

The cases were addressed to Charles Ward at his Pawtuxet bungalow, and State and Federal officials at once paid him a very forceful and serious call. They found him pallid and worried with his two odd companions, and received from him what seemed to be a valid explanation and evidence of innocence. He had needed certain anatomical specimens as part of a programme of research whose depth and genuineness anyone who had known him in the last decade could prove, and had ordered the required kind and number from agencies which he had thought as reasonably legitimate as such things can be. Of the *identity* of the specimens he had known absolutely nothing, and was properly shocked when the inspectors hinted at the monstrous effect on public sentiment and national dignity which a knowledge of the matter would produce. In this statement he was firmly sustained by his bearded colleague Dr. Allen, whose oddly hollow voice carried even more conviction than his own nervous tones; so that in the end the officials took no action,[a] but carefully set down the New York name and address which Ward gave them as a basis for a search which came to nothing. It is only fair to add that the specimens were quickly and quietly restored to their proper places, and that[b] the general public will never know of their blasphemous disturbance.

[a] action,] actions D
[b] that] *om.* D

On February[a] 9, 1928, Dr. Willett received a letter from Charles Ward which he considers of extraordinary importance, and about which he has frequently quarrelled with Dr. Lyman. Lyman believes that this note contains positive proof of a well-developed case of *dementia praecox,* but Willett on the other hand regards it as the last perfectly sane utterance of the hapless youth. He calls especial attention to the normal character of the penmanship; which[b] though shewing[c] traces of shattered nerves, is nevertheless distinctly Ward's own. The text in full is as follows:

"100 Prospect St.
Providence, R.I.,[d]
February[e] 8, 1928

"Dear[f] Dr. Willett:—

"I[g] feel that at last the time has come for me to make the disclosures which I have so long promised you, and for which you have pressed me so often. The patience you have shewn in waiting, and the confidence you have shewn[h] in my mind and integrity, are things I shall never cease to appreciate.

"And[i] now that I am ready to speak, I must own with humiliation that no triumph such as I dreamed of can ever be mine. Instead of triumph I have found terror, and my talk with you will not be a boast of victory but a plea for help and advice in saving both myself and the world from a horror beyond all human conception or calculation. You recall what those Fenner letters said of the old raiding party at Pawtuxet. That must all be done again, and quickly. Upon us depends more than can be put into words—all civilisation, all natural law, perhaps even the fate of the solar system and the universe. I have brought to light a monstrous abnormality, but I did it for the sake of knowledge. Now for the sake of all life and Nature[j] you must help me thrust it back into the dark again.

[a] February] ~~March~~ February A
[b] which] which, D
[c] shewing] showing D
[d] "100 . . . St. / . . . R.I.,] 100 . . . St., / . . . R. I., C; Providence, R.I., / 100 Prospect St., D
[e] February] March A, D
[f] "Dear] Dear C, D
[g] "I] I C, D
[h] shewn . . . shewn] shown . . . shown D
[i] "And] And C, D
[j] Nature] nature A, C, D

"I[a] have left that Pawtuxet place for ever,[b] and we must extirpate everything existing there, alive or dead. I shall not go there again, and you must not believe it if you ever hear that I am there. I will tell you why I say this when I see you. I have come home for good, and wish you would call on me at the very first moment that you can spare five or six hours continuously to hear what I have to say. It will take that long—and believe me when I tell you that you never had a more genuine professional duty than this. My life and reason are the very least things which hang in the balance.

"I[c] dare not tell my father, for he could not grasp the whole thing. But I have told him of my danger, and he has four men from a detective agency watching the house. I don't know how much good they can do, for they have against them forces which even you could scarcely envisage or acknowledge. So come quickly if you wish to see me alive and hear how you may help to save the cosmos from stark hell.

"Any[d] time will do—I shall not be out of the house. Don't telephone ahead, for there is no telling who or what may try to intercept you. And let us pray to whatever gods there be that nothing may prevent this meeting.

"In[e] utmost gravity and desperation,

"Charles Dexter Ward."[f]

"P.S. Shoot Dr. Allen on sight *and dissolve his body in acid.* Don't burn it."[g]

Dr. Willett received this note about 10:30 a.m.,[h] and immediately arranged to spare the whole late afternoon and evening for the momentous talk, letting it extend on into the night as long as might be necessary. He planned to arrive about four o'clock, and through all the intervening hours was so engulfed in every sort of wild speculation that most of his tasks were very mechanically performed. Maniacal as the letter would have sounded to a stranger, Willett had seen too much of Charles Ward's oddities to dismiss it as sheer raving. That something very subtle, ancient, and horrible was hovering about he felt quite sure, and the reference to Dr. Allen could almost be comprehended in view

[a] "I] I C, D
[b] for ever,] forever, A, C, D
[c] "I] I C, D
[d] "Any] Any C, D
[e] "In] In C, D
[f] "Charles Dexter Ward."] Charles Dexter Ward. C
[g] "P.S. . . . Don't burn it."] P. S. . . . *Don't burn it!* C; P.S. . . . *Don't burn it.* D
[h] 10:30 a.m.,] ten-thirty A.M., C; ten-thirty a.m., D

of what Pawtuxet gossip said of Ward's enigmatical colleague. Willett had never seen the man, but had heard much of his aspect and bearing, and could not but wonder what sort of eyes those much-discussed dark glasses might conceal.

Promptly at four Dr. Willett presented himself at the Ward residence, but found to his annoyance that Charles had not adhered to his determination to remain indoors. The guards were there, but said that the young man seemed to have lost part of his timidity. He had that morning done much apparently frightened arguing and protesting over the telephone, one of the detectives said, replying to some unknown voice with phrases such as "I am very tired and must rest a while",[a] "I can't receive anyone for some time, you'll have to excuse me",[b] "Please postpone decisive action till we can arrange some sort of compromise",[c] or "I am very sorry, but I must take a complete vacation from everything; I'll talk with you later".[d] Then, apparently gaining boldness through meditation, he had slipped out so quietly that no one had seen him depart or knew that he had gone until he returned about one[e] o'clock and entered the house without a word. He had gone upstairs, where a bit of his fear must have surged back; for he was heard to cry out in a highly[f] terrified fashion upon entering his library, afterward trailing off into a kind of choking gasp. When, however, the butler had gone to inquire what the trouble was, he had appeared at the door with a great show of boldness, and had silently gestured the man away in a manner that terrified him unaccountably. Then he had evidently done some rearranging of his shelves, for a great clattering and thumping and creaking ensued; after which he had reappeared and left at once. Willett inquired whether or not any message had been left, but was told that there was none. The butler seemed queerly disturbed about something in Charles's appearance and manner, and asked solicitously if there was much hope for a cure of his disordered nerves.

[a] while",] while," C
[b] me",] me," C
[c] compromise",] compromise," C
[d] later".] later." A, C
[e] one] 1 A
[f] highly] high C; high, D

For almost two hours Dr. Willett waited vainly in Charles Ward's library, watching the dusty shelves with their wide gaps where books had been removed, and smiling grimly at the panelled overmantel on the north wall, whence a year before the suave features of old Joseph Curwen had looked mildly down. After a time the shadows began to gather, and the sunset cheer gave place to a vague growing terror which flew shadow-like[a] before the night. Mr. Ward finally arrived, and shewed[b] much surprise and anger at his son's absence[c] after all the pains which had been taken to guard him. He had not known of Charles's appointment, and promised to notify Willett when the youth returned. In bidding the doctor goodnight he expressed his utter perplexity at his son's condition, and urged his caller to do all he could to restore the boy to normal poise. Willett was glad to escape from that library, for something frightful and unholy seemed to haunt it; as if the vanished picture had left behind a legacy of evil. He had never liked that picture; and even now, strong-nerved though he was, there lurked a quality in its vacant panel which made him feel an urgent need to get out into the pure air as soon as possible.

3.

The next morning Willett received a message from the senior Ward, saying that Charles was still absent. Mr. Ward mentioned that Dr. Allen had telephoned him to say that Charles would remain at Pawtuxet for some time, and that he must not be disturbed. This was necessary because Allen himself was suddenly called away for an indefinite period, leaving the researches in need of Charles's constant oversight. Charles sent his best wishes, and regretted any bother his abrupt change of plans might have caused. In listening to this message Mr. Ward heard Dr. Allen's voice for the first time, and it seemed to excite some vague and elusive memory which could not be actually placed, but which was disturbing to the point of fearfulness.

Faced by these baffling and contradictory reports, Dr. Willett was

[a] shadow-like] shadow-/like C; shadowlike D
[b] shewed] showed C, D
[c] absence] absence, D

frankly at a loss what to do. The frantic earnestness of Charles's note was not to be denied, yet what could one think of its writer's immediate violation of his own expressed policy? Young Ward had written that his delvings had become blasphemous and menacing, that they and his bearded colleague must be extirpated at any cost, and that he himself would never return to their final scene; yet according to latest advices he had forgotten all this and was back in the thick of the mystery. Common sense bade one leave the youth alone with his freakishness, yet some deeper instinct would not permit the impression of that frenzied letter to subside. Willett read it over again, and could not make its essence sound as empty and insane as both its bombastic verbiage and its lack of fulfilment would seem to imply. Its terror was too profound and real, and in conjunction with what the doctor already knew[a] evoked too vivid hints of monstrosities from beyond time and space[b] to permit of any cynical explanation. There were nameless horrors abroad; and no matter how little one might be able to get at them, one ought to stand prepared for any sort of action at any time.

For over a week[c] Dr. Willett pondered on the dilemma which seemed thrust upon him, and became more and more inclined to pay Charles a call at the Pawtuxet bungalow. No friend of the youth had ever ventured to storm this forbidden retreat, and even his father knew of its interior only from such descriptions as he chose to give; but Willett felt that some direct conversation with his patient was necessary. Mr. Ward had been receiving brief and non-committal typed notes from his son, and said that Mrs. Ward in her Atlantic City retirement had had no better word. So at length the doctor resolved to act;[d] and despite a curious sensation inspired by old legends of Joseph Curwen, and by more recent revelations and warnings from Charles Ward, set boldly out for the bungalow on the bluff above the river.

Willett had visited the spot before through sheer curiosity, though of course never entering the house or proclaiming his presence;[e] hence

---

[a] and . . . knew] and, . . . knew, D
[b] space] space, A, C, D
[c] week] week, D
[d] act;] act, D
[e] presence;] presence, D

knew exactly the route to take. Driving out[a] Broad Street one early afternoon toward the end of February in his small motor, he thought oddly of the grim party which had taken that selfsame[b] road a hundred and fifty-seven years before[c] on a terrible errand which none might ever comprehend.[d]

The ride through the city's decaying fringe was short, and trim Edgewood and sleepy Pawtuxet presently spread out ahead. Willett turned to the right down Lockwood Street and drove his car as far along that rural road as he could, then alighted and walked north to where the bluff towered above the lovely bends of the river and the sweep of misty downlands beyond. Houses were still few here, and there was no mistaking the isolated bungalow with its concrete garage on a high point of land at his left. Stepping briskly up the neglected gravel walk he rapped at the door with a firm hand, and spoke without a tremor to the evil Portuguese[e] mulatto who opened it to the width of a crack.

He must, he said, see Charles Ward at once on vitally important business. No excuse would be accepted, and a repulse would mean only a full report of the matter to the elder Ward. The mulatto still hesitated, and pushed against the door when Willett attempted to open it; but the doctor merely raised his voice and renewed his demands. Then there came from the dark interior a husky whisper which somehow chilled the hearer through and through[f] though he did not know why he feared it. "Let him in, Tony," it said, "we[g] may as well talk now as ever." But disturbing as was the whisper, the greater fear was that which immediately followed. The floor creaked and the

---

[a] out] out by D
[b] selfsame] self-same D
[c] before] before, C, D
[d] comprehend.] comprehend. Just beyond the Round-Top Church he looked back from the high-ground and surveyed the clustered roofs and domes and steeples of Old Providence in the glow of new spring sunlight. What lurking arcana of darkness lay beneath the surface of the centuried town, and from what lingering horror must its ancient hillside lanes and busy modern thoroughfares be saved? A [excised]
[e] Portuguese] Portugese A, C
[f] through] through, C, D
[g] "we] "We C

speaker hove in sight—and the owner of those strange and resonant tones was seen to be no other than Charles Dexter Ward.

The minuteness with which Dr. Willett recalled and recorded his conversation of that afternoon is due to the importance he assigns to this particular period. For at last he concedes a vital change in Charles Dexter Ward's mentality,[a] and believes that the youth now spoke from a brain hopelessly alien to the brain whose growth he had watched for six and twenty years. Controversy with Dr. Lyman has compelled him to be very specific, and he definitely dates the madness of Charles Ward from the time the typewritten notes began to reach his parents. Those notes are not in Ward's normal style; not even in the style of that last frantic letter to Willett. Instead, they are strange and archaic,[b] as if the snapping of the writer's mind had released a flood of tendencies and impressions picked up unconsciously through boyhood antiquarianism. There is an obvious effort to be modern, but the spirit and occasionally the language are those of the past.

The past, too, was evident in Ward's every tone and gesture as he received the doctor in that shadowy bungalow. He bowed, motioned Willett to a seat, and began to speak abruptly in that strange whisper which he sought to explain at the very outset.

"I am grown phthisical," he began, "from this cursed river air. You must excuse my speech. I suppose you are come from my father to see what ails me, and I hope you will say nothing to alarm him."

Willett was studying these scraping tones with extreme care, but studying even more closely the face of the speaker. Something, he felt, was wrong; and he thought of what the family had told him about the fright of that Yorkshire butler one night. He wished it were not so dark, but did not request that any blind be opened. Instead, he merely asked Ward why he had so belied the frantic note of little more than a week before.

"I was coming to that," the host replied. "You must know,[c] I am in a very bad state of nerves, and do and say queer things I cannot account

[a] mentality,] mentality D
[b] archaic,] archaick, C
[c] know,] know D

for. As I have told you often, I am on the edge of great matters;[a] and
the bigness of them has a way of making me light-headed. Any man
might well be frighted[b] of what I have found, but I am not to be put
off for long. I was a dunce to have that guard and stick at home; for
having gone this far, my place is here. I am not well spoke of by my
prying neighbours, and perhaps I was led by weakness to believe
myself what they say of me. There is no evil to any in what I do, so long
as I do it rightly. Have the goodness to wait six months, and I'll shew[c]
you what will pay your patience well.

"You may as well know I have a way of learning old matters from
things surer than books, and I'll leave you to judge the importance of
what I can give to history, philosophy, and the arts by reason of the doors
I have access to. My ancestor had all this when those witless peeping
Toms came and murdered him. I now have it again, or am coming very
imperfectly to have a part of it. This time nothing must happen, and least
of all through any idiot fears of my own. Pray forget all I writ you, Sir,
and have no fear of this place or any in it. Dr. Allen is a man of fine
parts, and I owe him an apology for anything ill I have said of him. I wish
I had no need to spare him, but there were things he had to do
elsewhere. His zeal is equal to mine in all those matters, and I suppose
that when I feared the work I feared him too as my greatest helper in it."

Ward paused, and the doctor hardly knew what to say or think. He
felt almost foolish in the face of this calm repudiation of the letter; and
yet there clung to him the fact that while the present discourse was
strange and alien and indubitably mad, the note itself had been tragic in
its naturalness and likeness to the Charles Ward he knew. Willett now
tried to turn the talk on early matters, and recall to the youth some past
events which would restore a familiar mood; but in this process he
obtained only the most grotesque results. It was the same with all the
alienists later on. Important sections of Charles Ward's store of mental
images, mainly those touching modern times and his own personal life,
had been unaccountably expunged; whilst[d] all the massed antiquarianism

---

[a] matters;] matters, D
[b] frighted] frightened D
[c] shew] show D
[d] whilst] while C, D

of his youth had welled up from some profound subconsciousness to engulf the contemporary and the individual. The youth's intimate[a] knowledge of elder[b] things was abnormal and unholy, and he tried his best to hide it. When Willett would mention some favourite object of his boyhood archaistic studies he often shed by pure accident such a light as no normal mortal could conceivably be expected to possess, and the doctor shuddered as the glib allusion glided by.

It was not wholesome to know so much about the way the fat sheriff's wig fell off as he leaned over at the play in Mr. Douglass'[c] Histrionick Academy in King Street on the eleventh[d] of February, 1762, which fell on[e] a Thursday; or about how the actors cut the text of Steele's "Conscious Lovers"[f] so badly that one was almost glad the Baptist-ridden legislature closed the theatre a fortnight later. That Thomas Sabin's Boston coach was "damn'd uncomfortable" old letters may well have told; but what healthy antiquarian could recall how the creaking of Epenetus Olney's new signboard (the gaudy crown[g] he set up after he took to calling his tavern the Crown Coffee House) was exactly like the first few notes of the new jazz piece all the radios in Pawtuxet were playing?

Ward, however, would not be quizzed long in this vein. Modern and personal topics he waved aside quite summarily, whilst regarding antique affairs he soon shewed[h] the plainest boredom. What he wished clearly enough was only to satisfy his visitor enough to make him depart without the intention of returning. To this end he offered to shew[i] Willett the entire house, and at once proceeded to lead the doctor through every room from cellar to attic. Willett looked sharply, but noted that the visible books were far too few and trivial ever to have filled the wide gaps on Ward's shelves at home, and that the meagre so-

[a] intimate] ultimate C, D
[b] elder] older D
[c] Douglass'] Douglass's C
[d] eleventh] 11th A
[e] on] of A, C
[f] Lovers"] Lover" A, C, D
[g] crown] Crown C, D
[h] shewed] showed D
[i] shew] show D

called "laboratory" was the flimsiest[a] sort of a blind. Clearly[b] there were a library and a laboratory elsewhere; but just where, it was impossible to say. Essentially defeated in his quest for something he could not name, Willett returned to town before evening and told the senior Ward everything which had occurred. They agreed that the youth must be definitely out of his mind, but decided that nothing drastic need be done just then. Above all, Mrs. Ward must be kept in as complete an ignorance as her son's own strange typed notes would permit.

Mr. Ward now determined to call in person upon his son, making it wholly a surprise visit. Dr. Willett took him in his car one evening,[c] guiding him to within sight of the bungalow and waiting patiently for his return. The session was a long one, and the father emerged in a very saddened and perplexed state. His reception had developed much like Willett's, save that Charles had been an excessively long time in appearing after the visitor had forced his way into the hall and sent the Portuguese[d] away with an imperative demand; and in the bearing of the altered son there was no trace of filial affection. The lights had been dim, yet even so the youth had complained that they dazzled him outrageously. He had not spoken out loud at all, averring that his throat was in very poor condition; but in his hoarse whisper there was a quality so vaguely disturbing that Mr. Ward could not banish it from his mind.

Now definitely leagued together to do all they could toward the youth's mental salvation, Mr. Ward and Dr. Willett set about collecting every scrap of data which the case might afford. Pawtuxet gossip was the first item they studied, and this was relatively easy to glean since both had friends in that region. Dr. Willett obtained the most rumours because people talked more frankly to him than to a parent of the central figure, and from all he heard he could tell that young Ward's life had become indeed a strange one. Common tongues would not dissociate his household from the vampirism of the previous summer, while the nocturnal comings and goings of the motor trucks provided

[a] flimsiest] filmsiest C
[b] Clearly] Clearly, C
[c] evening,] evening D
[d] Portuguese] Portugese A

their share of dark speculation. Local tradesmen spoke of the queerness of the orders brought them by the evil-looking mulatto, and in particular of the inordinate amounts of meat and fresh blood secured from the two butcher shops in the immediate neighbourhood. For a household of only three, these quantities were quite absurd.

Then there was the matter of the sounds beneath the earth. Reports of these things were harder to pin down, but all the vague hints tallied in certain basic essentials. Noises of a ritual nature positively existed, and at times when the bungalow was dark. They might, of course, have come from the known cellar; but rumour insisted that there were deeper and more spreading crypts. Recalling the ancient tales of Joseph Curwen's catacombs, and assuming for granted that the present bungalow had been selected because of its situation on the old Curwen site as revealed in one or another of the documents found behind the picture, Willett and Mr. Ward gave this phase of the gossip much attention; and searched many times without success for the door in the river-bank[a] which old manuscripts mentioned. As to popular opinions of the bungalow's various inhabitants, it was soon plain that the Brava Portuguese[b] was loathed, the bearded and spectacled Dr. Allen feared, and the pallid young scholar disliked to a profound extent. During the last week or two Ward had obviously changed much, abandoning his attempts at affability and speaking only in hoarse but oddly repellent whispers on the few occasions that he ventured forth.

Such were the shreds and fragments gathered here and there; and over these Mr. Ward and Dr. Willett held many long and serious conferences. They strove to exercise deduction, induction, and constructive imagination to their utmost extent; and to correlate every known fact of Charles's later life, including the frantic letter which the doctor now shewed[c] the father, with the meagre documentary evidence available concerning old Joseph Curwen. They would have given much for a glimpse of the papers Charles had found, for very clearly the key to the youth's madness lay in what he had learned of the ancient wizard and his doings.

[a] river-bank] river bank A, C, D
[b] Portuguese] Portugese A
[c] shewed] showed D

4.

And yet, after all, it was from no step of Mr. Ward's or Dr. Willett's that the next move in this singular case proceeded. The father and the physician, rebuffed and confused by a shadow too shapeless and intangible to combat,[a] had rested uneasily on their oars while the typed notes of young Ward to his parents grew fewer and fewer. Then came the first of the month with its customary financial adjustments, and the clerks at certain banks began a peculiar shaking of heads and telephoning from one to the other. Officials who knew Charles Ward by sight went down to the bungalow to ask why every cheque of his appearing at this juncture was a clumsy forgery, and were reassurred less than they ought to have been when the youth hoarsely explained that his hand had lately been so much affected by a nervous shock as to make normal writing impossible. He could, he said, form no written characters at all except with great difficulty; and could prove it by the fact that he had been forced to type all his recent letters, even those to his father and mother, who would bear out the assertion.

What made the investigators pause in confusion was not this circumstance alone, for that was nothing unprecedented or fundamentally suspicious; nor even the Pawtuxet gossip, of which one or two of them had caught echoes. It was the muddled discourse of the young man which nonplussed them, implying as it did a virtually total loss of memory concerning important monetary matters which he had had at his fingertips only a month or two before. Something was wrong;[b] for despite the apparent coherence and rationality of his speech, there could be no normal reason for this ill-concealed blankness on vital points. Moreover, although none of these men knew Ward well, they could not help observing the change in his language and manner. They had heard he was an antiquarian, but even the most hopeless antiquarians do not make daily[c] use of obsolete phraseology and gestures. Altogether, this combination of hoarseness, palsied hands, bad memory, and[d] altered

[a] combat,] combat D
[b] wrong;] wrong, D
[c] daily] *om.* D
[d] and] *om.* D

speech and bearing must represent[a] some disturbance or malady of genuine gravity, which no doubt[b] formed the basis of the prevailing odd rumours; and after their departure the party of officials decided that a talk with the senior Ward was imperative.

So on the sixth[c] of March, 1928, there was a long and serious conference in Mr. Ward's office, after which the utterly bewildered father summoned Dr. Willett in a kind of helpless resignation. Willett looked over the strained and awkward signatures of the cheques, and compared them in his mind with the penmanship of that last frantic note. Certainly, the change was radical and profound, and yet there was something damnably familiar about the new writing. It had crabbed and archaic[d] tendencies of a very curious sort, and seemed to result from a type of[e] stroke utterly different from that which the youth had always used. It was strange—but where had he seen it before? On the whole, it was obvious that Charles was insane. Of that there could be no doubt. And since it appeared unlikely that he could handle his property or continue to deal with the outside world much longer, something must quickly be done toward his oversight and possible cure. It was then that the alienists were called in, Drs. Peck and Waite of Providence and Dr. Lyman of Boston, to whom Mr. Ward and Dr. Willett gave the most exhaustive possible history of the case, and who conferred at length in the now unused library of their young patient, examining what books and papers of his were left in order to gain some further notion of his habitual mental cast. After scanning this material and examining the ominous[f] note to Willett[g] they all agreed that Charles Ward's studies had been enough to unseat or at least to warp any ordinary intellect, and wished most heartily that they could see his more intimate volumes and documents; but this latter they knew they could do, if at all, only after a scene at the bungalow itself. Willett now reviewed the whole case with febrile energy; it being at this time

---

[a] bearing must represent] bearing, represented D
[b] which no doubt] which, no doubt, C, D
[c] sixth] 6th A
[d] archaic] archaick C
[e] very . . . of a] *om.* D
[f] ominous] meaningless C; youth's D
[g] Willett] Willett, C, D

that he obtained the statements of the workmen who had seen Charles find the Curwen documents, and that he collated the incidents of the destroyed newspaper items, looking up the latter at the *Journal* office.

On Thursday, the eighth[a] of March, Drs. Willett, Peck, Lyman,[b] and Waite, accompanied by Mr. Ward, paid the youth their momentous call; making no concealment of their object and questioning the now acknowledged patient with extreme minuteness. Charles, though he was inordinately long in answering the summons and was still redolent of strange and noxious laboratory odours when he did finally make his agitated appearance, proved a far from recalcitrant subject; and admitted freely that his memory and balance had suffered somewhat from close application to abstruse studies. He offered no resistance when his removal to other quarters was insisted upon; and seemed, indeed, to display a high degree of intelligence as apart from mere memory. His conduct would have sent his interviewers away in bafflement had not the persistently archaic trend of his speech and unmistakable replacement of modern by ancient ideas in his consciousness marked him out as one definitely removed from the normal. Of his work he would say no more to the group of doctors than he had formerly said to his family and to Dr. Willett, and his frantic note of the previous month he dismissed as mere nerves and hysteria. He insisted that this shadowy bungalow possessed no library or laboratory beyond the visible ones, and waxed abstruse in explaining the absence from the house of such odours as now saturated all his clothing. Neighbourhood gossip he attributed to nothing more than the cheap inventiveness of baffled curiosity. Of the whereabouts of Dr. Allen he said he did not feel at liberty to speak definitely, but assured his inquisitors[c] that the bearded and spectacled man would return when needed. In paying off the stolid Brava who resisted all questioning by the visitors, and in closing the bungalow which still seemed to hold such nighted secrets, Ward shewed[d] no sign of nervousness save a barely noticed tendency to pause as though listening for something very faint.

[a] eighth] 8th A
[b] Lyman,] Lyman A, C, D
[c] inquisitors] visitors D
[d] shewed] showed D

He was apparently animated by a calmly philosophic resignation, as if his removal were the merest transient incident which would cause the least trouble if facilitated and disposed of once and for all. It was clear that he trusted to his obviously unimpaired keenness of absolute mentality to overcome all the embarrassments into which his twisted memory, his lost voice and handwriting, and his secretive and eccentric behaviour had led him. His mother, it was agreed, was not to be told of the change; his father supplying typed notes in his name. Ward was taken to the restfully and picturesquely situated private hospital maintained by Dr. Waite on Conanicut Island in the bay, and subjected to the closest scrutiny and questioning by all the physicians connected with the case. It was then that the physical oddities were noticed; the slackened metabolism, the altered skin, and the disproportionate neural reactions. Dr. Willett was the most perturbed of the various examiners, for he had attended Ward all his life and could appreciate with terrible keenness the extent of his physical disorganisation.[a] Even the familiar olive mark on his hip was gone, while on his chest was a great black mole or cicatrice which had never been there before, and which made Willett wonder whether the youth had ever submitted to any of the "witch markings" reputed to be inflicted at certain unwholesome nocturnal meetings in wild and lonely places. The doctor could not keep his mind off a certain transcribed witch-trial record from Salem which Charles had shewn[b] him in the old non-secretive days, and which read: "Mr. G. B. on that Nighte putt y[e] Divell his Marke upon Bridget S., Jonathan A., Simon O., Deliverance W., Joseph C., Susan P., Mehitable C., and Deborah B." Ward's face, too, troubled him horribly, till at length he suddenly discovered why he was horrified. For above[c] the young man's right eye was something which he had never previously noticed—a small scar or pit precisely like that in the crumbled painting of old Joseph Curwen, and perhaps attesting some hideous ritualistic inoculation to which both had submitted at a certain stage of their occult careers.

While Ward himself was puzzling all the doctors at the hospital[d] a

[a] disorganisation.] disorganization. D
[b] shewn] shown D
[c] For above] Above C, D
[d] hospital] hospital, C, D

very strict watch was kept on all mail addressed either to him or to Dr. Allen, which Mr. Ward had ordered delivered at the family home. Willett had predicted that very little would be found, since any communications of a vital nature would probably have been exchanged by messenger; but in the latter part of March there did come a letter from Prague for Dr. Allen which gave both the doctor and the father deep thought. It was in a very crabbed and archaic[a] hand; and though clearly not the effort of a foreigner, shewed[b] almost as singular a departure from modern English as the speech of young Ward himself. It read:

Kleinstrasse 11,
Altstadt, Prague,
11th Feby. 1928.

Brother in Almousin-Metraton:—[c]

I this day receiv'd y[r] mention of what came up[d] from the Salts[e] I sent you. It was wrong, and meanes clearly that y[e] Headstones had been chang'd when Barnabas[f] gott me the Specimen. It is often so, as you must be sensible of from the Thing you gott from y[e] Kings[g] Chapell ground in 1769 and what H.[h] gott from Olde Bury'g[i] Point in 1690, that was like to ende him. I gott such a Thing[j] in Aegypt 75 yeares gone, from the which came that Scar y[e] Boy saw on me here in 1924. As I told you longe ago, do not calle up That which you can not put[k] downe; either from dead Saltes or out of y[e] Spheres beyond. Have y[e] Wordes for laying at all times readie, and stopp not to be sure when there is any Doubte of *Whom* you have. Stones are all chang'd now in Nine groundes out of 10. You are never sure till you question. I this day heard from H., who has had Trouble with the Soldiers. He is like to be sorry Transylvania is pass'd from Hungary to Roumania,[l]

<hr>

[a] archaic] archaick C
[b] shewed] showed D
[c] Almousin-Metraton:—] Almousin-Metraton!— C, D
[d] up] upp D
[e] Salts] Saltes C, D
[f] Barnabas] Barnabus D
[g] Kings] King's C, D
[h] H.] ye D
[i] Bury'g] Bury's C
[j] Thing] thing D
[k] put] putt C
[l] Roumania,] Romania, D

and wou'd change his Seat if the Castel weren't so fulle of What we Knowe. But of this he hath doubtless writ you. In my next Send'g there will be Somewhat from a Hill tomb from ye East that will delight you greatly. Meanwhile forget not I am desirous of B. F. if you can possibly get him for me. You know G. in Philada.[a] better than I. Have him up firste if you will, but doe not use him soe hard he will be Difficult, for I must speake to him in ye End.[b]

Yogg-Sothoth Neblod Zin
Simon O.

To Mr. J. C. in
Providence.

Mr. Ward and Dr. Willett paused in utter chaos before this apparent bit of unrelieved insanity. Only by degrees did they absorb what it seemed to imply. So the absent Dr. Allen, and not Charles Ward, had come to be the leading spirit at Pawtuxet? That must explain the wild reference and denunciation[c] in the youth's last frantic letter. And what of this addressing of the bearded and spectacled stranger as "Mr. J. C."? There was no escaping the inference, but there are limits to possible monstrosity. Who was "Simon O.";[d] the old man Ward had visited in Prague four years previously? Perhaps, but in the centuries behind there had been another Simon O.—Simon Orne, alias Jedediah, of Salem, who vanished in 1771, *and whose peculiar handwriting Dr. Willett now unmistakably recognised from the photostatic copies of the Orne formulae which Charles had once shewn[e] him.* What horrors and mysteries, what contradictions and contraventions of Nature,[f] had come back after a century and a half to harass Old Providence with her clustered spires and domes?

The father and the old physician, virtually at a loss what to do or think, went to see Charles at the hospital and questioned him as delicately as they could about Dr. Allen, about the Prague visit, and about what he had learned of Simon or Jedediah Orne of Salem. To all

[a] Philada.] Philadelphia C, D
[b] End.] Ende. C, D
[c] denunciation] determination D
[d] O.";] O"; A; "O." D
[e] *shewn*] *shown* D
[f] Nature,] nature, A, C, D

these inquiries the youth was politely non-committal, merely barking in his hoarse whisper that he had found Dr. Allen to have a remarkable spiritual rapport with certain souls from the past, and that any correspondent the bearded man might have in Prague would probably be similarly gifted. When they left, Mr. Ward and Dr. Willett realised to their chagrin that they had really been the ones under catechism; and that without imparting anything vital himself, the confined youth had adroitly pumped them of everything the Prague letter had contained.

Drs. Peck, Waite, and Lyman were not inclined to attach much importance to the strange correspondence of young Ward's companion; for they knew the tendency of kindred eccentrics and monomaniacs to band together, and believed that Charles or Allen had merely unearthed an expatriated counterpart—perhaps one who had seen Orne's handwriting and copied it in an attempt to pose as the bygone character's reincarnation. Allen himself was perhaps a similar case, and may have persuaded the youth into accepting him as an avatar of the long-dead Curwen. Such things had been known before, and on the same basis the hard-headed doctors disposed of Willett's growing disquiet about Charles Ward's present handwriting, as studied from unpremeditated specimens obtained by various ruses. Willett thought he had placed its odd familiarity at last, and that what it vaguely resembled was the bygone penmanship of old Joseph Curwen himself; but this the other physicians regarded as a phase of imitativeness only to be expected in a mania of this sort, and refused to grant it any importance either favourable or unfavourable. Recognising this prosaic attitude in his colleagues, Willett advised Mr. Ward to keep to himself the letter which arrived for Dr. Allen on the second[a] of April from Rakus, Transylvania, in a handwriting so intensely and fundamentally like that of the Hutchinson cipher that both father and physician paused in awe before breaking the seal. This read as follows:

[a] second] 2nd A

Castle Ferenczy

7 March 1928.[a]

Dear C.:—[b]Hadd a Squad[c] of 20 Militia up[d] to talk about what the Country Folk say. Must digg deeper and have less Hearde. These Roumanians[e] plague me[f] damnably, being officious and particular where you cou'd buy a Magyar off with a Drinke and ffood.[g] Last monthe[h] M. got me ye Sarcophagus of y^e [i] Five Sphinxes from ye Acropolis where He whome I call'd up say'd it wou'd be, and I have hadde 3 Talkes with[j] *What was therein*[k] *inhum'd*. It will go to S. O. in Prague directly, and thence to you. It is stubborn but you know ye Way with Such. You shew Wisdom in having lesse about than Before; for there was no Neede to keep the Guards in Shape and eat'g off their Heads,[l] and it made Much[m] to be founde in Case[n] of Trouble, as you too[o] welle know. *You*[p] can now move and worke[q] elsewhere with no Kill'g Trouble if needful, tho'[r] I hope no Thing will soon force you to so Bothersome a Course. I rejoice that you traffick not so much with *Those Outside;*[s] for there was ever a Mortall Peril in it, and you are sensible what it did when you ask'd[t] Protection of One[u] not dispos'd to give it. You excel me in gett'g ye fformulae[v] so *another* may

[a] March 1928.] March, 1928. C; March 1928 D
[b] C.:—] C.:— ¶ C, D
[c] Squad] Squd A, C, D
[d] up] upp D
[e] Roumanians] Romanians D
[f] me] one C, D
[g] ffood.] food. C, D
[h] monthe] Monthe C, D
[i] got . . . y^e] gott me ye carcophagus of ye C; gott me the sarcophagus of the D
[j] with] *with* C, D
[k] *therein*] *therin* D
[l] Heads,] Heades, C, D
[m] Much] much C, D
[n] Case] case C, D
[o] too] two C, D
[p] *You*] You C, D
[q] worke] Worke C, D
[r] tho'] though C, D
[s] *Outside;*] *Outside,* D
[t] ask'd] asked C, D
[u] One] one C, D
[v] fformulae] formulae C, D

saye them with Success, but Borellus fancy'd it wou'd be so if just y[e] right Wordes were hadd. Does y[e] Boy use 'em often? I regret that he growes squeamish, as I fear'd he wou'd when I hadde him here nigh 15[a] Monthes, but am sensible you knowe[b] how to deal with him. You can't saye him down with y[e] fformula,[c] for that will Worke only upon such as y[e] other fformula[d] hath call'd up[e] from Saltes; but you still have strong Handes and Knife and Pistol, and Graves are not harde to digg, nor Acids loth to burne. O. sayes you have promis'd him B. F. I must have him after. B. goes to you soone, and may he give you what you wishe of that Darke Thing belowe Memphis. Imploy care in what you calle up,[f] and beware of y[e] Boy. It will be ripe in a yeare's time to have up[g] y[e] Legions from Underneath, and then there are no Boundes to what shal be oures. Have Confidence in what I saye, for you knowe O. and I have hadd these 150 yeares more than you to consulte these Matters in.

Nephren-Ka[h] nai Hadoth
Edw: H.

For J. Curwen, Esq.
Providence.

But if Willett and Mr. Ward refrained from shewing[i] this letter to the alienists, they did not refrain from acting upon it themselves. No amount of learned sophistry could controvert the fact that the strangely bearded[j] and spectacled Dr. Allen, of whom Charles's frantic letter had spoken as such a monstrous menace, was in close and sinister correspondence with two inexplicable creatures whom Ward had visited in his travels and who plainly claimed to be survivals or avatars of Curwen's old Salem colleagues; that he was regarding himself as the reincarnation of Joseph Curwen, and that he entertained—or was at least advised to entertain—murderous designs against a "boy" who could scarcely be other than Charles Ward. There was organised

---

[a] 15] fifteen C, D
[b] knowe] know D
[c] fformula,] Formula, A, C; Formulae, D
[d] fformula] Formula A, C; Formulae D
[e] up] upp D
[f] up,] upp, D
[g] up] upp D
[h] Nephren-Ka] Nephreu—Ka C, D
[i] shewing] showing D
[j] bearded] barded D

horror afoot;[a] and no matter who had started it, the missing Allen was by this time at the bottom of it. Therefore, thanking heaven[b] that Charles was now safe in the hospital, Mr. Ward lost no time in engaging detectives to learn all they could of the cryptic bearded doctor; finding whence he had come and what Pawtuxet knew of him, and if possible discovering his current whereabouts. Supplying the men[c] with one of the bungalow keys which Charles yielded up, he urged them to explore Allen's vacant room which had been identified when the patient's belongings had been packed; obtaining what clues they could from any effects he might have left about. Mr. Ward talked with the detectives in his son's old library, and they felt a marked relief when they left it at last; for there seemed to hover about the place a vague aura of evil.[d] Perhaps it was what they had heard of the infamous old wizard whose picture had once stared from the panelled overmantel, and perhaps it was something different and irrelevant; but in any case they all half sensed[e] an intangible miasma which centred in that carven[f] vestige of an older dwelling and which at times almost rose to the intensity of a material emanation.

V. A NIGHTMARE AND A CATACLYSM

1.

And now swiftly followed that hideous experience which has left its indelible mark of fear on the soul of Marinus Bicknell Willett, and has added a decade to the visible age of one whose youth was even then far behind. Dr. Willett had conferred at length with Mr. Ward, and had come to an agreement with him on several points which both felt the alienists would ridicule. There was, they conceded, a terrible movement alive in the world, whose direct connexion[g] with a

---

[a] afoot;] afoot, D
[b] heaven] Heaven A, C, D
[c] men] man C
[d] evil.] Evil. D
[e] half sensed] half-sensed A, C, D
[f] carven] craven C
[g] connexion] connection D

necromancy even older than the Salem witchcraft could not be doubted. That at least two living men—and one other of whom they dared not think—were in absolute possession of minds or personalities which had functioned as early as 1690 or before was likewise almost unassailably proved even in the face of all known natural laws. What these horrible creatures—and Charles Ward as well—were doing or trying to do seemed fairly clear from their letters and from every bit of light both old and new which had filtered in upon the case. They were robbing the tombs of all the ages, including those of the world's wisest and greatest men, in the hope of recovering from the[a] bygone ashes some vestige of the consciousness and lore which had once animated and informed them.

A hideous traffick[b] was going on among these[c] nightmare ghouls, whereby illustrious bones were bartered with the calm calculativeness of schoolboys swapping books; and from what was extorted from this centuried dust there was anticipated a power and a wisdom beyond anything which the cosmos had ever seen concentred[d] in one man or group. They had found unholy ways to keep their brains alive, either in the same body or different bodies; and had evidently achieved a way of tapping the consciousness of the dead whom they gathered together. There had, it seems, been some truth in chimerical old Borellus when he wrote of preparing from even the most antique remains certain "Essential Saltes" from which the shade of a long-dead living thing might be raised up. There was a formula for evoking such a shade, and another for putting it down; and it had now been so perfected that it could be taught successfully. One must be careful about evocations, for the markers of old graves are not always accurate.

Willett and Mr. Ward shivered as they passed from conclusion to conclusion. Things—presences or voices of some sort—could be drawn down from unknown places as well as from the grave, and in this process also one must be careful. Joseph Curwen had indubitably evoked many forbidden things, and as for Charles—what might one

---

[a] the] *om.* C, D
[b] traffick] traffic D
[c] among these] about those C; among those D
[d] concentred] concentrated C, D

think of him? What forces "outside the spheres" had reached him from Joseph Curwen's day and turned his mind on forgotten things? He had been led to find certain directions, and he had used them. He had talked with the man of horror in Prague and stayed long with the creature in the mountains of Transylvania. And he must have found the grave of Joseph Curwen at last. That newspaper item and what his mother had heard in the night were too significant to overlook. Then he had summoned something, and it must have come. That mighty voice aloft on Good Friday, and those *different* tones in the locked attic laboratory. What were they like, with their depth and hollowness? Was there not here some awful foreshadowing of the dreaded stranger Dr. Allen with his spectral bass? Yes, *that*[a] was what Mr. Ward had felt with vague horror in his single talk with the man—if man it were—over the telephone![b]

What hellish consciousness or voice, what morbid shade or presence, had come to answer Charles Ward's secret rites behind that locked door? Those voices heard in argument—"must have it red for three months"—Good God! Was not that just before the vampirism broke out? The rifling of Ezra Weeden's[c] ancient grave, and the cries later at Pawtuxet—whose mind had planned the vengeance and rediscovered the shunned seat of elder blasphemies? And then the bungalow and the bearded stranger, and the gossip, and the fear. The final madness of Charles neither father nor doctor could attempt to explain, but they did feel sure that the mind of Joseph Curwen had come to earth again and was following its ancient morbidities. Was daemoniac[d] possession in truth a possibility? Allen had something to do with it, and the detectives must find out more about one whose existence menaced the young man's life. In the meantime, since the existence of some vast crypt beneath the bungalow seemed virtually beyond dispute, some effort must be made to find it. Willett and Mr. Ward, conscious of the sceptical attitude of the alienists, resolved

[a] *that*] that C
[b] telephone!] telephone. D
[c] Weeden's] Bowen's A
[d] daemoniac] demoniac D

during their final conference to undertake a joint secret[a] exploration of unparalleled[b] thoroughness; and agreed to meet at the bungalow on the following morning with valises and with certain tools and accessories suited to architectural search and underground exploration.

The morning of April 6th[c] dawned clear, and both explorers were at the bungalow by ten o'clock. Mr. Ward had the key, and an entry and cursory survey were made. From the disordered condition of Dr. Allen's room it was obvious that the detectives had been there before, and the later searchers hoped that they had found some clue which might prove of value. Of course the main business lay in the cellar; so thither they descended without much delay, again making the circuit which each had vainly made before in the presence of the mad young owner. For a time everything seemed baffling, each inch of the earthen floor and stone walls having so solid and innocuous an aspect that the thought of a yawning aperture was scarcely to be entertained. Willett reflected that since the original cellar was dug without knowledge of any catacombs beneath, the beginning of the passage would represent the strictly modern delving of young Ward and his associates,[d] where they had probed for the ancient vaults whose rumour could have reached them by no wholesome means.

The doctor tried to put himself in Charles's place to see how a delver would be likely to start, but could not gain much inspiration from this method. Then he decided on elimination as a policy, and went carefully over the whole subterranean surface both vertical and horizontal, trying to account for every inch separately. He was soon substantially narrowed down, and at last had nothing left but the small platform before the washtubs, which he had tried once before in vain. Now experimenting in every possible way,[e] and exerting a double strength, he finally found that the top did indeed turn and slide horizontally on a corner pivot. Beneath it lay a trim concrete surface with an iron manhole, to which Mr. Ward at once rushed with excited

---

[a] secret] *om.* D
[b] unparalleled] unparallelled A
[c] 6th] sixth C, D
[d] associates,] associates D
[e] possible way,] way possible, D

zeal. The cover was not hard to lift, and the father had quite removed it when Willett noticed the queerness of his aspect. He was swaying and nodding dizzily, and in the gust of noxious air which swept up from the black pit beneath the doctor soon recognised[a] ample cause.

In a moment Dr. Willett had his fainting companion on the floor above and was reviving him with cold water. Mr. Ward responded feebly, but it could be seen that the mephitic blast from the crypt had in some way gravely sickened him. Wishing to take no chances, Willett hastened out to Broad Street[b] for a taxicab and had soon despatched[c] the sufferer home despite his weak-voiced protests; after which he produced an electric torch, covered his nostrils with a band of sterile gauze, and descended once more to peer into the new-found depths. The foul air had now slightly abated, and Willett was able to send a beam of light down the Stygian hole. For about ten feet, he saw, it was a sheer cylindrical drop with concrete walls and an iron ladder; after which the hole appeared to strike a flight of old stone steps which must originally have emerged to earth somewhat southwest[d] of the present building.

2.

Willett freely admits that for a moment the memory of the old Curwen legends kept him from climbing down alone into that malodorous gulf. He could not help thinking of what Luke Fenner had reported on that last monstrous night. Then duty asserted itself and he made the plunge,[e] carrying a great valise for the removal of whatever papers might prove of supreme importance. Slowly, as befitted one of his years, he descended the ladder and reached the slimy steps below. This was ancient masonry, his torch told him; and upon the dripping walls he saw the unwholesome moss of centuries. Down, down, ran the steps; not spirally, but in three abrupt turns; and with such narrowness that two men could have passed only with difficulty. He had counted about

[a] recognised] recognized D
[b] Street] Strreet C
[c] despatched] dispatched A, C, D
[d] southwest] southward C, D
[e] plunge,] plunge D

thirty when a sound reached him very faintly; and after that he did not feel disposed to count any more.

It was a godless sound; one of those low-keyed, insidious outrages of Nature[a] which are not meant to be. To call it a dull wail, a doom-dragged whine,[b] or a hopeless howl of chorused anguish and stricken flesh without mind would be to miss its most quintessential loathsomeness and soul-sickening overtones. Was it for this that Ward had seemed to listen on that day he was removed? It was the most shocking thing that Willett had ever heard, and it continued from no determinate point as the doctor reached the bottom of the steps and cast his torchlight around on lofty corridor walls surmounted by Cyclopean vaulting and pierced by numberless black archways. The hall in which he stood was perhaps fourteen feet high to the middle of the vaulting and ten or twelve feet broad. Its pavement was of large chipped flagstones, and its walls and roof were of dressed masonry. Its length he could not imagine, for it stretched ahead indefinitely into the blackness. Of the archways, some had doors of the old six-panelled[c] colonial type,[d] whilst others had none.

Overcoming the dread induced by the smell and the howling, Willett began to explore these archways one by one; finding beyond them rooms with groined stone ceilings, each of medium size and apparently of bizarre uses. Most[e] of them had fireplaces, the upper courses of whose chimneys would have formed an interesting study in engineering. Never before or since had he seen such instruments or suggestions of instruments as[f] here loomed up on every hand through the burying dust and cobwebs of a century and a half, in many cases evidently shattered as if by the ancient raiders. For many of the chambers seemed wholly untrodden by modern feet, and must have represented the earliest and most obsolete phases of Joseph Curwen's experimentation.[g] Finally there came a room of obvious modernity, or

[a] Nature] nature A, C, D
[b] whine,] whine D
[c] six-panelled] six panelled D
[d] type,] style, C
[e] uses. Most] uses; most C, D
[f] as] which D
[g] experimentation.] experimentations. D

at least of recent occupancy. There were oil heaters, bookshelves and tables, chairs and cabinets, and a desk piled high with papers of varying antiquity and contemporaneousness. Candlesticks and oil lamps stood about in several places; and finding a match-safe[a] handy, Willett lighted such as were ready for use.

In the fuller gleam it appeared that this apartment was nothing less than the latest study or library of Charles Ward. Of the books the doctor had seen many before, and a good part of the furniture had plainly come from the Prospect Street mansion. Here and there was a piece well known to Willett, and the sense of familiarity became so great that he half forgot the noisomeness and the wailing, both of which were plainer here than they had been at the foot of the steps. His first duty, as planned long ahead, was to find and seize any papers which might seem of vital importance; especially those portentous documents found by Charles so long ago behind the picture in Olney Court. As he searched he perceived how stupendous a task the final unravelling would be; for file on file was stuffed with papers in curious hands and bearing curious designs, so that months or even years might be needed for a thorough deciphering and editing. Once he found large packets[b] of letters with Prague and Rakus postmarks, and in writing clearly recognisable as Orne's and Hutchinson's; all of which he took with him as part of the bundle to be removed in his valise.

At last, in a locked mahogany cabinet once gracing the Ward home, Willett found the batch of old Curwen papers; recognising them from the reluctant glimpse Charles had granted him so many years ago. The youth had evidently kept them together very much as they had been when first[c] he found them, since all the titles recalled by the workmen were present except the papers addressed to Orne and Hutchinson,[d] and the cipher with its key. Willett placed the entire lot in his valise and continued his examination of the files. Since young Ward's immediate condition was the greatest matter at stake, the closest searching was done among the most obviously recent matter;

[a] match-safe] match safe A, C; box of matches D
[b] packets] jackets C
[c] first] *om.* D
[d] Hutchinson,] Hutchinson D

and in this abundance of contemporary manuscript one very baffling oddity was noted. That oddity was the slight amount in Charles's normal writing, which indeed included nothing more recent than two months before. On the other hand, there were literally reams of symbols and formulae, historical notes and philosophical comment, in a crabbed penmanship absolutely identical with the ancient script of Joseph Curwen, though of undeniably modern dating. Plainly, a part of the latter-day programme had been a sedulous imitation of the old wizard's writing, which Charles seemed to have carried to a marvellous state of perfection. Of any third hand which might have been Allen's there was not a trace. If he had indeed come to be the leader, he must have forced young Ward to act as his amanuensis.

In this new material one mystic formula, or rather pair of formulae, recurred so often that Willett had it by heart before he had half finished his quest. It consisted of two parallel columns, the left-hand one surmounted by the archaic symbol called "Dragon's Head" and used in almanacks to indicate the ascending node, and the right-hand one headed by a corresponding sign of "Dragon's Tail" or descending node. The appearance of the whole was something like this, and almost unconsciously the doctor realised that the second half was no more than the first written syllabically backward with the exception of the final monosyllables and of the odd name *Yog-Sothoth,* which he had come to recognise under various spellings from other things he had seen in connexion[a] with this horrible matter. The formulae were as follows—*exactly* so, as Willett is abundantly able to testify—and the first one struck an odd note of uncomfortable latent memory in his brain, which he recognised later when reviewing the events of that horrible Good Friday of the previous year.

☊	☋
Y'AI 'NG'NGAH,[b]	OGTHROD AI'F
YOG-SOTHOTH	GEB'L—EE'H
H'EE—L'GEB	*YOG-SOTHOTH*
F'AI THRODOG	'NGAH'NG AI'Y
UAAAH	*ZHRO*

[a] connexion] connection D
[b] Y'AI 'NG'NGAH,] Y'AI'NG'NGAH, D

So[a] haunting were these formulae, and so frequently did he come upon them, that before the doctor knew it he was repeating them under his breath. Eventually, however, he felt he had secured all the papers he could digest to advantage for the present; hence resolved to examine no more till he could bring the sceptical alienists en masse for an ampler[b] and more systematic raid. He had still to find the hidden laboratory, so leaving his valise in the lighted room he emerged again into the black noisome corridor whose vaulting echoed ceaselessly with that dull and hideous whine.

The next few rooms he tried were all abandoned,[c] or filled only with crumbling boxes and ominous-looking leaden coffins; but impressed him deeply with the magnitude of Joseph Curwen's original operations. He thought of the slaves and seamen who had disappeared, of the graves which had been violated in every part of the world, and of what that final raiding party must have seen; and then he decided it was better not to think any more. Once a great stone staircase mounted at his right, and he deduced that this must have reached to one of the Curwen outbuildings—perhaps the famous stone edifice with the high slit-like[d] windows—provided the steps he had descended had led from the steep-roofed farmhouse. Suddenly the walls seemed to fall away ahead, and the stench and the wailing grew stronger. Willett saw that he had come upon a vast open space, so great that his torchlight would not carry across it; and as he advanced he encountered occasional stout pillars supporting the arches of the roof.

After a time he reached a circle of pillars grouped like the monoliths of Stonehenge, with a large carved altar on a base of three steps in the centre;[e] and so curious were the carvings on that altar that he approached to study them with his electric light. But when he saw what they were he shrank away shuddering, and did not stop to investigate the dark stains which discoloured the upper surface and had spread down the sides in occasional thin lines. Instead, he found

[a] So] ¶ So D
[b] ampler] ample C, D
[c] abandoned,] abandoned C, D
[d] slit-like] slitlike A
[e] centre;] center; D

the distant wall and traced it as it swept round in a gigantic circle perforated by occasional black doorways and indented by a myriad of shallow cells with iron gratings and wrist and ankle bonds on chains fastened to the stone of the concave rear masonry. These cells were empty, but still the horrible odour and the dismal moaning continued, more insistent now than ever, and seemingly varied at times by a sort of slippery thumping.

3.

From that frightful smell and that uncanny noise Willett's attention could no longer be diverted. Both were plainer and more hideous in the great pillared hall than anywhere else, and carried a vague impression of being far below, even in this dark nether world of subterrene mystery. Before trying any of the black archways for steps leading further down, the doctor cast his beam of light about the stone-flagged floor. It was very loosely paved, and at irregular intervals there would occur a slab curiously pierced by small holes in no definite arrangement, while at one point there lay a very long ladder carelessly flung down. To this ladder, singularly enough, appeared to cling a particularly large amount of the frightful odour which encompassed everything. As he walked slowly about it suddenly occurred to Willett that both the noise and the odour seemed strongest directly above the oddly pierced slabs, as if they might be crude trap-doors leading down to some still deeper[a] region of horror. Kneeling by one, he worked at it with his hands, and found that with extreme difficulty he could budge it. At his touch the moaning beneath ascended to a louder key, and only with vast trepidation did he persevere in the lifting of the heavy stone. A stench unnamable[b] now rose up from below, and the doctor's head reeled dizzily as he laid back the slab and turned his torch upon the exposed square yard of gaping blackness.

If he had expected a flight of steps to some wide gulf of ultimate abomination, Willett was destined to be disappointed; for amidst that foetor and cracked whining he discerned only the brick-faced top of a

[a] to some still deeper] still deeper to some D
[b] unnamable] unnameable D

cylindrical well perhaps a yard and a half in diameter and devoid of any ladder or other means of descent. As the light shone down, the wailing changed suddenly to a series of horrible yelps; in conjunction with which there came again that sound of blind, futile scrambling[a] and slippery thumping. The explorer trembled, unwilling even to imagine what noxious thing might be lurking in that abyss,[b] but in a moment[c] mustered up the courage to peer over the rough-hewn brink;[d] lying at full length and holding the torch downward at arm's length to see what might lie below. For a second he could distinguish nothing but the slimy, moss-grown brick walls sinking illimitably into that half-tangible miasma of murk and foulness and anguished frenzy; and then he saw that something dark was leaping clumsily and frantically up and down at the bottom of the narrow shaft,[e] which must have been from twenty to twenty-five feet below the stone floor where he lay. The torch shook in his hand, but he looked again to see what manner of living creature might be immured there in the darkness of that unnatural well; left starving by young Ward through all the long month since the doctors had taken him away, and clearly only one of a vast number prisoned in the kindred wells whose pierced stone covers so thickly studded in the floor of the great vaulted cavern. Whatever the things were, they could not lie down in their cramped spaces; but must have crouched and whined and waited and feebly leaped all those hideous weeks since their master had abandoned them unheeded.

But Marinus Bicknell Willett was sorry that he looked again; for surgeon and veteran of the dissecting-room though he was, he has not been the same since. It is hard to explain just how a single sight of a tangible object with measureable[f] dimensions could so shake and change a man; and we may only say that there is about certain outlines and entities a power of symbolism and suggestion which acts frightfully on a sensitive thinker's perspective and whispers terrible

---

[a] scrambling] scrambing D
[b] abyss,] abyss; C, D
[c] moment] moment he D
[d] brink;] brink, D
[e] shaft,] shaft D
[f] measureable] measurable C

hints of obscure cosmic relationships and unnamable[a] realities behind the protective illusions of common vision. In that second look Willett saw such an outline or entity, for during the next few instants he was undoubtedly as stark mad as any inmate of Dr. Waite's private hospital. He dropped the electric torch from a hand drained of muscular power or nervous coördination,[b] nor heeded the sound of crunching teeth which told of its fate at the bottom of the pit. He screamed and screamed and screamed in a voice whose falsetto panic no acquaintance of his would ever have recognised;[c] and though he could not rise to his feet he crawled and rolled desperately away over the damp pavement where dozens of Tartarean wells poured forth their exhausted whining and yelping to answer his own insane cries. He tore his hands on the rough, loose stones, and many times bruised his head against the frequent pillars, but still he kept on. Then at last he slowly came to himself in the utter blackness and stench, and stopped his ears against the droning wail into which the burst of yelping had subsided. He was drenched with perspiration and without means of producing a light; stricken and unnerved in the abysmal blackness and horror, and crushed with a memory he never could efface. Beneath him dozens of those things still lived, and from one of the shafts the cover was removed. He knew that what he had seen could never climb up the slippery walls, yet shuddered at the thought that some obscure foothold might exist.

What the thing was, he would never tell. It was like some of the carvings on the hellish altar, but it was alive. Nature had never made it in this form, for it was too palpably *unfinished*. The deficiencies were of the most surprising sort, and the abnormalities of proportion could not be described. Willett consents only to say that this type of thing must have represented entities which Ward called up from *imperfect salts,* and which he kept for servile or ritualistic purposes. If it had not had a certain significance, its image would not have been carved on that damnable stone. It was not the worst thing depicted on that stone—but Willett never opened the other pits. At the time, the first

[a] unnamable] unnameable D
[b] coördination,] co-ordination, D
[c] recognised;] recognised, C, D

connected idea in his mind was an idle paragraph from some of the old Curwen data he had digested long before; a phrase used by Simon or Jedediah Orne in that portentous confiscated letter to the bygone sorcerer:[a] "Certainely, there[b] was Noth'g butt y[e] liveliest Awfulness[c] in that[d] which H. rais'd upp from What he cou'd gather onlie a part[e] of."

Then, horribly supplementing rather than displacing this image, there came a recollection of those[f] ancient lingering rumours anent the burned,[g] twisted thing found in the fields a week after the Curwen raid. Charles Ward had once told the doctor what old Slocum said of that object; that it was neither thoroughly human, nor wholly allied to any animal which Pawtuxet folk had ever seen or read about.

These words hummed in the doctor's mind as he rocked to and fro, squatting on the nitrous stone floor. He tried to drive them out, and repeated the Lord's Prayer to himself; eventually trailing off into a mnemonic hodge-podge like the modernistic "Waste Land" of Mr. T. S. Eliot and finally reverting to the oft-repeated dual formula he had lately found in Ward's underground library: *"Y'ai 'ng'ngah,*[h] *Yog-Sothoth"*, and so on till the final underlined *"Zhro"*.[i] It seemed to soothe him,[j] and he staggered to his feet after a time; lamenting bitterly his fright-lost torch and looking wildly about for any gleam of light in the clutching inkiness of the chilly air. Think he would not; but he strained his eyes in every direction for some faint glint or reflection of the bright illumination he had left in the library. After a while he thought he detected a suspicion of a glow infinitely far away, and toward this he crawled in agonised caution on hands and knees amidst the stench and howling, always feeling ahead lest he collide with the numerous great pillars or stumble into the abominable pit he had uncovered.

[a] sorcerer:] sorcerer: ¶ C, D
[b] there] ther D
[c] Awfulness] Awfullness C
[d] that] That C
[e] part] Part C
[f] those] these D
[g] burned,] burned and C, D
[h] *"Y'ai 'ng'ngah,*] *"Y'ai'ng'ngah,* D
[i] *Yog-Sothoth",* . . . *"Zhro".*] *Yog-Sothoth,"* . . . *"Zhro."* C
[j] him,] him C, D

Once his shaking fingers touched something which he knew must be the steps leading to the hellish altar, and from this spot he recoiled in loathing. At another time he encountered the pierced slab[a] he had removed, and here his caution became almost pitiful. But he did not come upon the dread aperture after all, nor did anything issue from that aperture to detain him. What had been down there made no sound nor stir. Evidently its crunching of the fallen electric torch had not been good for it. Each time Willett's fingers felt a perforated slab he trembled. His passage over it would sometimes increase the groaning below, but generally it would produce no effect at all, since he moved very noiselessly. Several times during his progress the glow ahead diminished perceptibly, and he realised that the various candles and lamps he had left must be expiring one by one. The thought of being lost in utter darkness without matches amidst this underground world of nightmare labyrinths impelled him to rise to his feet and run, which he could safely do now that he had passed the open pit; for he knew that once the light failed,[b] his only hope of rescue and survival would lie in whatever relief party Mr. Ward might send after missing him for a sufficient period. Presently, however, he emerged from the open space into the narrower corridor and definitely located the glow as coming from a door on his right. In a moment he had reached it and was standing once more in young Ward's secret library, trembling with relief, and watching the sputterings of that last lamp which had brought him to safety.

4.

In another moment he was hastily filling the burned-out lamps from an oil supply he had previously noticed, and when the room was bright again he looked about to see if he might find a lantern for further exploration. For racked though he was with horror, his sense of grim purpose was still uppermost;[c] and he was firmly determined to leave no stone unturned in his search for the hideous facts behind Charles

[a] slab] slat C
[b] failed,] failed C, D
[c] uppermost;] uppermost, C, D

Ward's bizarre madness. Failing to find a lantern, he chose the smallest of the[a] lamps to carry; also filling his pockets with candles and matches, and taking with him a gallon can of oil, which he proposed to keep for reserve use in whatever hidden laboratory he might uncover beyond the terrible open space with its unclean altar and nameless covered wells. To traverse that space again would require his utmost fortitude, but he knew it must be done. Fortunately neither the frightful altar nor the opened shaft was near the vast cell-indented wall which bounded the cavern area, and whose black mysterious archways would form the next goals of a logical search.

So Willett went back to that great pillared hall of stench and anguished howling; turning[b] down his lamp[c] to avoid any distant glimpse of the hellish altar, or of the uncovered pit with the pierced stone slab beside it. Most of the black[d] doorways led merely to small chambers, some vacant and some evidently used as storerooms;[e] and in several of the latter he saw some very curious accumulations of various objects. One was packed with rotting and dust-draped bales of spare clothing, and the explorer thrilled when he saw that it was unmistakably the clothing of a century and a half before. In another room he found numerous odds and ends of modern clothing, as if gradual provisions were being made to equip a large body of men. But what he disliked most of all were the huge copper[f] vats which occasionally appeared; these, and the sinister incrustations upon them. He liked them even less than the weirdly figured leaden bowls whose rims[g] retained such obnoxious deposits and around which clung repellent odours perceptible above even the general noisomeness of the crypt. When he had completed about half the entire circuit of the wall he found another corridor like that from which he had come, and out of which many doors opened.[h] This he proceeded to investigate;

[a] the] *om.* D
[b] howling; turning] howling, turned D
[c] lamp] lamps D
[d] black] *om.* D
[e] storerooms;] store rooms; C, D
[f] copper] cooper D
[g] rims] ruins C, D
[h] opened.] opened. ¶ C, D

and after entering three rooms of medium size and of no significant contents, he came at last to a large oblong apartment whose business-like[a] tanks and tables, furnaces and modern instruments, occasional books and endless shelves of jars and bottles proclaimed it indeed the long-sought laboratory of Charles Ward—and no doubt of old Joseph Curwen before him.

After lighting the three lamps which he found filled and ready, Dr. Willett examined the place and all its appurtenances with the keenest interest; noting from the relative quantities of various reagents on the shelves that young Ward's dominant concern must have been with some branch of organic chemistry. On the whole, little could be learned from the scientific ensemble, which included a gruesome-looking dissecting table; so that the room was really rather a disappointment. Among the books was a tattered old copy of Borellus in black-letter,[b] and it was weirdly interesting to note that Ward had underlined the same passage whose marking had so perturbed good Mr. Merritt at Curwen's farmhouse more than a century and a half before. That older copy, of course, must have perished along with the rest of Curwen's occult library in the final raid. Three archways opened off the laboratory, and these the doctor proceeded to sample in turn. From his cursory survey he saw that two led merely to small storerooms; but these he canvassed with care, remarking the piles of coffins in various stages of damage and shuddering violently at two or three of the few coffin-plates he could decipher. There was much clothing also stored in these rooms, and several new and tightly nailed[c] boxes which he did not stop to investigate. Most interesting of all, perhaps, were some odd bits which he judged to be fragments of old Joseph Curwen's laboratory appliances. These had suffered damage at the hands of the raiders, but were still partly recognisable as the chemical paraphernalia of the Georgian period.

The third archway led to a very sizeable chamber entirely lined with shelves and having in the centre a table bearing two lamps. These lamps Willett lighted, and in their brilliant glow studied the endless

[a] business-like] businesslike A, D; business-/like C
[b] black-letter,] black letter, D
[c] tightly nailed] tightly-nailed A, C, D

shelving which surrounded him. Some of the upper levels were wholly vacant, but most of the space was filled with small odd-looking leaden jars of two general types; one tall and without handles like a Grecian lekythos or oil-jug, and the other with a single handle and proportioned like a Phaleron jug. All had metal stoppers, and were covered with peculiar-looking symbols moulded in low relief. In a moment the doctor noticed that these jugs were classified with great rigidity; all the lekythoi being on one side of the room with a large wooden sign reading "Custodes" above them, and all the Phalerons on the other, correspondingly labelled with a sign reading "Materia".[a] Each of the jars or jugs, except some on the upper shelves that turned out to be vacant, bore a cardboard tag with a number apparently referring to a catalogue; and Willett resolved to look for the latter presently. For the moment, however, he was more interested in the nature of the array as a whole; and experimentally opened several of the lekythoi and Phalerons at random with a view to a rough generalisation. The result was invariable. Both types of jar contained a small quantity of a single kind of substance; a fine dusty powder of very light weight and of many shades of dull,[b] neutral colour. To the colours which formed the only point of variation there was no apparent method of disposal; and no distinction between what occurred in the lekythoi and what occurred in the Phalerons. A bluish-grey powder might be by the side of a pinkish-white one, and any one in a Phaleron might have its exact counterpart in a lekythos. The most individual feature about the powders was their non-adhesiveness. Willett would pour one into his hand, and upon returning it to its jug would find that no residue whatever remained on its[c] palm.

The meaning of the two signs puzzled him, and he wondered why this battery of chemicals was separated so radically from those in glass jars on the shelves of the laboratory proper. "Custodes",[d] "Materia"; that was the Latin for "Guards" and "Materials",[e] respectively—and

---

[a] "Materia".] "Materia." C, D
[b] dull,] dull C, D
[c] its] his C, D
[d] "Custodes",] "Custodes," C
[e] "Materials",] "Material," C; "Material", D

then there came a flash of memory as to where he had seen that word "Guards" before in connexion[a] with this dreadful mystery. It was, of course, in the recent letter to Dr. Allen purporting to be from old Edward Hutchinson; and the phrase had read: "There was no Neede to keep the Guards in Shape and eat'g off their Heads,[b] and it made Much[c] to be founde in case[d] of Trouble, as you too welle knowe."[e] What did this signify? But wait—was there not still *another* reference to "guards" in this matter which he had failed wholly to recall when reading the Hutchinson letter? Back in the old non-secretive days Ward had told him of the Eleazar Smith diary recording the spying of Smith and Weeden on the Curwen farm,[f] and in that dreadful chronicle there had been a mention of conversations overheard before the old wizard betook himself wholly beneath the earth. There had been, Smith and Weeden insisted, terrible colloquies wherein figured Curwen, certain captives of his, *and the guards of those captives.* Those guards, according to Hutchinson or his avatar, had 'eaten their heads off',[g] so that now Dr. Allen did not keep them *in shape.* And if not *in shape,* how save as the "salts" to which it appears this wizard band was engaged in reducing as many human bodies or skeletons as they could?

So *that* was what these lekythoi contained; the monstrous fruit of unhallowed rites and deeds, presumably won or cowed to such submission as to help,[h] when called up by some hellish incantation, in the defence[i] of their blasphemous master or the questioning of those who were not so willing?[j] Willett shuddered at the thought of what he had been pouring in and out of his hands, and for a moment felt an impulse to flee in panic from that cavern of hideous shelves with their silent and perhaps watching sentinels. Then he thought of the

[a] connexion] connection C, D
[b] Heads,] Heades, A, C, D
[c] Much] much A, C, D
[d] case] Case C
[e] knowe."] know." A; "Knowe." C, D
[f] farm,] farm D
[g] 'eaten . . . off',] "eaten . . . off," C; "eaten . . . off", D
[h] help,] help C, D
[i] defence] defense C
[j] willing?] willing! D

"Materia"—in the myriad Phaleron jugs on the other side of the room. Salts too—and if not the salts of "guards", then the salts of what? God! Could it be possible that here lay the mortal relics of half the titan thinkers of all the ages; snatched by supreme ghouls from crypts where the world thought them safe, and subject to the beck and call of madmen who sought to drain their knowledge for some still wilder end whose ultimate effect would concern, as poor Charles had hinted in his frantic note, 'all civilisation, all natural law, perhaps even the fate of the solar system and the universe'?[a] And Marinus Bicknell Willett had sifted their dust through his hands!

Then he noticed a small door at the farther end of the room, and calmed himself enough to approach it and examine the crude sign chiselled above. It was only a symbol, but it filled him with vague spiritual dread; for a morbid,[b] dreaming friend of his had once drawn it on paper and told him a few of the things it means in the dark abyss of sleep. It was the sign of Koth, that dreamers see fixed above the archway of a certain black tower standing alone in twilight—and Willett did not like what his friend Randolph Carter had said of its powers. But a moment later he forgot the sign as he recognised a new acrid odour in the stench-filled air. This was a chemical rather than animal smell, and came clearly from the room beyond the door. And it was, unmistakably, the same odour which had saturated Charles Ward's clothing on the day the doctors had taken him away. So it was here that the youth had been interrupted by the final summons? He was wiser than old Joseph Curwen, for he had not resisted. Willett, boldly determined to penetrate every wonder and nightmare this nether realm might contain, seized the small lamp and crossed the threshold. A wave of nameless fright rolled out to meet him, but he yielded to no whim and deferred to no intuition. There was nothing alive here to harm him, and he would not be stayed in his piercing of the eldritch cloud which engulfed his patient.

The room beyond the door was of medium size, and had no furniture save a table, a single chair, and two groups of curious

---

[a] 'all . . . universe'?] "all . . . universe"? C, D
[b] morbid,] morbid C

machines with clamps and wheels,[a] which Willett recognised after a moment as mediaeval instruments of torture. On one side of the door stood a rack of savage whips, above which were[b] some shelves bearing empty rows of shallow pedestalled cups of lead shaped like Grecian kylikes.[c] On the other side was the table; with a powerful Argand lamp, a pad and pencil, and two of the stoppered lekythoi from the shelves outside set down at irregular places as if temporarily or in haste. Willett lighted the lamp and looked carefully at the pad,[d] to see what notes young Ward might have been jotting down when interrupted; but found nothing more intelligible than the following disjointed fragments in that crabbed Curwen chirography, which shed no light on the case as a whole:

> "B. dy'd not. Escap'd into walls and founde Place below.
> "Saw olde V. saye y[e] Sabaoth and learnt y[e] Way.[e]
> "Rais'd *Yog-Sothoth* thrice and was y[e] nexte Day deliver'd.[f]
> "F. soughte to wipe out all know'g howe to raise Those from Outside."

As the strong Argand blaze lit up the entire chamber[g] the doctor saw that the wall opposite the door, between the two groups of torturing appliances in the corners, was covered with pegs from which hung a set of shapeless-looking[h] robes of a rather dismal yellowish-white. But far more interesting were the two vacant walls, both of which were thickly covered with mystic symbols and formulae roughly chiselled in the smooth dressed stone. The damp floor also bore marks of carving; and with but little difficulty Willett deciphered a huge pentagram in the centre, with a plain circle about three feet wide half way between this and each corner. In one of these four circles, near where a yellowish robe had been flung carelessly down, there stood a shallow kylix[i] of the sort found on the shelves above the whip-rack;

[a] wheels,] wheels C, D
[b] were] where D
[c] kylikes.] Kylikes. C, D
[d] pad,] pad C, D
[e] Way.] Way." D
[f] deliver'd.] deliver'd." D
[g] chamber] chamber, D
[h] shapeless-looking] shapeless looking A, C, D
[i] kylix] Kylix C, D

and just outside the periphery was one of the Phaleron jugs from the shelves in the other room, its tag numbered 118. This was unstoppered, and proved upon inspection to be empty; but the explorer saw with a shiver that the kylix[a] was not. Within its shallow area, and saved from scattering only by the absence of wind in this sequestered cavern, lay a small amount of a dry, dull-greenish efflorescent powder which must have belonged in the jug; and Willett almost reeled at the implications that came sweeping over him as he correlated little by little the several elements and antecedents of the scene. The whips and the instruments of torture, the dust or salts from the jug of "Materia",[b] the two lekythoi from the "Custodes" shelf, the robes, the formulae on the walls, the notes on the pad, the hints from letters and legends, and the thousand glimpses, doubts, and suppositions which had come to torment the friends and parents of Charles Ward—all these engulfed the doctor in a tidal wave of horror as he looked at that dry greenish powder outspread in the pedestalled leaden kylix[c] on the floor.

With an effort, however, Willett pulled himself together and began studying the formulae chiselled on the walls. From the stained and incrusted letters it was obvious that they were carved in Joseph Curwen's time, and their text was such as to be vaguely familiar to one who had read much Curwen material or delved extensively into the history of magic. One the doctor clearly recognised as what Mrs. Ward heard her son chanting on that ominous[d] Good Friday a year before, and what an authority had told him was a very terrible invocation addressed to secret gods outside the normal spheres. It was not spelled here exactly as Mrs. Ward had set it down from memory, nor yet as[e] the authority had shewn[f] it to him in the forbidden pages of "Eliphas Levi";[g] but its identity was unmistakable, and such words as *Sabaoth*,

---

[a] kylix] Kylix C, D
[b] "Materia",] "Materia," C
[c] kylix] Kylix D
[d] ominous] noxious D
[e] yet as] as yet D
[f] shewn] shown D
[g] Levi";] Levi; A

Metraton, Almousin,[a] and *Zariatnatmik* sent a shudder of fright through the searcher who had seen and felt so much of cosmic abomination just around the corner.

This was on the left-hand wall as one entered the room. The right-hand wall was no less thickly inscribed, and Willett felt a start of recognition as he came upon the pair of formulae so frequently occurring in the recent notes in the library. They were, roughly speaking, the same;[b] with the ancient symbols of "Dragon's Head" and "Dragon's Tail" heading them as in Ward's scribblings. But the spelling differed quite widely from that of the modern versions, as if old Curwen had had a different way of recording sound, or as if later study had evolved more powerful and perfected variants of the invocations in question. The doctor tried to reconcile the chiselled version with the one which still ran persistently in his head, and found it hard to do. Where the script he had memorised began *"Y'ai 'ng'ngah,*[c] *Yog-Sothoth",*[d] this epigraph started out as *"Aye, engengah,*[e] *Yogge-Sothotha";* which to his mind would seriously interfere with the syllabification of the second word.

Ground as the later text was into his consciousness, the discrepancy disturbed him; and he found himself chanting the first of the formulae aloud in an effort to square the sound he conceived with the letters he found carved. Weird and menacing in that abyss of antique blasphemy rang his voice;[f] its accents keyed to a droning sing-song either through the spell of the past and the unknown, or through the hellish example of that dull, godless wail from the pits whose inhuman cadences[g] rose and fell rhythmically in the distance through the stench and the darkness.

[a] *Almousin,*] *Almonsin,* C, D
[b] same;] same: D
[c] *'ng'ngah,*] *'Ng'ngah,* A
[d] *Yog-Sothoth",*] *Yog-Sothoth,"* C
[e] *engengah,*] *cngengah,* C, D
[f] voice;] voice, D
[g] cadences] coldness D

"Y'AI 'NG'NGAH,[a]
YOG-SOTHOTH
H'EE—L'GEB[b]
F'AI[c] THRODOG
UAAAH!"[x][d]

But what was this cold wind which had sprung into life at the very outset of the chant? The lamps were sputtering woefully, and the gloom grew so dense that the letters on the wall nearly faded from sight. There was smoke, too, and an acrid odour which quite drowned out the stench from the far-away wells; an odour like that he had smelt before, yet infinitely stronger and more pungent. He turned from[e] the inscriptions to face the room with its bizarre contents, and saw that the kylix[f] on the floor, in which the ominous efflorescent powder had lain, was giving forth a cloud of thick, greenish-black vapour of surprising volume and opacity. That powder—Great God! it had come from the shelf of "Materia"—what was it doing now, and what had started it? The formula he had been chanting—the first of the pair—Dragon's Head, *ascending node*—Blessed Saviour, could it be . . .[g]

The doctor reeled, and through his head raced wildly disjointed scraps from all he had seen, heard, and read of the frightful case of Joseph Curwen and Charles Dexter Ward. "I say to you againe, doe not call[h] up Any that you can not put[i] downe. . . . Have y[e] Wordes for laying at all times readie, and stopp not to be sure when there is any Doubte of *Whom* you have. . . . Three Talkes with *What was therein inhum'd*[j] . . ." *Mercy of heaven,*[k] *what is that shape behind the parting smoke?*

[a] 'NG'NGAH,] 'NG'NGAH C, D
[b] L'GEB] L'BEG D
[c] F'AI] F'AI' C, D
[d] *UAAAH!"*] UAAH!" A
[e] from] *om.* D
[f] kylix] Kylix C, D
[g] be . . .] be . . ." A
[h] call] calle C, D
[i] can not put] cannot put C; cannot putt D
[j] *was therein inhum'd*] was therein inhum'd A, C, D
[k] *heaven,*] Heaven, A, C, D

5.

Marinus Bicknell Willett has no hope that any part of his tale will be believed except by certain sympathetic friends, hence he has made no attempt to tell it beyond his most intimate circle. Only a few outsiders have ever heard it repeated, and of these the majority laugh and remark that the doctor surely is getting old. He has been advised to take a long vacation and to shun future cases dealing with mental disturbance. But Mr. Ward knows that the veteran physician speaks only a horrible truth. Did not he himself see the noisome aperture in the bungalow cellar? Did not Willett send him home overcome and ill at eleven o'clock that portentous morning? Did he not telephone the doctor in vain that evening, and again the next day, and had he not driven to the bungalow itself on that following noon, finding his friend unconscious but unharmed on one of the beds upstairs? Willett had been breathing stertorously, and opened his eyes slowly when Mr. Ward gave him some brandy fetched from the car. Then he shuddered and screamed, crying out, *"That beard ... those eyes.... God, who are you?"* A very strange thing to say to a trim, blue-eyed,[a] clean-shaven gentleman whom he had known from the latter's boyhood.

In the bright noon sunlight the bungalow was unchanged since the previous morning. Willett's clothing bore no disarrangement beyond certain smudges and worn places at the knees, and only a faint acrid odour reminded Mr. Ward of what he had smelt on his son that day he was taken to the hospital. The doctor's flashlight was missing, but his valise was safely there, as empty as when he had brought it. Before indulging in any explanations, and obviously with great moral effort, Willett staggered dizzily down to the cellar and tried the fateful platform before the tubs. It was unyielding. Crossing to where he had left his yet-unused[b] tool satchel the day before, he obtained a chisel and began to pry up the stubborn planks one by one. Underneath the smooth concrete was still visible, but of any opening or perforation there was no longer a trace. Nothing yawned this time to sicken the mystified father who had followed the doctor downstairs; only the

[a] blue-eyed,] blue-eyed A
[b] yet-unused] yet unused D

smooth concrete underneath the planks—no noisome well, no world of subterrene horrors, no secret library, no Curwen papers, no nightmare pits of stench and howling, no laboratory or shelves or chiselled formulae, no . . . Dr. Willett turned pale, and clutched at the younger man. "Yesterday," he asked softly, "did you see it here . . . and smell it?" And when Mr. Ward, himself transfixed with dread and wonder, found strength to nod an affirmative, the physician gave a sound half a sigh and half a gasp, and nodded in turn. "Then I will tell you," he said.

So for an hour, in the sunniest room they could find upstairs, the physician whispered his frightful tale to the wondering father. There was nothing to relate beyond the looming up of that form when the greenish-black vapour from the kylix[a] parted, and Willett was too tired to ask himself what had really occurred. There were futile, bewildered head-shakings from both men, and once Mr. Ward ventured a hushed suggestion, "Do you suppose it would be of any use to dig?" The doctor was silent, for it seemed hardly fitting for any human brain to answer when powers of unknown spheres had so vitally encroached on this side of the Great Abyss. Again Mr. Ward asked, "But where did it go? It brought you here, you know, and it sealed up the hole somehow." And Willett again let silence answer for him.

But after all, this was not the final phase of the matter. Reaching for his handkerchief before rising to leave, Dr. Willett's fingers closed upon a piece of paper in his pocket which had not been there before, and which was companioned by the candles and matches he had seized in the vanished vault. It was a common sheet, torn obviously from the cheap pad in that fabulous room of horror somewhere underground, and the writing upon it was that of an ordinary lead pencil—doubtless the one which had lain beside the pad. It was folded very carelessly, and beyond the faint acrid scent of the cryptic chamber bore no print or mark of any world but this. But in the text itself it did indeed reek with wonder; for here[b] was no script of any wholesome age, but the laboured strokes of mediaeval darkness, scarcely legible to the laymen who now strained over it, yet having combinations of symbols which

[a] kylix] Kylix C, D
[b] here] there D

seemed vaguely familiar. The briefly scrawled message was this, and its mystery lent purpose to the shaken pair, who forthwith walked steadily out to the Ward car and gave orders to be driven first to a quiet dining place and then to the John Hay Library on the hill.

Coruinuſ neandur eſt.
Cadauer aq̃ forti diſſoluendum
ne aliqd retinendum.
Tace ut poteſ.

At the library it was easy to find good manuals of palaeography, and over these the two men puzzled till the lights of evening shone out from the great chandelier. In the end they found what was needed. The letters were indeed no fantastic invention, but the normal script of a very dark period. They were the pointed Saxon minuscules of the eighth or ninth[a] century A.D.,[b] and brought with them memories of an uncouth time when under a fresh Christian veneer[c] ancient faiths and ancient rites stirred stealthily, and the pale moon of Britain looked sometimes on strange deeds in the Roman ruins at[d] Caerleon and Hexham,[e] and by the towers[f] along Hadrian's crumbling wall. The words were in such Latin as a barbarous age might remember— *"Corvinus[g] necandus est. Cadaver aq(ua) forti dissolvendum, nec aliq(ui)d retinendum. Tace ut potes."*—which may roughly be translated, "Curwen must be killed. The body must be dissolved in aqua fortis, nor must anything be retained. Keep silence as best you are able."

Willett and Mr. Ward were mute and baffled. They had met the unknown, and found that they lacked emotions to respond to it as they vaguely believed they ought. With Willett, especially, the capacity for receiving fresh impressions of awe was well-nigh exhausted; and both men sat still and helpless till the closing of the library forced them to

[a] eighth or ninth] 8th or 9th A
[b] A.D.,] A.D., D
[c] veneer] veneer, C
[d] at] of D
[e] Hexham,] Hexhaus, C, D
[f] towers] Towers C, D
[g] *"Corvinus*] *"Corwinus,* C; *"Corwinus* D

leave. Then they drove listlessly to the Ward mansion in Prospect Street, and talked to no purpose into the night. The doctor rested toward morning, but did not go home. And he was still there Sunday noon when a telephone message came from the detectives who had been assigned to look up Dr. Allen.

Mr. Ward, who was pacing nervously about in a dressing-gown,[a] answered the call in person; and told the men to come up early the next day when he heard their report was almost ready. Both Willett and he were glad that this phase of the matter was taking form, for whatever the origin of the strange minuscule message, it seemed certain that the "Curwen" who must be destroyed could be no other than the bearded and spectacled stranger. Charles had feared this man,[b] and had said in the frantic note that he must be killed and dissolved in acid. Allen,[c] moreover, had been receiving letters from the strange wizards in Europe under the name of Curwen, and palpably regarded himself as an avatar of the bygone necromancer. And now from a fresh and unknown source had come a message saying that "Curwen" must be killed and dissolved in acid. The linkage was too unmistakable to be factitious; and besides, was not Allen planning to murder young Ward upon the advice of the creature called Hutchinson? Of course, the letter they had seen had never reached the bearded stranger; but from its text they could see that Allen had already formed plans for dealing with the youth if he grew too 'squeamish'.[d] Without doubt, Allen must be apprehended; and even if the most drastic directions were not carried out, he must be placed where he could inflict no harm upon Charles Ward.

That afternoon, hoping against hope to extract some gleam of information anent the inmost mysteries from the only available one capable of giving it, the father and the doctor went down the bay and called on young Charles at the hospital. Simply and gravely Willett told him all he had found, and noticed how pale he turned as each description made certain the truth of the discovery. The physician

---

[a] dressing-gown,] dressing gown, D
[b] man,] man D
[c] Allen,] Allen D
[d] 'squeamish'.] 'squeamish.' C; "squeamish". D

employed as much dramatic effect as he could, and watched for a wincing on Charles's part when he approached the matter of the covered pits and the nameless hybrids within. But Ward did not wince. Willett paused, and his voice grew indignant as he spoke of how the things were starving. He taxed the youth with shocking inhumanity, and shivered when only a sardonic laugh came in reply. For Charles, having dropped as useless his pretence that the crypt did not exist, seemed to see some ghastly jest in this affair; and chuckled hoarsely at something which amused him. Then he whispered, in accents doubly terrible because of the cracked voice he used, "Damn 'em, they *do* eat, but they *don't need to!* That's the rare part! A month, you say, without food? Lud, Sir, you be modest! D'ye know, that was the joke on poor old Whipple with his virtuous bluster! Kill everything off, would he? Why, damme, he was half-deaf with the noise from Outside and never saw or heard aught from the wells![a] He never dreamed they were there at all! Devil take ye, *those cursed[b] things have been howling down there ever since Curwen was done for a hundred and fifty-seven years gone!*"

But no more than this could Willett get from the youth. Horrified, yet almost convinced against his will, he went on with his tale in the hope that some incident might startle his auditor out of the mad composure he maintained. Looking at the youth's face, the doctor could not but feel a kind of terror at the changes which recent months had wrought. Truly, the boy had drawn down nameless horrors from the skies. When the room with the formulae and the greenish dust was mentioned, Charles shewed[c] his first sign of animation. A quizzical look overspread his face as he heard what Willett had read on the pad, and he ventured the mild statement that those notes were old ones, of no possible significance to anyone not deeply initiated in the history of magic. "But,"[d] he added, "had you but known the words to bring up that which I had out in the cup, you had not been here to[e] tell me this. 'Twas Number 118, and I conceive you would have shook had you

---

[a] wells!] wells. C, D
[b] *those cursed*] those cursed D
[c] shewed] showed D
[d] "But,"] "But", A
[e] here to] hereto D

looked it up in my list in t'other room. 'Twas never raised by me, but I meant to have it up that day you came to invite me hither."

Then Willett told of the formula he had spoken and of the greenish-black smoke which had arisen; and as he did so he saw true fear dawn for the first time on Charles Ward's face. "It *came,* and you be here alive?"[a] As Ward croaked the words his voice seemed almost to burst free of its trammels and sink to cavernous abysses of uncanny resonance. Willett, gifted with[b] a flash of inspiration, believed he saw the situation, and wove into his reply a caution from a letter he remembered. "No. 118, you say? But don't forget that *stones are all changed now in nine grounds out of ten. You are never sure till you question!*" And then, without warning, he drew forth the minuscule message and flashed it before the patient's eyes. He could have wished no stronger result, for Charles Ward fainted forthwith.

All this conversation, of course, had been conducted with the greatest secrecy lest the resident alienists accuse the father and the physician of encouraging a madman in his delusions. Unaided, too, Dr. Willett and Mr. Ward picked up the stricken youth and placed him on the couch. In reviving, the patient mumbled many times of some word which he must get to Orne and Hutchinson at once; so when his consciousness seemed fully back the doctor told him that of those strange creatures at least one was his bitter enemy, and had given Dr. Allen advice for his assassination. This revelation produced no visible effect, and before it was made the visitors could see that their host had already the look of a hunted man. After that he would converse no more, so Willett and the father departed presently; leaving behind a caution against the bearded Allen, to which the youth only replied that this individual was very safely taken care of, and could do no one any harm even if he wished. This was said with an almost evil chuckle very painful to hear. They did not worry about any communications Charles might indite[c] to that monstrous pair in Europe, since they knew that the hospital authorities seized all outgoing mail for censorship and would pass no wild or outré-looking missive.

[a] alive?"] alive!" C, D
[b] with] wih D
[c] indite] write C, D

There is, however, a curious sequel to the matter of Orne and Hutchinson, if such indeed the exiled wizards were. Moved by some vague presentiment amidst the horrors of that period, Willett arranged with an international press-cutting bureau for accounts of notable current crimes and accidents in Prague and in eastern Transylvania; and after six months believed that he had found two very significant things amongst the multifarious items he received and had translated. One was the total wrecking of a house by night in the oldest quarter of Prague, and the disappearance of the evil old man called Josef Nadek,[a] who had dwelt in it alone ever since anyone could remember. The other was a titan explosion in the Transylvanian mountains east of Rakus, and the utter extirpation with all its inmates of the ill-regarded Castle Ferenczy, whose master was so badly spoken of by peasants and soldiery alike that he would shortly have been summoned to Bucharest for serious questioning had not this incident cut off a career already so long as to antedate all common memory. Willett maintains that the hand which wrote those minuscules was able to wield stronger weapons as well; and that while Curwen was left to him to dispose of, the writer felt able to find and deal with Orne and Hutchinson itself. Of what their fate may have been the doctor strives sedulously not to think.

6.

The following morning Dr. Willett hastened to the Ward home to be present when the detectives arrived. Allen's destruction or imprisonment—or Curwen's, if one might regard the tacit[b] claim to reincarnation as valid—he felt must be accomplished at any cost, and he communicated this conviction to Mr. Ward as they sat waiting for the men to come. They were downstairs this time, for the upper parts of the house were beginning to be shunned because of a peculiar nauseousness which hung indefinitely about; a nauseousness which the older servants connected with some curse left by the vanished Curwen portrait.

[a] Nadek,] Nadeh, C, D
[b] tacit] tactic D

At nine o'clock the three detectives presented themselves and immediately delivered all that they had to say. They had not, regrettably enough, located the Brava Tony Gomes as they had wished, nor had they found the least trace of Dr. Allen's source or present whereabouts; but they had managed to unearth a considerable number of local impressions and facts concerning the reticent stranger. Allen had struck Pawtuxet people as a vaguely unnatural being, and there was an[a] universal belief that his thick Vandyke[b] beard was either dyed or false—a belief conclusively upheld by the finding of such a false beard, together with a pair of dark glasses, in his room at the fateful bungalow. His voice, Mr. Ward could well[c] testify from his one telephone conversation, had a depth and hollowness that could not be forgotten; and his glance seemed malign even through his smoked and horn-rimmed glasses. One shopkeeper, in the course of negotiations, had seen a specimen of his handwriting and declared it was very queer and crabbed; this being confirmed by pencilled notes of no clear meaning found in his room and identified by the merchant.[d] In connexion[e] with the vampirism rumours[f] of the preceding summer, a majority of the gossips believed that Allen rather than Ward was the actual vampire. Statements were also obtained from the officials who had visited the bungalow after the unpleasant incident of the motor truck robbery. They had felt less of the sinister in Dr. Allen, but had recognised him as the dominant figure in the queer shadowy cottage. The place had been too dark for them to observe him clearly, but they would know him again if they saw him. His beard had looked odd, and they thought he had some slight scar above his dark spectacled[g] right eye. As for the detectives'[h] search of Allen's room, it yielded nothing definite save the beard and glasses, and several pencilled notes in a

---

[a] an] a C, D
[b] Vandyke] sandy D
[c] well] here D
[d] merchant.] merchant. ¶ C, D
[e] connexion] connection C, D
[f] rumours] ructions C, D
[g] dark spectacled] dark-spectacled D
[h] detectives'] *om.* C, D

crabbed writing[a] which Willett at once saw was identical with that shared by the old Curwen manuscripts and by the voluminous recent notes of young Ward found in the vanished catacombs of horror.

Dr. Willett and Mr. Ward caught something of a profound, subtle, and insidious cosmic fear from this data as it was[b] gradually unfolded, and almost trembled in following up the vague, mad thought which had simultaneously reached their minds. The false beard and glasses—[c] the crabbed Curwen penmanship—the old portrait and its tiny scar— *and the altered youth in the hospital with such a scar*—that deep, hollow voice on the telephone—was it not of this that Mr. Ward was reminded when his son barked forth those pitiable tones to which he now claimed to be reduced? Who had ever seen Charles and Allen together? Yes, the officials had once, but who later on? Was it not when Allen left that Charles suddenly lost his growing fright and began to live wholly at the bungalow? Curwen—Allen—Ward—in what blasphemous and abominable fusion had two ages and two persons become involved? That damnable resemblance of the picture to Charles—had it not used to stare and stare, and follow the boy around the room with its eyes? Why, too, did both Allen and Charles copy Joseph Curwen's handwriting, even when alone and off guard? And then the frightful work of those people—the lost crypt of horrors that had aged the doctor overnight; the starved monsters in the noisome pits; the awful formula which had yielded such nameless results; the message in minuscules found in Willett's pocket; the papers and the letters and all the talk of graves and "salts" and discoveries—whither did everything lead? In the end Mr. Ward did the most sensible thing. Steeling himself against any realisation of why he did it, he gave the detectives an article to be shewn[d] to such Pawtuxet shopkeepers as had seen the portentous Dr. Allen. That article was a photograph of his luckless son, on which he now carefully drew in ink the pair of heavy glasses and the black pointed beard[e] which the men had brought from Allen's room.

[a] writing] writing, C, D
[b] this data as it was] these data as they were D
[c] glasses—] glasses, C, D
[d] shewn] shown D
[e] beard] beard, C, D

For two hours he waited with the doctor in the oppressive house where fear and miasma were slowly gathering as the empty panel in the upstairs library leered and leered and leered. Then the men returned. Yes. *The*[a] *altered photograph was a very passable likeness of Dr. Allen.* Mr. Ward turned pale, and Willett wiped a suddenly dampened brow with his handkerchief. Allen—Ward—Curwen—it was becoming too hideous for coherent thought. What had the boy called out of the void, and what had it done to him? What, really,[b] had happened from first to last? Who was this Allen who sought to kill Charles as too 'squeamish',[c] and why had his destined victim said in the postscript to that frantic letter that he must be so completely obliterated in acid? Why, too, had the minuscule message, of whose origin no one dared think, said that "Curwen" must be likewise obliterated? What was the *change,* and when had the final stage occurred? That day when his frantic note was received—he had been nervous all the morning, then there was an alteration. He had slipped out unseen and swaggered boldly in past the men hired to guard him. That was the time, when he was out. But no—had he not cried out in terror as he entered his study—this very room? What had he found there? Or wait—*what had found him?* That simulacrum which brushed boldly in without having been seen to go—was that an alien shadow and a horror forcing itself upon a trembling figure which had never gone out at all? Had not the butler spoken of queer noises?

Willett rang for the man and asked him some low-toned questions. It had, surely enough, been a bad business. There had been noises—a cry, a gasp, a choking, and a sort of clattering or creaking or thumping, or all of these. And Mr. Charles was not the same when he stalked out without a word. The butler shivered as he spoke, and sniffed at the heavy air that blew down from some open window upstairs. Terror had settled definitely upon the house, and only the business-like[d] detectives failed to imbibe a full measure of it. Even they were restless, for this case had held vague elements in the background which pleased

[a] Yes. The] Yes, *the* C, D
[b] What, really,] What really C, D
[c] 'squeamish',] 'squeamish,' C; "squeamish", D
[d] business-like] businesslike A, C, D

358 COLLECTED FICTION: 1926–1930

them not at all. Dr. Willett was thinking deeply and rapidly, and his thoughts were terrible ones. Now and then he would almost break into muttering[a] as he ran over in his head a new, appalling, and increasingly conclusive chain of nightmare happenings.

Then Mr. Ward made a sign that the conference was over, and everyone save him and the doctor left the room. It was noon now, but shadows as of coming night seemed to engulf the phantom-haunted mansion. Willett began talking very seriously to his host, and urged that he leave a great deal of the future investigation to him. There would be, he predicted, certain obnoxious elements which a friend could bear better than a relative. As family physician he must have a free hand, and the first thing he required was a period alone and undisturbed in the abandoned library upstairs, where the ancient overmantel had gathered about itself an aura of noisome horror more intense than when Joseph Curwen's features themselves glanced slyly down from the painted panel.

Mr. Ward, dazed by the flood of grotesque morbidities and unthinkably maddening suggestions that poured in upon him from every side, could only acquiesce; and half an hour later the doctor was locked in the shunned room with the panelling from Olney Court. The father, listening outside, heard fumbling sounds of moving and rummaging as the moments passed; and finally a wrench and a creak, as if a tight cupboard door were being opened. Then there was a muffled cry, a kind of snorting choke, and a hasty slamming of whatever had been opened. Almost at once the key rattled and Willett appeared in the hall, haggard and ghastly, and demanding wood for the real fireplace on the south wall of the room. The furnace was not enough, he said; and the electric log had little practical use. Longing yet not daring to ask questions, Mr. Ward gave the requisite orders and a man brought some stout pine logs, shuddering as he entered the tainted air of the library to place them in the grate. Willett meanwhile had gone up to the dismantled laboratory and brought down a few odds and ends not included in the moving of the July before. They were in a covered basket, and Mr. Ward never saw what they were.

Then the doctor locked himself in the library once more, and by

---

[a] muttering] mutterings D

the clouds of smoke which rolled down past the windows from the chimney it was known that he had lighted the fire. Later, after a great rustling of newspapers, that odd wrench and creaking were heard again; followed by a thumping which none of the eavesdroppers liked. Thereafter two suppressed cries of Willett's were heard, and hard upon these came a swishing rustle of indefinable hatefulness. Finally the smoke that the wind beat down from the chimney grew very dark and acrid, and everyone wished that the weather had spared them this choking and venomous[a] inundation of peculiar fumes. Mr. Ward's head reeled, and the servants all clustered together in a knot to watch the horrible black smoke swoop down. After an age of waiting the vapours seemed to lighten, and half-formless sounds of scraping, sweeping, and other minor operations were heard behind the bolted door. And at last, after the slamming of some cupboard within, Willett made his appearance—[b]sad, pale,[c] and haggard, and bearing the cloth-draped basket he had taken from the upstairs laboratory. He had left the window open, and into that once accursed room was pouring a wealth of pure, wholesome air to mix with a queer new smell of disinfectants. The ancient overmantel still lingered; but it seemed robbed of malignity now, and rose as calm and stately in its white panelling as if it had never borne the picture of Joseph Curwen. Night was coming on, yet this time its shadows held no latent fright, but only a gentle melancholy. Of what he had done the doctor would never speak. To Mr. Ward he said, "I can answer no questions, but I will say that there are different kinds of magic. I have made a great purgation, and those[d] in this house will sleep the better for it."

7.

That Dr. Willett's "purgation" had been an ordeal almost as nerve-racking in its way as his hideous wandering in the vanished crypt is shewn[e] by the fact that the elderly physician gave out completely as

[a] venomous] venemous D
[b] appearance—] appearance, C, D
[c] pale,] pale A, C, D
[d] purgation, and those] purgation. Those C, D
[e] shewn] shown D

soon as he reached home that evening. For three days he rested constantly in his room, though servants later muttered something about having heard him after midnight on Wednesday, when the outer door softly opened[a] and closed with phenomenal softness. Servants' imaginations, fortunately, are limited, else comment might have been excited by an item in Thursday's *Evening Bulletin* which ran as follows:

North End Ghouls
Active Again[b]

After a lull of ten months since the dastardly vandalism in the Weeden lot at the North Burial Ground, a nocturnal prowler was glimpsed early this morning in the same cemetery by Robert Hart, the night watchman. Happening to glance for a moment from his shelter at about 2 a.m.,[c] Hart observed the[d] glow of a lantern or pocket torch not far to the northwest,[e] and upon opening the door detected the figure of a man with a trowel very plainly silhouetted against a nearby electric light. At once starting in pursuit, he saw the figure dart hurriedly toward the main entrance, gaining the street and losing himself among the shadows before approach or capture was possible.

Like the first of the ghouls active during the past year, this intruder had done no real damage before detection. A vacant part of the Ward lot shewed[f] signs of a little superficial digging, but nothing even nearly the size of a grave had been attempted, and no previous grave had been disturbed.

Hart, who cannot describe the prowler except as a small man probably having a full beard, inclines to the view that all three of the digging incidents have a common source; but police from the Second Station think otherwise on account of the savage nature of the second incident, where an ancient coffin was removed and its headstone[g] violently shattered.

The first of the incidents, in which it is thought an attempt to bury something was frustrated, occurred a year ago last March, and has been attributed to bootleggers seeking a cache. It is possible, says Sergt.[h] Riley,

---

[a] opened] opened, C, D
[b] Active Again] Again Active C, D
[c] 2 a.m.,] two A.M., C; two a.m., D
[d] the] a C, D
[e] northwest,] northward, C, D
[f] shewed] showed D
[g] headstone] headstones C
[h] Sergt.] Sergeant C, D

that this third affair is of similar nature. Officers at the Second Station are taking especial pains to capture the gang of miscreants responsible for these repeated outrages.

All day Thursday Dr. Willett rested as if recuperating[a] from something past or nerving himself for something to come. In the evening he wrote a note to Mr. Ward, which was delivered the next morning and which caused the half-dazed parent to ponder long and deeply. Mr. Ward had not been able to go down to business since the shock of Monday with its baffling reports and its sinister "purgation",[b] but he found something calming about the doctor's letter in spite of the despair it seemed to promise and the fresh mysteries it seemed to evoke.

> "10[c] Barnes St.,
> Providence, R.I.,
> April 12, 1928

"Dear Theodore:—[d]I feel that I must say a word to you before doing what I am going to do tomorrow. It will conclude the terrible business we have been going through (for I feel that no spade is ever likely to reach that monstrous place we know of),[e] but I'm afraid it won't set your mind at rest unless I expressly assure you how very conclusive it is.

"You[f] have known me ever since you were a small boy, so I think you will not distrust me when I hint that some matters are best left undecided and unexplored. It is better that you attempt no further speculation as to Charles's case, and almost imperative that you tell his mother nothing more than she already suspects. When I call on you tomorrow Charles will have escaped. That is all which need remain in anyone's mind. He was mad, and he escaped. You can tell his mother gently and gradually about the mad part when you stop sending the typed notes in his name. I'd advise you to join her in Atlantic City and take a rest yourself. God knows you need one after this shock, as I do myself. I am going south[g] for a while to calm down and brace up.

[a] recuperating] recuperatng D
[b] "purgation",] "purgation," C
[c] "10] 10 C, D
[d] "Dear Theodore:—] Dear Theodore:— ¶ C, D
[e] through (. . .),] through, (. . .) A
[f] "You] You C, D
[g] south] South A, C, D

"So[a] don't ask me any questions when I call. It may be that something will go wrong, but I'll tell you if it does. I don't think it will. There will be nothing more to worry about, for Charles will be very, very safe. He is now—safer than you dream. You need hold no fears about Allen, and who or what he is. He forms as much a part of the past as Joseph Curwen's picture, and when I ring your doorbell you may feel certain that there is no such person. And what wrote that minuscule message will never trouble you or yours.

"But[b] you must steel yourself to melancholy, and prepare your wife to do the same. I must tell you frankly that Charles's escape will not mean his restoration to you. He has been afflicted with a peculiar disease, as you must realise from the subtle physical as well as mental changes in him, and you must not hope to see him again. Have only this consolation—that he was never a fiend or even truly a madman, but only an eager, studious, and curious boy whose love of mystery and of the past was his undoing. He stumbled on things no mortal ought ever to know, and reached back through the years as no one ever should reach; and something came out of those years to engulf him.

"And[c] now comes the matter in which I must ask you to trust me most of all. For there will be, indeed, no uncertainty about Charles's fate. In about a year, say, you can if you wish devise a suitable account of the end;[d] for the boy will be no more. You can put up a stone in your lot at the North Burial Ground exactly ten feet west of your father's and facing the same way, and that will mark the true resting-place[e] of your son. Nor need you fear that it will mark any abnormality or changeling. The ashes in that grave will be those of your own unaltered bone and sinew—of the real Charles Dexter Ward whose mind you watched from infancy—the real Charles with the olive-mark on his hip and without the black witch-mark on his chest or the pit on his forehead. The Charles who never did actual evil, and who will have paid with his life for his 'squeamishness'.[f]

"That[g] is all. Charles will have escaped, and a year from now you can put up his stone. Do not question me tomorrow. And believe that the

---

[a] "So] So C, D
[b] "But] But C, D
[c] "And] And C, D
[d] end;] end, D
[e] resting-place] resting place D
[f] 'squeamishness'.] 'squeamishness.' C; "squeamishness." D
[g] "That] That C, D

honour of your ancient family remains untainted now, as it has been at all times in the past.

"With[a] profoundest sympathy, and exhortations to fortitude, calmness, and resignation, I am ever

Sincerely your friend,[b]

Marinus B. Willett"[c]

So on the morning of Friday, April 13, 1928, Marinus Bicknell Willett visited the room of Charles Dexter Ward at Dr. Waite's private hospital on Conanicut Island. The youth, though making no attempt to evade his caller, was in a sullen mood; and seemed disinclined to open the conversation which Willett obviously desired. The doctor's discovery of the crypt and his monstrous experience therein had of course created a new source of embarrassment, so that both hesitated perceptibly after the interchange of a few strained formalities. Then a new element of constraint crept in, as Ward seemed to read behind the doctor's mask-like[d] face a terrible purpose which had never been there before. The patient quailed, conscious that since the last visit there had been a change whereby the solicitous family physician had given place to the ruthless and implacable avenger.

Ward actually turned pale, and the doctor was the first to speak. "More," he said, "has been found out, and I must warn you fairly that a reckoning is due."

"Digging again, and coming upon more poor starving pets?" was the ironic reply. It was evident that the youth meant to shew[e] bravado to the last.

"No," Willett slowly rejoined, "this time I did not have to dig. We have had men looking up Dr. Allen, and they found the false beard and spectacles in the bungalow."[f]

"Excellent," commented the disquieted host in an effort to be wittily insulting, "and I trust they proved more becoming than the beard and glasses you now have on!"

[a] "With] With C, D
[b] friend,] friend D
[c] Willett"] Willett C, D
[d] mask-like] masklike A, C, D
[e] shew] show D
[f] bungalow."] bungalow!" C

"They would become you very well," came the even and studied response, *"as indeed they seem to have done."*

As Willett said this, it almost seemed as though a cloud passed over the sun; though there was no change in the shadows on the floor. Then Ward ventured:

"And is this what asks so hotly for a reckoning? Suppose a man does find it now and then useful to be twofold?"[a]

"No," said Willett gravely, "again you are wrong. It is no business of mine if any man seeks[b] duality; *provided he has any right to exist at all, and provided he does not destroy what called him out of space.*"

Ward now started violently. "Well, Sir, what *have* ye found, and what d'ye want with me?"

The doctor let a little time elapse before replying, as if choosing his words for an effective answer.

"I have found," he finally intoned, "something in a cupboard behind an ancient overmantel where a picture once was, and I have burned it and buried the ashes where the grave of Charles Dexter Ward ought to be."

The madman choked and sprang from the chair in which he had been sitting:

"Damn ye, who did ye tell—and who'll believe it was he after these full two months, with me alive? What d'ye mean to do?"

Willett, though a small man, actually took on a kind of judicial majesty as he calmed the patient with a gesture.

"I have told no one. This is no common case—it is a madness out of time and a horror from beyond the spheres which no police or lawyers or courts or alienists could ever fathom or grapple with. Thank God some chance has left inside me the spark of imagination, that I might not go astray in thinking out this thing. *You cannot deceive me, Joseph Curwen, for I know that your accursed magic is true!*

"I know how you wove the spell that brooded outside the years and fastened on your double and descendant; I know how you drew him into the past and got him to raise you up from your[c] detestable

---

[a] twofold?"] 'twofold'?" C
[b] seeks] seek D
[c] your] a C

grave; I know how he kept you hidden in his laboratory while you studied modern things and roved abroad as a vampire by night, and how you later shewed[a] yourself in beard and glasses that no one might wonder at your godless likeness to him; I know what you resolved to do when he balked at your monstrous rifling of the world's tombs, *and at what you planned afterward,* and I know how you did it.

"You left off your beard and glasses and fooled the guards around the house. They thought it was he who went in, and they thought it was he who came out when you had strangled and hidden him. But you hadn't reckoned on the different contents[b] of two minds. You were a fool, Curwen, to fancy that a mere visual identity would be enough. Why didn't you think of the speech and the voice and the handwriting? It hasn't worked, you see, after all. You know better than I who or what wrote that message in minuscules,[c] but I will warn you it was not written in vain. There are abominations and blasphemies which must be stamped out, and I believe that the writer of those words will attend to Orne and Hutchinson. One of those creatures wrote you once, 'do not call up any that you can not[d] put down'.[e] You were undone once before, perhaps in that very way, and it may be that your own evil magic will undo you all again. Curwen, a man can't tamper with Nature beyond certain limits, and every horror you have woven will rise up to wipe you out."

But here the doctor was cut short by a convulsive cry from the creature before him. Hopelessly at bay, weaponless, and knowing that any show of physical violence would bring a score of attendants to the doctor's rescue, Joseph Curwen had recourse to his one ancient ally, and began a series of cabbalistic[f] motions with his forefingers as his deep, hollow voice, now unconcealed by feigned hoarseness, bellowed out the opening words of a terrible formula.

"PER ADONAI ELOIM, ADONAI JEHOVA, ADONAI SABAOTH, METRATON. . . ."

---

[a] shewed] showed D
[b] contents] contacts C, D
[c] minuscules,] minuscule, D
[d] can not] cannot C, D
[e] down'.] down.' C
[f] cabbalistic] cabalistic A, C, D

But Willett was too quick for him. Even as the dogs in the yard outside began to howl, and even as a chill wind sprang suddenly up from the bay, the doctor commenced the solemn and measured intonation of that which he had meant all along to recite. An[a] eye for an eye—magic for magic—let the outcome shew[b] how well the lesson of the abyss had been learned! So in a clear voice Marinus Bicknell Willett began the *second* of that pair of formulae whose first had raised the writer of those minuscules—the cryptic invocation whose heading was the Dragon's Tail, sign of the *descending node—*

"OGTHROD AI'F
GEB'L—EE'H
YOG-SOTHOTH
'NGAH'NG AI'Y
ZHRO!"

At the very first word from Willett's mouth the previously commenced formula of the patient stopped short. Unable to speak, the monster made wild motions with his arms until they too were arrested.[c] When the awful name of *Yog-Sothoth* was uttered, the hideous change began. It was not merely a *dissolution,* but rather a *transformation* or *recapitulation;* and Willett shut his eyes lest he faint before the rest of the incantation could be pronounced.

But he did not faint, and that man of unholy centuries and forbidden secrets never troubled the world again. The madness out of time had subsided,[d] and the case of Charles Dexter Ward was closed. Opening his eyes before staggering out of that room of horror, Dr. Willett saw that what he had kept in memory had not been kept amiss. There had, as he had predicted, been no need for acids. For like his accursed picture a year before, Joseph Curwen now lay scattered on the floor as a thin coating of fine bluish-grey dust.

---

[a] recite. An] recite, an D
[b] shew] show D
[c] arrested.] wrested. D
[d] subsided,] subsided C

The Colour out of Space

West of Arkham the hills rise wild, and there are valleys with deep woods that no axe has ever cut. There are dark narrow glens where the trees slope fantastically, and where thin brooklets trickle without ever having caught the glint of sunlight. On the gentler slopes there are farms, ancient and rocky, with squat, moss-coated cottages brooding eternally over old New England secrets in the lee of great ledges; but these are all vacant now, the wide chimneys crumbling and the shingled sides bulging perilously beneath low gambrel roofs.

The old folk have gone away, and foreigners do not like to live there. French-Canadians have tried it, Italians have tried it, and the Poles have come and departed. It is not because of anything that can be seen or heard or handled, but because of something that is imagined. The place is not good for the[a] imagination, and does not bring restful dreams

Editor's Note: The story was first published in *Amazing Stories* (September 1927). It presumably followed a T.Ms. supplied by HPL; but there is some evidence that the surviving T.Ms. was not prepared by HPL, since there are a few errors that appear to be the result of the typist's inability to read HPL's handwriting. The existing T.Ms. is probably the one prepared by F. Lee Baldwin for his never-completed reprint of the story as a pamphlet. It is unclear whether Baldwin followed the original T.Ms. or the *Amazing Stories* appearance; I suspect the former. The T.Ms. bears numerous revisions by HPL. A handwritten note attached to the T.Ms. states: "Here you are! I think this is pretty nearly correct—but I'd like to read the proofs if possible. I have a letter-perfect copy to check up by. Anything overlooked now can be caught in the proofs."

It is not entirely clear what text Arkham House followed. It appears that it may have followed the original T.Ms. (now non-extant), since in at least three places it prints words or sentences (also found in the existing T.Ms.) that do not appear in the *Amazing Stories* appearance. But of course, no text prior to my 1984 edition prints the revisions found in the revised T.Ms.

Texts: A = *Amazing Stories* 2, No. 6 (September 1927): 557–67; B = T.Ms. (by F. Lee Baldwin?; revised by HPL); C = *The Dunwich Horror and Others* (Arkham House, 1963), 60–88. Copy-text: B.

[a] the] *om.* A, B [*revised by HPL*], C

at night. It must be this which keeps the foreigners away, for old Ammi Pierce has never told them of anything he recalls from the strange days. Ammi, whose head has been a little queer for years, is the only one who still remains, or who ever talks of the strange days; and he dares to do this because his house is so near the open fields and the travelled roads around Arkham.

There was once a road over the hills and through the valleys, that ran straight where the blasted heath is now; but people ceased to use it and a new road was laid curving far toward the south. Traces of the old one can still be found amidst the weeds of a returning wilderness, and some of them will doubtless linger even when half the hollows are flooded for the new reservoir. Then the dark woods will be cut down and the blasted heath will slumber far below blue waters whose surface will mirror the sky and ripple in the sun. And the secrets of the strange days will be one with the deep's secrets; one with the hidden lore of old ocean, and all the mystery of primal earth.

When I went into the hills and vales to survey for the new reservoir they told me the place was evil. They told me this in Arkham, and because that is a very old town full of witch legends I thought the evil must be something which grandams[a] had whispered to children through centuries. The name "blasted[b] heath" seemed to me very odd and theatrical, and I wondered how it had come into the folklore of a Puritan people.[c] Then I saw that dark westward tangle of glens and slopes for myself, and ceased to wonder at anything beside[d] its own elder mystery. It was morning when I saw it, but shadow lurked always there. The trees grew too thickly, and their trunks were too big for any healthy New England wood. There was too much silence in the dim alleys between them, and the floor was too soft with the dank moss and mattings of infinite years of decay.

In the open spaces, mostly along the line of the old road, there were little hillside farms;[e] sometimes with all the buildings standing,

[a] grandams] grandmas A
[b] name "blasted] name"blasted A
[c] people.] people C
[d] beside] besides A
[e] farms;] farms, B

sometimes with only one or two, and sometimes with only a lone chimney or fast-filling cellar. Weeds and briers reigned, and furtive wild things rustled in the undergrowth. Upon everything was a haze of restlessness and oppression; a touch of the unreal and the grotesque, as if some vital element of perspective or chiaroscuro were awry. I did not wonder that the foreigners would not stay, for this was no region to sleep in. It was too much like a landscape of Salvator Rosa; too much like some forbidden woodcut in a tale of terror.

But even all this was not so bad as the blasted heath. I knew it the moment I came upon it at the bottom of a spacious valley; for no other name could fit such a[a] thing, or any other thing fit such a name. It was as if the poet had coined the phrase from having seen this one particular region. It must, I thought as I viewed it, be the outcome of a fire; but why had nothing new ever grown over those five acres of grey desolation that sprawled open to the sky like a great spot eaten by acid in the woods and fields? It lay largely to the north of the ancient road line, but encroached a little on the other side. I felt an odd reluctance about approaching, and did so at last only because my business took me through and past it. There was no vegetation of any kind on that broad expanse, but only a fine grey dust or ash which no wind seemed ever to blow about. The trees near it were sickly and stunted, and many dead trunks stood or lay rotting at the rim. As I walked hurriedly by I saw the tumbled bricks and stones of an old chimney and cellar on my right, and the yawning black maw of an abandoned well whose stagnant vapours played strange tricks with the hues of the sunlight. Even the long, dark woodland climb beyond seemed welcome in contrast, and I marvelled no more at the frightened whispers of Arkham people. There had been no house or ruin near; even in the old days the place must have been lonely and remote. And at twilight, dreading to re-pass[b] that ominous spot, I walked circuitously back to the town by the curving road on the south. I vaguely wished some clouds would gather, for an odd timidity about the deep skyey voids above had crept into my soul.

In the evening I asked old people in Arkham about the blasted

[a] a] *om.* A
[b] re-pass] repass A, B, C

heath, and what was meant by that phrase "strange days" which so many evasively muttered. I could not, however, get any good answers, except that all the mystery was much more recent than I had dreamed. It was not a matter of old legendry at all, but something within the lifetime of those who spoke. It had happened in the 'eighties, and a family had disappeared or was killed. Speakers would not be exact; and because they all told me to pay no attention to old Ammi Pierce's crazy tales, I sought him out the next morning, having heard that he lived alone in the ancient tottering cottage where the trees first begin to get very thick. It was a fearsomely archaic[a] place, and had begun to exude the faint miasmal odour which clings about houses that have stood too long. Only with persistent knocking could I rouse the aged man, and when he shuffled timidly to the door I could tell he was not glad to see me. He was not so feeble as I had expected; but his eyes drooped in a curious way, and his unkempt clothing and white beard made him seem very worn and dismal.[b] Not knowing just how he could best be launched on his tales, I feigned a matter of business; told him of my surveying, and asked vague questions about the district. He was far brighter and more educated than I had been led to think, and before I knew it had grasped quite as much of the subject as any man I had talked with in Arkham. He was not like other rustics I had known in the sections where reservoirs were to be. From him there were no protests at the miles of old wood and farmland to be blotted out, though perhaps there would have been had not his home lain outside the bounds of the future lake. Relief was all that he shewed;[c] relief at the doom of the dark ancient valleys through which he had roamed all his life. They were better under water now—better under water since the strange days. And with this opening his husky voice sank low, while his body leaned forward and his right forefinger began to point shakily and impressively.

It was then that I heard the story, and as the rambling voice scraped and whispered on I shivered again and again despite the summer day. Often I had to recall the speaker from ramblings, piece

---

[a] archaic] ancient A, B [*revised by HPL*], C
[b] dismal.] dismal. ¶ A, C
[c] shewed;] showed; A, B, C

out scientific points which he knew only by a fading parrot memory of professors' talk, or bridge over gaps[a] where his sense of logic and continuity broke down. When he was done I did not wonder that his mind had snapped a trifle, or that the folk of Arkham would not speak much of the blasted heath. I hurried back before sunset to my hotel, unwilling to have the stars come out above me in the open; and the next day returned to Boston to give up my position. I could not go into that dim chaos of old forest and slope again, or face another time that grey blasted heath where the black well yawned deep beside the tumbled bricks and stones. The reservoir will soon be built now, and all those elder secrets will be[b] safe for ever[c] under watery fathoms. But even then I do not believe I would like to visit that country by night— at least,[d] not when the sinister stars are out; and nothing could bribe me to drink the new city water of Arkham.

It all began, old Ammi said, with the meteorite. Before that time there had been no wild legends at all since the witch trials, and even then these western woods were not feared half so much as the small island in the Miskatonic where the devil held court beside a curious stone altar older than the Indians. These were not haunted woods, and their fantastic dusk was never terrible till the strange days. Then there had come that white noontide cloud, that string of explosions in the air, and that pillar of smoke from the valley far in the wood. And by night all Arkham had heard of the great rock that fell out of the sky and bedded itself in the ground beside the well at the Nahum Gardner place. That was the house which had stood where the blasted heath was to come—the trim white Nahum Gardner house amidst its fertile gardens and orchards.

Nahum had come to town to tell people about the stone, and had[e] dropped in at Ammi Pierce's on the way. Ammi was forty then, and all the queer things were fixed very strongly in his mind. He and his wife had gone with the three professors from Miskatonic University who

[a] gaps] gaps, A, B [*revised by HPL*], C
[b] be] lie A
[c] for ever] forever A, B, C
[d] least,] least A, B [*revised by HPL*], C
[e] had] *om.* C

hastened out the next morning to see the weird visitor from unknown stellar space, and had wondered why Nahum had called it so large the day before. It had shrunk, Nahum said as he pointed out the big brownish mound above the ripped earth and charred grass near the archaic well-sweep in his front yard; but the wise men answered that stones do not shrink. Its heat lingered persistently, and Nahum declared it had glowed faintly in the night. The professors tried it with a geologist's hammer and found it was oddly soft. It was, in truth, so soft as to be almost plastic; and they gouged rather than chipped a specimen to take back to the college for testing. They took it in an old pail borrowed from Nahum's kitchen, for even the small piece refused to grow cool. On the trip back they stopped at Ammi's to rest, and seemed thoughtful when Mrs. Pierce remarked that the fragment was growing smaller and burning the bottom of the pail. Truly, it was not large, but perhaps they had taken less than they thought.

The day after that—all this was in June of '82—the professors had trooped out again in a great excitement. As they passed Ammi's they told him what queer things the specimen had done, and how it had faded wholly away when they put it in a glass beaker. The beaker had gone, too, and the wise men talked of the strange stone's affinity for silicon. It had acted quite unbelievably in that well-ordered laboratory; doing nothing at all and shewing[a] no occluded gases when heated on charcoal, being wholly negative in the borax bead, and soon proving itself absolutely non-volatile at any producible temperature, including that of the oxy-hydrogen blowpipe. On an anvil it appeared highly malleable, and in the dark its luminosity was very marked. Stubbornly refusing to grow cool, it soon had the college in a state of real excitement; and when upon heating before the spectroscope it displayed shining bands unlike any known colours of the normal spectrum there was much breathless talk of new elements, bizarre[b] optical properties, and other things which puzzled men of science are wont to say when faced by the unknown.

Hot as it was, they tested it in a crucible with all the proper reagents. Water did nothing. Hydrochloric acid was the same. Nitric acid and even

[a] shewing] showing A, B, C
[b] bizarre] bizzare C

aqua regia merely hissed and spattered against its torrid invulnerability. Ammi had difficulty in recalling all these things, but recognised[a] some solvents as I mentioned them in the usual order of use. There were ammonia and caustic soda, alcohol and ether, nauseous carbon disulphide and a dozen others; but although the weight grew steadily less as time passed, and the fragment seemed to be slightly cooling, there was no change in the solvents to shew[b] that they had attacked the substance at all. It was a metal, though, beyond a doubt. It was magnetic, for one thing; and after its immersion in the acid solvents there seemed to be faint traces of the Widmannstätten[c] figures found on meteoric iron. When the cooling had grown very considerable, the testing was carried on in glass; and it was in a glass beaker that they left all the chips made of the original fragment during the work. The next morning both chips and beaker were gone without trace, and only a charred spot marked the place on the wooden shelf where they had been.

All this the professors told Ammi as they paused at his door, and once more he went with them to see the stony messenger from the stars, though this time his wife did not accompany him. It had now most certainly shrunk, and even the sober professors could not doubt the truth of what they saw. All around the dwindling brown lump near the well was a vacant space, except where the earth had caved in; and whereas it had been a good seven feet across the day before, it was now scarcely five. It was still hot, and the sages studied its surface curiously as they detached another and larger piece with hammer and chisel. They gouged deeply this time, and as they pried away the smaller mass they saw that the core of the thing was not quite homogeneous.

They had uncovered what seemed to be the side of a large coloured globule imbedded[d] in the substance. The colour, which resembled some of the bands in the meteor's strange spectrum, was almost impossible to describe; and it was only by analogy that they called it colour at all. Its texture was glossy, and upon tapping it appeared to promise both brittleness and hollowness. One of the

[a] recognised] recognized A, B, C
[b] shew] show A, B, C
[c] Widmannstätten] Widmännstätten A, B [*revised by HPL*], C
[d] imbedded] embedded A, B [*revised by HPL*], C

professors gave it a smart blow with a hammer, and it burst with a
nervous little pop. Nothing was emitted, and all trace of the thing
vanished with the puncturing. It left behind a hollow spherical space
about three inches across, and all thought it probable that others
would be discovered as the enclosing substance wasted away.

Conjecture was vain; so after a futile attempt to find additional
globules by drilling, the seekers left again with their new specimen—
which proved, however, as baffling in the laboratory as its predecessor
had been.[a] Aside from being almost plastic, having heat, magnetism,
and slight luminosity, cooling slightly in powerful acids, possessing an
unknown spectrum, wasting away in air, and attacking silicon
compounds with mutual destruction as a result, it presented no
identifying features whatsoever; and at the end of the tests the college
scientists were forced to own that they could not place it. It was
nothing of this earth, but a piece of the great outside; and as such
dowered with outside properties and obedient to outside laws.

That night there was a thunderstorm, and when the professors went
out to Nahum's the next day they met with a bitter disappointment.
The stone, magnetic as it had been, must have had some peculiar electrical
property; for it had "drawn the lightning",[b] as Nahum said, with a singular
persistence. Six times within an hour the farmer saw the lightning strike
the furrow in the front yard, and when the storm was over nothing
remained but a ragged pit by the ancient well-sweep, half-choked[c]
with[d] caved-in earth. Digging had borne no fruit, and the scientists
verified the fact of the utter vanishment. The failure was total; so that
nothing was left to do but go back to the laboratory and test again the
disappearing fragment left carefully cased in lead. That fragment lasted
a week, at the end of which nothing of value had been learned of it.
When it had gone, no residue was left behind, and in time the
professors felt scarcely sure they had indeed seen with waking eyes that
cryptic vestige of the fathomless gulfs outside; that lone, weird message
from other universes and other realms of matter, force, and entity.

[a] predecessor had been.] predecessor. A, B [*revised by HPL*], C
[b] lightning",] lightning," A, B, C
[c] half-choked] half-chocked A
[d] with] with a C

As was natural, the Arkham papers made much of the incident with its collegiate sponsoring, and sent reporters to talk with Nahum Gardner and his family. At least one Boston daily also sent a scribe, and Nahum quickly became a kind of local celebrity. He was a lean, genial person of about fifty, living with his wife and three sons on the pleasant farmstead in the valley. He and Ammi exchanged visits frequently, as did their wives; and Ammi had nothing but praise for him after all these years. He seemed slightly proud of the notice his place had attracted, and talked often of the meteorite in the succeeding weeks. That July and August were hot,[a] and Nahum worked hard at his haying in the ten-acre pasture across Chapman's Brook; his rattling wain wearing deep ruts in the shadowy lanes between. The labour tired him more than it had in other years, and he felt that age was beginning to tell on him.

Then fell the time of fruit and harvest. The pears and apples slowly ripened, and Nahum vowed that his orchards were prospering as never before. The fruit was growing to phenomenal size and unwonted gloss, and in such abundance that extra barrels were ordered to handle the future crop. But with the ripening came sore disappointment, for of all that gorgeous array of specious lusciousness not one single jot was fit to eat. Into the fine flavour of the pears and apples had crept a stealthy bitterness and sickishness, so that even the smallest of[b] bites induced a lasting disgust. It was the same with the melons and tomatoes, and Nahum sadly saw that his entire crop was lost. Quick to connect events, he declared that the meteorite had poisoned the soil, and thanked heaven[c] that most of the other crops were in the upland lot along the road.

Winter came early, and was very cold. Ammi saw Nahum less often than usual, and observed that he had begun to look worried. The rest of his family,[d] too, seemed to have grown taciturn; and were far from steady in their churchgoing[e] or their attendance at the various

---

[a] hot,] hot; A, B, C
[b] of] *om.* C
[c] heaven] Heaven A, B, C
[d] family,] family A, B [*revised by HPL*], C
[e] churchgoing] church-going C

social events of the countryside. For this reserve or melancholy no cause could be found, though all the household confessed now and then to poorer health and a feeling of vague disquiet. Nahum himself gave the most definite statement of anyone when he said he was disturbed about certain footprints in the snow. They were the usual winter prints of red squirrels, white rabbits, and foxes, but the brooding farmer professed to see something not quite right about their nature and arrangement. He was never specific, but appeared to think that they were not as characteristic of the anatomy and habits of squirrels and rabbits and foxes as they ought to be. Ammi listened without interest to this talk until one night when he drove past Nahum's house in his sleigh on the way back from Clark's Corners. There had been a moon, and a rabbit had run across the road, and the leaps of that rabbit were longer than either Ammi or his horse liked. The latter, indeed, had almost run away when brought up by a firm rein. Thereafter Ammi gave Nahum's tales more respect, and wondered why the Gardner dogs seemed so cowed and quivering every morning. They had, it developed, nearly lost the spirit to bark.

In February the McGregor boys from Meadow Hill were out shooting woodchucks, and not far from the Gardner place bagged a very peculiar specimen. The proportions of its body seemed slightly altered in a queer way impossible to describe, while its face had taken on an expression which no one ever saw in a woodchuck before. The boys were genuinely frightened, and threw the thing away at once, so that only their grotesque tales of it ever reached the people of the countryside. But the shying of the[a] horses near Nahum's house had now become an acknowledged thing, and all the basis for a cycle of whispered legend was fast taking form.

People vowed that the snow melted faster around Nahum's than it did anywhere else, and early in March there was an awed discussion in Potter's general store at Clark's Corners. Stephen Rice had driven past Gardner's in the morning, and had noticed the skunk-cabbages coming up through the mud by the woods across the road. Never were things of such size seen before, and they held strange colours that could not be put into any words. Their shapes were monstrous, and the horse had

---

[a] the] *om.* A, C

snorted at an odour which struck Stephen as wholly unprecedented. That afternoon several persons drove past to see the abnormal growth, and all agreed that plants of that kind ought never to sprout in a healthy world. The bad fruit of the fall before was freely mentioned, and it went from mouth to mouth that there was poison in Nahum's ground. Of course it was the meteorite; and remembering how strange the men from the college had found that stone to be, several farmers spoke about the matter to them.

One day they paid Nahum a visit; but having no love of wild tales and folklore were very conservative in what they inferred. The plants were certainly odd, but all skunk-cabbages[a] are more or less odd in shape and odour[b] and hue. Perhaps some mineral element from the stone had entered the soil, but it would soon be washed away. And as for the footprints and frightened horses—of course this was mere country talk which such a phenomenon as the aërolite[c] would be certain to start. There was really nothing for serious men to do in cases of wild gossip, for superstitious rustics will say and believe anything. And so all through the strange days the professors stayed away in contempt. Only one of them, when given two phials of dust for analysis in a police job over a year and a half later, recalled that the queer colour of that skunk-cabbage had been very like one of the anomalous bands of light shewn[d] by the meteor fragment in the college spectroscope, and like the brittle globule found imbedded in the stone from the abyss. The samples in this analysis case gave the same odd bands at first, though later they lost the property.

The trees budded prematurely around Nahum's, and at night they swayed ominously in the wind. Nahum's second son Thaddeus, a lad of fifteen, swore that they swayed also when there was no wind; but even the gossips would not credit this. Certainly, however, restlessness was in the air. The entire Gardner family developed the habit of stealthy listening, though not for any sound which they could consciously name. The listening was, indeed, rather a product of

---

[a] skunk-cabbages] skunk-cabbags A
[b] and odour] *om.* A, B [*revised by HPL*], C
[c] aërolite] aerolite A, B [*revised by HPL*], C
[d] shewn] shown A, B, C

moments when consciousness seemed half[a] to slip away. Unfortunately such moments increased week by week, till it became common speech that "something was wrong with all Nahum's folks".[b] When the early saxifrage came out it had another strange colour; not quite like that of the skunk-cabbage, but plainly related and equally unknown to anyone who saw it. Nahum took some blossoms to Arkham and shewed[c] them to the editor of the *Gazette,* but that dignitary did no more than write a humorous article about them, in which the dark fears of rustics were held up to polite ridicule. It was a mistake of Nahum's to tell a stolid city man about the way the great, overgrown mourning-cloak butterflies behaved in connexion[d] with these saxifrages.

April brought a kind of madness to the country folk, and began that disuse of the road past Nahum's which led to its ultimate abandonment. It was[e] the vegetation. All the orchard trees blossomed forth in strange colours, and through the stony soil of the yard and adjacent pasturage there sprang up a bizarre growth which only a botanist could connect with the proper flora of the region. No sane wholesome colours were anywhere to be seen except in the green grass and leafage; but everywhere[f] those hectic and prismatic variants of some diseased, underlying primary tone without a place among the known tints of earth. The Dutchman's breeches[g] became a thing of sinister menace, and the bloodroots grew insolent in their chromatic perversion. Ammi and the Gardners thought that most of the colours had a sort of haunting familiarity, and decided that they reminded one of the brittle globule in the meteor. Nahum ploughed and sowed the ten-acre pasture and the upland lot, but did nothing with the land around the house. He knew it would be of no use, and hoped that the summer's strange growths would draw all the poison from the soil. He was prepared for almost anything now, and had grown used to the sense of something near him waiting to be heard. The shunning of his

[a] half] *om.* B
[b] folks".] folks." A, B, C
[c] shewed] showed A, B, C
[d] connexion] connection A, B, C
[e] was] was next A
[f] everywhere] everywhere were A, B [*revised by HPL*], C
[g] Dutchman's breeches] "Dutchman's breeches" A, B [*revised by HPL*], C

house by neighbours[a] told on him, of course; but it told on his wife more. The boys were better off, being at school each day; but they could not help being frightened by the gossip. Thaddeus, an especially sensitive youth, suffered the most.

In May the insects came, and Nahum's place became a nightmare of buzzing and crawling. Most of the creatures seemed not quite usual in their aspects and motions, and their nocturnal habits contradicted all former experience. The Gardners took to watching at night—watching in all directions at random for something . . .[b] they could not tell what. It was then that they all owned that Thaddeus had been right about the trees. Mrs. Gardner was the next to see it from the window as she watched the swollen boughs of a maple against a moonlit sky. The boughs surely moved, and there was no wind. It must be the sap. Strangeness had come into everything growing now. Yet it was none of Nahum's family at all who made the next discovery. Familiarity had dulled them, and what they could not see was glimpsed by a timid windmill salesman from Bolton[c] who drove by one night in ignorance of the country legends. What he told in Arkham was given a short paragraph in the *Gazette;* and it was there that all the farmers, Nahum included, saw it first. The night had been dark and the buggy-lamps faint, but around a farm in the valley which everyone knew from the account must be Nahum's[d] the darkness had been less thick. A dim though distinct luminosity seemed to inhere in all the vegetation, grass, leaves, and blossoms alike, while at one moment a detached piece of the phosphorescence appeared to stir furtively in the yard near the barn.

The grass had so far seemed untouched, and the cows were freely pastured in the lot near the house, but toward the end of May the milk began to be bad. Then Nahum had the cows driven to the uplands, after which the[e] trouble ceased. Not long after this the change in grass and leaves became apparent to the eye. All the verdure was going grey, and was developing a highly singular quality of brittleness. Ammi was

---

now the only person who ever visited the place, and his visits were becoming fewer and fewer. When school closed the Gardners were virtually cut off from the world, and sometimes let Ammi do their errands in town. They were failing curiously both physically and mentally, and no one was surprised when the news of Mrs. Gardner's madness stole around.

It happened in June, about the anniversary of the meteor's fall, and the poor woman screamed about things in the air which she could not describe. In her raving there was not a single specific noun, but only verbs and pronouns. Things moved and changed and fluttered, and ears tingled to impulses which were not wholly sounds. Something was taken away—she was being drained of something—something was fastening itself on her that ought not to be—someone must make it keep off—nothing was ever still in the night—the walls and windows shifted. Nahum did not send her to the county asylum, but let her wander about the house as long as she was harmless to herself and others. Even when her expression changed he did nothing. But when the boys grew afraid of her, and Thaddeus nearly fainted at the way she made faces at him, he decided to keep her locked in the attic. By July she had ceased to speak and crawled on all fours, and before that month was over Nahum got the mad notion that she was slightly luminous in the dark, as he now clearly saw was the case with the nearby vegetation.

It was a little before this that the horses had stampeded. Something had aroused them in the night, and their neighing and kicking in their stalls had been terrible. There seemed virtually nothing to do to calm them, and when Nahum opened the stable door they all bolted out like frightened woodland deer. It took a week to track all four, and when found they were seen to be quite useless and unmanageable. Something had snapped in their brains, and each one had to be shot for its own good. Nahum borrowed a horse from Ammi for his haying, but found it would not approach the barn. It shied, balked, and whinnied, and in the end he could do nothing but drive it into the yard while the men used their own strength to get the heavy wagon near enough the hayloft for convenient pitching. And all the while the vegetation was turning grey and brittle. Even the flowers whose hue[a] had been so strange were greying[b] now, and the fruit was coming out grey and dwarfed and tasteless. The asters and goldenrod[c] bloomed grey and distorted, and the roses and zinneas and hollyhocks in the front yard were such blasphemous-looking things that Nahum's oldest boy Zenas cut them down. The strangely puffed insects died about that time, even the bees that had left their hives and taken to the woods.

By September all the vegetation was fast crumbling to a greyish powder, and Nahum feared that the trees would die before the poison was out of the soil. His wife now had spells of terrific screaming, and he and the boys were in a constant state of nervous tension. They shunned people now, and when school opened the boys did not go. But it was Ammi, on one of his rare visits, who first realised[d] that the well water was no longer good. It had an evil taste that was not exactly foetid[e] nor exactly salty, and Ammi advised his friend to dig another well on higher ground to use till the soil was good again. Nahum, however, ignored the warning, for he had by that time become calloused to strange and unpleasant things. He and the boys continued to use the tainted supply, drinking it as listlessly and mechanically as they ate their meagre and ill-cooked meals and did their thankless and monotonous chores through the aimless days. There was something of stolid resignation about them all, as if they walked half in another world between lines of nameless guards to a certain and familiar doom.

Thaddeus went mad in September after a visit to the well. He had gone with a pail and had come back empty-handed, shrieking and waving his arms, and sometimes lapsing into an inane titter or a whisper about "the moving colours down there".[f] Two in one family was pretty bad, but Nahum was very brave about it. He let the boy run about for a week until he began stumbling and hurting himself, and then he shut him in an attic room across the hall from his mother's. The way they screamed at each other from behind their locked doors

[a] hue] hues A
[b] greying] graying A
[c] goldenrod] golden-rod C
[d] realised] realized A, B
[e] foetid] fetid A, B [*revised by HPL*], C
[f] there".] there." A, B, C

was very terrible, especially to little Merwin, who fancied they talked in some terrible language that was not of earth. Merwin was getting frightfully imaginative, and his restlessness was worse after the shutting away of the brother who had been his greatest playmate.

Almost at the same time the mortality among the livestock commenced. Poultry turned greyish and died very quickly, their meat being found dry and noisome upon cutting. Hogs grew inordinately fat, then suddenly began to undergo loathsome changes which no one could explain. Their meat was of course useless, and Nahum was at his wit's end. No rural veterinary would approach his place, and the city veterinary from Arkham was openly baffled. The swine began growing grey and brittle and falling to pieces before they died, and their eyes and muzzles developed singular alterations. It was very inexplicable, for they had never been fed from the tainted vegetation. Then something struck the cows. Certain areas or sometimes the whole body would be uncannily shrivelled or compressed, and atrocious collapses or disintegrations were common. In the last stages—and death was always the result—there would be a greying and turning brittle like that which beset the hogs. There could be no question of poison, for all the cases occurred in a locked and undisturbed barn. No bites of prowling things could have brought the virus, for what live beast of earth can pass through solid obstacles? It must be only natural disease—yet what disease could wreak such results was beyond any mind's guessing. When the harvest came there was not an animal surviving on the place, for the stock and poultry were dead and the dogs had run away. These dogs, three in number, had all vanished one night and were never heard of again. The five cats had left some time before, but their going was scarcely noticed since there now seemed to be no mice, and only Mrs. Gardner had made pets of the graceful felines.

On the nineteenth of October Nahum staggered into Ammi's house with hideous news. The death had come to poor Thaddeus in his attic room, and it had come in a way which could not be told. Nahum had dug a grave in the railed family plot behind the farm, and had put therein what he found. There could have been nothing from outside, for the small barred window and locked door were intact; but it was much as it had been in the barn. Ammi and his wife consoled the stricken man as best they could, but shuddered as they did so.

Stark terror seemed to cling round the Gardners and all they touched, and the very presence of one in the house was a breath from regions unnamed and unnamable. Ammi accompanied Nahum home with the greatest reluctance, and did what he might to calm the hysterical sobbing of little Merwin. Zenas needed no calming. He had come of late to do nothing but stare into space and obey what his father told him; and Ammi thought that his fate was very merciful. Now and then Merwin's screams were answered faintly from the attic, and in response to an inquiring look Nahum said that his wife was getting very feeble. When night approached, Ammi managed to get away; for not even friendship could make him stay in that spot when the faint glow of the vegetation began and the trees may or may not have swayed without wind. It was really lucky for Ammi that he was not more imaginative. Even as things were, his mind was bent ever so slightly; but had he been able to connect and reflect upon all the portents around him he must inevitably have turned a total maniac. In the twilight he hastened home, the screams of the mad woman and the nervous child ringing horribly[a] in his ears.

Three days later Nahum lurched[b] into Ammi's kitchen in the early morning, and in the absence of his host stammered out a desperate tale once more, while Mrs. Pierce listened in a clutching fright. It was little Merwin this time. He was gone. He had gone out late at night with a lantern and pail for water, and had never come back. He'd been going to pieces for days, and hardly knew what he was about. Screamed at everything. There had been a frantic shriek from the yard then, but before the father could get to the door,[c] the boy was gone. There was no glow from the lantern he had taken, and of the child himself no trace. At the time Nahum thought the lantern and pail were gone too; but when dawn came, and the man had plodded back from his all-night search of the woods and fields, he had found some very curious things near the well. There was a crushed and apparently somewhat melted mass of iron which had certainly been the lantern; while a bent

[a] horribly] horrible A
[b] lurched] burst A, B [*revised by HPL*], C
[c] door,] door A, C

bail[a] and twisted iron hoops beside it, both half-fused, seemed to hint at the remnants of the pail. That was all. Nahum was past imagining, Mrs. Pierce was blank, and Ammi, when he had reached home and heard the tale, could give no guess. Merwin was gone, and there would be no use in telling the people around, who shunned all Gardners now. No use, either, in telling the city people at Arkham who laughed at everything. Thad was gone, and now Mernie[b] was gone. Something was creeping and creeping and waiting to be seen and felt[c] and heard. Nahum would go soon, and he wanted Ammi to look after his wife and Zenas if they survived him. It must all be a judgment of some sort; though he could not fancy what for, since he had always walked uprightly in the Lord's ways so far as he knew.

For over two weeks Ammi saw nothing of Nahum; and then, worried about what might have happened, he overcame his fears and paid the Gardner place a visit. There was no smoke from the great chimney, and for a moment the visitor was apprehensive of the worst. The aspect of the whole farm was shocking—greyish withered grass and leaves on the ground, vines falling in brittle wreckage from archaic walls and gables, and great bare trees clawing up at the grey November sky with a studied malevolence which Ammi could not but feel had come from some subtle change in the tilt of the branches. But Nahum was alive, after all. He was weak, and lying on[d] a couch in the low-ceiled kitchen, but perfectly conscious and able to give simple orders to Zenas. The room was deadly cold; and as Ammi visibly shivered, the host shouted huskily to Zenas for more wood. Wood, indeed, was sorely needed; since the cavernous fireplace was unlit and empty, with a cloud of soot blowing about in the chill wind that came down the chimney. Presently Nahum asked him if the extra wood had made him any more comfortable,[e] and then Ammi saw what had happened. The stoutest cord had broken at last, and the hapless farmer's mind was proof against more sorrow.

---

[a] bail] pail A; handle B [*revised by HPL*], C
[b] Mernie] Merwin A, B [*revised by HPL*], C
[c] and felt] *om.* A, B [*revised by HPL*], C
[d] on] in A
[e] comfortable,] confortable, A

Questioning tactfully, Ammi could get no clear data at all about the missing Zenas. "In the well—he lives in the well—" was all that the clouded father would say. Then there flashed across the visitor's mind a sudden thought of the mad wife, and he changed his line of inquiry. "Nabby? Why, here she is!" was the surprised response of poor Nahum, and Ammi soon saw that he must search for himself. Leaving the harmless babbler on the couch, he took the keys from their nail beside the door and climbed the creaking stairs to the attic. It was very close and noisome up there, and no sound could be heard from any direction. Of the four doors in sight, only one was locked, and on this he tried various keys on[a] the ring he had taken. The third key proved the right one, and after some fumbling Ammi threw open the low white door.

It was quite dark inside, for the window was small and half-obscured by the crude wooden bars; and Ammi could see nothing at all on the wide-planked floor. The stench was beyond enduring, and before proceeding further he had to retreat to another room and return with his lungs filled with breathable air. When he did enter he saw something dark in the corner, and upon seeing it more clearly he screamed outright. While he screamed he thought a momentary cloud eclipsed the window, and a second later he felt himself brushed as if by some hateful current of vapour. Strange colours danced before his eyes; and had not a present horror numbed him he would have thought of the globule in the meteor that the geologist's hammer had shattered, and of the morbid vegetation that had sprouted in the spring. As it was he thought only of the blasphemous monstrosity which confronted him, and which all too clearly had shared the nameless fate of young Thaddeus and the livestock.[b] But the terrible thing about this[c] horror was that it very slowly and perceptibly moved as it continued to crumble.

Ammi would give me no added particulars to[d] this scene, but the shape in the corner[e] does not reappear in his tale as a moving object.

---

[a] on] of C
[b] livestock.] live-/stock. A; live-stock. C
[c] this] the A, B [*revised by HPL*], C
[d] to] of A
[e] corner] corners A

There are things which cannot be mentioned, and what is done in common humanity is sometimes cruelly judged by the law. I gathered that no moving thing was left in that attic room, and that to leave anything capable of motion there would have been a deed so monstrous as to damn any accountable being to eternal torment. Anyone but a stolid farmer would have fainted or gone mad, but Ammi walked conscious through that low doorway and locked the accursed secret behind him. There would be Nahum to deal with now; he must be fed and tended, and removed to some place where he could be cared for.

Commencing his descent of the dark stairs, Ammi heard a thud below him. He even thought a scream had been suddenly choked off, and recalled nervously the clammy vapour which had brushed by him in that frightful room above. What presence had his cry and entry started up? Halted by some vague fear, he heard still further sounds below. Indubitably there was a sort of heavy dragging, and a most detestably sticky noise as of some fiendish and unclean species of suction. With an associative sense goaded to feverish heights, he thought unaccountably of what he had seen upstairs. Good God! What eldritch dream-world was this into which he had blundered? He dared move neither backward nor forward, but stood there trembling at the black curve of the boxed-in staircase. Every trifle of the scene burned itself into his brain. The sounds, the sense of dread expectancy, the darkness, the steepness of the narrow steps—and merciful heaven! . . .[a] the faint but unmistakable luminosity of all the woodwork in sight; steps, sides, exposed laths, and beams alike![b]

Then there burst forth a frantic whinny from Ammi's horse outside, followed at once by a clatter which told of a frenzied runaway. In another moment horse and buggy had gone beyond earshot, leaving the frightened man on the dark stairs to guess what had sent them. But that was not all. There had been another sound out there. A sort of liquid splash—water—it must have been the well. He had left Hero untied near it, and a buggy-wheel[c] must have brushed the coping and

[a] heaven! . . .] Heaven!— A, B [revised by HPL to Heaven! . . .], C
[b] alike!] alike. A, B [revised by HPL], C
[c] buggy-wheel] buggywheel C

knocked in a stone. And still the pale phosphorescence glowed in that detestably ancient woodwork. God! how old the house was! Most of it built before 1670, and the gambrel roof not[a] later than 1730.[b]

A feeble scratching on the floor downstairs now sounded distinctly, and Ammi's grip tightened on a heavy stick he had picked up in the attic for some purpose. Slowly nerving himself, he finished his descent and walked boldly toward the kitchen. But he did not complete the walk, because what he sought was no longer there. It had come to meet him, and it was still alive after a fashion. Whether it had crawled or whether it had been dragged by any external force,[c] Ammi could not say; but the death had been at it. Everything had happened in the last half-hour, but collapse, greying, and disintegration were already far advanced. There was a horrible brittleness, and dry fragments were scaling off. Ammi could not touch it, but looked horrifiedly into the distorted parody that had been a face. "What was it, Nahum—what was it?" he[d] whispered, and the cleft, bulging lips were just able to crackle out a final answer.

"Nothin' . . . nothin' . . . the colour . . . it burns . . . cold an' wet, but it burns . . . it lived in the well . . . I seen it . . . a kind o'[e] smoke . . . jest like the flowers last spring . . . the well shone at night . . . Thad an' Mernie[f] an' Zenas . . . everything alive . . . suckin' the life out of everything . . . in that stone . . . it must a'[g] come in that stone . . . pizened the whole place . . . dun't know what it wants . . . that round thing them men from the college dug outen the stone . . . they smashed it . . . it was that same colour . . . jest the same, like the flowers an' plants . . . must a' ben more of 'em . . . seeds . . . seeds . . . they growed . . . I seen it the fust time this week . . . must a' got strong on Zenas . . . he was a big boy, full o' life . . . it beats down your mind an' then gits[h] ye . . . burns ye up . . . in the well water . . . you was right

[a] not] *om.* A [*see below*]; no C
[b] Most . . . 1730.] Most of it built before 1700. A
[c] force,] forces, A, B [*revised by HPL*], C
[d] he] He A, B, C
[e] o'] of C
[f] Mernie] Merwin A, B [*revised by HPL*], C
[g] a'] o' A
[h] gits] gets C

about that . . . evil water . . . Zenas never come back from the well . . .
can't git away . . . draws ye . . . ye know summ'at's comin',[a] but 'tain't[b]
no use . . . I seen it time an' agin senct[c] Zenas was took . . . whar's
Nabby, Ammi? . . . my head's no good . . . dun't know how long senct[d]
I fed her . . . it'll git her ef we ain't keerful . . . jest a colour . . . her face
is gettin'[e] to hev that colour sometimes towards night . . . an' it burns
an' sucks . . . it come from some place whar things ain't as they is here
. . . one o' them professors said so . . . he was right . . . look out,
Ammi, it'll do suthin' more . . . sucks the life out. . . ."

But that was all. That which spoke could speak no more because it
had completely caved in. Ammi laid a red checked tablecloth over
what was left and reeled out the back door into the fields. He climbed
the slope to the ten-acre pasture and stumbled home by the north road
and the woods. He could not pass that well from which his horse[f] had
run away. He had looked at it through the window, and had seen that
no stone was missing from the rim. Then the lurching buggy had not
dislodged anything after all—the splash had been something else—
something which went into the well after it had done with poor
Nahum. . . .

When Ammi reached his house the horse[g] and buggy had arrived
before him and thrown his wife into fits of anxiety. Reassuring her
without explanations, he set out at once for Arkham and notified the
authorities that the Gardner family was no more. He indulged in no
details, but merely told of the deaths of Nahum and Nabby, that of
Thaddeus being already known, and mentioned that the cause seemed to
be the same strange ailment which had killed the livestock.[h] He also
stated that Merwin and Zenas had disappeared.[i] There was considerable
questioning at the police station, and in the end Ammi was compelled

[a] comin',] comin' C
[b] 'tain't] tain't C
[c] senct] om. A
[d] senct] sence A; sense C
[e] getting'] gittin' A, C
[f] horse] horses A, B [revised by HPL], C
[g] horse] horses A, B [revised by HPL], C
[h] livestock.] live-/stock. A; live-stock. C
[i] disappeared.] dissappeared. A

to take three officers to the Gardner farm, together with the coroner, the medical examiner, and the veterinary who had treated the diseased animals. He went much against his will, for the afternoon was advancing and he feared the fall of night over that accursed place, but it was some comfort to have so many people with him.

The six men drove out in a democrat-wagon, following Ammi's buggy, and arrived at the pest-ridden farmhouse about four o'clock. Used as the officers were to gruesome experiences, not one remained unmoved at what was found in the attic and under the red checked tablecloth on the floor below. The whole aspect of the farm with its grey desolation was terrible enough, but those two crumbling objects were beyond all bounds. No one could look long at them, and even the medical examiner admitted that there was very little to examine. Specimens could be analysed, of course, so he busied himself in obtaining them—and here it develops that a very puzzling aftermath occurred at the college laboratory where the two phials of dust were finally taken. Under the spectroscope both samples gave off an unknown spectrum, in which many of the baffling bands were precisely like those which the strange meteor had yielded in the previous year. The property of emitting this spectrum vanished in a month, the dust thereafter consisting mainly of alkaline phosphates and carbonates.

Ammi would not have told the men about the well if he had thought they meant to do anything then and there. It was getting toward sunset, and he was anxious to be away. But he could not help glancing nervously at the stony curb by the great sweep, and when a detective questioned him he admitted that Nahum had feared something down there—so much so that he had never even thought of searching it for Merwin or Zenas. After that nothing would do but that they empty and explore the well immediately, so Ammi had to wait trembling while pail after pail of rank water was hauled up and splashed on the soaking ground outside. The men sniffed in disgust at the fluid, and toward the last held their noses against the foetor they were uncovering. It was not so long a job as they had feared it would be, since the water was phenomenally low. There is no need to speak too exactly of what they found. Merwin and Zenas were both there, in part, though the vestiges were mainly skeletal. There were also a small deer and a large dog in about the same state, and a number of bones of smaller[a] animals. The ooze and slime at the bottom seemed inexplicably porous and bubbling, and a man who descended on handholds[b] with a long pole found that he could sink the wooden shaft to any depth in the mud of the floor without meeting any solid obstruction.

Twilight had now fallen, and lanterns were brought from the house. Then, when it was seen that nothing further could be gained from the well, everyone went indoors and conferred in the ancient sitting-room while the intermittent light of a spectral half-moon played wanly on the grey desolation outside. The men were frankly nonplussed by the entire case, and could find no convincing common element to link the strange vegetable conditions, the unknown disease of livestock[c] and humans, and the unaccountable deaths of Merwin and Zenas in the tainted well. They had heard the common country talk, it is true; but could not believe that anything contrary to natural law had occurred. No doubt the meteor had poisoned the soil, but the illness of persons[d] and animals who had eaten nothing grown in that soil was another matter. Was it the well water? Very possibly. It might be a good idea to analyse[e] it. But what peculiar madness could have made both boys jump into the well? Their deeds were so similar—and the fragments shewed[f] that they had both suffered from the grey brittle death. Why was everything so grey and brittle?

It was the coroner, seated near a window overlooking the yard, who first noticed the glow about the well. Night had fully set in, and all the abhorrent grounds seemed faintly luminous with more than the fitful moonbeams; but this new glow was something definite and distinct, and appeared to shoot up from the black pit like a softened ray from a searchlight, giving dull reflections in the little ground pools where the water had been emptied. It had a very queer colour, and as all the men clustered round the window Ammi gave a violent start. For this strange beam of ghastly miasma was to him of no unfamiliar hue.

[a] smaller] small C
[b] handholds] hand-holds A, B, C
[c] livestock] live-stock C
[d] persons] person A
[e] analyse] analyze C
[f] shewed] showed A, B, C

He had seen that colour before, and feared to think what it might mean. He had seen it in the nasty brittle globule in that aërolite[a] two summers ago, had seen it in the crazy vegetation of the springtime, and had thought he had seen it for an instant that very morning against the small barred window of that terrible attic room where nameless things had happened. It had flashed there a second, and a clammy and hateful current of vapour had brushed past him—and then poor Nahum had been taken by something of that colour. He had said so at the last—said it was like the globule and the plants. After that had come the runaway in the yard and the splash in the well—and now that well was belching forth to the night a pale insidious beam of the same daemoniac[b] tint.

It does credit to the alertness of Ammi's mind that he puzzled even at that tense moment over a point which was essentially scientific. He could not but wonder at his gleaning of the same impression from a vapour glimpsed in the daytime, against a window opening on[c] the morning sky, and from a nocturnal exhalation seen as a phosphorescent mist against the black and blasted landscape. It wasn't right—it was against Nature—and he thought of those terrible last words of his stricken friend, "It come from some place whar things ain't as they is here . . . one o' them professors said so. . . ."

All three horses outside, tied to a pair of shrivelled saplings by the road, were now neighing and pawing frantically. The wagon driver started for the door to do something, but Ammi laid a shaky hand on his shoulder. "Dun't go out thar," he whispered. "They's more to this nor what we know. Nahum said somethin' lived in the well that sucks your life out. He said it must be some'at growed from a round ball like one we all seen in the meteor stone that fell a year ago June. Sucks an' burns, he said, an' is jest a cloud of colour like that light out thar now, that ye can hardly see an' can't tell what it is. Nahum thought it feeds on everything livin' an' gits stronger all the time. He said he seen it this last week. It must be somethin' from away off in the sky like the men from the college last year says the meteor stone was. The way it's made an' the way it works ain't like no way o' God's world. It's some'at from beyond."

[a] aërolite] aerolite A, B [*revised by HPL*], C
[b] daemoniac] demoniac A, B, C
[c] on] in A

So the men paused indecisively as the light from the well grew stronger and the hitched horses pawed and whinnied in increasing frenzy. It was truly an awful moment; with terror in that ancient and accursed house itself, four monstrous sets of fragments—two from the house and two from the well—in the woodshed behind, and that shaft of unknown and unholy iridescence from the slimy depths in front. Ammi had restrained the driver on impulse, forgetting how uninjured he himself was after the clammy brushing of that coloured vapour in the attic room, but perhaps it is just as well that he acted as he did. No one will ever know what was abroad that night; and though the blasphemy from beyond had not so far hurt any human of unweakened mind, there is no telling what it might not have done at that last moment, and with its seemingly increased strength and the special signs of purpose it was soon to display beneath the half-clouded moonlit sky.

All at once one of the detectives at the window gave a short, sharp gasp. The others looked at him, and then quickly followed his own gaze upward to the point at which its idle straying had been suddenly arrested. There was no need for words. What had been disputed in country gossip was disputable no longer, and it is because of the thing which every man of that party agreed in whispering later on[a] that the[b] strange days are never talked about in Arkham. It is necessary to premise that there was no wind at that hour of the evening. One did arise not long afterward, but there was absolutely none then. Even the dry tips of the lingering hedge-mustard, grey and blighted, and the fringe on the roof of the standing democrat-wagon were unstirred. And yet amid that tense, godless calm the high bare boughs of all the trees in the yard were moving. They were twitching morbidly and spasmodically, clawing in convulsive and epileptic madness at the moonlit clouds; scratching impotently in the noxious air as if jerked by some alien[c] and bodiless line of linkage with subterrene horrors writhing and struggling below the black roots.

Not a man breathed for several seconds. Then a cloud of darker depth passed over the moon, and the silhouette of clutching branches

[a] on] on, A, B [revised by HPL], C
[b] the] om. A
[c] alien] allied A, B [revised by HPL], C

faded out momentarily. At this there was a general cry; muffled with awe, but husky and almost identical from every throat. For the terror had not faded with the silhouette, and in a fearsome instant of deeper darkness the watchers saw wriggling at that treetop[a] height a thousand tiny points of faint and unhallowed[b] radiance, tipping each bough like the fire of St. Elmo or the flames that came[c] down on the apostles' heads at Pentecost. It was a monstrous constellation of unnatural light, like a glutted swarm of corpse-fed fireflies dancing hellish sarabands over an accursed marsh; and its colour was that same nameless intrusion which Ammi had come to recognise[d] and dread. All the while the shaft of phosphorescence from the well was getting brighter and brighter, bringing to the minds of the huddled men[e] a sense of doom and abnormality which far outraced any image their conscious minds could form. It was no longer *shining* out,[f] it was *pouring* out; and as the shapeless stream of unplaceable colour left the well it seemed to flow directly into the sky.

The veterinary shivered, and walked to the front door to drop the heavy extra bar across it. Ammi shook no less, and had to tug and point for lack of a[g] controllable voice when he wished to draw notice to the growing luminosity of the trees. The neighing and stamping of the horses had become utterly frightful, but not a soul of that group in the old house would have ventured forth for any earthly reward. With the moments the shining of the trees increased, while their restless branches seemed to strain more and more toward verticality. The wood of the well-sweep was shining now, and presently a policeman dumbly pointed to some wooden sheds and bee-hives[h] near the stone wall on the west. They were commencing to shine, too, though the tethered vehicles of the visitors seemed so far unaffected. Then there was a wild commotion and clopping in the road, and as Ammi quenched

---

[a] that treetop] the treetop A; that tree / top C
[b] unhallowed] unhalloed A
[c] came] come A, B [*revised by HPL*], C
[d] recognise] recognize B, C
[e] men] men, A, B [*revised by HPL*], C
[f] out,] out; A, C
[g] a] *om.* C
[h] bee-hives] beehives A

the lamp for better seeing they realised[a] that the span of frantic greys[b] had broken their sapling and run off with the democrat-wagon.

The shock served to loosen several tongues, and embarrassed whispers were exchanged. "It spreads on everything organic that's been around here,"[c] muttered the medical examiner. No one replied, but the man who had been in the well gave a hint that his long pole must have stirred up something intangible. "It was awful," he added. "There was no bottom at all. Just ooze and bubbles and the feeling of something lurking under there." Ammi's horse still pawed and screamed deafeningly in the road outside, and nearly drowned its owner's faint quaver as he mumbled his formless reflections. "It come from that stone . . .[d] it growed down thar . . .[e] it got everything livin' . . .[f] it fed itself on 'em, mind and body . . .[g] Thad an' Mernie,[h] Zenas an' Nabby . . .[i] Nahum was the last . . .[j] they all drunk the water . . .[k] it got strong on 'em . . .[l] it come from beyond, whar things ain't like they be here . . .[m] now it's goin' home. . . ."[n]

At this point, as the column of unknown colour flared suddenly stronger and began to weave itself into fantastic suggestions of shape which each spectator later described differently, there came from poor tethered Hero such a sound as no man before or since ever heard from a horse. Every person in that low-pitched sitting-room[o] stopped his ears, and Ammi turned away from the window in horror and nausea. Words could not convey it—when Ammi looked out again the hapless

---

[a] realised] realized A, B, C
[b] greys] grays A
[c] here,"] here." A
[d] stone . . .] stone— A, B [*revised by HPL*], C
[e] thar . . .] thar— A, B [*revised by HPL*], C
[f] livin' . . .] livin'— A, B [*revised by HPL*], C
[g] body . . .] body— A, B [*revised by HPL*], C
[h] Mernie,] Merwin, A, B [*revised by HPL*], C
[i] Nabby . . .] Nabby— A, B [*revised by HPL*], C
[j] last . . .] last— A, B [*revised by HPL*], C
[k] water . . .] water— A, B [*revised by HPL*], C
[l] 'em . . .] 'em— A, B [*revised by HPL*], C
[m] here . . .] here— A, B [*revised by HPL*], C
[n] home. . . ."] home—" A, B [*revised by HPL*], C
[o] sitting-room] sitting room A, B, C

beast lay huddled inert on the moonlit ground between the splintered shafts of the buggy. That was the last of Hero till they buried him next day. But the present was no time to mourn, for almost at this instant a detective silently called attention to something terrible in the very room with them. In the absence of the lamplight it was clear that a faint phosphorescence had begun to pervade the entire apartment. It glowed on the broad-planked floor and the fragment of rag carpet,[a] and shimmered over the sashes of the small-paned windows. It ran up and down the exposed corner-posts, coruscated about the shelf and mantel, and infected the very doors and furniture. Each minute saw it strengthen, and at last it was very plain that healthy living things must leave that house.

Ammi shewed[b] them the back door and the path up through the fields to the ten-acre pasture. They walked and stumbled as in a dream, and did not dare look back till they were far away on the high ground. They were glad of the path, for they could not have gone the front way, by that well. It was bad enough passing the glowing barn and sheds, and those shining orchard trees with their gnarled, fiendish contours; but thank heaven[c] the branches did their worst twisting high up. The moon went under some very black clouds as they crossed the rustic bridge over Chapman's Brook, and it was blind groping from there to the open meadows.

When they looked back toward the valley and the distant Gardner place at the bottom they saw a fearsome sight. All the farm was shining with the hideous unknown blend of colour; trees, buildings, and even such grass and herbage as had not been wholly changed to lethal grey brittleness. The boughs were all straining skyward, tipped with tongues of foul flame, and lambent tricklings of the same monstrous fire were creeping about the ridgepoles of the house, barn,[d] and sheds. It was a scene from a vision of Fuseli, and over all the rest reigned that riot of luminous amorphousness, that alien and undimensioned rainbow of cryptic poison from the well—seething, feeling, lapping, reaching,

[a] and the . . . carpet,] where the rag carpet left it bare, A
[b] shewed] showed A, B, C
[c] heaven] Heaven A, B, C
[d] barn,] barn A, B, C

scintillating, straining, and malignly bubbling in its cosmic and unrecognisable[a] chromaticism.

Then without warning the hideous thing shot vertically up toward the sky like a rocket or meteor, leaving behind no trail and disappearing through a round and curiously regular hole in the clouds before any man could gasp or cry out. No watcher can ever forget that sight, and Ammi stared blankly at the stars of Cygnus, Deneb twinkling above the others, where the unknown colour had melted into the Milky Way. But his gaze was the next moment called swiftly to earth by the crackling in the valley. It was just that. Only a wooden ripping and crackling, and not an explosion, as so many others of the party vowed. Yet the outcome was the same, for in one feverish,[b] kaleidoscopic instant there burst up from that doomed and accursed farm a gleamingly eruptive cataclysm of unnatural sparks and substance; blurring the glance of the few who saw it, and sending forth to the zenith a bombarding cloudburst of such coloured and fantastic fragments as our universe must needs disown. Through quickly re-closing vapours they followed the great morbidity that had vanished, and in another second they had vanished too. Behind and below was only a darkness to which the men dared not return, and all about was a mounting wind which seemed to sweep down in black, frore gusts from interstellar space. It shrieked and howled, and lashed the fields and distorted woods in a mad cosmic frenzy, till soon the trembling party realised[c] it would be no use waiting for the moon to shew[d] what was left down there at Nahum's.

Too awed even to hint theories, the seven shaking men trudged back toward Arkham by the north road. Ammi was worse than his fellows, and begged them to see him inside his own kitchen, instead of keeping straight on to town. He did not wish to cross the nighted,[e] wind-whipped woods alone to his home on the main road. For he had had an added shock that the others were spared, and was crushed for ever[f] with a brooding fear he dared not even mention for many years to

[a] unrecognisable] unrecognizable A, B, C
[b] feverish,] feverish A, B [*revised by HPL*], C
[c] realised] realized A, B, C
[d] shew] show A, B, C
[e] nighted,] blighted, A, B [*revised by HPL*], C
[f] for ever] forever B, C

come. As the rest of the watchers on that tempestuous hill had stolidly set their faces toward the road, Ammi had looked back an instant at the shadowed valley of desolation so lately sheltering his ill-starred friend. And from that stricken, far-away spot he had seen something feebly rise, only to sink down again upon the place from which the great shapeless horror had shot into the sky. It was just a colour—but not any colour of our earth or heavens. And because Ammi recognised[a] that colour, and knew that this last faint remnant must still lurk down there in the well, he has never been quite right since.

Ammi would never go near the place again. It is over half a century[b] now since the horror happened, but he has never been there, and will be glad when the new reservoir blots it out. I shall be glad, too, for I do not like the way the sunlight changed colour around the mouth of that abandoned well I passed. I hope the water will always be very deep—but even so, I shall never drink it. I do not think I shall visit the Arkham country hereafter. Three of the men who had been with Ammi returned the next morning to see the ruins by daylight, but there were not any real ruins. Only the bricks of the chimney, the stones of the cellar, some mineral and metallic litter here and there, and the rim of that nefandous well. Save for Ammi's dead horse, which they towed away and buried, and the buggy which they shortly returned to him, everything that had ever been living had gone. Five eldritch acres of dusty grey desert remained, nor has anything ever grown there since. To this day it sprawls open to the sky like a great spot eaten by acid in the woods and fields, and the few who have ever dared glimpse it in spite of the rural tales have named it "the blasted heath".[c]

The rural tales are queer. They might be even queerer if city men and college chemists could be interested enough to analyse[d] the water from that disused well, or the grey dust that no wind seems ever[e] to disperse. Botanists, too, ought to study the stunted flora on the borders of that spot, for they might shed light on the country notion

[a] recognised] recognized A, B, C
[b] over half a century] forty-four years A, B [*revised by HPL*], C
[c] heath".] heath." A, B, C
[d] analyse] analyze A, B, C
[e] ever] *om.* C

that the blight is spreading—little by little, perhaps an inch a year. People say the colour of the neighbouring[a] herbage is not quite right in the spring, and that wild things leave queer prints in the light winter snow. Snow never seems quite so heavy on the blasted heath as it is elsewhere. Horses—the few that are left in this motor age—grow skittish in the silent valley; and hunters cannot depend on their dogs too near the splotch of greyish dust.

They say the mental influences are very bad, too. Numbers[b] went queer in the years after Nahum's taking, and always they lacked the power to get away. Then the stronger-minded folk all left the region, and only the foreigners tried to live in the crumbling old homesteads. They could not stay, though; and one sometimes wonders what insight beyond ours their wild, weird stores[c] of whispered magic have given them. Their dreams at night, they protest, are very horrible in that grotesque country; and surely the very look of the dark realm is enough to stir a morbid fancy. No traveller[d] has ever escaped a sense of strangeness in those deep ravines, and artists shiver as they paint thick woods whose mystery is as much of the spirit[e] as of the eye. I myself am curious about the sensation I derived from my one lone walk before Ammi told me his tale. When twilight came I had vaguely wished some clouds would gather, for an[f] odd timidity about the deep skyey voids above had crept into my soul.

Do not ask me for my opinion. I do not know—that is all. There was no one but Ammi to question; for Arkham people will not talk about the strange days, and all three professors who saw the aërolite[g] and its coloured globule are dead. There were other globules—depend upon that. One must have fed itself and escaped, and probably there was another which was too late. No doubt it is still down the well—I know there was something wrong with the sunlight I saw above that[h]

---

[a] neighbouring] neighboring A, B [*revised by HPL*], C
[b] too. Numbers] too; numbers A, B [*revised by HPL*], C
[c] stores] stories A, B [*revised by HPL*], C
[d] traveller] traveler A, B [*revised by HPL*], C
[e] spirit] spirits A, B [*revised by HPL*], C
[f] an] *om.* A
[g] aërolite] aerolite A, B [*revised by HPL*], C
[h] that] the C

miasmal brink. The rustics say the blight creeps an inch a year, so perhaps there is a kind of growth or nourishment even now. But whatever daemon[a] hatchling is there, it must be tethered to something or else it would quickly spread. Is it fastened to the roots of those trees that claw the air? One of the current Arkham tales is about fat oaks that shine and move as they ought not to do at night.

What it is, only God knows. In terms of matter I suppose the thing Ammi described would be called a gas, but this gas obeyed[b] laws that are not of our cosmos. This was no fruit of such worlds and suns as shine on the telescopes and photographic plates of our observatories. This was no breath from the skies whose motions and dimensions our astronomers measure or deem too vast to measure. It was just a colour out of space—a frightful messenger from unformed realms of infinity beyond all Nature as we know it; from realms whose mere existence stuns the brain and numbs us with the black extra-cosmic gulfs it throws open before our frenzied eyes.

I doubt very much if Ammi consciously lied to me, and I do not think his tale was all a freak of madness as the townsfolk had forewarned. Something terrible came to the hills and valleys on that meteor, and something terrible—though I know not in what proportion—still remains. I shall be glad to see the water come. Meanwhile I hope nothing will happen to Ammi. He saw so much of the thing—and its influence was so insidious. Why has he never been able to move away? How clearly he recalled those dying words of Nahum's—"can't git away ...[c] draws ye ...[d] ye know summ'at's comin',[e] but 'tain't[f] no use...."[g] Ammi is such a good old man—when the reservoir gang gets to work I must write the chief engineer to keep a sharp watch on him. I would hate to think of him as the grey, twisted, brittle monstrosity which persists more and more in troubling my sleep.

---

[a] daemon] demon A, B, C
[b] obeyed] obeyed the C
[c] away ...] away— A, B [*revised by HPL*], C
[d] ye ...] ye— A, B [*revised by HPL*], C
[e] comin',] comin' C
[f] 'tain't] tain't C
[g] use...."] use—" A, B [*revised by HPL*], C

The Descendant

In London there is a man who screams when the church bells ring. He lives all alone with his streaked cat in Gray's Inn, and people call him harmlessly mad. His room is filled with books of the tamest and most puerile kind, and hour after hour he tries to lose himself in their feeble pages. All he seeks from life is not to think. For some reason thought is very horrible to him, and anything which stirs the imagination he flees as a plague. He is very thin and grey and wrinkled, but there are those who declare he is not nearly so old as he looks. Fear has its grisly claws upon him, and a sound will make him start with staring eyes and sweat-beaded forehead. Friends and companions he shuns, for he wishes to answer no questions. Those who once knew him as scholar and aesthete say it is very pitiful to see him now. He dropped them all years ago, and no one feels sure whether he left the country or merely sank from sight in some hidden byway. It is a decade now since he moved into Gray's Inn, and of where he had been he would say nothing till the night young Williams bought the "Necronomicon".[a]

Williams was a dreamer, and only twenty-three, and when he moved into the ancient house he felt a strangeness and a breath of cosmic wind about the grey wizened man in the next room. He forced his friendship where old friends dared not force theirs, and marvelled

Editor's Note: HPL's A.Ms. survives and was the basis of the first appearance, in *Leaves* (1938). At the bottom of the first page of the A.Ms., upside down, is the following sentence: "Writing on what the doctor tells me is my deathbed, my most hideous fear is that the man is wrong. I suppose I shall seem to be buried next week, but [. . .]" It is now my belief that this is either an incomplete initial draft of the current fragment or (more likely) an altogether unrelated fragment. It has been crossed out in the A.Ms.; the indication "*(foregoing deleted)*" is presented in *Leaves* but not in *Dagon and Other Macabre Tales.*

A = A.Ms. (JHL); B = *Leaves* 2 (1938): 107–10; C = *Dagon and Other Macabre Tales* (Arkham House, 1965), 336–39. Copy-text: A.

[a] "Necronomicon".] Necronomicon. A, B; *Necronomicon.* C

at the fright that sat upon this gaunt, haggard watcher and listener. For that the man always watched and listened no one could doubt. He watched and listened with his mind more than with his eyes and ears, and strove every moment to drown something in his ceaseless poring[a] over gay, insipid novels. And when the church bells rang he would stop his ears and scream, and the grey cat that dwelt with him would howl in unison till the last peal died reverberantly away.

But try as Williams would, he could not make his neighbour speak of anything profound or hidden. The old man would not live up to his aspect and manner, but would feign a smile and a light tone and prattle feverishly and frantically of cheerful trifles; his voice every moment rising and thickening till at last it would split in a piping and incoherent falsetto. That his learning was deep and thorough, his most trivial remarks made abundantly clear; and Williams was not surprised to hear that he had been to Harrow and Oxford. Later it developed that he was none other than Lord Northam, of whose ancient hereditary castle on the Yorkshire coast so many odd things were told; but when Williams tried to talk of the castle, and of its reputed Roman origin, he refused to admit that there was anything unusual about it. He even tittered shrilly when the subject of the supposed under crypts, hewn[b] out of the solid crag that frowns on the North Sea, was brought up.

So matters went till that night when Williams brought home the infamous "Necronomicon"[c] of the mad Arab Abdul Alhazred. He had known of the dreaded volume since his sixteenth year, when his dawning love of the bizarre had led him to ask queer questions of a bent old bookseller in Chandos Street; and he had always wondered why men paled when they spoke of it. The old bookseller had told him that only five copies were known to have survived the shocked edicts of the priests and lawgivers against it and that all of these[d] were locked up with frightened care by custodians who had ventured to begin a reading of the hateful black-letter. But now, at last, he had not only

---

[a] poring] pouring B
[b] under crypts, hewn] under-crypts, hwen B; under-crypts, hewn C
[c] "Necronomicon"] Necronomicon A, B; *Necronomicon* C
[d] these] them B, C

found an accessible copy but had made it his own at a ludicrously[a] low figure. It was at a Jew's shop in the squalid precincts of Clare Market, where he had often bought strange things before, and he almost fancied the gnarled old Levite smiled amidst tangles of beard as the great discovery was made. The bulky leather cover with the brass clasp had been so prominently visible, and the price was so absurdly slight.

The one glimpse he had had of the title was enough to send him into transports, and some of the diagrams set in the vague Latin text excited the tensest and most disquieting recollections in his brain. He felt it was highly necessary to get the ponderous thing home and begin deciphering it, and bore it out of the shop with such precipitate haste that the old Jew chuckled disturbingly behind him. But when at last it was safe in his room he found the combination of black-letter and debased idiom too much for his powers as a linguist, and reluctantly called on his strange,[b] frightened friend for help with the twisted, mediaeval Latin. Lord Northam was simpering inanities to his streaked cat, and started violently when the young man entered. Then he saw the volume and shuddered wildly, and fainted altogether when Williams uttered the title. It was when he regained his senses that he told his story; told his fantastic figment of madness in frantic whispers,[c] lest his friend be not quick to burn the accursed book and give wide scattering to its ashes.

* * *[d]

There must, Lord Northam whispered, have been something wrong at the start; but it would never have come to a head if he had not explored too far. He was the nineteenth Baron of a line whose beginnings went uncomfortably far back into the past—unbelievably far, if vague tradition could be heeded, for there were family tales of a descent from pre-Saxon times, when a certain Cnaeus[e] Gabinius Capito, military tribune in the Third Augustan Legion then stationed at

---

[a] ludicrously] ridiculously B, C

[b] strange,] strange B, C

[c] whispers,] whispers B, C

[d] * * *] om. C

[e] Cnaeus] Luneus B, C

Lindum in Roman Britain, had been summarily expelled from his command for participation in certain rites unconnected with any known religion. Gabinius had, the rumour ran, come upon a[a] cliffside cavern where strange folk met together and made the Elder Sign in the dark; strange folk whom the Britons knew not save in fear, and who were the last to survive from a great land in the west that had sunk,[b] leaving only the islands with the raths[c] and circles and shrines of which Stonehenge was the greatest. There was no certainty, of course, in the legend that Gabinius had built an impregnable fortress over the forbidden cave and founded a line which Pict and Saxon, Dane and Norman were powerless to obliterate; or in the tacit assumption that from this line sprang the bold companion and lieutenant of the Black Prince whom Edward Third created Baron of Northam. These things were not certain, yet they were often told; and in truth the stonework of Northam Keep did look alarmingly like the masonry of Hadrian's Wall. As a child Lord Northam had had peculiar dreams when sleeping in the older parts of the castle, and had acquired a constant habit of looking back through his memory for half-amorphous scenes and patterns and impressions which formed no part of his waking experience. He became a dreamer who found life tame and unsatisfying; a searcher for strange realms and relationships once familiar, yet lying nowhere in the visible regions of earth.[d]

Filled with a feeling that our tangible world is only an atom in a fabric vast and ominous, and that unknown demesnes press on and permeate the sphere of the known at every point, Northam in youth and young manhood drained in turn the founts of formal religion and occult mystery. Nowhere, however, could he find ease and content; and as he grew older the staleness and limitations of life became more and more maddening to him. During the 'nineties he dabbled in Satanism, and at all times he devoured avidly any doctrine or theory which seemed to promise escape from the close vistas of science and the dully unvarying laws of Nature. Books like Ignatius Donnelly's

[a] a] the C
[b] sunk,] sunken, A, B, C
[c] raths] roths B, C
[d] of earth.] of Earth. B; of the Earth. C

chimerical account of Atlantis he absorbed with zest, and a dozen obscure precursors of Charles Fort enthralled him with their vagaries. He would travel leagues to follow up a furtive village tale of abnormal wonder, and once went into the desert of Araby to seek a Nameless City of faint report, which no man has ever beheld. There rose within him the tantalising faith that somewhere an easy gate existed, which if one found would admit him freely to those outer deeps whose echoes rattled so dimly at the back of his memory. It might be in the visible world, yet it might be only in his mind and soul. Perhaps he held within his own half-explored brain that cryptic link which would awaken him to elder[a] and future lives in forgotten dimensions; which would bind him to the stars, and to the infinities and eternities beyond them.

[a] elder] Elder B, C

History of the "Necronomicon"

Original title "Al Azif"[a]—*azif*[b] being the word used by the Arabs to designate that nocturnal sound (made by insects) supposed[c] to be the howling of daemons.

Composed by Abdul Alhazred, a mad poet of Sanaá,[d] in Yemen, who is said to have flourished during the period of the Ommiade caliphs, circa A.D. 700.[e] He visited the ruins of Babylon and the subterranean secrets of Memphis and spent ten years alone in the great southern desert of Arabia—the Roba el Khaliyeh or "Empty Space" of the ancients—and[f] "Dahna" or "Crimson" desert of the modern Arabs,[g] which is held to be inhabited by protective evil spirits and

Editor's Note: The original A.Ms. was written on the back of a letter from William Bryant dated 27 April 1927. At some point HPL must have prepared another A.Ms. (or possibly a T.Ms.); he sent it to Wilson Shepherd in early 1937: "Since you seem to be interested, I'll enclose an outline copy of that 'history'—which is of course merely a lot of mock-scholarship cooked up about a book which does not exist" (HPL to Wilson Shepherd, 21 January 1937; ms., JHL). Wilson prepared his own T.Ms. (now at JHL), but it is full of errors. His published version duplicates these errors. Bookseller L. W. Currey once sold a T.Ms. that appears to have been prepared by HPL (it has his handwritten notation "please return" in the upper left-hand corner, and the typeface, so far as it is legible, appears to be his); but Currey reproduced only the first page of the T.Ms. on his website. This T.Ms. contains the two passages that are not present in the original A.Ms. Later publications use the title "History and Chronology of the *Necronomicon.*"

Texts: A = A.Ms. (JHL; also reproduced in facsimile in *Lovecraft at Last* [Arlington, VA: Carrollton-Clark, 1975], 104–5]); B = T.Ms. (formerly in the possession of L. W. Currey [p. 1 only]); C = *A History of the Necronomicon* (Oakman, AL: Rebel Press, [1937]). Copy-text: B (and A after B ends).

[a] "Al Azif"] *Al Azif* A, B, C
[b] *azif*] *Azif* B, C
[c] supposed] suppos'd A
[d] Sanaá,] Sanna, C
[e] A. D. 700] 700 A.D. A; A.D. 700. C
[f] ancients—and] ancients and B, C
[g] the Roba . . . Arabs,] (The Roba . . . Arabs) C

monsters of death. Of this desert many strange and unbelievable marvels are told by those who pretend to have penetrated it. In his last years Alhazred dwelt in Damascus, where the "Necronomicon" ("Al Azif")[a] was written, and of his final death or disappearance (A.D. 738)[b] many terrible and conflicting things are told. He is said by Ebn Khallikan (12th century biographer[c]) to have been seized by an invisible monster in broad daylight and devoured horribly before a large number of fright-frozen witnesses. Of his madness many things are told. He claimed to have seen the fabulous Irem, or City of Pillars, and to have found beneath the ruins of a certain nameless desert town[d] the shocking annals and secrets of a race older than mankind.[e] He was only an indifferent Moslem, worshipping unknown entities[f] whom he called Yog-Sothoth[g] and Cthulhu.[h]

In A.D.[i] 950 the "Azif",[j] which had gained a considerable though[k] surreptitious circulation amongst the philosophers of the age, was secretly translated into Greek by Theodorus Philetas of Constantinople under the title "Necronomicon".[l] For a century it impelled certain experimenters to terrible attempts, when it was suppressed and burnt by the patriarch Michael. After this it is only heard of furtively, but (1228) Olaus Wormius made a Latin translation later in the Middle Ages, and the Latin text was printed twice—once in the fifteenth[m]

---

[a] "Necronomicon" ("Al Azif")] Necronomicon (Al Azif) A, B; *Necronomicon (AL AZIF)* C
[b] (A.D. 738)] (738 A.D.) A; A. D. 738 C
[c] century biographer] cent. biographer A; century biography C
[d] town] city C
[e] mankind.] mankind. (Editors Note: A full description of the nameless city, and the annals and secrets of its one time inhabitants will be found in the story THE NAMELESS CITY, published in the first issue of Fanciful Tales, and written by the author of his outline). C
[f] entities] Entities C
[g] Yog-Sothoth] *Yog-Sothoth* C
[h] Cthulhu.] Cthuthu. C
[i] A.D.] A. D. C
[j] "Azif",] *Azif,* A, B, C
[k] considerable though] considerable tho' A; considerable, though C
[l] "Necronomicon".] *Necronomicon.* A, B, C
[m] fifteenth] 15th A, B, C

century in black-letter[a] (evidently in Germany) and once in the seventeenth (probably Spanish);[b] both editions being without identifying marks, and located as to time and place by internal typographical evidence only. The work, both Latin and Greek,[c] was banned by Pope Gregory IX.[d] in 1232,[e] shortly after its Latin translation, which called attention to it. The Arabic original was lost as early as Wormius' time, as indicated by his prefatory[f] note;*[g] and no sight of the Greek copy—which was printed in Italy between[h] 1500 and 1550—has been reported since the burning of a certain Salem man's library in 1692. A translation made by Dr. Dee was never printed,[i] and exists only in fragments recovered from the original manuscript.[j] Of the Latin texts now existing one (15th century[k]) is known to be in the British Museum under lock and key, while another (17th century[l]) is in the Bibliothèque[m] Nationale at Paris. A seventeenth-century[n] edition is in the Widener Library at Harvard, and in the library at[o] Miskatonic University at Arkham; also[p] in the library of the University of Buenos Aires.[q] Numerous other copies probably exist in

---

*There is, however, a vague account of a secret copy appearing in San Francisco during the present century, but later perishing by fire.

[a] black-letter] black letter B, C
[b] seventeenth (probably Spanish);] 17th—(prob. Spanish) A; 17th (probably Spanish); C
[c] work, . . . Greek,] work . . . Gr. A
[d] IX.] IX A, C
[e] 1232,] 1232 B, C
[f] prefatory] prefactory C
[g] note;*] note; A [*no footnote*]; note; [*footnote:* there is, . . . fire.] B; note; (there is however, a vague account of a secret copy appearing in San Francisco during the present century, but later perished in fire), C
[h] between] bet. A
[i] printed,] printed B
[j] original manuscript.] orig. MS. A
[k] century] cent. A
[l] century] cent. A
[m] Bibliothèque] Bibliotheque A, B, C
[n] seventeenth-century] 17th cent. A; 17th century B, C
[o] at] of A
[p] Arkham; also] Arkham. Also A
[q] Aires.] Ayres. A

secret, and a fifteenth-century[a] one is persistently rumoured[b] to form part[c] of the collection of a celebrated American millionaire. A still vaguer rumour[d] credits the preservation of a sixteenth-century[e] Greek text in the Salem family of Pickman; but if it was so preserved, it vanished with the artist R. U. Pickman, who disappeared early[f] in 1926. The book is rigidly suppressed by the authorities of most countries, and by all branches of organised[g] ecclesiasticism. Reading leads to terrible consequences. It was from rumours[h] of this book (of which relatively few of the general public know) that R. W.[i] Chambers is said to have derived the idea of his early novel "The King in Yellow".[j]

Chronology

"Al Azif"[k] written circa A.D. 730[l] at Damascus by Abdul Alhazred[m]
Tr. to[n] Greek A.D. 950 as "Necronomicon"[o] by Theodorus Philetas
Burnt[p] by Patriarch Michael 1050 (i.e.,[q] Greek text).[r] Arabic text now lost.[s]
Olaus[t] translates Greek[u] to[v] Latin 1228[w]

---

[a] fifteenth-century] 15th cent. A; 15th century B, C
[b] rumoured] rumored B, C
[c] part] a part C
[d] rumour] rumor B, C
[e] sixteenth-century] 16th cent. A; 16th [*end of p. 1*] B; 16th century C
[f] early] *om.* C
[g] organised] organized C
[h] rumours] rumors C
[i] R. W.] R W A
[j] "The . . . Yellow".] "THE KING IN YELLOW". C
[k] "Al Azif"] *Al Azif* A; One—*Al Azif* C
[l] A.D. 730] 730 A.D. A; A. D. 730 C
[m] Alhazred] Alhazred. C
[n] Tr. to] Two—Translated into C
[o] A.D. 950 . . . "Necronomicon"] 950 A.D. as *Necronomicon* A; as *Necronomicon*, A. D. 950 C
[p] Burnt] Three—Burnt C
[q] i.e.,] i. e. C
[r] text).] Text . . . C
[s] Arabic . . . lost.] (Arabic Text now lost). C
[t] Olaus] Four—Olaus C
[u] Greek] Gr. A
[v] to] into C
[w] Latin 1228] Latin, A. D. 1228 C

1232—Latin ed. (and Greek)[a] suppressed[b] by Pope[c] Gregory IX.[d]
14...[e] Black-letter printed edition (Germany)[f]
15...[g] Greek text printed in Italy[h]
16...[i] Spanish reprint[j] of Latin text[k]

[a] Latin . . . Greek)] Latin ed. (& Gr.) A; Five—Latin and Greek editions C
[b] suppressed] suppr. A
[c] Pope] *om.* C
[d] IX.] IX A; IX—A. D. 1232 C
[e] 14...] Six—14 . . ? C
[f] Black-letter . . . (Germany)] Black letter edition printed in Germany. C
[g] 15...] Seven—15 . . ? C
[h] Italy] Italy. C
[i] 16...] Eight—16 . . ? C
[j] reprint] translations C
[k] text] text. C

Ibid

("...—as Ibid says in his famous 'Lives of the Poets'."[a]
—From a student theme.)

The erroneous idea that Ibid[b] is the author of the "Lives"[c] is so frequently met with, even among those pretending to a degree of culture, that it is worth correcting. It should be a matter of general knowledge that Cf. is responsible for this work. Ibid's masterpiece, on the other hand, was the famous "Op. Cit."[d] wherein all the significant undercurrents of Graeco-Roman expression were crystallised once for all—and with admirable acuteness, notwithstanding the surprisingly late date at which Ibid wrote. There is a false report—very commonly reproduced in modern books prior to Von Schweinkopf's monumental "Geschichte der Ostrogothen in Italien"[e]—that Ibid was a Romanised[f] Visigoth of Ataulf's horde who settled in Placentia about 410 A.D.[g] The contrary cannot be too strongly emphasised; for Von Schweinkopf,

Editor's Note: This comic story was presumably included in or attached to a letter to Maurice W. Moe, probably in 1928. Moe refers to the piece as "that delightful Spectator paper on the marvellous history of old man Ibid" (M. W. Moe to HPL, 3 August 1928; ms., JHL). The A.Ms. does not appear to survive, and the first published text—in the amateur journal *O-Wash-Ta-Nong* (January 1938), edited by George W. Macauley—must serve as the basis of the text. (The story was reprinted in the *Phantagraph* [June 1940], but this is irrelevant to the textual history of the tale.)

Texts: A = *O-Wash-Ta-Nong* 3, No. 1 (January 1938): 11–13; B = *Beyond the Wall of Sleep* (Arkham House, 1943), 346–48. Copy-text: A.

[a] 'Lives of the Poets'." ¶] *Lives of the Poets.*" A, B
[b] Ibid] Ib B
[c] "Lives"] Lives A; *Lives* B
[d] "Op. Cit."] *Op. Cit.* A, B
[e] "Geschichte . . . Italien"] *Geschichte . . . Italien* A, B
[f] Romanised] Romanized A, B
[g] A.D.] A. D. B

and since his time Littlewit* and Bêtenoir,† [a] have shewn[b] with irrefutable force that this strikingly isolated figure was a genuine Roman—or at least as genuine a Roman as that degenerate and mongrelised age could produce—of whom one might well say what Gibbon said of Boethius, "that he was the last whom Cato or Tully could have acknowledged for their countryman." He was, like Boethius and nearly all the eminent men of his age, of the great Anician[c] family, and traced his genealogy with much exactitude and self-satisfaction to all the heroes of the republic. His full name—long and pompous according to the custom of an age which had lost the trinomial simplicity of classic Roman nomenclature—is stated by Von Schweinkopf** [d] to have been Caius Anicius Magnus Furius Camillus Æmilianus Cornelius Valerius Pompeius[e] Julius Ibidus; though Littlewit‡ rejects *Æmilianus* and adds *Claudius Decius Junianus;* whilst Bêtenoir§ [f] differs radically, giving the full name as Magnus Furius Camillus Aurelius Antoninus Flavius Anicius Petronius Valentinianus Aegidus[g] Ibidus.

The eminent critic and biographer was born in the year 486, shortly after the extinction of the Roman rule in Gaul by Clovis. Rome and Ravenna are rivals for the honour[h] of his birth, though it is certain that he received his rhetorical and philosophical training in the schools of Athens—the extent of whose suppression by Theodosius a century

*"Rome and Byzantium: A Study in Survival" (Waukesha, 1869), Vol. XX, p. 598. [Rome . . . study in Survival A; Rome . . . Study in Survival B]

†"Influences Romains dans le Moyen Age" (Fond du Lac, 1877), Vol. XV, p. 720. [Influence . . . Age A; Influences . . . Age B; due Lac, 1877) A]

**Following Procopius, *Goth.* x.y.z. [Goth. B]

‡Following Jornandes, Codex Murat. xxj. 4144. [Jornandeds A; xxi. B]

§After Pagi, 50–50.

[a] Bêtenoir,] Betenoir, A, B
[b] shewn] shown A, B
[c] Anician] Anican A
[d] stated . . . Schweinkopf] seated . . . Schweinkopf's A
[e] Pompeius] Pomeius A
[f] Bêtenoir] Betenoir A, B
[g] Aegidus] Ægidus B
[h] honour] honor A, B

before is grossly exaggerated by the superficial. In 512, under the benign rule of the Ostrogoth Theodoric, we behold him as a teacher of rhetoric at Rome, and in 516 he held the consulship together with Pompilius Numantius Bombastes Marcellinus Deodamnatus. Upon the death of Theodoric in 526, Ibidus retired from public life to compose his celebrated work[a] (whose pure Ciceronian style is as remarkable a case of classic atavism[b] as is the verse of Claudius Claudianus, who flourished a century before Ibidus); but he was later recalled to scenes of pomp to act as court rhetorician for Theodatus, nephew of Theodoric.

Upon the usurpation of Vitiges, Ibidus fell into disgrace and was for a time imprisoned; but the coming of the Byzantine-Roman[c] army under Belisarius soon restored him to liberty and honours.[d] Throughout the siege of Rome he served bravely in the army of the defenders, and afterward followed the eagles of Belisarius to Alba, Porto, and Centumcellae. After the Frankish siege of Milan, Ibidus was chosen to accompany the learned Bishop Datius to Greece, and resided with him at Corinth in the year 539. About 541 he removed to Constantinopolis, where he received every mark of imperial favour[e] both from Justinianus and Justinus the Second. The Emperors Tiberius and Maurice did kindly honour[f] to his old age, and contributed much to his immortality—especially Maurice, whose delight it was to trace his ancestry to old Rome notwithstanding his birth at Arabissus,[g] in Cappadocia. It was Maurice who, in the poet's[h] 101st year, secured the adoption of his work as a textbook in the schools of the empire, an honour[i] which proved a fatal tax on the aged rhetorician's emotions, since he passed away peacefully at his home

[a] work] word A
[b] atavism] stavism B
[c] Byzantine-Roman] Bzantine-Roman A
[d] honours.] honors. A, B
[e] favour] favor A, B
[f] honour] honor A, B
[g] Arabissus,] Arabiscus, A, B
[h] poet's] poets' A
[i] honour] honor A, B

near the church of St. Sophia on the sixth day before the Kalends of September, A.D. 587, in the 102nd[a] year of his age.

His remains, notwithstanding the troubled state of Italy, were taken to Ravenna for interment; but being interred in the suburb of Classe, were exhumed and ridiculed by the Lombard Duke of Spoleto,[b] who took his skull to King Autharis for use as a wassail-bowl. Ibid's skull was proudly handed down from king to king of the Lombard line. Upon the capture of Pavia by Charlemagne in 774, the skull was seized from the tottering Desiderius[c] and carried in the train of the Frankish conqueror. It was from this vessel, indeed, that Pope Leo administered the royal unction which made of the hero-nomad a Holy Roman Emperor. Charlemagne took Ibid's skull to his capital at Aix, soon afterward presenting it to his Saxon teacher Alcuin,[d] upon whose death in 804 it was sent to Alcuin's[e] kinsfolk[f] in England.

William the Conqueror, finding it in an abbey niche where the pious family of Alcuin[g] had placed it (believing it to be the skull of a saint* who had miraculously annihilated the Lombards by his prayers),[h] did reverence to its osseous antiquity; and even the rough soldiers of Cromwell, upon destroying Ballylough Abbey in Ireland in 1650 (it having been secretly transported thither by a devout Papist in 1539, upon Henry VIII's dissolution of[i] the English monasteries),[j] declined to offer violence to a relic so venerable.

It was captured by the private solder Read-'em-and-Weep Hopkins, who not long after traded it to Rest-in-Jehovah[k] Stubbs for a quid of

*Not till the appearance of Von Schweinkopf's work in 1797 were St. Ibid and the rhetorician properly re-identified. [von . . . reidentified B]

[a] 102nd] 102d B
[b] Spoleto,] Spolato, B
[c] Desiderius] Deniderius B
[d] Alcuin,] Alouin, B
[e] Alcuin's] Alouin's B
[f] kinsfolk] kinfolk A, B
[g] Alcuin] Alouin B
[h] prayers),] prayers) A, B
[i] of] to A, B
[j] 1650 (. . .),] 1650, (. . .) A
[k] Rest-in-Jehovah] Rest-in-Jehova A

new Virginia weed. Stubbs, upon sending forth his son Zerubbabel to
seek his fortune in New England in 1661 (for he thought ill of the
Restoration atmosphere for a pious young yeoman),[a] gave him St.
Ibid's—or rather Brother Ibid's, for he abhorred all that was Popish—
skull as a talisman. Upon landing in Salem Zerubbabel set it up in his
cupboard beside the chimney, he having built a modest house near the
town pump. However, he had not been wholly unaffected by the
Restoration influence; and having become addicted to gaming, lost the
skull to one Epenetus Dexter, a visiting freeman of Providence.

It was in the house of Dexter, in the northern part of the town
near the present intersection of North Main and Olney Streets, on the
occasion of Canonchet's[b] raid of March 30, 1676, during King Philip's
War; and the astute sachem, recognising[c] it at once as a thing of
singular venerableness and dignity, sent it as a symbol of alliance to a
faction of the Pequots in Connecticut with whom he was negotiating.
On April 4 he was captured by the colonists and soon after executed,
but the austere head of Ibid continued on its wanderings.

The Pequots, enfeebled by a previous war, could give the now
stricken Narragansetts no assistance; and in 1680 a Dutch fur-trader of
Albany, Petrus van Schaack, secured the distinguished cranium for the
modest sum of two guilders, he having recognised[d] its value from the half-
effaced inscription carved in Lombardic minuscules (palaeography, it
might be explained, was one of the leading accomplishments of New-
Netherland fur-traders of the seventeenth[e] century).[f]

From van Schaack, sad to say, the relic was stolen in 1683 by a
French trader, Jean Grenier, whose Popish zeal recognised[g] the
features of one whom he had been taught at his mother's knee to
revere as St. Ibide.[h] Grenier, fired with virtuous rage at the possession of

---

[a] 1661 (. . .),] 1661, (. . .) A
[b] Canonchet's] Cannonchet's A
[c] recognising] recognizing A
[d] recognised] recognized A
[e] seventeenth] 17th A, B
[f] century).] century). / [B *attempts to reproduce the purported inscription:* "*Ibidus rhetor romanus*"]
[g] recognised] recognized A
[h] Ibide.] Ibid. B

this holy symbol by a Protestant, crushed van Schaack's head one night with an axe and escaped to the north with his booty; soon, however, being robbed and slain by the half-breed voyageur[a] Michel Savard, who took the skull—despite the illiteracy which prevented his recognising[b] it—to add to a collection of similar but more recent material.

Upon his death in 1701 his half-breed son Pierre traded it among other things to some emissaries of the Sacs and Foxes, and it was found outside the chief's tepee a generation later by Charles de Langlade, founder of the trading post at Green Bay, Wisconsin. De Langlade regarded this sacred object with proper veneration and ransomed it at the expense of many glass beads; yet after his time it found itself in many other hands, being traded to settlements at the head of Lake Winnebago, to tribes around Lake Mendota, and finally, early in the nineteenth[c] century, to one Solomon Juneau, a Frenchman, at the new trading post of Milwaukee on the Menominee River and the shore of Lake Michigan.

Later traded to Jacques Caboche,[d] another settler, it was in 1850[e] lost in a game of chess or poker to a newcomer named Hans Zimmerman; being used by him as a beer-stein until one day, under the spell of its contents,[f] he suffered it to roll from his front stoop to the prairie path before his home—where, falling into the burrow of a prairie-dog, it passed beyond his power of discovery or recovery upon his awaking.

So for generations did the sainted skull of Caius Anicius[g] Magnus Furius Camillus Æmilianus Cornelius Valerius Pompeius Julius Ibidus, consul of Rome, favourite[h] of emperors, and saint of the Romish church, lie hidden beneath the soil of a growing town. At first worshipped[i] with dark rites by the prairie-dogs, who saw in it a deity

[a] voyageur] vogageur A
[b] recognising] recognizing A
[c] nineteenth] 19th A, B
[d] Caboche,] Cabocho, B
[e] 1850] 1860 B
[f] contents,] contents A, B
[g] Anicius] Anicus A
[h] favourite] favorite A, B
[i] worshipped] worshipt B

sent from the upper world, it afterward fell into dire neglect as the race of simple, artless burrowers succumbed before the onslaught of the conquering Aryan. Sewers[a] came, but they passed it by. Houses went up—2303[b] of them, and more—and at last one fateful night a titan thing occurred. Subtle Nature,[c] convulsed with a spiritual ecstasy, like the froth of that region's quondam beverage, laid low the lofty and heaved high the humble—and behold! In the roseal[d] dawn the burghers of Milwaukee rose to find a former prairie turned to[e] a highland! Vast and far-reaching was the great upheaval. Subterrene arcana, hidden for years, came at last to the light. For there, full in the rifted roadway,[f] lay bleached and tranquil in bland, saintly, and consular pomp the dome-like[g] skull of Ibid!

[a] Sewers] Sowers B
[b] 2303] 2,303 A
[c] Nature,] nature, A, B
[d] roseal] roseate B
[e] to] into B
[f] roadway,] roadway A, B
[g] dome-like] dome-/like A

The Dunwich Horror

"Gorgons, and Hydras, and Chimaeras[a]—dire stories of Celaeno and the Harpies—may reproduce themselves in the brain of superstition—*but they were there before*. They are transcripts, types—the archetypes are in us, and eternal. How else should the recital of that which we know in a waking sense to be false come to affect us at all? Is it that we naturally conceive terror from such objects, considered in their capacity of being able to inflict upon us bodily injury? O,[b] least of all! *These terrors are of older standing. They date beyond body*—or without the body, they would have been the same. . . . That the kind of fear here treated is purely spiritual—that it is strong in proportion as it is objectless on earth, that it predominates in the period of our sinless infancy—are difficulties the solution of which might afford some probable insight into our ante-mundane condition, and a peep at least into the shadow-land[c] of pre-existence."[d]

—*Charles Lamb*: "Witches and Other Night-Fears"[e]

I.

When a traveller[f] in north central Massachusetts takes the wrong fork at the junction of the Aylesbury pike just beyond Dean's Corners he comes upon a lonely and curious

Editor's Note: The A.Ms. does not survive, but the T.Ms., prepared by HPL, does. It was followed relatively accurately by *Weird Tales* (April 1929), aside from its usual customary changes in accordance with its house style. The Arkham House editions follow the T.Ms., hence are also quite accurate. There are, however, a number of small internal inconsistencies of usage that require correction.

Texts: A = T.Ms. (JHL); B = *Weird Tales* 13, No. 4 (April 1929): 481–508; C = *The Dunwich Horror and Others* (Arkham House, 1963), 160–202. Copy-text: A.

[a] Chimaeras] Chimeras B
[b] O,] Oh, B
[c] shadow-land] shadowland B, C
[d] "Gorgons, . . . pre-existence."] *Gorgons, . . . pre-existence.* C
[e] —*Charles* . . . Night-Fears"] —Charles Lamb: *Witches and Other Night-Fears.* B; — CHARLES LAMB: Witches and Other Night-Fears C
[f] traveller] traveler B

country. The ground gets higher, and the brier-bordered stone walls press closer and closer against the ruts of the dusty, curving road. The trees of the frequent forest belts seem too large, and the wild weeds, brambles, and grasses attain a luxuriance not often found in settled regions. At the same time the planted fields appear singularly few and barren; while the sparsely scattered houses wear a surprisingly[a] uniform aspect of age, squalor, and dilapidation. Without knowing why, one hesitates to ask directions from the gnarled, solitary figures spied now and then on crumbling doorsteps or on[b] the sloping, rock-strown[c] meadows. Those figures are so silent and furtive that one feels somehow confronted by forbidden things, with which it would be better to have nothing to do. When a rise in the road brings the mountains in view above the deep woods, the feeling of strange uneasiness is increased. The summits are too rounded and symmetrical to give a sense of comfort and naturalness, and sometimes the sky silhouettes with especial clearness the queer circles of tall stone pillars with which most of them are crowned.

Gorges and ravines of problematical depth intersect the way, and the crude wooden bridges always seem of dubious safety. When the road dips again there are stretches of marshland that one instinctively dislikes, and indeed almost fears at evening when unseen whippoorwills chatter and the fireflies come out in abnormal profusion to dance to the raucous, creepily insistent rhythms of stridently piping bull-frogs.[d] The thin, shining line of the Miskatonic's upper reaches has an oddly serpent-like[e] suggestion as it winds close to the feet of the domed hills among which it rises.

As the hills draw nearer, one heeds their wooded sides more than their stone-crowned tops. Those sides loom up so darkly and precipitously that one wishes they would keep their distance, but there is no road by which to escape them. Across a covered bridge one sees a small village huddled between the stream and the vertical slope of Round

[a] surprisingly] surprizing B
[b] on] in B
[c] rock-strown] rock-strewn C
[d] bull-frogs.] bullfrogs. B
[e] serpent-like] serpentlike B

Mountain, and wonders at the cluster of rotting gambrel roofs bespeaking an earlier architectural period than that of the neighbouring[a] region. It is not reassuring to see, on a closer glance, that most of the houses are deserted and falling to ruin, and that the broken-steepled church now harbours[b] the one slovenly mercantile establishment of the hamlet. One dreads to trust the tenebrous tunnel of the bridge, yet there is no way to avoid it. Once across, it is hard to prevent the impression of a faint, malign odour[c] about the village street, as of the massed mould[d] and decay of centuries. It is always a relief to get clear of the place, and to follow the narrow road around the base of the hills and across the level country beyond till it rejoins the Aylesbury pike. Afterward one sometimes learns that one has been through Dunwich.

Outsiders visit Dunwich as seldom as possible, and since a certain season of horror all the signboards pointing toward it have been taken down. The scenery, judged by any ordinary aesthetic[e] canon, is more than commonly beautiful; yet there is no influx of artists or summer tourists. Two centuries ago, when talk of witch-blood, Satan-worship, and strange forest presences was not laughed at, it was the custom to give reasons for avoiding the locality. In our sensible age—since the Dunwich horror of 1928 was hushed up by those who had the town's and the world's welfare at heart—people shun it without knowing exactly why. Perhaps one reason—though it cannot apply to uninformed strangers—is that the natives are now repellently decadent, having gone far along that path of retrogression so common in many New England[f] backwaters. They have come to form a race by themselves, with the well-defined mental and physical stigmata of degeneracy and inbreeding. The average of their intelligence is woefully[g] low, whilst their annals reek of overt viciousness and of half-hidden murders, incests, and deeds of almost unnamable violence and perversity. The old gentry, representing the two or three armigerous families which came from

[a] neighbouring] neighboring B
[b] harbours] harbors B
[c] odour] odor B
[d] mould] mold B
[e] aesthetic] esthetic B
[f] New England] New-England A, C
[g] woefully] wofully B

Salem in 1692, have kept somewhat above the general level of decay; though many branches are sunk into the sordid populace so deeply that only their names remain as a key to the origin they disgrace. Some of the Whateleys and Bishops still send their eldest sons to Harvard and Miskatonic, though those sons seldom return to the mouldering[a] gambrel roofs under which they and their ancestors were born.

No one, even those who have the facts concerning the recent horror, can say just what is the matter with Dunwich; though old legends speak of unhallowed rites and conclaves of the Indians, amidst which they called forbidden shapes of shadow out of the great rounded hills, and made wild orgiastic prayers that were answered by loud crackings and rumblings from the ground below. In 1747 the Reverend Abijah Hoadley, newly come to the Congregational Church at Dunwich Village, preached a memorable sermon on the close presence of Satan and his imps; in which he said:

> "It must be allow'd,[b] that these Blasphemies of an infernall Train of Daemons are Matters of too common Knowledge to be deny'd; the cursed Voices of *Azazel* and *Buzrael*, of *Beelzebub* and *Belial*, being heard now[c] from under Ground by above a Score of credible Witnesses now living. I my self[d] did not more than a Fortnight ago catch a very plain Discourse of evill Powers in the Hill behind my House; wherein there were a Rattling and Rolling, Groaning, Screeching, and Hissing, such as no Things of this Earth cou'd raise up, and which must needs have come from those Caves that only black Magick can discover, and only the Divell unlock."[e]

Mr. Hoadley disappeared soon after delivering this sermon; but the text, printed in Springfield, is still extant. Noises in the hills continued to be reported from year to year, and still form a puzzle to geologists and physiographers.

Other traditions tell of foul odours[f] near the hill-crowning circles of stone pillars, and of rushing airy presences to be heard faintly at certain hours from stated points at the bottom of the great ravines;

[a] mouldering] moldering B
[b] allow'd,] allow'd B
[c] now] *om.* B
[d] my self] myself B
[e] "It . . . unlock."] It . . . unlock. B, C
[f] odours] odors B

while still others try to explain the Devil's Hop Yard—a bleak, blasted hillside where no tree, shrub, or grass-blade will grow. Then[a] too, the natives are mortally afraid of the numerous whippoorwills which grow vocal on warm nights. It is vowed that the birds are psychopomps lying in wait for the souls of the dying, and that they time their eery cries in unison with the sufferer's struggling breath. If they can catch the fleeing soul when it leaves the body, they instantly flutter away chittering in daemoniac[b] laughter; but if they fail, they subside gradually into a disappointed silence.

These tales, of course, are obsolete and ridiculous; because they come down from very old times. Dunwich is indeed ridiculously old— older by far than any of the communities within thirty miles of it. South of the village one may still spy the cellar walls and chimney of the ancient Bishop house, which was built before 1700; whilst the ruins of the mill at the falls, built in 1806, form the most modern piece of architecture to be seen. Industry did not flourish here, and the nineteenth-century[c] factory movement proved short-lived. Oldest of all are the great rings of rough-hewn stone columns on the hilltops, but these are more generally attributed to the Indians than to the settlers. Deposits of skulls and bones, found within these circles and around the sizeable[d] table-like rock on Sentinel Hill, sustain the popular belief that such spots were once the burial-places of the Pocumtucks; even though many ethnologists, disregarding the absurd improbability of such a theory, persist in believing the remains Caucasian.

II.

It was in the township of Dunwich, in a large and partly inhabited farmhouse set against a hillside four miles from the village and a mile and a half from any other dwelling, that Wilbur Whateley was born at 5 a.m.[e] on Sunday, the second of February, 1913. This date was recalled

---

[a] Then] Then, B
[b] daemoniac] demoniac B
[c] nineteenth-century] Nineteenth Century B; nineteenth century C
[d] sizeable] sizable B
[e] a.m.] a. m. B; A.M. C

because it was Candlemas, which people in Dunwich curiously observe under another name; and because the noises in the hills had sounded, and all the dogs of the countryside had barked persistently, throughout the night before. Less worthy of notice was the fact that the mother was one of the decadent Whateleys, a somewhat deformed, unattractive albino woman of thirty-five,[a] living with an aged and half-insane father about whom the most frightful tales of wizardry had been whispered in his youth. Lavinia Whateley had no known husband, but according to the custom of the region made no attempt to disavow the child; concerning the other side of whose ancestry the country folk might—and did—speculate as widely as they chose. On the contrary, she seemed strangely proud of the dark, goatish-looking infant who formed such a contrast to her own sickly and pink-eyed albinism, and was heard to mutter many curious prophecies about its unusual powers and tremendous future.

Lavinia was one who would be apt to mutter such things, for she was a lone creature given to wandering amidst thunderstorms in the hills and trying to read the great odorous books which her father had inherited through two centuries of Whateleys, and which were fast falling to pieces with age and worm-holes. She had never been to school, but was filled with disjointed scraps of ancient lore that Old Whateley had taught her. The remote farmhouse had always been feared because of Old Whateley's reputation for black magic, and the unexplained death by violence of Mrs. Whateley when Lavinia was twelve years old had not helped to make the place popular. Isolated among strange influences, Lavinia was fond of wild and grandiose day-dreams and singular occupations; nor was her leisure much taken up by household cares in a home from which all standards of order and cleanliness had long since disappeared.

There was a hideous screaming which echoed above even the hill noises and the dogs' barking on the night Wilbur was born, but no known doctor or midwife presided at his coming. Neighbours[b] knew nothing of him till a week afterward, when Old Whateley drove his sleigh through the snow into Dunwich Village and discoursed

[a] thirty-five,] 35, A, B, C
[b] Neighbours] Neighbors B, C

incoherently to the group of loungers at Osborn's general store. There seemed to be a change in the old man—an added element of furtiveness in the clouded brain which subtly transformed him from an object to a subject of fear—though he was not one to be perturbed by any common family event. Amidst it all he shewed[a] some trace of the pride later noticed in his daughter, and what he said of the child's paternity was remembered by many of his hearers years afterward.

"I dun't keer what folks think—ef Lavinny's boy looked like his pa, he wouldn't look like nothin' ye expeck. Ye needn't think the only folks is the folks hereabaouts.[b] Lavinny's read some, an' has seed some things the most o' ye only tell abaout. I calc'late her man is as good a husban' as ye kin[c] find this side of Aylesbury; an' ef ye knowed as much abaout the hills as I dew, ye wouldn't ast no better church weddin' nor her'n. Let me tell ye suthin'—*some day yew folks'll hear a child o' Lavinny's a-callin' its father's name on the top o' Sentinel Hill!*"

The only persons who saw Wilbur during the first month of his life were old Zechariah Whateley, of the undecayed Whateleys, and Earl Sawyer's common-law wife, Mamie Bishop. Mamie's visit was frankly one of curiosity, and her subsequent tales did justice to her observations; but Zechariah came to lead a pair of Alderney cows which Old Whateley had bought of his son Curtis. This marked the beginning of a course of cattle-buying on the part of small Wilbur's family which ended only in 1928, when the Dunwich horror came and went; yet at no time did the ramshackle Whateley barn seem overcrowded with livestock. There came a period when people were curious enough to steal up and count the herd that grazed precariously on the steep hillside above the old farmhouse, and they could never find more than ten or twelve anaemic,[d] bloodless-looking specimens. Evidently some blight or distemper, perhaps sprung from the unwholesome pasturage or the diseased fungi and timbers of the filthy barn, caused a heavy mortality amongst the Whateley animals. Odd wounds or sores, having something of the aspect of incisions, seemed to afflict the

[a] shewed] showed B
[b] hereabaouts.] hereabouts. B, C
[c] kin] kin' C
[d] anaemic,] anemic, B

visible cattle; and once or twice during the earlier months certain callers fancied they could discern similar sores about the throats of the grey,[a] unshaven old man and his slatternly, crinkly-haired albino daughter.

In the spring after Wilbur's birth Lavinia resumed her customary rambles in the hills, bearing in her misproportioned arms the swarthy child. Public interest in the Whateleys subsided after most of the country folk had seen the baby, and no one bothered to comment on the swift development which that newcomer seemed every day to exhibit. Wilbur's growth was indeed phenomenal, for within three months of his birth he had attained a size and muscular power not usually found in infants under a full year of age. His motions and even his vocal sounds shewed[b] a restraint and deliberateness highly peculiar in an infant, and no one was really unprepared when, at seven months, he began to walk unassisted, with falterings which another month was sufficient to remove.

It was somewhat after this time—on Hallowe'en—that a great blaze was seen at midnight on the top of Sentinel Hill where the old table-like stone stands amidst its tumulus of ancient bones. Considerable talk was started when Silas Bishop—of the undecayed Bishops—mentioned having seen the boy running sturdily up that hill ahead of his mother about an hour before the blaze was remarked. Silas was rounding up a stray heifer, but he nearly forgot his mission when he fleetingly spied the two figures in the dim light of his lantern. They darted almost noiselessly through the underbrush, and the astonished watcher seemed to think they were entirely unclothed. Afterward he could not be sure about the boy, who may have had some kind of a fringed belt and a pair of dark[c] trunks or trousers on. Wilbur was never subsequently seen alive and conscious without complete and tightly buttoned attire, the disarrangement or threatened disarrangement of which always seemed to fill him with anger and alarm. His contrast with his squalid mother and grandfather in this respect was thought very notable until the horror of 1928 suggested the most valid of reasons.

The next January gossips were mildly interested in the fact that

[a] grey,] gray, B
[b] shewed] showed B
[c] dark] dark blue B

"Lavinny's black brat" had commenced to talk, and at the age of only eleven months. His speech was somewhat remarkable both because of its difference from the ordinary accents of the region, and because it displayed a freedom from infantile lisping of which many children of three or four might well be proud. The boy was not talkative, yet when he spoke he seemed to reflect some elusive element wholly unpossessed by Dunwich and its denizens. The strangeness did not reside in what he said, or even in the simple idioms he used; but seemed vaguely linked with his intonation or with the internal organs that produced the spoken sounds. His facial aspect, too, was remarkable for its maturity; for though he shared his mother's and grandfather's chinlessness, his firm and precociously shaped nose united with the expression of[a] his large, dark, almost Latin eyes to give him an air of quasi-adulthood and well-nigh preternatural intelligence. He was, however, exceedingly ugly despite his appearance of brilliancy; there being something almost goatish or animalistic about his thick lips, large-pored, yellowish skin, coarse crinkly hair, and oddly elongated ears. He was soon disliked even more decidedly than his mother and grandsire, and all conjectures about him were spiced with references to the bygone magic of Old Whateley, and how the hills once shook when he shrieked the dreadful name of *Yog-Sothoth* in the midst of a circle of stones with a great book open in his arms before him. Dogs abhorred the boy, and he was always obliged to take various defensive measures against their barking menace.

III.

Meanwhile Old Whateley continued to buy cattle without measurably increasing the size of his herd. He also cut timber and began to repair the unused parts of his house—a spacious, peaked-roofed affair whose rear end was buried entirely in the rocky hillside, and whose three least-ruined ground-floor rooms had always been sufficient for himself and his daughter. There must have been prodigious reserves of strength in the old man to enable him to accomplish so much hard

---

[a] of] on B

labour;[a] and though he still babbled dementedly at times, his carpentry seemed to shew[b] the effects of sound calculation. It had already[c] begun as soon as Wilbur was born, when one of the many tool-sheds[d] had been put suddenly in order, clapboarded, and fitted with a stout fresh lock. Now, in restoring the abandoned upper story of the house, he was a no less thorough craftsman. His mania shewed[e] itself only in his tight boarding-up of all the windows in the reclaimed section—though many declared that it was a crazy thing to bother with the reclamation at all. Less inexplicable was his fitting up[f] of another downstairs room for his new grandson—a room which several callers saw, though no one was ever admitted to the closely boarded[g] upper story. This chamber he lined with tall, firm shelving; along which he began gradually to arrange, in apparently careful order, all the rotting ancient books and parts of books which during his own day had been heaped promiscuously in odd corners of the various rooms.

"I made some use of 'em," he would say as he tried to mend a torn black-letter page with paste prepared on the rusty kitchen stove, "but the boy's fitten to make better use of 'em. He'd orter hev 'em as well sot[h] as he kin, for they're goin' to be all of his larnin'."

When Wilbur was a year and seven months old—in September of 1914—his size and accomplishments were almost alarming. He had grown as large as a child of four, and was a fluent and incredibly intelligent talker. He ran freely about the fields and hills, and accompanied his mother on all her wanderings. At home he would pore diligently over the queer pictures and charts in his grandfather's books, while Old Whateley would instruct and catechise[i] him through long, hushed afternoons. By this time the restoration of the house was finished, and those who watched it wondered why one of the upper

[a] labour;] labor; B
[b] shew] show B
[c] already] really B
[d] tool-sheds] tool sheds A, B, C
[e] shewed] showed B
[f] fitting up] fitting-up B
[g] closely boarded] closely-boarded A, B, C
[h] sot] so C
[i] catechise] catechize B

windows had been made into a solid plank door. It was a window in the rear of the east gable end, close against the hill; and no one could imagine why a cleated wooden runway was built up to it from the ground. About the period of this work's completion people noticed that the old tool-house, tightly locked and windowlessly clapboarded since Wilbur's birth, had been abandoned again. The door swung listlessly open, and when Earl Sawyer once stepped within after a cattle-selling call on Old Whateley he was quite discomposed by the singular odour[a] he encountered—such a stench, he averred, as he had never before smelt in all his life except near the Indian circles on the hills, and which could not come from anything sane or of this earth. But then, the homes and sheds of Dunwich folk have never been remarkable for olfactory immaculateness.

The following months were void of visible events, save that everyone swore to a slow but steady increase in the mysterious hill noises. On May-Eve[b] of 1915 there were tremors which even the Aylesbury people felt, whilst the following Hallowe'en produced an underground rumbling queerly synchronised[c] with bursts of flame—"them witch Whateleys' doin's"—from the summit of Sentinel Hill. Wilbur was growing up uncannily, so that he looked like a boy of ten as he entered his fourth year. He read avidly by himself now; but talked much less than formerly. A settled taciturnity was absorbing him, and for the first time people began to speak specifically of the dawning look of evil in his goatish face. He would sometimes mutter an unfamiliar jargon, and chant in bizarre rhythms which chilled the listener with a sense of unexplainable terror. The aversion displayed toward him by dogs had now become a matter of wide remark, and he was obliged to carry a pistol in order to traverse the countryside in safety. His occasional use of the weapon did not enhance his popularity amongst the owners of canine guardians.

The few callers at the house would often find Lavinia alone on the ground floor, while odd cries and footsteps resounded in the boarded-up second story. She would never tell what her father and the boy were

[a] odour] odor B
[b] May-Eve] May Eve A, B, C
[c] synchronised] synchronized B

doing up there, though once she turned pale and displayed an abnormal degree of fear when a jocose fish-peddler tried the locked door leading to the stairway. That peddler told the store loungers at Dunwich Village that he thought he heard a horse stamping on that floor above. The loungers reflected, thinking of the door and runway, and of the cattle that so swiftly disappeared. Then they shuddered as they recalled tales of Old Whateley's youth, and of the strange things that are called out of the earth when a bullock is sacrificed at the proper time to certain heathen gods. It had for some time been noticed that dogs had begun to hate and fear the whole Whateley place as violently as they hated and feared young Wilbur personally.

In 1917 the war came, and Squire Sawyer Whateley, as chairman of the local draft board, had hard work finding a quota of young Dunwich men fit even to be sent to a[a] development camp. The government, alarmed at such signs of wholesale regional decadence, sent several officers and medical experts to investigate; conducting a survey which New England newspaper readers may still recall. It was the publicity attending this investigation which set reporters on the track of the Whateleys, and caused the *Boston Globe* and *Arkham Advertiser* to print flamboyant Sunday stories of young Wilbur's precociousness, Old Whateley's black magic, the[b] shelves of strange books, the sealed second story of the ancient farmhouse, and the weirdness of the whole region and its hill noises. Wilbur was four and a half then, and looked like a lad of fifteen. His lips and cheeks[c] were fuzzy with a coarse dark down, and his voice had begun to break.[d]

Earl Sawyer went out to the Whateley place with both sets of reporters and camera men, and called their attention to the queer stench which now seemed to trickle down from the sealed upper spaces. It was, he said, exactly like a smell he had found in the tool-shed abandoned when the house was finally repaired;[e] and like the faint odours[f] which he sometimes thought he caught near the stone

[a] a] *om.* C
[b] the] and the C
[c] lips and cheeks] lip and cheek B
[d] break. ¶] break. B
[e] repaired;] repaired, B
[f] odours] odors B

circles[a] on the mountains. Dunwich folk read the stories when they appeared, and grinned over the obvious mistakes. They wondered, too, why the writers made so much of the fact that Old Whateley always paid for his cattle in gold pieces of extremely ancient date. The Whateleys had received their visitors with ill-concealed distaste, though they did not dare court further publicity by a violent resistance or refusal to talk.

IV.

For a decade the annals of the Whateleys sink indistinguishably into the general life of a morbid community used to their queer ways and hardened to their May-Eve[b] and All-Hallows[c] orgies. Twice a year they would light fires on the top of Sentinel Hill, at which times the mountain rumblings would recur with greater and greater violence; while at all seasons there were strange and portentous doings at the lonely farmhouse. In the course of time callers professed to hear sounds in the sealed upper story even when all the family were downstairs, and they wondered how swiftly or how lingeringly a cow or bullock was usually sacrificed. There was talk of a complaint to the Society for the Prevention of Cruelty to Animals; but nothing ever came of it, since Dunwich folk are never anxious to call the outside world's attention to themselves.

About 1923, when Wilbur was a boy of ten whose mind, voice, stature, and bearded face gave all the impressions of maturity, a second great siege of carpentry went on at the old house. It was all inside the sealed upper part, and from bits of discarded lumber people concluded that the youth and his grandfather had knocked out all the partitions and even removed the attic floor, leaving only one vast open void between the ground story and the peaked roof. They had torn down the great central chimney, too, and fitted the rusty range with a flimsy outside tin stovepipe.

[a] circles] circle C [s *added in pen in A*]
[b] May-Eve] May Eve A, B, C
[c] All-Hallows] All-Hallow B

In the spring after this event Old Whateley noticed the growing number of whippoorwills that would come out of Cold Spring Glen to chirp under his window at night. He seemed to regard the circumstance as one of great significance, and told the loungers at Osborn's that he thought his time had almost come.

"They whistle jest in tune with my breathin' naow," he said, "an' I guess they're gittin' ready to ketch my soul. They know it's a-goin' aout, an' dun't calc'late to miss it. Yew'll know, boys, arter I'm gone, whether they git me er not. Ef they dew, they'll keep up a-singin' an' laffin' till break o' day. Ef they dun't[a] they'll kinder quiet daown like. I expeck them an' the souls they hunts fer hev some pretty tough tussles sometimes."

On Lammas Night, 1924, Dr. Houghton of Aylesbury was hastily summoned by Wilbur Whateley, who had lashed his one remaining horse through the darkness and telephoned from Osborn's in the village. He found Old Whateley in a very grave state, with a cardiac action and stertorous breathing that told of an end not far off. The shapeless albino daughter and oddly bearded grandson stood by the bedside, whilst from the vacant abyss overhead there came a disquieting suggestion of rhythmical surging or lapping, as of the waves on some level beach. The doctor, though, was chiefly disturbed by the chattering night birds outside; a seemingly limitless legion of whippoorwills that cried their endless message in repetitions timed diabolically to the wheezing gasps of the dying man. It was uncanny and unnatural—too much, thought Dr. Houghton, like the whole of the region he had entered so reluctantly in response to the urgent call.

Toward one[b] o'clock Old Whateley gained consciousness, and interrupted his wheezing to choke out a few words to his grandson.

"More space, Willy, more space soon. Yew grows—an' *that* grows faster. It'll be ready to sarve ye soon, boy. Open up the gates to Yog-Sothoth with the long chant that ye'll find on page 751 *of the complete edition,* an' *then* put a match to the prison. Fire from airth can't burn it nohaow."[c]

---

[a] dun't] dun't, B
[b] one] 1 B
[c] nohaow."] nohaow!" B

He was obviously quite mad. After a pause, during which the flock of whippoorwills outside adjusted their cries to the altered tempo while some indications of the strange hill noises came from afar off, he added another sentence or two.

"Feed it reg'lar, Willy, an' mind the quantity; but dun't let it grow too fast fer the place, fer ef it busts quarters or gits aout afore ye opens to Yog-Sothoth, it's all over an' no use. Only them from beyont kin make it multiply an' work. . . . Only them, the old uns as wants to come back. . . ."

But speech gave place to gasps again, and Lavinia screamed at the way the whippoorwills followed the change. It was the same for more than an hour, when the final throaty rattle came. Dr. Houghton drew shrunken lids over the glazing grey[a] eyes as the tumult of birds faded imperceptibly to silence. Lavinia sobbed, but Wilbur only chuckled whilst the hill noises rumbled faintly.

"They didn't git him," he muttered in his heavy bass voice.

Wilbur was by this time a scholar of really tremendous erudition in his one-sided way, and was quietly known by correspondence to many librarians in distant places where rare and forbidden books of old days are kept. He was more and more hated and dreaded around Dunwich because of certain youthful disappearances which suspicion laid vaguely at his door; but was always able to silence inquiry through fear or through use of that fund of old-time gold which still, as in his grandfather's time, went forth regularly and increasingly for cattle-buying. He was now tremendously mature of aspect, and his height, having reached the normal adult limit, seemed inclined to wax beyond that figure. In 1925, when a scholarly correspondent from Miskatonic University called upon him one day and departed pale and puzzled, he was fully six and three-quarters feet tall.

Through all the years Wilbur had treated his half-deformed albino mother with a growing contempt, finally forbidding her to go to the hills with him on May-Eve[b] and Hallowmass; and in 1926 the poor creature complained to Mamie Bishop of being afraid of him.

"They's more abaout him as I knows than I kin tell ye, Mamie,"

---

[a] grey] gray B
[b] May-Eve] May Eve A, B, C

she said, "an' naowadays they's more nor what I know myself. I vaow afur Gawd, I dun't know what he wants nor what he's a-tryin' to dew."

That Hallowe'en the hill noises sounded louder than ever, and fire burned on Sentinel Hill as usual; but people paid more attention to the rhythmical screaming of vast flocks of unnaturally belated whippoorwills which seemed to be assembled near the unlighted Whateley farmhouse. After midnight their shrill notes burst into a kind of pandaemoniac[a] cachinnation which filled all the countryside, and not until dawn did they finally quiet down. Then they vanished, hurrying southward where they were fully a month overdue. What this meant, no one could quite be certain till later. None of the country folk seemed to have died—but poor Lavinia Whateley, the twisted albino, was never seen again.

In the summer of 1927 Wilbur repaired two sheds in the farmyard and began moving his books and effects out to them. Soon afterward Earl Sawyer told the loungers at Osborn's that more carpentry was going on in the Whateley farmhouse. Wilbur was closing all the doors and windows on the ground floor, and seemed to be taking out partitions as he and his grandfather had done upstairs four years before. He was living in one of the sheds, and Sawyer thought he seemed unusually worried and tremulous. People generally suspected him of knowing something about his mother's disappearance, and very few ever approached his neighbourhood[b] now. His height had increased to more than seven feet, and shewed[c] no signs of ceasing its development.

V.

The following winter brought an event no less strange than Wilbur's first trip outside the Dunwich region. Correspondence with the Widener Library at Harvard, the Bibliothèque[d] Nationale in Paris, the British Museum, the University of Buenos Ayres,[e] and the Library of

[a] pandaemoniac] pandemoniac B
[b] neighbourhood] neighborhood B
[c] shewed] showed B
[d] Bibliothèque] Bibliotheque A, B, C
[e] Ayres,] Aires, B

Miskatonic University at Arkham had failed to get him the loan of a book he desperately wanted; so at length he set out in person, shabby, dirty, bearded, and uncouth of dialect, to consult the copy at Miskatonic, which was the nearest to him geographically. Almost eight feet tall, and carrying a cheap new valise from Osborn's general store, this dark and goatish gargoyle appeared one day in Arkham in quest of the dreaded volume kept under lock and key at the college library—the hideous "Necronomicon"[a] of the mad Arab Abdul Alhazred in Olaus Wormius' Latin version, as printed in Spain in the seventeenth century.[b] He had never seen a city before, but had no thought save to find his way to the university grounds; where, indeed, he passed heedlessly by the great white-fanged watchdog that barked with unnatural fury and enmity, and tugged frantically at its stout chain.

Wilbur had with him the priceless but imperfect copy of Dr. Dee's English version which his grandfather had bequeathed him, and upon receiving access to the Latin copy he at once began to collate the two texts with the aim of discovering a certain passage which would have come on the 751st page of his own defective volume. This much he could not civilly refrain from telling the librarian—the same erudite Henry Armitage (A.M.[c] Miskatonic, Ph. D. Princeton, Litt. D.[d] Johns Hopkins) who had once called at the farm, and who now politely plied him with questions. He was looking, he had to admit, for a kind of formula or incantation containing the frightful name *Yog-Sothoth,* and it puzzled him to find discrepancies, duplications, and ambiguities which made the matter of determination far from easy. As he copied the formula he finally chose, Dr. Armitage looked involuntarily over his shoulder at the open pages; the left-hand one of which, in the Latin version, contained such monstrous threats to the peace and sanity of the world.

"Nor is it to be thought," ran the text as Armitage mentally translated it, "that[e] man is either the oldest or the last of earth's masters, or that the

---

[a] "Necronomicon"] *Necronomicon* A, B, C
[b] seventeenth century.] Seventeenth Century. B
[c] A.M.] A. M. B, C
[d] Litt. D.] Litt.D. C
[e] "Nor . . . thought," ran . . . it, "that] Nor . . . thought, [ran . . . it] that B, C

common bulk of life and substance walks alone. The Old Ones were, the Old Ones are, and the Old Ones shall be. Not in the spaces we know, but *between* them,[a] They walk serene and primal, undimensioned and to us unseen. *Yog-Sothoth* knows the gate. *Yog-Sothoth* is the gate. *Yog-Sothoth* is the key and guardian of the gate. Past, present, future, all are one in *Yog-Sothoth*. He knows where the Old Ones broke through of old, and where They shall break through again. He knows where They have trod earth's fields, and where They still tread them, and why no one can behold Them as They tread. By Their smell can men sometimes know Them near, but of Their semblance can no man know, *saving only in the features of those They have begotten on mankind;* and of those are there many sorts, differing in likeness from man's truest eidolon to that shape without sight or substance which is *Them*.[b] They walk unseen and foul in lonely places where the Words have been spoken and the Rites howled through at their Seasons. The wind gibbers with Their voices, and the earth mutters with Their consciousness. They bend the forest and crush the city, yet may not forest or city behold the hand that smites. Kadath in the cold waste hath known Them, and what man knows Kadath? The ice desert of the South and the sunken isles of Ocean hold stones whereon Their seal is engraven, but who hath seen the deep frozen city or the sealed tower long garlanded with seaweed and barnacles? Great Cthulhu is Their cousin, yet can he spy Them only dimly. *Iä!*[c] *Shub-Niggurath!* As a foulness shall ye know Them. Their hand is at your throats, yet ye see Them not; and Their habitation is even one with your guarded threshold. *Yog-Sothoth* is the key to the gate, whereby the spheres meet. Man rules now where They ruled once; They shall soon rule where man rules now. After summer is winter, and after winter summer. They wait patient and potent, for here shall They reign again."[d]

Dr. Armitage, associating what he was reading with what he had heard of Dunwich and its brooding presences, and of Wilbur Whateley and his dim, hideous aura that stretched from a dubious birth to a cloud of probable matricide, felt a wave of fright as tangible as a draught of the tomb's cold clamminess. The bent, goatish giant before him seemed like the spawn of another planet or dimension; like something only partly of mankind, and linked to black gulfs of essence

[a] them,] them. B
[b] *Them.*] *They.* B
[c] *Iä!*] *Iä* B
[d] again."] again. B, C

and entity that stretch like titan phantasms[a] beyond all spheres of force and matter, space and time.[b] Presently Wilbur raised his head and began speaking in that strange, resonant fashion which hinted at sound-producing organs unlike the run of mankind's.

"Mr. Armitage," he said, "I calc'late I've got to take that book home. They's things in it I've got to try under sarten conditions that I can't git here, an' it 'ud be a mortal sin to let a red-tape rule hold me up. Let me take it along, Sir,[c] an' I'll swar they wun't nobody know the difference. I dun't need to tell ye I'll take good keer of it. It wa'n't[d] me that put this Dee copy in the shape it is. . . ."

He stopped as he saw firm denial on the librarian's face, and his own goatish features grew crafty. Armitage, half-ready to tell him he might make a copy of what parts he needed, thought suddenly of the possible consequences and checked himself. There was too much responsiblity in giving such a being the key to such blasphemous outer spheres. Whateley saw how things stood, and tried to answer lightly.

"Wal, all right, ef ye feel that way abaout it. Maybe Harvard wun't be so fussy as yew be." And without saying more he rose and strode out of the building, stooping at each doorway.

Armitage heard the savage yelping of the great watchdog, and studied Whateley's gorilla-like lope as he crossed the bit of campus visible from the window. He thought of the wild tales he had heard, and recalled the old Sunday stories in the *Advertiser;* these things, and the lore he had picked up from Dunwich rustics and villagers during his one visit there. Unseen things not of earth—or at least not of tri-dimensional earth—rushed foetid[e] and horrible through New England's glens, and brooded obscenely on the mountaintops.[f] Of this he had long felt certain. Now he seemed to sense the close presence of some terrible part of the intruding horror, and to glimpse a hellish advance in the black dominion of the ancient and once passive

[a] phantasms] fantasms B
[b] time.] time. ¶ B
[c] Sir,] sir, B
[d] wa'n't] wan't A, C
[e] foetid] fetid B
[f] mountaintops.] mountain tops. A, B, C

nightmare. He locked away the "Necronomicon"[a] with a shudder of disgust, but the room still reeked with an unholy and unidentifiable stench. "As a foulness shall ye know them," he quoted. Yes—the odour[b] was the same as that which had sickened him at the Whateley farmhouse less than three years before. He thought of Wilbur, goatish and ominous, once again, and laughed mockingly at the village rumours[c] of his parentage.

"Inbreeding?" Armitage muttered half-aloud[d] to himself. "Great God, what simpletons! Shew[e] them Arthur Machen's Great God Pan[f] and they'll think it a common Dunwich scandal! But what thing—what cursed shapeless influence on or off this three-dimensioned earth— was Wilbur Whateley's father? Born on Candlemas—nine months after May-Eve[g] of 1912, when the talk about the queer earth noises reached clear to Arkham— What[h] walked on the mountains that May-Night?[i] What Roodmas horror fastened itself on the world in half-human flesh and blood?"

During the ensuing weeks Dr. Armitage set about to collect all possible data on Wilbur Whateley and the formless presences around Dunwich. He got in communication with Dr. Houghton of Aylesbury, who had attended Old Whateley in his last illness, and found much to ponder over in the grandfather's last words as quoted by the physician. A visit to Dunwich Village failed to bring out much that was new; but a close survey of the "Necronomicon",[j] in those parts which Wilbur had sought so avidly, seemed to supply new and terrible clues to the nature, methods, and desires of the strange evil so vaguely threatening this planet. Talks with several students of archaic lore in Boston, and letters to many others elsewhere, gave him a growing amazement

[a] "Necronomicon"] *Necronomicon* A, B, C
[b] odour] odor B
[c] rumours] rumors B
[d] half-aloud] half aloud B
[e] Shew] Show B
[f] Great God Pan] *Great God Pan* B
[g] May-Eve] May Eve A, B, C
[h] Arkham— What] Arkham—What A; Arkham—what B, C
[i] May-Night?] May Night? A, B; May night? C
[j] "Necronomicon",] *Necronomicon,* A, B, C

which passed slowly through varied degrees of alarm to a state of really acute spiritual fear. As the summer drew on he felt dimly that something ought to be done about the lurking terrors of the upper Miskatonic valley, and about the monstrous being known to the human world as Wilbur Whateley.

VI.

The Dunwich horror itself came between Lammas and the equinox in 1928, and Dr. Armitage was among those who witnessed its monstrous prologue. He had heard, meanwhile, of Whateley's grotesque trip to Cambridge, and of his frantic efforts to borrow or copy from the "Necronomicon"[a] at the Widener Library. Those efforts had been in vain, since Armitage had issued warnings of the keenest intensity to all librarians having charge of the dreaded volume. Wilbur had been shockingly nervous at Cambridge; anxious for the book, yet almost equally anxious to get home again, as if he feared the results of being away long.

Early in August the half-expected outcome developed, and in the small hours of the third Dr. Armitage was awakened suddenly by the wild, fierce cries of the savage watchdog on the college campus. Deep and terrible, the snarling, half-mad growls and barks continued; always in mounting volume, but with hideously significant pauses. Then there rang out a scream from a wholly different throat—such a scream as roused half the sleepers of Arkham and haunted their dreams ever afterward—such a scream as could come from no being born of earth, or wholly of earth.

Armitage, hastening into some clothing and rushing[b] across the street and lawn to the college buildings, saw that others were ahead of him; and heard the echoes of a burglar-alarm still shrilling from the library. An open window shewed[c] black and gaping in the moonlight. What had come had indeed completed its entrance; for the barking and the screaming, now fast fading into a mixed low growling and moaning,

---

[a] "Necronomicon"] *Necronomicon* A, B, C
[b] Armitage, hastening . . . rushing] Armitage hastened . . . rushed B
[c] shewed] showed B

proceeded unmistakably from within. Some instinct warned Armitage that what was taking place was not a thing for unfortified eyes to see, so he brushed back the crowd with authority as he unlocked the vestibule door. Among the others he saw Professor Warren Rice and Dr. Francis Morgan, men to whom he had told some of his conjectures and misgivings; and these two he motioned to accompany him inside. The inward sounds, except for a watchful, droning whine from the dog, had by this time quite subsided; but Armitage now perceived with a sudden start that a loud chorus of whippoorwills among the shrubbery had commenced a damnably rhythmical piping, as if in unison with the last breaths[a] of a dying man.

The building was full of a frightful stench which Dr. Armitage knew too well, and the three men rushed across the hall to the small genealogical reading-room whence the low whining came. For a second nobody dared to turn on the light,[b] then Armitage summoned up his courage and snapped the switch. One of the three—it is not certain which—shrieked aloud at what sprawled before them among disordered tables and overturned chairs. Professor Rice declares that he wholly lost consciousness for an instant, though he did not stumble or fall.

The thing that lay half-bent on its side in a foetid[c] pool of greenish-yellow ichor and tarry stickiness was almost nine feet tall, and the dog had torn off all the clothing and some of the skin. It was not quite dead, but twitched silently and spasmodically while its chest heaved in monstrous unison with the mad piping of the expectant whippoorwills outside. Bits of shoe-leather and fragments of apparel were scattered about the room, and just inside the window an empty canvas sack lay where it had evidently been thrown. Near the central desk a revolver had fallen, a dented but undischarged cartridge later explaining why it had not been fired. The thing itself, however, crowded out all other images at the time. It would be trite and not wholly accurate to say that no human pen could describe it, but one may properly say that it could not be vividly visualised[d] by anyone whose ideas of aspect and contour

---

[a] breaths] breath B
[b] light,] light; B
[c] foetid] fetid B
[d] visualised] visualized B

are too closely bound up with the common life-forms of this planet and of the three known dimensions. It was partly human, beyond a doubt, with very man-like[a] hands and head, and the goatish, chinless face had the stamp of the Whateleys upon it. But the torso and lower parts of the body were teratologically fabulous, so that only generous clothing could ever have enabled it to walk on earth unchallenged or uneradicated.

Above the waist it was semi-anthropomorphic; though its chest, where the dog's rending paws still rested watchfully, had the leathery, reticulated hide of a crocodile or alligator. The back was piebald with yellow and black, and dimly suggested the squamous covering of certain snakes. Below the waist, though, it was the worst; for here all human resemblance left off and sheer phantasy[b] began. The skin was thickly covered with coarse black fur, and from the abdomen a score of long greenish-grey[c] tentacles with red sucking mouths protruded limply. Their arrangement was odd, and seemed to follow the symmetries of some cosmic geometry unknown to earth or the solar system. On each of the hips, deep set in a kind of pinkish, ciliated orbit, was what seemed to be a rudimentary eye; whilst in lieu of a tail there depended a kind of trunk or feeler with purple annular markings, and with many evidences of being an undeveloped mouth or throat. The limbs, save for their black fur, roughly resembled the hind legs of prehistoric earth's giant saurians; and terminated in ridgy-veined pads that were neither hooves nor claws. When the thing breathed, its tail and tentacles rhythmically changed colour,[d] as if from some circulatory cause normal to the non-human side of its ancestry. In the tentacles this was observable as a deepening of the[e] greenish tinge, whilst in the tail it was manifest as a yellowish appearance which alternated with a sickly greyish-white[f] in the spaces between the purple rings. Of genuine blood there was none; only the foetid[g] greenish-yellow ichor which trickled

[a] man-like] manlike A, B, C
[b] phantasy] fantasy B
[c] greenish-grey] greenish-gray B
[d] colour,] color, B
[e] side . . . the] *om.* C
[f] greyish-white] grayish-white B
[g] foetid] fetid B

along the painted floor beyond the radius of the stickiness, and left a curious discolouration[a] behind it.

As the presence of the three men seemed to rouse the dying thing, it began to mumble without turning or raising its head. Dr. Armitage made no written record of its mouthings, but asserts confidently that nothing in English was uttered. At first the syllables defied all correlation with any speech of earth, but toward the last there came some disjointed fragments evidently taken from the "Necronomicon",[b] that monstrous blasphemy in quest of which the thing had perished. These fragments, as Armitage recalls them, ran something like *"N'gai, n'gha'ghaa, bugg-shoggog, y'hah; Yog-Sothoth, Yog-Sothoth. . . ."* They trailed off into nothingness as the whippoorwills shrieked in rhythmical crescendoes of unholy anticipation.

Then came a halt in the gasping, and the dog raised its head in a long, lugubrious howl. A change came over the yellow, goatish face of the prostrate thing, and the great black eyes fell in appallingly. Outside the window the shrilling of the whippoorwills had suddenly ceased, and above the murmurs of the gathering crowd there came the sound of a panic-struck whirring and fluttering. Against the moon vast clouds of feathery watchers rose and raced from sight, frantic at that which they had sought for prey.

All at once the dog started up abruptly, gave a frightened bark, and leaped nervously out of the window by which it had entered. A cry rose from the crowd, and Dr. Armitage shouted to the men outside that no one must be admitted till the police or medical examiner came. He was thankful that the windows were just too high to permit of peering in, and drew the dark curtains carefully down over each one. By this time two policemen had arrived; and Dr. Morgan, meeting them in the vestibule, was urging them for their own sakes to postpone entrance to the stench-filled reading-room till the examiner came and the prostrate thing could be covered up.

Meanwhile frightful changes were taking place on the floor. One need not describe the *kind* and *rate* of shrinkage and disintegration that occurred before the eyes of Dr. Armitage and Professor Rice; but it is

[a] discolouration] discoloration B
[b] "Necronomicon",] *Necronomicon,* A, B, C

permissible to say that, aside from the external appearance of face and hands, the really human element[a] in Wilbur Whateley must have been very small. When the medical examiner came, there was only a sticky whitish mass on the painted boards, and the monstrous odour[b] had nearly disappeared. Apparently Whateley had had no skull or bony skeleton; at least, in any true or stable sense. He had taken somewhat after his unknown father.

VII.

Yet all this was only the prologue of the actual Dunwich horror. Formalities were gone through by bewildered officials, abnormal details were duly kept from press and public, and men were sent to Dunwich and Aylesbury to look up property and notify any who might be heirs of the late Wilbur Whateley. They found the countryside in great agitation, both because of the growing rumblings beneath the domed hills, and because of the unwonted stench and the surging, lapping sounds which came increasingly from the great empty shell formed by Whateley's boarded-up farmhouse. Earl Sawyer, who tended the horse and cattle during Wilbur's absence, had developed a woefully[c] acute case of nerves. The officials devised excuses not to enter the noisome boarded place; and were glad to confine their survey of the deceased's living quarters, the newly mended sheds, to a single visit. They filed a ponderous report at the court-house[d] in Aylesbury, and litigations concerning heirship are said to be still in progress amongst the innumerable Whateleys, decayed and undecayed, of the upper Miskatonic valley.

An almost interminable manuscript in strange characters, written in a huge ledger and adjudged a sort of diary because of the spacing and the variations in ink and penmanship, presented a baffling puzzle to those who found it on the old bureau which served as its owner's desk. After a week of debate it was sent to Miskatonic University, together

---

[a] element] elements B
[b] odour] odor B
[c] woefully] wofully B
[d] court-house] court-/house B; courthouse C

with the deceased's collection of strange books, for study and possible translation; but even the best linguists soon saw that it was not likely to be unriddled with ease. No trace of the ancient gold with which Wilbur and Old Whateley[a] always paid their debts has yet been discovered.

It was in the dark of September 9th[b] that the horror broke loose. The hill noises had been very pronounced during the evening, and dogs barked frantically all night. Early risers on the tenth noticed a peculiar stench in the air. About seven[c] o'clock Luther Brown, the hired boy at George Corey's, between Cold Spring Glen and the village, rushed frenziedly back from his morning trip to Ten-Acre Meadow with the cows. He was almost convulsed with fright as he stumbled into the kitchen; and in the yard outside the no less frightened herd were pawing and lowing pitifully, having followed the boy back in the panic they shared with him. Between gasps Luther tried to stammer out his tale to Mrs. Corey.

"Up thar in the rud beyont the glen, Mis' Cory—they's suthin' ben thar! It smells like thunder, an' all the bushes an' little trees is pushed back from the rud like they'd a haouse ben moved along of it. An' that ain't the wust, nuther. They's *prints* in the rud, Mis' Corey—great raound prints as big as barrel-heads, all sunk daown deep like a elephant had ben along, *only they's a sight more nor four feet could make!*[d] I looked at one or two afore I run, an' I see every one was covered with lines spreadin' aout from one place, like as if big palm-leaf fans—twict or three times as big as any they is—hed of ben paounded daown into the rud. An' the smell was awful, like what it is araound[e] Wizard Whateley's ol' haouse. . . ."

Here he faltered, and seemed to shiver afresh with the fright that had sent him flying home. Mrs. Corey, unable to extract more information, began telephoning the neighbours;[f] thus starting on its rounds the overture of panic that heralded the major terrors. When she got Sally Sawyer, housekeeper at Seth Bishop's, the nearest place to Whateley's, it

[a] Whateley] Whateley had C [had *struck out in A*]
[b] 9th] ninth A, B, C
[c] seven] 7 B
[d] *make!*] *make.* B
[e] araound] around C
[f] neighbours] neighbors B

became her turn to listen instead of transmit; for Sally's boy Chauncey, who slept poorly, had been up on the hill toward Whateley's, and had dashed back in terror after one look at the place, and at the pasturage where Mr. Bishop's cows had been left out all night.

"Yes, Mis' Corey," came Sally's tremulous voice over the party wire, "Cha'ncey he just come back a-postin', and couldn't haff talk fer bein' scairt! He says Ol' Whateley's haouse is all blowed[a] up, with the[b] timbers scattered raound like they'd ben dynamite inside; only the bottom floor ain't through, but is all covered with a kind o' tar-like[c] stuff that smells awful an' drips daown offen the aidges onto the graoun' whar the side timbers is blowed away. An' they's awful kinder marks in the yard, tew—great raound marks bigger raound than a hogshead, an' all sticky with stuff like is on the blowed-up haouse. Cha'ncey he says they leads off into the medders, whar a great swath wider'n a barn is matted daown, an' all the stun walls tumbled every whichway[d] wherever it goes.

"An' he says, says he, Mis' Corey, as haow he sot to look fer Seth's caows, frighted ez he was; an' faound 'em in the upper pasture nigh the Devil's Hop Yard in an awful shape. Haff on 'em's clean gone, an' nigh haff o' them that's left is sucked most dry o' blood, with sores on 'em like they's ben on Whateley's cattle ever senct Lavinny's black brat was born. Seth he's gone aout naow to look at 'em, though I'll vaow he wun't keer ter git very nigh Wizard Whateley's! Cha'ncey didn't look keerful ter see whar the big matted-daown swath led arter it leff[e] the pasturage, but he says he thinks it p'inted towards the glen rud to the village.

"I tell ye, Mis' Corey, they's suthin' abroad as hadn't orter be abroad, an' I for one think that black Wilbur Whateley, as come to the bad eend[f] he desarved, is at the bottom of the breedin' of it. He wa'n't all human hisself, I allus says to everybody; an' I think he an' Ol' Whateley must a raised suthin' in that there nailed-up haouse as ain't even so human as he was. They's allus ben unseen things araound Dunwich—livin' things—

---

[a] blowed] bowed C
[b] the] *om.* C
[c] tar-like] tarlike B
[d] whichway] which way B
[e] leff] lef C
[f] eend] end C

as ain't human an' ain't good fer human folks.

"The graoun' was a-talkin' lass[a] night, an' towards mornin' Cha'ncey he heerd the whippoorwills so laoud in Col' Spring Glen he couldn't sleep nun.[b] Then he thought he heerd another faint-like[c] saound over towards[d] Wizard Whateley's—a kinder rippin' or tearin' o' wood, like some big box er crate was bein'[e] opened fur off. What with this an' that, he didn't git to sleep at all till sunup, an' no sooner was he up this mornin', but he's got to go over to Whateley's an' see what's the matter. He see enough, I tell ye, Mis' Corey! This dun't mean no good, an' I think as all the menfolks[f] ought to git up a party an' do suthin'. I know suthin' awful's abaout, an' feel my time is nigh, though only Gawd knows jest what it is.

"Did your Luther take accaount o' whar them big tracks led tew? No? Wal, Mis' Corey, ef they was on the glen rud this side o' the glen, an' ain't got to your haouse yet, I calc'late they must go into the glen itself. They would do that. I allus says Col' Spring Glen ain't no healthy nor decent place. The whippoorwills an' fireflies there never did act like they was creaters o' Gawd, an' they's them as says ye kin hear strange things a-rushin' an' a-talkin' in the air daown thar ef ye stand in the right place, atween the rock falls an' Bear's Den."

By that noon fully three-quarters of the men and boys of Dunwich were trooping over the roads and meadows between the new-made Whateley ruins and Cold Spring Glen, examining in horror the vast, monstrous prints, the maimed Bishop cattle, the strange, noisome wreck of the farmhouse, and the bruised, matted vegetation of the fields and roadsides. Whatever had burst loose upon the world had assuredly gone down into the great sinister ravine; for all the trees on the banks were bent and broken, and a great avenue had been gouged in the precipice-hanging underbrush. It was as though a house, launched by an avalanche, had slid down through the tangled growths of the almost vertical slope. From below no sound came, but only a

[a] lass] las' C
[b] nun.] none. B
[c] faint-like] faintlike B
[d] towards] toward A, C
[e] bein'] bin' C
[f] menfolks] men-folks A, C; men-/folks B

distant, undefinable foetor;[a] and it is not to be wondered at that the men preferred to stay on the edge and argue, rather than descend and beard the unknown Cyclopean horror in its lair. Three dogs that were with the party had barked furiously at first, but seemed cowed and reluctant when near the glen. Someone telephoned the news to the *Aylesbury Transcript;* but the editor, accustomed to wild tales from Dunwich, did no more than concoct a humorous paragraph about it; an item soon afterward reproduced by the Associated Press.

That night everyone went home, and every house and barn was barricaded as stoutly as possible. Needless to say, no cattle were allowed to remain in open pasturage. About two[b] in the morning a frightful stench and the savage barking of the dogs awakened the household at Elmer Frye's, on the eastern edge of Cold Spring Glen, and all agreed that they could hear a sort of muffled swishing or lapping sound from somewhere outside. Mrs. Frye proposed telephoning the neighbours,[c] and Elmer was about to agree when the noise of splintering wood burst in upon their deliberations. It came, apparently, from the barn; and was quickly followed by a hideous screaming and stamping amongst the cattle. The dogs slavered and crouched close to the feet of the fear-numbed family. Frye lit a lantern through force of habit, but knew it would be death to go out into that black farmyard. The children and the womenfolk[d] whimpered, kept from screaming by some obscure, vestigial instinct of defence[e] which told them their lives depended on silence. At last the noise of the cattle subsided to a pitiful moaning, and a great snapping, crashing, and crackling ensued. The Fryes, huddled together in the sitting-room, did not dare to move until the last echoes died away far down in Cold Spring Glen. Then, amidst the dismal moans from the stable and the daemoniac[f] piping of late whippoorwills in the glen, Selina Frye tottered to the telephone and spread what news she could of the second phase of the horror.

The next day all the countryside was in a panic; and cowed,

[a] foetor;] fetor; B; foeter; C

[b] two] 2 B

[c] neighbours,] neighbors, B

[d] womenfolk] women-folk A, C; women-/folk B

[e] defence] defense B

[f] daemoniac] demoniac B

uncommunicative groups came and went where the fiendish thing had occurred. Two titan swaths of destruction stretched from the glen to the Frye farmyard, monstrous prints covered the bare patches of ground, and one side of the old red barn had completely caved in. Of the cattle, only a quarter could be found and identified. Some of these were in curious fragments, and all that survived had to be shot. Earl Sawyer suggested that help be asked from Aylesbury or Arkham, but others maintained it would be of no use. Old Zebulon Whateley, of a branch that hovered about half way[a] between soundness and decadence, made darkly wild suggestions about rites that ought to be practiced[b] on the hilltops.[c] He came of a line where tradition ran strong, and his memories of chantings in the great stone circles were not altogether connected with Wilbur and his grandfather.

Darkness fell upon a stricken countryside too passive to organise[d] for real defence.[e] In a few cases closely related families would band together and watch in the gloom under one roof; but in general there was only a repetition of the barricading of the night before, and a futile, ineffective gesture of loading muskets and setting pitchforks handily about. Nothing, however, occurred except some hill noises; and when the day came there were many who hoped that the new horror had gone as swiftly as it had come. There were even bold souls who proposed an offensive expedition down in the glen, though they did not venture to set an actual example to the still reluctant majority.

When night came again the barricading was repeated, though there was less huddling together of families. In the morning both the Frye and the Seth Bishop households reported excitement among the dogs and vague sounds and stenches from afar, while early explorers noted with horror a fresh set of the monstrous tracks in the road skirting Sentinel Hill. As before, the sides of the road shewed[f] a bruising indicative of the blasphemously stupendous bulk of the horror; whilst the conformation of the tracks seemed to argue a passage in two

---

[a] half way] half-way B; half-/ways C
[b] practiced] practised B
[c] hilltops.] hill-tops. A, C
[d] organise] organize B
[e] defence.] defense. B
[f] shewed] showed B, C

directions, as if the moving mountain had come from Cold Spring Glen and returned to it along the same path. At the base of the hill a thirty-foot swath of crushed shrubbery and[a] saplings led steeply upward, and the seekers gasped when they saw that even the most perpendicular places did not deflect the inexorable trail. Whatever the horror was, it could scale a sheer stony cliff of almost complete verticality; and as the investigators climbed around to the hill's summit by safer routes they saw that the trail ended—or rather, reversed—there.

It was here that the Whateleys used to build their hellish fires and chant their hellish rituals by the table-like stone on May-Eve[b] and Hallowmass. Now that very stone formed the centre[c] of a vast space thrashed around by the mountainous horror, whilst upon its slightly concave surface was a thick and foetid[d] deposit of the same tarry stickiness observed on the floor of the ruined Whateley farmhouse when the horror escaped. Men looked at one another and muttered. Then they looked down the hill. Apparently the horror had descended by a route much the same as that of its ascent. To speculate was futile. Reason, logic, and normal ideas of motivation stood confounded. Only old Zebulon,[e] who was not with the group, could have done justice to the situation or suggested a plausible explanation.

Thursday night began much like the others, but it ended less happily. The whippoorwills in the glen had screamed with such unusual persistence that many could not sleep, and about 3 a.m.[f] all the party telephones rang tremulously. Those who took down their receivers heard a fright-mad voice shriek out, "Help, oh, my Gawd! . . ." and some thought a crashing sound followed the breaking off of the exclamation. There was nothing more. No one dared do anything, and no one knew till morning whence the call came. Then those who had heard it called everyone on the line, and found that only the Fryes did not reply. The truth appeared an hour later, when a hastily assembled group of armed men trudged out to the Frye place at the

[a] and] *om.* C
[b] May-Eve] May Eve A, B, C
[c] centre] center B
[d] and foetid] fetid B
[e] Zebulon,] Zebulon C
[f] a.m.] a. m. B; A.M. C

head of the glen. It was horrible, yet hardly a surprise.[a] There were more swaths and monstrous prints, but there was no longer any house. It had caved in like an egg-shell, and amongst the ruins nothing living or dead could be discovered. Only[b] a stench and a tarry stickiness. The Elmer Fryes had been erased from Dunwich.

VIII.

In the meantime a quieter yet even more spiritually poignant phase of the horror had been blackly unwinding itself behind the closed door of a shelf-lined room in Arkham. The curious manuscript record or diary of Wilbur Whateley, delivered to Miskatonic University for translation, had caused much worry and bafflement among the experts in languages both ancient and modern; its very alphabet, notwithstanding a general resemblance to the heavily shaded[c] Arabic used in Mesopotamia, being absolutely unknown to any available authority. The final conclusion of the linguists was that the text represented an artificial alphabet, giving the effect of a cipher; though none of the usual methods of cryptographic solution seemed to furnish any clue, even when applied on the basis of every tongue the writer might conceivably have used. The ancient books taken from Whateley's quarters, while absorbingly interesting and in several cases promising to open up new and terrible lines of research among philosophers and men of science, were of no assistance whatever in this matter. One of them, a heavy tome with an iron clasp, was in another unknown alphabet—this one of a very different cast, and resembling Sanscrit[d] more than anything else. The old ledger was at length given wholly into the charge of Dr. Armitage, both because of his peculiar interest in the Whateley matter, and because of his wide linguistic learning and skill in the mystical formulae of antiquity and the Middle Ages.[e]

Armitage had an idea that the alphabet might be something

---

[a] surprise.] surprize. B
[b] discovered. Only] discovered—only B
[c] heavily shaded] heavily-shaded A, C
[d] Sanscrit] Sanskrit B, C
[e] Middle Ages.] middle ages. A, C

esoterically used by certain forbidden cults which have come down from old times, and which have inherited many forms and traditions from the wizards of the Saracenic world. That question, however, he did not deem vital; since it would be unnecessary to know the origin of the symbols if, as he suspected, they were used as a cipher in a modern language. It was his belief that, considering the great amount of text involved, the writer would scarcely have wished the trouble of using another speech than his own, save perhaps in certain special formulae and incantations. Accordingly he attacked the manuscript with the preliminary assumption that the bulk of it was in English.

Dr. Armitage knew, from the repeated failures of his colleagues, that the riddle was a deep and complex one;[a] and that no simple mode of solution could merit even a trial. All through late August he fortified himself with the massed[b] lore of cryptography;[c] drawing upon the fullest resources of his own library, and wading night after night amidst the arcana of Trithemius' "Poligraphia",[d] Giambattista Porta's "De Furtivis Literarum Notis",[e] De Vigenère's[f] "Traité des Chiffres",[g] Falconer's "Cryptomenysis Patefacta",[h] Davys' and Thicknesse's eighteenth-century[i] treatises, and such fairly modern authorities as Blair, von Marten, and Klüber's "Kryptographik".[j] He interspersed his study of the books with attacks on the manuscript[k] itself, and in time became convinced that he had to deal with one of those subtlest and most ingenious of cryptograms, in which many separate lists of corresponding letters are arranged like the multiplication table, and the message built up with arbitrary key-words known only to the initiated. The older authorities seemed rather more helpful than the newer ones,

[a] one;] one, B
[b] massed] mass C
[c] cryptography;] cryptography, B
[d] "Poligraphia",] *Poligraphia*, A, B, C
[e] "De . . . Notis",] *De . . . Notis*, A, B, C
[f] Vigenère's] Vigenere's A, B, C
[g] "Traité . . . Chiffres",] *Traité . . . Chiffres*, A, B; *Traite . . . Chiffres*, C
[h] "Cryptomenysis Patefacta",] *Cryptomenysis Patefacta*, A, B, C
[i] eighteenth-century] Eighteenth Century B
[j] "Kryptographik".] *Kryptographik.* A, B; *om.* C [*see below*]
[k] "Kryptographik". . . . manuscript] script C

and Armitage concluded that the code of the manuscript was one of great antiquity, no doubt handed down through a long line of mystical experimenters. Several times he seemed near daylight, only to be set back by some unforeseen obstacle. Then, as September approached, the clouds began to clear. Certain letters, as used in certain parts of the manuscript, emerged definitely and unmistakably; and it became obvious that the text was indeed in English.

On the evening of September 2nd[a] the last major barrier gave way, and Dr. Armitage read for the first time a continuous passage of Wilbur Whateley's annals. It was in truth a diary, as all had thought; and it was couched in a style clearly shewing[b] the mixed occult erudition and general illiteracy of the strange being who wrote it. Almost the first long passage that Armitage deciphered, an entry dated November 26, 1916, proved highly startling and disquieting. It was written, he remembered, by a child of three and a half who looked like a lad of twelve or thirteen.

"Today learned the Aklo for the Sabaoth," it ran, "which[c] did not like, it being answerable from the hill and not from the air. That upstairs more ahead of me than I had thought it would be, and is not like to have much earth brain. Shot Elam Hutchins's collie Jack when he went to bite me, and Elam says he would kill me if he dast. I guess he won't. Grandfather kept me saying the Dho formula last night, and I think I saw the inner city at the 2 magnetic poles. I shall go to those poles when the earth is cleared off, if I can't break through with the Dho-Hna formula when I commit it. They from the air told me at Sabbat that it will be years before I can clear off the earth, and I guess grandfather[d] will be dead then, so I shall have to learn all the angles of the planes and all the formulas between the Yr and the Nhhngr. They from outside will help, but they cannot[e] take body without human blood. That upstairs looks it will have the right cast. I can see it a little when I make the Voorish[f] sign or blow the powder[g] of Ibn Ghazi at

[a] 2nd] second A, B, C
[b] shewing] showing B
[c] "Today . . . Sabaoth," it ran, "which] Today . . . Sabaoth, [it ran] which B; Today . . . Sabaoth (it ran), which C
[d] grandfather] Grandfather B
[e] cannot] can not B
[f] Voorish] Yoorish B
[g] powder] power B

it, and it is near like them at May-Eve[a] on the Hill. The other face may wear off some. I wonder how I shall look when the earth is cleared and there are no earth beings on it. He that came with the Aklo Sabaoth said I may be transfigured,[b] there being much of outside to work on."[c]

Morning found Dr. Armitage in a cold sweat of terror and a frenzy of wakeful concentration. He had not left the manuscript all night, but sat at his table under the electric light turning page after page with shaking hands as fast as he could decipher the cryptic text. He had nervously telephoned his wife he would not be home, and when she brought him a breakfast from the house he could scarcely dispose of a mouthful. All that day he read on, now and then halted maddeningly as a reapplication of the complex key became necessary. Lunch and dinner were brought him, but he ate only the smallest fraction of either. Toward the middle of the next night he drowsed off in his chair, but soon woke out of a tangle of nightmares almost as hideous as the truths and menaces to man's existence that he had uncovered.

On the morning of September 4th[d] Professor Rice and Dr. Morgan insisted on seeing him for a while, and departed trembling and ashen-grey. That evening he went to bed, but slept only fitfully. Wednesday—the next day—he was back at the manuscript, and began to take copious notes both from the current sections and from those he had already deciphered. In the small hours of that night he slept a little in an easy-chair in his office, but was at the manuscript again before dawn. Some time before noon his physician, Dr. Hartwell, called to see him and insisted that he cease work. He refused; intimating that it was of the most vital importance for him to complete the reading of the diary,[e] and promising an explanation in due course of time.[f]

That evening, just as twilight fell, he finished his terrible perusal and sank back exhausted. His wife, bringing his dinner, found him in a half-comatose state; but he was conscious enough to warn her off with a sharp cry when he saw her eyes wander toward the notes he had

[a] May-Eve] May Eve A, B, C
[b] transfigured,] transfigured C
[c] on."] on. B, C
[d] 4th] fourth A, B, C
[e] diary,] diary C
[f] time. ¶] time. C

taken. Weakly rising, he gathered up the scribbled papers and sealed them all in a great envelope, which he immediately placed in his inside coat pocket. He had sufficient strength to get home, but was so clearly in need of medical aid that Dr. Hartwell was summoned at once. As the doctor put him to bed he could only mutter over and over again, *"But what, in God's name, can we do?"*

Dr. Armitage slept, but was partly delirious the next day. He made no explanations to Hartwell, but in his calmer moments spoke of the imperative need of a long conference with Rice and Morgan. His wilder wanderings were very startling indeed, including frantic appeals that something in a boarded-up farmhouse be destroyed, and fantastic references to some plan for the extirpation of the entire human race and all animal and vegetable life from the earth by some terrible elder race of beings from another dimension. He would shout that the world was in danger, since the Elder Things wished to strip it and drag it away from the solar system and cosmos of matter into some other plane or phase of entity from which it had once fallen, vigintillions of aeons[a] ago. At other times he would call for the dreaded "Necronomicon"[b] and the "Daemonolatreia"[c] of Remigius, in which he seemed hopeful of finding some formula to check the peril he conjured up.

"Stop them, stop them!" he would shout. "Those Whateleys meant to let them in, and the worst of all is left! Tell Rice and Morgan we must do something—it's a blind business, but I know how to make the powder.... It hasn't been fed since the second of August, when Wilbur came here to his death, and at that rate . . ."

But Armitage had a sound physique despite his seventy-three years, and slept off his disorder that night without developing any real fever. He woke late Friday, clear of head, though sober[d] with a gnawing fear and tremendous sense of responsibility. Saturday afternoon he felt able to go over to the library and summon Rice and Morgan for a conference, and the rest of that day and evening the three men tortured their brains in the wildest speculation and the most

[a] aeons] eons B
[b] "Necronomicon"] *Necronomicon* A, B, C
[c] "Daemonolatreia"] *Daemonolatreia* A, B, C
[d] sober] sober, B

desperate debate. Strange and terrible books were drawn voluminously from the stack shelves and from secure places of storage; and diagrams and formulae were copied with feverish haste and in bewildering abundance. Of scepticism[a] there was none. All three had seen the body of Wilbur Whateley as it lay on the floor in a room of that very building, and after that not one of them could feel even slightly inclined to treat the diary as a madman's raving.

Opinions were divided as to notifying the Massachusetts State Police, and the negative finally won. There were things involved which simply could not be believed by those who had not seen a sample, as indeed was made clear during certain subsequent investigations. Late at night the conference disbanded without having developed a definite plan, but all day Sunday Armitage was busy comparing formulae and mixing chemicals obtained from the college laboratory. The more he reflected on the hellish diary, the more he was inclined to doubt the efficacy of any material agent in stamping out the entity which Wilbur Whateley had left behind him—the earth-threatening entity which, unknown to him, was to burst forth in a few hours and become the memorable Dunwich horror.

Monday was a repetition of Sunday with Dr. Armitage, for the task in hand required an infinity of research and experiment. Further consultations of the monstrous diary brought about various changes of plan, and he knew that even in the end a large amount of uncertainty must remain. By Tuesday he had a definite line of action mapped out, and believed he would try a trip to Dunwich within a week. Then, on Wednesday, the great shock came. Tucked obscurely away in a corner of the *Arkham Advertiser* was a facetious little item from the Associated Press, telling what a record-breaking monster the bootleg whiskey of Dunwich had raised up. Armitage, half stunned, could only telephone for Rice and Morgan. Far into the night they discussed, and the next day was a whirlwind of preparation on the part of them all. Armitage knew he would be meddling with terrible powers, yet saw that there was no other way to annul the deeper and more malign meddling[b] which others had done before him.

[a] scepticism] skepticism B, C
[b] meddling] muddling C

IX.

Friday morning Armitage, Rice,[a] and Morgan set out by motor for Dunwich, arriving at the village about one[b] in the afternoon. The day was pleasant, but even in the brightest sunlight a kind of quiet dread and portent seemed to hover about the strangely domed hills and the deep, shadowy ravines of the stricken region. Now and then on some mountaintop[c] a gaunt circle of stones could be glimpsed against the sky. From the air of hushed fright at Osborn's store they knew something hideous had happened, and soon learned of the annihilation of the Elmer Frye house and family. Throughout that afternoon they rode around Dunwich; questioning the natives concerning all that had occurred, and seeing for themselves with rising pangs of horror the drear Frye ruins with their lingering traces of the tarry stickiness, the blasphemous tracks in the Frye yard, the wounded Seth Bishop cattle, and the enormous swaths of disturbed vegetation in various places. The trail up and down Sentinel Hill seemed to Armitage of almost cataclysmic significance, and he looked long at the sinister altar-like[d] stone on the summit.

At length the visitors, apprised of a party of State Police which had come from Aylesbury that morning in response to the first telephone reports of the Frye tragedy, decided to seek out the officers and compare notes as far as practicable. This, however, they found more easily planned than performed; since no sign of the party could be found in any direction. There had been five of them in a car, but now the car stood empty near the ruins in the Frye yard. The natives, all of whom had talked with the policemen, seemed at first as perplexed as Armitage and his companions. Then old Sam Hutchins thought of something and turned pale, nudging Fred Farr and pointing to the dank, deep hollow that yawned close by.

"Gawd," he gasped, "I telled 'em not ter go daown into the glen, an' I never thought nobody'd dew it with them tracks an' that smell an' the whippoorwills a-screechin' daown thar in the dark o' noonday. . . ."

A cold shudder ran through natives and visitors alike, and every

---

[a] Rice,] Rice B
[b] one] 1 B
[c] mountaintop] mountain top A, B, C
[d] altar-like] altarlike B

ear seemed strained in a kind of instinctive, unconscious listening. Armitage, now that he had actually come upon the horror and its monstrous work, trembled with the responsibility he felt to be his. Night would soon fall, and it was then that the mountainous blasphemy lumbered upon its eldritch course. *Negotium perambulans in tenebris.* . . . The old librarian rehearsed the formulae he had memorised,[a] and clutched the paper containing the alternative one he had not memorised.[b] He saw that his electric flashlight was in working order. Rice, beside him, took from a valise a metal sprayer of the sort used in combating insects; whilst Morgan uncased the big-game rifle on which he relied despite his colleague's warnings that no material weapon would be of help.

Armitage, having read the hideous diary, knew painfully well what kind of a manifestation to expect; but he did not add to the fright of the Dunwich people by giving any hints or clues. He hoped that it might be conquered without any revelation to the world of the monstrous thing it had escaped. As the shadows gathered, the natives commenced to disperse homeward, anxious to bar themselves indoors despite the present evidence that all human locks and bolts were useless before a force that could bend trees and crush houses when it chose. They shook their heads at the visitors' plan to stand guard at the Frye ruins near the glen; and as they left, had little expectancy of ever seeing the watchers again.

There were rumblings under the hills that night, and the whippoorwills piped threateningly. Once in a while a wind, sweeping up out of Cold Spring Glen, would bring a touch of ineffable foetor to the heavy night air; such a foetor[c] as all three of the watchers had smelled once before, when they stood above a dying thing that had passed for fifteen years and a half as a human being. But the looked-for terror did not appear. Whatever was down there in the glen was biding its time, and Armitage told his colleagues it would be suicidal to try to attack it in the dark.

---

[a] memorised,] memorized, B, C
[b] memorised.] memorized. B, C
[c] foetor . . . foetor] fetor . . . fetor B

Morning came wanly, and the night-sounds ceased. It was a grey,[a] bleak day, with now and then a drizzle of rain; and heavier and heavier clouds seemed to be piling themselves up beyond the hills to the northwest. The men from Arkham were undecided what to do. Seeking shelter from the increasing rainfall beneath one of the few undestroyed Frye outbuildings, they debated the wisdom of waiting, or of taking the aggressive and going down into the glen in quest of their nameless, monstrous quarry. The downpour waxed in heaviness, and distant peals of thunder sounded from far horizons. Sheet lighting shimmered, and then a forky bolt flashed near at hand, as if descending into the accursed glen itself. The sky grew very dark, and the watchers hoped that the storm would prove a short, sharp one followed by clear weather.

It was still gruesomely dark when, not much over an hour later, a confused babel of voices sounded down the road. Another moment brought to view a frightened group of more than a dozen men, running, shouting, and even whimpering hysterically. Someone in the lead began sobbing out words, and the Arkham men started violently when those words developed a coherent form.

"Oh, my Gawd, my Gawd,"[b] the voice choked out. "It's[c] a-goin' agin, *an' this time by day!* It's aout—it's aout an' a-movin' this very minute, an' only the Lord knows when it'll be on us all!"

The speaker panted into silence, but another took up his message.

"Nigh on a haour ago Zeb Whateley here heerd the 'phone a-ringin', an' it was Mis' Corey, George's wife, that lives daown by the junction. She says the hired boy Luther was aout drivin' in the caows from the storm arter[d] the big bolt, when he see all the trees a-bendin' at the maouth o' the glen—opposite side ter this—an' smelt the same awful smell like he smelt when he faound the big tracks las' Monday mornin'. An' she says he says they was a swishin', lappin' saound, more nor what the bendin' trees an' bushes could make, an' all on a suddent the trees along the rud begun ter git pushed one side, an' they was a

[a] grey,] gray, B

[b] Gawd,"] Gawd!" B

[c] out. "It's] out, "It's A; out; "it's B

[d] arter] arten C

awful stompin' an' splashin' in the mud. But mind ye, Luther he didn't see nothin' at all, only just the bendin' trees an' underbrush.

"Then fur ahead where Bishop's Brook goes under the rud he heerd a awful creakin' an' strainin' on the bridge, an' says he could tell the saound o' wood a-startin' to crack an' split. An' all the whiles he never see a thing, only them trees an' bushes a-bendin'. An' when the swishin' saound got very fur off—on the rud towards Wizard Whateley's an' Sentinel Hill—Luther he had the guts ter step up whar he'd heerd it furst an' look at the graound. It was all mud an' water, an' the sky was dark, an' the rain was wipin' aout all tracks abaout as fast as could be; but beginnin' at the glen maouth, whar the trees had moved, they was still some o' them awful prints big as bar'ls like he seen Monday."

At this point the first excited speaker interrupted.

"But *that* ain't the trouble naow—that was only the start. Zeb here was callin' folks up an' everybody was a-listenin' in when a call from Seth Bishop's cut in. His haousekeeper Sally was carryin' on fit ter[a] kill—she'd jest seed the trees a-bendin' beside the rud, an' says they was a kind o' mushy saound, like a elephant puffin' an' treadin', a-headin' fer the haouse. Then she up an' spoke suddent of a fearful smell, an' says her boy Cha'ncey was a-screamin' as haow it was jest like what he smelt up to the Whateley rewins Monday mornin'. An' the dogs was all barkin' an' whinin' awful.

"An' then she let aout a turrible yell, an' says the shed daown the rud had jest caved in like the storm hed blowed it over, only the wind wa'n't strong enough to dew that. Everybody was a-listenin', an' we could hear lots o' folks on the wire a-gaspin'. All to onct Sally she yelled agin,[b] an' says the front yard picket fence hed jest crumpled[c] up, though they wa'n't no sign o' what done it. Then everybody on the line could hear Cha'ncey an' ol'[d] Seth Bishop a-yellin'[e] tew, an' Sally was shriekin' aout that suthin' heavy hed struck the haouse—not lightnin' nor nothin', but suthin' heavy agin'[f] the front, that kep' a-launchin'

---

[a] ter] to C
[b] agin,] again, C
[c] jest crumpled] just crumbled C
[d] ol'] old' C
[e] a-yellin'] a-yellin', B
[f] agin'] agin C

itself agin an' agin, though ye couldn't see nothin' aout the front winders. An' then . . . an' then . . ."

Lines of fright deepened on every face; and Armitage, shaken as he was, had barely poise enough to prompt the speaker.

"An' then . . . Sally she yelled aout, 'O help, the haouse is a-cavin' in' . . . an' on the wire we could hear a turrible crashin',[a] an' a hull flock o' screamin' . . . jest[b] like when Elmer Frye's place was took, only wuss. . . ."

The man paused, and another of the crowd spoke.

"That's all—not a saound nor squeak over the 'phone arter that. Jest still-like. We that heerd it got aout Fords an' wagons an' raounded[c] up as many able-bodied menfolks[d] as we could git, at Corey's place, an' come up here ter see what yew thought best ter dew. Not but what I think it's the Lord's jedgment[e] fer our iniquities, that no mortal kin ever set aside."

Armitage saw that the time for positive action had come, and spoke decisively to the faltering group of frightened rustics.

"We must follow it, boys." He made his voice as reassuring as possible. "I believe there's a chance of putting it out of business. You men know that those Whateleys were wizards—well, this thing is a thing of wizardry, and must be put down by the same means. I've seen Wilbur Whateley's diary and read some of the strange old books he used to read; and I think I know the right kind of spell to recite to make the thing fade away. Of course, one can't be sure, but we can always take a chance. It's invisible—I knew it would be—but there's a[f] powder in this long-distance sprayer that might make it shew[g] up for a second. Later on we'll try it. It's a frightful thing to have alive, but it isn't as bad as what Wilbur would have let in if he'd lived longer. You'll never know what the world has[h] escaped. Now we've only this one

[a] crashin',] crashin' C
[b] jest] jes C
[c] raounded] rounded C
[d] menfolks] men-folks A, B, C
[e] jedgment] judgment B
[f] a] *om.* C
[g] shew] show A, B, C
[h] has] *om.* C

thing to fight, and it can't multiply. It can, though, do a lot of harm; so we mustn't hesitate to rid the community of it.

"We must follow it—and the way to begin is to go to the place that has just been wrecked. Let somebody lead the way—I don't know your roads very well, but I've an idea there might be a shorter cut across lots. How about it?"

The men shuffled about a moment, and then Earl Sawyer spoke softly, pointing with a grimy finger through the steadily lessening rain.

"I guess ye kin git to Seth Bishop's quickest by cuttin' acrost the lower medder here, wadin' the brook at the low place, an' climbin' through Carrier's mowin' and the timber-lot beyont. That comes aout on the upper rud mighty nigh Seth's—a leetle t'other side."

Armitage, with Rice and Morgan, started to walk in the direction indicated; and most of the natives followed slowly. The sky was growing lighter, and there were signs that the storm had worn itself away. When Armitage inadvertently took a wrong direction, Joe Osborn warned him and walked ahead to shew[a] the right one. Courage and confidence were mounting; though the twilight of the almost perpendicular wooded hill which lay toward the end of their short cut, and among whose fantastic ancient trees they had to scramble as if up a ladder, put these qualities to a severe test.

At length they emerged on a muddy road to find the sun coming out. They were a little beyond the Seth Bishop place, but bent trees and hideously unmistakable tracks shewed[b] what had passed by. Only a few moments were consumed in surveying the ruins just around the bend. It was the Frye incident all over again, and nothing dead or living was found in either of the collapsed shells which had been the Bishop house and barn. No one cared to remain there amidst the stench and tarry[c] stickiness, but all turned instinctively to the line of horrible prints leading on toward the wrecked Whateley farmhouse and the altar-crowned slopes of Sentinel Hill.

As the men passed the site of Wilbur Whateley's abode they shuddered visibly, and seemed again to mix hesitancy with their zeal. It

[a] shew] show A, B, C
[b] shewed] showed B
[c] tarry] the tarry B

was no joke tracking down something as big as a house that one could not see, but that had all the vicious malevolence of a daemon.[a] Opposite the base of Sentinel Hill the tracks left the road, and there was a fresh bending and matting visible along the broad swath marking the monster's former route to and from the summit.

Armitage produced a pocket telescope of considerable power and scanned the steep green side of the hill. Then he handed the instrument to Morgan, whose sight was keener. After a moment of gazing Morgan cried out sharply, passing the glass to Earl Sawyer and indicating a certain spot on the slope with his finger. Sawyer, as clumsy as most non-users of optical devices are, fumbled a while; but eventually focussed[b] the lenses with Armitage's aid. When he did so his cry was less restrained than Morgan's had been.

"Gawd almighty, the grass an' bushes is a-movin'! It's a-goin' up— slow-like—creepin' up[c] ter the top this minute, heaven only knows what fur!"[d]

Then the germ of panic seemed to spread among the seekers. It was one thing to chase the nameless entity, but quite another to find it. Spells might be all right—but suppose they weren't? Voices began questioning Armitage about what he knew of the thing, and no reply seemed quite to satisfy. Everyone seemed to feel himself in close proximity to phases of Nature and of being utterly forbidden, and wholly outside the sane experience of mankind.

X.

In the end the three men from Arkham—old, white-bearded Dr. Armitage, stocky, iron-grey Professor Rice, and lean, youngish Dr. Morgan—[e]ascended the mountain alone. After much patient instruction regarding its focussing[f] and use, they left the telescope with the frightened group that remained in the road; and as they climbed

---

[a] daemon.] demon. B
[b] focussed] focused B
[c] creepin' up] creepin'—up C
[d] fur!"] fer!" B
[e] Morgan—] Morgan, A, C
[f] focussing] focusing B

they were watched closely by those among whom the glass was passed around. It was hard going, and Armitage had to be helped more than once. High above the toiling group the great swath trembled as its hellish maker re-passed[a] with snail-like deliberateness. Then it was obvious that the pursuers were gaining.

Curtis Whateley—of the undecayed branch—was holding the telescope when the Arkham party detoured radically from the swath. He told the crowd that the men were evidently trying to get to a subordinate peak which overlooked the swath at a point considerably ahead of where the shrubbery was now bending. This, indeed, proved to be true; and the party were seen to gain the minor elevation only a short time after the invisible blasphemy had passed it.

Then Wesley Corey, who had taken the glass, cried out that Armitage was adjusting the sprayer which Rice held, and that something must be about to happen. The crowd stirred uneasily, recalling that this[b] sprayer was expected to give the unseen horror a moment of visibility. Two or three men shut their eyes, but Curtis Whateley snatched back the telescope and strained his vision to the utmost. He saw that Rice, from the party's point of vantage above and behind the entity, had an excellent chance of spreading the potent powder with marvellous[c] effect.

Those without the telescope saw only an instant's flash of grey[d] cloud—a cloud about the size of a moderately large building—near the top of the mountain. Curtis, who had[e] held the instrument, dropped it with a piercing shriek into the ankle-deep mud of the road. He reeled, and would have crumpled[f] to the ground had not two or three others seized and steadied him. All he could do was moan half-inaudibly,[g]

"Oh, oh, great Gawd . . . *that . . . that . . .*"

There was a pandemonium of questioning, and only Henry Wheeler thought to rescue the fallen telescope and wipe it clean of

[a] re-passed] repassed B, C
[b] this] his C
[c] marvellous] marvelous B, C
[d] grey] gray B
[e] had] *om.* C
[f] crumpled] crumbled C
[g] half-inaudibly,] half-inaudibly: B; half-inaudibly. C

mud. Curtis was past all coherence, and even isolated replies were almost too much for him.

"Bigger'n a barn . . . all made o' squirmin' ropes . . . hull thing sort o' shaped like a hen's egg bigger'n anything,[a] with dozens o' legs like hogsheads that haff shut up when they step . . . nothin' solid abaout it—all like jelly, an' made o' sep'rit wrigglin' ropes pushed clost together . . . great bulgin' eyes all over it . . . ten or twenty maouths or trunks a-stickin' aout all along the sides, big as stovepipes,[b] an' all a-tossin' an' openin' an' shuttin' . . . all grey, with kinder blue or purple rings . . . *an' Gawd in heaven[c]—that haff face on top! . . .*"

This final memory, whatever it was, proved too much for poor Curtis;[d] and he collapsed completely before he could say more. Fred Farr and Will Hutchins carried him to the roadside and laid him on the damp grass. Henry Wheeler, trembling, turned the rescued telescope on the mountain to see what he might. Through the lenses were discernible three tiny figures, apparently running toward the summit as fast as the steep incline allowed. Only these—nothing more. Then everyone noticed a strangely unseasonable noise in the deep valley behind, and even in the underbrush of Sentinel Hill itself. It was the piping of unnumbered whippoorwills, and in their shrill chorus there seemed to lurk a note of tense and evil expectancy.

Earl Sawyer now took the telescope and reported the three figures as standing on the topmost ridge, virtually level with the altar-stone but at a considerable distance from it. One figure, he said, seemed to be raising its hands above its head at rhythmic intervals; and as Sawyer mentioned the circumstance the crowd seemed to hear a faint, half-musical sound from the distance, as if a loud chant were accompanying the gestures. The weird silhouette on that remote peak must have been a spectacle of infinite grotesqueness and impressiveness, but no observer was in a mood for aesthetic[e] appreciation. "I guess he's sayin' the spell," whispered Wheeler as he snatched back the telescope. The

[a] anything,] anything C

[b] stovepipes,] stove-pipes, C

[c] *heaven*] *Heaven* A, B, C

[d] Curtis;] Curtis, B

[e] aesthetic] esthetic B

whippoorwills were piping wildly, and in a singularly curious irregular rhythm quite unlike that of the visible ritual.

Suddenly the sunshine seemed to lessen without the intervention of any discernible cloud. It was a very peculiar phenomenon, and was plainly marked by all. A rumbling sound seemed brewing beneath the hills, mixed strangely with a concordant rumbling which clearly came from the sky. Lightning flashed aloft, and the wondering crowd looked in vain for the portents of storm. The chanting of the men from Arkham now became unmistakable, and Wheeler saw through the glass that they were all raising their arms in the rhythmic incantation. From some farmhouse far away came the frantic barking of dogs.

The change in the quality of the daylight increased, and the crowd gazed about the horizon in wonder. A purplish darkness, born of nothing more than a spectral deepening of the sky's blue, pressed down upon the rumbling hills. Then the lightning flashed again, somewhat brighter than before, and the crowd fancied that it had shewed[a] a certain mistiness around the altar-stone on the distant height. No one, however, had been using the telescope at that instant. The whippoorwills continued their irregular pulsation, and the men of Dunwich braced themselves tensely against some imponderable menace with which the atmosphere seemed surcharged.

Without warning came those deep, cracked, raucous vocal sounds which will never leave the memory of the stricken group who heard them. Not from any human throat were they born, for the organs of man can yield no such acoustic perversions. Rather would one have said they came from the pit itself, had not their source been so unmistakably the altar-stone on the peak. It is almost erroneous to call them *sounds* at all, since so much of their ghastly, infra-bass timbre spoke to dim seats of consciousness and terror far subtler than the ear; yet one must do so, since their form was indisputably though vaguely that of half-articulate *words*. They were loud—loud as the rumblings and the thunder above which they echoed—yet did they come from no visible being. And because imagination might suggest a conjectural source in the world of non-visible beings, the huddled crowd at the mountain's base huddled still closer, and winced as if in expectation of a blow.

[a] shewed] showed B

"Ygnaiih ... ygnaiih ... thflthkh'ngha ... Yog-Sothoth ..." rang the hideous croaking out of space. *"Y'bthnk ... h'ehye—[a]n'grkdl'lh. ...."*

The speaking impulse seemed to falter here, as if some frightful psychic struggle were going on. Henry Wheeler strained his eye at the telescope, but saw only the three grotesquely silhouetted human figures on the peak, all moving their arms furiously in strange gestures as their incantation drew near its culmination. From what black wells of Acherontic fear or feeling, from what unplumbed gulfs of extra-cosmic consciousness or obscure, long-latent heredity, were those half-articulate thunder-croakings drawn? Presently they began to gather renewed force and coherence as they grew in stark, utter, ultimate frenzy.

"Eh-ya-ya-ya-yahaah—[b]e'yayayayaaaa ... ngh'aaaa ... ngh'aaaa[c] ... h'yuh ... h'yuh[d] ... HELP! HELP! ... *ff—ff—ff*—FATHER! FATHER! YOG-SOTHOTH! ..."*

But that was all. The pallid group in the road, still reeling at the *indisputably English* syllables that had poured thickly and thunderously down from the frantic vacancy beside that shocking altar-stone, were never to hear such syllables again. Instead, they jumped violently at the terrific report which seemed to rend the hills; the deafening, cataclysmic peal whose source, be it inner earth or sky, no hearer was ever able to place. A single lightning-bolt[e] shot from the purple zenith to the altar-stone, and a great tidal wave of viewless force and indescribable stench swept down from the hill to all the countryside. Trees, grass, and underbrush were whipped into a fury; and the frightened crowd at the mountain's base, weakened by the lethal foetor[f] that seemed about to asphyxiate them, were almost hurled off their feet. Dogs howled from the distance, green grass and foliage wilted to a curious, sickly yellow-grey,[g] and over field and forest were scattered the bodies of dead whippoorwills.

[a] *h'ehye*—] *h'ehye ...* B
[b] *"Eh-ya-ya-ya-yahaah*—] *"Eh-ya-ya-ya-yahaah ...* B
[c] *ngh'aaaa ... ngh'aaaa*] *ngh'aaaaa ... ngh'aaa* C
[d] h'yuh ... h'yuh] *h'yuh ... h'yuh* C
[e] lightning-bolt] lightning bolt A, B, C
[f] foetor] fetor B
[g] yellow-grey,] yellow-gray, B

The stench left quickly, but the vegetation never came right again. To this day there is something queer and unholy about the growths on and around that fearsome hill. Curtis Whateley was only just regaining consciousness when the Arkham men came slowly down the mountain in the beams of a sunlight once more brilliant and untainted. They were grave and quiet, and seemed shaken by memories and reflections even more terrible than those which had reduced the group of natives to a state of cowed quivering. In reply to a jumble of questions they only shook their heads and reaffirmed one vital fact.

"The thing has gone for ever," Armitage said. "It has been split up into what it was originally made of, and can never exist again. It was an impossibility in a normal world. Only the least fraction was really matter in any sense we know. It was like its father—and most of it has gone back to him in some vague realm or dimension outside our material universe; some vague abyss out of which only the most accursed rites of human blasphemy could ever have called him for a moment on the hills."

There was a brief silence, and in that pause the scattered senses of poor Curtis Whateley began to knit back into a sort of continuity; so that he put his hands to his head with a moan. Memory seemed to pick itself up where it had left off, and the horror of the sight that had prostrated him burst in upon him again.

"*Oh, oh, my Gawd, that haff face—*[a]*that haff face on top of it . . . that face with the red eyes an' crinkly albino hair, an' no chin, like the Whateleys. . . . It was a octopus, centipede, spider kind o' thing, but they was a haff-shaped man's face on top of it, an' it looked like Wizard Whateley's, only it was yards an' yards acrost. . . .*"

He paused exhausted, as the whole group of natives stared in a bewilderment not quite crystallised[b] into fresh terror. Only old Zebulon Whateley, who wanderingly remembered ancient things but who had been silent heretofore, spoke aloud.

"Fifteen year' gone," he rambled, "I heerd Ol' Whateley say as haow some day we'd hear a child o' Lavinny's a-callin' its father's name on the top o' Sentinel Hill. . . ."

[a] *face—*] *face . . .* B
[b] crystallised] crystallized B, C

But Joe Osborn interrupted him to question the Arkham men anew.

"What was it anyhaow, an' haowever did young Wizard Whateley call it aout o' the air it come from?"

Armitage chose his words very[a] carefully.

"It was—well, it was mostly a kind of force that doesn't belong in our part of space; a kind of force that acts and grows and shapes itself by other laws than those of our sort of Nature. We have no business calling in such things from outside, and only very wicked people and very wicked cults ever try to. There was some of it in Wilbur Whateley himself—enough to make a devil and a precocious monster of him, and to make his passing out a pretty terrible sight. I'm going to burn his accursed diary, and if you men are wise you'll dynamite that altar-stone up there, and pull down all the rings of standing stones on the other hills. Things like that brought down the beings those Whateleys were so fond of—the beings they were going to let in tangibly to wipe out the human race and drag the earth off to some nameless place for some nameless purpose.

"But as to this thing we've just sent back—the Whateleys raised it for a terrible part in the doings that were to come. It grew fast and big from the same reason that Wilbur grew fast and big—but it beat him because it had a greater share of the *outsideness* in it. You needn't ask how Wilbur called it out of the air. He didn't call it out. *It was his twin brother, but it looked more like the father than he did.*"

---

[a] very] *om.* B

The Whisperer in Darkness

I.

B
ear in mind closely that I did not see any actual visual horror at the end. To say that a mental shock was the cause of what I inferred—that last straw which sent me racing out of the lonely Akeley farmhouse and through the wild domed hills of Vermont in a commandeered motor at night—is to ignore the plainest facts of my final experience. Notwithstanding the deep extent to which I shared the information and speculations of Henry Akeley, the[a] things I saw and heard, and the admitted vividness of the impression produced on me by these things, I cannot prove even now whether I was right or wrong in my hideous inference. For after all, Akeley's disappearance establishes nothing. People found nothing amiss in his house despite the bullet-marks on the outside and inside. It was just as though he had walked out casually for a ramble in the hills and failed to return. There was not even a sign that a guest had been there, or that those horrible cylinders and machines had been stored in the study. That he had mortally feared the crowded green hills and endless trickle of brooks among which he had been born and reared, means nothing at all, either; for thousands are subject to just such morbid fears. Eccentricity, moreover, could easily account for his strange acts and apprehensions toward the last.

Editor's Note: The original A.Ms. and the T.Ms. (prepared by HPL) survive. The latter was followed by *Weird Tales* (August 1931) with the usual editorial alter-ations, but on the whole the text was printed quite accurately. The Arkham House editions also followed the T.Ms., hence are comparatively accurate; but the 1963 edition omits some lines from previous Arkham House editions and makes other errors that result in confusion and incoherence.

Texts: A = A.Ms. (JHL); B = T.Ms. (JHL); C = *Weird Tales* 18, No. 1 (August 1931): 32–73; D = *The Dunwich Horror and Others* (Arkham House, 1963), 212–77. Copy-text: B.

[a] extent . . . the] *om.* D

The whole matter began, so far as I am concerned, with the historic and unprecedented Vermont floods of November 3, 1927. I was then, as now, an instructor of literature at Miskatonic University in Arkham, Massachusetts, and an enthusiastic amateur student of New England folklore. Shortly after the flood, amidst the varied reports of hardship, suffering, and organised[a] relief which filled the press, there appeared certain odd stories of things found floating in some of the swollen rivers; so that many of my friends embarked on curious discussions and appealed to me to shed what light I could on the subject. I felt flattered at having my folklore study taken so seriously, and did what I could to belittle the wild, vague tales which seemed so clearly an outgrowth of old rustic superstitions. It amused me to find several persons of education who insisted that some stratum of obscure, distorted fact might underlie the rumours.[b]

The tales thus brought to my notice came mostly through newspaper cuttings; though one yarn had an oral source and was repeated to a friend of mine in a letter from his mother in Hardwick, Vermont. The type of thing described was essentially the same in all cases, though there seemed to be three separate instances involved—one connected with the Winooski River near Montpelier, another attached to the West River in Windham County beyond Newfane, and a third centreing[c] in the Passumpsic in Caledonia County above Lyndonville. Of course many of the stray items mentioned other instances, but on analysis they all seemed to boil down to these three. In each case country folk reported seeing one or more very bizarre and disturbing objects in the surging waters that poured down from the unfrequented hills, and there was a widespread tendency to connect these sights with a primitive, half-forgotten cycle of whispered legend which old people resurrected for the occasion.

What people thought they saw were organic shapes not quite like any they had ever seen before. Naturally, there were many human bodies washed along by the streams in that tragic period; but those who described these strange shapes felt quite sure that they were not human, despite some superficial resemblances in size and general outline. Nor, said the witnesses, could they have been any kind of animal known to

[a] organised] organized C, D
[b] rumours.] rumors. C, D
[c] centreing] centering C, D

Vermont. They were pinkish things about five feet long; with crustaceous bodies bearing vast pairs of dorsal fins or membraneous[a] wings and several sets of articulated limbs, and with a sort of convoluted ellipsoid, covered with multitudes of very short antennae, where a head would ordinarily be. It was really remarkable how closely the reports from different sources tended to coincide; though the wonder was lessened by the fact that the old legends, shared at one time throughout the hill country, furnished a morbidly vivid picture which might well have coloured[b] the imaginations of all the witnesses concerned. It was my conclusion that such witnesses—in every case naive[c] and simple backwoods folk—had glimpsed the battered and bloated bodies of human beings or farm animals in the whirling currents; and had allowed the half-remembered folklore to invest these pitiful objects with fantastic attributes.

The ancient folklore, while cloudy, evasive, and largely forgotten by the present generation, was of a highly singular character, and obviously reflected the influence of still earlier Indian tales. I knew it well, though I had never been in Vermont, through the exceedingly rare monograph of Eli Davenport, which embraces material orally obtained prior to 1839 among the oldest people of the state. This material, moreover, closely coincided with tales which I had personally heard from elderly rustics in the mountains of New Hampshire. Briefly summarised,[d] it hinted at a hidden race of monstrous beings which lurked somewhere among the remoter hills—in the deep woods of the highest peaks, and the dark valleys where streams trickle from unknown sources. These beings were seldom glimpsed, but evidences of their presence were reported by those who had ventured farther than usual up the slopes of certain mountains or into certain deep, steep-sided gorges that even the wolves shunned.

There were queer footprints or claw-prints in the mud of brook-margins and barren patches, and curious circles of stones, with the grass around them worn away, which did not seem to have been placed or entirely shaped by Nature. There were, too, certain caves of problematical depth in the sides of the hills; with mouths closed by

[a] membraneous] membranous C, D
[b] coloured] colored C
[c] naive] naïve D
[d] summarised,] summarized, C, D

boulders in a manner scarcely accidental, and with more than an average quota of the queer prints leading both toward and away from them—if indeed the direction of these prints could be justly estimated. And worst of all, there were the things which adventurous people had seen very rarely in the twilight of the remotest valleys and the dense perpendicular woods above the limits of normal hill-climbing.

It would have been less uncomfortable if the stray accounts of these things had not agreed so well. As it was, nearly all the rumours[a] had several points in common; averring that the creatures were a sort of huge, light-red crab with many pairs of legs and with two great bat-like[b] wings in the middle of the back. They sometimes walked on all their legs, and sometimes on the hindmost pair only, using the others to convey large objects of indeterminate nature. On one occasion they were spied in considerable numbers, a detachment of them wading along a shallow woodland watercourse three abreast in evidently disciplined formation. Once a specimen was seen flying—launching itself from the top of a bald, lonely hill at night and vanishing in the sky after its great flapping wings had been silhouetted an instant against the full moon.

These things seemed content, on the whole, to let mankind alone; though they were at times held responsible for the disappearance of venturesome individuals—especially persons who built houses too close to certain valleys or too high up on certain mountains. Many localities came to be known as inadvisable to settle in, the feeling persisting long after the cause was forgotten. People would look up at some of the neighbouring[c] mountain-precipices with a shudder, even when not recalling how many settlers had been lost, and how many farmhouses burnt to ashes, on the lower slopes of those grim, green sentinels.

But while according to the earliest legends the creatures would appear to have harmed only those trespassing on their privacy; there were later accounts of their curiosity respecting men, and of their attempts to establish secret outposts in the human world. There were tales of the queer claw-prints seen around farmhouse windows in the morning, and of occasional disappearances in regions outside the obviously haunted areas. Tales, besides, of buzzing voices in imitation

[a] rumours] rumors C, D
[b] bat-like] batlike A, B, D
[c] neighbouring] neighboring C

of human speech which made surprising[a] offers to lone travellers[b] on roads and cart-paths in the deep woods, and of children frightened out of their wits by things seen or heard where the primal forest pressed close upon their dooryards. In the final layer of legends—the layer just preceding the decline of superstition and the abandonment of close contact with the dreaded places—there are shocked references to hermits and remote farmers who at some period of life appeared to have undergone a repellent mental change, and who were shunned and whispered about as mortals who had sold themselves to the strange beings. In one of the northeastern counties it seemed to be a fashion about 1800 to accuse eccentric and unpopular recluses of being allies or representatives of the abhorred things.

As to what the things were—explanations naturally varied. The common name applied to them was "those ones", or "the old ones",[c] though other terms had a local and transient use. Perhaps the bulk of the Puritan settlers set them down bluntly as familiars of the devil, and made them a basis of awed theological speculation. Those with Celtic legendry in their heritage—mainly the Scotch-Irish element of New Hampshire, and their kindred who had settled in Vermont on Governor Wentworth's colonial grants—linked them vaguely with the malign fairies and "little people" of the bogs and raths, and protected themselves with scraps of incantation handed down through many generations. But the Indians had the most fantastic theories of all. While different tribal legends differed, there was a marked consensus of belief in certain vital particulars; it being unanimously agreed that the creatures were not native to this earth.

The Pennacook myths, which were the most consistent and picturesque, taught that the Winged Ones came from the Great Bear in the sky, and had mines in our earthly hills whence they took a kind of stone they could not get on any other world. They did not live here, said the myths, but merely maintained outposts and flew back with vast cargoes of stone to their own stars in the north. They harmed only those earth-people who got too near them or spied upon them. Animals shunned them through instinctive hatred, not because of being hunted. They could not eat the things and animals of earth, but

---

[a] surprising] surprizing C
[b] travellers] travelers D
[c] ones", . . . ones",] ones", . . . ones," C; ones," . . . ones," D

brought their own food from the stars. It was bad to get near them, and sometimes young hunters who went into their hills never came back. It was not good, either, to listen to what they whispered at night in the forest with voices like a bee's that tried to be like the voices of men. They knew the speech of all kinds of men—Pennacooks, Hurons, men of the Five Nations—but did not seem to have or need any speech of their own. They talked with their heads, which changed colour[a] in different ways to mean different things.

All the legendry, of course, white and Indian alike, died down during the nineteenth century,[b] except for occasional atavistical flareups.[c] The ways of the Vermonters became settled; and once their habitual paths and dwellings were established according to a certain fixed plan, they remembered less and less what fears and avoidances had determined that plan, and even that there had been any fears or avoidances. Most people simply knew that certain hilly regions were considered as highly unhealthy, unprofitable, and generally unlucky to live in, and that the farther one kept from them the better off one usually was. In time the ruts of custom and economic interest became so deeply cut in approved places that there was no longer any reason for going outside them, and the haunted hills were left deserted by accident rather than by design. Save during infrequent local scares, only wonder-loving grandmothers and retrospective nonagenarians ever whispered of beings dwelling in those hills; and even such whisperers admitted that there was not much to fear from those things now that they were used to the presence of houses and settlements, and now that human beings let their chosen territory severely alone.

All this I had long known from my reading, and from certain folk-tales[d] picked up in New Hampshire; hence when the flood-time rumours[e] began to appear, I could easily guess what imaginative background had evolved them. I took great pains to explain this to my friends, and was correspondingly amused when several contentious souls continued to

[a] colour] color C
[b] nineteenth century,] Nineteenth Century, C
[c] flareups.] flare-ups. C
[d] folk-tales] folk tales A, B, C, D
[e] rumours] rumors C

insist on a possible element of truth in the reports. Such persons tried to point out that the early legends had a significant persistence and uniformity, and that the virtually unexplored nature of the Vermont hills made it unwise to be dogmatic about what might or might not dwell among them; nor could they be silenced by my assurance that all the myths were of a well-known pattern common to most of mankind and determined by early phases of imaginative experience which always produced the same type of delusion.

It was of no use to demonstrate to such opponents that the Vermont myths differed but little in essence from those universal legends of natural personification which filled the ancient world with fauns and dryads and satyrs, suggested the *kallikanzari*[a] of modern Greece, and gave to wild Wales and Ireland their dark hints of strange, small, and terrible hidden races of troglodytes and burrowers. No use, either, to point out the even more startlingly similar belief of the Nepalese hill tribes in the dreaded[b] *Mi-Go* or "Abominable Snow-Men" who lurk hideously amidst the ice and rock pinnacles of the Himalayan summits. When I brought up this evidence, my opponents turned it against me by claiming that it must imply some actual historicity for the ancient tales; that it must argue the real existence of some queer elder earth-race, driven to hiding after the advent and dominance of mankind, which might very conceivably have survived in reduced numbers to relatively recent times—or even to the present.

The more I laughed at such theories, the more these stubborn friends asseverated them; adding that even without the heritage of legend the recent reports were too clear, consistent, detailed, and sanely prosaic in manner of telling, to be completely ignored. Two or three fanatical extremists went so far as to hint at possible meanings in the ancient Indian tales which gave the hidden beings a non-terrestrial origin; citing the extravagant books of Charles Fort with their claims that voyagers from other worlds and outer space have often visited the earth. Most of my foes, however, were merely romanticists who insisted on trying to transfer to real life the fantastic lore of lurking "little people" made popular by the magnificent horror-fiction of Arthur Machen.

[a] *kallikanzari*] *kallikanzarai* D
[b] dreaded] dread C

II.

As was only natural under the circumstances, this piquant debating finally got into print in the form of letters to the *Arkham Advertiser;* some of which were copied in the press of those Vermont regions whence the flood-stories came. The *Rutland Herald* gave half a page of extracts from the letters on both sides, while the *Brattleboro Reformer* reprinted one of my long historical and mythological summaries in full, with some accompanying comments in "The[a] Pendrifter's" thoughtful column which supported and applauded my sceptical[b] conclusions. By the spring of 1928 I was almost a well-known figure in Vermont, notwithstanding the fact that I had never set foot in the state. Then came the challenging letters from Henry Akeley which impressed me so profoundly, and which took me for the first and last time to that fascinating realm of crowded green precipices and muttering forest streams.

Most of what I now[c] know of Henry Wentworth Akeley was gathered by correspondence with his neighbours,[d] and with his only son in California, after my experience in his lonely farmhouse. He was, I discovered, the last representative on his home soil of a long, locally distinguished line of jurists, administrators, and gentlemen-agriculturists. In him, however, the family mentally had veered away from practical affairs to pure scholarship; so that he had been a notable student of mathematics, astronomy, biology, anthropology, and folklore at the University of Vermont. I had never previously heard of him, and he did not give many autobiographical details in his communications; but from the first I saw he was a man of character, education, and intelligence, albeit a recluse with very little worldly sophistication.

Despite the incredible nature of what he claimed, I could not help at once taking Akeley more seriously than I had taken any of the other challengers of my views. For one thing, he was really close to the actual phenomena—visible and tangible—that he speculated so grotesquely about; and for another thing, he was amazingly willing to leave his conclusions in a tentative state like a true man of science. He

[a] "The] The D [*type may have dropped from original plate*]
[b] sceptical] skeptical C, D
[c] now] *om.* D
[d] neighbours,] neighbors, C

had no personal preferences to advance, and was always guided by what he took to be solid evidence. Of course I began by considering him mistaken, but gave him credit for being intelligently mistaken; and at no time did I emulate some of his friends in attributing his ideas, and his fear of the lonely green hills, to insanity. I could see that there was a great deal to the man, and knew that what he reported must surely come from strange circumstance deserving investigation, however little it might have to do with the fantastic causes he assigned. Later on I received from him certain material proofs which placed the matter on a somewhat different and bewilderingly bizarre basis.

I cannot[a] do better than transcribe in full, so far as is possible, the long letter in which Akeley introduced himself, and which formed such an important landmark in my own intellectual history. It is no longer in my possession, but my memory holds almost every word of its portentous message; and again I affirm my confidence in the sanity of the man who wrote it. Here is the text—a text which reached me in the cramped, archaic-looking scrawl of one who had obviously not mingled much with the world during his sedate, scholarly life.

R.F.D. #2,[b]
Townshend, Windham Co.,
Vermont.[c]

May 5, 1928.[d]
Albert N. Wilmarth, Esq.,
118 Saltonstall St.,
Arkham, Mass.,[e]

My dear Sir:—[f]
I have read with great interest the *Brattleboro Reformer's* reprint (Apr. 23, '28) of your letter on the recent stories of strange bodies seen floating in our flooded streams last fall, and on the curious folklore they so well agree with. It is easy to see why an outlander would take the position you take,

---

[a] cannot] can not C
[b] #2,] No. 2, C
[c] Townshend, . . . Vermont.] Townshend, Windham Co., Vermont, C; Townshend, Windham Co., Vermont. D
[d] 1928.] 1928 D
[e] Albert . . . Mass.,] ALBERT . . . MASS. D
[f] dear Sir:—] Dear Sir: C; Dear Sir:— D

and even why "Pendrifter" agrees with you. That is the attitude generally taken by educated persons both in and out of Vermont, and was my own attitude as a young man (I am now 57) before my studies, both general and in Davenport's book, led me to do some exploring in parts of the hills hereabouts not usually visited.

I was directed toward such studies by the queer old tales I used to hear from elderly farmers of the more ignorant sort, but now I wish I had let the whole matter alone. I might say, with all proper modesty, that the subject of anthropology and folklore is by no means strange to me. I took a good deal of it at college, and am familiar with most of the standard authorities such as Tylor, Lubbock, Frazer, Quatrefages, Murray, Osborn, Keith, Boule, G. Elliot[a] Smith, and so on. It is no news to me that tales of hidden races are as old as all mankind. I have seen the reprints of letters from you, and those arguing[b] with you, in the *Rutland Herald,* and guess I know about where your controversy stands at the present time.

What I desire to say now is, that I am afraid your adversaries are nearer right than yourself, even though all reason seems to be on your side. They are nearer right than they realise[c] themselves—for of course they go only by theory, and cannot[d] know what I know. If I knew as little of the matter as they, I would not[e] feel justified in believing as they do. I would be wholly on your side.

You can see that I am having a hard time getting to the point, probably because I really dread getting to the point; but the upshot of the matter is that *I have certain evidence that monstrous things do indeed live in the woods on the high hills which nobody visits.* I have not seen any of the things floating in the rivers, as reported, *but I have seen things like them* under circumstances I dread to repeat. I have seen footprints, and of late have seen them nearer my own home (I live in the old Akeley place south of Townshend Village, on the side of Dark Mountain) than I dare tell you now. And I have overheard voices in the woods at certain points that I will not even begin to describe on paper.

At one place I heard them so much that I took a phonograph there—with a dictaphone attachment and wax blank—and I shall try to arrange to have you hear the record I got. I have run it on the machine for some of

---

[a] Elliot] Elliott A, B, C, D
[b] arguing] agreeing D
[c] realise] realize C
[d] cannot] can not C
[e] not] *om.* D

the old people up here, and one of the voices had[a] nearly scared them paralysed[b] by reason of its likeness to a certain voice (that buzzing voice in the woods which Davenport mentions) that their grandmothers have told about and mimicked for them. I know what most people think of a man who tells about "hearing voices"—but before you draw conclusions just listen to this record and ask some of the older backwoods people what they think of it. If you can account for it normally, very well; but there must be something behind it. *Ex nihilo nihil fit,* you know.

Now my object in writing you is not to start an argument,[c] but to give you information which I think a man of your tastes will find deeply interesting. *This is private. Publicly I am on your side,* for certain things shew[d] me that it does not do for people to know too much about these matters. My own studies are now wholly private, and I would not think of saying anything to attract people's attention and cause them to visit the places I have explored. It is true—terribly true—that there are *non-human creatures watching us all the time;* with spies among us gathering information. It is from a wretched man who, if he was sane (as I think he was),[e] *was one of those spies,* that I got a large part of my clues to the matter. He later killed himself, but I have reason to think there are others now.

The things come from another planet, being able to live in interstellar space and fly through it on clumsy, powerful wings which have a way of resisting the ether but which are too poor at steering to be of much use in helping them about on earth. I will tell you about this later if you do not dismiss me at once as a madman. They come here to get metals from mines that go deep under the hills, *and I think I know where they come from.* They will not hurt us if we let them alone, but no one can say what will happen if we get too curious about them. Of course a good army of men could wipe out their mining colony. That is what they are afraid of. But if that happened, more would come from *outside*—any number of them. They could easily conquer the earth, but have not tried so far because they have not needed to. They would rather leave things as they are to save bother.

I think they mean to get rid of me because of what I have discovered. There is a great black stone with unknown hieroglyphics half worn away which I found in the woods on Round Hill, east of here; and after I took it home everything became different. If they think I suspect too much they

[a] had] has C
[b] paralysed] paralyzed C
[c] argument,] argument D
[d] shew] show B, C, D
[e] sane (. . .),] sane, (. . .) A; sane (. . .) B, C, D

will either kill me *or take me off the earth to where they come from.* They like to take away men of learning once in a while, to keep informed on the state of things in the human world.

This leads me to my secondary purpose in addressing you—namely, to urge you to hush up the present debate rather than give it more publicity. *People must be kept away from these hills,* and in order to effect this, their curiosity ought not to be aroused any further. Heaven knows there is peril enough anyway, with promoters and real estate men flooding Vermont with herds of summer people to overrun the wild places and cover the hills with cheap bungalows.

I shall welcome further communication with you, and shall try to send you that phonograph record and black stone (which is so worn that photographs don't shew[a] much) by express if you are willing. I say "try" because I think those creatures have a way of tampering with things around here. There is a sullen,[b] furtive fellow named Brown, on a farm near the village, who I think is their spy. Little by little they are trying to cut me off from our world because I know too much about their world.

They have the most amazing way of finding out what I do. You may not even get this letter. I think I shall have to leave this part of the country and go to[c] live with my son in San Diego, Cal.,[d] if things get any worse, but it is not easy to give up the place you were born in, and where your family has lived for six generations. Also, I would hardly dare sell this house to anybody now that the *creatures* have taken notice of it. They seem to be trying to get the black stone back and destroy the phonograph record, but I shall not let them if I can help it. My great police dogs always hold them back, for there are very few here as yet, and they are clumsy in getting about. As I have said, their wings are not much use for short flights on earth. I am on the very brink of deciphering that stone—in a very terrible way—and with your knowledge of folklore you may be able to supply[e] missing links enough to help me. I suppose you know all about the fearful myths antedating the coming of man to the earth—the Yog-Sothoth and Cthulhu cycles—which are hinted at in the "Necronomicon".[f] I had access to a copy of that once, and hear that you have one in your college library under lock and key.

---

[a] shew] show A, B, C, D
[b] sullen,] sullen D
[c] to] *om.* D
[d] Cal.,] Cal. A, B
[e] supply] supply the D
[f] "Necronomicon".] *Necronomicon.* A, B, C, D

To conclude, Mr. Wilmarth, I think that with our[a] respective studies we can be very useful to each other. I don't wish to put you in any peril, and suppose I ought to warn you that possession of the stone and the record won't be very safe; but I think you will find any risks worth running for the sake of knowledge. I will drive down to Newfane or Brattleboro to send whatever you authorise[b] me to send, for the express offices there are more to be trusted. I might say that I live quite alone now, since I can't keep hired help any more. They won't stay because of the things that try to get near the house at night, and that keep the dogs barking continually. I am glad I didn't get as deep as this into the business while my wife was alive, for it would have driven her mad.

Hoping that I am not bothering you unduly, and that you will decide to get in touch with me rather than throw this letter into the waste basket as a madman's raving, I am

Yrs. very truly,
HENRY W. AKELEY[c]

P.S. I[d] am making some extra prints of certain photographs taken by me, which I think will help to prove a number of the points I have touched on. The old people think they are monstrously true. I shall send you these very soon if you are interested. H. W. A.[e]

It would be difficult to describe my sentiments upon reading this strange document for the first time. By all ordinary rules, I ought to have laughed more loudly at these extravagances than at the far milder theories which had previously moved me to mirth; yet something in the tone of the letter made me take it with paradoxical seriousness. Not that I believed for a moment in the hidden race from the stars which my correspondent spoke of; but that, after some grave preliminary doubts, I grew to feel oddly sure of his sanity and sincerity, and of his confrontation by some genuine though singular and abnormal phenomenon which he could not explain except in this imaginative way. It could not be as he thought it, I reflected, yet on the other hand it could not be otherwise than worthy of investigation. The man seemed unduly excited and alarmed about something, but it was hard

[a] our] your D
[b] authorise] authorize C, D
[c] HENRY W. AKELEY] Henry W. Akeley. C; Henry W. Akeley D
[d] P.S. I] P. S.—I C; P. S. I D
[e] interested. H. W. A.] interested. / H. W. A. D

to think that all cause was lacking. He was so specific and logical in certain ways—and after all, his yarn did fit in so perplexingly well with some of the old myths—even the wildest Indian legends.

That he had really overheard disturbing voices in the hills, and had really found the black stone he spoke about, was wholly possible despite the crazy inferences he had made—inferences probably suggested by the man who had claimed to be a spy of the outer beings and had later killed himself. It was easy to deduce that this man must have been wholly insane, but that he probably had a streak of perverse outward logic which made the naive[a] Akeley—already prepared for such things by his folklore studies—believe his tale. As for the latest developments—it appeared from his inability to keep hired help that Akeley's humbler rustic neighbours[b] were as convinced as he that his house was besieged by uncanny things at night. The dogs really barked, too.

And then the matter of that phonograph record, which I could not but believe he had obtained in the way he said. It must mean something; whether animal noises deceptively like human speech, or the speech of some hidden, night-haunting human being decayed to a state not much above that of lower animals. From this my thoughts went back to the black hieroglyphed stone, and to speculations upon what it might mean. Then, too, what of the photographs which Akeley said he was about to send, and which the old people had found so convincingly terrible?

As I re-read the cramped handwriting I felt as never before that my credulous opponents might have more on their side than I had conceded. After all, there might be some queer and perhaps hereditarily misshapen outcasts in those shunned hills, even though no such race of star-born monsters as folklore claimed. And if there were, then the presence of strange bodies in the flooded streams would not be wholly beyond belief. Was it too presumptuous to suppose that both the old legends and the recent reports had this much of reality behind them? But even as I harboured[c] these doubts I felt ashamed that so fantastic a piece of bizarrerie as Henry Akeley's wild letter had brought them up.

In the end I answered Akeley's letter, adopting a tone of friendly

---

[a] naive] naïve D
[b] neighbours] neighbors C
[c] harboured] harbored C

interest and soliciting further particulars. His reply came almost by return mail; and contained, true to promise, a number of kodak views of scenes and objects illustrating what he had to tell. Glancing at these pictures as I took them from the envelope, I felt a curious sense of fright and nearness to forbidden things; for in spite of the vagueness of most of them, they had a damnably suggestive power which was intensified by the fact of their being genuine photographs—actual optical links with what they portrayed, and the product of an impersonal transmitting process without prejudice, fallibility, or mendacity.

The more I looked at them, the more I saw that my serious estimate of Akeley and his story had not been unjustified. Certainly, these pictures carried conclusive evidence of something in the Vermont hills which was at least vastly outside the radius of our common knowledge and belief. The worst thing of all was the footprint—a view taken where the sun shone on a mud patch somewhere in a deserted upland. This was no cheaply counterfeited thing, I could see at a glance; for the sharply defined pebbles and grass-blades in the field of vision gave a clear index of scale and left no possibility of a tricky double exposure. I have called the thing a "footprint",[a] but "claw-print" would be a better term. Even now I can scarcely describe it save to say that it was hideously crab-like,[b] and that there seemed to be some ambiguity about its direction. It was not a very deep or fresh print, but seemed to be about the size of an average man's foot. From a central pad, pairs of saw-toothed nippers projected in opposite directions—quite baffling as to function, if indeed the whole object were exclusively an organ of locomotion.

Another photograph—evidently a time-exposure taken in deep shadow—was of the mouth of a woodland cave, with a boulder of rounded regularity choking the aperture. On the bare ground in front of it one could just discern a dense network of curious tracks, and when I studied the picture with a magnifier I felt uneasily sure that the tracks were like the one in the other view. A third picture shewed[c] a druid-like circle of standing stones on the summit of a wild hill.

[a] "footprint",] "footprint," D
[b] crab-like,] crablike, A, B, D
[c] shewed] showed B, C, D

Around the cryptic circle the grass was very much beaten down and worn away, though I could not detect any footprints even with the glass. The extreme remoteness of the place was apparent from the veritable sea of tenantless mountains which formed the background and stretched away toward a misty horizon.

But if the most disturbing of all the views was that of the footprint, the most curiously suggestive was that of the great black stone found in the Round Hill woods. Akeley had photographed it on what was evidently his study table, for I could see rows of books and a bust of Milton in the background. The thing, as nearly as one might guess, had faced the camera vertically with a somewhat irregularly curved surface of one by two feet; but to say anything definite about that surface, or about the general shape of the whole mass, almost defies the power of language. What outlandish geometrical principles had guided its cutting—for artificially cut it surely was—I could not even begin to guess; and never before had I seen anything which struck me as so strangely and unmistakably alien to this world. Of the hieroglyphics on the surface I could discern very few, but one or two that I did see gave me[a] rather a shock. Of course they might be fraudulent, for others besides myself had read the monstrous and abhorred "Necronomicon"[b] of the mad Arab Abdul Alhazred; but it nevertheless made me shiver to recognise[c] certain ideographs which study had taught me to link with the most blood-curdling and blasphemous whispers of things that had had a kind of mad half-existence before the earth and the other inner worlds of the solar system were made.

Of the five remaining pictures, three were of swamp and hill scenes which seemed to bear traces of hidden and unwholesome tenancy. Another was of a queer mark in the ground very near Akeley's house, which he said he had photographed the morning after a night on which the dogs had barked more violently than usual. It was very blurred, and one could really draw no certain conclusions from it; but it did seem fiendishly like that other mark or claw-print photographed on the deserted upland. The final picture was of the Akeley place itself; a trim

---

[a] me] *om.* D

[b] "Necronomicon"] *Necronomicon* A, B, C, D

[c] recognise] recognize C

white house of two stories and attic, about a century and a quarter old, and with a well-kept lawn and stone-bordered path leading up to a tastefully carved Georgian doorway. There were several huge police dogs on the lawn, squatting near a pleasant-faced man with a close-cropped grey beard whom I took to be Akeley himself—his own photographer, one might infer from the tube-connected bulb in his right hand.

From the pictures I turned to the bulky, closely written[a] letter itself; and for the next three hours was immersed in a gulf of unutterable horror. Where Akeley had given only outlines before, he now entered into minute details; presenting long transcripts of words overheard in the woods at night, long accounts of monstrous pinkish forms spied in thickets at twilight on the hills, and a terrible cosmic narrative derived from the application of profound and varied scholarship to the endless bygone discourses of the mad self-styled spy who had killed himself. I found myself faced by names and terms that I had heard elsewhere in the most hideous of connexions[b]—Yuggoth, Great Cthulhu, Tsathoggua, Yog-Sothoth, R'lyeh, Nyarlathotep, Azathoth, Hastur, Yian, Leng, the Lake of Hali, Bethmoora, the Yellow Sign, L'mur-Kathulos, Bran, and the Magnum Innominandum—and was drawn back through nameless aeons[c] and inconceivable dimensions to worlds of elder, outer entity at which the crazed author of the "Necronomicon"[d] had only guessed in the vaguest way. I was told of the pits of primal life, and of the streams that had trickled down therefrom; and finally, of the tiny rivulet from one of those streams which had become entangled with the destinies of our own earth.

My brain whirled; and where before I had attempted to explain things away, I now began to believe in the most abnormal and incredible wonders. The array of vital evidence was damnably vast and overwhelming; and the cool, scientific attitude of Akeley—an attitude removed as far as imaginable from the demented, the fanatical, the hysterical, or even the extravagantly speculative—had a tremendous effect on my thought and judgment. By the time I laid the frightful letter aside I could understand the fears he had come to entertain, and was

[a] closely written] closely-written A, B, D
[b] connexions] connections C, D
[c] aeons] eons C
[d] "Necronomicon"] *Necronomicon* A, B, C, D

ready to do anything in my power to keep people away from those wild, haunted hills. Even now, when time has dulled the impression and made me half question[a] my own experience and horrible doubts, there are things in that letter of Akeley's which I would not quote, or even form into words on paper. I am almost glad that the letter and record and photographs are gone now—and I wish, for reasons I shall soon make clear, that the new planet beyond Neptune had not been discovered.

With the reading of that letter my public debating about the Vermont horror permanently ended. Arguments from opponents remained unanswered or put off with promises, and eventually the controversy petered out into oblivion. During late May and June I was in constant correspondence with Akeley; though once in a while a letter would be lost, so that we would have to retrace our ground and perform considerable laborious copying. What we were trying to do, as a whole, was to compare notes in matters of obscure mythological scholarship and arrive at a clearer correlation of the Vermont horrors with the general body of primitive world legend.

For one thing, we virtually decided that these morbidities and the hellish Himalayan *Mi-Go* were one and the same order of incarnated nightmare. There were[b] also absorbing zoölogical conjectures, which I would have referred to Professor Dexter in my own college but for Akeley's imperative command to tell no one of the matter before us. If I seem to disobey that command now, it is only because I think that at this stage a warning about those farther Vermont hills—and about those Himalayan peaks which bold explorers are more and more determined to ascend—is more conducive to public safety than silence would be. One specific thing we were leading up to was a deciphering of the hieroglyphics on that infamous black stone—a deciphering which might well place us in possession of secrets deeper and more dizzying than any formerly known to man.

[a] half question] half-question A, B, D
[b] were] was D

III.

Toward the end of June the phonograph record came—shipped from Brattleboro, since Akeley was unwilling to trust conditions on the branch line north of there. He had begun to feel an increased sense of espionage, aggravated by the loss of some of our letters; and said much about the insidious deeds of certain men whom he considered tools and agents of the hidden beings. Most of all he suspected the surly farmer Walter Brown, who lived alone on a run-down hillside place near the deep woods, and who was often seen loafing around corners in Brattleboro, Bellows Falls, Newfane, and South Londonderry in the most inexplicable and seemingly unmotivated way. Brown's voice, he felt convinced, was one of those he had overheard on a certain occasion in a very terrible conversation; and he had once found a footprint or claw-print near Brown's house which might possess the most ominous significance. It had been curiously near some of Brown's own footprints—footprints that faced toward it.

So the record was shipped from Brattleboro, whither Akeley drove in his Ford car along the lonely Vermont back roads. He confessed in an accompanying note that he was beginning to be afraid of those roads, and that he would not even go into Townshend for supplies now except in broad daylight. It did not pay, he repeated again and again, to know too much unless one were very remote from those silent and problematical hills. He would be going to California pretty soon to live with his son, though it was hard to leave a place where all one's memories and ancestral feelings centred.[a]

Before trying the record on the commercial machine which I borrowed from the college administration building I carefully went over all the explanatory matter in Akeley's various letters. This record, he had said, was obtained about 1 a.m.[b] on the first[c] of May, 1915, near the closed mouth of a cave where the wooded west slope of Dark Mountain rises out of Lee's Swamp.[d] The place had always been unusually plagued with strange voices, this being the reason he had brought the

[a] centred.] centered. C, D
[b] a.m.] a. m. C; A. M. D
[c] first] 1st A, B, C, D
[d] Swamp.] swamp. D

phonograph, dictaphone, and blank in expectation of results. Former experience had told him that May-Eve[a]—the hideous Sabbat-night of underground European legend—would probably be more fruitful than any other date, and he was not disappointed. It was noteworthy, though, that he never again heard voices at that particular spot.

Unlike most of the overheard forest voices, the substance of the record was quasi-ritualistic, and included one palpably human voice which Akeley had never been able to place. It was not Brown's, but seemed to be that of a man of greater cultivation. The second voice, however, was the real crux of the thing—for this was the accursed *buzzing* which had no likeness to humanity despite the human words which it uttered in good English grammar and a scholarly accent.

The recording phonograph and dictaphone had not worked uniformly well, and had of course been at a great disadvantage because of the remote and muffled nature of the overheard ritual; so that the actual speech secured was very fragmentary. Akeley had given me a transcript of what he believed the spoken words to be, and I glanced through this again as I prepared the machine for action. The text was darkly mysterious rather than openly horrible, though a knowledge of its origin and manner of gathering gave it all the associative horror which any words could well possess. I will present it here in full as I remember it—and I am fairly confident that I know it correctly by heart, not only from reading the transcript, but from playing the record itself over and over again. It is not a thing which one might readily forget!

(INDISTINGUISHABLE SOUNDS)[b]

(A CULTIVATED MALE HUMAN VOICE)[c]

. . . is the Lord of the Woods,[d] even to . . . and the gifts of the men of Leng . . . so from the wells of night to the gulfs of space, and from the gulfs of space to the wells of night, ever the praises of Great Cthulhu, of Tsathoggua, and of Him Who is not to be Named. Ever Their praises,

---

[a] May-Eve] May Eve A, B, C, D
[b] (INDISTINGUISHABLE SOUNDS)] (*Indistinguishable Sounds*) D
[c] (A . . . VOICE)] (*A Cultivated Male Human Voice*) D
[d] Woods,] Wood, A, B, C, D

and abundance to the Black Goat of the Woods. Iä! Shub-Niggurath! The Goat with a Thousand Young!

(A BUZZING IMITATION OF HUMAN SPEECH)[a]

Iä! Shub-Niggurath! The Black Goat of the Woods with[b] *a Thousand Young!*

(HUMAN VOICE)[c]

And it has come to pass that the Lord of the Woods, being . . . seven and nine, down the onyx steps . . . (tri)butes to Him in the Gulf, Azathoth, He of Whom Thou hast taught us marv(els) . . . on the wings of night out beyond space, out beyond th . . . to That whereof Yuggoth is the youngest child, rolling alone in black aether at the rim. . . .

(BUZZING VOICE)[d]

. . . go out among men and find the ways thereof, that He in the Gulf may know. To Nyarlathotep, Mighty Messenger, must all things be told. And He shall put on the semblance of men, the waxen mask and the robe that hides, and come down from the world of Seven Suns to mock. . . .

(HUMAN VOICE)[e]

. . . (Nyarl)athotep, Great Messenger, bringer of strange joy to Yuggoth through the void, Father of the Million Favoured[f] Ones, Stalker among . . .

(SPEECH CUT OFF BY END OF RECORD)[g]

Such were the words for which I was to listen when I started the phonograph. It was with a trace of genuine dread and reluctance that I pressed the lever and heard the preliminary scratching of the sapphire point, and I was glad that the first faint, fragmentary words were in a human voice—a mellow, educated voice which seemed vaguely Bostonian in accent, and which was certainly not that of any native of

---

[a] (A . . . SPEECH)] (*A Buzzing Imitation of Human Speech*) D
[b] *with*] *With* A, B, C
[c] (HUMAN VOICE)] (*Human Voice*) D
[d] (BUZZING VOICE)] (*Buzzing Voice*) D
[e] (HUMAN VOICE)] (*Human Voice*) D
[f] Favoured] Favored C
[g] (SPEECH . . . RECORD)] (*Speech Cut Off by End of Record*) D

the Vermont hills. As I listened to the tantalisingly[a] feeble rendering, I seemed to find the speech identical with Akeley's carefully prepared transcript. On it chanted, in that mellow Bostonian voice … "Iä! Shub-Niggurath! The Goat with a Thousand Young! …"

And then I heard *the other voice*. To this hour I shudder retrospectively when I think of how it struck me, prepared though I was by Akeley's accounts. Those to whom I have since described the record profess to find nothing but cheap imposture or madness in it; but *could they have heard*[b] *the accursed thing itself,* or read the bulk of Akeley's correspondence (especially that terrible and encyclopaedic[c] second letter),[d] I know they would think differently. It is, after all, a tremendous pity that I did not disobey Akeley and play the record for others—a tremendous pity, too, that all of his letters were lost. To me, with my first-hand impression of the actual sounds, and with my knowledge of the background and surrounding circumstances, the voice was a monstrous thing. It swiftly followed the human voice in ritualistic response, but in my imagination it was a morbid echo winging its way across unimaginable abysses from unimaginable outer hells. It is more than two years now since I last ran off that blasphemous waxen cylinder; but at this moment, and at all other moments, I can still hear that feeble, fiendish buzzing as it reached me for the first time.

"Iä! Shub-Niggurath! The Black Goat of the Woods with a Thousand Young!"

But though that voice is always in my ears, I have not even yet been able to analyse[e] it well enough for a graphic description. It was like the drone of some loathsome, gigantic insect ponderously shaped into the articulate speech of an alien species, and I am perfectly certain that the organs producing it can have no resemblance to the vocal organs of man, or indeed to those of any of the mammalia. There were singularities in timbre, range, and overtones which placed this phenomenon wholly outside the sphere of humanity and earth-life. Its

---

[a] tantalisingly] tantalizingly C
[b] *heard*] *om.* D
[c] encyclopaedic] encyclopedic C
[d] correspondence (. . .),] correspondence, (. . .) A, B, C; correspondence, (. . .), D
[e] analyse] analyze C

sudden advent that first time almost stunned me, and I heard the rest of the record through in a sort of abstracted daze. When the longer passage of buzzing came, there was a sharp intensification of that feeling of blasphemous infinity which had struck me during the shorter and earlier passage. At last the record ended abruptly, during an unusually clear speech of the human and Bostonian voice; but I sat stupidly staring long after the machine had automatically stopped.

I hardly need say that I gave that shocking record many another playing, and that I made exhaustive attempts at analysis and comment in comparing notes with Akeley. It would be both useless and disturbing to repeat here all that we concluded; but I may hint that we agreed in believing we had secured a clue to the source of some of the most repulsive primordial customs in the cryptic elder religions of mankind. It seemed plain to us, also, that there were ancient and elaborate alliances between the hidden outer creatures and certain members of the human race. How extensive these alliances were, and how their state today might compare with their state in earlier ages, we had no means of guessing; yet at best there was room for a limitless amount of horrified speculation. There seemed to be an awful, immemorial linkage in several definite stages betwixt man and nameless infinity. The blasphemies which appeared on earth, it was hinted, came from the dark planet Yuggoth, at the rim of the solar system; but this was itself merely the populous outpost of a frightful interstellar race whose ultimate source must lie far outside even the Einsteinian space-time continuum or greatest known cosmos.

Meanwhile we continued to discuss the black stone and the best way of getting it to Arkham—Akeley deeming it inadvisable to have me visit him at the scene of his nightmare studies. For some reason or other, Akeley was afraid to trust the thing to any ordinary or expected transportation route. His final idea was to take it across country to Bellows Falls and ship it on the Boston and Maine system through Keene and Winchendon and Fitchburg, even though this would necessitate his driving along somewhat lonelier and more forest-traversing hill roads than the main highway to Brattleboro. He said he had noticed a man around the express office at Brattleboro when he had sent the phonograph record, whose actions and expression had been far from reassuring. This man had seemed too anxious to talk with the clerks, and had taken the train on which the record was shipped. Akeley confessed that he had not felt strictly at ease about that record until he heard from me of its safe receipt.

About this time—the second week in July—another letter of mine went astray, as I learned through an anxious communication from Akeley. After that he told me to address him no more at Townshend, but to send all mail in care of the General Delivery at Brattleboro; whither he would make frequent trips either in his car or on the motor-coach line which had lately replaced passenger service on the lagging branch railway. I could see that he was getting more and more anxious, for he went into much detail about the increased barking of the dogs on moonless nights, and about the fresh claw-prints he sometimes found in the road and in the mud at the back of his farmyard when morning came. Once he told about a veritable army of prints drawn up in a line facing an equally thick and resolute line of dog-tracks, and sent a loathsomely disturbing kodak picture to prove it. That was after a night on which the dogs had outdone themselves in barking and howling.

On the morning of Wednesday, July 18, I received a telegram from Bellows Falls, in which Akeley said he was expressing the black stone over the B. & M. on Train No. 5508, leaving Bellows Falls at 12:15 p.m., standard time, and due at the North Station in Boston at 4:12 p.m. It ought, I calculated, to get up to Arkham at least by the next noon; and accordingly I stayed in all Thursday morning to receive it. But noon came and went without its advent, and when I telephoned down to the express office I was informed that no shipment for me had arrived. My next act, performed amidst a growing alarm, was to give a long-distance call to the express agent at the Boston North Station; and I was scarcely surprised[a] to learn that my consignment had not appeared. Train No. 5508 had pulled in only 35 minutes late on the day before, but had contained no box addressed to me. The agent promised, however, to institute a searching inquiry; and I ended the day by sending Akeley a night-letter outlining the situation.

With commendable promptness a report came from the Boston office on the following afternoon, the agent telephoning as soon as he learned the facts. It seemed that the railway express clerk on No. 5508

[a] surprised] surprized C

had been able to recall an incident which might have much bearing on my loss—an argument with a very curious-voiced man, lean, sandy, and rustic-looking, when the train was waiting at Keene, N.H.,[a] shortly after one[b] o'clock standard time.

The man, he said, was greatly excited about a heavy box which he claimed to expect, but which was neither on the train nor entered on the company's books. He had given the name of Stanley Adams, and had had such a queerly thick[c] droning voice, that it made the clerk abnormally dizzy and sleepy to listen to him. The clerk could not remember quite how the conversation had ended, but recalled starting into a fuller awakeness when the train began to move. The Boston agent added that this clerk was a young man of wholly unquestioned veracity and reliability, of known antecedents and long with the company.

That evening I went to Boston to interview the clerk in person, having obtained his name and address from the office. He was a frank, prepossessing fellow, but I saw that he could add nothing to his original account. Oddly, he was scarcely sure that he could even recognise[d] the strange inquirer again. Realising[e] that he had no more to tell, I returned to Arkham and sat up till morning writing letters to Akeley, to the express company,[f] and to the police department and station agent in Keene. I felt that the strange-voiced man who had so queerly affected the clerk must have a pivotal place in the ominous business, and hoped that Keene station employes[g] and telegraph-office records might tell something about him and about how he happened to make his inquiry when and where he did.

I must admit, however, that all my investigations came to nothing. The queer-voiced man had indeed been noticed around the Keene station in the early afternoon of July 18, and one lounger seemed to couple him vaguely with a heavy box; but he was altogether unknown, and had not been seen before or since. He had not visited the

[a] N.H.] N. H. A, B; New Hampshire, C; N. H., D
[b] one] 1 A, B
[c] thick] thick, C
[d] recognise] recognize C
[e] Realising] Realizing C
[f] company,] company A, B, C, D
[g] employes] employees D

telegraph office or received any message so far as could be learned, nor had any message which might justly be considered a notice of the black stone's presence on No. 5508 come through the office for anyone.[a] Naturally Akeley joined with me in conducting these inquiries, and even made a personal trip to Keene to question the people around the station; but his attitude toward the matter was more fatalistic than mine. He seemed to find the loss of the box a portentous and menacing fulfilment of inevitable tendencies, and had no real hope at all of its recovery. He spoke of the undoubted telepathic and hypnotic powers of the hill creatures and their agents, and in one letter hinted that he did not believe the stone was on this earth any longer. For my part, I was duly enraged, for I had felt there was at least a chance of learning profound and astonishing things from the old, blurred hieroglyphs. The matter would have rankled bitterly in my mind had not Akeley's immediately subsequent letters brought up a new phase of the whole horrible hill problem which at once seized all my attention.

IV.

The unknown things, Akeley wrote in a script grown pitifully tremulous, had begun to close in on him with a wholly new degree of determination. The nocturnal barking of the dogs whenever the moon was dim or absent was hideous now, and there had been attempts to molest him on the lonely roads he had to traverse by day. On the second[b] of August, while bound for the village in his car, he had found a tree-trunk laid in his path at a point where the highway ran through a deep patch of woods; while the savage barking of the two great dogs he had with him told all too well of the things which must have been lurking near. What would have happened had the dogs not been there, he did not dare guess—but he never went out now without at least two of his faithful and powerful pack. Other road experiences had occurred on August 5th and 6th;[c] a shot grazing his car on one occasion, and the barking of the dogs telling of unholy woodland presences on the other.

---

[a] anyone.] any one. C
[b] second] 2nd A, B, C
[c] 5th and 6th;] fifth and sixth; D

On August 15th[a] I received a frantic letter which disturbed me greatly, and which made me wish Akeley could put aside his lonely reticence and call in the aid of the law. There had been frightful happenings on the night of the 12–13th,[b] bullets flying outside the farmhouse, and three of the twelve great dogs being found shot dead in the morning. There were myriads of claw-prints in the road, with the human prints of Walter Brown among them. Akeley had started to telephone to Brattleboro for more dogs, but the wire had gone dead before he had a chance to say much. Later he went to Brattleboro in his car, and learned there that linemen had found the main telephone[c] cable neatly cut at a point where it ran through the deserted hills north of Newfane. But he was about to start home with four fine new dogs, and several cases of ammunition for his big-game repeating rifle. The letter was written at the post office in Brattleboro, and came through to me without delay.

My attitude toward the matter was by this time quickly slipping from a scientific to an alarmedly personal one. I was afraid for Akeley in his remote, lonely farmhouse, and half afraid for myself because of my now definite connexion[d] with the strange hill problem. The thing was *reaching out* so. Would it suck me in and engulf me? In replying to his letter I urged him to seek help, and hinted that I might take action myself if he did not. I spoke of visiting Vermont in person in spite of his wishes, and of helping him explain the situation to the proper authorities. In return, however, I received only a telegram from Bellows Falls which read thus:

APPRECIATE[e] YOUR POSITION BUT CAN DO NOTHING.[f] TAKE NO ACTION YOURSELF FOR IT COULD ONLY HARM BOTH.[g] WAIT FOR EXPLANATION.[h]

HENRY AKELY[i]

[a] 15th] fifteenth D
[b] 12–13th,] 12th–13th, C
[c] telephone] *om.* D
[d] connexion] connection C, D
[e] APPRECIATE] ¶ APPRECIATE C
[f] NOTHING.] NOTHING D
[g] BOTH.] BOTH D
[h] EXPLANATION.] EXPLANATION D
[i] APPRECIATE . . . AKELY] APPRECIATE . . . AKELY. C; APPRECIATE . . . AKELEY D

But the affair was steadily deepening. Upon my replying to the telegram I received a shaky note from Akeley with the astonishing news that he had not only never sent the wire, but had not received the letter from me to which it was an obvious reply. Hasty inquiries by him at Bellows Falls had brought out that the message was deposited by a strange sandy-haired man with a curiously thick, droning voice, though more than this he could not learn. The clerk shewed[a] him the original text as scrawled in pencil by the sender, but the handwriting was wholly unfamiliar. It was noticeable that the signature was misspelled—A-K-E-L-Y, without the second "E".[b] Certain conjectures were inevitable, but amidst[c] the obvious crisis he did not stop to elaborate upon them.

He spoke of the death of more dogs and the purchase of still others, and of the exchange of gunfire which had become a settled feature each moonless night. Brown's prints, and the prints of at least one or two more shod human figures, were now found regularly among the claw-prints in the road, and at the back of the farmyard. It was, Akeley admitted, a pretty bad business; and before long he would probably have to go to live with his California son whether or not he could sell the old place. But it was not easy to leave the only spot one could really think of as home. He must try to hang on a little longer; perhaps he could scare off the intruders—especially if he openly gave up all further attempts to penetrate their secrets.

Writing Akeley at once, I renewed my offers of aid, and spoke again of visiting him and helping him convince the authorities of his dire peril. In his reply he seemed less set against that plan than his past attitude would have led one to predict, but said he would like to hold off a little while longer—long enough to get his things in order and reconcile himself to the idea of leaving an almost morbidly cherished birthplace. People looked askance at his studies and speculations,[d] and it would be better to get quietly off without setting the countryside in a turmoil and creating widespread doubts of his own sanity. He had had enough, he admitted, but he wanted to make a dignified exit if he could.

---

[a] shewed] showed A, B, C, D
[b] "E".] "E." D
[c] amidst] amdist C
[d] speculations,] speculations B, C, D

This letter reached me on the twenty-eighth[a] of August, and I prepared and mailed as encouraging a reply as I could. Apparently the encouragement took[b] effect, for Akeley had fewer terrors to report when he acknowledged my note. He was not very optimistic, though, and expressed the belief that it was only the full moon season which was holding the creatures off. He hoped there would not be many densely cloudy nights, and talked vaguely of boarding in Brattleboro when the moon waned. Again I wrote him encouragingly,[c] but on September 5th there came a fresh communication which had obviously crossed my letter in the mails; and to this I could not give any such hopeful response. In view of its importance I believe I had better give it in full—as best I can do from memory of the shaky script. It ran substantially as follows:

Monday.[d]

Dear Wilmarth—

A rather discouraging P.S.[e] to my last. Last night was thickly cloudy— though no rain—and not a bit of moonlight got through. Things were pretty bad, and I think the end is getting near, in spite of all we have hoped. After midnight something landed on the roof of the house, and the dogs all rushed up to see what it was. I could hear them snapping and tearing around, and then one managed to get on the roof by jumping from the low ell. There was a terrible fight up there, and I heard a frightful *buzzing* which I'll never forget. And then there was a shocking smell. About the same time bullets came through the window and nearly grazed me. I think the main line of the hill creatures had got close to the house when the dogs divided because of the roof business. What was up there I don't know yet, but I'm afraid the creatures are learning to steer better with their space wings. I put out the light and used the windows for loopholes, and raked all around the house with rifle fire aimed just high enough not to hit the dogs. That seemed to end the business, but in the morning I found great pools of blood in the yard, besides pools of a green sticky stuff that had the worst odour[f] I have ever smelled. I climbed up on

[a] twenty-eighth] 28th A, B, C, D
[b] took] had D
[c] encouragingly,] encouragingly D
[d] Monday.] *Monday* D
[e] P.S.] P. S. C, D
[f] odour] odor C

the roof and found more of the sticky stuff there. Five of the dogs were killed—I'm afraid I hit one myself by aiming too low, for he was shot in the back. Now I am setting the panes the shots broke, and am going to Brattleboro for more dogs. I guess the men at the kennels think I am crazy. Will drop another note later. Suppose I'll be ready for moving in a week or two, though it nearly kills me to think of it.

Hastily—
AKELEY[a]

But this was not the only letter from Akeley to cross mine. On the next morning—September 6th—still another came; this time a frantic scrawl which utterly unnerved me and put me at a loss what to say or do next. Again I cannot do better than quote the text as faithfully as memory will let me.

Tuesday.[b]

Clouds didn't break, so no moon again—and going into the wane anyhow. I'd have the house wired for electricity and put in a searchlight if I didn't know they'd cut the cables as fast as they could be mended.

I think I am going crazy. It may be that all I have ever written you is a dream or madness. It was bad enough before, but this time it is too much. *They talked to me last night*—talked in that cursed buzzing voice and told me things *that I dare not repeat to you*. I heard them plainly above the barking of the dogs, and once when they were drowned out *a human voice helped them*. Keep out of this, Wilmarth—it is worse than either you or I ever suspected. *They don't mean to let me get to California now—they want to take me off alive, or what theoretically and mentally amounts to alive*—not only to Yuggoth, but beyond that—away outside the galaxy *and possibly beyond the last curved rim of space*. I told them I wouldn't go where they wish, *or in the terrible way they propose to take me*, but I'm afraid it will be no use. My place is so far out that they may come by day as well as by night before long. Six more dogs killed, and I felt presences all along the wooded parts of the road when I drove to Brattleboro today.

It was a mistake for me to try to send you that phonograph record and black stone. Better smash the record before it's too late. Will drop you another line tomorrow if I'm still here. Wish I could arrange to get my books and things to Brattleboro and board there. I would run off without anything if I could,[c] but something inside my mind holds me back. I can slip out to Brattleboro, where I ought to be safe, but I feel just as much a prisoner there as at the house. And I seem to know that I couldn't get much farther even if I dropped everything and tried. It is horrible—don't get mixed up in this.

Yrs—AKELEY[a]

I did not sleep at all the night after receiving this terrible thing, and was utterly baffled as to Akeley's remaining degree of sanity. The substance of the note was wholly insane, yet the manner of expression—in view of all that had gone before—had a grimly potent quality of convincingness. I made no attempt to answer it, thinking it better to wait until Akeley might have time to reply to my latest communication. Such a reply indeed came on the following day, though the fresh material in it quite overshadowed any of the points brought up by the letter it[b] nominally answered. Here is what I recall of the text, scrawled and blotted as it was in the course of a plainly frantic and hurried composition.

Wednesday.[c]

W—

Yr[d] letter came, but it's no use to discuss anything any more. I am fully resigned. Wonder that I have even enough will power[e] left to fight them off. Can't escape even if I were willing to give up everything and run. They'll get me.

Had a letter from them yesterday—R.F.D. man brought it while I was at Brattleboro. Typed and postmarked Bellows Falls. Tells what they want to do with me—I can't repeat it. Look out for yourself, too! Smash that record. Cloudy nights keep up, and moon waning all the time. Wish I dared to get help—it might brace up my will power[f]—but everyone[g] who would dare to come at all would call me crazy unless there happened to be some proof. Couldn't ask people to come for no reason at all—am all out of touch with everybody and have been for years.

But I haven't told you the worst, Wilmarth. Brace up to read this, for

---

[a] Yrs—AKELEY] Yrs—AKELEY. C; Yrs—Akeley D
[b] it] *om.* D
[c] Wednesday.] Wednesday B; *Wednesday* D
[d] Yr] Your D
[e] will power] will-power C
[f] will power] will-/power C
[g] everyone] every one C

COLLECTED FICTION: 1926–1930

it will give you a shock. I am telling the truth, though. It is this—*I have seen and touched one of the things, or part of one of the things.* God, man, but it's awful! It was dead, of course. One of the dogs had it, and I found it near the kennel this morning. I tried to save it in the woodshed to convince people of the whole thing, but it all evaporated in a few hours. Nothing left. You know, all those things in the rivers were seen only on the first morning after the flood. And here's the worst. I tried to photograph it for you, but when I developed the film *there wasn't anything visible except the woodshed.* What can the thing have been made of? I saw it and felt it, and they all leave footprints. It was surely made of matter—but what kind of matter? The shape can't be described. It was a great crab with a lot of pyramided fleshy rings or knots[a] of thick, ropy stuff covered with feelers where a man's head would be. That green sticky stuff is its blood or juice. And there are more of them due on earth any minute.

Walter Brown is missing—hasn't been seen loafing around any of his usual corners in the villages hereabouts. I must have got him with one of my shots, though the creatures always seem to try to take their dead and wounded away.

Got into town this afternoon without any trouble, but am afraid they're beginning to hold off because they're sure of me. Am writing this in Brattleboro P.O.[b] This may be goodbye—if it is, write my son George Goodenough Akeley, 176 Pleasant St., San Diego, Cal., *but don't come up here.* Write the boy if you don't hear from me in a week, and watch the papers for news.

I'm going to play my last two cards now—if I have the will power left. First to try poison gas on the things (I've got the right chemicals and have fixed up masks for myself and the dogs) and then if that doesn't work, tell the sheriff. They can lock me in a madhouse if they want to—it'll be better than what the *other creatures* would do. Perhaps I can get them to pay attention to the prints around the house—they are faint, but I can find them every morning. Suppose, though, police would say I faked them somehow; for they all think I'm a queer character.

Must try to have a state policeman spend a night here and see for himself—though it would be just like the creatures to learn about it and hold off that night. They cut my wires whenever I try to telephone in the night—the linemen think it is very queer, and may testify for me if they don't go and imagine I cut them myself. I haven't tried to keep them repaired for over a week now.

---

[a] knots] knot C
[b] P.O.] P. O. C, D

I could get some of the ignorant people to testify for me about the reality of the horrors, but everybody laughs at what they say, and anyway, they have shunned my place for so long that they don't know any of the new events. You couldn't get one of those run-down farmers to come within a mile of my house for love or money. The mail-carrier hears what they say and jokes me about it—God! If I only dared tell him how real it is! I think I'll try to get him to notice the prints, but he comes in the afternoon and they're usually about gone by that time. If I kept one by setting a box or pan over it, he'd think surely it was a fake or joke.

Wish I hadn't gotten to be such a hermit, so folks don't drop around as they used to. I've never dared shew[a] the black stone or the kodak pictures, or play that record, to anybody but the ignorant people. The others would say I faked the whole business and do nothing but laugh. But I may yet try shewing[b] the pictures. They give those claw-prints clearly, even if the things that made them can't be photographed. What a shame nobody else saw that *thing* this morning before it went to nothing!

But I don't know as I care. After what I've been through, a madhouse is as good a place as any. The doctors can help me make up my mind to get away from this house, and that is all that will save me.

Write my son George if you don't hear soon. Goodbye,[c] smash that record, and don't mix up in this.

Yrs—AKELEY[d]

The letter frankly plunged me into the blackest of terror. I did not know what to say in answer, but scratched off some incoherent words of advice and encouragement and sent them by registered mail. I recall urging Akeley to move to Brattleboro at once, and place himself under the protection of the authorities; adding that I would come to that town with the phonograph record and help convince the courts of his sanity. It was time, too, I think I wrote, to alarm the people generally against this thing in their midst. It will be observed that at this moment of stress my own belief in all Akeley had told and claimed was virtually complete, though I did think his failure to get a picture of the dead monster was due not to any freak of Nature but to some excited slip of his own.

---

[a] shew] show B, C, D

[b] shewing] showing B, C, D

[c] Goodbye,] Good bye, B; Good-bye, C

[d] Yrs—AKELEY] Yrs—AKELEY. C; Yrs—Akeley D

V.

Then, apparently crossing my incoherent note and reaching me Saturday afternoon, September 8th, came that curiously different and calming letter neatly typed on a new machine; that strange letter of reassurance and invitation which must have marked so prodigious a transition in the whole nightmare drama of the lonely hills. Again I will quote from memory—seeking for special reasons to preserve as much of the flavour[a] of the style as I can. It was postmarked Bellows Falls, and the signature as well as the body of the letter was typed—as is frequent with beginners in typing. The text, though, was marvellously[b] accurate for a tyro's work; and I concluded that Akeley must have used a machine at some previous period—perhaps in college. To say that the letter relieved me would be only fair, yet beneath my relief lay a substratum of uneasiness. If Akeley had been sane in his terror, was he now sane in his deliverance? And the sort of "improved rapport" mentioned . . . what was it? The entire thing implied such a diametrical reversal of Akeley's previous attitude! But here is the substance of the text, carefully transcribed from a memory in which I take some pride.

Townshend, Vermont,
Thursday, Sept. 6, 1928.

My dear Wilmarth:—

It gives me great pleasure to be able to set you at rest regarding all the silly things I've been writing you. I say "silly",[c] although by that I mean my frightened attitude rather than my descriptions of certain phenomena. Those phenomena are real and important enough; my mistake had been in establishing an anomalous attitude toward them.

I think I mentioned that my strange visitors were beginning to communicate with me, and to attempt such communication. Last night this exchange of speech became actual. In response to certain signals I admitted to the house a messenger from those outside—a fellow-human, let me hasten to say. He told me much that neither you nor I had even begun to guess, and shewed[d] clearly how totally we had misjudged and misinterpreted the purpose of the Outer Ones in maintaining their secret colony on this planet.

---

[a] flavour] flavor C
[b] marvellously] marvelously C
[c] "silly",] "silly," D
[d] shewed] showed A, B, C, D

It seems that the evil legends about what they have offered to men, and what they wish in connexion[a] with the earth, are wholly the result of an ignorant misconception of allegorical speech—speech, of course, moulded[b] by cultural backgrounds and thought-habits vastly different from anything we dream of. My own conjectures, I freely own, shot as widely past the mark as any of the guesses of illiterate farmers and savage Indians. What I had thought morbid and shameful and ignominious is in reality awesome and mind-expanding and even *glorious*—my previous estimate being merely a phase of man's eternal tendency to hate and fear and shrink from the *utterly different*.

Now I regret the harm I have inflicted upon these alien and incredible beings in the course of our nightly skirmishes. If only I had consented to talk peacefully and reasonably with them in the first place! But they bear me no grudge, their emotions[c] being organised[d] very differently from ours. It is their misfortune to have had as their human agents in Vermont some very inferior specimens—the late Walter Brown, for example. He prejudiced me vastly against them. Actually, they have never knowingly harmed men, but have often been cruelly wronged and spied upon by our species. There is a whole secret cult of evil men (a man of your mystical erudition will understand me when I link them with Hastur and the Yellow Sign) devoted to the purpose of tracking them down and injuring them on behalf of monstrous powers from other dimensions. It is against these aggressors— not against normal humanity—that the drastic precautions of the Outer Ones are directed. Incidentally,[e] I learned that many of our lost letters were stolen not by the Outer Ones but by the emissaries of this malign cult.

All that the Outer Ones wish of man is peace and non-molestation and an increasing intellectual rapport. This latter is absolutely necessary now that our inventions and devices are expanding our knowledge and motions, and making it more and more impossible for the Outer Ones' necessary outposts to exist *secretly* on this planet. The alien beings desire to know mankind more fully, and to have a few of mankind's philosophic and scientific leaders know more about them. With such an exchange of knowledge all perils will pass, and a satisfactory *modus vivendi* be established. The very idea of any attempt to *enslave* or *degrade* mankind is ridiculous.

As a beginning of this improved rapport, the Outer Ones have

[a] connexion] connection C, D
[b] moulded] molded C
[c] emotions] motions D
[d] organised] organized C
[e] Incidentally,] Incidently, D

naturally chosen me—whose knowledge of them is already so considerable—as their primary interpreter on earth. Much was told me last night—facts of the most stupendous and vista-opening nature—and more will be subsequently communicated to me both orally and in writing. I shall not be called upon to make any trip *outside* just yet, though I shall probably *wish* to do so later on—employing special means and transcending everything which we have hitherto been accustomed to regard as human experience. My house will be besieged no longer. Everything has reverted to normal, and the dogs will have no further occupation. In place of terror I have been given a rich boon of knowledge and intellectual adventure which few other mortals have ever shared.

The Outer Beings are perhaps the most marvellous[a] organic things in or beyond all space and time—members of a cosmos-wide race of which all other life-forms are merely degenerate variants. They are more vegetable than animal, if these terms can be applied to the sort of matter composing them, and have a somewhat fungoid structure; though the presence of a chlorophyll-like substance and a very singular nutritive system differentiate them altogether from true cormophytic fungi. Indeed, the type is composed of a form of matter totally alien to our part of space—with electrons having a wholly different vibration-rate. That is why the beings cannot be photographed on the *ordinary* camera films and plates of our known universe, even though our eyes can see them. With proper knowledge, however, any good chemist could make a photographic emulsion which would record their images.

The genus is unique in its ability to traverse the heatless and airless interstellar void in full corporeal form, and some of its variants cannot do this without mechanical aid or curious surgical transpositions. Only a few species have the ether-resisting wings characteristic of the Vermont variety. Those inhabiting certain remote peaks in the Old World were brought in other ways. Their external resemblance to animal life, and to the sort of structure we understand as material, is a matter of parallel evolution rather than of close kinship. Their brain-capacity exceeds that of any other surviving life-form, although the winged types of our hill country are by no means the most highly developed. Telepathy is their usual means of discourse, though they[b] have rudimentary vocal organs which, after a slight operation (for surgery is an incredibly expert and every-day thing among them),[c] can roughly duplicate the speech of such types of organism as still use speech.

[a] marvellous] marvelous C
[b] they] we D
[c] operation (. . .),] operation, (. . .) A, B

Their main *immediate* abode is a still undiscovered and almost lightless planet at the very edge of our solar system—beyond Neptune, and the ninth in distance from the sun. It is, as we have inferred, the object mystically hinted at as "Yuggoth" in certain ancient and forbidden writings; and it will soon be the scene of a strange focussing of thought upon our world in an effort to facilitate mental rapport. I would not be surprised[a] if astronomers became[b] sufficiently sensitive to these thought-currents to discover Yuggoth when the Outer Ones wish them to do so. But Yuggoth, of course, is only the stepping-stone. The main body of the beings inhabits strangely organised[c] abysses wholly beyond the utmost reach of any human imagination. The space-time globule which we recognise[d] as the totality of all cosmic entity is only an atom in the genuine infinity which is theirs. *And as much of this infinity as any human brain can hold is eventually to be opened up to me, as it has been to not more than fifty other men since the human race has existed.*

You will probably call this raving at first, Wilmarth, but in time you will appreciate the titanic opportunity I have stumbled upon. I want you to share as much of it as is possible, and to that end must tell you thousands of things that won't go on paper. In the past I have warned you not to come to see me. Now that all is safe, I take pleasure in rescinding that warning and inviting you.

Can't you make a trip up here before your college term opens? It would be marvellously[e] delightful if you could. Bring along the phonograph record and all my letters to you as consultative data—we shall need them in piecing together the whole tremendous story. You might bring the kodak prints, too, since I seem to have mislaid the negatives and my own prints in all this recent excitement. But what a wealth of facts I have to add to all this groping and tentative material— *and what a stupendous device I have to supplement my additions!*

Don't hesitate—I am free from espionage now, and you will not meet anything unnatural or disturbing. Just come along and let my car meet you at the Brattleboro station—prepare to stay as long as you can, and expect many an evening of discussion of things beyond all human conjecture. Don't tell anyone about it, of course—for this matter must not get to the promiscuous public.

---

[a] surprised] surprized C
[b] became] become D
[c] organised] organized C, D
[d] recognise] recognize C, D
[e] marvellously] marvelously C, D

The train service to Brattleboro is not bad—you can get a time-table in Boston. Take the B. & M. to Greenfield, and then change for the brief remainder of the way. I suggest your taking the convenient 4:10 p.m.[a]—standard—from Boston. This gets into Greenfield at 7:35, and at 9:19 a train leaves there which reaches Brattleboro at 10:01. That is week-days. Let me know the date and I'll have my car on hand at the station.

Pardon this typed letter, but my handwriting has grown shaky of late, as you know, and I don't feel equal to long stretches of script. I got this new Corona in Brattleboro yesterday—it seems to work very well.

Awaiting word, and hoping to see you shortly with the phonograph record and all my letters—and the kodak prints—

I[b] am

Yours in anticipation,

HENRY W. AKELEY.[c]

To Albert N. Wilmarth, Esq.,
Miskatonic University,
Arkham, Mass.[d]

  The complexity of my emotions upon reading, re-reading, and pondering over this strange and unlooked-for letter is past adequate description. I have said that I was at once relieved and made uneasy, but this expresses only crudely the overtones of diverse and largely subconscious feelings which comprised both the relief and the uneasiness. To begin with, the thing was so antipodally at variance with the whole chain of horrors preceding it—the change of mood from stark terror to cool complacency and even exultation was so unheralded, lightning-like, and complete! I could scarcely believe that a single day could so alter the psychological perspective of one who had written that final frenzied bulletin of Wednesday, no matter what relieving disclosures that day might have brought. At certain moments a sense of conflicting unrealities made me wonder whether this whole distantly reported drama of fantastic forces were not a kind of half-illusory dream created largely within my own mind. Then I thought of the phonograph record and gave way to still greater bewilderment.

---

[a] p.m.] p. m. C, D
[b] prints— / I] prints—I C
[c] HENRY W. AKELEY.] HENRY W. AKELEY. C; Henry W. Akeley D
[d] To . . . Mass.] TO . . . MASS. D

The letter seemed so unlike anything which could have been expected! As I analysed[a] my impression, I saw that it consisted of two distinct phases. First, granting that Akeley had been sane before and was still sane, the indicated change in the situation itself was so swift and unthinkable. And secondly, the change in Akeley's own manner, attitude, and language was so vastly beyond the normal or the predictable. The man's whole personality seemed to have undergone an insidious mutation—a mutation so deep that one could scarcely reconcile his two aspects with the supposition that both represented equal sanity. Word-choice, spelling—all were subtly different. And with my academic sensitiveness to prose style, I could trace profound divergences in his commonest reactions and rhythm-responses. Certainly, the emotional cataclysm or revelation which could produce so radical an overturn must be an extreme one indeed! Yet in another way the letter seemed quite characteristic of Akeley. The same old passion for infinity—the same old scholarly inquisitiveness. I could not for a moment—or more than a moment—credit the idea of spuriousness or malign substitution. Did not the invitation—the willingness to have me test the truth of the letter in person—prove its genuineness?

I did not retire Saturday night, but sat up thinking of the shadows and marvels behind the letter I had received. My mind, aching from the quick succession of monstrous conceptions it had been forced to confront during the last four months, worked upon this startling new material in a cycle of doubt and acceptance which repeated most of the steps experienced in facing the earlier wonders; till long before dawn a burning interest and curiosity had begun to replace the original storm of perplexity and uneasiness. Mad or sane, metamorphosed or merely relieved, the chances were that Akeley had actually encountered some stupendous change of perspective in his hazardous research; some change at once diminishing his danger—real or fancied—and opening dizzy new vistas of cosmic and superhuman knowledge. My own zeal for the unknown flared up to meet his, and I felt myself touched by the contagion of the morbid barrier-breaking. To shake off the maddening and wearying limitations of time and space and natural law—to be linked with the vast *outside*—to come close to the nighted and abysmal

[a] analysed] analyzed C

secrets of the infinite and the ultimate—surely such a thing was worth the risk of one's life, soul, and sanity! And Akeley had said there was no longer any peril—he had invited me to visit him instead of warning me away as before. I tingled at the thought of what he might now have to tell me—there was an almost paralysing[a] fascination in the thought of sitting in that lonely and lately beleaguered[b] farmhouse with a man who had talked with actual emissaries from outer space; sitting there with the terrible record and the pile of letters in which Akeley had summarised[c] his earlier conclusions.

So late Sunday morning I telegraphed Akeley that I would meet him in Brattleboro on the following Wednesday—September 12th—if that date were convenient for him. In only one respect did I depart from his suggestions, and that concerned the choice of a train. Frankly, I did not feel like arriving in that haunted Vermont region late at night; so instead of accepting the train he chose I telephoned the station and devised another arrangement. By rising early and taking the 8:07 a.m.[d] (standard) into Boston, I could catch the 9:25 for Greenfield; arriving there at 12:22 noon. This connected exactly with a train reaching Brattleboro at 1:08 p.m.[e]—a much more comfortable hour than 10:01 for meeting Akeley and riding with him into the close-packed, secret-guarding hills.

I mentioned this choice in my telegram, and was glad to learn in the reply which came toward evening that it had met with my prospective host's endorsement. His wire ran thus:

ARRANGEMENT[f] SATISFACTORY.[g] WILL MEET 1:08[h] TRAIN WEDNESDAY.[i] DON'T[j] FORGET RECORD AND LETTERS AND

---

[a] paralysing] paralyzing C
[b] lately beleaguered] lately-beleaguered A, B, C, D
[c] summarised] summarized C
[d] a.m.] a. m. C
[e] p.m.] p. m. C
[f] ARRANGEMENT] ¶ ARRANGEMENT C
[g] SATISFACTORY.] SATISFACTORY D
[h] 1:08] ONE EIGHT D
[i] WEDNESDAY.] WEDNESDAY D
[j] DON'T] DONT D

PRINTS.[a] KEEP DESTINATION QUIET.[b] EXPECT GREAT REVELATIONS.[c]

AKELEY.[d]

Receipt of this message in direct response to one sent to Akeley—and necessarily delivered to his house from the Townshend station either by official messenger or by a restored telephone service—removed any lingering subconscious doubts I may have had about the authorship of the perplexing letter. My relief was marked—indeed, it was greater than I could account for at that time; since all such doubts had been rather deeply buried. But I slept soundly and long that night, and was eagerly busy with preparations during the ensuing two days.

VI.

On Wednesday I started as agreed, taking with me a valise full of simple necessities and scientific data, including the hideous phonograph record, the kodak[e] prints, and the entire file of Akeley's correspondence. As requested, I had told no one where I was going; for I could see that the matter demanded utmost privacy, even allowing for its most favourable[f] turns. The thought of actual mental contact with alien, outside entities was stupefying enough to my trained and somewhat prepared mind; and this being so, what might one think of its effect on the vast masses of uninformed laymen? I do not know whether dread or adventurous expectancy was uppermost in me as I changed trains in Boston and began the long westward run out of familiar regions into those I knew less thoroughly. Waltham—Concord—Ayer—Fitchburg—Gardner—Athol—

My train reached Greenfield seven minutes late, but the northbound connecting express had been held. Transferring in haste, I felt a curious breathlessness as the cars rumbled on through the early afternoon

[a] PRINTS.] PRINTS D
[b] QUIET.] QUIET D
[c] REVELATIONS.] REVELATIONS D
[d] ARRANGEMENT . . . AKELEY.] ARRANGEMENT . . . AKELEY D
[e] kodak] Kodak D
[f] favourable] favorable C

sunlight into territories I had always read of but had never before visited. I knew I was entering an altogether older-fashioned and more primitive New England than the mechanised, urbanised[a] coastal and southern areas where all my life had been spent; an unspoiled, ancestral New England without the foreigners and factory-smoke, billboards[b] and concrete roads, of the sections which modernity has touched. There would be odd survivals of that continuous native life whose deep roots make it the one authentic outgrowth of the landscape—the continuous native life which keeps alive strange ancient memories, and fertilises[c] the soil for shadowy, marvellous,[d] and seldom-mentioned beliefs.

Now and then I saw the blue Connecticut River gleaming in the sun, and after leaving Northfield we crossed it. Ahead loomed green and cryptical hills, and when the conductor came around I learned that I was at last in Vermont. He told me to set my watch back an hour, since the northern hill country will have no dealings with new-fangled daylight time schemes. As I did so it seemed to me that I was likewise turning the calendar back a century.

The train kept close to the river, and across in New Hampshire I could see the approaching slope of steep Wantastiquet, about which singular old legends cluster. Then streets appeared on my left, and a green island shewed[e] in the stream on my right. People rose and filed to the door, and I followed them. The car stopped, and I alighted beneath the long train-shed[f] of the Brattleboro station.

Looking over the line of waiting motors I hesitated a moment to see which one might turn out to be the Akeley Ford, but my identity was divined before I could take the initiative. And yet it was clearly not Akeley himself who advanced to meet me with an outstretched hand and a mellowly phrased query as to whether I was indeed Mr. Albert N. Wilmarth of Arkham. This man bore no resemblance to the bearded, grizzled Akeley of the snapshot; but was a younger and more urban[g]

---

[a] mechanised, urbanised] mechanized, urbanized C
[b] billboards] bill-boards D
[c] fertilises] fertilizes C
[d] marvellous,] marvelous, C
[e] shewed] appeared A; showed B, C, D
[f] train-shed] train-/shed B; trainshed D
[g] urban] urbane D

person, fashionably dressed, and wearing only a small, dark moustache. His cultivated voice held an odd and almost disturbing hint of vague familiarity, though I could not definitely place it in my memory.

As I surveyed him I heard him explaining that he was a friend of my prospective host's who had come down from Townshend in his stead. Akeley, he declared, had suffered a sudden attack of some asthmatic trouble, and did not feel equal to making a trip in the outdoor air. It was not serious, however, and there was to be no change in plans regarding my visit. I could not make out just how much this Mr. Noyes—as he announced himself—knew of Akeley's researches and discoveries, though it seemed to me that his casual manner stamped him as a comparative outsider. Remembering what a hermit Akeley had been, I was a trifle surprised[a] at the ready availability of such a friend; but did not let my puzzlement deter me from entering the motor to which he gestured me. It was not the small ancient car I had expected from Akeley's descriptions, but a large and immaculate specimen of recent pattern—apparently Noyes's own, and bearing Massachusetts licence[b] plates with the amusing "sacred codfish" device of that year. My guide, I concluded, must be a summer transient in the Townshend region.

Noyes climbed into the car beside me and started it at once. I was glad that he did not overflow with conversation, for some peculiar atmospheric tensity made me feel disinclined to talk. The town seemed very attractive in the afternoon sunlight as we swept up an incline and turned to the right into the main street. It drowsed like the older New England cities which one remembers from boyhood, and something in the collocation of roofs and steeples and chimneys and brick walls formed contours touching deep viol-strings of ancestral emotion. I could tell that I was at the gateway of a region half-bewitched through the piling-up of unbroken time-accumulations; a region where old, strange things have had a chance to grow and linger because they have never been stirred up.

As we passed out of Brattleboro my sense of constraint and foreboding increased, for a vague quality in the hill-crowded countryside with its towering, threatening, close-pressing green and granite slopes

[a] surprised] surprized C
[b] licence] license B, C, D

hinted at obscure secrets and immemorial survivals which might or might not be hostile to mankind. For a time our course followed a broad, shallow river which flowed down from unknown hills in the north, and I shivered when my companion told me it was the West River. It was in this stream, I recalled from newspaper items,[a] that one of the morbid crab-like[b] beings had been seen floating after the floods.

Gradually the country around us grew wilder and more deserted. Archaic covered bridges lingered fearsomely out of the past in pockets of the hills, and the half-abandoned railway track paralleling[c] the river seemed to exhale a nebulously visible air of desolation. There were awesome sweeps of vivid valley where great cliffs rose, New England's virgin granite shewing[d] grey[e] and austere through the verdure that scaled the crests. There were gorges where untamed streams leaped, bearing down toward the river the unimagined secrets of a thousand pathless peaks. Branching away now and then were narrow, half-concealed roads that bored their way through solid, luxuriant masses of forest among whose primal trees whole armies of elemental spirits might well lurk. As I saw these I thought of how Akeley had been molested by unseen agencies on his drives along this very route, and did not wonder that such things could be.

The quaint, sightly village of Newfane, reached in less than an hour, was our last link with that world which man can definitely call his own by virtue of conquest and complete occupancy. After that we cast off all allegiance to immediate, tangible, and time-touched things, and entered a fantastic world of hushed unreality in which the narrow, ribbon-like road rose and fell and curved with an almost sentient and purposeful caprice amidst the tenantless green peaks and half-deserted valleys. Except for the sound of the motor, and the faint stir of the few lonely farms we passed at infrequent intervals, the only thing that reached my ears was the gurgling, insidious trickle of strange waters from numberless hidden fountains in the shadowy woods.

[a] items,] items D
[b] crab-like] crablike A, B, D
[c] paralleling] parallelling A, B
[d] shewing] showing B, C, D
[e] grey] gray C

The nearness and intimacy of the dwarfed, domed hills now became veritably breath-taking. Their steepness and abruptness were even greater than I had imagined from hearsay, and suggested nothing in common with the prosaic objective world we know. The dense, unvisited woods on those inaccessible slopes seemed to harbour[a] alien and incredible things, and I felt that the very outline of the hills themselves held some strange and aeon-forgotten[b] meaning, as if they were vast hieroglyphs left by a rumoured[c] titan race whose glories live only in rare, deep dreams. All the legends of the past, and all the stupefying imputations of Henry Akeley's letters and exhibits, welled up in my memory to heighten the atmosphere of tension and growing menace. The purpose of my visit, and the frightful abnormalities it postulated,[d] struck at me all at once with a chill sensation that nearly overbalanced[e] my ardour[f] for strange delvings.

My guide must have noticed my disturbed attitude; for as the road grew wilder and more irregular, and our motion slower and more jolting, his occasional pleasant comments expanded into a steadier flow of discourse. He spoke of the beauty and weirdness of the country, and revealed some acquaintance with the folklore studies of my prospective host. From his polite questions it was obvious that he knew I had come for a scientific purpose, and that I was bringing data of some importance; but he gave no sign of appreciating the depth and awfulness of the knowledge which Akeley had finally reached.

His manner was so cheerful, normal, and urbane that his remarks ought to have calmed and reassured me; but oddly enough, I felt only the more disturbed as we bumped and veered onward into the unknown wilderness of hills and woods. At times it seemed as if he were pumping me to see what I knew of the monstrous secrets of the place, and with every fresh utterance that vague, teasing, baffling *familiarity* in his voice increased. It was not an ordinary or healthy familiarity despite the thoroughly wholesome and cultivated nature of the voice. I somehow

[a] harbour] harbor C
[b] aeon-forgotten] eon-forgotten C
[c] rumoured] rumored C
[d] postulated,] postulated D
[e] overbalanced] over-balanced D
[f] ardour] ardor C

linked it with forgotten nightmares, and felt that I might go mad if I recognised[a] it. If any good excuse had existed, I think I would have turned back from my visit. As it was, I could not well do so—and it occurred to me that a cool, scientific conversation with Akeley himself after my arrival would help greatly to pull me together.

Besides, there was a strangely calming element of cosmic beauty in the hypnotic landscape through which we climbed and plunged fantastically. Time had lost itself in the labyrinths behind, and around us stretched only the flowering waves of faery and the recaptured loveliness of vanished centuries—the hoary groves, the untainted pastures edged with gay autumnal blossoms, and at vast intervals the small brown farmsteads nestling amidst huge trees beneath vertical precipices of fragrant brier and meadow-grass. Even the sunlight assumed a supernal glamour,[b] as if some special atmosphere or exhalation mantled the whole region. I had seen nothing like it before save in the magic vistas that sometimes form the backgrounds of Italian primitives. Sodoma and Leonardo conceived such expanses, but only in the distance, and through the vaultings of Renaissance arcades. We were now burrowing bodily through the midst of the picture, and I seemed to find in its necromancy a thing I had innately known or inherited,[c] and for which I had always been vainly searching.

Suddenly, after rounding an obtuse angle at the top of a sharp ascent, the car came to a standstill. On my left, across a well-kept lawn which stretched to the road and flaunted a border of whitewashed stones, rose a white, two-and-a-half-story house of unusual size and elegance for the region, with a congeries of contiguous or arcade-linked barns, sheds, and windmill behind and to the right. I recognised[d] it at once from the snapshot[e] I had received, and was not surprised[f] to see the name of Henry Akeley on the galvanised-iron[g] mail-box[h] near the road. For some

[a] recognised] recognized C
[b] glamour,] glamor, C
[c] inherited,] inherited B, C, D
[d] recognised] recognized C
[e] snapshot] snap-shot A, D; snap-/shot B
[f] surprised] surprized C
[g] galvanised-iron] galvanized-iron C
[h] mail-box] mailbox D

distance back of the house a level stretch of marshy and sparsely wooded[a] land extended, beyond which soared a steep, thickly forested[b] hillside ending in a jagged leafy crest. This latter, I knew, was the summit of Dark Mountain, half way[c] up which we must have climbed already.

Alighting from the car and taking my valise, Noyes asked me to wait while he went in and notified Akeley of my advent. He himself, he added, had important business elsewhere, and could not stop for more than a moment. As he briskly walked up the path to the house I climbed out of the car myself, wishing to stretch my legs a little before settling down to a sedentary conversation. My feeling of nervousness and tension had risen to a maximum again now that I was on the actual scene of the morbid beleaguering described so hauntingly in Akeley's letters, and I honestly dreaded the coming discussions which were to link me with such alien and forbidden worlds.

Close contact with the utterly bizarre is often more terrifying than inspiring, and it did not cheer me to think that this very bit of dusty road was the place where those monstrous tracks and that foetid[d] green ichor had been found after moonless nights of fear and death. Idly I noticed that none of Akeley's dogs seemed to be about. Had he sold them all as soon as the Outer Ones made[e] peace with him? Try as I might, I could not have the same confidence in the depth and sincerity of that peace which appeared in Akeley's final and queerly different letter. After all, he was a man of much simplicity and with little worldly experience. Was there not, perhaps, some deep and sinister undercurrent beneath the surface of the new alliance?

Led by my thoughts, my eyes turned downward to the powdery road surface which had held such hideous testimonies. The last few days had been dry, and tracks of all sorts cluttered the rutted, irregular highway despite the unfrequented nature of the district. With a vague curiosity I began to trace the outline of some of the heterogeneous impressions, trying meanwhile to curb the flights of macabre fancy

[a] sparsely wooded] sparsely-wooded B, C, D
[b] thickly forested] thickly-forested B, C, D
[c] half way] half-way C
[d] foetid] fetid C
[e] made] had made C

which the place and its memories suggested. There was something menacing and uncomfortable in the funereal stillness, in the muffled, subtle trickle of distant brooks, and in the crowding green peaks and black-wooded precipices that choked the narrow horizon.

And then an image shot into my consciousness which made those vague menaces and flights of fancy seem mild and insignificant indeed. I have said that I was scanning the miscellaneous prints in the road with a kind of idle curiosity—but all at once that curiosity was shockingly snuffed out by a sudden and paralysing[a] gust of active terror. For though the dust tracks were in general confused and overlapping, and unlikely to arrest any casual gaze, my restless vision had caught certain details near the spot where the path to the house joined the highway; and had recognised[b] beyond doubt or hope the frightful significance of those details. It was not for nothing, alas, that I had pored for hours over the kodak views of the Outer Ones' claw-prints which Akeley had sent. Too well did I know the marks of those loathsome nippers, and that hint of ambiguous direction which stamped the horrors as no creatures of this planet. No chance had been left me for merciful mistake. Here, indeed, in objective form before my own eyes, and surely made not many hours ago, were at least three marks which stood out blasphemously among the surprising[c] plethora of blurred footprints leading to and from the Akeley farmhouse. *They were the hellish tracks of the living fungi from Yuggoth.*

I pulled myself together in time to stifle a scream. After all, what more was there than I might have expected, assuming that I had really believed Akeley's letters? He had spoken of making peace with the things. Why, then, was it strange that some of them had visited his house? But the terror was stronger than the reassurance. Could any man be expected to look unmoved for the first time upon the claw-marks of animate beings from outer depths of space? Just then I saw Noyes emerge from the door and approach with a brisk step. I must, I reflected, keep command of myself, for the chances were that this genial friend knew nothing of Akeley's profoundest and most stupendous probings into the forbidden.

[a] paralysing] paralyzing C
[b] recognised] recognized C
[c] surprising] surprizing C

Akeley, Noyes hastened to inform me, was glad and ready to see me; although his sudden attack of asthma would prevent him from being a very competent host for a day or two. These spells hit him hard when they came, and were always accompanied by a debilitating fever and general weakness. He never was good for much while they lasted—had to talk in a whisper, and was very clumsy and feeble in getting about. His feet and ankles swelled, too, so that he had to bandage them like a gouty old beef-eater. Today he was in rather bad shape, so that I would have to attend very largely to my own needs; but he was none the less eager for conversation. I would find him in the study at the left of the front hall—the room where the blinds were shut. He had to keep the sunlight out when he was ill, for his eyes were very sensitive.

As Noyes bade me adieu and rode off northward in his car I began to walk slowly toward the house. The door had been left ajar for me; but before approaching and entering I cast a searching glance around the whole place, trying to decide what had struck me as so intangibly queer about it. The barns and sheds looked trimly prosaic enough, and I noticed Akeley's battered Ford in its capacious, unguarded shelter. Then the secret of the queerness reached me. It was the total silence. Ordinarily a farm is at least moderately murmurous from its various kinds of livestock, but here all signs of life were missing. What of the hens and the hogs? The cows, of which Akeley had said he possessed several, might conceivably be out to pasture, and the dogs might possibly have been sold; but the absence of any trace of cackling or grunting was truly singular.

I did not pause long on the path, but resolutely entered the open house door and closed it behind me. It had cost me a distinct psychological effort to do so, and now that I was shut inside I had a momentary longing for precipitate retreat. Not that the place was in the least sinister in visual suggestion; on the contrary, I thought the graceful late-colonial hallway very tasteful and wholesome, and admired the evident breeding of the man who had furnished it. What made me wish to flee was something very attenuated and indefinable. Perhaps it was a certain odd odour[a] which I thought I noticed—though I well knew how common musty odours[b] are in even the best of ancient farmhouses.

VII.

Refusing to let these cloudy qualms overmaster me, I recalled Noyes's instructions and pushed open the six-panelled,[c] brass-latched white door on my left. The room beyond was darkened, as I had known before; and as I entered it I noticed that the queer odour[d] was stronger there. There likewise appeared to be some faint,[e] half-imaginary rhythm or vibration in the air. For a moment the closed blinds allowed me to see very little, but then a kind of apologetic hacking or whispering sound drew my attention to a great easy-chair[f] in the farther, darker corner of the room. Within its shadowy depths I saw the white blur of a man's face and hands; and in a moment I had crossed to greet the figure who had tried to speak. Dim though the light was, I perceived that this was indeed my host. I had studied the kodak picture repeatedly, and there could be no mistake about this firm, weather-beaten face with the cropped, grizzled beard.

But as I looked again my recognition was mixed with sadness and anxiety; for certainly, this[g] face was that of a very sick man. I felt that there must be something more than asthma behind that strained, rigid, immobile expression and unwinking glassy stare; and realised[h] how terribly the strain of his frightful experiences must have told on him. Was it not enough to break any human being—even a younger man than this intrepid delver into the forbidden? The strange and sudden relief, I feared, had come too late to save him from something like a general breakdown. There was a touch of the pitiful in the limp, lifeless way his lean hands rested in his lap. He had on a loose dressing-gown,

[a] odour] odor C
[b] odours] odors C
[c] six-panelled,] six-paneled, C
[d] odour] odor C
[e] faint,] very faint, C
[f] easy-chair] easy-cair C
[g] this] his D
[h] realised] realized C

and was swathed around the head and high around the neck with a vivid yellow scarf or hood.

And then I saw that he was trying to talk in the same hacking whisper with which he had greeted me. It was a hard whisper to catch at first, since the grey moustache[a] concealed all movements of the lips, and something in its timbre disturbed me greatly; but by concentrating my attention I could soon make out its purport surprisingly[b] well. The accent was by no means a rustic one, and the language was even more polished than correspondence had led me to expect.

"Mr. Wilmarth, I presume? You must pardon my not rising.[c] I am quite ill, as Mr. Noyes must have told you; but I could not resist having you come just the same. You know what I wrote in my last letter—there is so much to tell you tomorrow when I shall feel better. I can't say how glad I am to see you in person after all our many letters. You have the file with you, of course? And the kodak prints and record?[d] Noyes put your valise in the hall—I suppose[e] you saw it. For tonight I fear you'll have to wait on yourself to a great extent. Your room is upstairs—the one over this—and you'll see the bathroom door open at the head of the staircase. There's a meal spread for you in the dining-room—right through this door at your right—which you can take whenever you feel like it. I'll be a better host tomorrow—but just now weakness leaves me helpless.

"Make yourself at home—you might take out the letters and pictures and record[f] and put them on the table here before you go upstairs with your bag. It is here that we shall discuss them—you can see my phonograph on that corner stand.

"No, thanks—there's nothing you can do for me. I know these spells of old. Just come back for a little quiet visiting before night, and then go to bed when you please. I'll rest right here—perhaps sleep here all night as I often do. In the morning I'll be far better able to go into the things

[a] grey moustache] gray mustache C
[b] surprisingly] surprizingly C
[c] rising.] rising, C
[d] record?] records? A, B, C, D
[e] suppose] supose C
[f] record] records C, D

we must go into. You realise,[a] of course, the utterly stupendous nature of the matter before us. To us, as to only a few men on this earth, there will be opened up gulfs of time and space and knowledge beyond anything within the conception of human science and philosophy.

"Do you know that Einstein is wrong, and that certain objects and forces *can* move with a velocity greater than that of light? With proper aid I expect to go backward and forward in time, and actually *see* and *feel* the earth of remote past and future epochs. You can't imagine the degree to which those beings have carried science. There is nothing they can't do with the mind and body of living organisms. I expect to visit other planets, and even other stars and galaxies. The first trip will be to Yuggoth, the nearest world fully peopled by the beings. It is a strange dark orb at the very rim of our solar system—unknown to earthly astronomers as yet. But I must have written you about this. At the proper time, you know, the beings there will direct thought-currents toward us and cause it to be discovered—or perhaps let one of their human allies give the scientists a hint.

"There are mighty cities on Yuggoth—great tiers of terraced towers built of black stone like the specimen I tried to send you. That came from Yuggoth. The sun shines there no brighter than a star, but the beings need no light. They have other,[b] subtler senses, and put no windows in their great houses and temples. Light even hurts and hampers and confuses them, for it does not exist at all in the black cosmos outside time and space where they came from originally. To visit Yuggoth would drive any weak man mad—yet I am going there. The black rivers of pitch that flow under those mysterious Cyclopean[c] bridges—things built by some elder race extinct and forgotten before the beings came to Yuggoth from the ultimate voids—ought to be enough to make any man a Dante or Poe if he can keep sane long enough to tell what he has seen.

"But remember—that dark world of fungoid gardens and windowless cities isn't really terrible. It is only to us that it would seem so. Probably this world seemed just as terrible to the beings when they

[a] realise,] realize, C
[b] other,] other D
[c] Cyclopean] cyclopean A, B, C, D

first explored it in the primal age. You know they were here long before the fabulous epoch of Cthulhu was over, and remember all about sunken R'lyeh when it was above the waters. They've been inside the earth, too—there are openings which human beings know nothing of—some of them in these very Vermont hills—and great worlds of unknown life down there; blue-litten K'n-yan, red-litten Yoth, and black, lightless N'kai. It's from N'kai that frightful Tsathoggua came—you know, the amorphous, toad-like god-creature mentioned in the Pnakotic Manuscripts[a] and the 'Necronomicon'[b] and the Commoriom myth-cycle preserved by the Atlantean high-priest Klarkash-Ton.

"But we will talk of all this later on. It must be four or five o'clock by this time. Better bring the stuff from your bag, take a bite, and then come back for a comfortable chat."

Very slowly I turned and began to obey my host; fetching my valise, extracting and depositing the desired articles, and finally ascending to the room designated as mine. With the memory of that roadside claw-print fresh in my mind, Akeley's whispered paragraphs had affected me queerly; and the hints of familiarity with this unknown world of fungous life—forbidden Yuggoth—made my flesh creep more than I cared to own. I was tremendously sorry about Akeley's illness, but had to confess that his hoarse whisper had a hateful as well as pitiful quality. If only he wouldn't *gloat*[c] so about Yuggoth and its black secrets!

My room proved a very pleasant and well-furnished one, devoid alike of the musty odour[d] and disturbing sense of vibration; and after leaving my valise there I descended again to greet Akeley and take the lunch he had set out for me. The dining-room was just beyond the study, and I saw that a kitchen ell extended still farther in the same direction. On the dining-table an ample array of sandwiches, cake, and cheese awaited me, and a Thermos-bottle[e] beside a cup and saucer testified that hot coffee had not been forgotten. After a well-relished meal I poured myself a liberal cup of coffee, but found that the culinary

[a] Pnakotic Manuscripts] *Pnakotic Manuscripts* D

[b] 'Necronomicon'] Necronomicon A, B, C; *Necronomicon* D

[c] *gloat*] gloat D

[d] odour] odor C

[e] Thermos-bottle] thermos-bottle C

standard had suffered a lapse in this one detail. My first spoonful revealed a faintly unpleasant acrid taste, so that I did not take more. Throughout the lunch I thought of Akeley sitting silently in the great chair in the darkened next room. Once I went in to beg him to share the repast, but he whispered that he could eat nothing as yet. Later on, just before he slept, he would take some malted milk—all he ought to have that day.

After lunch I insisted on clearing the dishes away and washing them in the kitchen sink—incidentally emptying the coffee which I had not been able to appreciate. Then returning to the darkened study I drew up a chair near my host's corner and prepared for such conversation as he might feel inclined to conduct. The letters, pictures, and record were still on the large centre-table,[a] but for the nonce we did not have to draw upon them. Before long I forgot even the bizarre odour[b] and curious suggestions of vibration.

I have said that there were things in some of Akeley's letters—especially the second and most voluminous one—which I would not dare to quote or even form into words on paper. This hesitancy applies with still greater force to the things I heard whispered that evening in the darkened room among the lonely haunted hills. Of the extent of the cosmic horrors unfolded by that raucous voice I cannot[c] even hint. He had known hideous things before, but what he had learned since making his pact with the Outside Things was almost too much for sanity to bear. Even now I absolutely refuse[d] to believe what he implied about the constitution of ultimate infinity, the juxtaposition of dimensions, and the frightful position of our known cosmos of space and time in the unending chain of linked cosmos-atoms which makes up the immediate super-cosmos of curves, angles, and material and semi-material electronic organisation.[e]

Never was a sane man more dangerously close to the arcana of basic entity—never was an organic brain nearer to utter annihilation in the chaos that transcends form and force and symmetry. I learned whence Cthulhu *first* came, and why half the great temporary stars of history had

[a] centre-table,] center-table, C
[b] odour] odor C
[c] cannot] can not C
[d] refuse] refused D
[e] organisation.] organization. C

flared forth. I guessed—from hints which made even my informant pause timidly—the secret behind the Magellanic Clouds and globular nebulae, and the black truth veiled by the immemorial allegory of Tao. The nature of the Doels was plainly revealed, and I was told the essence (though not the source) of the Hounds of Tindalos. The legend of Yig, Father of Serpents, remained figurative no longer, and I started with loathing when told of the monstrous nuclear chaos beyond angled space which the "Necronomicon"[a] had mercifully cloaked under the name of Azathoth. It was shocking to have the foulest nightmares of secret myth cleared up in concrete terms whose stark, morbid hatefulness exceeded the boldest hints of ancient and mediaeval mystics. Ineluctably I was led to believe that the first whisperers of these accursed tales must have had discourse with Akeley's Outer Ones, and perhaps have visited outer cosmic realms as Akeley now proposed visiting them.

I was told of the Black Stone and what it implied, and was glad that it had not reached me. My guesses about those hieroglyphics had been all too correct! And yet Akeley now seemed reconciled to the whole fiendish system he had stumbled upon; reconciled and eager to probe farther into the monstrous[b] abyss. I wondered what beings he had talked with since his last letter to me, and whether many of them had been as human as that first emissary he had mentioned. The tension in my head grew insufferable, and I built up all sorts of wild theories about the queer, persistent odour[c] and those insidious hints of vibration in the darkened room.

Night was falling now, and as I recalled what Akeley had written me about those earlier nights I shuddered to think there would be no moon. Nor did I like the way the farmhouse nestled in the lee of that colossal forested slope leading up to Dark Mountain's unvisited crest. With Akeley's permission I lighted a small oil lamp, turned it low, and set it on a distant bookcase beside the ghostly bust of Milton; but afterward I was sorry I had done so, for it made my host's strained, immobile face and listless hands look damnably abnormal and corpse-

[a] "Necronomicon"] Necronomicon A, B; *Necronomicon* C, D
[b] monstrous] montsrous C
[c] odour] odor C

like.[a] He seemed half-incapable[b] of motion, though I saw him nod stiffly once in a while.[c]

After what he had told, I could scarcely imagine what profounder secrets he was saving for the morrow; but at last it developed that his trip to Yuggoth and beyond—*and my own possible participation in it*—was to be the next day's topic. He must have been amused by the start of horror I gave at hearing a cosmic voyage on my part proposed, for his head wabbled violently when I shewed[d] my fear. Subsequently he spoke very gently of how human beings might accomplish—and several times had accomplished—the seemingly impossible flight across the interstellar void. It seemed[e] *that complete human bodies did not indeed make the trip,* but that the prodigious surgical, biological, chemical, and mechanical skill of the Outer Ones had found a way to convey human brains without their concomitant physical structure.

There was a harmless way to extract a brain, and a way to keep the organic residue alive during its absence. The bare, compact cerebral matter was then immersed in an occasionally replenished fluid within an ether-tight cylinder of a metal mined in Yuggoth, certain electrodes reaching through and connecting at will with elaborate instruments capable of duplicating the three vital faculties of sight, hearing, and speech. For the winged fungus-beings to carry the brain-cylinders intact through space was an easy matter. Then, on every planet covered by their civilisation,[f] they would find plenty of adjustable faculty-instruments capable of being connected with the encased brains; so that after a little fitting these travelling[g] intelligences could be given a full sensory and articulate life—albeit a bodiless and mechanical one—at each stage of their journeying through and beyond the space-time continuum. It was as simple as carrying a phonograph record about and playing it wherever a phonograph of the[h] corresponding

[a] corpse-like.] corpselike. A, B, D
[b] half-incapable] half incapable C
[c] a while.] awhile. A, B, D
[d] shewed] showed B, C, D
[e] It seemed] *It seemed* D
[f] civilisation,] civilization, C
[g] travelling] traveling C
[h] the] *om.* D

make exists. Of its success there could be no question. Akeley was not afraid. Had it not been brilliantly accomplished again and again?

For the first time one of the inert, wasted hands raised itself and pointed stiffly to a high shelf on the farther side of the room. There, in a neat row, stood more than a dozen cylinders of a metal I had never seen before—cylinders about a foot high and somewhat less in diameter, with three curious sockets set in an isosceles[a] triangle over the front convex surface of each. One of them was linked at two of the sockets to a pair of singular-looking machines that stood in the background. Of their purport I did not need to be told, and I shivered as with ague. Then I saw the hand point to a much nearer corner where some intricate instruments with attached cords and plugs, several of them much like the two devices on the shelf behind the cylinders, were huddled together.

"There are four kinds of instruments here, Wilmarth,"[b] whispered the voice. "Four kinds—three faculties each—makes twelve pieces in all. You see there are four different sorts of beings represented in those cylinders up there. Three humans, six fungoid beings who can't navigate space corporeally, two beings from Neptune (God! if you could see the body this type has on its own planet!),[c] and the rest entities from the central caverns of an especially interesting dark star beyond the galaxy. In the principal outpost inside Round Hill you'll now and then find more cylinders and machines—cylinders of extra-cosmic brains with different senses from any we know—allies and explorers from the uttermost Outside—and special machines for giving them impressions and expression in the several ways suited at once to them and to the comprehensions of different types of listeners. Round Hill, like most of the beings' main outposts all through the various universes, is a very cosmopolitan place![d] Of course, only the more common types have been lent to me for experiment.

"Here—take the three machines I point to and set them on the table. That tall one with the two glass lenses in front—then the box with the vacuum tubes and sounding-board—and now the one with the metal

[a] isosceles] isoceles A, B
[b] Wilmarth,"] Wilmarth" A; Wilmarth", B
[c] Neptune (. . .),] Neptune, (. . .) A, B
[d] place!] place. D

disc[a] on top. Now for the cylinder with the label 'B-67'[b] pasted on it. Just stand in that Windsor chair to reach the shelf. Heavy? Never mind! Be sure of the number—B-67. Don't bother that fresh, shiny cylinder joined to the two testing instruments[c]—the one with my name on it. Set B-67 on the table near where you've put the machines—and see that the dial switch on all three machines is jammed over to the extreme left.

"Now connect the cord of the lens machine with the upper socket on the cylinder—there! Join the tube machine to the lower left-hand socket, and the disc[d] apparatus to the outer socket. Now move all the dial switches on the machines over to the extreme right—first the lens one, then the disc[e] one, and then the tube one. That's right. I might as well tell you that this is a human being—just like any of us. I'll give you a taste of some of the others tomorrow."

To this day I do not know why I obeyed those whispers so slavishly, or whether I thought Akeley was mad or sane. After what had gone before, I ought to have been prepared for anything; but this mechanical mummery seemed so like the typical vagaries of crazed inventors and scientists that it struck a chord[f] of doubt which even the preceding discourse had not excited. What the whisperer implied was beyond all human belief— yet were not the other things still farther beyond, and less preposterous only because of their remoteness from tangible concrete proof?

As my mind reeled amidst this chaos, I became conscious of a mixed grating and whirring from all three of the machines lately linked to the cylinder—a grating and whirring which soon subsided into a virtual noiselessness. What was about to happen? Was I to hear a voice? And if so, what proof would I have that it was not some cleverly concocted radio device talked into by a concealed but closely watching[g] speaker? Even now I am unwilling to swear just what I heard, or just what phenomenon really took place before me. But something certainly seemed to take place.

[a] disc] disk C
[b] 'B-67'] "B-67" A, B
[c] testing instruments] testing-instruments C
[d] disc] disk C
[e] disc] disk C
[f] chord] cord A, B, C [B *corrected in pencil to read* chord, *but not in HPL's handwriting*]
[g] watching] watched D

To be brief and plain, the machine with the tubes and sound-box suddenly[a] began to speak, and with a point and intelligence which left no doubt that the speaker was actually present and observing us. The voice was loud, metallic, lifeless, and plainly mechanical in every detail of its production. It was incapable of inflection or expressiveness, but scraped and rattled on with a deadly precision and deliberation.

"Mr. Wilmarth," it said, "I hope I do not startle you. I am a human being like yourself, though my body is now resting safely under proper vitalising[b] treatment inside Round Hill, about a mile and a half east of here. I myself am here with you—my brain is in that cylinder and I see, hear, and speak through these electronic vibrators. In a week I am going across the void as I have been many times before, and I expect to have the pleasure of Mr. Akeley's company. I wish I might have yours as well; for I know you by sight and reputation, and have kept close track of your correspondence with our friend. I am, of course, one of the men who have become allied with the outside beings visiting our planet. I met them first in the Himalayas, and have helped them in various ways. In return they have given me experiences such as few men have ever had.

"Do you realise[c] what it means when I say I have been on thirty-seven different celestial bodies—planets, dark stars, and less definable objects—including eight outside our galaxy and two outside the curved cosmos of space and time? All this has not harmed me in the least. My brain has been removed from my body by fissions so adroit that it would be crude to call the operation surgery. The visiting beings have methods which make these extractions easy and almost normal—and one's body never ages when the brain is out of it. The brain, I may add, is virtually immortal with its mechanical faculties and a limited nourishment supplied by occasional changes of the preserving fluid.

"Altogether, I hope most heartily that you will decide to come with Mr. Akeley and me. The visitors are eager to know men of knowledge like yourself, and to shew[d] them the great abysses that most of us have had to dream about in fanciful ignorance. It may seem strange at first

[a] suddenly] *om.* D
[b] vitalising] vitalizing C
[c] realise] realize C
[d] shew] show B, C, D

to meet them, but I know you will be above minding that. I think Mr. Noyes will go along, too—the man who doubtless brought you up here in his car. He has been one of us for years—I suppose you recognised[a] his voice as one of those on the record Mr. Akeley sent you."

At my violent start the speaker paused a moment before concluding.

"So,[b] Mr. Wilmarth, I will leave the matter to you; merely adding that a man with your love of strangeness and folklore ought never to miss such a chance as this. There is nothing to fear. All transitions are painless, and there is much to enjoy in a wholly mechanised[c] state of sensation. When the electrodes are disconnected, one merely drops off into a sleep of especially vivid and fantastic dreams.

"And now, if you don't mind, we might adjourn our session till tomorrow. Good night[d]—just turn all the switches back to the left; never mind the exact order, though you might let the lens machine be last. Good night,[e] Mr. Akeley—treat our guest well! Ready now with those switches?"

That was all. I obeyed mechanically and shut off all three switches, though dazed with doubt of everything that had occurred. My head was still reeling as I heard Akeley's whispering voice telling me that I might leave all the apparatus on the table just as it was. He did not essay any comment on what had happened, and indeed no comment could have conveyed much to my burdened faculties. I heard him telling me I could take the lamp to use in my room, and deduced that he wished to rest alone in the dark. It was surely time he rested, for his discourse of the afternoon and evening had been such as to exhaust even a vigorous man. Still dazed, I bade my host good night[f] and went upstairs with the lamp, although I had an excellent pocket flashlight with me.

I was glad to be out of that downstairs study with the queer odour[g] and vague suggestions of vibration, yet could not of course escape a

[a] recognised] recognized C
[b] "So,] "So D
[c] mechanised] mechanized C
[d] Good night] Good-night C
[e] Good night,] Good-night, C
[f] good night] good-night C
[g] odour] odor C

hideous sense of dread and peril and cosmic abnormality as I thought of the place I was in and the forces I was meeting. The wild, lonely region, the black, mysteriously forested slope towering so close behind the house, the footprints[a] in the road, the sick, motionless whisperer in the dark, the hellish cylinders and machines, and above all the invitations to strange surgery and stranger voyagings—these things, all so new and in such sudden succession, rushed in on me with a cumulative force which sapped my will and almost undermined my physical strength.

To discover that my guide Noyes was the human celebrant in that monstrous bygone Sabbat-ritual on the phonograph record was a particular shock, though I had previously sensed a dim, repellent familiarity in his voice. Another special shock came from my own attitude toward my host whenever I paused to analyse[b] it; for much as I had instinctively liked Akeley as revealed in his correspondence, I now found that he filled me with a distinct repulsion. His illness ought to have excited my pity; but instead, it gave me a kind of shudder. He was so rigid and inert and corpse-like[c]—and that incessant whispering was so hateful and unhuman![d]

It occurred to me that this whispering was different from anything else of the kind I had ever heard; that, despite the curious motionlessness of the speaker's moustache-screened[e] lips, it had a latent strength and carrying-power remarkable for the wheezings of an asthmatic. I had been able to understand the speaker when wholly across the room, and once or twice it had seemed[f] to me that the faint but penetrant sounds represented not so much weakness as deliberate repression—for what reason I could not guess. From the first I had felt a disturbing quality in their timbre. Now, when I tried to weigh the matter, I thought I could trace this impression to a kind of subconscious familiarity like that which had made Noyes's voice so hazily ominous. But when or where I had encountered the thing it hinted at, was more than I could tell.

One thing was certain—I would not spend another night here. My

[a] footprints] footprint A, B, C, D
[b] analyse] analyze C
[c] corpse-like] corpselike A, B, D
[d] unhuman!] un-human! A, B, C, D
[e] moustache-screened] mustache-screened C
[f] seemed] semed C

scientific zeal had vanished amidst fear and loathing, and I felt nothing now but a wish to escape from this net of morbidity and unnatural revelation. I knew enough now. It must indeed be true that strange cosmic linkages do exist—but such things are surely not meant for normal human beings to meddle with.

Blasphemous influences seemed to surround me and press chokingly upon my senses. Sleep, I decided, would be out of the question; so I merely extinguished the lamp and threw myself on the bed fully dressed. No doubt it was absurd, but I kept ready for some unknown emergency; gripping in my right hand the revolver I had brought along, and holding the pocket flashlight in my left. Not a sound came from below, and I could imagine how my host was sitting there with cadaverous stiffness in the dark.

Somewhere I heard a clock ticking, and was vaguely grateful for the normality of the sound. It reminded me, though, of another thing about the region which disturbed me—the total absence of animal life. There were certainly no farm beasts about, and now I realised[a] that even the accustomed night-noises of wild living things were absent. Except for the sinister trickle of distant unseen waters, that stillness was anomalous—interplanetary—and I wondered what star-spawned, intangible blight could be hanging over the region. I recalled from old legends that dogs and other beasts had always hated the Outer Ones, and thought of what those tracks in the road might mean.

VIII.

Do not ask me how long my unexpected lapse into slumber lasted, or how much of what ensued was sheer dream. If I tell you that I awaked at a certain time, and heard and saw certain things, you will merely answer that I did not wake then; and that everything was a dream until the moment when I rushed out of the house, stumbled to the shed where I had seen the old Ford, and seized that ancient vehicle for a mad, aimless race over the haunted hills which at last landed me—after hours of jolting and winding through forest-threatened labyrinths—in a village which turned out to be Townshend.

[a] realised] realized C

You will also, of course, discount everything else in my report; and declare that all the pictures, record-sounds, cylinder-and-machine sounds, and kindred evidences were bits of pure deception practiced[a] on me by the missing Henry Akeley. You will even hint that he conspired with other eccentrics to carry out a silly and elaborate hoax—that he had the express shipment removed at Keene, and that he had Noyes make that terrifying wax record. It is odd, though, that Noyes has not even[b] yet been identified; that he was unknown at any of the villages near Akeley's place, though he must have been frequently in the region. I wish I had stopped to memorise[c] the licence-number[d] of his car—or perhaps it is better after all that I did not. For I, despite all you can say, and despite all I sometimes try to say to myself, know that loathsome outside influences must be lurking there in the half-unknown hills—and that those influences have spies and emissaries in the world of men. To keep as far as possible from such influences and such emissaries is all that I ask of life in future.

When my frantic story sent a sheriff's posse out to the farmhouse, Akeley was gone without leaving a trace. His loose dressing-gown,[e] yellow scarf, and foot-bandages lay on the study floor near his corner easy-chair, and it could not be decided whether any of his other apparel had vanished with him. The dogs and livestock were indeed missing, and there were some curious bullet-holes both on the house's exterior and on some of the walls within; but beyond this nothing unusual could be detected. No cylinders or machines, none of the evidences I had brought in my valise, no queer odour[f] or vibration-sense, no footprints[g] in the road, and none of the problematical things I glimpsed at the very last.

I stayed a week in Brattleboro after my escape, making inquiries among people of every kind who had known Akeley; and the results convince me that the matter is no figment of dream or delusion. Akeley's queer purchases of dogs and ammunition and chemicals, and the cutting

---

[a] practiced] practised C
[b] even] ever D
[c] memorise] memorize C, D
[d] licence-number] license number A; license-number B, C, D
[e] dressing-gown,] dressing gown, D
[f] odour] odor C
[g] footprints] foot-prints D

530   COLLECTED FICTION: 1926–1930

of his telephone wires, are matters of record; while all who knew him—including his son in California—concede that his occasional remarks on strange studies had a certain consistency. Solid citizens believe he was mad, and unhesitatingly pronounce all reported evidences mere hoaxes devised with insane cunning and perhaps abetted by eccentric associates; but the lowlier country folk sustain his statements in every detail. He had shewed[a] some of these rustics his photographs and black stone, and had played the hideous record for them; and they all said the footprints and buzzing voice were like those described in ancestral legends.

They said, too, that suspicious sights and sounds had been noticed increasingly around Akeley's house after he found the black stone, and that the place was now avoided by everybody except the mail man and other casual, tough-minded people. Dark Mountain and Round Hill were both notoriously haunted spots, and I could find no one who had ever closely explored either. Occasional disappearances of natives throughout the district's history were well attested, and these now included the semi-vagabond Walter Brown, whom Akeley's letters had mentioned. I even came upon one farmer who thought he had personally glimpsed one of the queer bodies at flood-time in the swollen West River, but his tale was too confused to be really valuable.

When I left Brattleboro I resolved never to go back to Vermont, and I feel quite certain I shall keep my resolution. Those wild hills are surely the outpost of a frightful cosmic race—as I doubt all the less since reading that a new ninth planet has been glimpsed beyond Neptune, just as those influences had said it would be glimpsed. Astronomers, with a hideous appropriateness they little suspect, have named this thing "Pluto".[b] I feel, beyond question, that it is nothing less than nighted Yuggoth—and I shiver when I try to figure out the real reason *why* its monstrous denizens wish it to be known in this way at this especial time. I vainly try to assure myself that these daemoniac[c] creatures are not gradually leading up to some new policy hurtful to the earth and its normal inhabitants.

But I have still to tell of the ending of that terrible night in the

[a] shewed] showed B, C, D
[b] "Pluto".] "Pluto." D
[c] these daemoniac] those demoniac C

farmhouse. As I have said, I did finally drop into a troubled doze; a doze filled with bits of dream which involved monstrous landscape-glimpses. Just what awaked me I cannot[a] yet say, but that I did indeed awake at this given point I feel very certain. My first confused impression was of stealthily creaking floor-boards in the hall outside my door, and of a clumsy, muffled fumbling at the latch. This, however, ceased almost at once; so that my really clear impressions begin with the voices heard from the study below. There seemed to be several speakers, and I judged that they were controversially engaged.

By the time I had listened a few seconds I was broad awake, for the nature of the voices was such as to make all thought of sleep ridiculous. The tones were curiously varied, and no one who had listened to that accursed phonograph record could harbour[b] any doubts about the nature of at least two of them. Hideous though the idea was, I knew that I was under the same roof with nameless things from abysmal space; for those two voices were unmistakably the blasphemous buzzings which the Outside Beings used in their communication with men. The two were individually different—different in pitch, accent, and tempo—but they were both of the same damnable general kind.

A third voice was indubitably that of a mechanical utterance-machine connected with one of the detached brains in the cylinders. There was as little doubt about that as about the buzzings; for the loud, metallic, lifeless voice of the previous evening, with its inflectionless, expressionless scraping and rattling, and its impersonal precision and deliberation, had been utterly unforgettable. For a time I did not pause to question whether the intelligence behind the scraping was the identical one which had formerly talked to me; but shortly afterward I reflected that *any* brain would emit vocal sounds of the same quality if linked to the same mechanical speech-producer; the only possible differences being in language, rhythm, speed, and pronunciation. To complete the eldritch colloquy there were two actually human voices—one the crude speech of an unknown and evidently rustic man, and the other the suave Bostonian tones of my erstwhile guide Noyes.

[a] cannot] can not C
[b] harbour] harbor C

As I tried to catch the words which the stoutly fashioned[a] floor so bafflingly intercepted, I was also conscious of a great deal of stirring and scratching and shuffling in the room below; so that I could not escape the impression that it was full of living beings—many more than the few whose speech I could single out. The exact nature of this stirring is extremely hard to describe, for very few good bases of comparison exist. Objects seemed now and then to move across the room like conscious entities; the sound of their footfalls having something about it like a loose, hard-surfaced clattering—as of the contact of ill-coördinated surfaces of horn or hard rubber. It was, to use a more concrete but less accurate comparison, as if people with loose, splintery wooden shoes were shambling and rattling about on the polished board floor. On[b] the nature and appearance of those responsible for the sounds, I did not care to speculate.

Before long I saw that it would be impossible to distinguish any connected discourse. Isolated words—including the names of Akeley and myself—now and then floated up, especially when uttered by the mechanical speech-producer; but their true significance was lost for want of continuous context. Today I refuse to form any definite deductions from them, and even their frightful effect on me was one of *suggestion* rather than of *revelation*. A terrible and abnormal conclave, I felt certain, was assembled below me; but for what shocking deliberations I could not tell. It was curious how this unquestioned sense of the malign and the blasphemous pervaded me despite Akeley's assurances of the Outsiders' friendliness.

With patient listening I began to distinguish clearly between voices, even though I could not grasp much of what any of the voices said. I seemed to catch certain typical emotions behind some of the speakers. One of the buzzing voices, for example, held an unmistakable note of authority; whilst the mechanical voice, notwithstanding its artificial loudness and regularity, seemed to be in a position of subordination and pleading. Noyes's tones exuded a kind of conciliatory atmosphere. The others I could make no attempt to interpret. I did not hear the familiar whisper of Akeley, but well knew that such a sound could never

[a] stoutly fashioned] stoutly-fashioned B, C, D
[b] On] Of C, D

penetrate the solid flooring of my room.

I will try to set down some of the few disjointed words and other sounds I caught, labelling[a] the speakers of the words as best I know how. It was from the speech-machine that I first picked up a few recognisable[b] phrases.

(THE SPEECH-MACHINE)[c]

". . . brought it on myself . . . sent back the letters and the record . . . end on it . . . taken in . . . seeing and hearing . . . damn you . . . impersonal force, after all . . . fresh, shiny cylinder . . . great God. . . ."

(FIRST BUZZING VOICE)[d]

". . . time we stopped . . . small and human . . . Akeley . . . brain . . . saying . . ."

(SECOND BUZZING VOICE)[e]

". . . Nyarlathotep . . . Wilmarth . . . records and letters . . . cheap imposture. . . ."

(NOYES)[f]

". . . (an unpronounceable word or name, possibly *N'gah-Kthun*) . . . harmless . . . peace . . . couple of weeks . . . theatrical . . . told you that before. . . ."

(FIRST BUZZING VOICE)[g]

". . . no reason . . . original plan . . . effects . . . Noyes can watch . . . Round Hill . . . fresh cylinder . . . Noyes's car. . . ."

(NOYES)[h]

". . . well . . . all yours . . . down here . . . rest . . . place. . . ."

---

[a] labelling] labeling C
[b] recognisable] recognizable C
[c] (THE SPEECH-MACHINE)] (*The Speech-Machine*) D
[d] (FIRST BUZZLING VOICE)] (*First Buzzing Voice*) D
[e] (SECOND BUZZING VOICE)] (*Second Buzzing Voice*) D
[f] (NOYES)] (*Noyes*) D
[g] (FIRST BUZZING VOICE)] (*First Buzzing Voice*) D
[h] (NOYES)] (*Noyes*) D

(SEVERAL VOICES AT ONCE IN INDISTINGUISHABLE
SPEECH)[a]

(MANY FOOTSTEPS, INCLUDING THE PECULIAR
LOOSE STIRRING OR CLATTERING)[b]

(A CURIOUS SORT OF FLAPPING SOUND)[c]

(THE SOUND OF AN AUTOMOBILE STARTING AND
RECEDING)[d]

(SILENCE)[e]

That is the substance of what my ears brought me as I lay rigid
upon that strange upstairs bed in the haunted farmhouse among the
daemoniac[f] hills—lay there fully dressed, with a revolver clenched in
my right hand and a pocket flashlight gripped in my left. I became, as I
have said, broad awake; but a kind of obscure paralysis nevertheless
kept me inert till long after the last echoes of the sounds had died
away. I heard the wooden, deliberate ticking of the ancient
Connecticut clock somewhere far below, and at last made out the
irregular snoring of a sleeper. Akeley must have dozed off after the
strange session, and I could well believe that he needed to do so.

Just what to think or what to do was more than I could decide.
After all, what *had* I heard beyond things which previous information
might have led me to expect? Had I not known that the nameless
Outsiders were now freely admitted to the farmhouse? No doubt
Akeley had been surprised[g] by an unexpected visit from them. Yet
something in that fragmentary discourse had chilled me immeasurably,
raised the most grotesque and horrible doubts, and made me wish
fervently that I might wake up and prove everything a dream. I think
my subconscious mind must have caught something which my

---

[a] (SEVERAL . . . SPEECH)] (*Several Voices at Once in Indistinguishable Speech*) D
[b] (MANY . . . CLATTERING)] (Many Footsteps, Including the Peculiar Loose
Stirring or Clattering) D
[c] (A . . . SOUND)] (*A Curious Sort of Flapping Sound*) D
[d] (THE . . . RECEDING)] (The Sound of an Automobile Starting and Receding) D
[e] (SILENCE)] (*Silence*) D
[f] daemoniac] demoniac C
[g] surprised] surprized C

consciousness has not yet recognised.[a] But what of Akeley? Was he not my friend, and would he not have protested if any harm were meant me? The peaceful snoring below seemed to cast ridicule on all my suddenly intensified fears.

Was it possible that Akeley had been imposed upon and used as a lure to draw me into the hills with the letters and pictures and phonograph record? Did those beings mean to engulf us both in a common destruction because we had come to know too much? Again I thought of the abruptness and unnaturalness of that change in the situation which must have occurred between Akeley's penultimate and final letters. Something, my instinct told me, was terribly wrong. All was not as it seemed. That acrid coffee which I refused—had there not been an attempt by some hidden, unknown entity to drug it? I must talk to Akeley at once, and restore his sense of proportion. They had hypnotised[b] him with their promises of cosmic revelations, but now he must listen to reason. We must get out of this before it would be too late. If he lacked the will power[c] to make the break for liberty, I would supply it. Or if I could not persuade him to go, I could at least go myself. Surely he would let me take his Ford and leave it in a garage at Brattleboro. I had noticed it in the shed—the door being left unlocked and open now that peril was deemed past—and I believed there was a good chance of its being ready for instant use. That momentary dislike of Akeley which I had felt during and after the evening's conversation was all gone now. He was in a position much like my own, and we must stick together. Knowing his indisposed condition, I hated to wake him at this juncture, but I knew that I must. I could not stay in this place till morning as matters stood.

At last I felt able to act, and stretched myself vigorously to regain command of my muscles. Arising with a caution more impulsive than deliberate, I found and donned my hat, took my valise, and started downstairs with the flashlight's aid. In my nervousness I kept the revolver clutched in my right hand, being able to take care of both valise and flashlight with my left. Why I exerted these precautions I do

[a] recognised.] recognized. C
[b] hypnotised] hypnotized C
[c] will power] will-power C

not really know, since I was even then on my way to awaken the only other occupant of the house.

As I half tiptoed[a] down the creaking stairs to the lower hall I could hear the sleeper more plainly, and noticed that he must be in the room on my left—the living-room I had not entered. On my right was the gaping blackness of the study in which I had heard the voices. Pushing open the unlatched door of the living-room I traced a path with the flashlight toward the source of the snoring, and finally turned the beams on the sleeper's face. But in the next second I hastily turned them away and commenced a cat-like[b] retreat to the hall, my caution this time springing from reason as well as from instinct. For the sleeper on the couch was not Akeley at all, but my quondam guide Noyes.

Just what the real situation was, I could not guess; but common sense told me that the safest thing was to find out as much as possible before arousing anybody. Regaining the hall, I silently closed and latched the living-room door after me; thereby lessening the chances of awaking[c] Noyes. I now cautiously entered the dark study, where I expected to find Akeley, whether asleep or awake, in the great corner chair which was evidently his favourite[d] resting-place. As I advanced, the beams of my flashlight caught the great centre-table,[e] revealing one of the hellish cylinders with sight and hearing machines attached, and with a speech-machine[f] standing close by, ready to be connected at any moment. This, I reflected, must be the encased brain I had heard talking during the frightful conference; and for a second I had a perverse impulse to attach the speech-machine[g] and see what it would say.

It must, I thought, be conscious of my presence even now; since the sight and hearing attachments could not fail to disclose the rays of my flashlight and the faint creaking of the floor beneath my feet. But in the end I did not dare meddle with the thing. I idly saw that it was

[a] half tiptoed] half-tiptoed A, B, C, D
[b] cat-like] catlike A, B, D
[c] awaking] awakening D
[d] favourite] favorite C, D
[e] centre-table,] center-table, C
[f] speech-machine] speech machine A, B, C, D
[g] speech-machine] speech machine A, B, C, D

the fresh,[a] shiny cylinder with Akeley's name on it, which I had noticed on the shelf earlier in the evening and which my host had told me not to bother. Looking back at that moment, I can only regret my timidity and wish that I had boldly caused the apparatus to speak. God knows what mysteries and horrible doubts and questions of identity it might have cleared up! But then, it may be merciful that I let it alone.

From the table I turned my flashlight to the corner where I thought Akeley was, but found to my perplexity that the great easy-chair was empty of any human occupant asleep or awake. From the seat to the floor there trailed voluminously the familiar old dressing-gown, and near it on the floor lay the yellow scarf and the huge foot-bandages I had thought so odd. As I hesitated, striving to conjecture where Akeley might be, and why he had so suddenly discarded his necessary sick-room garments, I observed that the queer odour[b] and sense of vibration were no longer in the room. What had been their cause? Curiously it occurred to me that I had noticed them only in Akeley's vicinity. They had been strongest where he sat, and wholly absent except in the room with him or just outside the doors of that room. I paused, letting the flashlight wander about the dark study and racking my brain for explanations of the turn affairs had taken.

Would to heaven[c] I had quietly left the place before allowing that light to rest again on the vacant chair. As it turned out, I did not leave quietly; but with a muffled shriek which must have disturbed, though it did not quite awake, the sleeping sentinel across the hall. That shriek, and Noyes's still-unbroken snore, are the last sounds I ever heard in that morbidity-choked farmhouse beneath the black-wooded crest of a[d] haunted mountain—that focus of trans-cosmic horror amidst the lonely green hills and curse-muttering brooks of a spectral rustic land.

It is a wonder that I did not drop flashlight, valise, and revolver in my wild scramble, but somehow I failed to lose any of these. I actually managed to get out of that room and that house without making any further noise, to drag myself and my belongings safely into the old Ford

---

[a] fresh,] fresh C, D
[b] odour] odor C
[c] heaven] Heaven A, B, C, D
[d] a] *om.* C, D [B *reads* thea, *with the* stricken *over with* x's]

in the shed, and to set that archaic vehicle in motion toward some unknown point of safety in the black, moonless night. The ride that followed was a piece of delirium out of Poe or Rimbaud or the drawings of Doré, but finally I reached Townshend. That is all. If my sanity is still unshaken, I am lucky. Sometimes I fear what the years will bring, especially since that new planet Pluto has been so curiously discovered.

As I have implied, I let my flashlight return to the vacant easy-chair after its circuit of the room; then noticing for the first time the presence of certain objects in the seat, made inconspicuous by the adjacent loose folds of the empty dressing-gown. These are the objects, three in number, which the investigators did not find when they came later on. As I said at the outset, there was nothing of actual visual horror about them. The trouble was in what they led one to infer. Even now I have my moments of half-doubt—moments in which I half accept[a] the scepticism[b] of those who attribute my whole experience to dream and nerves and delusion.

The three things were damnably clever constructions of their kind, and were furnished with ingenious metallic clamps to attach them to organic developments of which I dare not form any conjecture. I hope—devoutly hope—that they were the waxen products of a master artist, despite what my inmost fears tell me. Great God! That whisperer in darkness with its morbid odour[c] and vibrations! Sorcerer, emissary, changeling, outsider . . . that hideous repressed buzzing . . . and all the time in that fresh, shiny cylinder on the shelf . . . poor devil . . . "prodigious[d] surgical, biological, chemical, and mechanical skill" . . .[e]

For the things in the chair, perfect to the last, subtle detail of microscopic resemblance—or identity—were the face and hands of Henry Wentworth Akeley.

[a] half accept] half-accept A, B, D
[b] scepticism] skepticism C
[c] odour] odor C
[d] "prodigious] "Prodigious D
[e] skill" . . .] skill". . . . C; skill. . . ." D

CPSIA information can be obtained
at www.ICGtesting.com
Printed in the USA
BVHW04s0737140718
521445BV00005B/16/P